WAKE

This book is dedicated to Daniel.

Jem: January 19 to 23

Monday

Even sitting in the back corner of the room, in the farthest desk from student traffic and the teacher's line of sight, it is possible to be the center of attention. The curious thing about it is that I can be invisible at the same time.

No one likes to look at seriously ill people. It's awkward. It might be catching. It might happen to you some day, and that ruins the happy reality of your otherwise happy moment. That's the invisible bit. But every student in this class is hyperaware that I'm here, even if they don't look at or talk to me, because although they can't admit it, they're afraid I'm going to drop dead at any second.

Technically, I'm in remission. I say technically because I still feel like shit. Even after the cancer is gone, the bullshit doesn't end. Napalm-strength drugs damage practically everything, and even the most benign treatments are physically taxing.

I lay my head down on the desk. Class hasn't started yet, and none of my teachers tell me to straighten up and pay attention anymore, like lifting my head might kill me.

Fourth period Social Studies is my worst class. I didn't even want to take it, but I'm short on prerequisites and nothing else was available in this time slot. All the practical assignments are torture; most of these involve cooking, and the smell turns my stomach every time. This class is right after lunch, too, at the time of day when I'm sure to feel queasy or tired or both. That's part of the strategic appeal of the back corner seat: it's out of everyone's line of sight; it's right next to the window, so I can lay my head down on the table and nap in the sun; thirdly, there's a sink right behind me—lunch has reappeared a few times—and finally, it's farthest from the storage unit and fridge that I doubt has been cleaned since September.

Class starts right on the bell. We have a new student today, from St. John's, Newfoundland. Who in their right mind would willingly move to Smiths Falls?

I take my feet off the adjacent chair. New Girl is about to infringe on my nap zone, because this bird course is packed and the only other free seat is right in front of the teacher's desk. No one wants that seat, so she'll end up next to Cancer Boy.

I figure it'll be less awkward for her if we don't talk, so I don't even say hello. If I don't look at her, she won't stare at me. Luckily it's a lecture day and we don't have to work together on a practical assignment. We're given a series of transparencies to copy. I make an effort at the first two, and then give up and put my head down. I'll just read the textbook later. Maybe. If I get around to it. I'm pretty sure I'm failing this class already. I haven't completed an assignment yet.

I have my 'own' cot in the nurse's office, and it's there that I spend fifth period. I need a nap more than I need an English lecture. It seems too short a time before Elise is pulling my blanket off. My sister has a preternatural sense of when I'm having an awful day.

"Come on," she says. "Eric's illegally parked."

Tuesday

My morning starts off on a really annoying repetitive note. Luckily, alarm clocks are equipped with snooze buttons.

"Don't you dare hit snooze again!" Mom yells up the stairs.

I drag myself out of bed and head for the bathroom. I leave the light off and turn on the shower. I like to wash in the dark because it's like an extra five minutes of sleep. That, and it's easier on the ego.

This room used to be Elise's. Mine was down the hall and Eric and I shared an adjoining bathroom. The trade was her idea. She sensed how important it was to me to have a private bathroom when I got sick.

Bathing is a pain, even with a waterproof patch over my Hickman. I can't stand directly under the water, so I have to use a detachable showerhead to direct the spray and keep moisture away from my port—the first aggravation in what already promises to be a long day.

I get dressed without looking in the mirror. I don't need to see myself. No one else needs to, either, which is why I cover up my pale, hairless skin with long sleeves and clothes that used to fit but are now too loose.

It's a curious thing, what hair remains and what falls out after chemo. The obvious stuff went quick: head, eyebrows, eyelashes, facial hair. I lost my body hair in patches. The only hair that remains, like some sick joke, are the fine hairs on my second knuckles and enough stray pubic hairs to make me look like a thirteen-year-old boy.

I've got a drawer full of toques, mostly homemade. My crafty little sister knit me one during my first round of chemo and kept churning them out for weeks. I've got a toque in every color, and she gives me hell if I don't match the damn things to whatever I'm wearing. Today's selection is black, because I'm already in a bad mood and it's not even eight o'clock.

I'm feeling exactly like hell by the time I get to Social Studies. Lunch isn't sitting well. I hope we don't have a practical today. I just shut my eyes, try to remain completely still, block out the noise of the class, and recite a little mantra in my head that I don't vomit.

New Girl sits down next to me. Jeez, does she have to jostle the table like that?

"You alive?"

I crack an eyelid and glare at her. "You're funny." I want to close my eye again to make the room stop spinning, but that would ruin the effect of the glare.

"I'm Willa."

I turn and hurl into the sink. It feels like more comes back up than I swallowed today at lunch. How is that even possible?

The class shuts up faster than Jonas Brothers tickets sell out. People swivel in their seats to see what's going on, like they can't figure it out.

New Girl hands me paper towels and turns on the faucet. "Isn't this just fascinating?" she says brightly, and the other cretins all turn back to their own affairs with low noises of disgust.

"Peas?" she guesses.

"Lime Jell-O." Who asks a question like that?

This class isn't a practical, but I nearly wish it were. We're given our term assignments. We have to work in pairs over the next few months, so I can't ignore the girl who just watched me puke and then tried to talk about it.

Our assignment involves a joint paper and presentation about a social problem that affects the community we live in. This is going to be unbelievably dull.

Contrary to what Elise thinks, it's totally possible to tell when she's gone off her Ritalin. She can barely sit still and fiddles with her seatbelt on the ride home.

"So guess what?"

"Forty-two," Eric says. I suspect he might have cracked a book sometime in the past fortnight. Or it could just be a coincidence.

"Student Council picked a date for the winter formal." Elise is practically vibrating in the front seat. Should I tell her there's a Red Bull in the glove box?

She starts talking a mile a minute about themes and colors and stuff, so Eric turns on the radio. She makes a valiant attempt to talk over it, even when he maxes out the volume. The second we get home she puts on her hard-done-by whine and says, "*Mom*, Eric's being mean to me!"

"She's lying!"

"If nobody's bleeding, I don't want to know," Mom calls from the second floor. Got to love her parenting style. She thinks conflict is character building.

I write *Elise's Stupid Dance Thing* on the calendar in the kitchen. We'll do some character building tonight when she sees it.

Wednesday

Lunch is always boring. I sit with Elise most days, on the edge of her little group of friends. I don't talk much. We moveed to Smiths Falls just before I got sick, and I didn't meet a lot of people before treatment kept me out of school and I became the elephant in the room.

For the moment, I survive on water, fruit juice, yogurt and Jell-O. Everything else upsets my stomach and tastes like bitter cough syrup. Food tasted like metal during chemo, and now that it's over everything tastes too bitter or too sweet, so I can't eat much without feeling nauseated. Dad keeps nagging me to eat according to the plan the hospital dietician made for me, so every few days I force down something 'real' to appease him. Then I puke it right back up.

Which brings me to my current conundrum of which Jell-O cup to open first: cherry or lime?

"Just eat the cherry first, you know you want to," Elise says.

"Not hungry."

She tries to swipe my cherry Jell-O and I snatch it back. Her bullshit radar is entirely too good.

"I'll make milkshakes when we get home," she says. That makes me smile and takes the bitter edge off the Jell-O. Elise figured out a kick-ass mix for fruit and frozen yogurt milkshakes during my second round of napalm, and made an addict out of me. She uses them to bargain with me like I'm an unruly child. And I'm stupid enough to keep falling for it.

"I don't mind doing most of the work," the Newfie says. We're divvying up the workload for our term project. "But you're not allowed to be a jerk."

"Oh, anything but that." I really shouldn't push my luck with sarcasm. I'm fortunate not to have a grade-grubbing partner who would complain about me not pulling my weight. She's compassionate enough to take my fatigue into account, but it still feels lousy to be given an easy ride because she feels sorry for me.

"You're doing it again."

"You'd be in a bad mood too if you felt like shit."

"You have the worst attitude."

I hate it when strangers pretend to know me. It's so easy to be high and mighty about pain that isn't your own. I start to write stuff down on our proposal sheet as she flips through the textbook for project ideas. I don't believe she's really from Newfoundland. She doesn't even have an accent.

"Why are you staring at me?"

"Does it bother you?"

"Depends why you're staring."

"You're not really from Newfoundland, are you?"

"You don't really have cancer, do you?" That makes me smile, which throws her off.

"Actually, I don't."

She sizes me up like she thinks I'm full of it. I can't tell by her face if she believes me or not, but she smirks and tells me she likes my hat.

"I like your hair." I'm lying. She's blonde and will sooner or later prove to be a total ditz.

"You're trying to make this awkward on purpose, aren't you?"

"What gave you that idea?"

Newfie turns back to the textbook and tells me to start brainstorming. Why'd I have to get stuck in this stupid class? Why couldn't I have gotten into Chemistry, learned cool things about combustion? Making bombs could be a good use of my limited energy.

Thursday

Social Studies is starting to become a weird part of my day. I still feel tired and sick and cranky at the end of lunch, but my project partner is the only person besides Elise who talks to me at school. It's kind of nice, except for the fact that I can't stand her.

"You look better today."

"Do I?" Like I give a damn what she thinks. "Why do you say that?"

"You're sitting up, for one."

"Har har." *Bitch.*

Newfie starts to set up the equipment for today's practical. We're making enchiladas for our study of proper nutrition, since yesterday we learned all about making grocery lists and meal planning—a curriculum designed for glue-eaters. I just sit there and let her do all the work of setting up. She doesn't ask for help.

I've started to notice patterns with the Newfie. She never fails to show up to school in black and dark grey clothes, except for her gloves. This weirdo apparently owns an endless supply of fingerless gloves in any and all colors. I can't tell if she's trying to make a statement or just be ridiculous.

"I dare you to eat raw beef."

"After you." She pinches a piece of ground beef off the corner of our portion and holds it out to me. I want to do it just to be a smartass, but anything more solid than yogurt will cause serious pain. My stomach hurts just thinking about it.

"Maybe later."

She smirks and turns back to the practical setup. Damn it, she thinks she won. I'm sulking a bit as I write our information at the top of the worksheet. My normally dry hands are sweaty and the Newfie is stirring up odors by measuring out ingredients. I can already feel my stomach turning and we're not even cooking yet.

"I don't know if I'm gonna make it through class today."

"Will I get to guess what you had for lunch again?"

I don't have a good enough comeback for that one, so I just told my arms on the table and lay my head down. But the surface of the worktable smells like whatever they were using last period, and I sit right back up again. I just prop my head in my hands and lean my elbows on the tabletop. Breathe in—breathe out. Don't puke. Don't give her anything to guess at, like misery is a game.

The Newfie puts a hand on my back. "I can walk you to the nurse's office if you want."

"I'm alright." Actually, I don't trust myself to stand up right now. The Newfie opens the adjacent window to relieve some of the smell, which helps. She rubs little circles on my back with one hand and does our assignment with the other. It's just seasoning the meat in a frying pan and scooping it into the store-bought shells.

"You don't have to keep doing that," I say of her hand.

"Do you want me to knock it off?"

I don't answer, because asking her to keep going sounds pathetic. I miss being touched—at least in a way that doesn't involve needles or examinations. It gives me something to focus on besides the queasiness.

She takes her hand off me when Mrs. Hudson comes around to check our progress. She can see I'm not doing anything and suggests I go to the nurse's office.

"Maybe later."

I last through the rest of the day without retreating to the nurse's office, but I don't last the entire car ride home without getting sick. Thankfully I haven't got a big evening planned. Just three hours in a clinic recliner, hooked up to dialysis. Yes, I know, I lead a gripping life.

Friday

Thank God it's Friday, and thank Elise for delicious milkshakes. She made me a thermos-full for lunch today. It's worth noting that she only did it to apologize, though. I passed out on the couch last night and she drew eyebrows on me.

Is it pathetic that the high point of my day is a mango milkshake?

All of you is pathetic, idiot.

Elise's friends are all on the social planning committee. Lunch talk these days consists of the same things that go on in their official meetings: the upcoming dance, themes, budget, dress code, blah, blah, blah. Twenty minutes of this and I can't take it anymore.

"I'm going for a walk."

"Where?"

"Nowhere, *Mom*."

I go out to the parking lot end up sitting in the car with the heat running to avoid the cold.

Some walk.

Shut up.

Fuck you.

My iPod comes out and the earphones go in to tune out the world. I'd blast the radio, but Eric is very protective of the tuner in his car and earphones are much better for what I need right now: Tchaikovsky, the musical cure for deep-seeded bitterness. I hear the bell ring through my earbuds but make no move to get out of the car. The warning bell rings, and there's an annoying rap on the passenger window. I crack an eyelid and sure enough, it's Elise. She opens the door and looks down at me with a hand on her hip.

"Are you going to class or what?"

"But *Mom*."

She tugs at my sleeve. "Come on. You'll fail senior year and end up in my classes. Please, spare me the humiliation."

"I'm tired."

"No milkshakes for a week."

So I drag my ass out of the car. I really should hold her down one of these days and torture the recipe out of her—when I have the strength…six or seven months from now.

The Social Studies room smells like floor cleaner. It's the same industrial brand they use at the hospital, which, unfortunately, smells like home to me. I hate that.

I dump my books on the worktable and take my seat. I'm one of the last ones to arrive, but the Newfie isn't here yet. She'd better not be absent. Ripping on her is the only thing that makes this class worthwhile.

I should really stop thinking of her as *the Newfie*. I heard Chris I-am-such-a-twat Elwood call her 'St. Johnny' the other day like some sort of pet name. One: I will not sink to Elwood's level of wit. Two: if I think it, I might accidentally call her that one of these days, thereby violating my first reason for not thinking of her by her place of origin.

Do you ever think you might be over-thinking?

Willa makes it past the threshold at the exact moment the bell rings. Our assignment today is the write-up for yesterday's nutrition practical. I'll just fall asleep now and save the time, thanks.

Willa, as usual, takes the initiative. She opens her book and scribbles a few notes before asking, "So what are you doing this weekend?"

"What's it to you?"

"I'm being friendly."

"Well knock it off."

"Fuck you and your bad mood, Harper."

I hate to admit it, but that response has a nice ring to it.

"So what are *you* doing this weekend?"

She looks at me with that I-am-so-not-impressed expression. "Entertaining some friends. There's a basketball game on."

"Bullshit you're into basketball."

"No. But my brother is." She smirks at me. I don't like it. "Nice hat."

"Nice tits."

"You're such a shit."

"Are you going to buckle down and do our homework or what?" I nod to the open book on the table.

"I think a brain-damaged monkey could do this, so you definitely can too." She drops the textbook in front of me. "It's my turn to do nothing." Willa slouches down in her seat and begins to doodle on her notebook.

"You trust me with your grade?"

"No. I just relish the thought of your smug face twisted up in concentration."

"I'm not dumb, you know."

She gives me a skeptical look. I pull the book closer and take out a pen. I used to get straight As, damn it. I can pull off another one and show this cow.

Willa: January 25 to 30

Monday

It's easier to live with Frank than I'd anticipated. It's pretty much status quo from when we were growing up, given the seven-year age gap between us. I eat breakfast alone because he's already at work by the time I get up—Frank is a paramedic—and when he comes home we stay out of each other's way. I like this new arrangement. I can't tell if Frank does; he's hard to read.

Frank's home is exactly what you'd expect of a twenty-five-year-old man. He only moved out when Mom and Dad moved away to St. John's, and he bought this little Cape Cod house for himself. It's sparsely furnished, completely un-painted except for white primer, and the only attempt at personalized décor is a Habs magnet on the fridge. Our parents are paying him to take me off their hands for a few months, on the condition that I behave myself and pull my weight around the house.

My life here feels about as nondescript as Frank's walls. I did my freshman year in Smiths Falls before we moved away. I came back for a change from St. John's, only to find that everything is completely, depressingly, the same as when I left it. The people who I used to hang out with seem unevolved and insipid. There's Paige, still trying to be Miss Popularity—I'll admit that I was once an enthusiastic member of her entourage. Diane the bully and Hannah the sweet-heart are still among her faithful followers. Chris Elwood, the guy I knew as a pudgy dweeb in grade nine, has lost the baby fat and turned into a generically popular pretty-boy. Joey, who we all thought would grow up to discover the cure for cancer, has discovered his penis instead. At least Brian with the puppy eyes and Hannah the sweetheart are good people, so I can still have faith in my generation.

A little bit of that faith dies when I enter the school parking lot. Frank is let-ting me borrow his bike until I can find a car at a decent price—the sooner the better, in this weather—and I pull up just in time to see a group of boys throw that kid from my math class into one of the trash cans. They roll him down the sidewalk and drop him off the curb, much to everyone's delight. I share oxygen with these morons.

I lock Frank's bike up and tread through the mush toward the school. Twenty meters ahead, a short girl is skating on a patch of black ice. She's spinning and hopping along, only to get hit in the face by a snowball. She gives a shriek of indignation. "Jem!"

I didn't notice before, but now that she's yelled at him, I see my project part-ner walking along the line of cars. He's clearly the culprit; he's still wiping snow off his gloves. The bastard doesn't look a bit sorry, either. He's grinning like an idiot.

Holy shit, he can *smile*?

The little skater begins to stomp off in the direction of the side entrance. A second snowball hits her between the shoulder blades. That one was thrown by a stocky guy in a letterman jacket.

The little skater waves a pink-gloved bird at the two of them and disappears into the building.

⟿

I don't see the Axis of Annoying until after lunch. He's already at the table when I enter for Social Studies, staring out the window like the parking lot is fascinating. Despite the cold, it's sunny today, and the light on his face makes him look worse. He's extremely pale and those dark circles under his eyes make his illness obvious.

I wonder what he meant when he said he didn't have cancer.

"How was your weekend?"

Harper doesn't even look away from the window. "I solved world hunger."

"Yeah, right."

"Oh, ye of little faith."

"You realize that solving world hunger would mean you'd be doing something good for a change?"

"Ah, but there's the kicker: I destroyed my solutions." He finally looks away from the window and gives me this cocky smirk. "Malevolence 101, Kirk."

"Did you finish the write-up from Friday?"

He opens his under-used notebook and takes out a few typewritten pages. I skim them as we wait for class to start.

Wow, the jackass might actually have a brain. This isn't half bad.

Tuesday

Jem and I have yet to agree on a topic for our term project. All the other groups have already submitted proposals and started their research. Mrs. Hudson is getting impatient with us, so she gives us a library pass for fourth period. We have to go to the Social Sciences section and find something to write about.

Harper is content to let me do all the work, as usual. He condescendingly informs me that I should write the proposal because I need to practice my penmanship, and claims that my messy writing is a direct corollary of having 'freakishly' small hands.

"You're such a jerk." I wouldn't mind doing the majority of the work if he wasn't so nasty about it. I can have compassion for his illness, but my patience is in limited supply.

"No, really," he says. "If your tits were just a few sizes bigger, you'd have a promising porn career."

"I hope you choke on your own vomit." For some reason he finds that funny.

I'm not going to give him the pleasure of asking why, but he reads the question in my face and informs me that it's a sign I'm running out of comebacks when I go for the obvious insult.

"That wasn't obvious." I grab the nearest book of the shelf. "Want to write about drug addiction?" Jem just scoffs, which irritates me even more. "Obvious is calling you Uncle Fester."

He doesn't have a comeback for that one. Either he's run out of material, or I've hit a sore spot.

"Maybe we should write about acute illness."

Jem turns away from the shelf looking like he wants to hit me. "Your gloves are ridiculous."

"So is that comeback."

Wednesday

Frank isn't a social butterfly. He only has one really good friend, Doug Thorpe, who he hangs out with on a regular basis. They're a lot alike—reserved, deliberate, and outdoorsy. They go camping and hunting whenever they can get away, and when they can't, they park themselves in front of the same TV with a few beers.

The more time goes by, the more I suspect that Frank and Doug are more than just buddies. My brother has never had a girlfriend—something I've always chalked up to social ineptitude or shyness before now, but now that I look at it, my brother doesn't seem that interested in finding a woman. I'm not going to ask, though. Frank is a very private person, and there's no making him talk if he doesn't want to.

Doug is coming over tonight. Frank tells me this over breakfast and I ask if he wants me to get out of the house. "No girls at a guys' night, right?" That sounds better than offering to give maybe-lovers some privacy.

Frank clears his throat. "No, you can stay. Maybe you can cook dinner?" That explains why I'm welcome. "I'll ask Doug to bring Luke," he offers in consolation. Luke is the younger Thorpe brother, close to my age.

"Sure."

I pull some steaks out of the freezer for tonight and head to school. The prospect of company has put me in a good mood. I don't know Luke very well, which means there's a chance that he's one of the few things that have changed in this town since I've been away. Not even Social Studies with my twat of a project partner can sully my good mood, though he makes every effort. Jem is still sulking about yesterday's spat, but thankfully he gives up halfway through the period and falls asleep on the table. I don't bother to wake him up when the bell rings.

Luke is nothing like I remember. Last time I saw him, he was a gangly fourteen-year-old with braces and a buzz cut. Three years have allowed him to grow into his bones and grow out his hair, which is long enough to tie back now. Doug takes one look at us, blond and curly-haired, and remarks that we could be siblings.

Luke still grins easily. Those blue eyes make him look far too innocent, even when he clearly has mischief on his mind. I like him, and I wish we could hang out more. Unfortunately he attends school in Perth, so we'll only cross paths when our brothers give us an excuse.

Luke and I end up carrying the conversation over dinner, since Frank and Doug are about as verbose as houseplants in groups larger than two people. They leave us at the end of dinner to go watch the game, so Luke and I do the dishes. We're discussing Three Days Grace when he interrupts to ask, "So what are you doing this weekend?"

"Homework. Housework. What else is there in this town?"

Luke hums in agreement, and we wash in silence for a few minutes before he prompts me, "Well?"

"Well what?"

"You're not going to ask me what I'm doing?" He shakes his head with feigned disappointment. "And I thought Mrs. Kirk raised you to have manners." His sarcasm earns him an elbowing.

"What are you doing this weekend?" I ask. The question reminds me of Harper, and I have to shake the thought away.

"What was that?"

"Nothing. Just reminded of something my project partner said."

"What'd she say?"

"My partner's a he. And a jerk. He said I had porn star hands the other day." I put down the drying towel to extend my fingers and Luke pretends to inspect them.

"He might have a point," he teases. I swat his shoulder.

"I got the last word in, though. It doesn't matter much, I guess, because his attitude isn't going to improve any. I do most of our work because he's tired a lot. He's got cancer."

Luke's eyebrows go up. "You're not talking about Dr. Harper's kid, are you?"

"Jem Harper, yeah. You know him?"

Luke shrugs. "I know of him. Your brother's mentioned Dr. Harper a few times—they work at the same hospital. I think his kid's been sick since they moved here."

"When did they move here?" It could have been any time in the last three years, conceivably, since I didn't know Jem Harper before I moved away.

"Last summer, I think," Luke says. He flicks my face with water. "Want to go tobogganing this weekend?"

Thursday

"This is such bullshit," Jem complains as he fills in the little boxes on our work-sheet. I've forced him to take a turn at doing the practical report while I wash the pan and utensils we used to make macaroni and cheese. It was his idea that I do that part. The skin on his hands is really dry and he has lots of little cuts and cracks on his fingers—bad idea to handle food. He wanted me to do it all, but I'm having none of that today.

"Hey, if you don't have cancer, how come you're getting sick all the time?"

"Because," he says scathingly, "the fun doesn't stop just because the cancer's gone."

"What kind of cancer did you have, anyway?"

"None of your damn business, that's what kind."

I can ask my friends later. They must have heard it through the grapevine by now.

"So how long does it take to get back to normal?"

"Depends on the treatment," he answers vaguely. "A few days. A few weeks. Maybe a few months."

"When will your hair grow back?"

He glares at me bitterly. "Fuck off, Kirk."

Friday

My new car is an absolute piece of junk, and I love it. It's a '94 Toyota Tercel with non-original doors and bumper. The emissions test cost more than the car itself. Frank loaned me the money to put winter tires on it. The mechanic tried to sell me hubcaps to go along with the tires, but my little shitbox doesn't need anything fancy.

One of my favorite things about her is the sound system. The speakers still work perfectly, and she's only set up to play radio and cassettes. Passengers can forget about trying to control the music. But the absolute best thing about this car is that it has a manual transmission. Nobody will want to borrow it.

I lock her up before school as Jem crosses the parking lot to say good morn-ing—or some snarky equivalent, knowing him. He looks at my car with disdain and says, "Would it kill you to buy domestic?"

Lunch is going to be tricky for the next few weeks. The posters announcing the winter formal went up today and the people I sit with at lunch are excited about it. I hate school functions.

Paige, Hannah and Diane are into it. They're already making plans to go shopping. I'm trying to hide by slouching so low in my chair that I'm practically under the table. Maybe they won't see me and I won't be roped into shopping or, worse, attending this stupid thing. If I wanted to get that close to someone and grind against him, I'd do it in private and there would be a lot less clothing involved.

I could just focus on my guy friends, but they're equally enthusiastic. Just trying to get laid, I think, and taking the most inefficient route. Chris Elwood asks me if I'm thinking of going. He makes a point of leaning in toward me, speaking like we're the only two people in the room. I'm not keen on this sort of attention, and Chris has been doing it since my first day. I'm sure he's a nice guy, but I don't date anymore.

"I'm busy that night."

"With what?"

Rude much? "I'm visiting my grandma." I could always make real plans with her for an excuse. She told me to get in touch with her 'once I get settled,' but the woman is insane so I've been putting it off.

"You can't see her some other time?"

"No. It's her birthday." I have to derail this conversation before the lie gets out of hand. "I take it that you're going?"

Chris shrugs. "I was thinking about it. But if you want some company, I could visit your grandma with you."

I wonder if he's so obvious with every girl he's trying to move on. Visiting my grandma with me? Come on.

"No, thanks."

"You sure?"

"I wouldn't have said it if I wasn't."

"Well, maybe I'll see you after." This guy does not give up. I guess he never learned how to take a hint.

"Maybe." I turn back to my food, but a snicker from the next table distracts me. I look over and see Harper about ten feet away, eating with the little ice skater. He sees me looking at him and winks. Damn it, Soc is going to suck.

The first words my partner says to me when I get to class are, "Grandma's birthday? You couldn't come up with anything better than that?"

"It is her birthday."

"You're lying, Kirk."

"Chris bought it."

Harper looks at me with this condescending smirk and shakes his head. "He wanted to buy it. It's easier on his ego than the alternative."

"I hate you."

"Because I'm right."

I don't get a chance to respond to that before Mrs. Hudson calls the class to order, and the jerk beside me smiles smugly. It's only after we're doing independent seatwork that I get a chance to make another jab at him. I start to hum the *Addams Family* theme song low enough so that only we can hear. He pulls his hat lower over his ears, trying to block me out, but I can tell I'm getting to him. It doesn't make me feel any better.

Jem: January 30 to February 6

Friday

When we get home I don't even bother to say hello to Mom before going to my room. I crawl across the duvet and collapse into the pillows. I've been craving this since I got up this morning. Mom must have washed my sheets today, because they're smooth and smell like the inside of the dryer. Three days from now they'll have the smell of dead skin and stale chemical on them.

I don't like the silence of my room, so I roll over to turn on some music. My CD player beeps to let me know the tray is empty. I live with a thief. Elise insults my taste in music one day and steals my CDs the next.

Maybe I'll play my own music. I haven't practiced in a few days. But first a hot shower is in order. My joints are aching.

I strip down and go to the closet for my bathrobe. There's a mirror on the inside of the closet door and the guy staring back at me looks like the pictures of Auschwitz inmates in my History textbook. It's easy to believe that isn't me because he looks so different. He's thirty pounds lighter than I am. I've got thick hair with serious cowlicks, and he's got none at all. I don't have a Hickman sticking out of my chest, but this sad bastard does. I'm good looking. I'm popular. This guy looks like a stiff breeze could kill him and he has to sit with his little sister at lunch for company.

The only things that look the same are the eyes, which I ignore. They're a little yellow around the sclera, but still the only evidence of the real me inside this impostor.

Who are you kidding?

I close the closet and go to use the washroom. My penis hangs between my legs like a limp slug. I don't think the rest of the treatment's side effects would seem so bad if I still had some semblance of a sex drive. A five second orgasm would be a welcome break during the day, but I haven't wanted to chase after one for a while, and I certainly haven't had the energy. Just the thought of any kind of repetitive motion makes me queasy.

Maybe it's a blessing that treatment chased my sex drive away. It would be awful to be horny and trapped in a body that looks like Uncle Fester on a hunger strike. No one would be interested in screwing a guy like that.

You mean like you, genius.

There's a knock at the door. Elise is on the other side, rocking back and forth on her feet.

"I'm making milkshakes. Do you want peach or raspberry?"

"Whatever. Doesn't matter."

She looks me up and down from bald head to bare toes. I'm swimming in a bathrobe that used to fit. She looks at me like she knows exactly what's on my mind and opens her arms with a sad expression.

"Don't do that," she says with a pout in her voice. Her short arms can wrap all the way around my middle with extra left over.

"What?"

"You're not ugly," she scolds me.

"Who said I was?"

"You were beating yourself up. I know you were." She taps me between the eyes like a dog. "Is this about Soc?"

"Did you steal my Tea for the Tillerman CD?"

"Maybe, possibly, probably, sort of."

"Don't get cocky with my things just because you make a good milkshake."

Elise smiles and lets go of my waist. "I'll make raspberry." She skips away down the hall toward the kitchen, and I go for a shower. By the time I turn the water off she has returned my CD and pressed play. The first thing I hear is a guitar riff and the end of the chorus of "Don't Be Shy." My sister has good timing.

I wake up in the middle of the night feeling like I'm not alone. This happens once or twice a week. When Mom can't sleep she comes in here and watches me. I pretend I don't know because then we don't have to talk about it. It sucks knowing that I'm a high on her list of reasons why she can't sleep. My illness took her time and her money and broke her heart many times over, and even though it's over now, it still robs her of sleep. I just lay there and breathe deeply, letting her think that I'm asleep until I actually am. When I wake up in the morning, she's back in her own bed, cuddled next to Dad while he sleeps off the fatigue of a night shift at the hospital.

Saturday

I feel the need to mention that the only thing my dad knows how to cook is pancakes. Honestly. I don't mean pancakes are the only thing he cooks well, I mean pancakes are the only thing he cooks, full stop. I've seen him screw up boiled hotdogs. When we were kids and Mom had to go out in the evenings, we always had pancakes for dinner, unless Mom took pity on us and put leftovers aside. Dad can safely work a microwave—most days. It should also be noted that this is the same man who has a license to perform complex internal surgeries. He's a trauma surgeon, Mom's a freelance architect, and our house in Smiths Falls is their idea of blissful escape from the city.

Saturday mornings are Dad's day to make breakfast. By the time I get downstairs, Eric is already on his seventh pancake. He pauses to chew every two bites. Dad's gotten fancy today and decided to add blueberries.

"You up for a pancake?" he asks me. I shake my head and grab the yogurt out of the fridge.

After breakfast I lay on the couch in the den and wait for the nausea-inducing sugar crash. My days are just one never-ending cycle of feeling awful and waiting to feel awful, courtesy of transplant drugs and some serious painkillers. Elise has the TV on. It's set to the morning news, but she's not paying attention; she's browsing for a movie to watch.

"If you put Harry Potter on again, I will kill you."

"Did I ask for your input?"

Elise sewed herself a set of Hogwarts robes last year 'for Halloween' and says it 'helps her concentrate' to fiddle about with a toy wand. I'd be willing to overlook those eccentricities without teasing her if she didn't play the movies at least twice a week, reciting every line in sync with the actors.

Eventually Elise selects a movie and fast-forwards through the previews. When she presses play a familiar, comically eerie theme song is playing. She chose *Addams Family Values*.

"Come here so I can strangle you."

"You reminded me of it the other day," she says, and flops down on the loveseat. "I haven't seen this in forever."

"Elise."

"Shush."

"I'll sit through the Harry Potter movies with you if you just turn this crap off."

"You used to like this movie."

"Turn it off."

She hums along with the theme song and snaps her fingers. "You don't really look like Uncle Fester," she observes. "Your head isn't round enough."

I get off the couch and leave the living room. It would be a much more impressive exit if I had the energy to do more than shuffle my feet across the rug.

"Jemmy?"

"I'm shredding your Snape poster."

"You wouldn't." She feels secure in the family's love for her as the baby and only daughter and maker of milkshakes. She doesn't think I'd seriously screw with her.

"You should talk to your project partner," she says. "Be assertive, or whatever."

That's the last time I confide in her about school and feelings and crap.

I go into Mom's office and plug in the shredder. I grab a bunch of scrap paper out of the recycle box and start to feed it through the blades. Elise shrieks at the sound and comes tearing out of the living room in full-blown meltdown mode.

Only Eric thinks my joke is funny.

I spend the rest of the morning in my room. Mom has banished Elise and I to opposite ends of the house. She's probably clutching her stupid poster, rocking back and forth wearing wizard robes for comfort. I share DNA with that.

What she did was not cool, though. *Addams Family Values* is one thing, but then she had to go and call me *Jemmy*. I hate that name, and I hate that she had a point. Kirk's snotty remarks wouldn't bother me so much if I just told her off. I've let a girl I can't stand get under my skin. I ought to drive over to her place right now and chew her out, just so she can stew in guilt all weekend.

So do it, tough guy.

Nah, I'm all right.

Buk buk buk b-kok!

I hate you.

I am you.

I put on real clothes and borrow the keys to Eric's car. The phonebook helpfully provides Willa's address. The Kirks live a stone's throw from the hardware store.

I think through what I'll say to her while I drive. It's rare that anyone says something nasty about my disease right to my face. Mostly they just ostracize me and talk behind my back. I guess it's either guilt or fear that keeps them from teasing me outright—Chris please-punch-me-in-the-face Elwood is the notable exception.

When I turn onto Willa's street, I start to think that this might be a bad idea. When I find the house I'm tempted to drive right by, but instead I pull into the driveway and turn off the car. It's a quiet neighborhood. The drapes on the front window are shut. I could probably leave right now and she would never know I was here.

You are such a chickenshit.

I get out of the car and make my way to the front door to ring the bell. No one answers. I know she's home. That hunk of rusted metal she drives is parked out front. I ring the bell a few more times without an answer. Maybe she's around back.

I look over the gate at the side of the house and find her in the backyard.

"Hey, Kirk."

She looks over her shoulder at me. "Harper. What are you doing here?"

"I want to talk to you."

"The latch is on the right side."

I reach over the gate and let myself in. Willa is in a middle of filling a plastic bird feeder, but she stops when I approach and looks at me expectantly. This isn't going to work. She's being too welcoming. If she were grouchy about me showing up unannounced on a Saturday, it would be easy to tell her off.

"What do you want to talk about?" Willa prompts me when the silence stretches too long. I shrug. She closes the bag of birdseed and makes a vaguely welcoming hand gesture.

"Come inside. It's too cold out here for chit-chat."

We enter through the back door. The Kirk house is just a small Cape Cod, and it doesn't look very lived in. The walls are unpainted and bare. None of the furniture matches. The only personal item I can see is a fridge magnet.

We hang our coats on the back of kitchen chairs and Willa leads the way through to a sparse living room.

"Still moving in?" I venture.

"My brother's had the house for about three years."

Now it feels even weirder that the place is so bare. Maybe he's one of those serial killers that keep no personal possessions.

"What about your parents?"

"They still live in St. John's." She gathers some homework and a book off the couch to make room for sitting. The book has an image of a sad-faced kid on the cover.

"What are you reading?"

"Have a seat." She pats the cushion beside her.

I sit and she opens her book.

"Let me know when you're ready to tell me why you're really here."

I almost get up and leave. This is downright embarrassing. But then I'd have to face her on Monday, and I didn't drive all the way over here to give up and retreat like a loser. No more letting her under my skin.

I look at the cover of her book. It's a Charles Dickens novel. "Is that for English?"

"Nope."

"You read Dickens for fun, you dork?"

"You didn't come over here to talk about my leisure reading."

"For all you know."

"Are you trying to be friendly, Harper?" she says with amusement.

"Of course not, it's *you*."

Willa chuckles at that and flips the page. I just sit there and mentally kick myself. There is no good way to segue into what I came here to say. *So, remember the other day when you compared me to Fester Addams? Yeah? Well, piss off and die.* I could just come right out any say it, but then I'd look like a jerk. I came here to make her feel like one, not be one myself. I slouch down lower on the couch.

"Is this really what you do on weekends?"

"Yes. And before you try any other small talk: yes, I really did move here from Newfoundland; no, you may not borrow my car, homework, or money; black is my favorite color and the Stones feed it to the Beatles. Okay?"

Her little rant makes me snort in a most undignified way. "You like the Stones?"

"If you're a Beatles fan, get out of my house."

I chuckle while she deadpans. Willa goes back to reading her book and leaves me hanging. I'm never going to get a chance to chew her out if she keeps making me laugh.

Willa starts tapping her toe and humming the tune of "Stealing My Heart." Hell, if this chick wasn't so annoying she might actually be cool. I shut my eyes and tap along with her. I wonder if she likes Santana…

⊷

I'm awake before I realize I was ever asleep. The sun is beyond the front window now, and Willa is sitting in the easy chair across from the couch. I don't remember laying down, but I'm on my side and covered with an afghan.

That was nice of her.

Shut up. If she was nice you wouldn't be here.

I sit up and push back the blanket. My mouth is dry. "What time is it?"

Willa closes her book. "Time to start dinner." She stands up and tosses Dickens aside. "Come to the kitchen. You can stall some more in there."

She walks toward the door without waiting to see if I'll follow. I can't leave yet, so I fold the blanket and follow her.

The Kirk kitchen is small and bare, just like the rest of the house. I take a seat in one of the dining chairs and watch Willa take ingredients for baked chicken out of the fridge. We coexist in silence while she breads chicken and a headache builds at my temples.

"We don't have any Jell-O," she says as she slides the pan into the oven. "What else do you eat?"

"You don't have to feed me." I can't accept her hospitality when I fully intend to chew her out. That's just bad manners.

"Harper," she says with a tone that tells me her patience is limited, "what can you eat?"

"Got any yogurt?"

"No." She opens the fridge and studies its contents. "What about tomato soup?" Too much acid.

"No, thanks."

"Scrambled eggs?" Don't even mention eggs.

"No. Thanks."

Willa shuts the fridge

"Are you going to make me keep guessing?"

"I told you that you didn't have to feed me."

Willa fiddles with the fridge magnet. "Do you have stomach cancer?"

"I don't have cancer."

"What stage?"

"Did you hear me? I said I don't have cancer."

Willa opens the fridge and takes out carrots, peas, a jar of honey, and a carton of milk. She turns her back on me and starts peeling carrots over the sink. It bodes well for me that she's irritated. This might be the opening I've been waiting for. I'm just about to say something when the phone rings. Willa answers and talks with the handset tucked under her chin, still peeling carrots. I can't tell who it is from her half of the conversation. Willa answers the caller's questions with yeses and no's, with a quick 'see you' before hanging up.

"Here." Willa fills a cup with tap water and hands it to me. "You're dehydrated." The backs of her fingers brush my cheek after she sets the cup down on the table, and I flinch away. She thinks it's okay to touch me, does she?

"Drink."

The water does make me feel better. I drain my cup and rest with my head and arms on the table until the pain recedes to a dull ache. When I lift my head there are two pots of boiling water on the stove. I smell vegetables.

"Do you need more water?"

"No, I'm fine."

Willa refills my cup anyway. I drink it—not that she was right, or anything.

"So listen."

"So talk."

"I am, if you'll just listen and not interrupt."

"Hey, do your parents know you're here?"

"Quit trying to change the subject."

She begins to set up a blender. The chicken needs basting. Willa knows her way around a kitchen, I'll give her that. Now would be a great time for some smartass remark about knowing her place as a woman.

"So Mrs. Hudson called me aside the other day," Willa says with affected casualness. "She wanted to talk to me."

"What about?" This bodes ill for me.

"She wanted to let me know that she's thinking of grading us separately on our term project because you're 'not as active a participant.'"

"Whatever." It's only fair, even if it sucks.

"I told her not to."

"Why not?"

Willa sets a strainer in the sink for the vegetables. "I'm a team player," she answers sarcastically. She's not going tell me the real reason.

She pities you, you idiot.

"So listen."

"Listening." The vegetable water splashes in the sink.

"About why I came over…"

She dumps the carrots and peas into the blender.

"Yeah?"

"It's about something you said in class."

"What's that?"

Willa puts a big dollop of honey and a splash of milk into the blender jug with a dash of some spice I can't identify.

"Look, it was totally not cool when you—" Willa starts the blender and cuts off the rest of my sentence. She looks over at me with Bambi-eyes and switches it off.

"What?"

"When you—"

She does it again.

"Did you say something?"

"Stop being a twat, Kirk."

"Spit it out, Harper."

"I—"

She fires up the blender again.

"I swear to God, Kirk…"

She just smirks and turns the damn blender back on. She lets it run for more than five seconds this time and takes out a soup bowl. I wonder how hard she'd struggle if I tried to strangle her…

Willa pours her orange concoction out into the bowl and sets it in front of me with a tall glass of milk and a spoon.

"I'm not hungry." But it does smell good. The steam feels nice on my face.

"Try it."

The soup won't look any better coming back up. "I'd rather not."

"You're half a foot taller than me and we weigh about the same."

"You don't have cancer."

"Apparently you don't either."

Damn it, I should have just said she had a fat ass or something. But she doesn't. She has a nice ass, actually.

"Try one bite."

So I do. I coat my spoon with a fine layer of soup and lick it, waiting for the bitterness. Good Lord, it's good. Nothing tastes good anymore. I take a full bite. It's still good. I forgot what hot food tastes like after all this yogurt and Jell-O.

"It can't be throat cancer," Willa muses aloud. "Your voice is still smooth. Not lung cancer, either—you don't cough."

I'm too busy enjoying my soup to tell her to shut up and stop guessing.

"You're in the right age bracket for testicular cancer."

"My balls are none of your business, Kirk."

There's the click of a key in the front door and a moment later her brother steps in. He calls out his sister's name and she replies that she's in the kitchen.

"The chicken will be ready in five."

He comes into the kitchen and I stand up to say hello. I recognize his EMT uniform, and hope that he doesn't recognize me. He looks from me to his sister with a totally readable expression: *What is Cancer Boy doing in my kitchen?*

"We got company for dinner?"

"It's a pleasure to meet you." I hold out my hand and he shakes it like I'm made of glass.

"Frank Kirk." He, like most other people, is uncomfortable looking at me for more than three seconds, and quickly turns away to get himself a drink. I sit back down and return to my soup.

Willa fills in the awkward blank: "Jem's in my Social Studies class."

"Yeah? You guys working on homework?"

I haven't turned in a piece of homework since last semester.

"Yeah, our term project," Willa says.

"I'll keep the TV down."

"Can we work upstairs?"

Frank looks over at me under his lashes and clears his throat. I guess he has a rule about no boys on the second floor, or in the general vicinity of his sister altogether. But Cancer Boy isn't a threat. Who would want to fool around with him? And surely he's too weak and pathetic to force himself on her.

Stop talking about yourself in the third person, you twit.

"Okay. Not too late, though."

Willa's room isn't quite messy, but it isn't clean either. There are shoes and books scattered all over the floor and her desk is buried under paper. It's the only part of the house that looks lived-in. She leaves the door ajar and invites me to sit wherever.

"If you feel sick, the bathroom is the next door down the hall."

"I'm all right." The soup is sitting comfortably, even after two helpings. I feel full for the first time in awhile, and it's not painful like it used to be. Frank even remarked on my appetite over dinner. It didn't occur to me until he said something that I was eating at an embarrassing speed.

"Where'd you learn to make that stuff?"

"I had the recipe lying around."

Willa takes a seat at her desk chair and puts her feet up on the footboard. Her socks don't match. They're also the only colorful thing I've seen her wear besides the gloves, which she never takes off. Today's pair is pink.

"Could I get the recipe?"

"If you want." Willa takes a pad of paper out of her desk drawer and locates a stray pen amid the mess. She writes it all down for me quickly and tears the page out.

"So why'd you come here?" Willa folds the paper carefully, taking her time. Aw, hell, she's ransoming the damn thing.

"I wanted to talk to you."

"So you said."

"You kept changing the subject."

"Talk now."

"It's about something you said last week."

"Just say it, Harper."

I take a deep breath. "Suffice it to say, I like ripping on you. And I'm pretty sure you like ripping on me. We wouldn't have anything to say to each other if we didn't."

"Now say something interesting."

"There are things that are off limits, Kirk."

She makes a prompting hand motion to show that she's listening.

"We can only rip on each other for stuff we can control, all right?"

"Is this about the lime Jell-O?"

"No, it's about you calling me Uncle Fester."

Willa smiles and I ask her what's so damn funny. "You spent four hours here trying to work up the nerve to tell me not to razz you for being bald? Jeez, save yourself the effort and just text me next time."

"We're agreed, though? No more insults about stuff we can't control?"

She hands over the soup recipe. "Agreed—unless you really tempt me."

Sunday

I have zero energy and my joints ache, but for the first time in a long time, I'm excited to get out of bed. I'm eager to get down to the kitchen and eat. Soup can be a breakfast food, right?

Mom is the only one in the kitchen when I get downstairs. Dad is still at the hospital and my siblings aren't awake yet. She has the Sunday paper spread out in front of her and a steaming mug of coffee in her hand.

"Morning, sweetie," she says.

"Morning." My cheerful tone throws her and she looks up to see me taking carrots and peas out of the fridge. "Do we have any honey?"

"You want food?" She says it like the notion is absurd to the nth degree.

"I found a recipe that doesn't upset my stomach."

Mom leaves her paper and comes to look over the recipe. She quietly assembles the rest of the ingredients while I wash and peel carrots.

"What's this?" Mom points to the last ingredient on Willa's list. It's simply *The Secret Ingredient*. Damn it.

I take the page from Mom and get the phonebook out of the desk. I find the Kirks' listing and dial. It doesn't occur to me until the phone rings that her brother might not take kindly to being woken up early on a Sunday.

Willa answers the phone with a tired mumble that passes for 'hello.'

"What's the secret ingredient, Kirk?"

"Who is this?" She clears her throat of sleep.

"It's Jem. What's the secret ingredient?"

"Any excuse to call me, eh Harper?"

"Don't be difficult. Just tell me so I can eat."

"Meditate. It'll come to you."

"You enjoy screwing with me, don't you?"

"Nah, you're too boney. Screwing with you might cause a fire."

I curl my hands into fists and count to ten very slowly. "*Please*, Kirk."

"It's fresh ginger. Or dried, if you don't have fresh."

"Honestly?"

"Would I screw with you?" Evidently not.

"Why didn't you just write that?"

"Your frustration amuses me."

"You're sick."

"We match."

I hang up on her. Another second of that and I'd be tempted to commit a very messy homicide.

It's not like I want to screw her either.

Is that so?

Monday

I wonder what Chris Elwood sees in Willa. She's such a bitch. And yet there he is, flirting with her again and again no matter how many times she shuts him down. I guess she's polite about it, but still.

I wonder what she doesn't see in him. He's good looking, I guess, and popular. Hell if I understand why. I don't think he's funny and he's not all that bright or good at sports. I guess he's the mediocre everyman. Apparently Willa doesn't like that.

She's too quick for him, anyway. He couldn't handle her. Getting involved with Willa is like playing with fire.

Social Studies is simple today. I don't even have to talk to Willa. Mrs. Hudson puts on a movie for us. It's a documentary about international development projects in Africa. The lights go off, my head goes down, and I doze. The scraping of chairs across the floor wakes me up at the end of class, and I trudge off to English.

Elise catches up to me outside the languages wing after the final bell. She puts on her sweet voice and tries to borrow money from me.

"What did you blow yours on?"

"Nothing. I'm trying to put together enough to buy an outfit for winter formal."

"So ask Mom."

"I did. She suggested that I just alter the dress I wore at Christmas."

"Sounds like a good idea."

She rolls her eyes at me with a long-suffering sigh. "You're such a guy."

We have to wait for Eric, so Elise and I chill in the car while the parking lot empties around us. This is a great vantage point to people-watch, but the most interesting specimen is sitting in the seat directly in front of me. A group of seniors walk by and Elise leans forward, craning her neck to keep them in view until they're gone. Could she be a little more obvious?

"Do seniors ever think about dating juniors?" she says. I reach over the front seat and pat her spiky, over-gelled head.

"Keep dreaming, jail bait."

Tuesday

I balance my notebook on my knee and try to find something non-boring in this textbook. Willa did all the work of watching yesterday's movie and writing our report on the subject, so it's my turn to contribute and prepare our proposal for the term project. Mrs. Hudson wants us to design an in-depth analysis of a social issue in our community and prepare a mock grant proposal for imaginary study funding. "No, you will not actually get paid for this," she told the class. The cretins in the room laughed. Willa was one of them. Suck up.

The nurse makes another round of the dialysis patients, checking connections and equipment. I've got another hour here before I can go home. I want to finish this proposal in that time so I never have to look at it again.

I hear the squeaky wheels of the book cart coming down the hall beyond the curtain that divides me from the patient in the next recliner. The hospital has volunteers walk up and down the place, offering magazines, reading material, and chewing gum to patients. The volunteers are always either old people (visiting their friends or staking out a bed for when they end up here), or they're students trying to earn enough volunteer hours to merit a scholarship.

The squeaky cart stops in front of me. "Harper."

I look up. It's Willa, wearing a green volunteer vest.

"What the hell are you doing here?" Must I see her smirking face everywhere? Must she see me hooked up to a machine like some sort of freak?

She taps the volunteer tag on her vest in answer. "Care for something to read?" she says, and looks at the textbook on my knee. "How's it coming?"

"Boring as hell."

"Just pick one of the chapter questions and design a topic around that."

"Is part of your job to harass patients?"

"It's just one more service I offer." She starts to push the book cart away to the next cubicle. "Later, Harper."

Wednesday

I am awesome. Mrs. Hudson approved my proposal and told five other groups to refine theirs. Okay, so it's *our* proposal, but it's my genius.

"Soil pollution and pesticides? Really? There's so much other cool stuff we could have done with this. And why'd you pick snapdragons as an experimental model?"

"My mom grows them. The sample group is in her planters. The project is half-done already."

"I underestimated your laziness."

"It's pronounced *intelligence*, Kirk."

Thursday

"You should think about going," Elise says.

I slouch in the chair outside the fitting rooms and ponder insanity. Mom roped me into this shopping trip. She said she's tired of seeing me walk around in clothes three sizes too big. I told her that I don't want to waste money on clothes that will only fit until I gain the weight back, but she managed to bully me into buying one shirt and one pair of pants, which is how I ended up in the chair outside the fitting rooms, waiting for Elise to choose a dress for the stupid winter formal.

"Not going," I reply.

"You don't have enough fun." She opens the changing room door.

"That dress is way too short."

Mom comes back from browsing the racks just in time to undermine my opinion.

"Ooh, sweetie, turn around. That looks great on you."

Damn it, I don't want to see my little sister's *legs*. No one else should want to either. As far as I'm concerned it'd be better if she went to this dance in a nun's habit.

"Can we go yet?"

"Just be patient."

"If I vomit, can we go?"

Willa: February 7 to 14

Friday

Paige asked Chris to winter formal. I couldn't possibly care less, aside from the pleasant bonus of having an excuse not to see him before or after 'visiting my grandma.' Unfortunately, Chris has to ambush me by my locker at the end of lunch. He tries to talk me into joining a group to attend winter formal together. I guess he doesn't want to be tied to Paige all evening. Can't say I blame him. Paige can be a little needy.

"Yeeeah, Grandma's birthday is sort of a non-negotiable date."

"I get that. It's just…maybe I'll see you at an after-party? A bunch of us were going to go to Joey's place and hang out."

"I'll think about it." Maybe I can get Luke to come along as a friend-date. That might spare me from being hit on. Chris promises to send me an invite to the Facebook event, and I gladly slip away to go to class.

Jem is already at the worktable when I slide into my seat. He's staring out the window again, too absorbed in the view of the parking lot for a hello.

"You look different."

"Do I?" He doesn't care what I think, but to hell with it.

"Yeah, your clothes fit." I can actually see where his shoulders are and his pants fit all the way down his leg, not just at the waist where his belt cinches. I can even see the line between his ribs and hipbone. He's so thin, but it's nice to see the real shape of him. Even emaciated and pale, he's still sort of good looking.

Without thinking I touch the line between ribs and hip. Jem looks down at my hand and then gives me the strangest look.

Don't touch me.
What are you doing?
Why are you touching me?
You're touching me!
Piss off, Kirk.
You haven't let go yet.
Don't push your limits or I'll push mine.
Please push your limits.

I let go and turn to my book. Man, that guy's got intense eyes. I can feel him staring at me with that weird look that makes me feel like a circus freak.

"Books away! Pop quiz!"

Thank God—I won't have to talk to him.

Saturday

My brother has always been the helpful sort. That's why he became a paramedic.

33

Today, he decided to 'help' me make friends by accepting Paige's invitation to go shopping on my behalf. Apparently he can't just take a phone message like a normal person. This was not how I wanted to spend my Saturday, helping Paige and Hannah choose outfits for winter formal.

I leave the fitting room area to browse the cottons section. There's a sale on undershirts. I'm going through packs of Fruit of the Loom looking for Frank's size when an annoyingly familiar voice appears at my shoulder.

"Boxers or briefs?" Even for Elwood that's a lame pickup line.

"I don't think much about what my brother keeps his bits in."

I grab a pack of medium undershirts from the back of the rack. Elwood is still smiling. He has a dress shirt in his hand. I guess he's shopping for a formal outfit too.

"You're here alone? I thought girls always shopped in groups."

"Paige and Hannah are trying on dresses." I gesture vaguely in the direction of ladies formalwear.

"What about you? Still thinking about coming after you visit with family?"

I deliberately didn't respond to the Facebook invite. It would mean too much to Chris. "I'll come to the after party at Joey's."

"Sweet." Man, I hate that grin. There's something so grasping and affected about Elwood that I can't help but dislike him, even when he's being friendly. Then I feel guilty because I know he doesn't deserve to be disliked. He's trying to be nice, and it's not Chris's fault that I can't see him as anything other than the pudgy dork he used to be. He pats my shoulder and says he'll see me at school.

It's unfair of me to expect my old friends to have changed the same way I have, but it's still disappointing.

Sunday

Frank's house might look barren, but that doesn't mean it's clean, and that becomes my project for the day. I start with my room and when that's done, I break for breakfast. Next on the agenda are the kitchen cupboards. I'm sure there are cans of soup in there that my brother bought when he first moved in. Frank notices my activity and takes a crack at the garage. When I go out there with sandwiches for lunch I can tell exactly where he got bored and quit to wash his car instead.

If Frank can take a break, I can too. I take my lunch in front of my computer and write an email to my mother between bites.

I tell Mom about school and my new/old friends, about Luke and Doug, and living peacefully with Frank. I tell her about my project partner, and about the term project and gardening.

Her reply email consists of one sentence: *This project partner, is he cute?* That's a loaded question. She knows I've sworn off dating. Maybe she's just trying to judge my level of temptation—there is none where Jem Harper is concerned.

After lunch I make a surprise visit to Oma's house. She tells me how grown up I look. I tell her that she still looks good; for a sixty-eight-year-old smoker, she does. She lights up over coffee and doesn't say anything when I join in the activity. That's what I like best about Oma: she doesn't ask questions. We don't have to talk about family or school or my plans for the future. We chat about her garden ('Always plant your seeds on Good Friday'), the cost of heating, and whether I'll go to Ottawa for Winterlude.

Finally, she asks, "Is it easier, being back here?"

I shrug. "Not really, it's just different."

"You weren't wrong," Oma says levelly. I want to get off this topic. Every time it comes up I'm sure she's going to ask me to make the same mistake twice.

"I should go. Homework and stuff."

"Mmmm. Smart girl." I'm really not. I wouldn't make such bad decisions if I were.

Monday

I have to hide behind my textbook during at lunch. My friends are talking about pooling the cost of a limo or, failing that, carpooling to the dance and then to Joey's. I scribble a memo-to-self on the back of my hand: *Call Luke—Sat. JM's @ 11 pm*. I don't think to hide it and Chris sees the note. I'm going to pay for that later.

With his supernatural annoying powers, Jem grabs my wrist the second I sit down in Soc and reads the memo on the back of my hand.

"Luke? You got a boyfriend, Kirk, or is that just to crush Elwood's ego?"

I yank my wrist out of his grip. "None of your business, Harper."

He chuckles at me.

"He's not going to give up easily, you know. If he thinks you've got a boyfriend he'll only see it as a challenge and try harder."

"I didn't realize you were such an expert on the psychology of Chris Elwood."

"He's boring and predictable. That's why you don't like him, isn't it?"

I'm spared the trouble of answering by Mrs. Hudson, who tells us to come to the front to collect ingredients and worksheets for today's practical.

Jem fills out the worksheet and I begin to set up the assignment with my porn star hands. "You didn't answer my question," he says quietly.

"Because it's a stupid question."

Jem turns to me with a strange look. His eyes seem more expressive for the fact that they don't have lashes.

"Don't give me that look."

"What look?"

"You know the one."

"Obviously not, or I wouldn't have asked."

"Just measure the damn ingredients, Harper."

Tuesday

There's still a faint outline of my note-to-self on my hand after my morning shower. Should I leave it? Should I bug Elwood and give him another opportunity to ask uncomfortable questions? Should I give Jem another opportunity to razz me?

So I scrub my hand raw. It doesn't help much, because at lunch Paige asks me if I'll be bringing anyone to the party. Maybe Chris said something to her.

"Yep. His name's Luke."

Paige grins. "Are you guys a thing?" Whatever the hell that means.

I just roll my eyes playfully and say, "Come on, Paige, you're not gonna embarrass me, are you?"

She squeals with delight, but promises to be cool. She says she can't wait to meet him. A few tables over, I see Jem arguing quietly with the little ice skater. I wonder how they know each other, because from here it doesn't look like they have much in common. She's flamboyantly dressed, with gelled hair that's barely longer than a buzz cut. I don't even know her name but I decide that I like her, because she seems to be holding her own against Harper. Maybe he'll be too pissed off about that to harass me in class today.

"Hey, Paige?"

"Mmmh?"

"Who's the girl with the short hair, talking to Harper?" Paige leans over to see who I'm talking about.

"Oh, that's just Elise. She's on the social planning committee. That's her brother she's talking to." The way Paige's voice pitches down implies *the guy with cancer*.

Wednesday

Doug comes over to visit Frank before dinner, and Luke tags along. It's at this point that I realize I don't have enough food left in the fridge to feed four, so a quick trip to the grocery store is in order. Luke offers to come with me, and we leave our brothers to watch the sportscast—or so they claim.

Once we're alone in the car Luke informs me that he told a few people about the party at Joey's this Saturday.

"Just two," he says when he sees I'm concerned about this party getting out of hand. "Good friends of mine—Jake and Phil. All I had to do was mention girls." That makes me laugh.

"Only a few of them are single, you know." This does nothing to dampen Luke's enthusiasm.

We don't talk about Saturday again until he ambushes me with the subject in the condiments aisle.

"So I was wondering, are we supposed to be going *together* or as friends?"

"As friends. You're free to chase the single girls."

"Aren't you a single girl?"

"Yeeeah…"

Luke smiles as though this isn't at all uncomfortable. "Don't worry, I'll protect you from any guy who gets the wrong idea about you."

"Thanks. He's tall and annoying and his voice goes high when he's angry."

Luke snorts. "You're a magnet for losers, aren't you?"

"Patent pending."

Thursday

It's a quiet day in Social Studies. Jem is absent. I enjoy the peace and quiet, but it's sort of dull when he isn't around to annoy me.

As I walk to French for my last class of the day, I pass through the English department and notice Jem sitting in one of the classrooms. He has his head down on the desk, pillowed on skinny arms, and looks distinctly green. I bet he spent fourth period in the nurse's office. Why he didn't stay there is a mystery, because he looks like hell.

Chris catches up with me in the hall. All thought of my project partner drifts away in conversation with him. He wants me to bring my iPod to the after party; apparently he thinks I have good taste in music. I'm starting to think that he's looking forward to the after party more than the dance, even though Joey hasn't secured a source of alcohol yet, and there's no guarantee that he will.

On my way out to the parking lot, bored and tired, I see Harper walking with his little sister. She has a hand on his back for support and they're moving pretty slowly.

I guess my day wasn't so bad.

Friday

It's St. Valentine's Day. A lot of people are wearing pink or red and the cafeteria food is themed today. Spaghetti and garlic bread, red Jell-O or chocolate cake for dessert, and fish sticks dyed with red food coloring. The latter turn everybody's lips scarlet and Paige tries unsuccessfully to cover hers with lip gloss.

In Social Studies, Mrs. Hudson has a pot of mini-roses on the front lab table. Jem tells me happy Valentine's Day as I take my seat. That's the first friendly thing he's said all week.

"Nice hat." It's red, of course. I didn't figure him as the type to dress according to holiday, especially a mushy holiday.

We're copying overhead transparencies about the food pyramid today. It's silent work and it doesn't take long for note passing to start.

Who's your imaginary boyfriend today? Harper writes on the torn corner of his page. I can see him smirking out of the corner of my eye.

You're in a good mood today, I write back.

He hesitates before writing: *Who would be unhappy on a holiday that involves excessive amounts of sugar consumption?*

Because junk food is what you need. Don't you ever get tired of puking?

All the time, he writes.

You're in remission?

Yeah.

How long?

I see Jem tap his fingertips on the lab table one after the other. He's counting.

Forty-nine days.

Damn. That's barely longer than I've been back in Smiths Falls.

Jem: February 14 to 22

Friday

Basketball season is almost over, but the boys' and girls' varsity teams are holding an exhibition game in the gym as part of a fundraiser. I'm not sure what it's for—I didn't read the posters—but the proceeds are going to whichever disease, natural disaster, or impoverished country they've chosen to take pity on.

During lunch period the basketball teams put on their uniforms and set up a ticket/donations table in the lunchroom. I get to the cafeteria just in time to see Elise being canvassed by one of the seniors she was openly ogling the other day. I hope it isn't too late for her to avoid putting her foot in her mouth.

I head over to the fundraiser table to save Elise from herself. I don't know the guy she's talking to, but he's really tall, which makes her seem even shorter and me feel more protective of her. I watch them exchange money for game tickets and kick myself. If she doesn't embarrass herself here, she will at that game.

"Hang onto the stubs, 'cause the girls' team is holding a draw for door prizes. Doors open at six-thirty, game starts at seven."

Elise nods along with wide-eyed wonder like he's telling her the secrets of the universe. He politely pretends not to notice her stare.

"Yeah, so, we're selling tickets at the door, too, so bring your family, friends… girlfriend?"

Elise's intense smile disappears. I push past Chris shit-for-brains Elwood and try to grab Elise's arm, but she darts away before I can. The basketball player looks a little horrified, watching her run away in tears.

"Dude," is all I can say to him. I turn to follow Elise. She has a good head start, and I hope she hasn't gone into the girls' bathroom or some other place where I can't get to her.

Her ego is going to be bruised for weeks. If that guy she likes thinks she's gay, there's no way he's interested in her, and Elise isn't going to take that well. And that stereotyping jerk had to blurt out his assumption in front of a group of people—I can already hear what uncreative taunts they'll have for her by Monday morning. It's not like her hair will grow to out by then. I'm sure that's why he thought she was a lesbian. Why else would a girl have such short hair, right?

I feel even worse because it's my fault her hair is short to begin with. She collected sponsorships to shave her head last fall and donated the money to cancer research projects. Girly little Elise wouldn't have done anything like that unless someone close to her had cancer—me.

I find her curled up on the backseat of Eric's car, holding her knees and crying. She's locked all the doors.

"Open up." I tap on the window and she gives me the finger.

"Come on, open up. I'll take you for ice cream or something." That's the universal comfort food for girls, right?

"Go *away!*"

I give her some time and space to calm down, but when I return to the car after fourth period, she's still sitting in the back seat. She only opens the door when I suggest that we cut classes for the rest of the day and go home early. When Mom and Dad come home they find us on the couch in the den, watching *Harry Potter*. They take one look at Elise—full Hogwarts uniform, round glasses, wand in hand—and say, "Bad day, sweetie?"

Saturday

I wake up to find Elise in my room, standing in front of my closet mirror with one of my hats on.

"What are you doing?"

She tugs the toque off and her hair sticks up in all directions. We both inherited that unfortunate genetic trait. "Do you think it would look good if I dyed my hair blonde?"

"No. You'd get called a blonde ditz all the time and your Harry Pothead costume would look even dumber."

"Only if I kept wearing Gryffindor colors." She twists a short lock of her hair around her finger, frowning. "Maybe I'll dye it red like yours."

"What the hell do you mean, like mine?"

Elise huffs. "You're so sensitive."

"Put my hat back where it belongs."

I roll over and drop the pillow over my head to broadcast 'go away.' It doesn't work. A few seconds later I feel the mattress dip as Elise climbs on.

"Forget dyeing it," she says. "Maybe I should go with extensions."

"Elise, you seem to be laboring under the delusion that I am your sister. If you want to talk about girly shit like your hair, go to Mom."

"But Jemmy," she whines, and flops down on the pillows next to me. "Mom's busy. And you're honest."

I hold the pillow tighter over my face to muffle my groan. "Don't get extensions. Your hair's too short; it'll look like shit."

I shouldn't have encouraged her. She snuggles up to me and asks more of my opinion. "Maybe I'll just dye the front part? I could do something edgy like blue."

"Or you could act your age and get a boyfriend." She makes injured puppy sounds at that. Elise has mastered the art of being the spoiled youngest child. She can play us all like violins.

"Sorry."

"But while we're on the subject, you could use a girlfriend."

I yawn. "Yeah, right. Know anyone interested in emaciated bald guys?"

"Your personality is the bigger turn-off," she says, patting my head. Fucker.

✎

I get up and take a shower as an excuse to make Elise leave me alone. A big day of nothing stretches in front of me. The school dance is tonight, but hell if I'm going. It'll be a quiet evening without Elise for once.

By the time I get out of the shower I can hear *Harry Potter* playing downstairs. I need to get out of here. I get dressed and ask to borrow Mom's car.

"Where are you going?"

"Visiting some friends."

I can see *what friends?* written on her face before Eric tactfully blurts it out.

"School friends."

"Did you grow this friend in a petri dish in Bio?"

I take off my shoe and throw it at him.

"Eric, that's enough."

"He threw a shoe at me!"

Mom gives me a disapproving look, but she's been prone to letting my shenanigans slide since I got sick. I get off with just an apology to Eric, but I know he's going to mess with my stuff while I'm gone as payback.

Mom sighs and tells me to have the car back by seven. It's loaned to me on the condition that I drive Elise and her friends to the dance.

At first I just drive around Smiths Falls with no destination in mind. I stop at the store for a cup of yogurt, and then carry on driving around aimlessly. I end up sitting in the school parking lot, eating strawberry yogurt and watching the streamers for tonight's dance flap in the wind.

I really need to work on making some friends. I had a good group of friends back in Ottawa, before we moved. I haven't heard from Emily in awhile. Her emails have been sparse since Christmas. I guess I've fallen a few places on her priority list now that she has a boyfriend, whatever the hell his name is.

A girlfriend might be a good idea too. Not that Elise was right, or anything. It's just a thought.

Really? And how much would you pay her to pretend to be attracted to you?

Maybe I'll get lucky and find a blind asexual girl to go out with. Or maybe a chick with dementia that can't compare me to other guys and realize I'm rather inadequate.

When I get sick of my own thoughts I turn on the radio to fill the silence. "Ruby Tuesday" by the Stones is playing, and I'm reminded of Willa. Maybe I'll drop by unannounced to bother her again. I could make it a Saturday tradition, since I have nothing else to do with my weekends.

✎

When I get to the Kirk house, Willa is shoveling the driveway. She asks me what the hell I'm doing there and I ask her if she wants help clearing snow off the cars. She hands me a brush.

"You're not getting ready to drive to the dance, are you?"

"I don't do stuff like that."

"So what are you doing tonight?"

"Your mom."

I didn't know anyone over the age of ten still made 'your mom' jokes.

"No, really."

Willa shrugs. "Hanging out. Going down to Joe Moore's house tonight."

"What's at his house?" I thought Elwood was trying to get into her pants. Did I miss that dunce Moore's attempts to do the same? Does she keep turning down Elwood because she's into Moore?

"A small after party with people from school, and some of my friends from Port Elmsley."

"So you don't dance, but you'll go to an after party with the jackasses from school?"

"You visit a classmate you can't stand on a Saturday. You don't have anything better to do, do you?"

I toss the brush back to her and turn to leave.

"Harper."

"Piss off, Kirk."

"Do you want to come to the party tonight?"

I half-turn to look at her incredulously. That was one hell of a mood swing. One minute she's insulting me and the next she's inviting me out with her friends.

"What time?" Shut up, I'm lonely.

"Eleven."

"I'll meet you here and follow you."

"Fine."

When Mom hears that I made plans tonight, she offers to drive me. I think she just wants to see if I imagined the whole thing or if I'm telling the truth.

Three of Elise's friends are over. I can hear them giggling and chattering in her room as they get ready for the dance. Maybe it's not too late to convince Elise to wear a more modest dress. Or a tarp. And a chastity belt. And blinders so she can't ogle the seniors.

She comes downstairs with glitter in her spiked hair—seriously, *glitter*—and asks Mom to borrow some lipstick.

"What do you need lipstick for? It's just a school dance." Both Mom and Elise roll their eyes at me. Damn it all. I remember making mud pies with Elise and pulling her pigtails. Now she's getting all slutted up to go to a dance, and I'm chauffeuring her there. I should have bought a ticket so I could chaperone her, too.

"She's really growing up, isn't she?" Dad says when he sees the look on my face.

"Yeah. Is there a drug that can stop that?"

He laughs at me. "I know, it's hard. But she's lucky she's got two older brothers to look out for her."

Not that she makes it easy.

"How come you're not going to the dance?"

"Because it's dumb."

"You might try to have a little more fun, Jem," he tells me. "You're so serious. You'll get old before your time."

Too late.

⊖

I arrive to pick Elise up half an hour before the end of the dance and send a text to let her know I'm here. She doesn't answer, and I fidget impatiently. She'd better not make me late to meet Willa. Elise stays until the last possible second. By the time I get to Willa's house, she's already in her car, waiting for me. We exchange waves and then I follow her out of the neighborhood.

It's about a forty-minute drive to Joe Moore's house, adding the time spent on a detour. Willa heads toward Port Elmsley first and stops to pick up three teenage boys at a little white house nestled against the woods. I wonder if one of them is Luke.

It's eleven-thirty by the time we get to Moores' house. A few people are already there, sitting around the woodstove in the enclosed porch. Elwood waves to Willa through the wide porch window before either of us is even parked.

"Wait up."

Willa explains me to her friends as I make my way over. She introduces us— this *is* the mysterious Luke; he does exist—and we head inside. A few of the kids from Willa's lunch table are already here. I recognize Paige Holbrook, Hannah Whatever, and who could forget Chris shit-for-brains Elwood? The rest I know by face but not by name.

A boy with thick glasses whose name escapes me has brought a guitar. Bowls of chips are being passed around, and a few people are roasting marshmallows next to the wood stove. Willa, in typical weirdo fashion, has brought healthy food. She's got fruit, veggie sticks and hot cocoa in her backpack. She pulls out a second thermos and hands it to me with a spoon.

I'd be lying if I said I wasn't intrigued. Last time she cooked for me, I didn't eat anything else for three days. I open the thermos and steam rises up to meet me. This stuff smells good. It isn't the carrot and pea soup, but I do detect a hint of ginger in the aroma.

"What's in it?"

"Nothing you can't eat."

Good Lord, it's good. It's some sort of puree of broccoli and honey and a dozen other things I can't identify. I thank her between bites and she responds by slipping a folded piece of paper into my jacket pocket. I bet that's the recipe.

It's kind of nice being here, even though I don't know half the people. It's like being part of a group of friends again. Most of them don't look at me, as usual, because my appearance makes them uncomfortable. The only people who look at me and talk to me are Willa and her friend Luke, who doesn't seem to find anything out of the ordinary with my appearance. For the first time in a long time, I'm having fun.

Everyone is hungry after the dance, so the first part of the evening is spent snacking and roasting marshmallows. Paige Holbrook starts a game of Never-Have-I-Ever, and when that gets old What's-his-nuts brings out the guitar. He's not bad with that thing, but I still can't help wanting him to stop playing—the impromptu sing along has given Luke an excuse to cozy up to Willa's side and put a hand on her knee. She doesn't seem to mind. What is he, sixteen?

It isn't until well after midnight that the group concedes that the temperature has dropped too low to keep sitting on the enclosed porch, and we move inside. Paige suggests getting another group activity together soon. She proposes ice-skating and manages to get almost everyone on board.

Willa turns to me. "Care to join in, Harper?"

I shrug. "I might not feel up to it." There are a lot of things to consider, like what time of day they'll be going and how that will affect my stomach and energy level.

"You could meet us at the rink if we decide to go out after." She's trying, which is more than most people do for me, so I offer her a smile.

"I'd like that."

It's two o'clock in the morning by the time I get home. I walk in the front door to find Mom and Elise on the couch with hot chocolate, waiting up for me.

"You have a curfew young man," Mom says.

"Sorry." I lean over to give her a goodnight kiss and she less-than-subtly smells my jacket. I smell like smoke from the wood-burning stove, and I hurry to explain myself before she jumps to the more obvious conclusion.

"You really went out," she says with surprise. Always good to know she has faith in me. "Did you make friends?"

"Good night, Mom."

"Tell me what happened."

"*Good night*, Mom."

"Jem!"

Sunday

Sunday is sleep-in day at the Harper house. By the time I wake up the sun is shining across my bed and it's blissfully warm. I just lay there for a few moments, listening to the sounds of a sleeping house, before I bother to take stock of my body. When I do get around to it, I notice I'm hungry—that's been happening more and more this past week. My hand, as usual, has made its way into my pants of its own accord while I slept. The difference is, I wake up hard today. Last time that happened, there were still Halloween decorations around town. I smile and start to move my hand. This has got to be my favorite sign of recovery.

I miss this, is my first thought, right before I notice that it doesn't feel the same as it used to. I keep moving my hand, varying strokes and pressure, but there's no build. The sensation never gets more intense. The urge to come never arrives, and after five minutes of pumping fruitlessly my erection starts to wilt in my hand.

"Come on, you bastard."

Mom knocks on the door. The jig is up. So much for starting the day on a high note.

"Sweetie? Do you want breakfast?"

At least I've got a new soup recipe from Willa. That's sort of a positive start to the day. I still would have preferred an orgasm.

Monday

I think about sitting with Willa's crowd at lunch, even though it involves Chris bullshit-extraordinaire Elwood. But I do need to work on the whole 'friends' thing, and everyone was pretty cool on Saturday. They weren't outright repulsed by me, anyway. Maybe with time they'll get used to the elephant that follows me into every room, and I can be part of a social group again.

You know, I think I saw a flying pig out back.

Oh shut up, you.

You mean me?

I'm not having this argument with myself.

I follow behind Willa and her friends, keeping a bit of distance. Maybe I'll just go up to them once they've found a table and ask if this seat is taken. Or maybe that will make them feel guilty and obliged to tolerate my presence. Should I just sit down and let them make what they will of it?

As I'm debating this they find a table. I look around for a seat to occupy, but they're all full.

So much for that.

I turn and make my way toward Elise's table, trying to make it look like I'm not retreating. When I sit down Elise gives me a strange look. She thought I would sit with other people today too. I just shake my head and turn to my Jell-O cup, and she—mercifully—lets it slide.

⬥

You're an idiot, Harper.

  Why'd I want to be friends with her anyway? She's a bitch.

She's sort of hot.

  That's enough out of you.

Like it matters, limp-dick.

  Shut up.

She only invited you along to screw with your head.

  She's not totally incapable of being nice.

Look! The pig flew by again!

Willa spares me from my mental dialogue by pulling her chair back from the table loudly. She sits down with a nod hello and opens her books.

"Why'd you invite me to hang out with your friends?"

Now would also be a good time to blurt out that you're failing three of four classes and can't get it up, moron. Go on, share with the class.

Willa looks at me calmly. "Why do you think?"

"You like this snippy banter, don't you? On some level you enjoy hanging out with me because you get to be wittier than you can be with any of the other cretins in this place."

She smirks. "I felt sorry for you. Dude, you showed up at my house with nothing better to do than help me shovel snow. Come on."

I could have guessed that. But I didn't want to.

"That's some bit of brutal honesty."

"True friends stab you in the front."

I bet she thinks it makes her witty to quote Wilde's platitude. It disgusts me almost as much as her statement confuses me.

"We're not friends."

"If you say so."

"I take it back."

She laughs. "You're pathetic."

"You're not friends with pathetic people?"

"I'd be willing to make an exception, as long as there's a good reason why we should be friends."

I bite the inside of my cheek as I turn that over in my head. Brutal honesty might actually work here. "Because I'm lonely."

Willa smiles just slightly. Then she shakes her head. "Not good enough."

"Books open to page 245, class," Mrs. Hudson announces over the chatter. "I've got an in-class assignment for you today. All the info you need to answer the questions is on that page."

46

Assignment papers begin to circulate from the front of the room.

I turn to Willa. "Think about it? Please?"

She drops her voice to a murmur. "I think it's a bad idea. You don't really want to be friends with someone like me." Well, that's a convenient way of phrasing rejection.

"Why not?" Go on; tell me off to my face.

"Because I kill people like you."

Now that I didn't expect.

⤙⤚

That conversation distracts me for the rest of the day. I barely absorb a word of my English lecture. I wonder what she meant when she said she kills 'people like me.' What kind of people? Cancer patients? Flagrant assholes? She can't have been speaking literally. It bothers me so much that I can't let her leave school without confronting her. I follow Willa to her car after English and tap on the driver's side glass.

She rolls down the window. "What do you want, Harper?"

"It doesn't matter. I'm living like I'm already dead."

Willa smirks like I've said something funny. "Why me? There are plenty of nicer people in this school. Why not ask them to be your friends?" She gestures to the throngs of students milling around the parking lot.

"Because you're not scared to look at me."

I can't read the look on her face. Is she impressed?

"Get in."

⤙⤚

The Kirk kitchen still seems cryptically bare. Willa whips up a soup made of asparagus and chickpeas that tastes fantastic.

"Where'd you learn to cook like this?"

"My grandma."

"The one whose birthday was on Saturday?"

Willa doesn't bother to contradict the lie. "Yeah. She's a good cook. I made a lot of soup for my sister before she died."

Now I feel like a jerk for bringing it up.

"I'm sorry."

Willa shrugs. She doesn't seem upset that I've touched that topic. Maybe it's been so long that she's in a comfortable place with her grief.

"When did she die?"

"Two years ago. Cancer." Willa gets up and opens the cupboard next to the fridge. There are a few cookbooks in there, but she pulls out a binder and sets it on the table. The cover has her name on it. It's full of pages torn out of other

47

cookbooks and recipe clippings from magazines and newspapers. She stops on a recipe I recognize—the carrot and pea soup—and points to the title on the page header. She tore that page out of *Living with Cancer: Diet and Nutrition*. She's been serving me her sister's cancer food. That's so genuinely kind and accommodating I don't know what to say without sounding stupid.

"Were you guys close?"

"Not really. She was nine when I was born. We got closer after her diagnosis."

"Smoker?"

"Yep."

Willa gets up for another serving of soup. I wonder what it tastes like to someone with a strong stomach and functional taste buds.

"So are you ever going to tell me what kind of cancer you had?"

"Some other time."

For once, Willa leaves it without prodding.

Tuesday

We have a work period for the term project in Social Studies, but nerdy Willa has ensured that we're ahead of the game, so there's not much work for us to do. We fill the time by playing X's and O's on her notebook cover. Her gloves are yellow today.

"Do you ever take those off?"

"Sure," she says, and leaves it at that. "Are you eighteen yet?"

"Yeah. You?"

Willa asks me for my birth date—January tenth—and rolls her eyes at my answer.

"What?"

"We share a birthday."

I'm too competitive to let that slide, so I question her until we determine that I'm actually six hours older than she is. And I'll never let her forget it.

"So how old is your brother?"

"Damn it," she says as I win another tic-tac-toe match. "He's twenty-five."

"Is he a step-brother or were you an accident?"

"Shut up. At least I don't have Middle Child Syndrome." Willa gives me the eye.

"What's that supposed to mean?"

"How old are your siblings, anyway?"

I'm not happy about having my question dismissed, but settle for coming back to it later. "Eric is nineteen; doing a victory lap because he couldn't decide about university. Elise will be seventeen soon."

"So did she cut her hair short like that or did she have cancer too?"

"No, she shaved her head to raise funds for cancer research."

"What kind of research?"

"Research for a cure. Duh."

"No, what kind of cancer?"

"Kirk," I scold her. She wins her first match. The score is still ten to one in my favor.

"Do you have any hair at all under that hat?"

"Inappropriate question."

"Did you shave it before treatment? Or did you wait for it to dry out and fall away on its own?"

"Jesus, Kirk."

"Am I being too forthright?"

"Nosey is what it is."

"My sister had me shave her head," Willa says with a fond smile. "She had long, thick black hair. Barely even waited for it to thin; just invited me into the bathroom and handed me a razor."

"Creepy."

"Nah." Willa shakes her head. "She was still beautiful."

Wednesday

I'm washing the supper dishes with Eric when Mom comes into the kitchen with the cordless phone in her hand. She looks at me as if she's seriously concerned and says, "The phone is for you."

"Who is it?"

"It's a *girl*." Again, it's good to know Mom has faith in me. Eric sniggers at her surprise. I dry my hands and take the phone into the other room.

"Hello?"

"Hey. How's my partner?"

"Fine. Why are you calling?"

"We need to set a time to work on phase two of the term project. You told your mom you chose her snapdragons, right? She isn't going to catch us digging up her plants and freak out?"

"Yeah, I told her." I should really tell her.

"You free Saturday?"

"No, Kirk, my weekends are fully booked."

"Two o'clock?"

"Make it two-thirty."

"Address?"

Thursday

When I walk into the cafeteria I see Elise's friends huddled near the food line, giggling and whispering conspiratorially. What the hell? I find Elise at the usual table, talking to a senior. It's the guy she's been crushing on—the one who embarrassed her and made her cry. He'd better be apologizing.

Elise's friends practically hiss at me not to interrupt as I make my way over. I want to hear what this jackass has to say. I hear Elise giggle and realize they're having a pleasant conversation.

"Hey." I pull out a chair and sit across from her. Elise gives me a not-so-subtle 'go away' signal. Nice try.

"Well, I should get going," Douchebag says. He sounds uncomfortable. Maybe my stare bothers him. Or maybe it's the aura of death that people perceive around me.

Elise gets this panicked look on her face. "Oh…okay. Maybe I'll talk to you again sometime?"

Desperate, much?

"Sure. I'll see you around."

Elise turns right around in her chair to watch him leave. She only turns back to the table when he's taken a seat across the room with his friends.

"You're such a jerk." She kicks me under the table.

"Jesus, Lise." That's going to bruise.

"Why'd you have to go and ruin it? He was actually *talking* to me."

"Did he apologize for calling you a dyke?"

Elise growls and kicks me again.

"I'm just looking out for you."

"Well knock it off! You never want me to meet anybody or have any fun."

Now that the senior is gone, Elise's friends descend upon the table and demand to know every single detail of what was said. Their chatter derails our conversation, and I leave to go sit with Willa and Co. Elise and I will talk later. We each know where the other lives.

Friday

Today at lunch I try eating something other than soup, yogurt or Jell-O: a cup of tapioca pudding from the cafeteria cooler. It goes down okay, but my stomach starts to hurt by the end of the period.

"Don't piss me off today," I tell Kirk as she sits down at the table. "Or I'll readily puke on you."

"You can do it on cue?" she says with false admiration. She turns off the smartass and offers me a mint to suck on.

"Why did you come to class? Just go to the nurse's office if you're feeling sick."

I would, but then I'd miss the only part of my day where I get to have conversations with someone who isn't a member of my immediate family. I can't tell her that, of course. It would over-inflate her sense of self-worth.

And make you look pathetic.

"I don't want to deprive you of the chance to guess what I had for lunch."

"You're such an ass." She shakes her head and turns her attention to her work.

After five minutes, I've sucked my mint down to nothing and I ask her for another one.

"That was my last."

"What good are you?"

She casually elbows me in the side, and that slight jab is enough to make me gag. As I lean over the sink at the back of the room, I regret that I didn't aim for Willa instead. That would teach her.

Saturday

Willa's car is in desperate need of a new muffler. I can hear her coming from the end of the block. She's right on time. I can't believe I'm about to let that snarky bitch into my house. Mom had better not embarrass me. She works mostly from home, and even though it's two in the afternoon she's probably still in sweats with three or four drafting pencils sticking out from her ponytail.

I subtly close her office door as a preemptive measure, and then go to open the front door before Willa can ring the bell and tip Mom off to the presence of company.

"Nice house," Willa says by way of greeting.

"Thanks. Nice shirt."

"Stop staring at my tits, Harper."

"Easy. There's hardly anything to stare at." That makes her laugh. It's sort of nice that she can take a joke about her own body. I'm still trying to train Elise to do that. Over-sensitive teenage girls are annoying.

Who can't take a joke about their body?

    Oh shut up.

"The snapdragons are in the kitchen." I lead the way through the front room, down the hall towards the kitchen and our project planters. We pass by a row of family photos and Willa stops by one. It's the only picture of *before* that Mom wouldn't let me temporarily take down: the last one before we left Ottawa, when we went for an outing as a family. Elise had long hair then, and Eric's idea of an appropriate pose for a family photo had been to pretend to crush her like the Hulk.

Willa gapes at the photo. "You're a ginger?"

"Kirk."

"Oh you poor, soulless bastard."

I grab her by the upper arm and tow her away. I drag her into the kitchen and deposit her on one of the stools facing the island. "Stay."

"Do you treat all women like dogs?"

"Only the bitches."

I sit down and open my textbook. I've taken Mom's snapdragon planters away from the windows for this and lined them up along the island. We've got three pots of soil to play with; more if we separate the plants even further. The goal is to construct a microcosm of pollution before we compare it to actual pollution in the area. We have to do the math for our hypothesis and projections before we can decide how to violate the soil and in what order. I term that process 'plant raping' and Willa asks if tampering with the seeds counts as child molestation.

Elise overhears the question and stops in front of the kitchen door. "What are you talking about?" she demands shrilly.

"Church."

"*Jem.*" She stamps her little foot.

"Go away."

She gives me and Willa this narrow look and traipses into the kitchen to get a snack with conspicuous slowness. About halfway she gives up on giving me a dirty look and simply glares at Willa.

"Call me if you want milkshakes," she says, and with her current expression even the kind offer sounds like a threat. I smirk and thank her and tell her to get the hell out.

"Sorry," I say when she's out of earshot. "Elise is…protective."

Willa nods. "She knows I'll kill you."

Willa: February 22 to 28

Saturday

The Harper house has a pretty sweet setup. I guess they're affluent, him being a doctor. The house shows signs of being newly built. It's missing some of the final touches on the exterior, and the interior fixtures are still shiny with newness.

I fall in love with their kitchen the minute I see it. Granite countertops, a huge fridge, an island with a separate sink, cupboard space that goes on forever, and a gas range that looks pristine. They have a dishwasher too! If I lived here I would never leave this room. I have to focus on homework to keep from gawking at their appliances—their toaster looks high-tech enough to launch its own space program.

Jem and I are narrowing our hypotheses when a tall woman with black hair and more pencils than hands comes down the hall toward the kitchen. Three of these pencils are sticking out of her hair, one is behind her ear and another juts out of her pocket. She yells, "Are you kids getting hungry?" up the stairs, and when she turns she jumps at the sight of me.

"You didn't tell me we had company," she scolds Jem.

"She doesn't count. Just pretend she's part of the chair."

"It's nice to meet you. I'm Willa Kirk." I lean over the island and hold out my hand to shake. Mrs. Harper has a writer's bump the size of a grape.

"Call me Ivy. Would you like a sandwich?"

Ivy declines any help to make sandwiches for an afternoon snack, but watching her go about it, I notice that she's sort of scatterbrained. She loses her butter knife three times and mixes up what kind of sandwich she's making for whom, but blunders through it with a smile on her face.

"Mom's got a one-track mind," Jem says. "Architecture and nothing else."

"Oh hush," she scolds him fondly. She slides a sandwich to me across the island. "What are you guys working on?"

"Soc project."

Ivy's eyes go wide. "So *you're* his partner. We've heard so much about you."

"Really?" I look at Jem out of the corner of my eye. He's concentrating awfully hard on his homework, but he still looks ready to die of embarrassment.

"You're the one with all the soup recipes, right?"

"That's me."

On that note, she invites me to work magic in her fantastic kitchen. I don't even care that I'm making cancer food for my project partner—she has Wusthof knives! And her blender isn't missing a blade! And good Lord, you could store five dead penguins in that fridge!

"It's very irresponsible of you to distract a dedicated student, Mom," Jem says. He's still bent over our term project.

I give him a look of warning. "Don't you dare kill my buzz."

53

"Are you tired, honey?" Ivy puts a hand on Jem's forehead. He leans away from her and insists he's fine.

"Your sister and her buddies are going to a basketball game tonight. I was going to get you or Eric to take her, but if you're not feeling well…"

"I'll take her," Jem declares firmly. There's an edge of something like panic in his tone.

"Is she an avid basketball fan?" I ask.

"This week," Ivy says with a laugh. "She's trying to define herself."

Jem mutters something under his breath about hippies. He watches me from under lashless lids as I pour cooked vegetables and seasoning into the blender to puree. "What's in this one?"

"I'll tell you after you eat it." People carry far too many prejudices about food. They like much more than they think they do, if they don't know what they're eating.

"I can't believe he wants to eat," Ivy says with a smile. She pinches her son's side playfully and tells me that he's put on three pounds. Jem's face flushes with a patchy blush of embarrassment. What does Ivy expect me to say? *Three pounds? Really? What does he weigh now, ten altogether?*

I slide a bowl of spinach soup his way and he mutters, "Thank you."

For some reason, Jem is really eager to drive Elise and her friends to the basketball game at the school tonight. They've been doing fundraising for this thing all week. The donations are going toward literacy projects in Africa.

"Mind if I tag along?"

"Fine, whatever," he answers distractedly. "Go put on a sweater," he barks at Elise.

"I'm not hot." February is pretty early in the year to be wearing a tank top and short shorts.

"I'm not taking you out like that."

"It's the only thing I have in our school colors."

"Mom! Tell Elise to put on a sweater!"

I sneak out the front door and head to my car. I'll meet them at the game.

When Jem, Elise, and two of her friends arrive at the school, she's wearing a sweater and he looks thoroughly annoyed. I wave and they make their way up the bleachers to the row of seats I've staked out for us.

I'm not a big basketball fan. I'm just really, really bored with small town life. And four dollars of my ticket price goes to illiterate kids living in poverty, so why not?

"Who the hell are you waving at?" Jem demands of his sister. It's hard to believe, but I think he might be an even bigger jerk to her than he is to me.

"You don't know him."

"Him?"

"Number twenty-three," her friend says slyly. Elise elbows her. Jem and I both start looking around for number twenty-three. He's the guy with blond hair that is in desperate need of a trim and has the captain's armband around his bicep.

"Latham?" Jem reads off the back of his jersey.

"I told you that you didn't know him."

"What's his first name?"

"Kipp."

"His parents gave him a dog's name?"

"You're so mean," Elise says with a pronounced pout. "Just stop talking. No one wants to hear your negativity."

I laugh and Jem starts sulking.

It's an exhibition game for charity, which means there isn't a lot in the way of actual game play. The boys' and girls' varsity teams are playing each other, but their plays consist of poking fun at the other side. Occasionally a few of the cheerleaders step in for players on either team, only to switch sides without warning. Whenever someone scores, the sound crew blasts music through the overhead speakers and the scoring team has to do a ten second victory dance. Cheating is encouraged. At one point there are two balls in play, and the ref hands out penalties in the form of entertaining punishments. Lucy Walker's penalty is to crab-walk around the court to the sound of Depeche Mode, courtesy of a sadistic sound crew. This might have actually been worth the five bucks.

Jem tries to hustle us out of the gym immediately after the game. I'm in no hurry and neither are Elise and her friends.

"Let's hang out awhile," she says. The sound crew is still playing upbeat music and the fundraising people are walking around with bins to collect additional last-minute donations.

"No. Come on, let's go."

"Just wait," I say. "The parking lot is going to be chaos anyway."

He sulkily returns to his seat. Elise says she's going to use the restroom.

"Shit," Jem mutters as she skips away down the bleacher stairs.

Elise takes a pretty circuitous route to the washroom, stopping to say hello and congrats to a few of the players first. Particularly the captain of the boys' team. From this range it looks like she's trying to flirt. She's laughing too hard and 'casually' touches his sweaty arm.

"Great, she's never going to wash that hand again," Jem says.

"Is that why you gave her a hard time tonight? She likes that guy?"

"She's obsessed," Elise's mousy little friend (whose name I can't remember) interjects. "Like, *obsessed.*"

"Like, more than she is with Harry Potter," the other chimes in.

Jem leans back in his seat and rests his feet on the empty row of chairs in front of us. "You're so lucky you don't have younger siblings."

Sunday

When I wake up, Frank is gone and there's a note on the fridge about snowmobiling with his buddies. I check the contents of the fridge and find all the lunchmeat and four of the rolls gone. He plans to be away all day, then. I shower, set up my homework at the kitchen table, and turn on the TV for background noise.

Trigonometry blows. I'm saved from problem four, which looks more like a riddle to the universe than a math problem, by the phone. I lean back in my chair and grab the handset off the wall.

"Kirk residence."

"Willa?"

"Oh no."

"Bad time?"

"I'm doing math."

"So you won't mind being disturbed." I can hear Jem's smirk over the phone. I'm going to become rich and famous after I invent a device that allows you to remotely punch people in the face.

"What do you want, Harper?"

"My mom told me to call you. She wants to invite you over for lunch."

"To cook or to eat?"

"Both."

Hmm, another day in Jem's company…but his mom has a KitchenAid mixer.

"Yeah, alright."

I show up at the Harper house with a few recipes folded in my pocket. Ivy lets me in and we go to her kitchen to start lunch. This house just exudes intelligence, from the prints on the walls to the classical music playing in the background. Ivy gives me free reign over the fridge and cutting boards.

Today's recipes are a protein-heavy soup for Jem, and spanakopita with goat cheese tartlets for those of us with adequate stomach strength.

"What kind of dough do you use?" Ivy asks. She seems to genuinely interested in everything people say to her. It's sort of nice. And her short attention span for everything non-architectural means that conversation is pleasantly varied.

We set up the sheets of phyllo dough in a minimuffin tray. Ivy fills them with goat cheese, feta, cherry tomato, and rosemary with balsamic vinaigrette. Meanwhile, I boil down beef stock for Jem's soup. I try not to feel relieved that I haven't seen him yet. Too much happiness tempts the Fates.

Ivy and I are portioning goat cheese and feta into little pieces when the classical music falters and then re-starts. I thought it was a CD playing somewhere else in the house, but now I think it's a real person playing. It must be—I only hear a piano.

We have a bit of a wait while the spanakopita bakes and the soup continues to simmer, so we start to clean up the kitchen.

"It's so nice that Jem has a friend like you," Ivy says as we load the dishwasher. "He had a hard time making friends when we moved here, being out of school so often."

His attitude can't have helped any.

"He's in the living room," she continues. "Why don't you go say hi before lunch?"

She directs me down the hall towards the living room—which, I'm given to understand, is different from their 'front room.' This house goes on forever. I wonder if Ivy designed it.

I peek around the doorframe and see Jem sitting at an upright piano with his back to me. It's an old instrument, the kind that looks like it's been handed down a few generations. The scrollwork on it is beautiful and the restoration isn't bad. The innards of the piano are obviously newer than its exterior, because the sound quality is pristine for an upright.

For a complete asshole, Jem plays notably well. The light, mellow song doesn't match my idea of Jem Harper, smartass extraordinaire.

I tiptoe into the living room. He doesn't notice me until I sit down next to him on the bench, and then he startles so badly he jumps back and strikes six different keys at once.

"What are you doing, sneaking around like that?" he demands.

"I'm not sneaking. You're just oblivious."

He glares at me and begins to pack up the sheet music he was using.

"You don't have to stop."

"I'm done."

I'm in a taunting mood, so I use three fingers and pluck out a simple version of the *Addams Family* theme song. Jem threatens to slam the key cover down on my fingers.

"I didn't know you played."

"Yeah, well, you don't know me that well, do you?" He's on the defensive, and I know from experience that this will quickly descend into a sulk fest.

"How long have you been playing?"

"A while." He tries to close the key cover but I hold it open.

"Show me."

"No."

I have some knowledge of music that I picked up at work, which my boss would teach me during the slow hours. But that was just guitar, and I never owned my instrument. I know even less about how to play the piano. I know part of one song, and that's it, and I only memorized the finger placement, not the notes.

I start to pluck out my homely little song and Jem frowns. My left hand doesn't want to cooperate. After a minute he pinches my ring finger and moves it over to the next key. My incompetence must irk him.

"Bach is rolling over in his grave right now."

"This is Bach?"

Jem shakes his head at me. He can't resist my blundering forever. After a few minutes he starts to play along with me. His version sounds better.

"Lunch smells good," he says quietly. I do believe that might have been a compliment.

"Don't do that. When you're nice it screws up the whole dynamic of this friendship."

Jem snorts with amusement. He does that a lot. I bet his full-blown hysterical laugh is just a series of increasingly obnoxious snorts.

"It's a new soup today," I tell him. He smiles with genuine pleasure. "Lots of protein. See if you can't gain another three pounds."

Jem's smile fades to a look of chagrin. "Oh shut up," he mutters.

"How much do you weigh?"

"Inappropriate question."

It's almost time to take the tartlet shells out and check the soup. I slowly stop playing and take my hands off the keys.

"I gotta get back to the kitchen."

"'Kay." He doesn't look up when I leave the bench and walk away. He just keeps playing Bach much better than I ever could. I'm almost at the door when he stops suddenly and calls my name—my first name.

I stop and turn halfway.

"One-eighteen."

I don't say anything. I don't even nod. He turns back to his piano, and I turn back to the kitchen. Between the two of us there's a six-inch height difference, but the weight difference is barely the mass of a healthy newborn.

Ten minutes later, we all sit down to lunch. The food is a big hit—even the soup.

While we eat Jem condescends to tell me, "Ten years for piano, eight for cello."

Now, was that so hard?

Monday

I visit Oma after school. We bake cookies, and it feels just like being five years old again, only this time I'm tall enough to reach the mixer. I bring a plate of cookies home to share with Frank. Before he even takes one bite he pauses and looks at me suspiciously.

"Why do you smell like smoke?"

"I was at Oma's house."

Frank eyes the cookie in his hand. "Are you sure? These aren't *special*, are they?"

"Do they smell like weed? I don't do that anymore."

I can't fault him for being on his guard, but it still annoys me to be questioned like a delinquent.

"Sorry." He shrugs. "You've been all right so far, I guess. Your school hasn't called me yet, so…"

I have the urge to lower his expectations by telling him that it's only a matter of time.

Tuesday

I try to volunteer at least once a week, and the hospital is my first choice of locations. I go to the volunteer station in the hospitality office to grab my green vest and check in with the coordinator. For the past few weeks I've been assigned to read books to the kids on the pediatric floor, which is great as far as I'm concerned. I'd much rather do that than push the squeaky book cart along the other wards. I might run into Jem again and have to deal with his bad attitude in class.

I step into the elevator to go up to pediatrics. On the second floor the doors open and none other than Dr. Harper steps on. He's scrolling through his Blackberry and doesn't immediately notice me. I don't say anything because he looks busy. Dr. Harper is the kind of person that looks permanently pinched until he smiles. I have to look very hard to find a trace of Jem in him.

We both get off on the fourth floor. It looks like a clean break free of awkwardness, until he notices me out of the corner of his eye.

"Willa?"

"Hi, Dr. Harper."

"I didn't know you were a volunteer."

"Yeah. I'm on my way to Pediatrics."

He smiles and says the more he hears about me the better I seem. When the hell has he heard about me? What has he heard?

Dr. Harper's phone beeps and we exchange a short goodbye before he hurries off to answer that emergency. I have half a mind to visit the Dialysis Clinic, just to see if Jem is in and to find out what he's been telling people about me.

Wednesday

If I ask Jem what he said about me, he won't give a straight answer. He'll dodge the question or insult me, and that's just counterproductive.

"Why are you looking at me like that?" he demands during Soc.

"I'm stealing your thoughts."

Jem leans in and stares right back, mocking me. Our noses are only an inch apart. His breath smells like mint and lime, and is surprisingly warm. I tend to think of Jem as cold—pale, anemically chilly hands, icy personality, etc. There are flecks of green in his blue irises.

"Hey, your eyelashes are growing back."

Jem rears away from me as though I've just spit in his face. He turns back to his work and rests the side of his face on his hand, blocking me from looking at him too closely.

"I saw your dad last night."

Jem peaks over his hand like he's afraid of what he'll hear.

"He seems to be under the impression that I'm a good person."

Jem smirks without humor and gives a soft snort. "My mom must have said something."

Yes, he is indeed behind it.

Thursday

It's entirely Luke's fault that I have to do yesterday's homework at lunch. I was doing it last night like a good student, and then he called. Two hours of conversation later, when I realized what time it was, it was far too late to get everything done.

I like talking to Luke. He's interesting and takes a genuine interest in people. Chris teasingly scolds me when he notices I'm doing math at the lunch table, and it's difficult not to flip him off. Paige takes this opportunity to arrange a study date with Chris. I wasn't aware that either of them was registered for practical Biology this semester, but I'm sure a little studying can't hurt.

I'm not making enough headway on this assignment. It's too loud in here, and I have to turn this in by the end of the day. I take my books out of the cafeteria and find a quiet place to work. I end up in the stairwell behind the auditorium, sitting on the floor and listening to closing doors echo above.

I've got twenty minutes to finish four more math problems. At five minutes each, I can probably get this done and make it to class on time.

The stairwell door opens from the auditorium and Jem sighs impatiently when he sees me. "Kirk."

"Harper." I move my books and papers to make room. He doesn't take a seat.

"I was looking for you."

"Okay."

"You know, most people work in the library."

"Okay."

Jem huffs. I think my non-answers irritate him. "Math homework?" he says stiffly.

My math textbook is clearly visible right next to me. "No, French."

Jem gives me that cocky smirk that I hate so much. He folds his arms across his chest, watching me.

"You got any plans this weekend?" he asks.

"My brother and I are supposed to spend time together tomorrow."

Frank has been feeling guilty about not spending enough time with me. Tomorrow we're supposed to go to the Thorpes' house for dinner, because even quality time with my brother can't be spent one-on-one. We have almost nothing to say to each other. I summarize my plans for Jem while I conclude another math problem.

"Friday isn't part of the weekend." His voice is a little tense. He follows that up with, "So do you go to Port Elmsley often?"

I shrug. What does 'often' really mean, anyway?

"Seriously, what are you doing this weekend?"

"If I tell you, I'd be taking all the effort out of stalking me."

Jem snorts wryly. He doesn't have a comeback, and we're silent for the time it takes me to complete another math problem. Jem picks up the completed pages of my assignment and looks them over.

"If you need more time for this, I can cover for you. I'll tell Hudson you went to the nurse's office or something."

"No, I'm almost done."

"But some of these are wrong."

I snatch the papers out of his hand. I don't need an A+ in math; I just need to pass with a decent grade. "Bugger off, Harper."

He doesn't. He rudely grabs the pencil right out of my hand before snatching my assignment back.

"You factored wrong." He erases the work for three problems and redoes them in an impersonation of my handwriting. It takes him just three minutes, and then he gives back the pages and puts back my pencil.

"See you in class."

"Thank you."

"You owe me."

I'm going to regret this.

Friday

I don't think the potato salad is going to make it to the Thorpes' house. Frank has been eyeing it all evening. We're heading to Port Elmsley at five to have dinner and spend the evening. There's probably a game on that Frank and Doug will watch. Mr. Thorpe will be there of course, and Luke's little sister Briana.

It's weird, but going to Port Elmsley feels more like going home than any place else; like Frank and I belong there, in the Thorpes' house. I was worried I wouldn't feel like that anymore when I decided to move back to Smiths Falls, but I'm glad I do.

Jokes about the appetites of teenage boys practically write themselves. Two burgers and six hotdogs later, Luke and I are in the kitchen washing dishes. ESPN is on in the other room, and Briana is blasting music upstairs. She's changed, just like her brother. Her clothes are pretty tight and her makeup is awfully heavy for a fourteen-year-old.

"Want to take a walk when we're done?" Luke says. "It's a full moon tonight. We might be early enough to see it rise."

We finish cleaning up and walk down to the edge of a ravine that runs behind the house. I can hear moving water down below; it hasn't completely re-frozen from the afternoon melt.

"How have you been?" Luke casually takes my hand and I slowly pull it away. It might be warmer with my little hand wrapped up in his big mitten, but I don't do hand-holding. Luke's brows draw together; it's the only outward signal that he's miffed.

"Better. I'm more settled at school now."

"Making friends?"

"I don't think I'm fit company for anyone just yet."

"Sure you are," Luke says, and shoves my shoulder—it's a little more than a playful push. He has no idea, and I don't feel like talking about it, so I change the subject. I tell him about my plans to apply for a job in town. He tells me about a recent pep rally at his school where a cheerleader fell off the stage. I remind him of the tentative plan to go skating, and that improves his tender mood.

"Let me know when."

Jem: March 2 to 9

Sunday

Around ten, I borrow Mom's car and drive over to Willa's house. Neither of the Kirks' cars is at the house, so I sit on the front porch and wait for her to get home. It's Smiths Falls on a Sunday, what could she possibly be doing that would take more than an hour? She's probably just at the grocery store or something. I don't immediately consider the possibilitiy that she might have made plans with other friends—especially the friend that lives in Port Elmsley, the one that thinks it's okay to touch her whenever he feels like it.

It starts to drizzle so I sit in the car instead and listen to music for a while. The clock slowly creeps closer to noon. Where the hell is she? Maybe she's out with her other friends, Paige Holbrook and Hannah Trilby and whoever else.

Not Chris Elwood, anyone but Elwood. Even that baby-face Luke is preferable.

I should go home. I can hang out with Elise and Eric and pretend I was never here at all.

When I get home I park Mom's car by the garage, get out, and stand there staring at Willa's car. She was here all along. Now I need a cover story for when she asks where I've been for the past two hours. I can't admit to a girl that I've been loitering on her porch all morning.

The house smells like sugar and warm chocolate. Mom is laughing in the kitchen and Elise is chirping away about something. I can't tell what because she talks so fast the words run together.

"Sothenhesaid—"

"C'mere, Jem," Mom says when she sees me, and offers a beater for me to lick. Willa is up to her elbows in flour, rolling out dough for cookies. It smells like Christmas in here. While she rolls and cuts, Elise is decorating the cookies with squeeze-tube icing and chocolate chips.

"Where were you?" Mom leans in to kiss my cheek. She smells like cinnamon.

"At the library."

"Sothenhesaid 'maybe I'll see you around' andIwaslike, 'okay' andhewaslike, 'cool,'" Elise continues to chatter in Willa's ear. Willa has her smirk on; I think she's sort of enjoying Elise's one-woman catastrophe.

"She got her crush's email address," Mom informs me, sotto voce. "They were chatting online."

Oh crap. There's a whole arena of interactive space where I can't watch over her and counsel her not to make a fool of herself.

Willa puts the last cookie cutouts in the oven and begins to clean up the counter. Elise is still talking.

"Imeanthat'scool, right? Iwas, like, justtryingtoplay, y'know, laidback or cool-orwhatever—"

"Yeah, wonderful," Willa agrees when Elise pauses for breath.

63

"You think so?"

"How old are you again?"

"I'll be seventeen in two weeks."

"And how old is he?"

"So do you think it's too…I don't know, *eager* for a girl to ask a guy out? Or should I just ask? Or is that too pushy?"

Willa looks at me helplessly and I try, once again, to sell Elise on the idea of the Order of St. Clare. "You'd make a really cute nun," I tell her.

She stamps her foot. "I am not a frigid lesbian!"

"Elise!" Mom scolds her. "Why don't you give Willa a tour of the rest of the house?" Mom says to me. She's just trying to break Elise and I up so I'll stop torturing her.

"I'm sure she's sick of the kitchen."

"Oh, never." Willa grins. It's weird.

"Come on." I get off the island stool and lead the way through the rest of the ground floor. "The bedrooms and the library are on the second floor."

"You have a *library*?" She says it as though I've just informed her that we have a dungeon.

"Yeah, it's sort of an all-purpose office space with lots of bookshelves."

"Can I see it?"

I'm leading the way upstairs when Willa stops on the third step and grabs my sleeve. Something outside has her attention. When I step down to look through the window I see Eric and Celeste in the backyard, making a snowman.

"Is that his girlfriend?" she asks.

I snort. Right, like those two would ever date. "Of course not. That's Celeste. She's down from Ottawa for the weekend."

"Is she your cousin or something?"

"Nah, she and Eric have been friends since kindergarten. Lord knows why."

"But they aren't dating?" Willa cocks her head to the side as if the situation is puzzling. What's so complicated about it? It's just Eric and Celeste, best friends, building a lopsided snowman with tits.

"She has a boyfriend in Ottawa."

Willa smirks. "That's nice."

"She's not."

Celeste and I have never gotten along. She thinks of herself as assertive, but in reality she's an aggressive harpy, which explains her entourage of frenemies back home. Celeste is one of those girls that other girls love to hate. She's got so much going for her: amazing body, brains to go with it, popularity, an affluent family, and a boyfriend that completes the image of upper-middle class perfection—key word being 'image.' Celeste has an empty life, but she still likes to rub it in everyone's faces.

I take Willa up to the library and she immediately gravitates towards the bookshelves. Eric's homework lays abandoned on one of the desks.

"Wow, it's really organized," she says of the shelves. All the books are grouped by subject: medicine, architecture, fiction, music, art, etc. Willa pulls down *The Canterbury Tales*. I don't think that book has been opened since Mom completed her English requirement as an undergrad.

"Do you like Chaucer?" she asks me.

Until she mentioned his name, I had no idea who wrote the book.

"He's okay."

"You seem like The Miller's Tale type."

"What's that supposed to mean?"

"I think you'd get the most pleasure out of laughing at those characters' stupidity and hedonism."

"I'm only an asshole from nine to five, you know."

"This totally is your kind of humor." She starts reading aloud from the book and I don't catch a word.

"Is that written in Elvish?"

Willa just smiles and shelves the book. "The cookies will be done soon."

Monday

Last summer, my first round of chemo turned me into a night owl. Between fatigue and nausea I felt best between midnight and four a.m., and Mom and I ended up sitting awake a lot, drinking tea and talking. She's been a chronic insomniac for years. She used to take sleeping pills for it, but she stopped when she had kids because she wouldn't wake up if we cried in the night. She had only been back on the drug for a few years when I got sick and she immediately quit again. She was terrified that something would go wrong in the night and no one would be able to wake her up. Sometimes she still takes them on the nights that Dad is home, but if he's on call or on night shift she goes without and stays awake.

We would sit in the kitchen—the farthest room from the bedrooms—and talk about stuff. She told me about how she almost switched her major from Architecture to Women's Studies as an undergrad.

"Give me a break," she said when I expressed my disgust. "I was young and idealistic. I grew up in the seventies, for crying out loud."

She told me about deciding to study for her Masters right before she got married, because she wanted to keep at least one area of her life open for new possibilities.

"I thought you and Dad got married when you were already working?" They were living in Ottawa at the time and Mom worked for Simons & Co.—I knew that for a fact—and she did her Masters in Toronto.

"Mmm-hmm." She sipped her tea. "I meant my first marriage." That was the first time that she ever mentioned being with anyone other than my dad. I couldn't picture it.

"We met through mutual friends," she said with a smile I couldn't read. "We started dating, and we dated some more, and the rest just sort of…happened. We were happy together, but the love was shallow."

"How old were you?"

"I was twenty-four."

"And then what happened?"

"Well, marriage is difficult," she said vaguely. Mom got up to pour herself another mug of tea and when she came back to the table she told me that her first husband—she didn't call him by name—had wanted her to drop out of grad school and get a full time job.

"I was only working part time, you see. And when I got pregnant he hounded me day and night to stop working and stay home. He had it in his head that he could boss me around now that we were married."

The latter half of her explanation was lost on me. I was hung up on the part where she got pregnant.

"Let's not tell your brother and sister about this conversation, all right?" she said when I asked about it. "My first husband and I had a little boy about two years after we got married." I scrambled to do the mental math. Given her age, that would have been three years before Eric was born. It floored me that I had a sibling that I never knew about, old enough to have finished university, possibly living in Toronto with his dad.

"He doesn't live in Toronto," Mom corrected me. "He's buried in Oakville, though." In less than three minutes she had informed me of the existence of a brother and then of his death. She said his name had been Eliot, and that he had died of SIDS just two months after being born, and the day after his burial she had filed for divorce.

"I celebrated you guys' second birthdays with such relief," she said. "I'd gotten you through infancy in one piece. I just didn't know that there were bigger problems waiting to come along."

She reached over and ran a hand through my thinning hair.

"I'm sorry, Mom."

She acted like she hadn't heard me.

⟷

Before I leave for school, I make Mom's favorite breakfast and leave it on her desk with a cup of coffee. She always gets up, goes into her office, and works for an hour or two before considering food or a shower. Today, she's getting taken care of.

Today's her firstborn's birthday. She doesn't know I know. It took me awhile to find out, going through online records of marriage licenses to find out her first married name, and then through birth announcements in the newspaper archives. There was even a picture. Eliot was a pretty cute kid. I think. All newborns look the same to me: pink and flat-nosed.

"What are you sucking up to Mom for?" Elise asks with a shrewd look as we get into the car to go to school.

"Nothing. Just a feeling."

"What feeling?"

"That she's going to have a hard day."

"What did you do, Jem?"

"Nothing."

"Whatever you did wrong, Mom's gonna find it. She has a sixth sense for bullshit," Eric says. He doesn't say it like a warning, more like he's gleefully anticipating my head on a platter by dinnertime.

"I didn't do anything."

"Yeah, right."

Tuesday

It's a blissfully sunny day in Smiths Falls, and unseasonably warm to boot. The sunshine perks everybody up and the warm weather means t-shirts for the optimists. I don't hold out hope that the sunshine will last until noon.

Willa shows up to school in a warm-weather skirt and tee—all black, of course, except for her forearm-length purple gloves. It's sort of weird to see her shins and arms.

"Aren't you hot in that?" she asks.

"No." Long sleeves work well for me in all climates, at least until I look human again.

Willa gets a lot of compliments on her outfit over lunch, both from the girls and from Elwood and Joey Moore. They both have dirty fantasies about the easy access that skirt offers written all over their faces. Just shoot me.

Willa reintroduces the topic of getting a group together to go skating. The rink is open for public skating tonight. Chris immediately accepts the invite.

"I'll pick you up at four," she says. I hate the way that sounds.

"Mind if I tag along?"

Willa shrugs. "Whatever."

Whatever? Maybe that's her polite way of telling me to piss off. Nah, she's probably willing to say that to my face. Willa is blunt like that. Still, 'whatever' is so dismissive…

"If you don't want me to go, I won't."

The other people at the table look down at their plates. They all secretly want to exclude me. This excursion is no different—Chris is going, which means Diane will go to see him break a limb (ideally all four) and Paige will tag along to worship him. Hannah might come, and Brian follows her around like a puppy. So where does Cancer Boy fit in?

"Don't be so sensitive, Harper," Willa tells me. "It's narcissistic and boring."

See? She really is that blunt.
　Shut up.

✧

After school, I ride back to the Kirk house with Willa. I'll carpool with her and Chris to the rink.

"Do you skate much?" she says as we drive to Chris's house.

"No, I'll probably end up watching. Do me a favor and make sure Elwood bruises something, okay?"

Willa rolls her eyes. "Designated Pessimist; got it."

I'm annoyed that she didn't explicitly promise that Elwood would end up injured.

Willa's car doesn't have a back seat, so when Chris gets in I have to slide over to the middle of the bench, which worsens Chris' mood. He has designs on Willa, and doesn't like Cancer Boy getting in the way.

You really need to stop referring to yourself in the third person. It's narcissistic and boring.
　At least she doesn't like him back.

Chris starts to talk about some TV show that neither of us has heard of, so Willa turns on the stereo the second he pauses for breath. Her car is so old that the sound system only plays cassettes and radio. "She's So Cold" by the Rolling Stones comes on. Perfect.

"You know this song?" Willa says when she sees me grinning. We both start to sing along with the chorus. Elwood doesn't know the words. That dipshit. He tries to talk during the instrumental bridge, so Willa turns up the volume and drums on the steering wheel. This chick is awesome when she's annoying someone who isn't me.

Chris is good and pissed by the time we arrive at the rink. Paige's car is already here, and Willa recognizes her friend from Port Elmsley's truck. We go our separate ways in the lobby—Chris to the changing benches, and Willa and I to the skate rental counter. Willa gets a pair of boy's hockey skates.

"Are figure skates a threat to your masculinity?" I ask as she pays the clerk.

Willa gives me the eye. "They squeeze the *balls* of my feet."

She takes her skates away to the benches before I have a chance to return the riposte. I'll get her back later.

Hannah and Paige are already on the ice, skating slow laps. They're talking to Luke and two of his friends. I'm sure I met them that night at Joey's house, but their names escape me. They're flirting with the girls, but not having much luck. Or maybe that's wishful thinking. Misery loves company.

Neither Willa nor Elwood wait for me to finish lacing my skates, but at least Willa tosses me a, "See you out there." She does a quick warm-up lap and skates over to Luke for a hello hug.

I'd hate to be Elwood right now—cold-shouldered by the chick he wants to move on and supplanted by Cancer Boy and a sixteen-year-old. Maybe he'll get struck by lightning, too.

I follow them into the ice. It feels indecently cold in here, so I push through a lap to warm up. It's still really freaking cold. I catch up to Willa and her friends, who have broken off into two groups: those that want a slow, leisurely skate, and those that want to race. I stick with the slow pokes, but eventually they all get into the racing spirit until it's just Hannah and me.

"You don't have to stay with me. I'm not very good at this," she says.

Hannah has had a few stumbles so far, but she hasn't fallen down. She seems to think that I'm skating with her out of pity, and I don't tell her that it's only because I'm in no condition to be tearing around a rink.

"You're doing great." I give her my arm to steady her. Hannah's hand feels awfully light on my elbow, as though she doesn't want to touch me too forcefully. She doesn't look at me either, but that could be because she's focused on staying upright on her skates.

As we glide along slowly, something occurs to me: no one is staring. It's been months since I could go out in public without getting curious looks from strangers. When everyone is bundled up in a cold rink, my hat doesn't stand out so much. I seem normal, unless the other patrons look closely enough to notice my lack of eyebrows, not that any of them do.

"Cold?" Hannah can feel me shivering.

"One more lap."

I'm not ready to let go of my pretend normalcy yet. Up ahead of us, Elwood sneaks up on Paige and grabs her around the waist. He fails to see the six-year-old in front of her, though, and they both fall down in an attempt to avoid bumping the kid. Elwood lands on his shoulder and lays there whining and crying like a baby. That's going to make it really hard for Paige to worship him.

Why am I surrounded by sluts and morons?

Paige volunteers to take Elwood in for x-rays. He's convinced that he broke his 'shoulder bone.' He clearly has no idea what he's talking about and the fact that he keeps repeating it is embarrassing.

As soon as Paige and the moron drive away, everyone drops the somber act and starts making plans. Joey suggests a trip to the diner around the corner for an early dinner. Willa declines to go. There's no point hanging out with these people if she isn't around, so I pass on the invite as well.

"Are you okay with driving me home? I can call my brother if you're not."

Willa gestures to her crappy car. "Get in. I'll even let you control the music since you went a whole hour and a half without whining today."

"I don't whine that much."

"Just did. I'm revoking your tuner privileges."

When we get into the car I try to control the stereo anyway. Willa slaps my hand.

"Pass me 'Decent Day.'" She points to the glove box. Turns out that compartment is jam-packed with homemade mixed tapes, all with stupid labels: *Hungry; Blue Days; Whining Scene Bands; Creepy Lead Singers; Attitude Adjustment.*

"I assume there's a system."

Willa cranks the volume. "I label the tapes like theme music. Today was a decent day."

"Just decent?"

"Good days are just bad days waiting to happen. Decent is as good as it gets."

That's a horrible outlook on life, but I don't tell her so. I'm hardly an optimistic person either. Besides, this mix tape isn't bad. It's all acoustic folk with some top-forties, and when we pull into my driveway she lets "Beautiful Thing" by Slaid Cleaves finish before turning off the car.

"It was kinda cool, you coming out today," she says. "Did you have fun?"

"It was interesting." I wasn't part of the group, precisely, but I managed to blend in for once.

"You should come out with us more often."

I agree for the sake of agreeing and invite Willa in for dinner.

"Thanks, but I have to go feed my brother."

Willa wishes me a good night. I like the way she says goodnight, like by wishing it on me she can actually will the night to be good. Then she reaches out and gives me a sideways hug across the seat.

Willa doesn't hug me like I'm made of glass. She wraps her arms tight around me and holds me like she wants me there. She throws herself into it and genuinely lends me her body for the space of that embrace.

"Now get out of my car."

Elise has her face pressed to the front window as I walk up to the porch. I bet she watched that hug. Now I'm never going to hear the end of it.

Wednesday

Willa and I spend the Social Studies period making graphs to chart the progress of our soil contamination project to date. She has *call Luke* written on the back of her hand again. She just saw him yesterday; what could she possibly have to say to him already? I make the mistake of asking and Willa deadpans, "We talk about you behind your back." Her sarcasm does wonders for my mood.

Thursday

I habitually panic every time I hear the squeaky wheels of the book cart coming through the dialysis clinic. Then I see it's an old man in a green volunteer vest today, and I relax. I haven't seen Willa here for a while. It was embarrassing to be seen just the once. I didn't know how to deal with it; I had no visitors other than family when I was sick, and it's hard to prepare for an awkward meeting like that.

I cling to the numbers the doctors and nurses give me on my blood tests, watching my kidney function fluctuate between sixty and eighty percent. My renal system was shot to shit by last November, and I was staring a kidney transplant in the face. I got lucky: once the chemo was over my kidneys bounced back a little bit. I've been getting better, slowly. Maybe I won't need dialysis in a few months.

Mom tosses aside her magazine and turns to me for conversation. "How was school?"

"Fine."

"How are your friends?"

"They're okay."

"Elise is sure getting close with that boy she's been mooning over."

Jesus Christ, I thought that phrase died with the dinosaurs.

"Is she?"

Maybe that's why Elise hasn't been hanging around me lately, demanding attention; she has someone else to fix her annoying energies on. I'm almost hurt by that.

"Do you know him?" Mom asks.

"No."

"Have you heard anything? Does he seem like a good kid?"

"You know he's eighteen, right?"

"Age is just a number."

"Not when your sixteen-year-old daughter is involved."

Mom smiles condescendingly and strokes my cheek with the backs of her fingers. "You worry so much for such a young man," she says. "You always were like that; an old soul, I guess."

"Mom."

She chuckles at me. "When you were a baby the slightest things used to upset you. You were such a sensitive child."

Time for a subject change.

"Are you really going to let Elise go out with that guy?"

"He hasn't asked her out yet."

"That doesn't answer my question."

"Your dad and I haven't discussed it."

Dad will never go for it. Elise is a Daddy's Girl; he'll tell her to wait before dating... hopefully until she's thirty.

Friday

We have a work period in Social Studies, and after she finishes the assigned questions, Willa begins to make a grocery list in her notebook. When she's done that she starts making a list of stuff that can be found at the hardware store.

"Building something?"

"Yeah," she answers absently.

"What?"

"Doing this project…"

"What is it?"

She's so distracted that a noncommittal grunt is the only answer I receive. I prod her again and she adds, "With Frank and Luke."

She's been hanging out with Luke a lot. He smiles at her too much. And touches her too often. I bet he has designs on her, too. Every guy seems to.

Do you?

> *Shut up.*

She'd never go for it.

> *I don't think of her like that.*

Right.

> *She's annoying.*

I bet she's a moaner…

> *Jesus Christ.*

"Your shirt looks nice."

"Eyes off the tits, Harper."

"What tits?"

Perfectly palm-sized tits.

> *Will you shut the hell up?*

She sees through you, you know.

> *She doesn't know a goddamn thing about me.*

That terrified, are you?

Willa puts a hand on my face and physically turns my head to get me to stop staring.

It's Dad's day off today, and he suggests we go to dinner as a family. I feel tired and my head hurts, but stuff like this means a lot to him. I'll probably end up ordering the Jell-O dessert off the kids' menu, but I can play along and pretend to have a good time.

We go to Swiss Chalet. Elise snags a children's menu and a pack of crayons from the hostess station—she could have a promising career as a pickpocket— and orders the sorbet and Jell-O dessert so I don't have to. The waitress has the nerve to give her a judgmental look.

"I bet she thinks I'm anorexic or something," Elise says when the waitress leaves. I ordered the spring rolls on Elise's behalf. She insists on keeping the kids' menu, and colors the cartoons while we wait for food. She's half-finished with the duck on skis when she very suddenly quits and folds the menu away into her coat pocket.

"Did you suddenly remember your age?"

Elise completely ignores my question and leans back in her chair. I follow her gaze and see a table of teenagers across the dining room. Her favorite basketball player is among them. Mom notices too and smirks at Elise's behavior.

For the next five minutes, Elise covertly watches the other table from around Eric's shoulder. She looks a little peeved when the waitress flirts with them—only trying to improve her tip—and begins to fidget while we wait for food. Now is a really bad time for her to have forgotten her Ritalin.

"I have to use the restroom." She pushes her chair back and gets up. It takes me a second to realize that the path to the restrooms will take her right by the other table.

"Me too."

Elise doesn't immediately notice me following her, but when she gets close to the other table her pace slows a bit, as if she's planning to stop and try the 'I didn't see you there' line. My hand on her shoulder solves that problem as I march her forward to the restrooms at the end of the hall.

"Jem!" she hisses.

"Please, we're in public—and you look desperate and stupid when you try to flirt."

She gapes at me for a few seconds, and then the water works start. She kicks me in the shin and whirls away into the women's restroom. I can hear her crying from the hallway. Shit.

I limp back to the table just in time for the food to arrive.

"Where's Elise?"

"Restroom."

I don't have much of an appetite, but Eric is already laying into his chicken and I told myself I'd play along tonight. I pick at the Jell-O and sorbet Elise ordered. Mom knows something is up. She quietly slips away from the table a few minutes later and heads toward the restrooms. She's gone for twenty minutes.

"What happened? Where's Elise?" Dad asks when Mom finally gets back to the table.

"She wasn't feeling well. I took her home."

Aw, hell.

When we get home I try to apologize to Elise, but she won't open her bedroom door and yells some very colorful things at me when I try to apologize.

"Let her cool off until morning," Mom says.

I wonder how much Elise told her about what happened.

Saturday

I wake up to a note on my pillow: *You're a jerk.*

I write *I know. Sorry*, on it and slip it under Elise's door. Mom is at work in her office already. The rest of the house is still asleep, so I seek out a solitary breakfast.

I don't even think about my plans before I jump in the shower. Today is Saturday, so, naturally, I will go to the Kirk house to harass my friend and project partner. That's just the way weekends work now.

I pinch myself as I shower, trying to judge where the weight is gaining back. My thighs seem to have gained the most, but my midsection is a close second. It's still only eight pounds; not even enough to keep my hipbones from poking out. The only significant improvement is that my lowest ribs aren't as obvious through the skin anymore. I can't wait until I can get rid of the stupid Hickman.

I wonder who the hell that guy is as I pass the mirror on my way to get dressed. I throw on my one shirt and pair of jeans that actually fit. These clothes have the odd illusion of making me look *less* thin, which is weird. I guess it's because I don't swim in them. This is the shirt that made Willa touch me that one time, when I was feeling awful. She had the most disconcerting look of unguarded desire on her face. It turned my whole day around.

I'm digging through my drawer for my black toque when Elise knocks on the doorframe. She doesn't look happy.

"Are you going out?"

"Yeah."

"Could you drop me off at Carey's house on your way?" I owe her, but...

"I'm headed in the opposite direction."

"Where are you going?"

"Willa's."

Mom should be able to give her a ride to her friend's house. I'm probably the last person Elise wants to be alone in a car with right now; she only asked out of convenience. I grab my shoes out of the closet and straighten up to find her giving me a shrewd look.

"You're not falling for her, are you?"

"For Willa? What planet are you on?"

Elise smiles with satisfaction. "Good. Sorry, it was just an errant thought."

"Well keep those to yourself."

I put my shoes on and make myself scarce before she remembers to ask about a ride again.

⊷

When I get to Willa's house, the garage door is open and she's working in an oversized plaid shirt. The garage floor is covered in a rough grid of two-by-fours. She walks around them with a measuring tape and pencil, marking the wood.

"Hi."

"You again?" she says without looking up. "What time is it?"

"About eleven-thirty."

"How long are you here for?"

I shrug. "Whatever."

"Have you eaten?"

"Sort of."

"Want to help me measure the frame?"

"Is this the project you're doing with Luke?"

"Part of it."

She can never answer a question with a complete answer, can she? It's like her mission in life is to thwart my curiosity at every possible opportunity

"I'll help you."

"Soup first," she declares. "Want to help?"

We leave the wooden skeleton in the garage and go inside. We chop and boil and measure out the seasonings for the original carrot and pea soup.

Willa catches me licking honey off my finger and smiles.

"You've got a dirty mind, Kirk."

She scoffs. "You're sweet, not sexy." And my ego crawls away to die.

"I think you're a pretentious bitch."

"I think you're a narcissistic asshole."

You know, I'm kind of glad we got that out of the way. It eases the tension.

Willa reaches up on her toes to grab the blender off the top shelf and the highest button on her shirt pops open. She glares at me accusatorily and tells me to stop undressing her with my eyes. I burst out laughing while she deadpans.

"Don't die laughing," she says as she plugs in the blender. "I had a much more dramatic murder in mind for you."

"Still planning to kill me, are you?" I tease her.

She points a spatula at me like a gun and tells me to count on it.

I put the boiled vegetables in the blender jug while Willa measures out the seasonings and honey.

"Do you have anything important to say?" she asks with her finger hovering over the power button.

"Actually—"

She starts the blender and cuts me off.

The phone rings and Willa goes into the living room to answer it while the blender runs. Her side of the conversation is all yeses and nos, except for the "Hey Luke," at the beginning. What the hell does he want now? He's already got her involved in some project that has taken over the whole Kirk garage. And Willa doesn't strike me as the kind of girl to like construction—I bet she has an ulterior motive for helping him.

While she's on the phone, I take bowls and spoons out for serving. It's a short call, and when she hangs up the first thing she says is, "Let's eat."

I grab the blender handle to pour the soup into bowls. The heat of the glass takes me by surprise and I drop it with a curse. Steaming hot soup spills down the front of my shirt and all over the counter.

"Shit!"

Willa grabs me by the arm and tows me down the hall into the laundry room.

"Take your shirt off, I'll wash it right away."

It's so uncomfortably hot that I pull it over my head without protest and hand it to her. She tosses it in the washbasin and runs hot water over it. Most of the soup comes off, but there's a big orange stain that she covers with spray-on stain remover. Mom is going to give me hell for ruining a new shirt.

"Are you burnt?"

Willa looks over at me for the first time and her eyes settle on the middle of my chest. I look down. The outline of my Hickman is visible through my undershirt. I turn my back to her and stupidly clap a hand over it, as though hiding works retroactively.

Willa leaves the basin and goes to one of the baskets of folded laundry. "Here." She passes a faded polo over my shoulder. "It's my brother's. It might not fit, but…"

"Thanks." I pull it over my head.

As I'm buttoning it up to the collar, Willa leans close to my shoulder and whispers, "I don't think it's weird or disgusting."

Shoot me. I leave the laundry room without a word and start to clean up the orange puddle on the kitchen floor.

Lunch is ruined, but Willa dismisses it readily.

"Second shelf of the fridge," she says, and waves me away from the kitchen so she can mop the worst of it up. When I try to help she banishes me to the table and reiterates her statement about the fridge.

I open the door to find little Tupperwares of green Jell-O stacked and waiting.

"Kirk…"

"Just shut up and eat. You need to keep your energy up."

I hate being reminded how fragile I am. Nonetheless, I take a cup of Jell-O and sit down to eat it.

"Thank you."

"You're welcome."

❧

Willa's project with Luke involves framing a greenhouse. Frank has been looking into reasonably priced glass for the walls and ceiling. The plan is to erect it in her grandma's garden. It's not Luke's project after all, but the fact that he's involved still makes me suspicious.

"So is Luke helping to be a kiss-ass?"

"He likes building things. He gave my car a tune-up when I bought it."

"Have you ever thought about saving up to buy a car that was built in this decade?"

"Cars today aren't built to last," she says. "Sales are leases in disguise. That car is older than your sister and it runs like a dream."

"A really slow, loud dream with low fuel economy?"

She mutters something under her breath that sounds rude and shoves a notebook and pen into my hands. "Make sure we're following he blueprint."

We go up and down the loose beams, verifying that she's measured all her markings correctly. All that's left to do it screw it together. Her brother doesn't have an electric drill, so Willa has to do it by hand. Every hour or so she gets up and comes back with another Jell-O cup.

"I'm not going to pass out," I assure her the third time she does it. "It's not like I'm diabetic or anything."

"You know you'll get sick less if you graze."

I have nothing to say to that, so I just eat the Jell-O and pass her screws. It takes us three hours to get one side of the greenhouse framed. Willa plans to store it in the shed out back, to make room to frame the other walls on the garage floor.

We have to move some stuff around in the shed to make room for the frame. The shed smells like stale fishing tackle and wet wood. It's not insulated, with just plywood walls and a sheet metal roof. We've just got all the stuff put away when the sky opens and hail starts pouring down.

"Aw, hell," Willa says. We stand back from the door and wait for the storm to let up before venturing back across the lawn. It can't hold out long at this rate. The shed is too musty to close the door, so we leave it open and watch the hail fall.

Willa leans against the shelf and twists her hair around her finger absent-mindedly.

"At least it's not as bad as Newfoundland," she says.

"Are you and Luke a thing?"

Dude, you really need to work on delivery of extremely dumb questions.

Willa looks at me with raised eyebrows. "Inappropriate question."

"Fine. He just seems a little young, is all."

She doesn't say anything. I can't stand the silence.

"What is he, sixteen?"

"What kind of cancer did you have?"

"Brain tumor."

She laughs in my face. "You are so full of shit."

"Are you calling me a liar?"

"You are a liar."

"Why would I lie about that?"

"You are lying." She grabs my wrist and shakes my hand between us like a puppet. "Those scars on your hands are from graft-versus-host."

I yank my hand away from her and pull my cuffs down over my palms. "What are you, a doctor?"

"You had some kind of transplant, and it wasn't for a new brain. That might have helped though, come to think of it."

"Go to hell."

"Shouldn't have lied about it."

When is this hail going to let up?

"And no," she says calmly, "Luke and I are not a thing. Our families are very close."

Oh, how I hate her. I hate her smirk and the way she looks at my hands like she knows something. I hate it that she won't let me lie to her and I hate how exposed she can make me feel without giving away any of her own insecurities in return.

"Did your sister die of cancer? Or did she kill herself when it became inevitable?"

Willa looks at me with haunted eyes and doesn't say anything. After a minute she doesn't seem so haunted anymore—it feels more like she can see right through me and all the bullshit that surrounds this messed up situation.

"Thought about that, have you?" she murmurs. "Pills or rope? Or do your parents have a gun? Were you going to asphyxiate in that nice car your dad drives? It would take awhile, in that big three-car garage. Wrist-cutting is too dramatic, even for you." She says all this in a slow whisper like she's lulling a child to sleep on promises of sweet dreams. "No," she says. "You were never going to kill yourself; you don't have it in you."

I feel like I'm about five inches tall and naked in front of a crowd. How dare she pretend that she knows me? Why can't she just tell me to piss off when I'm an asshole, like a normal person would, instead of pushing back and digging into painful places?

"You don't know a goddamn thing," I whisper back.

She smirks sadly. "Pills were your first choice. Your mom's an insomniac. She told me. You were going to attempt suicide like a woman so someone could have time to find you and rescue you and fawn over you some more."

I shove her back against the shelves in a knee-jerk reaction. Willa goes limp and absorbs the blow with her shoulders. I shouldn't have done that.

She rights herself and rolls her shoulders. "Did you have a cancer with a low cure rate? Let me guess: lymphoma."

"Will you stop asking me about what I had?" I say through clenched teeth.

The hail has slowed to a sporadic patter. I can't stand to be in here anymore, so I march across the lawn to get away from her. The back door leads to the kitchen, and once there I stop and debate whether I should stay and fight with her some more. She can't just say shit like that and get away with it.

Willa stops in the threshold of the back door and watches me with a grim expression. "Just tell me."

"It's irrelevant, Kirk," I growl at her. "I don't have it anymore."

Willa folds her arms over her chest and shakes her head slowly. "It's not irrelevant. It's still killing you faster than I ever could." Hearing that makes me feel cold in an entirely unpleasant way. It's the fear of imminent death, creeping back from its recent dormancy.

"Do you ever say anything that isn't total bullshit?"

"Why does it bother you so much that I want to know what kind of cancer you had? How come you never want to talk about it?"

"Because!"

She's pissed me off to bad I can't help but shout. Raising my voice is the only way I can keep myself from tearing her head off.

"It's the most obvious fucking thing about me! It's what everybody notices! I was a *person* before, God damn it, not a fucking diagnosis! I don't want you to have any details because I don't want you to think of me in terms of my illness! Do you know how humiliating it is to be reduced to numbers and labels and a fucking progress chart, taking poison for medicine and feeling like shit all the time?"

I kick the nearest thing—a dining chair—and it goes flying across the kitchen tiles. Willa jumps back to avoid it.

"You think it's a big joke, making light every time I puke in class or miss lectures to crash in the nurse's office. Fuck you. You have no idea what I put up with, and on top of it there's your stupid questions and remarks about how I look and you think you know everything about me. You don't know a *single* thing, Kirk. You're such a—!"

There is no word for how much I hate her right now. I abandon the search for the right insult and yell 'Fuck you!' at her.

I turn on my heel and march out through the living room. It's drizzling again as I cross the driveway and slide into the car. Jesus, my stomach hurts. It's knotted up with stress and my hands are shaking as I try to put the key in the ignition slot. I drop the key in the dark around my feet.

"Shit."

The passenger door opens and Willa slips into the seat beside me. *What else you got?* her face says.

Nothing. I have nothing left. You've taken it all.

I have no more energy left to fight her. I spent it all in the shed and kitchen and now I'm just sore and miserable and want nothing more than to crawl away to lick my wounds.

My head falls forward until my forehead rests on the steering wheel. My stomach hurts. My head hurts. I can't believe I said those things to her. Why did I kick her furniture like a kid throwing a fit? How could I have asked that about her dead sister? What the hell is wrong with her that she comes back for more abuse?

This is possibly the most ashamed I have ever felt in my entire life. I curl my arms up around the steering wheel and dash, surrounding my throbbing head.

I feel Willa's hand on my back.

"Come inside," she says. "You shouldn't drive when you're this upset."

"I'm fine." I slowly straighten up. I am *so* not fine.

"If you're leaving, I'm coming with you," she states calmly. "Or you can stay here a while longer. Come inside. I'll make us tea. We can talk."

Her hand is still on my back.

"Please don't touch me."

She takes her hand away. The moment it's gone I almost wish I had it back. Almost.

I open the door and step out. "I'm sorry—about your sister."

Willa laughs and closes the car door. "She would have hated you."

"Do you?"

"You're growing on me."

⊕

I warm my hands around my mug while Willa puts the milk back in the fridge. I've straightened up her kitchen and apologized for kicking the chair. She accepted it graciously. Willa is being nice for once.

She brings her mug to the kitchen table and takes the seat adjacent to mine. She sits in it sideways, facing me, and moves her hand gently around the back of my collar.

I mumble an excuse about needing to use the bathroom. Once removed from her, shut up in that private little room, I hang my head in my hands and wonder how the hell I got into this mess.

I regularly fight with my only friend. I'm sure everyone wonders why she bothers to hang out with me. She must wonder, too. It's only a matter of time before she begins to dodge me.

You've got a thing for her, you know. It wouldn't matter so much, otherwise.

Hell, if Elwood was the one hanging out with her every weekend he'd have her on the couch downstairs by now, breathless from making out and her clothes stretched out of shape from being groped.

But does she want to be treated that way?

It's a nice mental picture…of her, anyway.

And me? What do I do? I pick a fight with her and then insult her dead sister. In theory, I wouldn't even do that to someone I really hated.

Willa opens the bathroom door and I lift my head out of my hands. "Can't you knock?"

"Knock knock."

"Jesus, Kirk."

I hang my head again and pray for the strength to deal with her ridiculous bullshit.

"Knock knock," she repeats more insistently.

"Who's there?"

"You look like you need a hug."

"That's not a joke."

She comes in and takes a seat next to me on the edge of the tub. This is starting to feel like an intervention.

"I wasn't going to kill myself."

She wraps an arm around my back. "I know. I said I knew you didn't have it in you."

"You make it sound like a weakness."

Willa chuckles darkly. "I think you've got more optimism in you than you let on. You wouldn't give up on something unless it was really and truly hopeless—but that doesn't mean you didn't think about it."

"Don't pretend you know me."

She smiles to herself. "I don't know why Paige thinks you're hard to read. Everything you think shows in your hands." She pokes my third knuckle. "Must be because you're a musician."

"You talk to Paige about me?"

"She brought it up."

"Did you encourage her?"

"She thinks you're cute."

"Really?"

"Actually, she thinks you're a creep." Willa winks.

I shrug her arm off and she lets go without protest.

"I can't wait to get out of here."

"Of this house, or this town?" she asks.

"Out of Smiths Falls."

"Where would you go?"

I shrug. "Probably back to Ottawa."

"It'd never be the same. That's why in books 'you can't go home again.' I did and I hate it."

"So go back to St. John's."

"That wouldn't solve the problem either. No matter where you are, you have to live with yourself," she says.

"But you fit in there."

"No, I didn't. And even if I did, I don't like to repeat experiences."

"You're crazy."

"You're a little desperate."

I hate that she says shit like that, especially because she's right.

"Wouldn't you be?"

"I don't know." Willa knits her fingers together over her knees. "You don't really want to go back to Ottawa, though. You just want to go back to a time when things were easier, and that time was in Ottawa. It's misplaced desire."

"Thank you, Freud."

She puts on a fake Austrian accent and asks if I've screwed my mother yet. This girl can make me laugh when I feel like doing anything but.

"What was your sister's name?"

"Thomasina. We called her Tessa."

"That's a charitable nickname."

"It's a family tradition, giving the girls boys' names."

"Willa is pretty feminine."

"It's Wilhelmina Joanne."

I can't help it, I laugh. Willa elbows me lightly but lets my rudeness slide.

"Let's go back and finish our tea."

"I think I should probably go home. Eric might need his car tonight."

We head downstairs and exchange trite goodbyes in the foyer. I'm just about to step out when she tells me to wait and heads down the hall to the laundry room. We almost forgot about my shirt.

Willa gives me my laundered shirt and says I can give Frank's back to her at school on Monday. I thank her and say goodbye, but just as I turn to leave I think better of it and stop.

I lean in to whisper in her ear, "It *is* weird and disgusting."

I'm halfway across the driveway to my car when she calls after me with a sultry smile in her voice, "You're full of it, Harper."

I crawl across the bed and starfish with my head in the pillow. Once home and nested, something inside me relaxes and tears well without intention or effort. I just lay there quietly while my eyes water and my throat aches.

Elise slips in quietly and lays down with me. She wraps her little arms around me and pillows her head between my shoulder blades.

"I hate it that she hurts you," she murmurs.

"She doesn't, Lise; I'm already hurting."

She whimpers like a wounded puppy and squeezes me harder.

"I'm sorry—about that guy."

"It's okay," she says. "It takes too much energy to be mad at you. I've got better things to do."

"I screwed up."

"It's okay."

"Lise."

"Do you not want me to forgive you?"

"Can you please just be mad at me?"

"Would it make you feel better?"

"Yes."

"I love you," she says. "Strange brother o'mine." She kisses my shoulder and gets off the bed. "I'm not mad, but I will make you a milkshake."

Elise makes the milkshakes extra thick. We need spoons to eat them, slouched and comfy on the couch.

"Feeling better now?"

I nod and take another bite of peach milkshake. There's a bitter aftertaste to this one; she used too much sugar product. I don't tell her that, though, because it might diminish the gesture.

"What happened?" Elise asks.

"I dunno."

"Did she say something?"

"Yeah, but I started it."

"Tell me."

"Nah."

Elise pouts. When that trick fails to work its magic, she makes her lip tremble and whimpers.

"I think you might have been right about her."

Elise immediately snaps out of her fake whimpering. "What?"

"I might like her."

"I thought so. You're always going over to her house and when Mom asks about your day you talk about lunch and Social Studies and—"

"Will you shut up?"

"I made you a milkshake—share your drama with me, damn it."

Her petty demand is actually kind of amusing.

"Fine. You know how when you're talking to Willa she can make you feel like you're the only person in the world?"

"Yeah."

"She can turn that around and make you feel very small and insignificant, too."

"Is that what happened tonight?"

I turn a bite of milkshake over in my mouth while I think about my answer. "Not entirely."

Willa did build me back up again after she tore me down, and I incurred her wrath entirely through my own fault.

Elise impatiently prompts me to continue with a circular hand gesture.

"It feels like she can see right through people."

"And you like her?"

"Maybe."

"Why?"

Because I haven't been seen the way she sees me for so long.

"Why do you like that guy you've been chasing?" It's the perfect subject change. Elise goes all dreamy and slouches down on the couch like her bones have turned to goo.

"Because, because, because," she murmurs like that's a complete answer, with a little 'mmh!' of pleasure on the end.

"Do you really think he's interested in you?" The question isn't an insult this time. I'm genuinely wondering.

Elise makes a face. "No. He has a girlfriend."

"Anyone I know?"

She gives me a look that reads *Who* do *you know?*

"Point taken."

Elise huffs. "Her name's Nina. And of course she just has to be freaking gorgeous."

"Is she that girl who ran for class president?"

"No, you're thinking of Mina Soto. *Nina* looks nothing like her. She's got long dark hair and she's curvy and she's from Argentina so she has that stupid sexy Latin thing going for her." Elise stabs her milkshake with her spoon.

"I guess they're pretty serious?"

Elise only groans and buries her spiky little head in the crook of my shoulder. Poor kid. I guess it was inevitable that eventually she'd learn how bad unrequited love sucks. I'm sorry to say it, but I'm actually kind of glad that she feels it now, before anything happened with that guy, than if she had been allowed to become attached and lose her adorable innocence.

"You're better off without him, Lise." I give her a squeeze. "Think about it: if you started dating now he'd graduate in three months, and then you'd only have the summer together before he goes off to college. You're a little young to have a long-distance relationship."

"If he goes to school in Ottawa we might be able to visit on weekends."

Yeah, and he can cheat on her with college chicks every other day of the week.

"I think you're better off not touching this one. You'll find another guy to crush on and make an ass out of yourself for."

"What about you and Willa?"

"What about it?"

"Are you going to ask her out?"

"No."

"Why not?" she whines.

"Because she's neither blind nor insane, and would therefore never date me."

"She's sort of friends with you."

"That's different."

Elise snorts like she doesn't believe me and mutters 'chicken' under her breath. Her Ron Weasley poster has a date with a Sharpie.

Sunday

I'm making soup for brunch when Willa calls. We have to do the weekly measurements for the Soc project. I don't think the snapdragons have undergone any big changes and would fudge the numbers under other circumstances, but Willa wants to come over. I'm not about to say no to that.

"I'm on my way," she says before hanging up.

Shit.

I dash upstairs to shower and pretend that I didn't sleep until eleven o'clock.

⚘

The Social Studies work takes exactly five minutes to complete. "I brought something for you," Willa says as we pack up our books. She sees my eager look before I can moderate my reaction and teases me, "No, it isn't food."

"Why the hell not?"

"Because I have better things to do with my day than cook for a jerk like you and watch you stuff your face."

"You feminist," I say with affected disgust.

Willa crams her books back into her bag and then opens the foremost pocket. "This is what I brought."

She takes out a scrapbook with a yellow cover and sunflower stickers on the corners. The date on the front is from two years ago.

"I wanted to show you this, since we talk about her so much."

She opens the book and shows me photos mounted on the black pages. The first one is a graduation photo of a woman with thick, dark hair and delicate features. She and Willa have the same mouth.

"That's Tessa."

I've never lost anyone dear to me. I don't know how to respond to the picture or how to empathize with Willa's situation. I study the studio portrait and nod.

"You must really miss her."

Willa's sister looks like the kind of woman people can't help but notice—kind of like Willa herself, even though they don't look much alike. Willa's hair is curly and wild, and it's a deceptively angelic golden blonde. She's not as delicate as Thomasina and her grey eyes give nothing away.

Willa smiles at the picture. "I miss talking to her."

She flips the page and shows me photos taken earlier, when Thomasina had long braids and Willa was just a baby on her lap. In subsequent photos, Thomasina's long hair is gone. She's bald and pale with dark circles under her eyes, but that spark is still in them. She's still trying to tempt people to her, sick as she is.

"What was she like?"

"Fiery," Willa says with a smile. "My mom is a lot like her, but more frenetic. Tessa was sort of disappointed that I was always so serious. When she got sick she sort of got determined to make me live a little more—she thought wildness was healthy." Willa sighs with pleasurable reminiscence. "We had such great talks, that last year."

She looks at me sideways with a smile like Thomasina's.

"You know," she says, "she told me a lot about the stuff I wasn't allowed to know as a kid. We talked about love and money and sex, and how it's so hard to have all three in balance." Willa takes my hand almost unconsciously and strokes the back of my palm with her thumb.

"She told me to sleep around," Willa says with a laugh. "She told me to figure out what I want. Tessa thought that waiting for marriage was the worst idea ever."

"You talked about all this with your sister?"

"Yeah. It was nice. There was nothing that was off limits. You know how when you're fifteen, you think of yourself as grown up and it's irritating how everyone still talks to you like you're a kid? She made me feel like I was grown up and worthy of her confidence."

Willa flips the page and shows me another photo. This one is of a young man, standing by a fence and smiling nervously.

"Is that her boyfriend?"

"No. That was the guy she had the best sex of her life with—when she was a virgin."

"If she was still a virgin then it isn't sex."

"It's a little more complex than that. To the day she died he remained her best lay—and they only hooked up once, and didn't do what we think of as 'sex.' He was our next door neighbor."

"So if he was such a good lay why didn't she date him?"

"He moved after high school. Last I heard he was doing a tour in Afghanistan." Willa shrugs at this scanty knowledge. "He and Tessa wrote a few times."

"Did you save the letters, too?"

Willa nods. "She left me all kinds of stuff like that. I haven't worked up the guts to read them yet."

We go through the rest of Thomasina's pictures. Willa is just a little girl in some. She was a pretty cute kid. In the course of our perusal Willa informs me that I'm the only friend to whom she's ever shown this book.

This is an extremely personal offering she's making. Thomasina was undoubtedly important in her life, and she trusts me enough to expose some of the happiest moments of her life as well as the subject of her deepest grief. And after what happened yesterday, I can hardly argue that she isn't my closest friend. I've told her things I haven't even told my family.

"It's nice that you have such good memories of her."

Willa smiles at the photos, but it's a shaky expression that hints at some greater underlying emotion. "Take the good with the bad, I guess."

There's plenty she's not saying. Willa never gives a straight answer.

Frank: March 10 to 13

March Break: Day One

I hadn't noticed it before, but Willie has a lot in common with the dog I had for a week when I was ten. It was an abused stray, skittish and vulnerable. Sometimes that dog would be as docile as a lamb, and just when I began to think there was no fight left in her, she lashed out and went for the throat. Mom made me get rid of that dog, and now she's gotten rid of Willie.

I booked the week of her March Break off to spend it with her. To be honest, I feel guilty about spending so little time with Willie, but after today I think it's safe to say she doesn't want to spend time with me. We haven't had much to say to each other since she moved in. Willie is conscientious and tidy, just like always. She pitches in around the house and makes good food, and I'm mostly glad to have her here. But now that I see her properly, I see that I'm living with a stranger, not my little sister.

Things are getting complicated. I don't like her volunteering at the hospital. It gives me a bad feeling—being around places like that might remind her of Tessa, of why Willie fell off the wagon to begin with. Not that arguing with her does any good. Months of telling her to stop, and she still goes back to that place every week.

March Break: Day Two

Willie and I spend the morning at the sugar bush. This place seemed way more fun when we were little, and Willie keeps giving me that pained look that us kids used to give Dad when he made us do things we'd outgrown. We stay for pancakes and then head home. Willa makes maple chicken for dinner with the fresh syrup we bought. Takes her gloves off to handle the meat and I don't remember the scar being that bad. It's a miracle that girl has her thumb. I ask her how it feels and she says she still doesn't grip well with her left hand. I suggest referring her to Jack in the PT department at the hospital, and Willie tells me not to bother.

"Just leave it alone, okay?"

March Break: Day Three

After supper I get a phone call from a boy asking for Willie. I don't want to give her the phone but she picks up the other handset before I can lie to the guy about her not being home. Willie's had enough trouble from boys; she doesn't need another one to crash through her life. It's only later that I realize I should have written down his number and screened his calls.

"Who was that boy that called earlier?"

"A serial rapist."

And she used to be the good child.

March Break: Day Four

I want to trust Willie, but she makes it hard. The boy that phoned yesterday is in my house, and he's not just any boy—he's Dr. Harper's kid. Now Willie's doing a school project with a cancer patient? He's currently sitting in my living room drinking mint tea, and I don't hear them talking about schoolwork, either.

After dinner I talk to Mom and Dad about it. They agree that the situation has bad news written all over it. Talking to Willie about it is an exercise in futility.

"I can't get rid of him," she says. "We're doing a project together."

"It didn't sound like schoolwork this afternoon."

"If I was going to murder him, I wouldn't do it with you plainly eavesdropping in the next room, Frank."

She doesn't seem to grasp that it's my job to eavesdrop. Mom and Dad tasked me with taking care of her. I *know* this kid she's hanging out with. He ended up in the back of my ambulance last fall—twice—and I know that he has some serious issues weighing on his body. Willie doesn't need to lose anybody else. She's dealt with enough death.

When Willie goes to the hospital to volunteer, I head over to Doug's house. Luke is asleep on the couch when I get there, but Doug dismisses his company.

"He sleeps like a log."

Doug hands me a beer and steals a quiet kiss. Luke doesn't stir in the other room.

"Willie's giving me trouble."

"Coloring on the walls?"

Doug smirks and sips his beer. He's teasing me. My sister hasn't been 'Willie' since she was five, but having her here, being protective of her in a whole new way... the old name fits, even though I don't dare call her that to her face.

"Hanging out with a damned cancer patient, now. She's trying to give me an ulcer, I swear."

"So tell her not to invite him around."

"They're assigned to do a school project together."

"Call the teacher?"

I shrug. Doug's suggestion has merit.

"Frank...do you think that maybe Willa's learned her lesson? You really think she'd hurt this kid?"

"I'm more worried about her than that other kid. She wouldn't hurt him; I'm sure of that. But if she gets attached and something happens to him, she won't be able to deal with it. Again."

"She keeping clean?"

"She is. And she thinks good behavior entitles her to pull a stunt like this."

Doug runs a hand through my hair, trying to comfort me.

"Relax," he says. "You're supposed to be on vacation." Doug thinks I have cabin fever from sitting around babysitting teenagers all day, and that it's only fuelling my paranoia about the Harper kid.

"She'll be fine," Doug says. "Willie knows what she can handle and what she can't."

Jem: March 14

I love having a week off school to sleep in. I wake up at ten and head downstairs for breakfast, but when I get to the kitchen I can hear Dad on the phone. He's talking about platelets, so I turn around and head for the front door. Maybe Willa will take pity on me and provide breakfast.

I didn't tell her where I was for the first three days of March Break, and she didn't ask. Dad took me to Ottawa to see some of his specialist colleagues at CHEO. He wants a second opinion on my condition every so often, so we spent the days in hospital rooms and the nights at my grandparents' house in Nepean. It's dehumanizing, waiting in cold exam rooms to be prodded and exposed. Then I showed up at Willa's house to do homework yesterday and the first thing she said to me was, "Please tell me you saw Tosh.O this week." Normal, and perfectly so.

I knock on the Kirks' front door. Willa answers in her pajamas.

"You a bible salesman?" she deadpans.

"Feed me?"

Willa rolls her eyes and opens the screen door. "Now I'll never get rid of you."

Turns out Willa was already cooking. The blender is set up and four kinds of peeled fruit cover the cutting board. I steal a piece of kiwi to suck on while she works.

"What are you making?"

"Popsicles."

I grin from ear to ear. "Yeah, you're never getting rid of me."

Would she try?

  Duh.

"How's your week so far?" Willa asks.

"Shitty."

I hope she'll let me hang out here for a while, because I know a conversation about platelets is waiting for me at home.

"Well, that's a kick in the teeth." She doesn't sound the least bit sympathetic. I kind of like it.

I reach for another piece of fruit and she slaps my hand away.

"Bitch, I'm hungry."

"Be patient."

I make a point of glaring at her while she purées the fruit for popsicles. It seems to work, because she gives me some puree mixed with extra orange juice for breakfast.

"Hey," I ask as she pours the rest into molds, "how do you keep from getting fruit juice on your gloves?" Even though she's in pajamas, Willa has her trademark fingerless gloves on, and they're spotless.

"I'm not a slob."

"Do you sleep with those things on?"

"Yes."

"Really?"

Willa snorts. "No. Ever heard the story about the girl with the green ribbon?"

I haven't, so Willa enlightens me. It's one of those old ghost stories, about a girl who always wore a green ribbon around her neck. She grew up and married her childhood sweetheart, and whenever he asked about it she refused to remove the ribbon. Until she got sick, that is, and then she asked him to untie it. Her head fell off.

"So your gloves keep your hands from falling apart?"

"Something like that."

"I don't get you."

"Your hat keeps the sky from falling."

"It does not."

Willa smirks at me. I don't like it. "Whatever, Harper."

Willa: March 17 to 23

Sunday

I'm just putting away the breakfast dishes when the front door opens and Luke strolls in. The benefit of being like family: he makes himself at home.

"You look good."

He's joking. I'm wearing clothes that I can get dirty in: torn jeans and the plaid button-down that Mom used to wear during her stint as a house painter.

"You ready to go?"

I lock up the house and we get into Mr. Thorpe's truck to drive back to Port Elmsley. Luke wouldn't let me meet him there. He insisted on surprising me and told me to wear old clothes.

"So where are we going?"

"Disneyland."

I swat his shoulder and he laughs at me.

"Okay, fine, we're not going to the happiest place on earth—but it's still a pretty sweet spot."

"You're not going to tell me anything, are you?"

"Nope." He flashes a cheesy grin.

Luke takes the road toward the Perth Golf Course, but then makes a right onto an unpaved road that looks more like a driveway. The spruce trees encroach on it from all sides, brushing against the doors.

"I usually come here by bike," Luke says. When the path gets too narrow to drive we leave the truck and start walking. I can hear moving water not far off.

"No one knows about this place, okay? It's our secret."

"Sure."

By 'no one' I'm pretty sure he means all his friends already know. He's probably found a great spot for bush parties.

Luke takes my hand and pulls me into the trees. We both have to walk bent-double to pass under the lowest branches. Little flecks of light are all that make it through the foliage, and the space we pass through is dark and damp and starting to smell like spring. Luke smells like that sometimes, under the scent of teenage boy.

"How often do you come here?"

"Whenever." He's dodging, but it's not worth it to push.

When we step out of the trees, we're on a sloping ridge of rock that breaks away into a pebble beach around a slow-moving stream.

"Over here."

Luke pulls me farther along the shore, across a fallen log and over the lip of the opposite bank. It's rockier on the other side of the river, where large chunks of granite rise out of the Canadian Shield.

"What do you think?"

We're standing in a small cave, sheltered by smooth rocks as tall as Luke. The gap between two pieces of granite is almost ten feet wide, with a clear view of the pines above. It's so quiet in here—no forest sounds and I can hardly hear the water nearby.

"It's beautiful, Luke."

It takes a great deal of trust to share a spot like this with someone and count on it remaining private.

I notice a marking low on the rock wall. It's marker ink, written on the rock in the form of a date.

"I camped here, once," Luke says. "Marked the event."

There's something quietly thrilling about the fact that only Luke and I know about this place. We take some time to explore the surrounding rocks, caves, and crevices. Luke puts his hands on my waist and lifts me up to sit on one of the high rocks.

"You can see all the way to the stream." He points it out over the top of our sheltered little spot.

"How often do you really come here?"

Luke shrugs. I'm making him uncomfortable.

"I'd come here every day in warm weather."

He chuckles. "You'd get eaten alive in the summer."

Luke hops up next to me on the rock. It's so peaceful here, and I'm happy having this time with him. One thought keeps intruding, unbidden: *I'd like to bring Jem here.* He could use a little peace and beauty in his life—but not here. This is an unadulterated spot, just for Luke and me.

Jem wouldn't appreciate it properly, anyway.

Monday

Madame Bizot has a new game for the class to play. It's supposed to help us remember the conjugation of French verbs. I think it will only succeed in making me hate this class even more. She produces a rubber ball, borrowed from the gym, and explains that the object is to toss the ball around until all forms of a verb have been conjugated, and then the next person gets to change the verb. She even makes us arrange our chairs into a circle.

I'm the oldest person in this class. I postponed my grade nine French credit in favor of Visual Arts, and when took it in grade eleven, at my new school, I blew off most of the classes and failed. Madame Bizot knows this and is prone to eyeing me like I'm a total screw-up.

I zone out of the game, completely bored, only to get hit in the face by the stupid ball.

"Son of a bitch."

A few people ask if I'm okay.

"What the hell, man?" I ask the kid who threw it at me, even though I know it's not his fault. I feel my nose dripping and sure enough, it's blood. I'm actually inclined to consider the nosebleed as a worthwhile excuse to get out of class.

I go to the nurse's office to clean up and get an icepack. She takes one look at me and asks me if I've hit just my nose, or my head in general.

"I took a rubber ball to the face. I'm pretty sure it's just my nose."

The nurse gives me a wet towel for my neck, a box of Kleenex, an icepack, and sits me down in a chair by the sink. When she leaves to note this accident in the main office's records, the white screen that divides the cot from the rest of the room moves.

"What the hell did you do?" Jem asks dryly. I can see the top half of his head in the narrow gap between the wall and the curtain. If his lids were any heavier, they'd be made of concrete.

"Occupational hazard of learning French."

Jem looks at me as though I'm a complete idiot.

"Feeling sick?"

"More tired than sick," he says. "Are you gonna be okay?"

"It's just a nosebleed."

"Do you need any help? She'll be gone awhile." He nods in the direction of the office door, where the nurse left. She and the secretary are talking, and it sounds like they're gossiping.

"I'm okay."

Jem still gets up and comes around to my side of the divider. He moves slowly, like a man exhausted, and he's in socked feet. He takes the plastic chair next to mine and adjusts the cool cloth on the back of my neck.

"Did you even go to English today?"

"No. I barely made it through Soc."

I stand over the sink and try removing the wad of tissues from under my nose. It's still bleeding pretty badly. I replace the Kleenex and rinse the sink where I bled on it.

Jem is smirking at me. "Does your nose bleed easily?"

"No. This was a random attack by a rabid freshman."

He chuckles tiredly at that. "I used to get nosebleeds so bad I'd have to go to the ER."

"Before or after you got sick?"

"After, dummy."

I put on a tone of fake hopefulness. "So if I were to punch you right now, would you bleed to death?"

"Nah, I'd survive just to spite you."

He leans his shoulder against the sink, slouching like he has a bad hangover.

"As soon as I can stand upright I'll help you back to the cot."

I test my nose again. Still bleeding. I'm stuck bent over the sink for a few more minutes.

"I don't need your help."

"You look exhausted. You should be in bed."

"But I want to be here," he says simply. "I think you need it."

He takes a Kleenex and catches a drip of blood as it runs past my handful of tissue, over my upper lip.

"I guess you do owe me."

He smiles sadly. "That I do, Kirk."

Tuesday

I turn in our progress report for the soil pollution project. Jem is absent today. It's going to be a long, boring period without my smartass project partner, but at least I can get some work done.

Mrs. Hudson announces that we're going to be moving on to the Family Life unit. She hands out the syllabus for the next three weeks. It includes fertility and reproduction, infant care, parenting and attachment theories, and an 'egg project.' I need someone to remind me why I took this crappy elective.

Jem calls me after school to 'find out what he missed.' I didn't think he was that dedicated a student. But it would be mean to call bullshit on him, so I tell him about the new study theme.

"Do you think we'll have to watch that birthing video they show to the Health classes?"

"God, I hope not. Once was enough."

Like the truly insensitive jerk he is, Jem takes this opportunity to remind me that I have the fuzzy end of the lollipop when it comes to reproduction. I encourage him not to breed, lest idiocy be genetic.

I end the call when Frank gets home. Time to prepare dinner. He casually informs me that our parents called to check in today. Apparently my progress report was good.

"They're starting to relax about you being here, I think."

"They made it sound worse than it was at home, didn't they?"

Frank doesn't answer, but I feel a soft touch on the back of my head. He pets my hair once and murmurs, "I'm glad you're all right," on his way out. End of discussion.

Wednesday

I buy a relatively small turkey for Easter, since we won't have to feed many people. Apart from cooking, Easter Sunday is going to be a pretty quiet day. Frank and I are nominally Presbyterian because our dad was raised that way, but we haven't practiced for as far back as I can remember. In the Kirk house, Easter is four days off work to watch TV and eat turkey. It's fairly low key, except for Sunday dinner, when Oma (lapsed Catholic) will probably get plastered, take her teeth out, and prank-call the pizza place. Don't even get me started on

Christmases with her. On Canada Day she smokes weed on the front porch.

"Hey Willa," Cody Russell greets me at the checkout counter. He's a friend of Chris's and we run in similar circles, but I don't know him very well. He asks me if I'm cooking for a big crowd as he rings up the turkey. It's only a seventeen-pounder.

"Not so big, no."

"Family in town?"

"Not really."

Mom and Dad are staying in Newfoundland for the holiday, so it will just be Oma, Frank and me.

Cody says, "You're such a healthy girl," as he checks and bags all the fruit and vegetables. He says it sweetly, like a responsible diet is adorable.

"Are you hanging out with Paige and the usual crowd this weekend?" he asks.

"Maybe. I don't have any definite plans."

"It would be cool if you did."

The printer chugs out the receipt very slowly, as if it's trying to trap me in this conversation.

"You're into group things, aren't you?"

"Uh, yeah?" What is that supposed to mean?

"You should have come to the dance. We all went as a group, anyway."

"Oh."

I drop my bags back in the cart as quickly as I can without being rude. I shouldn't have given him the opportunity to start this conversation, because it's too tempting to be scathing in return.

"Are you going to the grad dance?"

"It's not really my thing." Not to mention that I won't be graduating this year.

"It can be fun; depends who you're with." He smiles and winks at me. The hell? "Later, Willa."

I can't help but look back over my shoulder as I leave. Cody waves, and I start to wonder if he's a few bricks shy of a full load. Or was that flirting? How do normal people come on to each other?

Thursday

Jem is in an especially bad mood today. He picks a fight with Paige at lunch over *Harry Potter*, for Christ's sake. They can't agree on who played Dumbledore in the first two films. What kind of dork is he that he knows that?

Paige is getting pissed, which means she'll soon get catty. I know Jem's moods well enough to know that he won't take that in stride.

"Come on." I nudge Jem's shoulder. "Let's go for a walk. You two can settle this later."

He seethes quietly all the way out of the cafeteria. I ask him who pissed on his parade and he tells me to shut up.

"Change your tampon or something, Christ…"

"I told you to shut up."

"Why are you so tense?"

"I am n—" He cuts himself off with a lurch and brings a hand up to his mouth. Jem shuts his eyes and swallows with great difficulty. Damn, he's so worked up he's making himself sick.

"Are you okay?"

Jem cautiously lowers his hand. "I'm fine."

"Did you eat too much?"

"I said I'm fine."

"Easy, now." I don't want him to work himself up if he's going to lose his lunch over it.

"Don't tell me what to do."

"Fine, puke your guts out."

"To hell with you." He shoves my shoulder. Not very hard, just enough to make me take a step back. "You think—" He cuts himself off again. One hand goes to his mouth and the other around his middle, and he bolts. Luckily, we're not more than ten feet from the boys' washroom.

"Shit."

I dig through my pockets for mints. I have a couple for him. I should stock up before Social Studies. I think Jem is going to be in there for a while, so I go back to the cafeteria and buy a bottle of water for him.

When Jem does come out, he does so like he's trying not to be seen. He notices me waiting nearby and stops. "Were you out here the whole time?"

I pass him the bottle of water and neglect to answer. I drop a couple of mints into his palm and suggest he cut class to go to the nurse's office.

"Thanks."

"I have to go."

The bell is about to ring and I don't have anything I need for my next class. I step around Jem and he grabs my wrist. His hands are sweaty.

"Wait. I'm sorry."

"Yeah, great, forgiven." I don't have time for a feel-good conversation right now.

"No."

Jem tugs me back when I try to pull away. He's embarrassed, and talks so lowly that I have no choice but to lean in to hear him. He smells like vomit and soap.

"I'm really sorry. You were trying to be nice. I shouldn't have said that stuff."

"Jem, all's forgiven, okay?" I pat his flushed cheek. "Try to chill out, eh?"

I slip out of his grasp and jog back to my locker. I'll have to sprint to class, now.

Jem misses Soc, and I assume he's either resting in the nurse's office or that he went home early to recover there. There is nothing to suggest otherwise until after school, when I go out to my car and find a damp sheet of lined paper tucked under my windshield wiper. I grab it and get into my car. The sky is threatening rain.

Happy Easter, Kirk.

Friday

I sleep in to get the long weekend started off right. I follow that up with a long, thorough shower and one of my favorite books over a bowl of Fruit Loops. I plan to do absolutely nothing remotely resembling work today. You have to be dedicated to appreciate long weekends.

Paige calls around noon to make plans to hang out. Hannah can't come because her family is pretty religious and actually observes Good Friday, but the rest of us go to a movie and dinner at McDonald's. For a few hours it almost feels like nothing has changed, like I didn't move away and have my entire life turned upside down. I'm not sure I like it, but it's a temporary relief.

When I get home I check the answering machine. Nothing from Frank, who picked up a holiday shift for the extra pay, and nothing from Jem, either.

Saturday

I set up my homework on the kitchen table, even though I know it will be interrupted. I even prop the front door open, and not just to let fresh air in through the screen. Maybe Jem will take the hint and just welcome himself in. Who knows? He's weird about boundaries. They move according to his moods, and he's quite a moody bastard.

By one o'clock I've finished my homework and move on to the prep for tomorrow's dinner. I mix the stuffing in advance and set peeled potatoes in water. The turkey is thawing in the fridge.

By the time I'm done with Easter dinner prep, it's time to start today's dinner. The sun is set and I haven't seen or heard from Jem, which is pretty weird for a Saturday. Or maybe not—it's a holiday weekend, after all. Maybe he has family obligations. Maybe he's in Ottawa to see relatives.

It's ten o'clock at night, well past the socially acceptable hour for phone calls, when I can't stand any more speculation about Jem. He could be with family, yes, but he could also be really sick. He could be pulling some moody cold-shoulder stunt because I didn't take his side in that stupid argument with Paige on Thursday. I take the phone and curl up on my bed with it, half-expecting to get the answering machine—proof that the Harpers are out of town.

Ivy answers the call with a polite but muted 'hello.' I apologize for calling at such a late hour and she ignores me to divine the reason for my call: "You want to talk to Jem."

"I was just wondering how he's doing. I haven't heard from him in a few days."

"I'll see if he's still awake," she says.

"Thank you."

"I'm glad you called, Willa," she says quietly. "He's had quite a day."

I ask her what she means, but she won't elaborate. "Let him tell you."

Jem: March 21 to 29

Thursday

"Don't gnaw the whole thing off," Eric tells me as he looks over to change lanes.

I stop biting my thumbnail and slouch down in the passenger seat, sulking a little. It's Easter weekend, and Eric and I are driving up to Ottawa. Celeste's family isn't religious and Emily is Jewish, so Easter is just a four day weekend for them—and a great opportunity to visit. The plan is to drive up today, spend the night at Celeste's house, and then drive back to Smiths Falls tomorrow morning with Celeste and Emily.

I'm a little nervous. I haven't seen Emily since last June, except in pictures. A year can really change people. I don't even look like the same person.

Emily used to have a crush on me, back in grade ten. It was really sweet and I tried to like her back, but it just wasn't there, so we went back to being friends. Or at least I did, and she tried to keep her desires under wraps. It hit her harder than any of my other friends when I moved away. She took it the worst when I told her about my diagnosis. Emily used to send me cards and stuff when I was in the hospital, and then she saw a photo of what cancer had done to me and she took a giant leap back as though I was a leper. I think that photo killed whatever romantic feeling she had towards me. Who could love this? Who would want this?

"Dude," Eric scolds me. I take my thumbnail out of my mouth. "What's the matter? You nervous?"

"No." That's a lie. I've been snapping at everybody since I woke up and my stomach is still in knots from the episode at lunch.

"It's been awhile since you've seen Em, hasn't it?"

"Yeah."

Eric reaches over and rubs my head roughly. "Trying to soften the shock?" he says.

My toque is rust-colored today. It's the first one Elise made for me. She chose this yarn because it's similar to my hair color. And yes, I'm wearing it to make myself look more like the Jem that Emily used to know.

"It's just a hat."

"You're tense, bro."

"Just restless." We've only been driving for thirty minutes.

"If you don't want to see her we can cancel." He gestures to the cell phone plugged into the dashboard charger.

"Of course I want to see her."

It was Mom's idea that I invite Emily, after Eric asked to invite Celeste. It was sort of a last minute thing. Celeste and her boyfriend are on the rocks (when *aren't* they?) and she was looking for a chance to get out of town.

I'm not looking forward to a night at the Harcourt house, but it's the only thing I have to delay seeing Emily. Odds are, my time at there will be tense or boring. Eric will do the best friend thing and comfort Celeste about her stupid boyfriend, nurturing her self-absorption or distracting her as only Eric can, and I'll be left to hang out with her parents or occupy myself. We're not picking Emily up until tomorrow morning. She can still cancel our plans. I almost expect her to.

I get a sneer and glance from Celeste when we get to the house, before she ignores me and monopolizes my brother. Mr. and Mrs. Harcourt are polite but distant. They don't know what to make of me, what to say or what to offer in the way of hospitality. These are people who value perfection, which means that in their eyes, I'm practically worthless.

"Are you feeling any better?" Mr. Harcourt says.

"Every day." Complete lie.

We're still making awkward conversation when Celeste and Eric come down to the kitchen in search of food. Celeste pays us no mind, still talking—nay, bitching—about her boyfriend.

"What's your boyfriend's name again?" I ask. I already know his name; I'm just trying to piss her off. Implying that the isn't the center of the universe will do that.

"It's Bentley," Celeste says coldly. She's offended that I interrupted her running stream of blah blah blah.

"Is his sister named Mercedes?"

She gives me a withering look. "Jem."

"Maybe a brother named Porsche?"

Mr. Harcourt thinks my joke is funny. Celeste turns her narrowed eyes on him instead of me for having the nerve to chortle. Who names a kid *Bentley*, anyway? Rich people with fatter egos than wallets, that's who. Figures Celeste would go for a guy like that—and still feel dissatisfied.

The Harcourts give Eric and I the queen-sized guest bed to share. Eric offers to take the couch but Mrs. Harcourt waves away his 'gallantry' and insists that the bed is big enough for two. I bet she thinks he'll drool on her nice throw cushions if she lets him have the couch. The Harcourts are weird about their possessions—their house looks like a museum or a magazine photo; not quite lived in, somewhat staged, and emotionally void.

As soon as Mrs. Harcourt leaves, Eric tells me to take the bed. We use the extra pillows and a spare blanket from the closet to make up a cot on the floor, and Eric sleeps there. I would share the bed with him gladly, but it's a risk. Eric is a wild sleeper and if he hits me during the night it would cost me more than a bruise. There's also the fact that my immune system is still weak. I shouldn't be sharing close quarters with anyone right now.

"Wake me if you need anything, eh?"

"Sure."

I don't get much sleep anyway, the way my brother snores.

101

Friday

Around nine o'clock we leave the bourgeoisie neighborhood the Harcourts reside in for the more unassuming suburb that Emily calls home. I'm sweating by the time Eric pulls onto her street. I've been waiting for her to call and bail, but the only response to my text that we were on our way was a smiley face. What the hell does that mean? Stupid noncommittal emoticons.

Eric parks along the curb in front of her house and I get out of the car. He joins me, which is a surprise, but a nice gesture nonetheless.

"You look sick, bro."

For a second I wonder if my 'sickness' is enough to get away with waiting in the car for Emily, for not going inside to see her parents, but that would be terribly rude.

"Come on."

Eric puts a hand on my shoulder and pushes me forward, up the front walk and onto the low porch. He rings the bell while I panic inside like a five-year-old girl.

"Relax, it's Emily, not the Inquisition," he whispers.

"You did your History homework."

"All one-third of it," he says proudly.

Emily answers the door with a giddy smile on her face. "Hi guys." She steps aside and holds the door open for us. Eric and I walk in amid an exchange of hellos, and I notice Emily giving me the once-over. She seems to be having trouble holding her smile.

"Still cheerleading?" Eric asks.

"I made captain."

"Congratulations."

They exchange a friendly one-armed hug. Emily looks at me as though she isn't sure if she's obligated to touch me now, too. Two years ago she had no problem sticking her tongue down my throat and inviting me to grope her.

I make it easy for her, looking the other way and asking politely if her parents are home.

"Mom's out, but my dad is home."

Emily goes upstairs to get her overnight bag while Eric and I make conversation with her father. It's easier for Eric—they talk sports. Emily's dad does that thing that everybody does these days: looks away from me when he's speaking because it's too awkward otherwise.

"Ready to go?" Emily says with forced cheerfulness. I bet she's regretting this already.

On the way to the car she studies me some more and says, "You look pretty good."

Pretty good? That's a left-handed compliment if I ever heard one.

❧

The drive back to Smiths Falls is filled with friendly but unsubstantial conversation. Celeste and Eric have their talk in the front seat, Emily and I have ours in the back, and occasionally the subjects cross to include everyone. For the most part, Celeste isn't interested in talking to Emily or me. She dislikes me for a variety of reasons and disdains Emily on principle. I've heard Emily referred to as 'that cheerleader' when she isn't around. Celeste considers herself so beautiful that she doesn't have to 'put herself on display like that,' to use her phrase.

"Are you really okay?" Emily asks lowly as we drive through Kanata.

"Yeah. I'm getting better."

"Ask him how much he weighs now," Eric says with a stupid grin.

I kick the back of his seat. Emily looks out the window uncomfortably. He got that idea from Mom, who has been bragging to anyone who will listen about how I've been gaining pounds by eating soup.

"Thanks," I tell him.

"If I guess right, will you tell me?" Celeste says with a mean smirk.

"Piss off, Barbie."

"Show her how they jack you into the Matrix," Eric says. I kick his seat again.

When we arrive at the house, Mom meets us at the car and gathers Emily into a hug of welcome. Eric unlocks the trunk to get Emily and Celeste's bags, and I corner him to demand what the hell he was trying to do to me back there.

"You two were so painfully awkward," he says with a nod in Emily's direction. "Just talk about it and demystify the whole thing before it wrecks your weekend."

When Eric sounds wise, you know you're screwed.

Elise accosts Emily in the foyer with giggly demands for updates on all the friends she left back in Ottawa when we moved. Emily obliges as best she can, and we somehow end up on the couch watching *Harry Potter* with my sister. Elise is trying to hide her dorkiness, but every so often I catch her mouthing the dialogue out of the corner of my eye.

In the kitchen, Mom is trying to cook a special meal in honor of our guests. A jar of Willa's homemade soup for me is on to heat, and Mom is making an attempt at kosher food for Emily. Her parents are strict about stuff like that. They make her do all sorts of volunteer work at her synagogue or she doesn't get to stay in cheerleading.

When the kosher meal is ready, I'm glad I don't have to eat it. Mom isn't a great cook when it comes to recipes she's done a million times, never mind new ones. She's too scatterbrained and 'as long as it's edible' is her philosophy.

I smugly eat my soup while the others force their way through dinner. Elise wipes her mouth a lot and crumples at least a dozen napkins. I wonder if she swallowed anything at all. The food is so bad that not even Celeste tries to be a kiss-ass by complimenting it. When everyone quits trying to choke it down, Elise offers to make milkshakes.

"How's your soup?" Emily asks as Elise sets up the blender. I'm practically licking the bowl—it's that good and I want to rub it in.

"It's ok."

"His friend makes it for him," Dad chimes in. "She's a very good cook."

"I guess you eat it a lot," Emily says jokingly.

I can't see what's funny about that exactly, but I smile anyway.

"It's all he *can* eat," Celeste interjects, and I'm not smiling anymore. She must be fondly remembering my first round of chemo, when she was in town and I almost threw up in her car. I still regret asking her to pull over. I should have barfed on that bitch's nice leather seats.

"He's a sucker for milkshakes, too," Elise says. "You're going to love these, Emily. Do you want raspberry or peach?"

Despite her talent for annoying me, my little sister knows how to pleasantly divert an uncomfortable conversation. I don't even mind that I owe her one now.

Saturday

Dad has the day off, and he proposes a trip to the Rideau Trail, since the weather is going to be nice. It's one of Eric's favorite places to hike, but I've never been. We head out after breakfast, Mom and Dad in the Audi and the five kids in Eric's Neon. Elise claims the middle seat as the littlest person, but sandwiched between me and Emily, she seems like a protective placeholder, as though she doesn't want anyone getting too close to me.

Rideau Trail Association organizes activities year-round. Right now we have the option to hike or snowshoe along the trail around Perth. Sections of the trail include a wide gravel path, while others are just trodden ground.

"Only three quarters of a kilometre to the first rest stop," Elise notes aloud as she flips through the brochure. Her pink-gloved hand slips into mine and squeezes. That's longer than I've walked in a while. I'm not going to fail at this, though, especially in front of Emily. I don't even want to contemplate how embarrassing that would be.

Emily hasn't looked at me all day, except from under her lashes when she thinks I'm not looking. I'm making her uncomfortable just by the way I look and my silence on the subject, but I don't know how to initiate a conversation of that sort. Lucky for me, Elise is good at chatter, and she fills the silence along the trail. She stops to take photos a lot, and I take each opportunity to rest on a rock or fallen log.

"Are we moving too fast?" Dad asks.

"Not at all." My joints are going to hurt tonight.

It's almost noon when we get to the first rest area. It took us twice as long to walk the first leg of the trail as it usually takes Eric when he comes here alone. Blame it on Elise's photo taking and Mom's bird watching and my growing fatigue.

We stop at the rest area for a picnic lunch—no kosher food this time; Mom's given up already. Emily sticks to vegetables and dip and I eat a Jell-O cup. Eric eats four sandwiches and Elise loses half of hers by dropping it on the ground. Eric dares her to eat it anyway.

The walk back to the cars is even slower than our walk into the forest. Emily hangs back with me, acting as if my slow pace is normal, and we talk comfortably for the first time in months. She's stressing over what to do this summer. Her dad wants her to go to Torah camp again, but she wants to stay in Ottawa and get a job—and be near her boyfriend.

"Aren't you old enough to be a counselor at that camp now?"

Emily wrinkles her nose. "Probably. But it's in Montreal. I don't want to be so far away again."

Her parents have signed her up for camp without asking her opinion on the matter for eight years running.

"Maybe your boyfriend could mysteriously end up at the same camp."

"He isn't Jewish."

That makes me laugh. "What does your dad think of that?"

"He doesn't know."

This guy is doomed. The two weeks that Emily and I tried to date were punctuated by no less than five attempts by her parents to set her up with nice Jewish boys, hoping to divert her interest away from the likes of me.

"Let me know when your dad finds out. I'll swing by for the funeral." I laugh, but Emily gasps and looks at me as though I've said something blasphemous.

"What?"

"Nothing."

She buries her hands in her coat pockets and picks up her pace a little.

You idiot.

She spent half of last year anticipating a funeral notice—mine.

Emily takes the middle seat on the way home. I have a headache building, so I lean my head back and close my eyes. After about twenty minutes my pose is mistaken for sleep and they start to whisper about me.

Emily asks Elise if I'm really looking better. She has no personal experience to draw a comparison.

"Yeah, he does," Elise whispers back. "The sores have healed, and his stomach isn't upset as much anymore. He's got color again. He used to be so pale he looked green." She paints a nice picture, doesn't she? Whatever; it's the truth.

"He's so thin."

"He's gained weight," Eric chimes in.

"I heard you were his donor," Emily says to Elise.

"Yeah."

"Do you have a scar?"

"I have a few." She says it with such pride, like the complications of the procedure didn't come close to killing her.

"I'm doing a presentation for my drama class—it's a monologue about the satisfaction of being an organ and tissue donor." She never told me that...

"Did he tell you he's taken up knitting?" she says innocently. That little witch knows I'm awake.

"I thought it was macramé?" Celeste interjects.

"To hell with all of you," I mutter. "Except you," I say to Emily, and crack an eyelid to give her a sideways look. She's as red as an overripe tomato; she was probably the only one who genuinely thought I was sleeping. Talk about a social gaffe.

"Sorry."

"Let's play the license plate game," Elise says, and grabs Emily's hand excitedly. Either she's forgotten her Ritalin again, or she is an angel.

⊷

It's about an hour after dinner when Emily works up the guts to talk to me openly about... things. She sits cross-legged on my bed like a kid sitting down for a campfire story, and doesn't protest when I take the desk chair instead of sitting with her. I prop my feet up on the edge of the bed and slouch comfortably.

"Did your mom give you the email I sent when you were in isolation?"

"Yeah, she did."

"You didn't write back."

"I was in isolation."

"I mean after."

"It seemed stupidly belated to answer."

"I wouldn't have cared."

"I called you."

Emily grimaces sadly. "You could barely talk, your voice was so hoarse."

"I still had sores."

Emily scoots forward on the bed until she's sitting right on the edge, leaning in toward me. "Can I see you without your hat?"

"Why?"

Emily shrugs. "I'm curious." Her tone makes it sound like an apology.

"You said the photo I sent you was weird, and that was when I still had some hair."

"I didn't say it was weird. I said it made me *feel* weird."

"Weird how?"

"I dunno." She shrugs and looks away uncomfortably. "Guilty, maybe? Freaked out? Like all of a sudden it was real and you were seriously sick?"

"Why do you want to see more of that?"

It was probably to everyone's benefit that I didn't receive treatment in Ottawa; friends would have felt obligated to visit me, and that would have been torture for us all.

"Because it is real."

I can't argue with that. I've lived it. So I take off my hat.

Emily stares. She stands up and touches my head. She moves the skin around under the pads of her fingers as though she's never seen human flesh before.

"Do you think your hair will grow back the same color? I've heard it changes sometimes, after chemo."

"I don't know."

She runs a finger over the ridge of bone where my eyebrow used to be. "Are you totally hairless?"

"Almost."

Emily pushes up my sleeve without asking permission and studies my smooth forearm.

"What's almost?"

"I have hair here." I direct her attention to the fine hairs on the backs of my second knuckles. Those are the only ones fit for polite discussion.

"Just there?"

I can see she's wondering about the parts that aren't open for polite discussion.

"Not *just* there."

"What happened to your hands?"

"It's a side effect of the transplant. Perfectly normal." And perfectly hideous.

"Will it go away?"

"Eventually. Like a sunburn." But not completely.

"I heard chemo feels cold going in."

"They have to keep the drugs at a certain temperature."

"Does it make your arm go numb?"

"It doesn't go in through the arm. I've got a tube in my chest for that."

There's a reason I didn't tell Emily all this stuff as it was happening. It would have freaked her out, as it does now when I explain what a Hickman is.

"Can I see it?"

"No." I put my hat back on.

"Why?"

"It's private."

Palming my bald scalp is one thing. Staring at the port in my boney, hairless chest is another. My ego can't take that kind of negative scrutiny.

"That's why Eric calls it my connection to the Matrix," I offer by way of lame humor. Emily laughs sweetly.

"Come here."

I grab her around the waist, teasing her like I used to, and pull her onto my lap. I twist her long dark hair around my hand like a rope and say 'gotcha' in her ear.

Emily rolls her eyes at me. She always did. She's the kind of girl who pretends to hate attention until she can't stand to fake it anymore.

"You're so immature."

"And?" I chuckle. She tries to stand up and I pull her back. "Where you going?"

"I'm not too heavy?"

"I think you weigh all of fifty pounds when wet."

Emily sticks her tongue out at me. She loves it.

"I mean, I'm not hurting you, right?"

A year ago she tackled me onto a couch with absolutely no mind for gentleness—just passionate making out in her parents' basement. Now she's afraid to sit on my lap.

"I'm not made of glass, you know."

"I know, but you're so thin…"

"I'm fine. Relax."

I pull her back against me and slouch again. We both put our feet on the bed, nudging toes. It's a familiar pose. We were cuddle-friends even before I knew she had a crush on me, before she had a boyfriend. That's why I don't feel bad about holding another guy's girl; I was there first, technically.

"I can feel it," she says quietly.

"What?"

"Against my shoulder."

She flexes slightly in demonstration. She's talking about my Hickman. She can feel the catheter tips through our shirts.

"Sorry."

I let go and help her sit up.

"I don't mind."

Elise interrupts the moment by bursting into my room with the force of a small bomb. The door bangs back on its hinges as she launches herself onto the bed and bounces there on her knees.

"Guess what? Guess what?" she squeals.

"Rowling is writing an eighth Potter book?" What else could reduce Elise to the level of an over-emotional four-year-old so quickly?

Elise stands up and starts jumping on my bed, talking between bounces in a voice breathless with excitement. "I sent him an email about the party Mom said I could have and he said—"

"Jesus Christ, Lise."

"—Yeeeees!" she sings, and jumps off my bed with a flourish. "He's coming to my party. And he's not going to blow me off at the last second, either, so don't even say it, Mr. Pessimist." She jabs a finger at me. Emily laughs.

I can see a million ways this can go wrong. But Elise is happy, and damn it if I can stand to contemplate all the ways she could be hurt. It's not as simple to get a smile like that out of her anymore—at one point all it took was a chocolate chip cookie.

Elise squeals again and skips out of my room. "I have to call Carey!"

Emily smiles. "She hasn't changed a bit, has she?"

"Of course she has."

This last year as seen plenty of change in her: she has boobs now (gross) and is chasing after a jock like some horny teenaged airhead (grosser).

"I meant her enthusiasm," Emily clarifies. "But you're right, the boobs are an improvement."

"Oh shut up."

Emily finds it easier to talk when she doesn't have to look at me, so she stays on my lap for a while. We turn on the computer and creep her boyfriend's Facebook page. She shows me the photos of her winter formal—it looks like she had a fun time—and it occurs to her to ask if I've made any new friends here.

"A few." Okay, one.

"Anyone interesting?"

"Not really." Only a riddle of a girl.

"Are you lying to me?"

She looks at me over her shoulder with a teasingly shrewd expression. I just chuckle and tell her of course not.

"You smell different," she says suddenly. I don't know why, but I can feel my face go hot at her inconsequential comment.

"Just my soap, I guess."

But the soap I use is unscented, hypoallergenic stuff from the pharmacy, formulated to keep my skin from peeling off in sheets and breaking out in blisters.

"You don't smell like a brand scent," she continues. "You smell like…I don't know what."

So I come right out and say it.

"I smell like drugs."

Emily flinches.

"They've got me on so much strong stuff that my skin is soaked with it. I've got opiates in my sweat. The chemo smell was worse."

Emily is about as rigid as a statue. Mom calls up the stairs that dinner is ready, and Emily practically runs from my room.

You shouldn't have scared her like that

She needed to hear it.

Gently, you jerk.

How do you gently tell someone that you smell like a cancer patient?

⌘

After dinner, Elise starts a game of War with three decks of cards. She must have blackmail on Eric, because he and Celeste join in instead of going off on their own. The three of them keep Emily distracted while I slip away to discreetly vomit upstairs. All I ate for dinner was soup. Willa's soup has never made me sick, or even queasy. Maybe the milk was bad.

Everything comes back up—why does it always feel like I puke three times as much as I eat?—and when the nausea passes I feel hungry again. I wash up, brush my teeth to hide the smell of vomit, and go downstairs to seek out a cup of yogurt.

"Help Elise," Eric says when I enter the kitchen. "She's losing, hard."

Elise kicks him under the table as hard as she can, and he barely flinches. I just laugh and grab a yogurt cup before sitting down beside her.

The point of this game is to gain all the cards in the decks. Each person sets down one card at a time, and the person with the highest card claims all the others. It takes a long time to play, with great ebb and flow between streaks of luck. That's if we play by the rules. It's a tradition among us kids to cheat as much as possible, and if you catch someone cheating, you get to punch them in the shoulder.

"Jem's on my team."

"We're not playing in teams," Celeste says.

"Donor and recipient can be counted as a single person, then," Elise says, and sticks her tongue out at Celeste, who sniffs in response.

Elise scoots onto my knee and plays an ace. She really is getting clobbered. I make all the snatches, even the cheat ones, since her reflexes are horrible. She takes all the punches when we get caught, though. That's my tough little Elise, taking the beatings she knows I can't.

You've reached a new level of pathetic.

   And you owe her a big thank-you.

Maybe I'll put Gryffindor-colored M&Ms in her pancakes tomorrow.

When she finally catches Eric cheating, Elise gets up and walks around the table to give him as good a punch as her scrawny arms will deliver. She pushes back against me to move the chair, and the slight weight of her back against my front sets something off. I try to swallow to forestall the sensation, but it's no good. The yogurt is coming back up.

I practically trip over Elise in my haste to get to the sink—there's no way I'm making it to the bathroom.

"Crap." Elise drops her cards and grabs a roll of paper towels from under the sink for me. Eric asks if I'm okay and Celeste sighs loudly.

"Jeez, Jem," she complains.

Elise turns around and stamps her foot. "He didn't do it on purpose, Cee!" Her voice is beyond shrill with indignation.

"Shut up, Elise."

She turns to look at me with surprise, and then with hurt. She throws the rest of the paper towels down next to me.

"Fine," she hisses, and storms away.

She was only trying to defend you.

> *Because a guy like you needs his shrimp of a sister to fight his battles for him.*

You need to apologize.

> *You need to grow a pair.*

"Let's put on a movie," Eric says, trying to divert our guests' focus. He, Celeste and Emily abandon the cards on the table and go to the living room. Emily hangs back, though.

"Do you need any help?" she asks as I turn on the tap to rinse the sink.

"No. I'll meet you in there."

She goes without any further encouragement. I think she understands why it takes me an hour to show my face in the living room.

↭

I'm tired as all hell by ten, but I stay up because everyone else is still awake. Normally I would go to bed whenever my body tells me to quit, but Emily's presence gives me social obligations as her host. She comes into my room before bed, dressed in pajama pants and a tank top, and says she's going to have bruises on her shoulders by tomorrow.

"Well if you didn't cheat so much…" I tease her, but the joke falls flat.

"Do you still feel sick?" Emily asks. She's standing back farther than normal, holding her arms defensively around her middle. Like I'm catching. Like I might puke on her.

"I'm okay now. I got sick really suddenly, is all. It doesn't happen that much anymore."

"It used to?"

"During chemo it could happen without warning."

She doesn't like my direct honesty nearly as much as Willa does. Why can't she take it? Whatever she's imagining can't be nearly as bad as going through it yourself or with a loved one, like Willa has.

What a wimp.

> *Be nice. She's still your friend too, and you have a limited supply of those.*

Emily steps up to me vcautiously, as though she isn't sure if I'll bite. She reaches up and pulls my hat off.

"It's less weird that way," she says.

"What?"

"When your hat is on I can't help picturing you with hair. It's like watching

111

someone wear sunglasses indoors." She bites her lower lip and shrugs. "This is…you."

I don't want this to be me.

Emily sets my hat aside on the dresser. We sit on the bed and talk about tomorrow's plans. Dad wants to go to church, and Emily and Celeste are free to come if they want. Easter breakfast is always a big deal, and Eric still puts on an egg hunt for Elise even though Mom and Dad insist she's too old for it. We're discussing plans for an afternoon walk when Mom knocks on the door.

"Can I come in?"

I jam my hat back down on my head. Emily might like to look at me this way, but it's enough to make Mom cry. She'll lose more sleep if I upset her right before bed.

Mom knocks softly on the door before poking her head in. "The phone is for you, Jem. Do you want to take it or are you too tired?"

"I'll take it."

I accept the cordless phone from Mom and ask Emily to excuse me before taking it into the hall. I shut the bedroom door behind me. Mom slips away down the hall with a smile and a wave goodnight.

"Hello?"

"Hi." Willa's voice is soft and sort of dreamy, as if she's about to whisper a fond secret.

"Hey. What's up?"

It's a relief to talk to someone who isn't weird about…well, *me*.

"I missed you today."

I should probably say it back, but all I can do it smile from ear to ear.

"You too good to hang out with me now, or something?" she teases.

"No. No, I've just had company today." I have to speak lowly for Emily's sake.

"I worried about you. It's been awhile since you've been MIA on a Saturday."

"I'm sorry."

It's a warming but guilty feeling, knowing that she cares enough about me to worry when I'm not around and don't call.

"You were with family today?"

"No. A friend came down from Ottawa."

"Did you have fun?"

"She's in town all weekend."

"Don't think I didn't notice that you dodged the question, Harper."

I rest my back against the wall and slide down to sit on the floor. I set my elbows on bent knees and seriously consider her question.

"No, actually."

"Why not?"

I swallow. "I might have to answer your question with a question."

"Okay."

"What…um…you know how…?"

"Go ahead," she prompts me softly.

I hang my head. "How can you stand to look at me?"

She's silent. I hear her shift positions on the other end of the line. "That's a complicated question."

"I might need to hear an actual answer."

"You've got such nice eyes…" she trails off thoughtfully. "They suck me in." I hear the rustle of fabric near the phone. "And you've got these really interesting hands. I like to watch them."

My chest feels tight and my stomach has butterflies. The feeling is reminiscent of that time in fourth grade when Bette Lapalme pantsed me after gym class, even though we were alone packing up equipment and she was the only one who saw my underwear.

"And sometimes when you come to class you've got Jell-O coloring on your teeth."

I snort.

"I look at you because I like to."

"And it doesn't bother you?"

"Sometimes," she admits. "But *you* don't bother me."

For some reason, I don't doubt her.

"I want to show you something. When you have time," she says.

"Alright."

"Are you going to bed soon?"

"Maybe. Are you?" I don't want to hang up yet, but if she's tired…

"I'm in bed."

I smile at the thought of her curled up in that narrow bed I sat on a few weeks ago. The one with the soft sheets that smells like Willa. I could live in that bed—provided she was in it too, of course.

"Goodnight." It is good, Willa.

"Sweet dreams."

She hangs up first. I sit there with the phone to my ear until I hear the dead line tone. I get up, set the phone on the shelf, and go back to Emily. She glances up when I enter but can't hold her gaze.

"Maybe we should go to bed."

"Okay," she readily agrees. She throws in a fake yawn for my benefit.

I walk her down the hall to the guest room and say goodnight.

I return to my bed and tally up how long I have to wait before I'll see Willa again.

Sunday

Elise spends fifteen minutes looking for her Ritalin (lost the bottle again) when she wakes up. She's going to need it today. Easter breakfast is generally sugar-heavy: scones, croissants, bacon, eggs, and muffins with jam. And then there's the egg hunt Eric has planned. I saw him come home from the grocery store last week with two shopping bags full of chocolate eggs. I won't be the only one with a sore stomach today if he plans on hiding all that.

The eggs are already hidden when we wake up in the morning. Elise finds three on her way downstairs—her genuine, innocent smile brightens my day tenfold—and tucks them away in her pajama pockets. She prowls around the house for more while the rest of the family puts breakfast together. Eric watches Elise hunt and calls out 'warmer, colder' to her as she crawls around, looking under the furniture for sweets.

"Aw, Eric!" she complains when she realizes he's hidden six eggs on top of the blades of the ceiling fan. Eric never half-asses a game. Then she finds an egg in the sugar bowl, and four in Mom's flowerpots. She's got quite the haul by the time breakfast is served.

She bounces in her seat when she sees the red and yellow M&Ms in her pancakes.

This is why Elise can never grow up. She brings so much sunshine to this house. If she wasn't such a little girl, she couldn't do that.

"Whose idea was the M&Ms?" she says around a full mouth of pancake.

"Mine," I say.

"Will you do it for me on my birthday, too? I know you're too cheap to get me a present," she teases.

She just had to remind me that she's going to be seventeen soon—too old for such things. But it's Elise, and I'm a complete sucker for her sweet requests, so I say yes.

"But this means I'm returning your gift."

"No!"

"I wonder if Dollarama gives store credit…"

"Jem," she complains, but she's laughing too hard to pull it off. I mess up her bed head some more and she tells me to bugger off.

I get up, still chuckling, and go to the fridge to grab a cup of Jell-O. I catch Emily looking at me like she's pleasantly surprised.

"What?"

She shrugs and smiles. "You haven't changed a bit."

❧

The day goes by at a lazy pace. Everyone is a little bit food-drunk, except for Elise, who has apparently become immune to Ritalin's effects. Dad practically forces her to play a game on the Wii to keep her focused and burn off her sugar high.

"Sorry," I say to Emily. She smiles and shrugs.

"I like it."

She's an only child, and lonely a lot, I guess. Emily is more than happy to get sucked up into the Harper family dynamic—so much so that I actually have time to slip away and call Willa after lunch. It goes to voicemail. This disappoints me far more than it should, given the circumstances.

I wait all day for her to call me back, but she doesn't. I thought she had some kind of sixth sense for when I need her, like Elise does—she's always handing me mints for my stomach, and she called last night when I was feeling down.

You don't need her right now, idiot.

You just want to hear her voice.

Monday

Mom drives Celeste and Emily back to Ottawa. Eric would have done it, but Mom found out that he hasn't done any homework all weekend. He's been banished to the library until it's done. Emily and I part with a gentle hug, as if her little arms might break me.

"Say hi to everyone for me."

"I will."

She waves and slides into the backseat. When she drives away, I don't miss her.

I hate her a little bit. She made me feel visible, but not in a good way—not like Willa does. Emily made me feel visible for all the reasons I wish I could hide. I wasn't Jem, the friend she's known since preschool; I was a set of symptoms to be watched and scrutinized. It took her three days in my company to see me as just Jem.

I go back inside and shut the door behind me.

"Want to play?" Elise calls as I pass the living room, holding out a Wii controller.

"Not now, Lise."

She drops the remote and scampers after me. She throws her arms around my waist from behind and damn it, she's heavier than I remember.

"Elise." I try to walk but she keeps her feet planted, dragging along behind me. "You're such a child."

"What's wrong?" She pouts.

"I'm tired and I feel like shit, that's what's wrong. Now let me go."

She releases me, but continues to follow me upstairs in complete violation of my personal space.

"Will you lay off?"

She grabs the cordless phone off the side table. "I'll call Willa."

Like Willa is supposed to fix everything?

"I'll do it."

I reach for the phone and Elise scurries away, dialing madly. I grab the back of her shirt before she can descend the stairs and she curls into a ball, playing keep-away with the phone.

"Willa?"

"Give me the phone."

"It's Elise—aah!" She shrieks as I pick her up under the arms and try to set her on her feet. She goes limp from the waist down.

"Can you—"

"Give me the friggin' phone!"

I try to grab it and Elise elbows me in the chest. We're both so boney that it hurts like hell.

"Can you come over this afternoon?" she asks Willa calmly as I cough next to her. I make another half-hearted grab for the phone and Elise stomps on my foot. I swear, I'll snap her wand in half.

"Okay, great. See you then." She hangs up and hands me the phone.

"You bitch," I growl at her.

Elise isn't perturbed by my tone. "She's coming over in an hour, but she can only stay till four. She has to volunteer tonight."

"Next time, just give me the phone."

Elise rolls her eyes. "I did you a favor. If you had called, it would have taken you an hour just to work up the guts to ask her over."

Maybe I'll burn her wand instead. Just *try* scotch-taping that back together.

"Love you," she says sweetly, and skips down the stairs.

⌖

I have about forty-five minutes before Willa is due to arrive. Time enough for a power-nap. The doorbell will wake me up if Willa's crappy muffler doesn't.

The depth of my desire to see her surprises me. It's been a rough weekend, and she knows how to make me feel better—when she isn't making me feel like an asshole.

I don't know what I want to do with her today. Maybe we'll go for a walk. Maybe we'll fumble through Bach again at the piano. Maybe we'll cook one of her recipes and her face will light up like it does when food just comes together exactly as planned.

The thought of that smile comforts me to sleep.

⌖

The need to use the bathroom wakes me up. I push the pillow away groggily and sit up. My joints ache and my limbs feel like lead. I hope this is just from sleeping in one position too long and not the early signs of muscle fatigue.

Then I notice that it's dim in my room. The sun has shifted away from my bedroom window, around the corner of the house. I look at the clock and realize it's almost four.

"Shit."

Elise laughs downstairs, and I'm fairly sure that's Willa, not another of my sister's friends, laughing along with her. I get out of bed, wobbling slightly on sore joints, and use the bathroom as quickly as possible before heading downstairs.

I have to take the stairs slowly. My knees and ankles protest every step, but gradually loosen with more motion. I follow the sounds of life to the kitchen, where Elise and Willa are bent over a magazine, chatting happily.

I brace my forearms on the doorframe as Willa looks up.

"When did you get here?"

"About two hours ago."

I've slept away practically all the time I had with her today.

"Why didn't you wake me up?"

"You need your rest," Elise says, and I shoot her the look. She knows the kind: the I-will-torch-your-Hogwarts-robes one. I hate her even more right now because she's right. I can feel fatigue creeping up the muscles in my back and legs, even though I just had a nap.

"I've gotta get going," Willa says.

She grabs her purse from under the table and her jacket off the back of the chair. Watching her do it makes me angry. I haven't had my time with her yet. She was supposed to come visit with me, not Elise.

"Sorry we didn't get time to talk," Willa says as we walk to the front door. "If you're up for it, give me a call tonight. Or we'll talk tomorrow."

I want to ask her to blow off volunteer work to stay with me, but she'd never do it. Willa takes her commitments seriously.

"What time do you get off?"

"Eight."

"Maybe you could come back here after?"

"It's a school night."

"One of your brother's rules?"

"No, one of mine."

"Oh."

Personal principle or not, it stings that she doesn't want to spend time with me. After the weekend I've had, any small rejection feels particularly wounding.

"She got you good, didn't she?" Willa says with a casual study of my face. "Can't let her do that, man. It gives the demons too much power."

She claps me on the shoulder—*ow*—and turns away. She gets into her car and I'm walking as fast as I can to catch her before she leaves. My growing fatigue makes my feet feel heavier than they ought.

Willa's eyebrows go up as I climb into the passenger seat beside her.

"How?"

"Uh…"

"Tell me. I honestly want to know how you do it."

She smiles like she's not sure if I'm joking. "You serious?"

"Yes."

"Are you high?" My eyes must be bloodshot, if she's asking.

"No."

"Let's go inside." She looks concerned. I probably look like shit. I certainly feel like it.

Willa gets out of her car and I follow. These doors are really heavy. I lean a bit on her hood as I walk back to the house, and Willa graciously offers her arm. I don't want to take it, but I need it. When cancer-fatigue (which is different from regular fatigue, by the way) sets in, it's swift and feels like walking through semi-set cement. The three steps up to the porch might as well be Mount Everest.

Eric appears in the front door. "Aw, jeez," he mutters. He probably thinks that Willa's departure has been thwarted by my inability to get back inside unassisted.

Eric comes down the steps and puts an arm under my shoulder. He gets me up the steps and into the house.

"When did you last eat?"

"I'm not going to pass out," I tell him. "Just sore."

He helps me up to the second floor and into my room. I'm lucky to have a brother like him; Eric knows how to be discreet when it counts. He takes my shoes off, knowing I don't have the energy to lift my feet up to do it myself, and gets a pair of pajamas out of the drawer.

"He'll be all right," Eric says to Willa in a dismissive sort of way. He's giving her permission to leave.

She hangs back in the threshold.

"He'll sleep it off." He pats my head roughly. The noogies are going to start again as soon as my hair grows back.

"We'll talk tomorrow," she promises me.

"Wait. We can still talk—I'm just…sluggish."

That's one of the worst things about cancer-fatigue: I can be completely physically drained and still be mentally wide-awake.

"Get comfy," she says, and closes the bedroom door.

Eric helps me change and tucks me into bed.

"Don't tell Mom." She'll worry, and I'll probably feel better by the time she gets back from Ottawa.

"Sure, bro." I'm certain he's lying to me.

Eric leaves and shuts the door behind him. Willa doesn't immediately come back, and I wonder if she changed her mind. Or maybe I misinterpreted her words, and she never meant to stay. Maybe she'll come back after volunteering, only it's a school night… I'm waiting for the sound of her tires on the gravel driveway when the door opens.

"Are you sure you want to talk? This can wait."

"Come in. I'm sure."

Willa steps into my room and closes the door behind her. Tucked up in bed like this I feel like such a…such a….*cancer patient*. It's stupid, but I like to appear healthier than I am, especially in front of her. I don't want to be disgusting and fragile.

Willa puts down her bag, toes off her shoes, and crawls across my bed towards me. I could get used to the look of that.

She sits cross-legged beside me and sets a spare pillow across her lap.

"You still want to talk about demons?" Maybe she is willing to blow off her shift.

"Yeah, I do."

If it'll make her stay.

Willa reaches over me and grabs the container of medicinal cream off the nightstand. She pulls off her right glove—the hand doesn't fall apart—and takes my scarred, dry hand into her lap. She rubs lotion into my palm while she talks. These personal liberties she's wont to take are at once endearing and frightening.

"It depends what you do with your pain," she says thoughtfully. "I ignored mine until it broke me."

"When you were mourning, you mean?"

"I didn't mourn properly. I missed Tessa like she had gone on vacation, until about a month later when the reality of it hit me like a transport truck and her absence became real. And even if you don't really mourn, there's other shit to deal with."

"You seem to have dealt with it ok."

Willa gives me a hard look. "You don't know how I dealt with it."

The words hang there for a beat. She seems to sense that they're cryptic and changes tack.

"Emotional pain is a sensation that your body can't sustain forever—you start to break down; it becomes a physical problem. Eventually, if you're determined to resolve that feeling, it becomes something less haunting. You become thankful for what happened and how bad it sucked by refusing to weigh the negatives and only focusing on the positives."

"You sound like one of those self-help charlatans."

"That'll be five hundred bucks, please."

She spreads the cream right down my wrist, massaging it into the skin with her thumbs.

"When it hit me all at once like that, I snapped and threw a brick through the kitchen window. It didn't make me feel any better."

Her mouth twitches into a fleeting grimace.

"But seriously, yeah, my sister is gone, and in some ways it's a good thing. She isn't hurting anymore. Her disease made us closer than we would have been otherwise. If I hadn't been there through her illness, I wouldn't have been able to give you that soup recipe." She smiles at me and then goes back to being serious. "I might have been skittish around you, like Emily is."

I would have been happy to keep this conversation all about her.

"I don't blame Emily."

"What was the demon this weekend?"

Willa sets down my right hand and reaches out to take my left.

"Were you being serious when you said you liked my hands? Or were you telling me what you thought I wanted to hear?"

The skin on my hands is perpetually dry and cracking around the knuckles. Willa runs her thumb around the edge of the white scar on my palm from graft-versus-host disease. These aren't pretty hands.

"When do I ever just tell you what you want to hear?"

"Fair point."

Willa laces her fingers with mine, spreading lotion between my knuckles. Her hands are so small.

"The demon?"

"There are a few."

"Tell me."

"It's no big deal."

"Misery shared is misery halved."

"Another time, ok?"

"I already know one," Willa says. "You feel self-conscious that she couldn't look at you."

"Kind of." Emily did look, eventually. She just saw everything that isn't me.

"Did she ask uncomfortable questions about your illness, like I do?" Willa smirks.

"Yes. More than you do, actually. She's known me longer, I guess. She thought she was entitled to answers."

"Is that a positive or a negative?"

"It doesn't matter. I only told her what I wanted to tell."

"What's the worst thing about having cancer?"

I don't even think to stop her when she pushes my sleeve up and massages the lotion into my forearm. I should. There's a reason why I wear long sleeves all the time.

"That it takes away so much more than just physical function."

"You mean like Emily's approval?"

I pull my lip between my teeth. It's somewhat easier that she isn't looking at me. She's focused on the skin under her hands.

"Yeah. Plus, my parents' money, and time. It made Elise sick. It ruined my senior year—I'm going to have to repeat classes instead of graduating. My average has gone to shit because I'm tired all the time. And the worst part of it all is that it took away my status as a person—as a guy."

"Will the fatigue wear off eventually?"

"It's supposed to. It's the transplant, and the drugs I still take for it."

She doesn't ask what I got from Elise. Thank God. We don't need to have that conversation right now.

"Does it hurt?"

"Sometimes."

My joints still hurt in the mornings, and then there's the stomach upsets that my plethora of drugs makes me sensitive to.

"And how long until it's 'supposed to' stop zapping your energy? Is there a common recovery time for most patients?"

Of course, she doesn't know about cancer recovery. She knows about treatment and death. Her sister never made it to the other side of the slope.

"Up to a year. For some, much less."

Willa nods acceptingly.

"It's been almost five months."

"I guess you're pretty tired of being tired?"

"Don't you dare imagine that was clever."

Willa looks up at me and chuckles. "I'm sorry you're tired."

"I don't need your pity."

"Did I say I pitied you?"

"You were thinking it."

"Don't pretend you know me," she says in a cheesy imitation of my voice. I flick the hand that's massaging mine.

"That's not funny."

"I'm not a clown," she says.

"Right, you're a demon guru."

Willa presses her hands together and bows like a yogi. She checks her watch and says she has to go.

"But before I do…"

She goes to my desk and grabs a pad of Post-Its and a pen out of the drawer. She writes on two of the sticky notes, folds them, and puts them on opposite sides of the room, equal distance from my bed.

"What are you doing?"

"Read them when you feel well enough to get up," she says. Her eyes light on the whiteboard above my desk.

"What are you looking at?"

Willa doesn't answer, but she picks up the dry erase marker. She looks around my room like she's lost.

"Willa?"

She opens my closet. Willa uncaps the marker and starts writing on my mirror.

"What do you think you're doing?"

"For later," she says, and keeps writing. When she's done she closes the closet door, picks up her purse, and tells me to feel better. "See you tomorrow."

She kisses my cheek, and then she's gone. A few minutes later, I can hear her pull out of the gravel drive.

My cheek tingles a little bit where she kissed it.

You are such a chick sometimes.

    Shut up.

Fine. Your balls and I will be over here. Join us when you're through.

    I'll do that.

Fine.

    Fine.

It's nine o'clock by the time I feel well enough to get up. I shuffle towards the dresser and the first of Willa's notes. I unfold it and turn on the lamp to read.

You're amazing just the way you are. You are you.

This feels bitterly nice, knowing she left that for me. She was just trying to make me feel better, but the white lie still warms me. I re-fold it and put the paper in the bottom of my sock drawer for safekeeping.

The other note is on my bookshelf. I make my way over to it and untwist her second paper.

Ask me what I think about before I fall asleep.

Under that, in parentheses and tiny lettering, she's written: *There's another note in the mailbox.*

I consider looking at what Willa left in my closet, but the possibilities make me nervous, so I put it off. I put on my slippers instead and go downstairs to check the mailbox. It's chilly tonight, and I don't linger on the porch as I grab her third note and take it back upstairs. I shut the door behind me for privacy and lean back against the wood. Why didn't she leave this one out in the open? I have to be careful not to tear the paper in my haste to unfold it.

Made you look. Sucker.

Tuesday

When I open my closet to get dressed I'm blindsided by a mirror covered in blue marker. I forgot about Willa's note, the one that I decided to avoid when I went to bed. She covered my entire mirror in ink.

I'm not invisible. I have desires. I want to be touched and held and told that I'm worth something. I am not pitiful. I am better than you can imagine. I have talents. I have successes and failures. I love my life. I sometimes feel dissatisfied with the world. I come from a place of love, not death. I am special. I matter. I can be the most interesting person in the room. I can blend in and that's okay. I'm a somebody. I'm a nobody. I feel deeply and I want to be allowed to show it. I don't want to be judged. I can be judgmental. When you give me platitudes you belittle my feelings. I'm brave. I'm scared. I'm wandering. I have plans. I will be the best me I can be. I am not who I think I am; I am not who you think I am; I am who I think you think I am, so think well of me, please.

I grab the first clothes my hands touch and slam the closet door. I feel completely bare in a way that has nothing to do with nudity. I hurry to dress for school, feeling the need to get away from the closet as fast as possible. The fact that words on a mirror have me so on edge makes me angry—what's wrong with me that Willa can put me so off balance? How could she write that in my room and let it blindside me? A little warning would have been nice, if she's going to poke into private things I'd rather not think about. And furthermore… how did she know?

The dynamic of this friendship is screwed up beyond repair. Willa casually hands me a mint as she doodles on the margins of her page. She just *knows* when I'm not feeling well, like Elise does. This is the girl who's seen me puke, rage, come close to tears, and laid up in bed like the sick bastard I am, and she still hangs out with me.

"You're staring."

"What are you doing tonight?"

"Girls' night out with Paige and Hannah."

Why is it so hard to get a bit of her time these days? I feel like I have to schedule an appointment with her three weeks in advance.

She's popular, you idiot.

"You're not avoiding me, are you?"

Willa looks at me sideways and quirks an eyebrow, as if she's waiting for me to realize how stupid my question is.

"Well, you didn't wake me up yesterday," I retort quietly.

"You were sleeping so soundly."

She saw me sleeping? Elise didn't just tell her that I was napping? My own unwitting vulnerability irks me, but then my stupid brain catches up.

She's seen you puke on multiple occasions.

 Don't forget the crying.

Or the shuffling around like an old man.

 Shut up!

"What do girls do on a night out?"

"That's classified information," she says seriously.

"Can I come?"

Willa rolls her eyes at me. It was worth a try.

 You take desperate to a level not worth naming.

Wednesday

I think I'm actually getting dumber by taking this class. Mrs. Hudson hands out raw eggs to each of the seated pairs and explains that these will be our 'infants' until Friday, when the unit on human reproduction ends. Can't we just break it now and get it over with? Willa picks the stupid egg up and draws a face on it with her pen.

"You are such a twit."

"I'm naming him Egbert."

"The hell you are; he's *ours*. We're supposed to name him together."

"It's just an egg."

"It's Steve."

"No." The finality of Willa's tone surprises me.

She looks away, slightly pink in the cheeks, and mutters, "Whatever, just not Steve."

I relent. "Fine, we'll call it Egbert. But it's still a dumb name."

↝

Willa has yogurt in her fridge. I wonder....

I put together a snack for us while Willa sets up our homework. This egg project is heavy on dead trees. We have to come up with a whole parenting plan—how we propose to discipline our egg, educate it, give it siblings, keep it healthy, etc. When I come back from the kitchen, Willa is doing our homework with one hand and casually spinning Egbert with the other. I lay down on the couch and get comfy.

"Do you believe in spanking?" she asks.

"Real children or eggs?"

"Useless," she mutters.

It's actually a careful strategy to avoid working on this dumb assignment.

I turn on the TV and start channel surfing. I pause on Animal Planet for half a second too long and Willa calls me a pervert. This channel has forever been ruined by creeps who like to watch animals screw.

"So did we adopt this egg or did you lay it?"

Willa reaches out and sets Egbert on my chest. Her hand comes dangerously close to grazing my hardware.

"Spend some time with your kid. And *you* laid him, jackass."

I buk at her. I don't think Willa is amused. I leave Animal Planet on just to be facetious. It's a show about ostriches and I explain to Egbert that he will never hatch and grow up to be such a big, ugly bird.

"Are you talking to the egg?"

I mimic her voice. "Are you talking to the egg?"

"Shut up."

"Make me." I stick my tongue out at her and Willa turns back to her work, quietly giving me the finger. I send it right back at her and get up off the couch. It's almost six; I need to take my meds.

"Do you want a drink?" I call to Willa.

124

"No, thanks." At least she answered; I haven't annoyed her *too* badly.

I pour myself a glass of water and take my medication out of my back pocket. I carry around one of those plastic pill-sorters like an old man. In the afternoon slot there are five pills: one for pain, two Gravol—which are partly for show, considering their efficacy—and magnesium and famotidine. I take three at once and then wait a minute before taking the Gravol. Half the time the stuff doesn't work at countering the nausea caused by my other drugs.

I turn to put the water pitcher back in the fridge when Willa laughs suddenly in the other room. I shut the fridge and go see what's so funny. A young ostrich is harassing a cameraman, pecking at the Jeep door. Willa finds this absolutely hysterical.

"Okay, it's funny, take it easy, psycho."

I sit down on the couch and change the channel. She doesn't protest.

Willa checks her watch and mutters something about starting dinner. I keep flipping channels. She's gone for a few minutes before I realize I left my meds— and Egbert—on the counter. Oh shit.

I very quietly make my way to the kitchen door. Maybe she didn't notice. I left the container over by the toaster, after all.

No such luck. Willa's back is to me. She rests her hands against the counter next to the toaster, looking down. All the compartments on my sorter are open. I didn't leave it that way.

Willa notices my presence and jumps. She looks away hurriedly, wipes a hand across her cheeks, and awkwardly remarks, "OxyContin is a bitch, eh?" She knows what the drug looks like by the sight of the pills alone—that's a little messed up.

I quietly pack up the sorter and pocket it. Willa is still facing away from me. She's unusually quiet and every few minutes she runs a hand over her face, wiping away tears.

It's bizarrely entrancing, watching her cry. For one, I didn't know she even had tear ducts, being made of granite and all. For another...I feel slightly compelled to do something about it.

"Do you want me to go?"

"Uh...no."

"Do you need a minute?"

Willa turns and leans back against the counter with her arms folded. Her eyelashes are stuck together with tears and her lids are red-rimmed. She bites her lower lip and looks me up and down, studying me.

"Are you in a lot of pain?"

"Sometimes."

My answer stirs up some disturbing memory for her; I can see it in her face.

"It's just a maintenance dose. You can't just go off opiates all at once. When I'm actually in pain I take two tablets."

Why am I telling her this?

"My sister took Percocet. But it made her sick, so they put her on Oxy," Willa says.

I smirk. OxyContin is responsible for most of my stomach upsets, but it's the gentlest of several options. Percocet messes me up too. I was so high I couldn't move except to throw up—and I did a lot of that.

Willa sucks in a deep breath, holds it, and says, "I need to start dinner" on the exhalation. She steps away from the counter and opens the fridge.

"I should go."

"You're not staying for dinner?"

"I should be getting back, and you'd need to make a separate meal for me anyway." She doesn't need that trouble. I turn to go.

"Harper," Willa tiredly calls me back. "Come here. I have another recipe I want to show you."

Damn it, she knows my weakness.

Willa puts a frozen lasagna in the oven to bake and then begins to pull ingredients for my meal. She makes me help this time and promises I won't get burnt.

"This is a cold dish."

The end result is a tart that has the consistency of cheesecake, but without the flaky crust. It's low in acid, sugar-free, and creamy as pudding: the brilliant combination of cream cheese, vanilla and berry yogurt, and honey.

"I might have to steal your recipe binder."

"It doesn't contain all my recipes." She smirks and taps her temple smugly.

"I might have to blackmail you, then."

Willa laughs and leaves me to eat this amazing tart.

"Hey," I interrupt her as she checks the readiness of the lasagna. "I meant to ask you yesterday—what do you think about before you go to sleep?"

"Shouldn't you first give me a hard time about the note I left in your mailbox?"

"Just tell me."

"Or the one I left in the umbrella stand?"

"You left one in the umbrella stand?"

"And in your jacket pocket."

I get up and go to the foyer where my jacket hangs on a peg. I rifle through the side pockets and front pockets, finding only mint wrappers.

"The *inner* pocket, genius," she calls from the kitchen.

The note is folded up so small it's the size of a pencil eraser. I unfold it and take it back to the kitchen to read her scrawl under proper light.

I think about music.

And all I can think is, *Well that was anticlimactic.*

    What were you hoping for?

Nothing.

    You were hoping she thought about you, like you think about her.

No I don't.

"I've been listening to Bach."

That perks me up. "Yeah?" She plays his music horribly, but it's one of the few weak points of connection we share.

"I think I like Wagner better."

I hate Wagner.

When I get home I check the umbrella stand in the foyer. Willa's note has fallen right to the bottom with the dust bunnies and a few of Elise's stray mittens.

It says: *That's twice now. Sucker.*

Thursday

Elise's birthday dinner is fairly low-key. It's just family tonight. Mom and Dad are letting her throw a party with friends later this spring, when the weather is more favorable.

Mom bought a *Harry Potter* themed ice cream cake from the store, but it looks like the clerk thought the cake was for a seven-year-old, not a seventeen-year-old, because Mom has added the 1 with raspberry jam. Elise barely notices.

"Open mine first." Eric lobs Elise's present at her across the table.

Elise shakes the box before opening it and there's a clanking sound. She broke it. "Oh no!" Elise tears off the wrapping and opens up a shoebox.

It's full of broken bottle glass.

"Just kidding," Eric says. "Here's your real one."

He throws a much smaller box at her. He's given her a pair of earrings

"You threw a box of broken glass at her?" I say quietly as Elise crumples up the used paper.

"It was wrapped. Perfectly safe."

I suppose he's right, but I can't help but think of the Christmas he gave me a pet rock. The thing fell through the bottom of the box and broke my toe.

Elise receives a new skirt and blouse from Mom and Dad, and a card with cash from our grandparents. I got her a stuffed plush owl. I really shouldn't enable her childish obsession with *Harry Potter*, but the way her face lights up when she sees it can't compete with any logical reasoning.

"It's Hedwig!"

She bounces around the table to give me a hug, chanting 'thank you' over and over. I inform her that it's actually a puppet and she practically blows a happy fuse. She shoves her hand up its butt and finds the second part of her gift. It's a much smaller brown owl.

"Pig!"

"No, *owl*, silly," Eric says.

"No, his name is Pigwidgeon." And it's a finger puppet.

Elise puts an owl on each hand and starts a conversation between them.
Dad chuckles and stands up to clear away the dirty ice cream plates.
"We're never going to get that off her hand," he says.
Crap. He's right. What have I done?

Friday

Mornings after dialysis are like hangovers in reverse. I go to bed feeling groggy
and sluggish and wake up feeling alive, at least until the rest of my medication
catches me up and I crash again. From the first round of dialysis, I noticed
its tendency to screw with my energy cycles and sex drive. I'd get these weird
bursts of energy that would promptly be shot down by fatigue. I'd be horny
as hell but have little inclination or privacy to masturbate. It got better when I
started to receive dialysis as an outpatient, because I could go home and sleep it
off, and I had the option to jerk off fruitlessly in the morning.

Today is one such morning. I wake up starfished across my bed with my pillow at my feet—I'm a restless sleeper after dialysis, but I never feel more rested
than the morning after. I could flail all night and never feel a thing. I contemplate reaching down to retrieve my pillow, but decide it's hardly worth it.

Sandwiched comfortably between my body and the mattress is a promising
start to the day. I get out of bed and turn on the shower. I'm really recovering
now; my body is going to cooperate this time.

I strip in the dark and step into the warm shower. I angle the showerhead
toward the inner wall and lean against the tiles so that the water runs down my
back. The steam feels like hot breath on my skin, and for a split second I'm
reminded of the way Emily used to breathe across my neck when she kissed it.

I can't think about her right now, and push that thought away as quickly as I
can. Images from various porn sites take her place, but no matter what I think
about—her parts, her revealing clothes, her positions—the girl in my head always turns into a petite blonde.

Don't over-think that—not now.

I bend and twist the girl in my mind—the one with fair skin and curly hair
and a tempting look in her eye. The idea of her gets me harder than I've been
in awhile, and as I move my hand and the water runs down my back, I feel the
familiar weightlessness of a building climax.

My hip begins to cramp from leaning against the shower wall. I ignore it at
first, too afraid that the slightest pause will make this wonderful feeling disappear. But then my knees start to shake, and I kneel down on the floor of the tub,
taking the weight off my back and legs.

Relax. You're making yourself too tense.

I'm so afraid of not coming that I'm psyching myself out, and then I can't.
It's a vicious cycle. I focus on the blonde, on the fantasy of bending her over in
this very tub. She'd brace her hands against the slippery sides, with water run-

ning down her back and my hands around her hips. She'd be tight as hell and have a goddamned dirty mouth...

Suddenly I feel like I've been kicked in the balls and the stomach at once. I curl reflexively around my abdomen with a grunt of pain as my cock twitches in my hand. Thin strings of semen dribble pathetically out of my penis. I'm ejaculating, but where the hell is the orgasm? Why did that hurt so much?

I rest a hand between my hips. It feels like I pulled a muscle, and the pain radiates all the way along my groin.

You pulled a muscle just by coming, it's been so long.

This is how ninety-year-old men must feel.

I rest my head against the shower wall and sigh. It felt so good, and then...

"Fuck!" I slam my fist against the side of the bathtub in frustration.

"Jem?"

I freeze as Mom knocks on the bathroom door. She must have come in to wake me up. How much did she hear?

"Are you all right?"

Before I can answer she opens the bathroom door.

"Mom!"

"Why is it dark in here?"

"Because the lights are off. Get out!" I stand up and hold the edges of the shower curtain shut.

She turns on the bathroom light. I'm screwed.

"I heard a thump. Did you fall?"

"No! I dropped a bottle. *Get out*, please."

"It sounded heavier than that."

Her fingers slip around the edge of the curtain, ready to push it back.

I slap her hand away. "Mom! Get out!"

"Are you bleeding?"

"No!"

Elise's slippers make a slapping sound on the floor as she crosses my bedroom to stand in the bathroom door. "What's going on in here?" she asks.

"Everyone is going to *get out, now!*"

"Did you bump yourself against the shower? Why on earth would you shower in the dark, anyway? Are you bruising?" Mom persists.

Maybe I'll put the plug in the drain and drown myself.

"Yeah, Jem," Elise interjects. "Is it swollen?"

She walks away with a giggle, and the plug becomes irrelevant. I am going to die of embarrassment long before the tub could fill enough to drown in.

Mom mutters something about breakfast and bagels, sounding nearly as embarrassed as I feel, and the bathroom door shuts sharply behind her. Breakfast is going to be awkward.

As I towel off, I hear Eric's booming laugh and know that it's going to be a very long drive to school.

Willa: March 29 to April 8

Friday

On humid days like this, the cafeteria is too stuffy for comfort, and Paige keeps trying to talk to me about Chris's proficiency as a kisser. Hell no. I drift away from the group more or less silently. It's not until I'm past the main office that I notice I'm not alone. Jem follows just slightly behind me, hands in his pockets.

"Totally airless in there," he says.

"You read my mind."

Jem and I go out to the parking lot to sit on one of the picnic tables, resting our feet on the bench. The lot is quiet apart from the infrequent cries of seagulls. There's harsh weather coming in if the gulls are hanging out inland.

The silence between me and Jem is comfortable. He usually feels the need to fill these, but today he doesn't. He just rests his elbows on his knees, twines his fingers together, and watches the seagulls scavenge for food around the trashcans.

"Who do you think would win in a fight over garbage—a seagull or a raccoon?" he says suddenly.

"Raccoons. They're smarter, can hunt in packs, and have claws."

"But the seagull can shit on a whim."

I laugh without meaning to. "How is that relevant?"

"Even if it doesn't get the garbage, it can get revenge. So who wins?"

"What would you rather have—food or vengeance?"

He thinks about that for a moment. "Food."

As if on cue, one of the gulls takes a dump on Elwood's windshield. Jem laughs, but I limit myself to a smile.

"Screw it," he says. "Vengeance is better, but only if you have an army of seagull minions to carry it out."

I shake my head. "Why do I know you?"

Jem turns to me with that sideways smile. "You could be my second in command. We could take over Greenland."

"Greenland?"

"No one would expect it."

I smile. "Fine. Greenland it is."

Jem's mood is unusually good today. It lends him a buoyancy, an ease of movement, that isn't typical of him. He smiles easily instead of wryly or reluctantly. When he jokes, he isn't insulting anybody or self-deprecating. He's… happy.

Some of Jem's paleness is starting to fade. Healthy color is coming back into his face and hands. His lips don't blend in with the rest of his face anymore. Looking at his skin in the sunlight, it looks like he might have shaved this morning, and I wonder if his hair is starting to grow back enough for that. Maybe it's just the color coming back into his skin that gives it a new texture.

I wonder about him. He was so put off balance by Emily this past weekend— he must value her opinion highly. He called her his friend, but perhaps that's a new label on their relationship. Maybe they were something else entirely. Maybe that's why he took it so hard.

I can't picture Jem dating anyone. Then again, I also can't really picture him as the red-haired teenager I've seen in photos. I've only known this incarnation of him—this oversensitive, loveable asshole. Maybe I don't know him well enough to know his romantic predilections. Maybe Emily wasn't it, but someone else was. Jem isn't exactly vocal about the past. I don't know if he's ever dated, much less whom, or if he has a type. Even the broad categories like orientation have never come up in conversation. I'll keep him filed under 'ambiguous' for now.

"Why are you staring at me like that?"

The happiness in his eyes dims with suspicion. Jem gets so defensive over the smallest things. I can't even have the pleasure of looking at him without an excuse.

"Aren't you used to it?"

Jem's face goes blank, but his hands clench into fists before he gets up off the picnic table and storms away.

"Wait."

Jem ignores me. I knew better than to say that, and now I need to apologize.

I get up and take my time crossing the parking lot. Jem is marching toward his car, pissed off as he is. I know he's sensitive about his appearance and others' reactions to him. He says he likes me for not being afraid to look, but I he doesn't really want anyone to look at him, even himself.

Jem gets into the driver's seat and leans over to check the glove box for a spare key. I open the passenger door and slide in.

"Piss off," he growls at me.

"I'm sorry."

"Get out."

"At least let me apologize. I was out of line."

"Damn right you were." He slams the glove box closed. His palms come down heavily on the steering wheel as he blows out an angry breath. I watch his knuckles turn white as he grips the wheel.

"Can we talk?"

"What the hell is there to talk about?"

He won't look at me. I must have stepped farther over the line than I thought.

"Why I was staring at you." That gets his attention. He looks at me like I just threatened to set off a firecracker in the car.

"Why?" he finally asks.

"I was thinking about Elise."

A little crease appears between Jem's eyebrows. I don't think he was expecting that, and can't see how it all adds up to the look I was giving him.

"About her and that guy she's crushing on. The basketball player."

"What about them?"

"Does romance weird you out? Or is it just Elise?"

"Just Elise. She's my baby sister, for crying out loud. She isn't supposed to be interested in that kind of crap."

His fingers, which were beginning to relax on the steering wheel, tense again. "Mmmh. I see."

"No you don't, your brother isn't a sixteen-year-old girl."

"Isn't that a little sexist? You wouldn't be tweaking if Elise was a boy."

Jem sighs irritably and ignores my question. "Was that really all you were thinking?" he demands.

"More or less."

"What does that mean?"

"I was also kind of wondering, if it wasn't just Elise that bugged you, but romance in general—if you were some kind of closet case or asexual."

Jem looks at me expectantly, as if I haven't finished my sentence. When I don't continue after ten seconds he bursts out laughing. The sudden noise makes me jump, and I sit there watching him rock in his seat with bitter laughter.

"You are so…!" He cuts himself off to think of the right word. "So…insane. You don't think clearly. Who else would jump to such a stupid conclusion but you?"

He has no idea how right he is.

"Well, you roll your eyes at Paige and Diane whenever they talk about dating, and you're downright mean to Elise whenever she shows interest in a guy. You're cynical about Celeste's boyfriend. You never show interest in any of the girls at school, and you're oddly fixated on Elwood—it's not such a wild conclusion, when you really think about it."

"Paige and Diane talk about petty high school drama. It's juvenile. And I've already explained Elise. Celeste's relationship is a joke, Elwood is a complete tool, and what good does it do me to be interested in any girl here—*who the hell would go out with me?*"

"You're right." That takes him aback. "You're an absolute asshole. Any girl with half a brain would avoid you."

Jem adjusts his face into a more neutral expression and turns away. He slouches down in the driver's seat, looking thoughtful. Stray raindrops begin to hit the windshield.

"Why don't you avoid me?" he murmurs.

"You've grown on me."

"Like a tumor."

"Jem." He absolutely has to ruin everything with bitterness and morbidity, doesn't he?

He mutters an apology and sighs. "Can we just forget about this?"

"No. You've made me curious."

"I'm not going to tell you what kind of cancer I had."

"Not about that. *Is* there anyone you're interested in?"

Lord have mercy on the girl he chooses to pursue. He'd probably be all creepy and melodramatic about it, like Van Gogh.

Jem looks at me out of the corner of his eye. The movement is just a flicker, gone before I can be sure I've seen it, and he sighs. "No."

⤙

It's the last day of the egg project. We hand in the assignment and show Mrs. Hudson the egg to prove that it's still 'alive.' When she sends us back to our seats Jem asks what we should do with the thing. What a stupid question.

I take it out of his hand and lob it toward the trash can. It cracks on the far side and yellow goo runs down the black bag, into the bin.

Jem is looking at me like I just murdered a kitten. "What?"

"What is the matter with you?"

"Dude, it's an egg."

Jem refuses to talk to me for the rest of the period. I don't get it. He wasn't even interested in this assignment.

Saturday

The gulls made good on their prophecy. It rained hard all night, with hail to punctuate the Devil's Hour. The storm carries over into the morning, bringing down blustery winds and flirting with sleet. On an especially nasty day like today it's hard to do anything. Of course, some people can't be deterred.

Luke calls at nine o'clock and persuades me to drive out to Port Elmsley to spend the day in his garage. He was deeply offended when he heard that I didn't know how to do basic stuff to my car like change a tire or check the oil. So we scheduled this little meeting to 'make me less of a girl.' I'm not sure if that's sexist or just true.

I spend the morning in the Thorpe garage and stay for lunch. Luke wants to spend the afternoon together too, but I beg the excuse of homework. When I get back to Smiths Falls and decent cell reception, my phone buzzes with three missed calls and a text message. The calls were from Jem. How the hell did he get my number? I certainly did not give it to him. He must have swiped my phone while he was over and programmed his info into it.

The text message is from him too: *Where are you?* It's been five hours since he sent that text.

You're not the only one who is allowed to be MIA on a Saturday.

Jem gets back to me right away: *I reserve the right to monopolize your attention next Saturday.*

We'll see.

Are you home now? What are you doing?
Your mom.

I don't hear from him again until late at night, just as I'm crawling into bed. I've gotten into the habit of putting headphones on to fall asleep lately. It helps to drown out the sound of the frigid wind blowing over the roof. Luckily Jem's text arrives before I press play, or I wouldn't have noticed the buzzing.

What are you thinking about tonight?

I keep it simple: *Music. Santana.* He made a reference to one of their songs yesterday at school and I've had the melody stuck in my head since.

I can't sleep.
Tough break.
Are you listening to Santana now?
Yeah. "Into the Night."
Can I listen with you?

Before I can reply, my phone rings. That's not my usual ringtone. It's a short recording of Jem saying, "Pick up, it's me." A picture of his stupid smirking face replaces my wallpaper. Not only did he steal my number, he programmed himself into my phone, created an annoying ringtone, and took a picture to go with it. That douche.

"We need to have a talk about boundaries," I say in place of 'hello.'

He giggles like a little kid who has managed to pull off a lame prank successfully. "I thought it was pretty stealthy."

"You are such an ass."

"Did you have a good day?" There's a hopeful undercurrent in his voice, as though he genuinely wants me to be happy. What a weirdo.

"It was decent."

"Did you and Frank do something?"

"No, I was in Port Elmsley all day."

"Oh." He doesn't like that. And it's too late in the day for me to even consider dealing with his sulky moods.

"Do you want Santana or not?"

"Yeah, please."

I leave one earphone in and place the other over my cell phone mic on my pillow. I listen to "Into the Night" with Jem, a song that sounds sort of like a lullaby despite the electric guitars.

"Goodnight," I say when the song ends.

He doesn't answer me, but I hear slow breathing on the other end of the line. So much for insomnia.

Sunday

I set today aside for errands. I make a quick stop at the bank and then it's on to the grocery store. I'm choosing apples from the bin when a pair of hands grabs my waist suddenly.

"Gotcha."

I jump. I can't help it. And when I turn around, guess who's the culprit?

"Are you seriously stalking me now?"

"It's a nice Sunday morning hobby." Jem takes the bag of apples from me and ties it off. "What next?"

He pushes the cart farther down the aisle toward the nectarines and oranges. I guess he's shopping with me, then.

"Fresh ginger," I say, and Jem gives me a strange look. His expression is almost happy, somewhat satisfied, and a little bit suspicious. Let him wonder.

⊷

In complete violation of common sense, I bring my stalker home with me. He helps me put the groceries away and then I sit down to plan four days' worth of frozen meals. I figure two lasagnas and two casseroles should do the trick. I'll make those this afternoon.

In the meantime, I show my stalker how to make green tea sweetened with fresh ginger.

"You should be a chef," he tells me. "You love cooking so much."

"Maybe."

"Lucky for me you do." Jem nudges my shoulder teasingly. "I was getting sick of puking up green Jell-O."

"So you're glad to have a variety of things to puke back up?" That might be the strangest compliment ever given to anyone, anywhere.

"No," he says, suddenly serious. "Your food has never made me sick. Well, there was one time, but I was pretty tense so it probably wasn't the food."

"I'm glad to hear it."

"How do you know?"

I look up from the simmering pot of ginger on the stove to find him giving me a searching look.

"Know what?"

"Just what to make, when. You never make something I can't handle, and that changes hour-by-hour."

I didn't even realize I was doing it, but now that he's asked, the answer springs to mind with the obviousness of plain truth: "I watch you. When you're sluggish you need sugars. When you're cranky you need protein. You suck on the inside of your lip when you're in the mood for something sweet. If you keep very still or flex your hands a lot, I go heavy on the mint and ginger." I shrug. "You're an open book, Harper."

Jem frowns just slightly and slips his hands into his pockets. "Thank you, for...caring enough to notice all that."

"It's habit."

"Your sister?"

"Everyone. I like to cook, remember? It involves pleasing an audience." But that's only partly true. He had it right with his first guess. Cooking for my sister made me feel a little less helpless.

Monday

Jem writes the next progress report for our Soc project. We've successfully killed six snapdragons in illustration of the effects of pollution on local vegetation. I'll do the next phase of the report—probably about community clean-up initiatives.

At night Jem calls me up before bed and requests "Bitch" by Meredith Brooks. "Why?" And why am I pandering to his requests like a DJ?

"It reminds me of you."

"Go to hell."

"I'm not calling you a bitch," he protests in that persuasive tone that I've come to think of as his form of whining. It sounds nicer, but it's whining nonetheless, because most of the time it works on me.

I ignore his request and put on "Possibility" by Sierra Noble—another lullaby song. It's my go-to music on nights I can't sleep. This time, Jem is awake when the song ends.

"Why did you pick that one?" he says quietly.

"It relaxes me."

He doesn't say anything, but I can hear the faint rustle of bedding as he adjusts his position on the other end of the line.

"Goodnight."

"Goodnight, Willa."

He hangs up before I do. His parting tone was sad. Thinking about that keeps me awake longer than it ought.

Tuesday

Frank plans to put in the weekly call to Mom and Dad with my progress report after dinner, so I make myself scarce. Holed up in my room, I try to get some homework done, and after four hours this essay for Geography is driving my insane.

The phone rings. Thank God. Even if it's Paige calling to gush about Elwood, it'll rescue me from this project. More likely it's Luke, calling to work out plans for this weekend like we said we would. I leap across the room to grab it off my dresser and answer without checking the caller ID.

"Thank God you called."

An altogether too smug chuckle greets me. "Happy to hear from me?"

"Oh, crap, it's *you*."

Jem laughs at me.

"What do you want?"

"Isn't this your bedtime?" he says.

I look over at the clock on my nightstand. It's half past ten, the approximate time when I usually go to sleep.

"I'm pulling an all-nighter."

"Whatever," he says with a smile. "Who were you expecting a call from this late?"

"My mom. She keeps odd hours." I'm not sure why I'm lying to him.

"I thought of another song that reminds me of you."

"What?"

"You know that one 'Beautiful Girl'?"

"Did you just compare me to a Beatles song?"

"It's just George Harrison."

"You're dead to me."

Jem snorts softly. I don't know what to say next.

"Are there any songs that remind you of me?" he asks suddenly.

"Maybe."

"Play one for me?"

"Hold on." I flop down on the bed and scroll through my playlists, looking for an appropriate tune. It takes me a few minutes to settle on one, and then I set the phone up next to my earphone and press play. Tonight he gets "Troublemaker" by Weezer. Perfect for him.

Wednesday

Frank is volun-telling me for stuff again. Mr. Thorpe has been asking his sons to spend some time with their bratty sister, and according to Frank we can't let our friends suffer Briana's shenanigans alone. As it stands, on Saturday Luke, Briana, and I are going to the movies.

Jem calls promptly at ten-thirty. I skip the hello because it's irrelevant and open with, "Do you have nothing better to do with your night?"

He ignores my question, I guess because he finds it irrelevant. "Have you ever heard 'The Gambler' by Kenny Rogers?"

"Country?"

"Yeah. It reminds me of your demons spiel."

"Sorry, I don't have any Kenny Rogers." He's got me thinking, though. "Do you know 'Hard Road' by Sam Roberts?"

"No."

"It reminds me of my demon spiel too."

I skip the headphones tonight and prop my phone up next to my laptop speakers. While it plays we both listen to it and I quietly compile a playlist of other songs that might come up one night—the ones that remind me of Jem. Just for comparison, I do a 'Luke' playlist too. He has a lot more happy songs than Jem does.

"Don't bring a lunch tomorrow," I tell Jem before we say goodbye.

"Why?"

"I'm bringing soup."

"Really?" He sounds so excited. "A new one or an old one?"

"A new one."

"What kind?"

"You'll find out tomorrow."

Jem whines my name. I tell him to shut up and let it be a surprise.

"Thanks. You don't have to do this, you know."

"I want to." I want him to eat. When he eats he's happy, and when he's happy he can really be himself. The real Jem Harper isn't as big a drag as the starving, bitter boy who takes over his body periodically.

"And you won't even give me a hint?"

"Lentils."

"Lentils?"

"Yes."

"And I'll get it before school tomorrow?"

"No, you'll get it at lunch, you greedy bastard. I'm not going to give it to you in the morning so you can eat it all too early and be a hungry, cranky jerk by Soc."

Jem chuckles at my rant and puts on that persuasive tone, trying to sway me to his way of thinking.

"No. You get it at noon."

"Fine." He manages to make pouting audible over the phone.

"Don't make me regret this," I threaten him.

"Noon is fine," he agrees with newfound cheerfulness. He really wants a new soup. We say goodnight—he reminds me not to forget the soup—and hang up.

Downstairs, the ingredients are already chopped and measured, ready to be boiled down tomorrow morning before school. I think he's really going to like this one.

Thursday

When the bell rings at the start of lunch, I make my way to my locker and find Jem already there waiting for me, arms folded and tapping his toe impatiently.

"Can I have it *now*?"

I pretend to consult my watch. Lunch period goes from 11:45 to 12:30, and we agreed on noon. "Well…"

"Kirk."

I open my locker and give him the thermos of soup. Jem unscrews the lid immediately and takes a sniff. He smiles and sips right out of the thermos neck.

"Care for a spoon?" I offer him one, and although he takes it, Jem keeps sipping right from the source as we walk to the cafeteria.

"I like it." He practically inhales the soup and scrapes the sides of the thermos with his spoon when there's no more left to drink. It's satisfying to make someone's day, especially with something as simple as homemade soup.

"You're annoying as hell, Harper," I tell him. "But I like you. Sort of."

He grins and tells me the feeling is mutual.

⌁

Tonight is a big night for music. I stay up later than normal, listening to pertinent songs with Jem. Tonight the focus is on songs that remind me of him: "Imaginary Bars" by Great Lake Swimmers; "Here's to the Halcyon" by The Old 97's; "Barrett's Privateers" by Stan Rogers. Jem is barely awake by the end of that last one.

"What does that have to do with anything?" he mumbles sleepily.

"Life didn't go the way he thought it would. The guy got screwed over hard and was permanently disfigured by it."

"And that's how you think of me?"

"*Your* physical state isn't permanent. Hair grows back. Severed legs don't."

"No," he says quietly. "Time won't fix it all. I'll always be scarred. You're right."

"I didn't say that."

"Go to sleep, Willa," he says sadly.

Jem hangs up and the line goes dead. The hell? That's a new level of moody sensitivity for him. I call him back immediately—he can't just hang up without letting me explain.

Jem answers on the second ring and skips the hello. "You know, when people hang up on you, it's because they don't want to talk to you anymore."

"Dude, stop wallowing. It's just a song."

"Just forget it."

"Jem, I don't think of you as scarred and disfigured," I say slowly and clearly. He's playing dense, so I might as well play along and talk to him like a simpleton. "You know what I think of you."

"That I'm a narcissistic, boring asshole."

"Right now you're like the man on the dock: there's hope in front of you but you can't see it. So quit wallowing."

This time, I hang up on him. He doesn't call back with a snarky riposte. Either he's wallowing, or he's sleeping on it. Smart money is on wallowing.

Friday

Frank is acting weird. When he got home from work he changed out of his uniform into black jeans and a nice button-down shirt, of all things. That's about as dressed up as Frank ever gets, but he keeps insisting that he has no plans when I ask. The question of my plans, however, is one in which Frank is very interested. He encourages me to go out—immediately, if possible.

"Do you have a date you don't want me to know about?"

Frank sidesteps the question. "It's a Friday night, you should go do something." He's been saying that for the better part of an hour.

"Why do I have to leave? So I won't see you leaving for your date? Or are you meeting here?"

Frank gives me a disgruntled look and I ask if I should spend the night at Oma's house. "You know, in case your date comes home with you." I swear, my brother's eye twitches at the offer.

"You don't have to do that."

"Your date lives alone, eh?" Yep, his eye definitely twitches.

Frank grabs his jacket and marches out the front door.

"Call me if you go out," he says.

"I won't wait up," I call back.

Frank slams the front door behind him. It's weird, but I think this is the first time I've ever seen my twenty-five year-old brother go out on a date. Maybe it's an anniversary.

I take out my phone and send a text to Luke: *Warn your brother to expect a cranky boyfriend tonight.*

It's slightly satisfying to receive, *Lol, will do,* from Luke. Apparently I'm not the only one who suspects a relationship; or maybe Doug is out to his family. I don't think Frank will ever do that. He values his privacy too highly.

Saturday

Today could have gone better. Mr. Thorpe is looking for good influences for his daughter, because by the look of her, she has plenty of bad ones. Briana's barely into high school and just a hop, skip and a jump away from solving her problems with meaningless sex and substance abuse, if she isn't there already. She reminds me of myself, and I'm a little peeved that her dad thought an afternoon at the movies with 'wholesome' people would help her. I could see uneasiness written all over Frank's face too, but he kept his mouth shut. That's my brother's specialty.

My annoyance with the situation keeps me awake long past my usual hour. It's nearly midnight when Jem calls, which is unusual. If he's going to call, he usually does it by ten-thirty.

I really have to change Jem's ringtone. "Pick up, it's me" is starting to get annoying.

"Why are you calling so late?" I say, because 'hello' has ceased to become a part of our phone conversations.

"Where were you today?" Jem's short tone surprises me. My automatic reaction is to become defensive, just like I did whenever Mom and Dad asked me that question.

"What's it to you?"

"Tell me."

"I was out with friends, you ass."

"Paige?"

"No, some friends from Port Elmsley. We went to a movie."

"Why didn't you invite me?"

"We had a full car already."

"Did it completely slip your mind that we had plans today?"

"We did?"

"Just forget it." Jem hangs up on me, and I'm left wondering what the hell just happened. He and I never made any plans this weekend. The only mention of anything weekend-related was the text he sent me days ago: *I reserve the right to monopolize your attention next Saturday.* That does *not* count as making plans. What's in it for me? And I never agreed.

I drop my phone on the nightstand, roll over, and hope that he gets over his hissy fit by Monday.

Sunday

Frank and I head over to Oma's house after breakfast. Doug is meeting us there, and we're going to surprise Oma with the new greenhouse. We still have to assemble it, and there's the issue of putting shelving on the inside, but she should have a place to keep her seedlings within the month.

My phone keeps chirping with texts from Paige. Frank is annoyed by the sound. He's been annoyed with me in general since I mouthed off on Friday night, and tells me to turn off my phone.

"You're with family today, all right? Be present, for once."

I stand there with a framing hammer in my hand and stare at him.

"For once?"

I was more present for the big events in our family than he has been for the past four years. I picked up my whole life and moved for our sister, to say nothing of what happened after. Framing a greenhouse doesn't compare, and if he's annoyed by my ringtone he can just say so.

Frank looks away uncomfortably and mumbles an apology.

"I'll turn my phone off."

"Okay then."

Compromise doesn't have to be *that* hard.

✥

Erecting the greenhouse takes all day, and Oma invites us to stay for dinner. On the way home I ask Frank if I can turn my phone on, and he has the good grace to look chagrined when he tells me yes. My phone starts buzzing with backlogged texts, and they're not all from Paige.

The first one from Jem came at eleven: *I'm sorry I snapped at you yesterday. Can we talk?*

And fifteen minutes later: *Please answer your phone. This is childish.*

I leave my inbox and check the log for missed calls. I have four. All from him. Needy or what?

At twelve: *I'm on my way over, since you won't answer.*

And at twelve-thirty: *I can see your car in the driveway, genius. Answer the door.*

I chuckle humorlessly. Of course my car is still in the driveway; I drove to Oma's house with Frank in his car. I can picture Jem standing on my porch, hammering on the door with his usual lack of patience, thinking himself ignored.

He clearly gave up on my door sometime between twelve-thirty and three, because the next message is: *Call me at home when you get this, please. I left you a voicemail.*

I wait until Frank and I get home to dial into my voicemail inbox. I take my phone up to my room first and close the door for privacy.

Jem wasn't precisely truthful when he said he left me a voicemail. He left two. The first one begins without a hello: "Look, I know you're mad at me. I shouldn't have snapped on you like that. I was just mad that you made plans and didn't say anything when we usually do stuff on Saturdays. I know I shouldn't have assumed but… Okay, will you just answer your phone? I feel like an idiot talking to your answering machine. And—" The message ends abruptly.

I press play on the second message.

"Shit reception," he says by way of explanation for the way his last message ended. "I was going to say we should make plans. If you want to. I could make up for being rude to you the other night."

There's a long pause where he doesn't say anything.

"Did you really have a full car yesterday? No, never mind, it's not important. Sorry."

The message ends.

Well, at least he apologized. I don't like the way he thinks he can put dibs on my time, though. We hang out on a few Saturdays and he thinks he owns that day now? His over-sensitive temper is troublesome, too. Jem picks fights more than I do.

One of my sister's favorite phrases was, *If you didn't want trouble, why did you invite it?* Did I give Jem the impression that he could treat me like this? As far as

I can tell, I didn't give him the impression that he could boss me around, but I did give the impression of availability and accessibility. I take entirely too much interest in him, and he took that as an invitation to insinuate himself into my life. If I'd known he would become possessive, I would have been on my guard from the first. I'm in no state to have anyone lean on me.

Once again, I'm uncomfortably conscious of how much I stare at him—study him, really. I watch Jem's hands for clues to what he's thinking or feeling or craving to eat. I watch his face for signs of health and I could probably list the colors of the toques he's worn over the past three school days. I know what and how much he eats during lunch, even on the days we don't sit at the same table. On Friday I took one of his earphones out without asking, just because I wanted to see what he was listening to. It was "Friday I'm in Love" by the Cure and he got all embarrassed and changed the song. Next to Vivaldi, The Cure isn't all that embarrassing. But when I got home that night, I listened to the entire album and it reminded me of him.

I take far too much interest in Jem for his good or mine. I don't get attached to people anymore. I don't do intimacy in any form and haven't for years. There is a big thick boundary line between my emotions and others' and I have no intention of crossing it.

This has to stop. Precisely because I like it and I think about him far too much. Tessa always said that if something feels good it must be wrong, unless it's so wrong it can only feel good. Of course, she meant that as encouragement—she wanted me to get out of my over-cautious rut and be bad for a change. The words also serve as a damn good warning: take a big leap back, Kirk, because you know Jem well enough to know that he's not the right kind of guy to get close to. He gets attached, and you don't. He's manipulative and sneaky, too. Just look at the caller ID on your phone.

Speaking of my phone… I turn it off for the night instead of calling him back. That boy needs to learn that he doesn't own me and has no right to boss me around.

Jem: April 9 to 13

Monday

I text Willa when I get up—she still hasn't gotten in touch with me—but she doesn't answer that message, either. I wonder if something happened to her. Maybe she had an accident of some sort, or maybe she's got troubles at home to keep her occupied.

I'm relieved when I see her car in the parking lot at school, but I don't have time to seek her out before the start of first period—thank you, Elise, you lazy dawdler.

I don't have a chance to see Willa until lunch. I get to the cafeteria and find her without trouble, like she's a homing device sending out a signal. To my surprise, Elise is sitting with her and the usual group. I slide into a nearby seat in time to hear Elise inviting her over this Friday.

"It's a small birthday thing. Just a few friends."

"I thought your birthday was a few weeks ago?"

"It was, but it was so close to the school dance and the weather was so crummy, I decided to put off a little celebration until things were calmer around here. And the sun will be out, of course—good weather gives a party atmosphere. It's supposed to be nice this Friday."

Willa agrees to attend and Elise gives her a quick hug before skipping away to her regular table to join her friends.

Paige draws Willa into conversation next, and I have no opportunity to get a word in edgewise, the way Paige babbles. As usual, everyone else at the table ignores me out of discomfort.

Hannah takes pity on me by the end of the hour. "So, did you have a good weekend?" she says shyly.

I don't think I've ever spoken two words to her before, but I know she's a good person by what I've seen and heard.

"It was pretty quiet." In other words, my only friend ditched me—twice—so I sat at home and moped over music. "You?"

"It was okay."

I don't know her well enough to know what else to ask about her weekend. So we drift off into awkward silence until the bell rings.

⌇

Willa is ignoring me. She's about as unenthused about the Soc term project as I am, and yet here she is, too dedicated to the assignment to give me the time of day. Every time I try to start a conversation she answers me in clipped monosyllables without looking away from her paper.

"Are you still mad at me? You got my message apologizing, right?"

"Harper," she says, voice thick with irritation. It's a *screw off* in disguise.

I let her be. Maybe she's just stressed about her half of the project (I should probably put some thought into the project too, come to that), and doesn't really care about this weekend anymore.

"Everyone ready to discuss the term presentation rubric with your partner?" Mrs. Hudson asks the class. She takes the sound of shuffling papers for a yes and tells us to start brainstorming plans for our group presentations.

Willa ignores me, which hardly seems possible given that we're working on a joint assignment. She just reads over Mrs. Hudson's guidelines and says, "I think we can just wing this." Apparently that's the end of the discussion.

For the rest of the period she barely talks to me, and only when I talk to her first and ask point-blank questions, which she answers as curtly as possible. She won't look at me, either, and that unsettles me more.

"Look at me."

Willa lifts her head and looks over at me with a tightly controlled expression. Her face doesn't offer softness or compassion, or any other inviting emotion.

"Why are you looking at me like that?"

"You told me to look at you."

"Not like that."

She turns away with a huff. "Make up your mind."

Something happened this weekend. Maybe my rudeness was just the cherry on a shit sundae, but I thought I had fixed this with an apology. I guess not.

After an unbearably silent Soc period—Willa doesn't look at me again—I spend most of my English class writing her a proper apology note. Maybe my phone message didn't cut it. I fold the note and slip it under her windshield wiper before the end of the day. I'll call her again tonight.

Willa doesn't answer her phone. I call every hour and it consistently goes to voicemail. I try her house line and Frank says that she's busy.

"Oh. Is she volunteering tonight?"

He hesitates just slightly. "Yeah. She's at the hospital."

She's at home, dodging my calls.

Tuesday

Willa manages to look right past me as she asks what she should get Elise for her birthday. Her face is turned in my general direction, but the focus of her gaze is somewhere over my left shoulder, looking out the window. I lean over to be in her line of sight and she looks down at her book instead.

"Anything Harry Potter-related would be a hit."

Willa hums in agreement.

"Mom will be happy to see you. She was asking last night why you haven't been around lately."

"I've been busy."

"Been working on the next project report?"

"Ugh, don't remind me."

Willa folds her arms on the lab table and lays her head on them, shutting herself away.

"Are you not feeling well?"

I put a hand on her back and she flinches away. She really looks at me for the first time in days—to glare at me.

I take my hand off her and murmur 'sorry.' We don't talk for the rest of the period.

↬

Elise makes me a milkshake without me having to ask.

"Bad day?" Dad asks when he sees me nursing the milkshake and watching *Harry Potter* with Elise. Dad's not great with the emotional stuff. That's more Mom's area of expertise. Dad is good for injuries, business advice, and grand philosophical questions about the nature of the universe. If I told him that my only friend, who, coincidentally, is also the girl I'm crushing on, is mad at me and has been for days, he'd stare at me like I'd ceased to speak English and maybe tell me to keep my chin up. So I change the subject.

"I need to refill my prednisone prescription soon."

Dad nods. "I'll pick it up tomorrow after work. How's your pain management working out?"

"Fine."

"Keep trying to follow the dietician's plan, okay?"

"Sure." I might glance at it, later.

Dad asks us if we want pancakes. We both say no but Eric shouts a resounding "YES!" from the second floor. I think that boy eats his own bodyweight in food every day.

"Cheer up," Elise says as Dad walks away to make pancakes. She tugs on my ear and I tell her to knock it off.

"Not until you smile."

She tugs on my earlobe again with a smirk. When she was a baby she had this weird thing about sucking on my ears—just mine, Eric's wouldn't do. She wouldn't take a soother, but she'd willingly follow me around, arms locked around my head, gumming my ears. I was so young myself that I just took her abuse as normal.

"Well cheer me up, then," I complain.

I pull my hat down over my ears to keep her from teasing them.

"Want to tell me what happened at school today?" Elise tactfully mutes the movie, which is a big deal because she's usually incapable of turning her attention away from the screen for even a nanosecond while this is on.

"No."

"Was it Willa?"

I suck back more milkshake instead of answering.

Elise sits up so fast she almost falls off the couch. "She's still coming on Friday, right?"

"Yeah, she asked me what to get you for your birthday."

"That was sweet of her. So come on, did you guys fight or something? Or was it a stupid spat like the Uncle Fester thing?"

"She just hasn't been in a talking mood lately."

Elise shrugs at that. "Give her space. She'll be fine." And I would give her space, but I'm paranoid.

By the time I retreat to my room to escape the smell of burnt pancakes (way to go, Dad), I'm thinking about this weekend. Willa has been hanging out a lot with other friends lately. Maybe she was distancing herself before I even knew it.

It's physically painful to think that she might be giving into peer pressure and permanently ditching me. She might be consciously and deliberately cutting me out of her life, and not bit-by-bit so I have time to land on my feet, but all at once—cold turkey with no notice.

I get up and turn on my laptop and speakers. I play the angriest music I own at top volume. It doesn't help. I try to vent into my cello, which usually cures all, but it hurts my hands too much and I have to stop. The piano is no better. *Everything* reminds me of Willa. She's in every room of this house—in my very own bed, where she comforted me; at my piano where we played Bach; in the kitchen where she neatly insinuated herself into the fold of my mother's society and Elise's confidence; in the library where she gushed over Chaucer. There is absolutely nothing I can do and *not* think of her.

I fucking hate her. And I want to fall on my knees and beg her to keep me around.

At six I have to head over to the Dialysis Clinic for my weekly appointment. I bring a book for the long wait, but I don't feel much like reading. I just sit there and stare at the page and wonder what Willa is doing right now. I think about calling or texting her, but the nurses are Nazis about cell phone use in the hospital. Maybe I'll get lucky and Willa will be volunteering tonight. Or maybe that's no luck at all—maybe she won't look at me even if we do bump into each other. She could pretend not to know me, like I'm just another patient. Or, worst of all, seeing me hooked up to a machine might remind her of why she's dodging me to begin with.

If I met myself, I wouldn't be friends with me. I'm a drag to be around, always tired or sick or cranky. Whoever I hang out with will get stared at because I'm with them. People feel the need to watch what they say around me. Willa isn't one of those people—or at least she wasn't. Keeping her other friends is probably more important to her than keeping my pathetic ass around, and it's no secret that the other kids in her clique don't like me.

I can't control how people see me, but I can control what they think of me as a person by being friendly, and I don't even do that well. That's why Willa's friends can't get over the fact that I look diseased: I'm too standoffish. But with Willa I figured things were different, because nastiness was the status quo and she said it screwed up the whole dynamic of the friendship when I was nice. I took that as license to unload who I really was instead of hiding behind a veneer of false happiness. I could be myself around her.

But that gets old. She's done with me. She's moving on to normal friends.

I lay my book on my lap and hang my head in my hands. This shouldn't hurt so much. I got along just fine without her for seven months. I was doing okay before she showed up. The fact that I'm addicted to her company is embarrassing.

Could she really never look at me again?

It's not like she even likes you back. Parting is easy for her. She barely knows you. Do you really know her?

She was only hanging out with you because she felt sorry for you. Pity only goes so far.

And you are pitiful.

Seriously, what did you think you had to offer that would tempt her to put up with your sorry ass?

By the time I get home my stomach is twisted into painful knots. Figures, my body can't even get heartache right. I call Willa again, but she doesn't answer.

Elise tries to comfort me. I'm not in the mood, so she just returns my headphones and two CDs—all taken without permission—and leaves me to myself. I take a hefty dose of Benadryl to crash; awful, I know, considering I just came back from getting my blood cleansed of toxins. It knocks me out, and the deep sleep after dialysis takes me too far under to even dream.

The Benadryl only keeps me under until three o'clock in the morning, and I wake up feeling hot and groggy with a hand down my pants. The migration of said hand is a matter of course, really, but whatever I don't remember dreaming about seems to have been a turn-on.

I don't even bother to get out of bed. The simple act of rolling over to grab the Kleenex box is a difficult one to wrap my head around as I push my sweatpants down. I'm still dozy from the Benadryl and the vague promise of pleasure is the only conscious thought I am capable of.

My hands move to no effect. There's stimulation, but no build. I shake off the drug haze and move my hand harder, faster, trying everything to make my body cooperate with my urge to achieve release. I even bring in the image of the petite blonde, but skilful as she is—and is she ever—I can't coax my body into submission.

I'm just about to give up when a painful spasm creeps up the back of my spine and I arch involuntarily. I fall back onto my pillow with the eye-watering pain in my abdomen that feels just like last time; like someone has cut through the length of my crotch with a hot serrated knife. I bite the pillow to keep quiet and curl around my sore center.

Why did you even bother?

It takes almost forty minutes for the pain to fade this time; way longer than it did in the shower. When I can move again I reach for the Kleenex to clean myself up, but realize there's nothing to clean. I even turn on the lamp and stand up to inspect my clothes and the bed. Nothing. I didn't even ejaculate this time.

I crawl back into bed, more defeated than I've felt in awhile, and bury my head in the pillow. What if this problem never goes away? What if I can never get off again? What if I can't ever have sex because of this? That would really scare a girl off—a guy who screams in agony and has to lay in the fetal position for an hour every time he nearly-comes.

My sleep is restless for the remainder of the night, and I get up with sore joints and a pounding head. I think the Benadryl was a bad idea.

Wednesday

I've been out of bed for exactly thirty seconds and my day has already gone to shit. My piss is cloudy. I don't have an infection and it doesn't hurt to pee, which leaves one obvious solution: retrograde ejaculation. Damn it. Do you know who does that? Paraplegics and old guys with no bladder control left, that's who. I'm supposed to be in recovery and my body just keeps finding new ways to betray me.

I try to rub one out in the shower in an attempt to power-trip on my own body; show it who's boss, and all. I can't even get hard enough to call it a semi. I think I'll just crawl back into bed.

↢

We're a little early for school. Elise insisted on leaving early so she could 'drop something off at the social planner's office.' That's probably total bullshit, considering that the basketball team had a seven a.m. practice and she's still pining for that guy who's no good for her.

I don't want to go into the school yet. I have no one to hang out with and chat to before class, and standing around like a loner is tough on the ego. So I lay down on the backseat and try to get an extra fifteen minutes of sleep before going in for first period. I hear the telltale rumbling of Willa's lousy muffler and sit bolt upright. She's early too.

I get out of the car and head toward her car. Willa is still sitting in the front seat, holding a notebook up against the steering wheel. She must have some last-minute homework to finish.

I open the driver's side door and say hello. Willa's speakers are playing "(I Can't Get No) Satisfaction" by The Rolling Stones at a low volume. She's listening to the soundtrack of my night.

"Morning."

She looks at me like she can't believe I have the nerve to talk to her, and then at my hand where it rests on the edge of her car door.

"Uh, I guess you want to be left alone?"

"What do you want?"

She's doing that thing again—the thing that makes me feel very small and insignificant and helplessly in the wrong.

"Just to see how you are."

"I have to finish this." She gestures to her homework and closes the car door firmly.

I stand there like the idiot I am, watching her work while she doesn't even spare me a glance.

How can she just blow me off like that? I have the sudden urge to pound on her window and ask her what the hell is up her ass, but that would only worsen her mood. I shove my hands in my pockets and head inside.

She's not just being cold and ignoring anymore—she's being downright mean.

Elise makes me a milkshake without having to ask for the second time this week. My night turns around: in sweats by five, sitting down to a milkshake and bowl of homemade soup for a snack.

"Why don't you invite Willa over for dinner?" Mom says. "I haven't seen her all week."

"I'll call her." And just like that, my day is shit again.

I call Willa's cell and house lines, but she won't answer either one. I tell Mom that she's busy tonight. By her worried expression, I get the sense that she doesn't entirely believe me. Willa's absence has been noted.

Thursday

My alarm clock goes off unreasonably early. Before I even open my eyes or roll over to switch it off, three thoughts surface from beneath the haze of sleep: *It's Thursday. It's a school day. I can't do this.*

I roll over and shut off my alarm. My day hasn't even started and I feel completely, utterly defeated. Why should I bother to get up and go to school? No one there cares that I even exist. I don't feel like eating. I don't feel like doing anything. I spend five whole minutes debating whether it's worth the trouble to get up to pee.

Mom pokes her head in and tells me to get a move on.

"I'm not going in today."

"Why not?" She steps into my room and puts a hand on my forehead. I'm not sick. Not in that way, at least.

"I'm not up to it."

She studies me for a moment, and it looks like she's about to say something when she turns and leaves without a word. She comes back a minute later with a glass of water and a reminder to take my meds.

"I'll call the school and tell them you won't be in."

"Thanks, Mom."

When she leaves I burrow deeper into my blankets and go back to sleep. It's about as numb as I can get without a morphine drip.

⌖

Tom Petty wakes me up. The hell? I lift my head—the clock says it's ten-thirty—and look over my shoulder at my speaker setup. The thing doesn't just turn on by itself.

There's a blue-haired freak standing by my speakers, dancing unabashedly. She hasn't changed a bit. The blue of her hair matches the bullring in her nose and the stud in her eyebrow, because she likes to coordinate like that.

Ava catches my eye and smiles. "Hey slut."

She takes a run at the bed and leaps toward me. She lands above me on all fours with a wicked grin on her face.

"Check it out." She sticks her tongue out to show me a new piercing. I'm not surprised. Ava's primary motivation for most things is 'because it would piss my dad off.'

"I'm thinking of getting my lip done, too."

She kisses my forehead—shit, I'm not wearing a hat—and then sits back on her heels, balancing above my waist. I'm so thin that there's actually room between her butt and my stomach.

"Good idea. Your dad'll have a stroke." I sit up on my elbows. "What are you doing here?"

"Nice to see you too, bitch." She teasingly brushes her hand across my face in an approximation of a slap. "Your mom called me this morning. She wanted me to call you and cheer you up or some shit. But this is better, even if it is a long-ass drive."

"It's a school day."

"A what?" She blinks at me. "Screw that. You're my excuse to get out of Gym class." Ava pulls back my blanket and waves me up. "Come on, get up. Emily said you were getting your energy back. We're doing shit today."

"She said stuff about me?"

I swing my legs out of bed, but stop there. I'm dreading her answer. If it's bad I'll just crawl back into bed and bury my head in the sand.

"Not 'said' exactly."

Ava goes to my drawers and starts rifling through them. She throws articles of clothing at me as she finds them—socks, underwear, shirt, sweatpants. Then she opens the drawer I keep my toques in and throws her hands up. "Dude, it looks like a yarn factory threw up in here."

"Just tell me what she said."

Ava huffs "Caitlin wanted to know how her weekend was and before Emily even said anything she started bawling like a fucking baby." Ava slams the drawer and makes a disgusted sound in the back of her throat. "She can be such a whiny little priss sometimes."

"I'm telling her you said that."

"Speaking of—" Ava whirls on me. "How come you invited her for Easter and not me?"

"It was Mom's idea."

Mom likes Ava, but only in small doses. She couldn't do an entire weekend with her as a guest. Ava has a mouth like a teamster, no sense of appropriate timing, and no verbal filter on her thoughts. She can be absolutely hilarious or embarrassing as all hell.

"So what is there to do in this town?"

"Nothing."

"Come on, there has to be something."

"Nope. It's Smiths Falls."

"Don't kids usually go cow-tipping or something in small towns?"

That makes me laugh. "Did you pass many cow pastures along the road?"

Ava heaves a long-suffering sigh. She's a city girl to the core.

"I brought Shelby with me in case you weren't up to going out. But since there's nothing to go out and do…"

Shelby is Ava's violin. She plays nearly as seriously as I do cello. We weren't really friends until we were in the same music classes. My hands are too sore join her on strings, but there's always the piano.

"Bring her in."

It's been awhile since Ava played classical. She isn't signed up for Music at school this semester, and if the school or music camps aren't forcing her to play classical, she attaches an amp to her violin and creates her own sound. These past few years she's been flirting with death metal. If I'd seen her band play before I knew her, I'd have totally stalked her.

"You're such a goody-two-shoes," Ava complains as she rifles through my sheet music, looking for something worth playing. My collection is entirely classical. I did aspire to play professionally, a lifetime or more ago.

"Just pick one."

Ava pulls a blue folio out of the stack and smirks. "Okay, you're taste isn't *totally* pathetic."

She pulls out the sheet music and slaps *Das Wohltemperierte Klavier, Prelude in G Major* down on the music stand. Kill me now.

"I'm sick of Bach."

"Well you're short on Apocalyptica, so this'll have to do," Ava says.

She tests the tune of her instrument before launching into the opening bars without me.

"Ava."

She stops and looks at me archly. "It's this or cow-tipping."

God damn it, why couldn't she have just called like Mom asked her to? I turn to the keyboard and shift reluctantly through the notes. It's like walking, just one key after the other. Keep moving, because it hurts too much to stay put. It's the illusion that I'm going somewhere, or going away from something. I'm moving, so I must be alive. I can't die, because music isn't really alive. It's an equation; a sensation; a fleeting thought that runs through my head too fast to be heard; an idea that lingers and drives me insane until I have to play it. To move is to blur the line between self and song.

Willa likes this song. She hates me, but she likes this. Willa falls asleep to this song. I wonder if she ever thinks of the time we played it together. Does she ever think of me at all without disgust? I bet her other friends keep her too busy to spare me much thought. It's not like I have anything to offer that she would miss.

The faster I play the faster it will end and I can get her out of my head.

Yeah right.

Ava lowers her bow and flicks my ear. "Stop messing up the tempo."

"Sorry."

We start again from the beginning. So much for getting this over faster. But this is supposed to be a light, mellow song. To adjust its speed is to corrupt its tone. I block out the thoughts of Willa and the aches in my joints and the niggling hunger in my stomach, and just listen to it. I haven't played like this in ages. It's effortless, weightless. It breathes. Time becomes irrelevant and the room could go up in flames without my noticing. When I run out of notes to play I'm not quite sure what to do. My hand lingers on the final key, drawing out the note unnecessarily. Ava gets fed up with the pointless noise and grabs me by the wrist to lift my hand away.

That's when we both notice that my hands are shaking. I curl my fingers into fists to make it stop, but the tremor only gets worse. It's hard to get a good breath.

"Jesus, boy," Ava says, and grabs my hands. She turns me away from the keyboard and forces me to put my head between my knees. "You okay?"

"Yeah. Sorry. Just…got a little lost."

She knows what I mean, the way music can transport you to such an *other* place. Down the rabbit hole, with no clear way of how to get back when the song ends.

"You, my friend," she says, "are more messed up than I first fucking suspected."

I hang my head. That is such an Ava thing to say. What's weird is that I know exactly what she means by it, and it isn't cruel.

Ava crouches down in front of me to be on eye-level. "Who is she?"

"Who?"

"It's always a girl."

"What's always a girl?" I pull my hands away and sit up.

"There are times," Ava says seriously, pointing a finger at me, "that you get this look on your face. It's like your making love to the goddamned piano, and I know it's the doing of some chick you're all lovesick and blue-balled about." She smirks and shakes her head. "You're really quite a musical pervert."

"This coming from the girl who lines her violin case with Georgia O'Keefe prints?"

"You were fingering the bejesus out of that piano."

"I was not."

Ava presses the nearest key she can reach, keening in time with it. Her voice pitches up with each key press and she sets an almost frantic tempo. She makes my piano sound like a girl about to come.

"Damn it." I grab her hand off the keyboard and she laughs at me.

"It's really cruel to tease her like that," Ava informs me seriously. "It didn't even look like she came when you were giving her Bach."

"I can't do this."

I pack up the sheet music and close the key cover. That's quite enough of music and my playing habits for one day.

Ava quickly resumes her original plan. "Let's go out."

⊕

Ava's car is a lemon yellow Gremlin that she won off her brother. Well, it's mostly yellow, in between the rust spots. He bet this piece of shit on a football game and she took him up on it. Ava loves this car, even though it's fuck-ugly, falling apart, and can barely pass emissions testing.

We have no idea where we're going when we pull out of the driveway. There's nothing to do, so we'll just drive around 'until we find trouble,' as Ava so touchingly puts it.

She turns on the radio and searches for a station with good reception. She settles on an obscure AM station without too much static. They're broadcasting "Cecelia" by Simon and Garfunkel. Ava turns it up and sings along.

I change the station.

"My car, my music." She changes it back.

"I hate this song."

"Nobody hates this song."

"I do."

"I can see broken-hearted depressives hating it, but come on. It's a great song. And adultery is natural, don't you think?"

I don't say anything. We travel for a few more minutes without conversation, listening to this annoying song. When it ends, Ava switches the radio off entirely and asks, "Who?"

"What?"

"Who broke your heart?"

"No one."

"Give me a name so I have an excuse to crack her skull."

"Ava," I complain. I don't need to involve her in this.

She smiles with surprise. "It's not a she?"

Typical Ava. She lives in fear of being stereotyped as 'the gay friend,' even though she plays both sides.

"I'm not gay." Though it's the second time in two weeks that I've been asked. "And I'm not seeing anyone, and haven't been since I moved here. No broken heart, so lose that theory, okay?"

Ava mulls that over for a few seconds. "Yeah, bullshit."

"It's not bullshit."

"Emily didn't mention anything about a girlfriend, but she's always been such a spazz around you that it's no wonder she'd leave out that little detail. So come on, who is she?"

"No one." I need to change the subject before Ava really gets pushy. "Are you still with that guy? The dipshit with the ponytail and the GreenPeace shirt?"

"Phil? Eh." Ava shrugs. "He's a little political. Keeps blowing me off to do *important* shit like protest for PETA. Fuck'm."

"Good." I never particularly liked him. He was always pushing some agenda. I wonder if he's ever had an original thought, because all I've ever heard from him are the platitudes and PR bullshit that he gets from environmental groups.

"So who's the girl?"

"God damn it, Ava, I said there is no girl."

"I'll ask Elise. She'll blab."

She's right. Elise will talk about anything with minimal prompting.

"She's just a friend."

Ava laughs, gleeful that I've given in. "A fuck-friend? Or a friend you want to fuck?"

"Neither."

"I watched you do her in your head while playing Bach."

"Ava," I complain. Worse than being caught at it is the way she describes it.

"Does she like you back?"

"No."

"Why not? You're adorable." Ava reaches over and taps my nose. Great. Because every guy aspires to be 'adorable.' Nobody wants to date guys like that. They're the poor schmucks that continually get sorted under 'friend.'

"I pissed her off."

"That is a habit of yours."

"Shut up."

"Remember—"

"No."

"Or—"

"*No.*"

"And the time that—"

"Will you be quiet?"

Ava blows a raspberry at me. "When are you going to learn to stop pissing off the girls you want? This is so fourth grade."

"It's more complicated than that."

"You're a guy. How complicated can it be?"

I end up telling her the whole story in all its pathetic detail. How I hated Willa's guts at first, but was too lonely to pass up trading insults with her. How she made me soup and slowly brought me around to thinking that she was a nice person, she just had a short temper and a lot of anger. How she was nice to me and invited me places and my family liked her. I even tell Ava about the music late at night and how I can't sleep if I don't talk to her first.

"Fucking hell, you've got it bad," Ava says with an appreciative chuckle.

"She hates my guts right now."

"Of course she does. You're a chronic fuck-up."

"I told you this was different."

"How?"

"We usually do stuff on Saturdays. She made plans last weekend and didn't tell me, and I snapped at her for blowing me off."

"That doesn't mean she hates you. She's just sore about it. Girls hold grudges like that."

"I apologized for snapping on her. She won't even look at me."

"Did she apologize for blowing you off?"

"We didn't exactly have firm plans..."

"So which is it? She blew you off or she didn't?"

"It's complicated."

Ava rolls her eyes. "Your life is fucked, my friend."

We stop near one of the rocky beaches on Lower Rideau Lake and sit on the hood of the car, watching the waves and clouds roll in. I tell Ava about the get-together after the school dance, the first time since moving here that I've felt normal. She thinks it's hilarious that a school dance is the highlight of the social calendar here.

I'm not mad at Willa because she didn't include me in last weekend's plans. I can't change the past, so it's useless to dwell on a weekend with her that I'll never get back. She probably did have a full car, considering how many friends she has. That is why I resent her: she has people she can be with. I only have two, and one is my little sister.

"This bullshit has changed you," Ava says, and rubs my head. I think she means my cancer. "You've gotten used to being taken care of. You used to be so full of initiative."

"I am not used to being taken care of."

"Yeah you are. It's to be expected, I guess, after all that time in the hospital, and your mom looking after you, and Elise."

"It's not like that. You have no idea. We haven't seen each other since last June."

"That's a lot to put on a girl. I assume you've been chasing her, since you've already fucked up, and probably not by accident."

"I'm not chasing her. I know it's not fair to her." It wouldn't be fair to put any girl to the choice of being with me, and I couldn't stand the humiliation of having her say no.

"Maybe when you recover a little more."

"This whole thing will blow over by then. It's just a stupid crush."

Ava laughs out loud like she's just heard the funniest joke in the world. "No way that is a crush," she cackles.

"Shut up. You know jack shit, all right?"

"When you have a crush on someone you're infatuated—you see all the person's good traits but none of their flaws. You like the idea of the person more than the actual person. This chick is different—you notice everything about her, including the unpleasant things." Ava playfully nudges my shoulder. "You're falling for her."

"I am not."

"Have you written her a song yet? That's always your go-to when you're really into a girl."

"I haven't written her a song, damn it." Well, not really. The fact is that Willa sounds like a cello, and I can't play mine right now, so writing any music about her consists of doodling staves on napkins. But that does *not* mean I'm falling in love with her. I just like to…y'know, do her in my head and think about her all the fucking time and orchestrate little gestures to make her smile.

"Do you ever meet a person and swear you can hear, like, theme music around them? Like they have their own special tune?" Ava says.

157

"Yeah, I know what you mean."

"You sound like Haydn's *Pereira*."

Typical Ava.

"You're cheating on Phil with a cellist, aren't you?"

"That is entirely, completely…beside the point."

I snicker and she punches my shoulder. Not as hard as she used to, because I look breakable now, but hard enough to let me know she's annoyed.

"Is your girl into music?"

"Yeah, but she doesn't play."

"That's a shame."

The wind is starting to pick up along the beach. I can smell rain moving in, so I suggest we go home. There really is nothing to do in Smiths Falls, after all.

On the drive home, Ava tells me about her plans to go back to music camp for another crack at some scholarship money. Hearing about her plans and being excited with her is almost enough to make me forget about Willa. Almost.

When Elise gets home from school, she sees Ava's car in the driveway and comes tearing up the stairs chanting "Ava! Ava!" in a voice that could strip wallpaper. She bursts into my room and throws herself on Ava.

"My little whore," Ava greets her warmly.

Elise beams like that's a glowing compliment.

"You been using that trick I taught you?"

Oh God, what trick?

Elise nods like her head is on a spring. "When did you get here? How long are you staying?"

Ava laughs at Elise's enthusiasm. "I got here this morning."

"You've been here all freakin' day and didn't tell me?" Elise stamps her foot.

"I had to cheer this twat up," Ava says of me, and rubs my head roughly. "I can't stay much longer; have to get back to the city."

Mom calls up the stairs to Elise and she drags her feet along the carpet with a huff. "Coming!" She points a finger at Ava. "And don't you dare leave without saying goodbye."

"I won't," Ava promises.

The second Elise is out of earshot, she turns to me and says, "Dude, your sister turned hot."

"Don't you fucking dare."

Ava leaves around four o'clock to be back in Ottawa by dinnertime. After Elise squeezes the hell out of her, we hug goodbye on the porch and she claps me on the shoulder.

"I'll see you soon. Try not to suck too much cock before then; you'll injure yourself."

Ava descends the porch steps and waves over her shoulder.

"Later, slut."

It's hard to believe, but I actually missed her.

Friday

It's Elise's birthday party tonight. Mom and Dad will be out of the house for the evening in what I think is a remarkable display of trust, and Eric and I will be 'supervising' the party. Nonetheless, Mom and Dad aren't idiots. Mom locks her office, Dad hides the box of cigars he normally keeps on the mantle, and they lock the liquor cabinet. They also place a fire extinguisher on the kitchen counter 'because accidents happen.' Mom is a hippie with more wayward youth stories than she cares to divulge, so it's Dad that reads us the riot act before they leave: no smoking, drinking, nudity, drugs or 'ingenious' pranks while they're gone.

Eric asks for a full breakdown of what falls under the ban of 'ingenious pranks.' It's quite a long list.

Dad is just getting to the part about no water balloons in the house when Mom comes in with her purse, ready to leave, and says, "I'm not condoning anything, but if circumstances require it, there are condoms in the bathroom cabinet."

Excuse me while I go hang myself.

I'm putting chips into serving bowls when Elise comes downstairs, dressed up for the party. She has on this black knee-length dress with lace in layers around the skirt and along the collar. She makes a lot of own clothes, and this dress must have taken her weeks. It's extremely detailed and fits perfectly. She's sculpted her hair into loose ringlets, made her eyes dark and smoky, and donned a red beret that slouches over her left ear. She looks like *the other woman* in a 1950s movie, dangerous and beautiful and charming.

"You look good."

She giggles with delight and the image is broken. She's still my little Elise, even if that dress does make her boobs look…there.

"I'm gonna go start the music." She begins to skip away, and then remembers that she's dressed nicely and puts on a flirty little swagger instead. Where the hell did she learn to do that?

Eric and I are still setting up in the kitchen when the first of Elise's guests arrive. Figures Carey would be the first to show up. She squeals over Elise's outfit and then they start to whisper frantically in the foyer. What the hell are they planning?

Eric breaks me out of my reverie by loudly dumping a bin of ice cubes into the sink. We fill the sink with ice and pop, guestimating how much we'll need. Elise invited about twenty people. Some of those might bring unexpected dates. This house could get pretty crowded by the end of the night.

The guests arrive in twos and threes, in the carpooling nature of teenagers. Some I recognize from the social planning committee, or from clubs and teams at school. Elise is quite the social butterfly, after all.

By eleven the party is in full swing. I hang back a little, drifting from room to room. No one talks to me and they avert their eyes when I pass by. I bet if this wasn't my house they'd be whispering, "Who invited *him*?"

Out on the porch, I notice Carey flirting with a tall, dark-haired guy who looks too old for her. It takes me a few seconds to place his face: he's on the basketball team. What is it with these girls? Is it some sort of fad to date a basketball player this week?

I go to the kitchen for another ginger ale. As I cross the front hall the door opens and another cluster of guests welcome themselves in and Fuck. It's. Him. I didn't think he'd actually show. I mean, a party is a party, but what self-respecting senior has the time of day for a pipsqueak like Elise?

Speaking of Elise, she's doomed. The chick this asshole brought with him turns more heads in three seconds than any other girl has all night. She's sexy. She's dark. She's charismatic. The only justice in this world would be if she were as dumb as a rock.

Elise comes dancing across the house to greet this particular guest. Kipp tells her happy birthday and gives her a one-armed hug—his girlfriend is holding his other hand.

"I'm glad you could make it." Elise surprises me by giving Nina a hug too. Either she's a better person than I thought, or she is *way* better at this game than I first suspected.

Again, who the *hell* taught her to do that?

The happy couple gives Elise a CD wrapped in yellow paper. She opens it in front of them and seems genuinely excited about the gift. When she tilts the case I can see the cover art—it's a Kimya Dawson CD.

"Just your taste," I say.

Elise looks over her shoulder and jumps a little when she sees how close I am. I know I'm thin, but for crying out loud, I've been standing right next to the stairs the whole time.

"You guys know my brother, right?" she says to them.

"Yeah, I know him. I'm Kipp—" I know who he is. He's the dickhead who has possessed my little sister. "—and this is Nina." He nods to his girlfriend, the girl who probably exists in voodoo doll form up in Elise's room.

I complete my half of the introductions and walk away to the kitchen. People part in front of me like the waters of the Red Sea; like I'm a leper and they'd better not get too close.

By the time I get to the kitchen I can't remember why I wanted to come here. I clean a few empty cans off the counters and put more ice in the sink, but I'm running on autopilot. There is no one here I want to talk to. No one here wants to talk to me. I wish they would all just leave. The sanctuary of my home, where no one stares anymore, has been ruined for tonight.

I'm considering going into the living room to try to talk to my sister's friends from drama club when I hear Elise's distinct chirp: "Willa! What took you so long?"

The universe narrows to a single fact: She's here, in my house.

Then my focus broadens, and I remember that there are a lot of people in my house.

People to see how she won't give you the time of day anymore. To see you be well and truly ignored in your own home.

And it'll be okay for everyone else to do the same.

"Who've you brought with you?" Elise asks warmly. Oh God. Willa brought a *date*? I don't even have to wonder who it is. I know.

I slip away from the kitchen, down the hall to the laundry room. It's a cramped space, and all alone I wait and listen until I'm sure she's well within the house. The sound of her voice follows Elise to the kitchen, chatting happily. It seems Willa brought food as a hostess gift, because Elise tells her that whatever she brought looks really good and does it need to warm up in the oven first?

I wonder if it's something I can eat...

So not worth the humiliation to find out.

I wait until their voices fade to leave my hiding spot. I head upstairs to my room and close the door behind me.

You are such a coward.

It's for the best. She probably doesn't want to see you.

I fall face down on my bed like a starfish and groan. That girl has an almost supernatural ability to reduce me to my absolute worst without lifting a finger. You'd think she'd been doing it for years.

I'm gone for an hour before anyone notices. Elise knocks on my door and I tell her that I'm not feeling well.

"I could send them all home if you need to rest," she offers. Because I want to ruin her birthday party on top of everything else I've cost her.

"No, don't. Just let me stay up here awhile, and I'll come down again later."

"Okay."

She gives me a hug and a kiss and goes back down to her party. She looks so pretty tonight, dressed up and in her element, surrounded by people. What I'd give to keep her that way: small and happy and quirky as only Elise can be.

I will never be able to pay her back for what she's given me. And she just keeps giving. No matter how bad it gets, or how much it costs her, she never hesitates, and no amount of red and yellow M&Ms or stuffed owls will make up for her fearlessness and dedication.

That jackass better not break her heart. If he does it just proves what an ass-hole he is, because her heart is too big and too fierce to be broken easily.

I wonder if his left or right leg would snap more easily...

Decisions, decisions.

The first time my throat got too sore to even talk was during my initial rounds of radiation. Elise made me a chart with boxes to point to, each with a common phrase in it. She knew just what to put on it: the usual things, of course, like, *Drink please; Food please; I'd like to sit up; I'd like to lay down; I'm hot; I'm cold;* etc. A box for each physical need. Right after that she put *I need a hug*, and *I need a kiss*. And most understandingly, the capped the list off with: *I need to be alone*.

The stiff paper she wrote it on (and laminated, in case I puked or bled on it) is pretty worn around the edges now. It's been folded and marked on and caught in the car door and tacked to the wall beside my bed a couple of times. I run my finger across the last option on the list. I need to be alone. I don't think that one is necessary anymore. I can't bear another day of isolation, of walking around like the ghost that everybody can see but pretends to not to notice.

I call Emily. Bizarre impulse, I know, but I'm lonely and she knew me before I was hollowed out by disease. The phone rings three times before her mom answers, and when I ask for Emily I'm told she's out with friends from school.

"Okay. Thanks anyway."

"Shall I tell her you called?"

"No, it's okay. Don't bother." I say goodbye and toss the phone on my night-stand.

It's childish and ridiculous, but it feels like Emily abandoned me. I waste half an hour being mad at her, because it feels slightly more productive than being mad at myself, before I pick up the phone again and try my other friends.

Morgan is grounded and can't come to the phone. Ava is out with Emily tonight, according to her brother, and when I try her cell she doesn't answer. She probably lost it again. Ava is perpetually losing small objects. Caitlin actually answers her phone, but all I can hear is shitty techno playing in the background at top volume. She's out clubbing tonight.

"Can you hear me?" She can't, so I ditch the effort and hang up. The only good friend left to try is Kyle, but he's unreachable at the best of times. He doesn't have a cell phone because 'their radiation kills bees' and his house line is sketchy because his grandma forgets to pay the bill sometimes. Even if I can get through, I'd have to talk to Grandma May for twenty minutes first while she confuses me with her long-lost fuck up of a son, Richard.

With nothing to do and no one to do it with, I just lay back across the foot of my bed and stare at the ceiling. Music and the noise of the party come through the walls, invading my bubble of privacy. I know this song. I know Willa knows this song.

I dare you to go a whole minute without thinking about her.

    Fine. I can do that. Easy.

My stomach growls in hunger.

    I wonder what Willa brought…

Damn it!

    That wasn't even ten seconds.

Shut up.

Make me.

I don't want to go downstairs to find food. I'm not that hungry; just peckish. I lay there at the foot of the bed, listening and brooding and wishing that one of my friends had answered my call. I've passed out of their lives completely— I'm no longer around, and no longer worrying them with my illness. No need to spare any thought for Jem anymore.

I'm still mad about it when I drift off to sleep in the wee hours of the morning. I don't sleep long before Elise wakes me up with a hand on my cheek.

"W'time is it?"

I try to stretch and then think better of it. My joints ache.

"Almost three."

She slips my hat off and sets it aside. I seem to be wrapped up in a blanket. I didn't fall asleep that way.

"You never came down," she says sadly.

"Stomachache."

Elise nods acceptingly and gives me a hug. "Sorry you had to miss it."

"Did you have a good time?"

Elise grins. She pulls her hands in toward her chest and spins on one foot. It's such a romantically giddy move.

"When he said happy birthday he gave me a hug and he smells so…*ugh*. If only they bottled that smell."

"Gross, Lise."

She blows a raspberry at me.

"Tell Carey about that shit, not me."

"I'm going to bed." She pulls her beret off and stifles a yawn. "Goodnight." Elise bends over to give me a kiss on the cheek.

"Thanks for the blanket."

"You already had it on."

"Oh."

Elise shrugs in a dismissive sort of way. She calls goodnight over her shoulder as she leaves, shutting the door behind her.

Did Willa…?

> *Don't even think it.*

But—

> *Don't. Hell would freeze over.*

I find myself sniffing the corner of the blanket for traces of her scent, to prove that it's not just wishful thinking. Maybe she came up here looking for me. Maybe she wanted to talk—shit, and I missed her.

> *Do I have to* explain *the concept of hell freezing over?*

> *Shut up.*

Quit sniffing the blanket, you're not a friggin' dog.

> *She's starting to come around.*

Yes, joy—she took thirty seconds away from her time with baby-face Luke to bundle you up like an invalid.

Eric passes my door on his way to bed. He belches loudly and all at once I feel like an idiot. He probably covered me up. He must have come looking for me, wondering where the other 'supervisor' of this party was, and found me asleep.

I didn't think my night could get any worse, but it has. False hope stings. Sleep is a long time coming.

Willa: April 11 to 17

Wednesday

I park myself in front of the TV after school and don't budge for hours. It's up to Frank to make dinner tonight, so it's frozen pierogies and bacon. My phone rings "pick up, it's me" while I'm watching TV. Jem is beginning to rival Chris Elwood for persistence. I don't answer the call. I can't deal with him right now.

He complains that I won't look at him, as if he truly wants to be seen. I have my doubts about that. And he rarely pauses to consider what it might cost me to look at him; that it might invite things I don't want or am not ready for, or it might remind me of watching my sister's descent into illness. That day in the shed when he asked me about suicide… that hurt more than he knew, because part of it was true.

Pills were Jem's first choice, too—or they would have been, if he had ever come to that. Pills don't require elaborate planning, see, and complex plans are difficult for a seriously ill person. All one needs is a room with a lock—most bathrooms have one—and a bottle of pills. Swallow, lay down on the floor to avoid alerting others with the sound of a crash, and wait for the bright light at the end of the tunnel. He had access to sleeping pills; little chance of vomiting, like he would with Oxy, just a guarantee of respiratory and cardiac arrest as the depressant flowed through him.

Not that he would have done it.

I'm scheduled to volunteer tonight, and though I'd rather just stay in and be by myself, I can't shirk a commitment like that. It's nice to feel needed, even though I just hand out magazines and read to kids. It keeps me together. Sort of.

Volunteer work is a challenge today. The coordinator puts me in the oncology ward, handing out chewing gum and magazines. This ward feels bizarrely familiar, with its sounds and smells, and brings back memories I'd rather not revisit too frequently. I half-expect to see the people I met while Tessa was in treatment. Some of those people are probably dead now. It's almost surprising how little that idea bothers me, but I've worked so hard to numb those memories that it's no great wonder.

The one person I do consider with genuine curiosity, though, is the guy Tessa briefly shared a room with. He was only seventeen, just barely old enough for a bed on the adult ward, and dying slowly. He had a rare disorder that caused tumors to grow indiscriminately all over his body. They pushed on his organs and nerves, causing pain and interrupting normal function. The first time I saw him he completely freaked me out. Luckily he was asleep at the time, so he didn't witness my poor reaction. The whole left side of his face and eyelid were swollen with a massive tumor. He looked like something out of a horror movie. I avoided looking at him whenever I went to visit Tessa, because I didn't think I could control my expression enough not to offend him.

I remember very clearly the first time I ever spoke to him, because I was terrified to do it. I was sitting by Tessa while she slept, reading a book. School was out and I had no homework left to keep me occupied. The curtains around both beds were closed, but in the silence I heard a plop and a splash, followed by a quiet, "Damn."

I peeked under the curtains and saw a juice box on the floor on its side, leaking slowly. I wasn't sure if I should pick it up. I went out to the orderlies' station first and grabbed a juice box off the tray to replace the dropped one. By the time I got back to the room I was antsy with nerves.

I 'knocked' before stepping around the curtain. That sort of threw him. He was so used to being in hospitals with no privacy and bustling nurses who had no time to knock.

"I, uh, brought you a new one." I held up the juice box lamely.

"Thanks."

I threw the old box in the garbage and cracked open the new one for him. His hands creeped me out more than his face—they were covered with little bumps that were tumors under the skin, and he was missing two fingers that had been removed along with more troublesome growths. I tried not to flinch when I realized he needed help holding the juice box. His hands were next to useless from nerve damage.

I couldn't help staring at him while he drank. The unusual swell of his face looked so painful, and his left eye was nearly swollen shut. His healthy eye stared right back at me.

"Your eyes are really pretty."

I turned beet red the second after I blurted that out. I wasn't lying—he had gorgeous blue eyes with long dark lashes—only I was worried that he would take my remark the wrong way. But he just said 'thank you' after a moment and told me that he liked my hair. I don't think a stranger had ever said he looked nice before.

I'm still not sure how it happened, really, since we didn't discuss it or even talk much that first day, but for the rest of the summer, whenever I went to visit Tessa, I would visit him too. We talked of mundane things, of heavy things. He didn't belittle my sadness and anger at what was happening to Tessa, even though he had his own heap of troubles to contend with. That was the summer I grew boobs and hips and lost my childish gangliness. He taught me how to flirt, the way we would banter back and forth with my sister asleep just a few feet away. Or at least I thought she was asleep. He was my first kiss, just days before Tessa came home to die. I told him the plan to move her and that I wouldn't be coming around the hospital anymore. We exchanged phone numbers that neither of us would ever call, and as I hugged him goodbye he said, "What, no kiss?" To this day I'm not sure if he was being serious or not, but I kissed him anyway. He was warm and his lips tasted like morphine and orange juice. I'm almost certain he's dead now.

Trying not to think about that period winds me up, and when I leave the hospital I don't go straight home: I go to the Thorpe house.

Mr. Thorpe isn't home when I get there, but there's a light on in the living room. I let myself in and Luke looks up from the couch where he lays, watching TV.

"I didn't know you were coming over." He sounds pleasantly surprised. That's good, because it didn't occur to me to call ahead.

"I had a rough day."

I drop my purse by the door, slip out of my shoes, and sit down on the couch. Luke puts a gentle hand on my shoulder and pulls me down next to him.

"Relax," he says. "You've earned it."

Spooning on the couch isn't half bad. Luke's like a big, warm, cuddly teddy bear, and I could use one right now.

"What happened?"

"Shit shift volunteering." And Frank is just waiting for me to crack. And Jem keeps bugging me with possessive bullshit. And Chris Elwood is a persistent pain in my ass.

…and yesterday Jem was keeping so still and only ate half a Jell-O cup at lunch, and I intended to tape a mint to his locker for after but I didn't have any stored up to give him. And Elise looked like she was talking to herself in the car after school, but he was there, in the back seat, too sick to sit up.

I notice far more about him than I should.

"You got through it," Luke says, and pulls me tighter against him with an arm around my waist. We spoon for a while, watching the badly dubbed made-for-TV martial arts movie Luke had on when I got here.

"You can change the channel if you like."

"I don't care."

Luke turns the volume down a few notches until it's just background noise. He runs his fingers through my hair, humming softly.

"What song is that?"

"Un Canadien Errant. One of those old folk tunes, y'know?"

"Can I hear it?"

His mouth is right behind my ear, and his warm breath tickles me softly as he sings the deep, liquid words. It seems more soothing, not knowing what all the words mean. Luke's hand slips under the front of my shirt as he sings, resting against my bare stomach. I'm not sure I like it but I'm too lazy to move his hand.

"What does it mean?" I ask when he finishes the last verse.

"It's about exile," he answers vaguely. I like that.

"It sounds nice."

The hand on my belly flexes slightly, gripping the skin and releasing quickly. "You're soft," Luke whispers.

"Okay." I'm not in the mood for affection or compliments.

"I can turn this off if you want," he whispers.

"No. Leave it."

His fingers begin to trace little circles on my stomach. The largest of these go low enough to brush against the waistband of my jeans, and high enough to touch my second rib. For a second I wonder if he's consciously doing that, but his movement is too even and calculated to be accidental. He's trying to feel me up, testing the waters before he goes for it. I should tell him to stop. I should react in some way to put him off the idea. But I don't. I lay there and watch this stupid movie while his hand moves around under my top.

Luke's hand moves slowly, coming down from where it edged around my bra to rest on my lower abdomen. Slowly, like I won't notice, he slips his little finger under the waistband of my jeans. He finds the edge of my underwear—and goes beneath it.

"Willa?" It's weirding him out that I haven't reacted in any way.

"Yeah, Luke?" I want to hear what brilliant argument for sex he has prepared.

Luke sits up on his elbow, leaning over me to study my face. A piece of his hair falls over my forehead and he brushes it away.

I grab the lock back and twist it around my finger. The innocent look of him comforts me, even though I know he's anything but.

Like most guys, he needs only the slightest invitation to bend down and kiss me. I wasn't asking for it. I wasn't thinking about it. But he's warm and I feel so small next to him. It's like curling up in a favorite blanket as he turns me toward him with the arm under my shoulders.

Luke is a very thorough kisser. He leaves no part of my lips unattended to, even if he is a little heavy-handed and forceful about it. The fingers just beyond my waistband are migrating again, moving lower.

He has no idea what he's doing down there. I don't think he's going to admit it or ask directions, either, by the way he kisses me more determinedly—as if I can be distracted from what's going on elsewhere, just until he figures things out.

The couch is narrow and uncomfortable. Luke rolls on top of me for a better angle and I'm surrounded by a curtain of hair as he kisses me. He smells like Cheetos and wood shavings and he's pressing his groin against my thigh like that on purpose.

I know the drill; how these things always go. My mind is a blank space as I reach down to his waistband and pop the button on his pants. He raises his hips slightly to give me enough room to lower the fly, and my hand slips inside. Under his boxers, between his legs. It takes only the slightest movement and pressure to make him lurch against my hand and moan into my mouth. The hand down my pants stumbles with distraction and his eyes flutter closed. I guess he's new at this; multitasking pleasurable things takes practice.

And just like any other guy, a little moan in return is enough to remind him that his hand should be doing something back. I prefer these things without discussion. Luke has large hands, but he isn't clumsy—just inexperienced. I think his finger slips inside me purely by accident, because he looks completely surprised.

"I'm not hurting you, am I?" So close to my face, his voice is little more than a husky whisper against my lips. I don't want to talk, so instead of answering I stroke him more insistently and lift my hips against his hand. Luke takes the hint. Guys aren't that stupid when it comes to sex. Millions of years of instinct trump conscious thought.

I rock back and forth in the narrow space between the couch and his hips. His finger is a nice counterpoint to move against. I'm getting close, and so is he, rubbing each other off to the cadence of fake punches and attack screams on TV. Luke's arm tightens around the back of my shoulders, pressing our chests together. I know the harsh tone of his breathing, the absence of little whimpers that mean he's entered the home stretch. I watch his face with a sense of detachment: eyes closed, swollen lips parted, resting his forehead against mine as he pants with pleasure.

He stops breathing just before he comes. A shudder ripples down his throat and back, and his eyes open. I'm fucking paralyzed by such openness as he looks me right in the eye and falls the fuck apart on top of me. I can't look away. He bares himself to me in a wholly unfamiliar act of intimacy that I couldn't have prepared myself for even if I'd known it was coming, and it makes me feel entirely exposed.

Luke's hand brushes my hair. He places a shaky kiss on my lips and whispers, "Willa."

I try to move too quickly and end up on the floor. I just lay there on my back with my legs still pinned under his, and decide it's not worth it to move any farther just yet.

"Are you okay?" He reaches out to grab me but I put my hands up. Distance is good right now.

Luke hesitates, kneeling on the couch on all fours, still winded from our romp. He eases off my legs and my feet fall limply to the floor.

"Willa?"

"Shit." I sit up.

Luke looks at me unsurely.

"I shouldn't have done that."

He gives me this confused, somewhat wounded expression. God damn it, he has sex hair right now.

"I don't do this kind of shit with friends." Especially not friends as un-complicated as Luke. I've messed up a good thing. I shouldn't know what my friend looks like when he comes. "We're not friends who do that. I shouldn't have let this shit happen."

"You didn't *let* anything happen."

"This was a one-off, okay?"

Telling myself that it will never happen again alleviates some of the guilt from my broken promise to Mom and Dad—I said I was done screwing around with boys when I moved here.

Luke wipes his hand on his jeans. Oh God. His pants are still undone. So are mine.

"Did you like it?" he asks a little shyly.

"This never happened."

"Are you going to be weird now?" he says with a smirk and a scolding tone.

I know that look in his eye. At first glance it's friendly chiding, but underneath that is a firm demand for the desired response—or else.

I stand up and fasten my pants. "Don't tell our brothers about this either."

"I won't," he promises quietly.

I grab my purse and shoes and prepare to leave. Luke walks me to the door and tells me to drive safely like he means the exact opposite.

"No weirdness," he reminds me as I descend the front steps.

"Weirdness about what?"

Luke huffs, and as I drive away I can still see him in my rearview mirror, watching me with crossed arms. I don't know what Luke thinks he can get from me, but I'm certain I'm not in a position to give it.

I eat a piece of leftover lasagna, blow off homework, and crawl into bed.

I can't sleep.

I put on really angry music and count sheep and meditate and I'm still awake. I think about calling Jem and then I kick myself. This week has been horrible enough, trying to put distance between him and myself, especially because he's so lonely and I'm a sucker for lost causes.

I shouldn't have done that with Luke.

Done what?

Damn straight.

It's past eleven o'clock when my cell rings. It's Jem again, smirking up at me from the screen. And in a moment of weakness, I answer. I press the phone to my ear and listen to the static silence. It doesn't occur to me to say anything.

His voice creeps across the line after a few seconds, shy and slightly hopeful: "Willa?"

I hang up. I shouldn't have answered to begin with. I toss the phone to the foot of my bed and curl away from it like it's a snake.

What the hell is the matter with me that I have such a hard time ignoring him, even when I know better than to involve myself? After a few minutes of indecision and much self-flagellation, I sit up and retrieve my phone. He gets a text message—nothing more.

Do you want music?

Yes, please.

He gets "Life Starts Now" by Three Days Grace, and I relax for the first time tonight, watching the twin glows of my phone and iPod. He only gets one song because I'm trying not to involve myself, and I text *Goodnight* instead of saying it over the phone.

Jem replies: *I had a dream about you the other night.*

Since when does 'goodnight' invite conversation? I don't reply but he sends another text anyway.

You were accusing me of stealing your mallard duck.

I can't help but smile at the image.

I reply: *Sounds like something you'd do. Did you give it back?*

Of course :)

I put my phone aside and roll over, ready for sleep. It buzzes again.

Are we okay now?

Don't get any ideas.

Jem would take the slightest invitation to make himself entirely too welcome in my life. I can't abide that. The borderline-insanity of being apart from him is better than the insanity of being around him. There's no one but me to witness, this way.

Can I call you? We need to talk.

Jesus Christ, that sounds like something a boyfriend would say. My gag reflex isn't strong enough for this.

There's nothing to say.

There isn't anything I want to hear, anyway. I turn off my phone for the night in the hope of sparing my last shred of sanity—if I can find that much left in the recesses of my weary brain. Somehow, I doubt it.

Thursday

In my dreams Tessa always has long hair. This time she stands in front of the mirror with her hair undone, brushing it out before bed. My reflection doesn't appear in the mirror, but she sees me behind her and smiles. She hands me the hairbrush.

As I brush her long hair, strands fall away in clumps, just as they did when I shaved her head. I brush until there is nothing left but her smooth scalp and the web of veins underneath.

"Do you regret it?" she asks. "Regrets are heavy things, Will."

I watch her face in the mirror as she watches me.

"You're going to regret that boy."

She isn't beautiful anymore, like she was when I started to brush her hair. Her skin is grey and papery and her eyes are red with burst blood vessels. Tessa grins at me and her teeth are stained with blood.

"Have you killed him, yet?" When she speaks more blood seeps from between her teeth. It drips over her lips and runs down her chin, onto the bathroom counter. A slow trickle runs from her left ear.

I tell her I never meant to hurt anybody. She chuckles at me, the same way she used to when I was little and being silly.

"Dying is easier than breathing." She winks. "But I think you know that already."

The blood flows faster. It comes out of her nose, too, and forms a steady drip.

"Still," she turns away and makes a flippant hand gesture, "if you're going to kill that boy, do it quick, one way or another. He's already dying, and you know how fast a body can go."

"I know."

A blinding pain in the side of my head wakes me up. I rolled out of bed in my sleep and railed my head on the nightstand. Frank comes in to investigate why I'm taking the Lord's name in vain so loudly this early in the morning.

"Are you bleeding?" he checks my scalp and says it looks okay. "You might have a bit of a bump, but you didn't hit it hard enough to concuss yourself."

"Great."

It's still only five o'clock, so after he determines that I'm fine and helps me off the floor, Frank says goodnight and goes back to bed.

Shit.

I hang my head between my knees and breathe deeply.

"Have you killed him, yet?"

I have my phone in my hand and Jem's number selected (he put himself on my speed dial, too) before I catch myself. I shouldn't call him. For one, it's five o'clock in the freaking morning. For another, he's probably fine. He's not dying that fast.

What do you care? You're not involving yourself, remember?

Maybe so, but advice from beyond the grave is difficult to ignore. Tessa said to kill him one way or another.

She's dead. It was a dream.

I'm really starting to lose my shit.

I bury my head under my pillow and count the minutes until I have to get up for school. I don't sleep a wink.

✐

School is like a minefield. I almost make myself late so I won't have to run into any of the Harpers in the hallway, and during Math Paige chats my ear off about Chris's general indecisiveness. Apparently he won't commit to being in an exclusive relationship with her. I don't blame him—it's Paige and it's only been a few weeks.

"Just give him some space." I don't know if that's good advice or not; I just like the sound of it at the moment.

"You think so?"

I shouldn't have said anything. Now if this goes rotten, I'm the one who touched it last.

"Scratch that, just follow your heart." Paige is one for platitudes. She often mistakes them for deep philosophy.

"Maybe I should try to make him jealous."

Be a good friend. Be a good friend. "That's an excellent idea, Paige." *A* good *friend!* The little devil on my shoulder is entirely too persuasive sometimes.

Paige sighs tiredly and changes the subject by asking me how my night was.

"Completely uneventful, actually."

Clearly her mind is still on her own romantic woes, because she immediately switches the subject back to Chris. "He's so...he never wants to do anything with me! Is Luke like that?"

"What?" Did she just assume we're in the same category as her and Chris?

"Like that time he came skating with us. You guys do stuff together, right?"

Yeah, like fool around on his dad's couch.

"We have our shared hobbies. We're not dating, though."

"You should. He's really cute."

I think of that look on his face last night. Luke Thorpe is anything but 'cute.'

"He's only sixteen."

"You're blushing!"

I turn away and mutter lamely about how hot it is in here.

Jem isn't in Social Studies today. I take careful notes that he probably won't ask to copy. He only cares about this course when it suits him. At the end of the hour I swing by the nurse's office on my way to French. He isn't there either.

"Are you looking for your friend?" the nurse says to me. I guess for how often Jem is in here, she's noticed that I'm the only one besides his family that talks to him.

"He's not been in today," she says. If he's not in class and he's not here, he's probably at home. I thank the nurse and head off to class.

Jem hasn't been sick enough to miss a whole day in awhile. I tell myself that I'm not supposed to care this much, but I'm curious about what happened to him and vaguely annoyed that we can't be on speaking terms without him getting clingy.

I put Jem out of my mind. It's not healthy to get this attached to such a fragile friend.

Friday

When I get to Social Studies, Jem is already seated, arms folded on the table and head pillowed on top. His face is turned to the side, watching me as I take my seat and arrange my books.

"Hey," he murmurs quietly, as though he's expecting rebuff.

"Hi."

He watches me for the rest of the period, but I can't stand to look at him. He looks so *sad*, and the new pallor in his face worries me. I shouldn't involve myself in that. It's bad for me, if past experience is anything to judge by, and probably bad for him too.

He could really use a bowl of chickpea and kidney bean soup. I hate myself for noticing that.

When class ends I get up to leave and Jem grabs my sleeve. I look over to see what he wants, but he looks just as bewildered as I feel to find his hand on my shirt. He lets go like the fabric is hot and walks away with his eyes on the floor.

I catch a glimpse of him on my way to French. He's leaning against his locker door and visibly trying not to be sick. Poor guy. He sees me looking at him and gives me a glare that makes me truly glad that looks cannot kill.

I deserve that.

⊷

I can't decide if I should go to Elise's party tonight. I said I would and I already bought her gift, but Jem will be there. It takes about twenty minutes of pacing to come to the conclusion that it's Elise's party, and that my problems with Jem shouldn't interfere with making tonight special for her. I have no issues with Elise, after all.

And looks can't *really* kill.

I make garlic knots as a hostess gift, five of which fall victim to Frank's appetite before I manage to pack them up to take with me. As I clean up the mess from preparing garlic knots, I consider what else I could bring. Jem ate yogurt at lunch today, but didn't finish his juice. He barely drank half of it. His lips were dry today in Soc and he was breathing slower than normal.

Peeled, seeded cucumbers find their way into the blender with vanilla yogurt, honey and lots of milk. Tessa always wanted cinnamon with her Dehydration Shakes, as she called them—can his stomach handle that? Jem generally does well with barely spiced foods, so I play it safe and season with a few tablespoons of orange juice to bring out the sweetness of the cucumber.

I pour the shake into a thermos for the road, and go upstairs to get ready. Shower, dress, a touch of makeup, and I'm out of reasons to stall. Why am I going to his house again?

Because Elise is too much of a sweetheart to skip out on.

I still feel weird about going. I don't know many of Elise's other friends. What if I have no one to talk to, and Jem uses that as an excuse to corner me? He would rather sequester me alone with him than crawl out of his shell, and the thought of an entire evening in his company makes me nervous. I can't stand to be around him that long. He…upsets me.

I pick up the phone and consider whom to call. It doesn't take long to come up with a suitable friend, and I dial. The phone rings five times before I get an answer.

"Hello?"

"Want to come to a party with me tonight?"

The line of parked cars stretches from the Harpers' front porch, down the long driveway, and out onto the shoulders of the road. I guess 'just a few friends' is relative to someone as social as Elise.

"I've always wanted to see the inside of this house," Hannah says as I find a place to park. "It looks so nice from outside."

"It's gorgeous inside, too."

Hannah smiles. "I'm not surprised you've been inside."

I can't put my finger on exactly why that remark irritates me. It's unsettling to not know the origins of my own moods.

When we enter the front hall, Elise skips through the crowd—there must be fifty people here—to welcome us.

"Willa!" she sings. "What took you so long?"

It's only ten-thirty, but judging by the noise level, Hannah and I are a little late.

"Who've you brought with you?" Elise asks as she folds Hannah's hand between hers in welcome. I introduce Hannah.

I give Elise her birthday gift right then, since it might actually work with what she's already wearing. Her gift is small enough to fit in my pocket: it's an ebony wood ring with a lion's head carved into the upper half. Word has it Gryffindor is her favorite Hogwarts house.

Elise is pleased with the ring and garlic knots. She leads the way to the kitchen and even gives me a serving tray to put them out on.

"Do they have to warm up in the oven?"

"They're good warm, but they don't have to be."

I put Jem's thermos in the fridge to keep cool while Elise and Hannah start putting the knots on the tray. Elise notices my other 'gift.'

"He's around."

I was just about to be glad that I haven't run into Jem yet, because it's going to be extremely awkward when I do.

It might even break me.

I don't regret my decision to bring Hannah along. We find seats on the porch, and though I don't know many people here, she knows a few people from the drama club's stage crew. We hang out with them, and it is so sweet to watch the way Hannah looks at the puppy-eyed kid, Brian. She regards him with genuine affection, not just lust.

"I'm surprised you're not on stage crew," I say to Hannah. "You're so organized."

Brian takes the bait and looks up from his drink. "Yeah, it's not too late to join. The school play isn't till May, and we always need extra hands."

Hannah flushes at the attention.

"Tall people always come in handy on the crew," he concludes. I want to kick him.

Hannah hunches down a little, conscious of her height. She's tall for a girl, but not freakishly so.

"I wish I had long legs like yours."

We three look down at Hannah's legs, casually extended in front of her and crossed at the ankle. She really does have beautiful legs.

Hannah blushes and mumbles "Thanks."

Brian doesn't say anything, but he's giving her this weird, eager smile. If they weren't so cute, they'd be kind of dorky.

It's after midnight when Hannah finally works up the guts to just ask Brian to dance. I quickly make an excuse to go inside for another drink, to give them some privacy.

Jem's thermos is still in the fridge. I haven't seen him all night. Granted, I've been out on the porch and it's probably too chilly out there for him.

I take the thermos out of the fridge and go to look for him. I try the obvious places first: living room, front room, hallway, and backyard—nothing. I even check unlikely places, like the laundry room and garage, but he isn't there either.

I run into Elise near the stereo—she's giggling her way through some sort of partnered dance with a Latina girl whose name I don't know—and ask if she's seen Jem around.

"He went upstairs for a bit."

In the spirit of wishful thinking, I check the library first. I really don't want to have to knock on Jem's bedroom door. That would imply that I want to spend one-on-one time with him, and just the thought of that creeps me out. But he isn't in the library.

"Damn it."

I weigh the thermos in my hand, considering whether I should just leave it in the fridge. But he looked dehydrated this afternoon…

I walk softly down the hall to Jem's room, like a thief trying not to get caught, and knock on his door. Maybe I should just leave the thermos on the carpet and run.

Jem doesn't answer. I put my ear to the door and listen. Nothing. Maybe he went back downstairs…

The soft thump of a small object on carpet changes my mind. I knock again and he still doesn't answer.

I test the door handle. It isn't locked. I slide the door open a crack and peer into the dim room. Jem is asleep, but it doesn't look like he planned it. He's laying across the foot of the bed, for one, and still fully clothed, for another. His left arm hangs over the edge of the mattress. He's going to get pins and needles like that.

The object I heard fall turns out to be his cell phone. It rests just under his limp arm, glowing up at me. The screen reads *No New Messages*. I wonder whom he was trying to contact.

I pick up the phone and place it on his nightstand. His arm is trickier. I have to move it very slowly and gently to lay it across his chest without waking him, and then remove his watch so carefully you'd think I was trying to steal it. It's hard to tell with only the small amount of light coming up the stairs, but he still looks dehydrated and ill. A big part of me wants to wake him up and offer him the thermos, but I don't know where that gesture will lead, and I'm not exactly up for an early morning heart-to-heart in his bedroom. I fold Jem's comforter in half to keep him warm and close the door softly behind me.

I want to go home.

I find Hannah with Brian in the living room and tell her that I'm going to take off.

"Oh…okay," she says unsurely. I know she wants to stay with Brian. She wants to dance some more and talk to him and maybe even sneak a kiss or two.

"Maybe Brian can drive you home? You guys look like you're having fun."

Hannah and Brian exchange questioning looks.

"Uh…sure I can take her home."

Hannah blushes a little. I hug her goodbye and leave her to an evening of romantic possibilities.

That night I dream of a highway surrounded by tall firs. I'm home. There is no sun, no rain, no wind; only the highway and the smell of gasoline and the vibration of tires under my body. I was never any good at running away. I always drove.

Saturday

I wake up numb. It feels good. I throw on the first clothes I find and drag my feet down to the kitchen. I need to do groceries today.

We need the usual stuff: eggs, milk, butter, and bread. I make a list of vegetables I feel like using and check the freezer to determine our meat supply. I open the cupboard to check our stock of oatmeal and cereal, and find the honey jar almost empty. I can't have used that much already…

But I did. Two months of making soups and drinks for Jem adds up. I take the empty jar down from the shelf and stare at it. Should I buy more? Should I keep making him food? He needs it. I enjoy doing it. I worry about him when I don't do it. But does that mean I *should?*

I end up buying honey. And ginger. And rice flour. And after I'm done checking out, I hate myself. I'm a foolish masochist, revisiting all the painful shit in my life just so he can gain a pound or two. I should stop. Let him eat Jell-O and fend for himself.

But then I'd really hate myself.

When I get home from the grocery store there is a box of hinges on the porch. A note rests on top, penned in Luke's wide, sprawling hand.

I told Frank I'd drop these off for the greenhouse windows. Sorry I couldn't stick around. Dad needs my help today. — Luke

He's drawn a big 'O' underneath and filled it with X's. How downright cheeky of him.

I change into my plaid work shirt and head through the garage toward the shed with the new box of hinges. It can go on one of the overburdened shelves with Frank's tools and the rest of the greenhouse parts.

When I open the door at the side of the garage and nearly walk into the bumper of a blue Neon. I didn't even hear him arrive. Jem steps out of his brother's car, watching me intently, as I kick the side door shut behind me.

"You could have called before coming over."

"You could have answered."

He notices the box in my hands and frowns.

I walk away, through the side gate and toward the back shed. Jem follows me slowly, quietly, as though he's trying not to be intrusive. That's a new thing for him.

I put the box inside with all the other crap and step back into the wan light of day. Jem studies me with a scowl as I replace the padlock on the shed door.

"Why are you here?"

"Are you still mad at me?" he demands.

"Yes." Not for the reasons he's probably thinking, but that wasn't the question. He asked if I was mad, and I am.

Jem steps forward and stands close enough to invade my personal space. He corners me between the shed wall and his tall frame, looming over me like a bully spoiling for a fight.

"And you won't even listen to an apology?" he snarls.

"Piss off, Harper." I put my hands on his shoulders and push him back. "You have no right to intimidate me like that."

"Why won't you look at me?" he demands.

"Why does it matter?"

He takes another step in my direction and I back away. Space is a very good thing right now. Last time he lost his temper, he shoved me into shelves hard enough to cause bruises and kicked a chair. I don't want to be the thing he lashes out against this time, and I don't want to have to hit him back when I know he's still unwell.

"You know why it's important to me," he snaps. That selfish ass. All he thinks about is his own ego and emotional wellbeing. It never occurs to him that it might be difficult for me to look at him, no matter what my reason.

"No, why is it important to *me?*"

It occurs to him now, but as usual, he twists it with selfishness. Jem gapes at me with a wounded look and takes a step back. All he perceives is rejection, with no thought spared for what's going on in my head. He tries and fails to compose his face into blankness before turning away and walking toward the gate. He folds his arms around his front as he goes.

Fuck him, I think, and lean back against the shed door. Jem has a way of sucking all the energy out of me. Since I met him all he's done is take from me and give barely anything in return. I'm crazy to hang out with him. The entire dynamic of this friendship is downright unhealthy.

He didn't latch the gate properly when he left. I slowly make my way across the muddy lawn to close it, and when I get close I see the front bumper of the Neon around the corner of the house, still in the driveway. He hasn't left yet.

I feel like a bitch just for contemplating it, but I know that I should stick up for myself and run him off. If he's loitering around waiting for me to cave and give him what he wants, he can forget it.

I march around the side of the house to tell Jem off, but I can't hold onto my resolve once I get a look at him. At first the only thing I see is the top of his hat above the steering wheel, on which he rests his forehead. I step slowly around the side of the car and see him clutching his arms around his middle like he's in pain.

My first thought is that something is physically wrong with him—that he's sick and needs medical attention. Then I pause to take a closer look at him through the window. I didn't see it at first with his head bent like that, but his face is twisted up in pain and he's crying.

The cold, calculating part of my brain wonders whether I should call the hospital or his parents first. I reach for my cell phone and open the car door to get a better look at him.

Jem startles and flinches away from the door. I hold a hand up for calm. "It's okay."

"I'm sorry." Jem turns away and wipes his cuff over his eyes with embarrassment.

"Do you want me to call someone?"

Jem shakes his head. I reach out to touch his shoulder and he grabs my hand so hard it hurts. I guess I have a spare, but damn…

"Please." His free hand fists around my shirt and his head tips to rest against my front. I put an arm around his shoulders—he's trembling with tears that he's shamefully trying to quiet.

"Don't cut me out," he says shakily. I wish he wouldn't beg. "I've been a really shitty, fucking awful friend, but *please*..." A little sob escapes and fuck if that doesn't make my traitor heart melt.

I dislodge my hand from his grip and he backs up. He's got that wounded look of rejection again.

"Calm down."

sI wrap both arms around his shoulders. Jem practically falls into the hug with a grateful little whimper, holding onto my middle so hard I can barely breathe.

"I didn't mean to upset you like this," I say as he hiccups and gasps. I had banked on him feeling anger and resentment, not falling to pieces in my drive-way.

"I didn't mean to m-make you mad," he answers with a thin voice. "You just...I reacted badly, and I couldn't make it right..." His face twists in pain again and I tug on his shoulders before the water works can gear up again.

"Come inside."

↤

I give Jem a cup of cool water that he's shaking too badly to drink, and sit him down in the kitchen with his head between his knees and a cool cloth across his neck. He's shaking and breathing like he just ran a marathon in cold weather.

"You're all right," I encourage him, rubbing circles on his back.

"You must think I'm such a pussy," he says lowly, sniffing back snot.

"You have no idea what I think." Neither do I. My indecision bothers me.

Jem sits up slowly and takes the towel off his neck. His thinly lashed eyes are swollen and his cheeks are stained. "Why wouldn't you let me apologize?"

"Because I didn't want to fix it."

That was precisely the wrong thing to say. He presses his lips together and stops breathing. At first I think he's angry, and watch as he lowers his head again and replaces the cold towel. He doesn't make a sound, but little drops begin to strike the tiles. It's not the towel that's dripping.

"Jem."

"You're my only friend," he says quietly. "We can't—? I won't hang around if you don't want me to." He tries to stand up but I grab him by the shoulders and sit him right back down.

"You have no idea what I want." Coincidentally, neither do I, apparently.

"You don't want me around."

"Let's talk about this when you've calmed down a little." I take the towel off his neck and brush it across his cheeks. "Lay down on the couch for a bit, ok?"

Jem lays down on his side, still breathing shakily, and tucks one of the throw pillows under his head. There are spots of color on his cheeks, whether from exertion or embarrassment, I can't tell. Maybe it's a little of both.

Jem grimaces and points at my front. I look down and see a big, smeared string of snot on my shirtfront from when I hugged him in the car.

"I'm sorry." He reaches for the Kleenex box but I hold out a hand to stop him.

"That'll just smear it around." I turn to go change out of this shirt and Jem sits up as I leave. I point a finger at him and say, "Lay down."

He wisely obeys, but there's a distrustful look in his eye, as though he doesn't want to let me out of his sight.

So I don't go upstairs. I go across the hall to the laundry room and take a clean t-shirt off the top of the basket. I bring it back to the living room—because I know if I was gone for more than fifteen seconds he would get up to follow me like a puppy. Jem looks up when I come back in, plainly trying to read my face.

I toss the t-shirt on the recliner and take a seat. I have to unbutton the plaid shirt carefully to avoid touching the snot, but I get it off without smearing. My bra today is a tired, well-loved one: old white cotton, as modest coverage as they make, with sweat stains under the arms that even bleach won't take care of. I pull my t-shirt over my head and straighten it around my shoulders.

Jem is glaring at me.

"What?"

"You don't think of me as a real guy, do you?"

"What are you talking about?"

"You wouldn't have just taken your shirt off in front of Chris Elwood." His tone is accusatory, which sets me on edge.

"A gentleman would have looked away."

"A lady wouldn't have taken her shirt off in the first place."

I grab the snotted-up plaid and stand up with a huff. "There's always something up your ass," I complain, and march off to the laundry room to wash the plaid. I throw it in the washer with a load of dirty dishtowels, still ruminating on what an oversensitive prick Jem can be. He's right, I probably wouldn't take my shirt off in front of Elwood, but that's because Chris would read it as an invitation. Under any other circumstances, I wouldn't mind being shirtless at all. This bra covers way more than the average bathing suit, so it's hardly pushing the bounds of modesty to show it off, not to mention it's probably the least sexy thing I own. It's not like I flashed him.

When I return to the living room Jem is sitting sideways on the couch with his knees bent, arms resting over them, looking contrite. "I'm sorry," he says.

I know it's emotional blackmail, but it's sort of nice how politely he speaks to me now. He's terrified of doing anything that might dissolve our friendship even further.

I stand over him and bury my hands in my pockets. "I'm sorry I didn't talk to you before I cold-shouldered you."

Jem looks down at his lap and smiles sadly. "Why'd you do it?"

"I told you from the start I'd be a bad friend. I intend to kill you, remember?"

He looks up at me with squinty eyes, as though he's irritated but trying to hide it. Eventually Jem looks away and shrugs dismissively. I watch him flex his hands around his knees. His knuckles dig into the denim, tightening and releasing, before he knits his hands together and looks up at me. If his hands are an obvious indicator of his thoughts, his eyes are even more so.

"Are we still friends?"

"Can you handle me?"

"Can you handle *me*?" he returns quietly but earnestly.

"Maybe. Do you have it in you to stop being so pessimistic all the time, and to be a little less possessive?"

"I shouldn't have snapped on you," he murmurs.

"Yeah," I agree with a nod. "I get it that you were mad, but there's shit you just don't do. I don't call you Uncle Fester, you don't steal my phone and mess with it, or get pissed off that I have a life outside of this." I gesture between us. Whatever 'this' is.

"You don't cut me out like that again," he adds.

"I won't. And will you please quit calling all the time and asking Frank where I am? He thinks I have a stalker."

"I'll cut back. A little. You could just, y'know, answer your phone."

"I'll work on it."

"So…friends?"

The word sounds wrong; frightening, strangely pleasant, and somehow not enough. I feel like I know him better than that. I've shared my memories of my happiest and hardest days with this guy. I'm not 'friends' with Jem the same way I am with Paige or Hannah. Or Luke.

"I'm not a good person."

"I'm not either."

"Okay then."

"Okay, friends?"

"Okay, we'll call it even. I guess that's as good a foundation for friendship as any other." That gets a smirk out of him. Hail the return of the smartass.

Jem excuses himself to use the washroom and I go upstairs. There's something I want to show him. I brought very few books with me to Frank's house, but the one I couldn't do without was Darrell Epp's *Imaginary Maps*. I thumb through the worn pages for the poem I have in mind. By the time I find it I can hear Jem calling for me nervously on the ground floor, like I would take off and ditch him in my own house.

"Coming."

He meets me halfway up the stairs. He's got that frightened puppy look again.

"For you." I hand him the book with the cover folded back and he takes it like it's a death warrant. Hardly. Jem reads "For A Sick Friend" through a few times, standing below me on the stair. I've never seen him from this angle before.

Standing on the upper stair, we're almost equal height.

The poem is one about the helplessness of watching a loved one deal with sickness, and the contradiction of both needing and failing to express what that means. It was always good at making me feel a little less alone.

"Is that how you see me?" he asks, looking up at me from under red lids.

"I figured you'd get it."

He turns back to the page. "So..."

He struggles for a few seconds, blowing sighs out through his nose and fiddling with his hat and rubbing the back of his neck.

"Is that why you...y'know, ditched me? It was too much to handle...with your sister. And...stuff. I mean, I know what everyone thinks—were you tired of being stared at?"

"If I had a problem with you having cancer I wouldn't have been decent to you in the first place. It's not like it's something you have to disclose." I gesture up and down to his tall, thin frame. He looks absolutely sallow in the late afternoon light.

Jem looks down and nods uncomfortably. He knows how he looks.

"This," I flick the poem, "is my side of things. Can you appreciate that maybe you remind me of some very painful shit that happened in my life? I mean in addition to being a jerk."

"Are you sure you don't want me to leave you alone?"

"I want you to admit that your feelings aren't the only ones that matter."

"I'm sorry. You do matter. You matter a lot."

He reaches out to grab the railing suddenly and sways a little.

"Are you okay?"

"Just got lightheaded there for a minute." He turns and sits down on the stair before he can fall down.

"Do you need food? Juice?"

"No."

I take a seat beside him and he snorts self-deprecatingly. "You know, I was so nervous to come over here and talk to you that I made myself sick."

"Jeez, Harper." I rub slow circles on his back. Jem carefully closes the cover on *Imaginary Maps*.

"Is it okay with you if I lay on the couch awhile longer?"

"Do you want my bed? That couch sags like ninety-year-old tits and the bed closer to the bathroom if you feel sick."

Jem quietly accepts the offer and we head upstairs. On second thought, I go back downstairs to grab the mop bucket out of the laundry room. If he's dizzy as well as nauseated it'd be better if he didn't have to try to run to the bathroom.

I sit on the desk chair, facing Jem where he's curled up on his side. He barely fits length-wise in my twin bed.

"Why weren't you at Elise's party last night?" I don't think he came downstairs the whole night.

"I was. I drifted in and out. Eric and I were supposed to be supervising, but it seemed like he had a handle on it."

"What did you do?"

"I called some friends. Caught up with them and stuff." That explains the cell phone on his floor.

"Sounds like fun."

Jem snorts. "More like an exercise in jealousy."

"How's that?"

"They have lives. Places to go, people to see. I live in *Smiths Falls* and have no social life."

"I take it you didn't always scare people away?"

Jem scowls at me. "You know why people avoid me."

"I know why you *think* they do." Jem gives me a dry look, which I ignore. "You think you look creepy and that it puts people off. And yeah, you're right, maybe it does freak a few people out, but that's not enough to make you a complete pariah. People avoid you because you push them away with moodiness and jackassery."

Jem stares at me for a few seconds, as though I haven't got to the point yet, and then closes his eyes and sighs through his nose. "I wish I could have known you before I got sick."

I have never felt more compelled to smack this boy. I tell him that's a stupid thing to wish.

"I know. Can't turn back time." He can be so dense it's unbelievable.

"Everything I know about you from before points to the fact that I wouldn't have liked you had I known you then, and you probably wouldn't have liked me, either."

"You like me now?" Always with the difficult questions.

"You're not unlikeable."

"But do you?" he pushes quietly.

"Yes."

The corner of his mouth lifts in a small smile. "I like you too."

There's an awkward silence where I don't know if I'm supposed to say something back. We both get a little shifty-eyed; studying benign objects around the room in between the searching glances we throw at each other.

He breaks the silence first. "Can you...?"

"What?"

"Can you come sit over here? I mean...your hand on my back felt really nice." He seems so embarrassed just to ask.

I can't think of a reason why not, so I leave the chair and sit behind him on the bed, between his back and the wall. He relaxes just a little as I make circles on his back. The arms he has wrapped around his middle shift slightly, so he's holding them up around his chest.

"Thanks." He smiles sadly and snorts like something is funny in a pathetic

184

sort of way.

"What was that for?"

"Yesterday you weren't even willing to look at me, and today you're being nice and touching me."

"You're being nice too."

Jem reaches out and picks up my iPod off the nightstand. He holds it out to me questioningly, and I take it. We each take an earphone and I scroll through my playlists for an appropriate song. I choose "One Week" by the Barenaked Ladies. It's apt. Jem picks the next one, "Iris" by The Goo Goo Dolls, and he drifts off to my second pick: "In the Sun" by Joseph Arthur.

Jem's sleep is swift and sound. He's exhausted in so many ways. I take the earphone out gently when he begins to snore and sit back with my music, watching him sleep. When he begins to shiver slightly I get up and fold the blanket over him like a human burrito. That settles him for a little while, but then he begins to shake again and makes mewling sounds under his breath.

"Shh," I whisper, like he's a restless child. I put an arm over him and adjust the edge of the blanket to keep the cooler air away from him. Jem curls further into himself, pressing his back against my front. Some part of his unconscious mind realizes I'm warm, and he turns his head toward me in sleep. His neck is going to cramp like that.

"Lift your head," I encourage him, even as I do it for him. I slip the pillow under his head and bundle the blanket a little tighter. Jem's eyelids flutter.

He groans and I sit up on my elbow. "Go back to sleep. I've got you."

Jem licks his lips and forces his eyes open. He has a hell of a time of it, blinking tiredly as he tries to focus.

"I forgot my meds."

It feels like all the air has gone out of the room at once. I haven't felt that in awhile. It's a sensation whose absence I never lament.

"Fuck."

I fling back the edge of the blanket and pat down his pockets, looking for the little pill sorter I know he keeps. I find it in his front left pocket. There's still a familiar pill in the 'afternoon' slot.

"I'll get you some water."

I take the stairs two at a time. I am such a screw up—to upset him so badly is one thing, but to upset him to the point where he forgets important medication is quite another. He wasn't shivering in his sleep; he wasn't cold—he was in pain and starting to withdraw a little bit. It's a nasty business to miss a dose of opiates after prolonged use.

I take the cup of water upstairs and help Jem sit up. His hands are shaking, so I slip the pill past his lips and help him steady the cup at his mouth.

"I'm sorry," he says.

"You're *sorry*? I don't care if you're sorry—are you okay?"

"You look worried." He tilts his head to the side curiously, as though I'm the one being the idiot here.

"I look worried…" I shake my head. "I ought to bubble-wrap you, Harper."

"I'll be fine."

"Lay down."

He obeys like he's scared of what I'll do if he doesn't.

"Are you hurting?"

"Kirk," he scolds me softly. I must be over-reacting. I do that when people mess with my head. I have serious issues with watching people endure pain.

"Sorry." I set the pill sorter down on the nightstand and set myself down on my desk chair. "I'm sorry I messed you up so bad."

"I've lived through worse."

I have to bite the inside of my cheek to keep from yelling at him: *Stop saying shit like that! Your entire life isn't a fucking disease!* But I've frightened him enough for one day, so I let it be.

"Okay then," I say. "But I still intend to kill you."

Jem stays for dinner. I make beet soup with fresh mint leaves. It's a starter for Frank and I, and a main course for Jem. I've got mararoni in the oven and vegetables on the stove for the entrée.

We're just sitting down to eat when Luke shows up unexpectedly and lets himself in. He takes a chair as though his presence is nothing out of the ordinary, and Frank asks him how Doug is doing. I wonder if he drove all this way for a meal or if he was in Smiths Falls already on some errand.

"Not bad," Luke says. He lifts the cover on the soup pot and smells the contents. "Looks good."

He takes a helping and gets red lips along with the rest of us.

"Okay, where's the real food?" he says when I get up to clear away three soup bowls. He jumps up to help me take the pork out of the oven and serve it.

Jem's face is practically buried in his bowl. It would be easy to mistake his posture for eagerness to eat, but he's spooning his soup slowly and his shoulders are hunched. Just working his way through his 'fake' food, I guess.

"How's the soup?" I slide a serving of pork Frank's way.

"It's good. Thank you," he says quietly.

Luke tries to make conversation by asking Jem how he's been since they last met, that night at Joe Moore's house.

"Fine. Did you have fun last night?"

The question perplexes Luke. He looks to me for help, and I can only shrug. I don't know what Jem is referring to.

"The party," he says, as though we're the slow ones.

"What party?" Luke elbows me.

"It was his sister's birthday last night," I tell Luke, and elbow him back.

"Cool. Sorry I missed it."

Jem looks like he couldn't possibly disagree more.

"Hannah and I ended up going together," I say.

Jem looks from me to Luke with something like curiosity, or maybe suspicion. Luke steals a cherry tomato off my plate and Frank, who is never good at making conversation, asks Jem how Dr. Harper has been lately.

When the meal is done, I pack up a container of the leftover soup for Jem to take home. He might need a filling snack later to balance the strain of a trying day.

After the day I've had, I'm emotionally exhausted, but Luke is a bundle of energy, and it's contagious. He helps me with the dishes while Jem hangs back, quietly putting the dry dishes away. He watches me intently out of the corner of his eye, looking for something. Luke, in turn, is eying Jem. The way he does it makes me think that he wants Jem to leave. Clearly Jem thinks that too, because the moment the last dish is put away he quietly announces his intention to go home.

"I'll walk you out."

We hug goodbye in the foyer. Jem makes another unnecessary apology and says, "Thanks for the blanket last night." He's got this look on his face like he isn't sure he phrased that right.

"You're welcome."

The corner of his mouth twitches up. There's nothing left to say, so he quietly takes his leave. I stand by the screen door, watching him go to his car. He drives away quickly.

"You doing anything tonight?" Luke says from *right* behind me. I jump and he chuckles.

"You're gangly as hell; how can you walk so softly?"

"It's a gift." He smiles cheekily. "There's a bonfire at my place tonight."

It's a Saturday and I've had a hard week. A night out of the house might actually be a good idea. I grab my jacket, shout my plans across the house to Frank, and we're off.

The bonfire is an excuse to dispose of the dead brush that the Thorpes have pruned from around their property, and is attended by a few of Luke's friends, his sister Briana, Doug, and Mr. Thorpe. Everyone is in good spirits besides Briana, who maintains a sullen glare in between biting comments to the rest of the company.

"She's been a real pain in the ass lately," Luke says to me.

"Shut your stupid mouth, Luke," she barks at him.

"Don't listen."

"I'll leave if you don't want me here."

"No you won't," he laughs. "It's your mission in life to annoy the crap out of people."

So she stays, sitting like a bump on a log, sullenly tossing twigs into the fire. I don't like to look at Briana. She's stained and starving in places that can only be seen if you know what to look for. It gives me shivers. Luke mistakes these for cold and puts an arm around me. He's getting touchy, but he's warm, and we're supposed to pretend that nothing happened, so I let him.

Luke drives me home when Frank calls to tell me that it's getting late. It's not, really, but he's concerned and the Thorpes respect my brother too much to keep me here longer.

"Sorry about Briana," Luke says as we pull out of the driveway.

"She's alright." I ask Luke what happened to her, and he tells me about Briana getting involved with the wrong people at school. She's on probation for possession until July. Not so bad in the general scheme of things, but disturbing when I consider that she's only fourteen.

"She'll be okay."

"I hope so. Her attitude is getting old."

When Luke drops me off he tries to kiss me. I don't let him.

"That stuff on the couch doesn't mean anything, you know."

Luke kisses my cheek instead. "Yet."

That cocky, is he?

Sunday

I wake up at six and can't fall back to sleep, so I get up and take a shower. I eat a big breakfast, read the morning paper, and barely wait till eight o'clock before getting in my car and heading over to the Harper house.

Ivy is awake when I get there—go figure. She lets me in and we chat over coffee while we wait for everyone else to wake up. Dr. Harper comes downstairs first and offers to make pancakes. Ivy declines. Elise drifts in next, bleary-eyed with wild bed-head and pajama pants about six inches too long. She pours herself a giant cup of coffee and tries to drown herself in it before saying good morning.

"How'd you sleep?" Ivy asks her.

Elise grunts dully. "Did he wake you up?"

Ivy's smile fades to a look of worry. "Again?"

Elise nods and lifts her mug. "And he *never* has nightmares after dialysis. Every freaking night now."

"Shit, I know," Eric concurs loudly as he enters the kitchen. "How'd you hear him? Your room is all the way down the hall."

"Light sleeper, remember?"

Eric opens the breadbox and Elise leans back on her chair legs, arm extended. He tosses her a muffin without looking.

"I think it's the prednisone," she says.

The Harpers are such gossips. They talk so casually behind Jem's back and justify it with love.

The object in question this morning appears at the kitchen door just as Elise pours her second mug of coffee and Eric goes for a fourth muffin. Jem looks like hell; the circles under his eyes couldn't possibly get any darker and he shuffles his feet instead of walking.

"Morning, sweetie," Ivy says.

Jem doesn't respond. He just stands in the door like an idiot and stares at me. "Hi."

"Hi." He looks at the breakfast table suspiciously, as if this is all an elaborate ruse to conceal some ulterior motive.

"Sit down," Eric says. So he does. Slowly, like he's wary of his own family.

"Plans for today?" I ask. Jem studies my face and shakes his head no. "We'll stay here, then."

Jem nods and Elise slides the tub of yogurt his way for breakfast. It takes him a few minutes, eating plain yogurt amid his family's morning chatter, but eventually a smile does creep onto his face.

We spend the day on his turf, moving at his pace. Most of the morning is wiled away at the piano, messing around together or listening to him play. He's totally transported when he plays. Something about music takes him to a higher plane while I stay below, watching him float with that special smile on his face. When I ask Jem where he 'goes' when he plays, his face turns red and he shrugs.

"Nowhere, I guess."

I let him have his secret.

"Can I hear you play your cello some time?"

"I haven't really played it since last fall." Jem extends his hand to me, palm up, and shows me the damage to his skin from graft-versus-host. "It hurts to depress the strings for more than a few minutes."

"You'll get back to playing eventually."

Jem shrugs as though he doesn't care, but his eyes are sad. He misses it.

After lunch, Jem and I go for a walk. The rain holds off long enough for us to stroll to the corner and back, discussing bands. He likes The Eels but can't stand Spiral Beach. He knows Great Big Sea but has never heard of Spirit of the West (how is that even possible?) and he thinks that *Beggar's Banquet* is the best of the Stones' albums.

"Nuh-uh, 'Exile on Main Street.' Maybe 'Emotional Rescue' as a close second, but only maybe."

"Oh what do you know?" he dismisses me with a scoff. "I bet you can't stand Neil Young too, right?"

"Are you nuts? Who doesn't like Neil Young? I bet you think Wintersleep is fluff."

"Nuh-uh. The Tragically Hip are over-rated, right?"

"If you honestly think that you're a stunned twat, Harper."

When we get back to the house, Ivy is singing country music in her office. The night of rough sleep and an active morning have tired Jem, so we go into the living room and put on a movie. He chooses *Addams Family Values*.

"Seriously?"

"Why not?" He smiles. I sit at the end of the couch while he lays down on his side. He curls up at first, trying to give me space, but he looks so cramped that I take his ankles and pull his feet onto my lap.

"Do you mind?"

"Not at all."

I'm probably spoiling him, giving him a day of my undivided attention and a foot rub too, but I really should make up for trying to cut him out last week. He basks so sweetly in the attention that I can't help but give him more.

"Thanks," he murmurs as I massage his soles. I try to pull his sock off but Jem draws his foot back to stop me.

He winces at my questioning look and says, "I'm anemic. My feet are always cold."

"Okay. Socks stay on."

Jem has very ticklish feet. I have to massage slowly and carefully or he spazzes all over the couch and makes the funniest little 'ack!' sound. I don't do it on purpose…much.

Jem is fighting to keep his eyes open when the movie ends, but he tries to stay awake and be a good host. I offer to leave.

"No, stay, please. Do you want to look around the library?"

He knows how to tempt me.

When we go upstairs I head straight for Dickens. Ivy's anthology has better footnotes than my second-hand novels, with beautiful prints of important scenes inserted throughout the chapters. It's a lovely book, with a leather cover and strong spine.

"You're quite an adorable nerd," Jem tells me. He slouches against the bookcase, smirking at me. The poor guy looks ready to drop.

"You need a nap."

Jem's smirk falters, but he doesn't argue outright. "I'll be okay."

I can't decide if it's sweet or stupid of him to lie just because I'm a guest.

"Come on." I link my arm with his. "I'll read in your room."

⚭

I make myself comfy against the headboard while Jem excuses himself to the washroom. Beyond the bathroom door I can hear the sound of a pill sorter being opened and a cup filling at the tap. He doesn't want to take his medication in front of me. I guess I owe him one now, since he's being so considerate. He understands that it flips a switch in me to know what poisons he's taking.

When Jem comes out of the bathroom he tries to sit next to me against the headboard.

"Your neck will cramp if you fall asleep like that."

He grimaces. "You don't mind if I sleep a little bit?"

"Of course not. You need it. And I've got Pip and Company for entertainment." I tap the cover of the collection. I decided on *Great Expectations* while arranging the pillows.

Jem lays down on his side, facing me, and folds his arms loosely around his front. He closes his eyes and sighs purposefully, but the silence is awkward.

"You don't have to stay in here if you don't want to," he offers.

It would be rude to say, "Shut up, you goof," so I open the book to the first chapter of *Great Expectations* and read aloud. He's asleep in less than five minutes. Absolutely no appreciation for classic literature....

I read the first few chapters of *Great Expectations* before my back starts to cramp from sitting against the headboard. I close the book and very carefully move off the bed to stretch. Jem slumbers on without the slightest hint that he registered my movement.

I don't want to disturb him by climbing back onto the mattress, so I pull out his desk chair and turn it around so I can watch him sleep. I enjoy doing that far too much.

The first time I watched Jem sleep, it was on the couch that first Saturday he showed up at my house. His feet twitched in his sleep and his mouth fell open slightly. He looked like a little boy, tuckered out and bundled up. Then there was Easter weekend, when he had the blankets pulled up to his chin and his cheek squished against the pillow. I thought it was funny that he napped with his hat on, but Jem is so self-conscious that I shouldn't have been surprised. He probably only takes his hat off to bathe and sleep through the night.

"What a strange creature you are," I whisper to his sleeping back. His breath comes softly through parted lips.

The last time I watched Jem sleep, just this past Saturday, he did so with the defeat and peace of a dead man. He didn't twitch or stir, except to whimper in pain. His cheeks were still lined with red tracks from crying—it's the poisons in him; his own tears are enough to burn the skin slightly. The tracks ran directly down both cheeks from his lids because his sparse, fledgling lashes weren't enough to funnel the moisture out the corners of his eyes.

Jem's fingers twitch. Maybe he's dreaming about music. They flutter and relax several times, but he doesn't wake.

His breathing changes after a while. No longer quite even, he makes little snuffling sounds when his fingers twitch. When his hands quit, his feet start. They tremor just slightly and his toes curl. I wonder if he's a sleep-walker, because most people can't even twitch in deep sleep.

"What are you dreaming about?" I whisper with a smile. If I asked waking Jem, he probably wouldn't tell me. He would call me nosey and demand to know why I was watching him like some sort of creep. Maybe I am a creep. I do enjoy watching him sleep. When his face is relaxed it's easy to see what he must have looked like as a little boy.

As long as I'm being a creep, I might as well make it worthwhile. I open the drawer of his nightstand and peek at the contents. Harper is quite the packrat. I carefully sift through three half-empty medication bottles, a lot of crumpled receipts, notes-to-self composed in acronyms and half-sentences, and elastic bands of all shapes and sizes. There's also a postcard wedged in the back of the drawer. It's one of those generic ones with a picture of a sunset over the beach and *Wish you were here!* on the front. I flip it over and find a short note in very feminine penmanship:

Hey, Cancer! Give up while you still can! You're never going to beat him. He's too strong for you!

I throw the postcard back in the drawer and shut it tight. Jesus Christ…

Jem snuffles again and I lean over him to make sure the pillow isn't blocking his airway. His jaw is relaxed, but his eyes are tight and worried-looking. His fingers twitch again. Whatever he's dreaming doesn't seem pleasant.

I put a hand around his shoulder and call his name softly.

Jem wakes with a gasp and jerks his arm up, as though I'm a threat that needs to be pushed away. I grab his wrist before he can hit me in the face and push it back down.

"You're okay. It's me."

He still isn't quite awake. I hold both his wrists against his front like a human straightjacket.

"You were dreaming."

"Shit," he whispers, and pulls in several deep breaths as though he's been starving for air.

"Nightmare?" Elise said he'd been having them lately.

Jem makes a hum that passes for yes.

"What was it about?"

"Drowning," he answers shortly, and sucks in a steadying breath.

"It's okay. I've got you. You're alive and well."

Jem turns his head to look at me over his shoulder. "I'm not well." He says it with the surprise and disappointment of a kid learning that Santa isn't real. Break my heart, why doesn't he?

"Regardless, I've still got you." I give him a little squeeze to prove it.

Jem turns his face away again, but squeezes me back where our arms overlap across his front.

"You must have been cold. You're more likely to have nightmares when you are. I'm sorry I didn't realize—I would have covered you up."

"Why are you so fucking nice to me?" he says bitterly.

I smile at the back of his head and nudge his temple with my nose. "Because you're such a fucking peach."

That deflates him a little. "Sorry."

"Don't worry about it."

Jem dislodges my arms and sits up. He scrubs a hand over his face to clear his eyes and pulls his hat lower over his ears. "How long was I out?"

"I don't know. I wasn't keeping track."

Jem swings his legs out of bed and stops there. For a moment he just sits there and studies me, frowning slightly, as though there's something puzzling about the way I look. He reaches out and grabs the sleeve of my sweater. Jem pulls on me so hard that I practically fall off the chair and onto his lap. He couldn't just ask for a hug like a normal person—if this can be called a hug. It feels more like he's trying to squeeze the living breath out of me.

"Air!" I gasp, and he lets go all at once. I lose my balance and fall flat on my ass.

"Shit! I'm so sorry." Jem puts a hand on my arm to help me up but I brush him off.

"Screw it." I lay back on the floor to regain my breath. "I'll be down here."

"Are you okay?"

"Fine. My ass broke my fall."

He doesn't appreciate my attempt at humor. He looks sick with worry, which makes me laugh.

"It's not funny."

"Sure it is."

"Let me help you up."

I allow it this time. He refuses to try to sleep some more, but he's too tired for us to do much. We end up playing crazy eights on his bed. It's the dorkiest, most calming afternoon I've had in quite some time.

We play for about an hour before Jem's eyes really start to droop again. I talk less, wondering if he might fall asleep without conversation to keep him awake. His is a subtle transition between waking and sleeping. His eyelids close, but he holds onto his cards awhile before his wrist relaxes and they slip through his fingers. I gather up the cards and set them on the nightstand. He doesn't need more nightmares, so I cover him up too.

I consider seeking the company of Ivy or Elise while Jem sleeps, but I don't really want to leave this room. Jem has a knack for objects. He knows how to arrange otherwise random, meaningless things to reflect his personality. Why should a scattered collection of bottle caps on his dresser say *Jem*? I don't know, but it does. So I study the room, studying him.

He isn't big on books, but there are a lot of notebooks on his shelf. They're the kind designed for music students, with blank staves instead of lines. I flip through a few and find compositions I can't read. The pages are thin from countless erasings and there are slash marks across sections that he scrapped in a rush. I wish I could read this. I want to know what kind of sounds creep through his mind when he's in a creative mood.

Then I find the black notebook. It's set up like a day calendar. It started last July, and on each day he has kept a record of what medications he took, how much and what he ate, and his symptoms. I shut the book as fast as I can and put it back on the shelf. Mom kept a book like that for Tessa, to show the doctors what was happening when they weren't around. I don't want to look at his book, and I bet Jem doesn't either. That part is behind him.

I take Jem's desk chair into the corner, where the sun shines in warmly, and open his nightstand drawer. I bet I can make a ball the size of a plum with all the stray elastic bands he has in here.

↬

It's almost an hour later that Jem wakes with a yawn. He looks around the room blearily, moving his eyes from the deck of cards on the opposite nightstand to the closed door, and sits up on his elbow with a defeated look.

"Do you need more sleep?"

Jem jumps when he realizes that I'm in the corner behind him. "Shit, Kirk," he curses. He looks at the ball in my hands and says, "What are you doing?"

"Playing with rubbers." My little joke gets a smile out of him. "Did you think I left?" I nod to the door. He was practically pouting in that direction a moment ago.

Jem nods. "Yeah. Sorry I dozed off. I'm not very interesting company."

He sits up and swings his legs out of bed, rolling his shoulders to slowly stretch.

"Thanks for staying."

Jem gives me a small smile that reveals way more gratitude than I can handle. He's still waiting for me to run off again while he isn't looking.

"Do I owe you an explanation for…you know?"

"Last week?"

"Yeah."

Jem shifts slightly, contemplating. "If you don't want to…"

"But I should."

"It would be…appreciated," he says, choosing his words carefully. I can see why the subject makes him skittish. I might talk myself into cutting him out again.

I put the rubber band ball back in his drawer and stand up. My first thought is to sit next to him on the bed, but then I think better of it. I don't want to give this conversation the feel of a mushy heart-to-heart. I want to just explain my issues and get it over with.

After a few seconds Jem catches on that I'm just going to stand here like an idiot without sitting down. He reaches out for my hand and jostles it a little.

"Tell me."

His hand is warm and slightly sticky from sleep.

"I don't... I don't like it when people try to control me. Or manipulate me. Or when people try to pull shit over on me. It..." I drop his hand and run mine through my hair. "This isn't coming out right. This is the worst explanation ever."

Jem smirks. "I can imagine worse." He snorts softly and his smirk fades. "Are you sure you don't want me to leave you alone?"

"That's the thing, I don't."

Jem tries and fails to hide his sense of relief.

"But you scare the shit out of me."

"I'm sorry I worried you. I don't usually forget me meds like that."

"I don't mean that. But as long as we're on the subject, don't do that again." He chuckles at me. "I'll try not. Is it the dying part that scares you?"

I try not to think about the fact that he could easily relapse at any time. That is an 'if' that I don't have enough energy to panic about from moment to moment.

"No."

"So what did you mean?" An automatic hunch creeps over his shoulders. He's so self-conscious that he's conditioned to brace for pain.

"It's frightening that...that if you asked nicely I'd probably give you anything you wanted; even the things I don't want to give."

He swallows and curls his fingers on his knees.

"You have the power to suck me dry and I absolutely hate you for it. I don't want to go back to living like that."

Jem takes my hand and turns it over, brushing his thumb across my palm. "I won't, you know. I wouldn't do that to you."

I try to smile, but all I can manage is a spasm of my upper lip.

"You know..." He turns my hand again, studying my fingernails like they're really interesting. "Good people don't suck each other dry. They give as much as they take. Friends do that." He looks up at me as though I'm supposed to say something back.

"I'm not good with stuff like that."

"You'll learn," Jem says, and squeezes my hand. "It's okay to take, too, Willa. You don't have to give all the time."

The clock on his nightstand beeps to announce the turnover of the hour. It's five o'clock.

"I should go. I have to make dinner for Frank."

I slip my hand out of his grasp and his hovers there for a few seconds, as if he wants me to put mine back. Jem reluctantly says goodbye to me—after extending an invitation to dinner no less than three times.

"Would you like to have dinner with us tomorrow?" he says when all attempts to get me to stay tonight fail.

"I can't," I tell him as he walks me to the door. "I made plans with Hannah."

"Oh, okay. Some other time, maybe." He almost manages to hide his disappointment, too.

I can't help but think *poor guy* as I give him a one-armed hug goodbye. He might be in better shape if he'd gotten sick in Ottawa, where he had friends to rally around him. This perpetual loneliness isn't good for him—it's made him a philosopher on ideal friendship, of all things. Like such a thing even exists. It didn't in St. John's, and it won't in Smiths Falls. Not for me, and not for him either, judging by the way people treat him at school.

No one appreciates Jem properly, anyway. All they see is his disease. He's beautiful, and you don't have to look that closely to see it. You just have to look.

Monday

I have to study for French today at lunch, because I can't possibly cram enough for this test. I scarf down half a sandwich en route to the library. Mrs. Gilmore gives me a dirty look when I walk in still chewing the last of it, so I stand in the vestibule and glare at her until I swallow. Nitpicky librarians…

The carrels are all full, so I circle around to the area of worktables. These aren't used as much because Domme Gilmore watches them like a hawk and chews out anybody who raises their voice above a whisper to speak to their colleagues around the table. I park myself at an empty table and set my books up across the surface, taking up as much space as possible to throw people off the idea of sitting near me—I need to study.

I feel a tug at the back of my head and a twist as a lock of my hair gets wrapped around a finger. Ugh. Paige greeted me like this last week, when she was entertaining thoughts of giving me a new haircut for fun. Flattery is always the best way to distract Paige, so I say, "Hey Gorgeous."

My hair stops twisting. I look over my shoulder and instead of petite Paige Holbrook standing there, it's Jem. Damn it all to hell, he's going to tease the crap out of me for saying hello like that.

"Uh, hi."

He stares at me for a few seconds, slowly unwinding my hair from his index finger, before he pulls out the adjacent seat and sits down.

"Hey Beautiful," he says quietly, not looking at me. I can't decide if he's trying to embarrass, guilt, or tease me.

Jem reaches under the table for my backpack. "I'm borrowing your Soc notes."

Normally I would be annoyed by the fact that he didn't ask before taking, but part of my grade is tied to his, so I let him catch up on the material without complaint. As long as he copies my notes quietly and doesn't interrupt my cram session, I will abide his presence.

"Who did you think I was?" he asks as he flips through my notebook.

"Paige."

"Reeeally?"

"Bugger off."

Jem smirks as he copies my diagram of human fertilization. He starts to sing under his breath, "Willa and Paige, sitting in a tree—" My partner has the intellect of a third grader. I haven't heard that song since primary school.

"Shut up." I bump my shoulder against his. Jem bumps me back.

"F–u–c–k–i–n–g," he continues, trying not to laugh. "First comes love, then comes a civil union at the courthouse, then comes…" He pauses to think. "Baster babies?"

"You are a moron, Harper," I say slowly.

"But I can still set up a camera in the corner, right?"

It's unbelievably difficult to resist the urge to bitch-slap him with my notebook. But I can't let him get a rise out of me. Then he wins.

"Fine, set up a camera."

Jem laughs at me.

"I need to study."

Jem steals my book from under my elbow and flips through it. I just lost my page.

"You really suck at this subject, don't you?"

I lean over to grab my book back and Jem scoots his chair sideways, holding the book out of my reach.

"Harper," I warn him.

"Want me to quiz you?"

"No, I want you to give me my book back and shut the hell up so I can *learn* this garbage."

He doesn't listen. "Comment ça va?"

"I'm ready to punch you, that's how I am."

Jem smirks and shakes his head. "Non, à la français."

"This isn't an oral test, it's a written one. Give me the book."

"You'll remember it better if you speak it." Still, he hands my book back. I start flipping to find my original page and he says, "Je souhaite que tu saches comment je t'aime."

I'm not going to give him the satisfaction of watching me look up what the hell that means. Stupid smug polyglots.

To his credit, Jem dutifully shuts up and lets me work for the rest of the period. He copies my Soc notes, getting sidetracked every now and then to doodle in his margins. At the end of the hour he packs up my notes and puts them back in my bag.

"Why do you keep all this crap in here?" he says when he opens my backpack. I don't think I've cleaned that thing out since sixth grade. Atlantis could be buried at the bottom for all I know.

"It's a necessary mess," I tell him. I just don't feel like cleaning it. Someday the problem will get so bad that I'll just have to give up and torch the whole backpack.

Jem starts going through my mess, picking and reading scraps of notes taken Lord knows when. He finds about six empty pens, a few dead batteries, band-aids for gym class, and a crumpled bag of mints.

"And I thought my sister's purse was bad," he mutters.

"Oh shut it."

Jem pulls out a piece of folded notepaper and pauses. He studies it for a second, peeking past the corner, and then looks over at me. "Did you even read it?"

I snatch the note out of his hand and stuff it down my shirt. I did read his apology note, thank you very much. And I hung onto it too.

"Willa?"

"I read it, okay? Bugger off."

"How come—"

I clap a hand over his mouth.

"We're not going to talk about this right now."

Jem mumbles something behind my hand that sounds like, "When?"

Uh, never? When I'm drunk? When the Wizard of Oz beams down and puts a watchamacallit in my chest?

"When we're a hundred and five, okay? Save the date." I take my hand off his face, grab my books and my backpack off his lap, and bolt.

☙

Sometimes I wonder why Hannah hangs out with Paige and Diane—she's so genuine and they're so not. Her parents are out of town for the evening and she asked me to help her watch her little brothers; a favor I wouldn't do for anyone else. But Hannah is an angel, and it turns out the Trilby boys are extremely well behaved.

She asks me how Jem is as we put together supper for the kids. For a second I panic—does she know about the fight on Saturday? Did she notice I avoided him all week? Does she know about the note on my windshield? Or is she referring to the whole day I spent with him yesterday? But then I realize that these worries are senseless. No one notices Jem, except in a bad way, and he's the only other person who could have spread the news of our fight. Who would he have told?

"He's okay."

"Just okay?"

"He's better than he was."

Hannah nods. "He can be really sweet, can't he?"

"When he wants to be, yeah."

Hannah smiles and slathers more peanut butter on a celery slice. She's making frogs on a log with raisins. "I think you two would be a really cute couple." The way she says it surprises me more than the statement itself; she's not scheming or giggly or sarcastic. She says it like she means it. And as for the statement itself—for some reason it doesn't surprise me. It feels natural, which is completely weird.

"I don't think that either of us is in a relationship mindset."

Hannah shrugs. "It was just a thought. You two seem like really good friends."

We are. And it works that way. Perfectly.

Right?

Tuesday

Jem and I manage to spend the entire Soc period arguing over how to organize the results of our experimental model for the term project. Hannah was wrong. We wouldn't be a cute couple. If we can argue for over an hour about bar versus line graphs, we'd be that couple that annoys each other to death. We only work as friends.

But hate sex has its merits…

That night, Jem doesn't text me about music like he usually does, so I assume he's tired and went to bed early. That's fine by me. He hasn't been sleeping well, anyway.

But just in case, I send him a *Goodnight* text. He doesn't get back to me. Poor guy must be out cold.

↔

My ringtone is in my dream. I claw my way to the surface of consciousness and roll over, taking my time about it. It's nearly midnight. This better be good.

"Hello?"

"Willa?" I notice the difference in Jem's voice immediately. It isn't smooth or sleepy or hopeful, like it usually is when he calls me at night—it's low and shaky and distant.

"What's wrong?" The way he breathes makes it sound like he's shivering. I sit up and draw my knees in, ready to swing them out of bed and…what? Drive over there in the middle of the night?

"Not feeling well." His voice is so tight that it trembles with the effort to remain level.

"Are your parents home?"

"They know," he assures me. "I told them to leave me alone. They can't help."

"What's the matter?"

"Stomach." I can hear his wince over the phone. And he doesn't show pain willingly unless he's in serious agony.

"I know it sounds counterproductive, but sometimes the best thing when you feel sick is to try to puke."

Jem groans softly on the other end of the line. "I did. A lot. There's nothing to bring up anymore, but I still feel horrible." And he was feeling so well just this morning.

"You took two Oxy, didn't you?"

"Yeah," he admits with defeat. "I was hurting…"

"You don't have to justify it to me."

Jem blows out a fortifying sigh. "Can you…just talk to me? Please?"

"Uh…Paige is trying to get me to go to prom?"

Jem snorts. "Why?"

"A bigger group makes a limo cheaper."

"Do you want to go?"

"Absolutely not. Come on, it's *prom*."

"We'll make plans that night," Jem promises quietly. "Give you an excuse not to go."

"Thanks." His quick breathing turns sharp. "Jem?"

"It hurts," he murmurs. I can just picture him curled up in the fetal position, holding his stomach and sweating in pain. And he sent everyone away—he wanted to suffer this alone. When there is nothing anyone can do, and attendance would make others fret, it's best to beg for solitude.

"Are you in bed right now?" I use that slow, sleepy voice that parents of young children use to coax their little ones to bed.

"Yeah."

"Can you feel your heart beating?"

"What?"

"Without touching your chest—are you aware of your heart beating?"

For a few seconds the only sound on the line is his shallow breathing. It slows just slightly before he whispers, "Yes."

"And can you feel the soles of your feet? Are they cold or hot?"

"Cold."

"Do you feel your heartbeat there?"

This time it takes him longer to answer.

"Yes."

"Feel it in your ankles."

His breaths turn long and deep as he moves the sensation from feet to ankles; ankles to calves; calves to knees. He breathes in time with his pulse without realizing it, and it calms him.

"Can you feel the blood leaving your heart? Picture it flowing through your arteries, directly to your lungs."

He pulls in a deep breath.

"Feel how smoothly your diaphragm moves?"

"Yeah." He breathes it so softly I can barely hear him.

"Feel it pushing the air up and up, into your throat?"

He makes a hum that sounds like a yes.

"Can you feel your heartbeat in your nose?"

"Mmm."

"In your gums?"

"Uh-huh." He's gotten quick at locating his heartbeat in remote places. He's in tune with his body instead of fighting with it.

"Your eyes are closed, aren't they?"

"Yeah."

"What do the insides of your lids look like?"

"Dark." He adds a timid, "I like it," a moment later.

"Do you hear blood in your ears?"

"Yes."

"What does it say?"

Jem hesitates over that one. "I…I don't know."

"But it's a nice sound, isn't it?"

"Yeah."

"It's okay to fall asleep."

"I know."

"Can you?"

"I don't want to."

"Why?"

His breathing is slow, sleepy, and it takes him nearly ten seconds to answer my question. "I don't want to be alone."

"You're not. It's you, your heartbeat, and me. And I'll be here until you fall asleep."

He breathes a little sigh of relief. "Thank you."

Jem: April 18 to 22

Wednesday

I wake up on my side, dozy and achy, to find Elise sleeping next to me. She must have crawled in sometime after I fell asleep talking to Willa. She's curled up to save space, tucked in under the afghan from the couch, and cradling the phone close to her chest. She must have pulled it out of my hand while I was passed out.

Poor Lise. She looks so tired and worried. I softly run a hand across her short hair and she wakes with a start.

"W'as wrong?" she says sleepily. She isn't even really awake yet.

"Nothing. You're just tired. Go back to sleep."

I open an arm to her and she crawls into the crook of my chest and shoulder. She's so small and light-boned, like a little bird. It only takes her a few seconds to slip into sleep again, and though I feel guilty for making her worry, I'm too tired to stay awake to dwell on it for long.

I find Willa first thing when I get to school. She's got her locker open (it's a complete mess) and is holding a pen between her teeth and a book under her arm while she rifles through her backpack.

"What are you digging for this time?"

"China," she says around the pen. "Screw it." She spits out the pen and throws her backpack in her locker.

I nudge her shoulder to get her to look at me. "Thanks," I tell her. "For... last night." I make sure to say it quietly so that people won't overhear and make assumptions about the new girl and Cancer Boy. Such a rumor would be humiliating for her by default, and humiliating for me when everyone learns that it isn't true.

"No problem."

"Where'd you learn that?"

"It's a useful little survival skill," she answers vaguely. Willa never can give a straight answer.

"I have lunch for you today," she offers.

My eyes immediately flit to her locker and she shifts in front of it, blocking me. "No, you can't have it now."

I laugh and tell her that I'll just break into her locker while she's in class. Willa rolls her eyes at me.

"It's good for aches as well as your stomach."

My eyes shift to her locker again before settling back on her face. She went out of her way this morning to make sure I don't have a repeat of last night.

"Thank you."

Willa smiles, but she doesn't look happy. She shuts her locker and says, "See you at lunch."

I don't pay much attention to my first lecture. I'm too busy wondering whether I messed things up by calling Willa last night. Did I stir up some painful memory? Did I hurt her? Did I take too much, again?

It's not like I asked her to make me food, either. I mean, of course I'll still scarf it down at lunch like it's the last remaining food on earth, but she didn't have to make it....

I try to apologize to Willa when she hands over the thermos at lunch, but she won't hear it.

"The last thing you need is a guilt complex about food on top of everything else."

"So forgive me."

Willa sighs tiredly. "Fine. I forgive you for accepting a gift you didn't ask for."

"Now you're just trying to guilt me."

She tries to take the thermos back and I hold it out of her reach. It's *mine*, damn it.

"Please, just eat."

It's a smoothie today: raspberry yogurt, buttermilk, and mint. It tastes like fresh sorbet mated with a cheesecake. I want to bathe in this stuff.

"Can I have the recipe?"

"What if I said no?"

"You wouldn't."

"Wouldn't I?"

I try pouting and she tells me there's something wrong with my lip.

"Is it working?"

"Nope."

"What about if I just do this all through lunch and Soc?" I nudge her repeatedly with my boney elbow—not hard enough to hurt, but persistent enough to be really annoying.

Willa takes a folded piece of notebook paper out of her pocket and holds it up. I snatch it from her fingers before she can change her mind and retract it, and she laughs at my eagerness.

It isn't until I get home and unfold the paper that I realize it doesn't have the recipe on it. It says, *You pick the music tonight.* I'd be entirely peeved about the recipe rip-off if she didn't already have me thinking through potential playlists for tonight.

❧

I call Willa around ten o'clock and immediately forget to give her shit for gypping me out of a recipe—it's entirely her fault. She distracts me with the way she answers the phone: "Hey. Hang on a second, ok?"

"Sure. Everything all right?"

"Yeah. I wasn't expecting you to call yet. I only have half a pair of pajamas on." And she feels the need to just casually reveal that to me? Like I'm not going to picture it and turn into an incoherent mess?

Willa sets aside her phone and I can hear the soft sounds of her pulling on clothes nearby. I wonder if she was missing her pants or shirt….

"What are we listening to tonight?" she asks.

"See if you can name them."

I play her "Comes a Time," by Neil Young, because she reminded me of it last weekend. She names that one without trouble, including the album it was released on.

"Why don't you play an instrument? You're so invested in music."

"I can sort of play guitar, but not very well. What else you got?"

I give her "Picking up the Pieces" by Blue October.

She's surprised that I own any of their music. "I didn't think they were your style."

"My tastes are wide and varied." And the album was a gift, anyway.

I try to lighten the mood with the cheesy pop song "Every Other Time" by LFO. Willa practically busts a gut laughing and says she hopes I bought that CD before I hit puberty, because anything else is just sad.

"Alright, fine, smartass." I continue in the same vein with "Absolutely" by Nine Days. Willa approves of that one more, but only slightly. We cap off the evening with "Old Habits Die Hard" by Mick Jagger.

"Tomorrow it's my turn," she says before we say goodnight.

"Make it good."

"You doubt me?"

"Never."

"Sweet dreams."

She hangs up without properly saying goodbye. I try not to take offense to that, but the fact that the call ended is enough to bother me either way. I never want to end a call with her.

Thursday

The guy staring back at me in the bathroom mirror looks like hell. He looks like he hasn't slept well and hasn't had a decent meal in months. Sounds like someone I know.

I splash cool water over my face to wake up. I slept, sure, but I don't feel rested. I've been having nightmares on a regular basis lately, even after dialysis, which usually puts me too far under to dream. Maybe it's the meds, or the food. It could be a fucking brain tumor for all I know, but my regular blood work would have shown that.

I'm reluctant to blame it on the meds entirely, because it's always the same nightmare. If it was creepy dreams in general, sure. But the same one over and over again must mean something.

I dream of Willa drowning. The first time it happened I was in the public garden Mom that helped design when I was a kid, and I was holding a duck under my arm like a football. The duck just hung there limply and let me carry him around, quacking occasionally. There wasn't even much point to the dream until Willa showed up. She said the duck was hers and I should give it back, so I did. She took it with her into one of the park ponds, swimming and diving below the murky surface. The duck kept swimming. Willa never came back up.

The dreams are always different, but she always drowns: a surfing accident; unconscious at the bottom of a swimming pool; as a little kid alone in a bathtub; swept out to sea in a riptide. Every single time, I stand there watching her die, unable to do anything about it or even to reach out and retrieve her body.

Last night she drowned in a car that had crashed into a creek. I stood on the bridge and watched the air pockets in the car rise to the surface until the water became still, and all I could see was the outline of the bumper beneath the current.

I suppose I should be glad she hasn't pulled a Virginia Woolf in my dreams yet. You know, in the spirit of optimism and all.

Willa takes one look at me when I get to school, before I can even tell her good morning, and says, "You look like you slept under a bus."

"I did, actually. I clung to the underside like a bat and dozed."

She cracks a smile. Today isn't going to be so bad after all. I've got a good feeling about this one.

⌁

I barely have time to close the car door before Elise turns around in the front seat and practically shouts, "I sat with him at lunch today!"

"Are you deaf, too?" I yell back.

Elise grins and flaps her hands like a demented circus monkey.

"He's planning to work at Camp Concord this summer. Isn't that sweet? He said—"

I don't care what he said. I hate him already. People work at Camp Concord when they want to put brownie points for their scholarship applications—it's one of those 'inclusive' camps that caters to disabled kids. A scholarship committee will eat that shit up faster than if he wrote, *I saved a box of puppies from a burning building* on his application.

"Does his girlfriend work there too?" I ask.

Elise's face falls just a little at the mention of Nina. "No. She works at the grocery store."

"Gotta save for college somehow."

"I've been thinking of where to apply for summer work."

Please—God, Buddha, Allah, Krishna—*not* Camp Concord.

"Maybe Dad could put in a good word for you at the hospital cafeteria."

Elise makes a face. She's about as sick of hospitals as I am. "Maybe I'll end up at the grocery store."

What the hell is she playing at?

⮞

I miss the latter half of Willa's playlist tonight. Her first pick is "Weighty Ghost" by Wintersleep, which is sort of a relaxing song, and I can't keep my eyes open for most of "Hey Man" by the Eels. I lose consciousness during the opening rift of a song I don't recognize by a band I've never heard before. Tonight I don't dream.

Friday

I am so bored. The homework I brought to the clinic for the three-hour wait has long since been finished, and the volunteer with the book cart had no good magazines to offer. It was a choice between *Teen Vogue* and *Fisherman's Quarterly*. Pass.

I'm busy counting the ceiling tiles when the curtain around my chair shifts. Willa slips into the cubicle in an oversized grey sweatshirt with the hood pulled up, as though she's trying not to be seen, and takes up the visitor's chair.

"What are you doing here?"

"Visiting." She adjusts her sweater around her. "Had to borrow this from one of the cafeteria workers. If people see the green vest they ask me to do stuff."

"Did you know I'd be here?"

"Gerald tipped me off that you were still here," she says of the old man who pushed the book cart down this ward twenty minutes ago. "But your mom was the one who told me you had an appointment tonight." Willa chuckles to herself. "I think that woman is determined to get you laid. She'll sell your merits to anyone who will listen."

"Kirk," I complain. She shouldn't talk about anybody's mom like that and my (lack of) sex life is no one's business but my own.

"We had a nice chat."

Willa pulls a can of pop out of one of the sweater's oversized pockets, cracks it and takes a sip. She offers it to me but I decline.

"What did you talk about?" Please, in the name of all that is holy, don't let Mom have embarrassed me. It's embarrassing enough to be seen receiving treatment.

Willa looks once at the tubes that enter above the collar of my hospital gown, and tries not to look at them again. If I'd known she was coming I would have asked the nurse for a blanket or something to hide this.

"She told me that you used to win awards for music."

"It was just a stupid music camp certificate."

"So you didn't win some competition to play with the Ottawa Philharmonic when you were like, fifteen?"

Why did Mom have to go and tell her that? She probably bragged about it, too.

"I don't play that seriously anymore."

"Why not?"

"Chemo."

"I thought you were done?"

"No, chemo messed up my hands, like it did my taste buds." I extend my scarred hand to her in illustration. "Chemo kills a lot of cells that are actually useful. I lost feeling in my fingers and freaked out, so my doctor told me to drink a lot of water. I was chugging something like eight liters a day. Not all the feeling came back, though. I can't play as well as I used to. And GVH made my hands so sore that I couldn't play for weeks at a time."

"You still play very beautifully."

"Like you're such an expert."

"Your mom said you used to compose, too."

"A little."

"Will you show me an original piece sometime?"

"Maybe."

"Harper," she says severely. Her tone is weird because she's smiling.

"Fine. I'll show you some time."

Willa nods with satisfaction. She takes a long sip of ginger ale and then gives me that devilish smirk that I don't trust for shit.

"So, you went to music camp?"

"So?"

"Touchy."

"It was one summer."

"Or five."

Damn it, Mom!

"Are you going this summer?"

"I'll be in summer school, catching up on all the stuff I missed."

"That's a shame."

I shrug. "It's no big deal."

"Elise said it used to be the highlight of your year. 'Bigger than Christmas,' she said."

"You talked to Elise about me too?"

"You talk to them about me."

"That's different."

"Why?"

"They're *my* family."

"And they care about you very much—enough to gossip freely, anyway."

"Music just isn't a big part of my life anymore. Did they tell you that?"

"Jem," Willa said calmly. Uh-oh. She's first-naming me. "That is complete and utter bullshit."

"Stop acting like you know everything. You know shit about my music."

"Were you in a band?" she teases. "Bunch of classical nerds together in a garage—cello, oboe, euphonium—"

She knows what a euphonium is?

"All you'd need are a couple of bowties and you're set."

"Yeah? Well…"

Willa looks at me expectantly while I fish for a riposte.

"Damn it, you don't have any dorky hobbies."

"Ha!"

"But reading Dickens for fun is still nerdy as shit."

"So are you not as dexterous anymore or what?" She reaches out and picks up my hand where it sits on the armrest of the recliner. She turns it over in her hand and runs her thumb along my palm.

"I've still got full movement." I wiggle my fingers to show her. "I just can't moderate how hard or soft I touch things, sometimes. Music takes that kind of finesse."

"So what's your favorite song to play?"

"I dunno. It changes to whatever I feel like at the moment, I guess, or whatever piece I'm working on. I used to practice a lot more than I do now. I had a lot of free time on my hands before we started hanging out."

Willa smirks. That last sentence reveals too much, and my face betrays me by turning red.

"I had a lot of superficial friends before I met you," she says.

"Are you calling me ugly?"

"I'm saying you get me."

"I do?"

Willa shrugs. This woman is frustrating as hell. "Do you think you get me?"

"I don't understand a single word that comes out of your mouth."

She laughs and tells me I'm full of shit.

Saturday

Elise makes a crack at me for running late on a Saturday as I rush around the house getting ready. Shower, clothes, breakfast, missing keys—all annoying little things that get in the way of me going over to the Kirk house.

"What time will you be home?" Elise asks, following me around like a puppy. If she's going to do that, she could at least help me look for the car keys.

"I don't know."

"Maybe we can do something tonight?"

"We'll see."

"Jem," she whines.

"What?"

"You don't want to spend time with me?"

"Maybe tomorrow. Call Carey or something."

"She's busy."

"So am I." Where the hell could Mom have put those keys?

"Can I come?"

"No."

"Why not? Willa likes me."

"I said no, Lise."

"Fine. Hmph."

She sits cross-legged on the kitchen floor and folds her arms, pouting profusely. She's about ten years too old to be pulling this shit. I set a cup of water and a bag of Bits'n'Bites next to her, because "Pouting is tiring work," and leave her to sulk. She'll get over it.

When I walk up to the Kirks' porch the door is open and there's a sticky note attached to the screen: *Just come in, Harper.* I like how she expects me now.

I step inside and follow the sound of the Stones' "Everybody Getting High." From the foyer I see Willa slide across the kitchen tiles on socked feet, singing along loudly. She's in her standard weekend outfit: torn black jeans, oversized plaid shirt (probably either stolen or a hand-me-down) and holey socks. I can't imagine how she could look any better.

Willa turns the music down when she sees me and says good morning.

"Good morning to you too."

She turns away and walks into the living room, so naturally I follow. Willa has three laundry baskets on the couch and chairs and has organized the wash into several different piles on the floor and coffee table. The whole room smells of warm laundry and I just want to get comfy and breathe it in. I have a thing about the scent of fresh laundry. I used to crawl into the dryer when I was a kid. Mom has pictures of me napping in the dryer barrel on a pile of warm towels.

Willa takes a stack of folded dishtowels to the kitchen. I contemplate burying my face in a nearby pile of t-shirts, but she might catch me and freak.

"Want to go for a walk?" Willa calls from the other room. "It's a nice day and I need air."

"Okay."

"We won't go far," she promises as she comes back to the living room. She grabs Frank's piles of shirts, socks, and jeans and loads them all into one of the baskets.

"If you need air we'll go as far as you want."

"Can you handle it?"

I give her a look and take the basket from her. "I'll be fine."

⌐

It's a nice day for April. The sun makes more of an impression through the cloud cover than usual, and there's a slight breeze. Willa and I stroll down her block slowly.

She looks over at me and smiles. "Nice hat."

"Thanks." It's blue today. Elise took one look at me when I came downstairs this morning, sighed ruefully, and said, 'At least it matches your eyes.'

"You look healthier today."

"Yeah?" That's a real compliment, coming from her and considering that I look the way I do.

"Am I still not allowed to ask about your cancer?"

"You just said I look healthy; can't we leave it at that?"

"Sure."

We walk in silence for a few minutes. Willa swings her arms slowly by her sides. I've got my hands in my pockets, as usual. I got into the habit as a way to hide the scars. I do it around Willa as a matter of routine, even though she said she likes my hands. Whether or not that's true is an open question.

"I have a similar but related question," Willa says after awhile.

"What?" I'm curious to know what it is, even though I may choose not to answer.

"How'd it feel to find out you had cancer?"

I snort. "Like a bomb went off in the middle of my life. It's enough to make your skin crawl, knowing there's something living inside you that can kill you—that *is* killing you."

"But it didn't."

"I got lucky—a lot."

"Hot nurses?"

It takes me a second to get it, and then I tell her to bugger off even as I chuckle. "Nice nurses, but not many hot ones. I had some cool roommates, though."

"Anyone interesting?"

"My first roommate was a year older than me—Evan—and he'd been sick a few times. Lost his eyes to cancer as a kid, and shit. He had this massive stack of Braille books on the side table and he used to read them out loud, except when I knew him he had a brain tumor and he'd have these weird spells where he'd forget stuff and read the same passage over and over again."

"Did that bug you?"

"No, actually. He was just this guy who had it so much worse than me, but he was still knew who he was and enjoyed his hobbies in spite of all the shit. I liked to think that I got him in a way that the nurses and everyone else didn't, 'cause I was sick too."

"Did he know he was repeating passages?"

I shrug. "I never told him. I don't think any of the nurses did, either. He didn't have visitors very often, to tell him he was losing his mind."

Willa stops and looks at me searchingly. "He's dead now, isn't he?"

"Yeah. He had a grand mal and went into a coma. His family pulled the plug after a few days."

"Was it scary to watch that, being so ill yourself?"

"I only saw him seize; they took him to the ICU after that. I found his obit later, and nobody dies *that* fast in a coma unless someone yanks the power on their ventilator."

"He did have a brain tumor. That could have killed him. They wouldn't have let the family withdraw his vent if he wasn't already brain dead."

"Doesn't matter; I prefer to think of his barely-there family as a bunch of assholes that didn't want him hanging around on life support."

"Would you want to hang around on life support?"

"I wouldn't want to die alone."

"You don't know that he did."

"His obit said that he 'passed away peacefully in the care of hospital staff.' I bet his family just phoned in the order to stop wasting the insurance coverage and called the funeral home while he was still plugged in."

"Did it make you feel lucky?" she asks. "That you have such a caring family, I mean."

"Yeah. It did."

"Did you go to his funeral?"

"I couldn't, but Mom did. They cremated him."

"My sister was, too. I read up on it after—it's a sick process. They put the bodies in these cardboard boxes and slide them into giant ovens so their sternum is centered, and then they burn the shit out of the body and roll what's left around in a mixer with ball bearings to reduce it to dust."

Uh, gross. And I need to know that why?

"Only you would do research instead of grieving."

She chuckles. "Hey now, I had a bomb go off in the middle of my life, too. Mine just had a timer on the detonator."

"It's not the same. Having your own body turn against you and having a loved one die are different kinds of catastrophes."

"Did I tell you what Tessa had? It started with lymphoma, but by the time she died it was all through her abdomen. Her stomach was so swollen that she looked pregnant."

"Jesus, Kirk."

"There's nothing graceful about dying. A catastrophe is a catastrophe, no matter what your role is in it."

I nod in agreement because I don't have any argument left, and we'll never see eye-to-eye on this issue anyway. I can't live her experience any more than she can live mine.

"We talk about the weirdest shit."

Willa giggles. "Imagine if we were set up on a blind date or something. It would be the most depressing first impression."

"But would you call back?"

"This is hypothetical."

"Spare my ego, Kirk."

"Oh, not the fragile ego," she says with a roll of her eyes.

"Seriously." I nudge her with my elbow and smile to show I'm teasing. "Would you?"

Willa sighs thoughtfully. "But this *is* hypothetical, right?"

"You're stalling."

She elbows me. "It depends. Are we both at the same school in this scenario?"

"Sure."

"Is it a dinner date?"

"If you like."

"Would you try for a kiss at the end of the night?"

I try and fail to read the desired answer on her face. "No?"

Willa wrinkles her nose and shrugs. "I'd probably file you under 'friend.' That scenario is over-traditional and has the potential to get messy. If we're at the same school and it doesn't work out, we'd still have to see each other every day."

"And what about the real-life scenario?"

"We're speaking hypothetically."

"Real life is infinitely messier. And what's wrong with a dinner date?"

"It's so conventional. It's like something out of a bad sitcom."

"Have you ever been on a dinner date?"

Willa mumbles noncommittally. That's a no.

"You should go on one before you judge. I'll take you out sometime."

"No."

"In the interest of research."

"Not interested."

"In dinner, or dinner with me?"

"Both."

"Why?" I'm a sucker for punishment. I have this compulsive need to hear her list in great detail each and every specific reason for rejecting me.

"Besides the fact that we'd have to go to a vegan restaurant for you to be able to order anything?"

"Very funny."

"I like cooking."

"You deserve a night off once in awhile."

"Not to eat tofu with my asshole project partner on a pretend date—a date which will, if the hypothetical proves an accurate model for reality, end with no action to make it worthwhile."

"See, I would kiss you on this never-gonna-happen date, but that vitriol you keep in your mouth would probably burn my face off."

"Chicken."

"What?"

Willa begins to buk at me. For a few seconds I just stare at this girl doing a bird impression—flapping wings and all—and a thought sneaks into my head like a ninja with Tourette's: *Grab her tit. She'll never expect it.*

Willa's not wearing a bra under that shirt.

"Harper!" She slaps my hand away and glares at me.

"Uh, sorry."

"Dude."

"You said you wanted action."

"You are such a shit."

"Really, I'm sorry. It was a stupid impulse."

"Fine, apology accepted," she says stiffly. I still suspect she'll kick me when I'm not looking.

"I'll treat you better when I take you out for dinner."

"We're not going out for dinner."

"We will even if I have to kidnap you." I smile in the hope that she'll relax a little and joke with me. I'm not joking about dinner, though—I'm taking her out.

"This isn't a date."

"So I can't grab your tit again?"

She takes a swing at me and I dodge her little fist, laughing.

"Hey, don't hit the cancer patient."

Willa lowers her fist. "You did *not* just play that card."

"You weren't really gonna hit me." I wink at Willa and her eyes narrow.

"For all you know." Willa mutters something that doesn't sound kind and resumes her stroll with a wary eye trained in my direction.

"I won't grab you again, I promise."

She snorts incredulously and looks the other way. She's going to hold this over me like she did when I messed with her phone.

"Hey." I put a hand on her shoulder to turn her toward me. "Honestly, I'm sor—"

Willa lunges at me unexpectedly. She doesn't weigh much, but she catches me off guard and I step backwards. One of her arms winds around my waist, turning me away as I struggle for balance. And the other hand? It tickles me. *Everywhere.* I spazz and flail like a moron, trying to throw her off or grab hold of her hands.

She's the first to fall on the slick grass of her neighbor's lawn, and she pulls me down with her. I land on top and she makes the quietest little 'oof!' sound, like a kitten being squished.

"Are you okay?"

"Peachy." She lets go of me and I roll off her. "You all right?"

"You *tickled* me."

"Is there a rule against tickling cancer patients?" She laughs. It's a sound I've never heard from her before—it's childish and pleasure-filled, with no sarcasm or wryness.

I roll over and kneel above her legs, pinning her down on the damp lawn while I return the favor. She makes this strangled 'gah!' sound and thrashes like a fish out of water.

God, she's soft.

This is the closest you're ever going to get to really touching her.

I give her a break when she turns red in the face. She's got grass on her hair and she's panting from exertion and her loose shirt is twisted around her body. She looks at me with a smile that says, 'You win.'

"You're beautiful."

Oh snap.

If she suddenly went temporarily deaf just now, there must be a God.

Dude, think before you talk!

Willa pauses for the space of two breaths. "So are you."

I awkwardly climb off her and stand up. I extend a hand to help her to her feet, but Willa ignores it. Her back is wet from the grass and stray blades stick to her hair and clothes. She brushes them off forcefully and turns back toward the house at a brisk pace.

You screwed up, Harper.

I start after her. "Hey." I reach out to take her arm and she throws my hand off.

"Don't." She holds a finger up in warning. I wouldn't put it past her to rap me between the eyes with it. I hold my tongue, and after a few seconds she lowers her finger and marches away.

I follow at a slower pace, and by the time I get back to the Kirk house Willa is parked in front of the TV, channel surfing.

"Do you want to talk?"

"Do I look like I'm in a talking mood?"

"Point taken."

I'm about to sit down in the easy chair across from the couch when Willa tells me to look in the freezer.

"What?"

"Look in the freezer."

I get up and go open the freezer. The cloud of condensation takes a second to dissipate, and *holy shit yogurt pops!*

"Did you just hop?"

"No."

"I distinctly saw a hop—two of them, actually."

"No you didn't." I grab a yogurt pop out of the fridge and unwrap it. Excited or not, I most certainly did *not* hop.

Willa smirks.

"I didn't, damn it."

She lets me sit next to her on the couch, and even though she isn't in a talking mood, she rests her head on my shoulder while we watch cartoons. Her only remark is to tease me for the four yogurt pops I eat in the space of fifteen minutes.

"Do I need to explain how awesome these things are?"

"No. I'm just glad you're eating."

"Are you still going to care when my stomach gets better?"

Willa sighs. Her face changes as she mulls that one over. "Yeah," she says. "I think I will."

⁂

It's approaching four o'clock when my phone rings. I check the caller ID while Willa flips through her recipe binder, considering what to make for dinner. It's Ava.

"Hello?"

"Bitch, pack your shit. We'll pick you up around six."

"What?"

"I cleared it with your Mom. You're coming to Ottawa tonight."

I look over at Willa, brow furrowed and flipping pages with a shrewd eye. I didn't actually say I was staying for dinner. Is it implied at this point? Should I tell her that I have plans with others? Should I invite her along?

She invited you out when no one else would.

But Ava did consider cracking her skull last week…

"Um…"

"Dude, you're not backing down from this. We're already on our way to your podunk town."

"We?"

"Emily and me."

Do I want to spend two hours in a car with Emily? I could definitely do it with just Ava…but I want to see the others tonight, too.

"Alright, I'll come."

"Try not to sound so enthusiastic."

"Shut up."

"Slut."

"Cocktease." I hang up and Willa gives me a sideways look for the way that call ended. "That was, uh…"

"Let me guess—Eric."

That makes me snort. "No, um, I've got company coming to the house to-night."

"Cool." She sounds like she doesn't really care.

"I have to take off soon to meet them."

"Sure."

"And I probably won't get a chance to call you tonight."

"Okay."

"I don't know if I'll be able to see you tomorrow, either."

"That's fine."

Is it so hard to *pretend* that she's going to miss me?

"Sleep well, okay Kirk?" She accepts a one-armed hug and agrees that she will. Willa offers no similar wish in return.

As I leave the house I call back down the hall to her, "I'll make that dinner reservation."

Willa answers with a skeptical "Ha!"

I get the sense that she hasn't been treated well before; at least not romantically. That can be remedied.

By you?

Shut up.

✢

When I get home I find Elise in my bedroom, arranging clothes across my bed and folding them into an overnight bag.

"What are you doing?"

"Oh, you'd just pack anything," she says. "It's nice when things match some-times, you know. I'm putting together an outfit for—" She looks up and sees how dangerously close she is to having her neck wrung. "Er…do you want to bring your blue shirt or the grey one?"

I point to the door and she drops my clothes with a huff.

"You're *welcome*," she says moodily.

"Thank you. But get the hell out." I shut the door and she blows a raspberry at me from the hall.

I fold and place the change of clothes she gave me in my overnight bag, along with an extra shirt and a pair of pajamas. Then the real packing starts. I fill a smaller bag with medication bottles, clean syringes, swabs, tape, gauze, and hypoallergenic toiletries. The gear it takes to keep me alive weighs about as much as my normal luggage. I throw the bag of toiletries in with my clothes and zip it up.

When I go downstairs I find Eric in the kitchen with a packed bag of his own. He's cramming snacks for the road into the last remaining spaces.

"Are you going somewhere?"

"Ava said she'd give me a ride to Ottawa." Of course, he wants to see Celeste. I have no idea why he would want to do anything other than punch her in the face, ever, but everyone has their quirks.

It's five-thirty by the time Ava and Emily get here. They're driving Emily's mom's minivan, which is a lot comfier and smells better than Ava's Gremlin. Not that I don't appreciate the suspicious stains all over Ava's car, or anything.

Eric and I throw our bags in the trunk and pile into the backseat. Ava drove here, so Emily is driving back while Ava plays DJ with the sound system.

"So we're dropping you off at Celeste's house?" Emily confirms with Eric as we head toward the 416.

"Much appreciated."

Ava makes a disgusted noise in her throat as she flips through a CD wallet. "I don't understand that bitch," she says. Ava would think nothing of referring to someone as a bitch in casual conversation with the person's best friend.

"What are you talking about?" Eric demands. He knows to take Ava with a grain of salt (lime and tequila optional), but he's loyal enough not to let a remark about Celeste slide.

"All the attention she gets. I guess she's hot and all, but girls that prissy never know what to do with a guy." Ava turns around in the front seat and flicks her tongue past her lips suggestively, showing off her new stud. The piercing sits forward on her tongue—she didn't get that with Phil in mind.

Eric laughs at Ava. "Is somebody bitter? You know she'd turn you down if you ever asked."

"I wouldn't ask." Ava turns around in the front seat and chooses a CD. She slides Rammstein into the CD player and Emily makes a little sound of displeasure. She's more of an R&B girl; any kind of metal doesn't do it for her.

"Oh come on, what did the Germans ever do to you?"

Ava smiles so sweetly in the face of Emily's glare.

Morgan, Kyle and Caitlin are already at Ava's house when we get there. When we come in the front door Ava's brother bellows from across the house, "Where the fuck did you put the Pop-Tarts?"

Ava screams back: "Up your ass, you stunned twat!" which is pretty much the normal way these two hold a civilized conversation. Kyle takes the box of Pop-Tarts off the coffee table and hides it under one of the throw pillows in the couch.

Caitlin gets up to give me a hug. She's dressed to go out: short skirt, low cut top, too much makeup, and ridiculously high heels. "Geez, you're thin," she says as she lets go the hug.

"It's the chemo diet."

She laughs and says she has to tell her fat bitch boss about that one. Caitlin isn't exactly the sensitive type. She oversubscribes to the idea that whatever doesn't kill us makes us stronger.

Ava disappears into her bedroom with Emily, and I take a seat on the chair across from the others. They're all dressed for a night out. I'm not.

"Plans for tonight?"

"Ava got us tickets to a gig," Kyle says. It's been forever since I've felt up to going out on a weekend, never mind the way we six used to. I'm not exactly prepared for it, but I want to do it anyway. I miss the sense of normalcy I get from hanging out with these people.

Ava's brother comes in, eating out of the box of Cap'n Crunch, and flops down on the couch next to Caitlin. He doesn't say a word to anyone, but turns on the TV and changes the channel to Spike.

Then he notices me. "Who are you?"

"Jem Harper. We've met." Hundreds of times.

Both his eyebrows go up. "Oh. Shit. Didn't recognize you, dude."

Ava (sort of) spares me from the awkward moment by returning to the living room in an obscenely revealing blue dress. "Is this merely slutty or full-on whorish?" she asks. Her brother doesn't even look up from the TV. If Elise tried that shit, Eric and I wouldn't let her out the door.

"You know what would go well with that?" Kyle says. "A pearl necklace."

Ava takes her shoe off and whips it at him.

"Easy, you'll scare away your customers."

Everyone but Ava laughs—including her brother. She gives Kyle the finger and retrieves her shoe from the living room floor.

"To hell with you all, I'm wearing it."

As she slips her spike heel back on, she turns to me and asks if that's what I'm wearing tonight. I have on a pair of jeans and a long-sleeved cotton tee. It's a 'sit at home and do nothing' outfit, not a 'go out and get wasted' ensemble.

"Uh, yeah."

"I'm lending him one of your shirts," Ava says to her brother, who grunts at her through a mouthful of Cap'n Crunch. The shirt Ava finds in his room is too big, but it'll work for one night.

"Where are we going, anyway?" The usual haunts are dive concert halls. Live music is essential to a good night out for us.

"The Plains. Biocide is playing."

I have a feeling that Ava has a *special* relationship with the band's drummer, but I don't want to ask.

‹›

We're all underage in Ontario, but four of us are legal in Quebec, so we'll be going to Hull tonight. Caitlin and Morgan will have to rely on fake IDs. As is traditional, we pre-drink at Ava's house because it would piss her dad off if he ever found out.

Kyle sets up six shot glasses along the coffee table and uncaps a bottle of tequila.

"Just five," I tell him as he's about to pour.

"Are you the driver tonight? You can have a small one, man."

"I can't. It screws with the meds."

"Not even a little bit?"

"Nope."

Kyle shakes his head. "You don't even sound disappointed. Small town life—makes people boring and complacent."

Emily punches him in the shoulder. "Shut the hell up, Kyle. He has *cancer*."

"No I don't."

There's an awkward pause before Ava grabs the bottle from Kyle and starts pouring out shots. "None of this cancer bullshit," she says. "We're all gonna live forever. Sláinte!"

They all toss their shots back. Emily is trying to look anywhere but at me, and I'm doing the same with Ava. I thought she was just being Ava last time I saw her, but this clinches it: she can't let go of the old me; the one that Emily couldn't find. She wants to continue to live the uncomplicated existence of a normal teenager, and for me to be a part of that again. I can't. Life doesn't work backwards.

They pre-drink awhile longer. As the only sober one, I end up being the driver as we all pile into the minivan. We'll have to park at least three blocks from The Plains because this setup screams *high schoolers*.

The usual Saturday crowd is out and in fine form. Ava knows the bouncer from her last gig here, and manages to get us inside without too much of a wait. It's nice to know people in low places, because I'm not exactly keen on standing out in the frigid night air for long. I don't tolerate extreme temperatures very well.

Inside, The Plains is one of those places that has clearly seen better days. That's what we like about it. The floorboards are scratched and rotting, the graffiti on the walls and fixtures is full of outdated cultural references, the paint is peeling, the furniture is broken, and the lights are *supposed* to flicker like that. The only part of the place that doesn't predate the birth of most patrons is the owner's pride and joy: a state-of-the-art sound system—what makes The Plains such a hidden gem.

Kyle heads to the bar while the rest of us hunt for a booth near the back. He comes back with a tray of drinks.

"I just got you a ginger ale," he says, passing the glass to me. Ginger ale is probably the gentlest option on the menu, but I still drink it cautiously. I haven't had a carbonated drink in a long time. Refined sugars taste bitter to me now.

Ava and I always come to these types of places for the same reason: to get caught up in the sound until nothing else can possibly exist. We all have our pleasures—Caitlin comes to dance, Kyle likes to get wasted, and Emily is a flirt. Morgan always manages to meet the most interesting people on random nights out. She attracts oddballs—that's how the six of us became friends, in her orbit.

"We're dancing. Now," Ava says when she's finished her drink. She grabs my hand and tows me away from the booth. We pass by Emily, who is talking sweetly to a guy wearing sunglasses indoors, and Ava says, "You have a boy-friend, you whore." She scurries away before Emily can give her hell for ruining her conquest.

As I follow Ava to the centre of the crowded dance floor, I can't help think-ing this is a bad idea. I don't have the energy for stuff like this. I'm going to be black and blue by midnight. But… I miss this. I miss going out and not giving a shit and getting buzzed on cheap drinks and raw music. I miss Ava being a cocktease (she doesn't screw friends) and sneaking home at three o'clock in the morning and trying to convince Mom that I'm sober.

It's no secret that Ava wants to pick up tonight. She'll be with me until the second set ends, and then she'll go corner the drummer and they'll go fool around in the bathroom. Typical Saturday night, really. I savor the time we have together, just the two of us; we're both convinced that only true musicians re-ally get the feeling of being completely swept up in the crowd and the music. It moves us, and pretty soon I don't care about the sweet pounding in my ears or the elbows in my sides or the smell of spilt beer and sweat. I'm so busy ignoring all the shit that has no place here tonight that I don't immediately understand the look of fear that Ava gives me when the second set finishes.

"Dude." She grabs my arm with concern. I look down and realize I'm shak-ing. She pulls me to the side of the building, away from the press of bodies, and without the heat of the other patrons around me I suddenly feel cold.

"You look ready to pass out." She puts a hand to my clammy forehead and offers to get me a bottle of water.

"No, no. I just need air."

Ava purses her lips and nods. She doesn't offer to come with me like Emily would, because she doesn't like to cozy up to the idea that I'm really ill.

I make my way out the side door, into the alley. I lean against the opposite wall and try to get a decent breath. Everything hurts and my ears are ringing. My entire body feels like lead. Without the distractions of the club, all I can feel is the pain and the mingled scents of spilt booze, sweat, and nearby trashcans. The shirt Ava loaned me is soaked through with perspiration and I'm starting to shiver. There's a crowd out front, so I head in the opposite direction. It doesn't even occur to me where I'm going until I'm halfway there, but I end up back at the minivan.

There are worse places to crash. I get in and angle the driver's seat back as far as it will go, trying to relax my sore body. I am going to have so many bruises tomorrow. Elise is going to scream me stupid.

I can't decide if tonight was worth it or not. Maybe if I had been well enough to actually do all the things I used to love, I would enjoy a night out. This just feels like I'm imitating the life of someone I don't even know anymore.

The clock on the dashboard says it's one o'clock. It'll be at least another hour before the others decide to pack it in. I don't know if I'm up for anything else. I might just stay in the car and sleep a little, waiting for them.

That is such a lonely thought.

I call Willa, only half expecting her to answer her phone at this hour. It takes four rings, and when she does pick up she whines sleepily, "Whaaaat?"

"The Stones broke up."

"You're so full of shit," she slurs. Even half asleep, she knows how these conversations usually go. The familiarity of her response makes me smile.

"What are you doing?"

"Sleeping, dickhead. Don't tell me this is a social call."

"I just wanted to see how your night went."

"I cooked. I cleaned up. I did homework. I went to bed. 'Kay?"

"Aren't you going to ask about my night?"

"You don't sound happy, so you're probably calling to complain." The blankets rustle as she resituates herself in bed.

I chuckle dryly at her assumption. "It was a good night out."

"You went out?"

"I'm in Hull."

"How is it?"

I pause to think about that. The streetlamp throws an orange glow across the raindrops on the windshield. The Ottawa lights across the river make an impression on the cloudy sky. This city used to seem so alive. Now it just seems…cold. Like someone I used to know a long time ago, and kept fondly in memory, but now it seems ugly and standoffish. Or maybe that's me.

"I hate it."

Willa hums, amused. "That's why in books you can't go home again."

"I should have brought you with me."

"Don't be such a stick-in-the-mud. Let your friends show you a good time."

"Yeah, I know. But you make things…nicer." She would have come with me to get some air, at least. Ava's probably got her tongue down that drummer's throat by now.

"Is Emily being mean to you again?"

"She's okay." Emily can't help the way she is around me. I don't like it, but I forgive her for it.

"Stick it out. You'll be back tomorrow."

"I know." I let out a sigh and try not to think about how many hours exist between now and then. "Thanks for talking to me."

"I'll be waiting for you when you get back."

"Thanks." That just turned my whole night around.

"Goodnight."

"Sleep well."

I wait for her to hang up first, but then she says, "Oh, Jem?"

"Yeah?"

"If you ever call me at one o'clock in the morning again for anything *less* than the Stones breaking up, you're getting kicked in the balls. Hard."

I laugh and she hangs up. I feel better, but I don't want to go back to The Plains. I want to sit here and be alone with my thoughts. I turn on the radio and doze against the headrest. A knock on the window interrupts me.

Kyle opens the car door and looks in on me with concern. He sways a little bit and can't focus his eyes. "You alright man?" His words run together and his breath reeks of rum.

"Yeah. Just taking a break. I'll meet you back in there."

Kyle shuts the car door, but he doesn't go back to The Plains. He walks around the passenger side and gets in next to me. "I'll wait with you."

"You don't have to." I'm not exactly eager for his company when he's been drinking. This isn't even Kyle the Shitfaced Asshole yet. This is merely Kyle the Drunken Moron. The difference is about two drinks and one minor injury.

Kyle looks over at me with a sad smile. "You've been alone too long, man," he says. "I still talk to your sister, you know. She said…nah, never mind." He turns to look out the windshield with a burdened expression.

"When were you talking to Elise?" Kyle is a great guy, but he's not the sort of person I want lurking around my little sister. His reputation of bullshit and whimsy precedes him.

He shrugs. "On Facebook. I would have come out to see you more—during, I mean—but this whole not having a car thing limits my range." He takes a cigarette out of his pocket and sets it between his lips. I grab it from him and throw it out of the car before he can locate his lighter.

"Hey," he whines.

"Cancer patient," I tell him slowly and loudly. "Are you that dense?"

"It's not like it was lung cancer," he complains. Kyle sets his lighter on the dash and pats his pockets for another smoke. I take his lighter and whip it over my shoulder into the back seat.

"Good luck finding it."

"That wasn't even my lighter!"

"Your problem, not mine."

Kyle turns around in his seat and seethes like a bratty child. We don't say anything else for a while. He takes out a stick of gum and chews loudly, and I just let my thoughts drift to the sound on the radio.

"A few people recognized you in there, you know."

"What?"

"Some people saw you with Ava and asked if it was you."

"Who asked?"

Kyle shrugs. He isn't going to give me an honest answer. "Kids from around school. Nobody important."

It doesn't even matter because I don't go to school here anymore, but it bothers me that on Monday morning people are going to be murmuring in the hallways about what a shell Jem Harper has become. It's enough to make me glad that I moved away before getting sick. Being invisible in Smiths Falls is better than falling from my place on the social ladder in Ottawa.

I lean back and close my eyes. Kyle offers to drive me back to Ava's house and then come back for the others.

"You've been drinking."

Kyle sighs and gets out of the car, stumbling a little. I assume he's going back inside, but then there's a click and a draft as the back hatch of the van opens to the night.

"Come here, man."

I go around to the back of the van and find Kyle folding the last row of seats down. There is a sleeping bag rolled up in the back with a pillow tucked underneath.

"We planned for such a contingency."

I stay out of Kyle's way while he sets up a cot in the van. He pulls a water bottle from the center console between the front seats and says there's Jell-O in there too if I need it. I don't know what to say to him.

"Whose idea was this?"

"Emily's. You know how she worries." Kyle mimics Emily's high-pitched 'worry voice' and gestures to the cot. "Get in, I'll close the tailgate."

The bump of a pothole wakes me up. I open my eyes to find Ava in the adjacent seat, watching me. Caitlin is nowhere to be found. Kyle is riding shotgun, and Emily is driving. Morgan I find behind me, sandwiched between my back and the side of the car. Her sturdy arm is wrapped around my front, compensating for the instability of the seatbelt that has been stretched across our hips.

"You're bruising," Ava says. She pushes back my sleeve to reveal a purpling blotch on my arm.

"It happens."

"Why didn't you say something, you idiot?"

"I was having a good time."

"Don't ruin it, Ava," Kyle says quietly.

I don't fit in here anymore. They don't know how to deal with my problems. They shouldn't have to.

Morgan gives me a little squeeze. I ask her whom she met tonight, and she quietly tells me about the couple passing through on a road trip from Toronto to Hull for a wedding. She'll probably keep in touch with them, too; that's just

Morgan.
But she didn't keep in touch with you.

Sunday

I wake up in Ava's bed. Everything hurts. As I sit up a casual study of my arms and shoulders reveals a series of bruises that will take a week or more to fade.

"Hey bitch," Ava says from the doorway. She's wearing nothing but an over-sized t-shirt and holding a steaming mug of coffee. She looks surprisingly rested after a night on the couch. Ah, to be young and healthy.

"Hey slut," I reply tiredly, and swing my legs out of bed.

Ava studies my bruises and says she's going to have a hard time busting me out of Smiths Falls again.

"Your mom isn't going to let you play rough with us again any time soon." That might be a wise decision on Mom's part. I bet she was banking on me having better judgment than to go out on a Saturday night and party like any other eighteen-year-old boy.

"Will you drive me home after breakfast?" It seems rude to leave so early, but I want to get home. I need to rest up for school on Monday, and Willa said she would be waiting for me.

"Sure," Ava says. "We can eat on the road, if you like."

I expect her to leave, to let me get dressed and to hunt down something more substantial than coffee for herself, but she steps into the room and closes the door instead.

"What are you doing?"

Ava places a hand on my forehead and runs it back, over my scalp and down the slope of my neck. She could at least ask before making a freak of me, like Emily did.

"How's that girl of yours?" she asks.

"She's not mine."

"You said you hadn't dated since moving away."

"No."

"Must be lonely." Ava runs a hand along my jaw, feeling the place where the bone juts out for lack of fat. I'm considering all the snarky ways to answer her dumb question when she leans down and kisses me.

Ava never does this with friends.

She sets her coffee cup aside without breaking the kiss and pushes me back onto the bed. The weight of her stings the bruises a little as she crouches over me, touching my neck and shoulders, but it's difficult to care. It's been awhile since I did this with anyone—since anyone wanted to do this with me. And even though we both have morning breath and definitely need to shower, I enjoy her. It's even a little flattering that she's willing to break her I-don't-screw-friends rule for me.

A piece of blue hair falls in our way and I brush it back. There was a time when I often entertained fantasies of doing this with her. I liked the idea of Ava before I really knew her. Even though she doesn't feel quite right in my hands, she's warm and horny beggars can't be choosy.

Ava shifts so that more of her weight rests against me and I wince before I can stop myself. She lifts herself up on her arms.

"Too much?" she asks.

I grab Ava by the back of her head and pull her down. She is *not* going to treat me like I'm made of glass, damn it. But she's wary now, and holds herself slightly above me on her elbows and bent knees. Our fronts touch, but I bear none of her weight.

Ava offers to let me be on top and I don't know how to explain that I'm too sore and too weak to hold myself above her for very long.

"I like you on top," I say. That's good enough for Ava.

I reach under her nightshirt, running my hands up her sides until I get to her chest. Her shirt rides up along my forearms, showing off her skin. Her tits seem too large all of a sudden—too much for one handful, and I feel like an incompetent little boy trying to properly grope her. I prefer smaller chests, like W—

"Been awhile for you, hasn't it?" she says against my lips. She's got her wicked smirk on, mocking me.

"Oh shut up."

Ava's hand suddenly leaves the mattress and slips between my thighs. Shit. I expected a little more in the way of foreplay. Her hand runs up my thigh, trying to tease me, until her fingers cross paths with my dick.

And she's disappointed.

The first time a girl has touched me there in months, and I don't meet her expectations. Ava cups my balls and limp dick in her hand and says, "If you're not into it, we can stop. I won't be offended."

I pull her back for another kiss. "Really, I want to." Her hand starts stroking me through my pajama pants while her other hand tries to negotiate the worn tie at my waist. I kiss her neck and bite her ears and pull her hair a little—all things she used to bitch about her boyfriend never doing—but she won't be distracted from my failure to respond to her hand. No matter how she touches me, it stubbornly remains soft.

"Are you sure—?"

"*Yes*." Just be patient with me, damn it.

"Is this not doing it for you?"

"You're doing fine."

I go to kiss her again and she rolls her eyes before complying. "What are you, gay?" she mutters against my lips.

I put my hands on her shoulders and shove her back. Ava falls on her ass, stunned, and I sit up and pull away from her.

"I'm *sick*."

I have never seen Ava look so dumbfounded. She has always been the badass with a smart remark handy and unwavering composure, but now she just sits there and gapes at me.

Ava rights her twisted nightshirt and gets off the bed. She apologizes quietly and shrugs. "You know saying the right thing isn't my forté."

I let her off the hook. I don't want to make this more awkward than it already is. "Don't worry about it."

Ava leaves to eat and I get into the shower. I have to do it with the light on because I don't know Ava's bathroom well enough to navigate in the dark. I hate looking at myself. After a few minutes I give up on really showering and just stand there, studying my body. Thank God Ava didn't get far enough to see the scars, or the worst of the bruises, or my conspicuous lack of body hair, or the bones sticking out, or the central line in my chest. The whole thing could have gone so much worse.

The fact that I couldn't satisfy her is going to haunt me. She was willing to overlook the low body weight and the baldness, but my limp dick offended her. I'm useless. I'm not fun to be around anymore, even as her friend, and I couldn't rise to the occasion for a goddamned pity fuck. I wouldn't be surprised if she doesn't get in touch with me for a long, long time.

I feel like shit by the time I'm showered and dressed. Ava, on the other hand, has decided to act as if nothing happened—sort of the way she acts about my disease in general. She offers me a four-pack of Jell-O cups to eat on the road, and drives me home with a smile on her face. Even before we pick up Eric and have to act cool for the benefit of his ignorance, she talks about mundane crap as though nothing happened this morning.

"You weren't too hard on my little brother, were you?" Eric asks teasingly when we stop to pick him up from Celeste's house.

"Nah, I was good to him," she says. Too bad I couldn't return the favor.

When we pull into the driveway I see Elise on the porch swing with Willa, chatting happily. They look up and wave at us. Eric gets out of the car, and no sooner has he shut the door behind him than Ava teases me: "You're fucked."

Shit, was I grinning?

"Shut up."

She laughs at me.

I toss a, "Thanks, slut," over my shoulder as I grab my bag, and she replies, "You're welcome, whore."

As I ascend the porch steps I can hear Elise whispering Ava's general story to Willa—the electric violin; the hook ups; that time in Montreal…

"Hey." I drop my bag next to the porch swing and sit down beside Elise. She promptly scoots over onto my lap. "Did you miss me?"

"Pfft. No." She wraps my arms around her waist and fiddles with the strap on my watch. She totally missed me.

I turn to Willa "What about you?"

"I know how to keep myself occupied." Her tone is strange. Is she being coy? I can't tell if she missed me or not.

You're a fool to hope, Harper.

    Of course she'd never just tell you she did and put you out of your misery.

"I worry about you," Elise says casually, and reaches back to pat my cheek. "Did you sleep okay?"

"Like the dead."

She cranes her neck to look at me over her shoulder. "Do you want a milk-shake?"

"Yes, please."

Elise gets up and skips away into the house, singing "Do Your Ears Hang Low?" as she goes.

Willa stifles a giggle.

"Go ahead and laugh. She thrives on any sort of attention."

"Just like you."

"Nuh-uh."

Willa stands up and grabs the handle of my bag. "Come on." She nods to the front door. "You can brag to me about your night in Hull."

I go to the laundry room to deposit the weekend's clothes in the washing ma-chine, and Willa goes to the kitchen. I can hear her whispering with Elise from here.

"What are you talking about?" I call down the hall.

"Milkshakes!" Elise yells back.

That is so not fair. I've been trying to weasel that recipe from Elise for months. What kind of justice is this, that Willa can just stroll in and sweet-talk the secret out of her?

I enter the kitchen to find Elise putting the lid on the blender and Willa put-ting the milk away. They're like cockroaches in the light, hiding their method from me. Elise fires up the blender and I fetch glasses down from the cupboard.

Willa and I take seats at the island while Elise winds the blend speed back and forth, getting the froth just right on the milkshakes. She knows how to get them perfectly smooth every time.

I have to work to speak over the sound of the blender, but I tell Willa about The Plains and the live music. Some of my favorite CDs were purchased out of the back of the bands' vans directly after shows there, because The Plains supports a lot of unsigned artists. The idea of new music piques Willa's interest.

"Come up, I'll show you." I nod to the stairs.

"Wait, milkshakes," Elise calls after us. She pours three tall glasses of raspberry goodness and passes two across the island. "I'll clean up and meet you upstairs."

Did I say I wanted to host a little powwow in my room? I thought I invited Willa upstairs. I want her to myself. Elise notes the look on my face and realizes she isn't exactly welcome.

"Well fine," she snaps, and snatches the glass out of my hand. She upends the milkshake over the sink. "Get me to make you a milkshake and then expect me to bugger off, huh?"

"You *offered* to make milkshakes." I point to the melting mess in the sink. I was looking forward to that, damn it.

"No, I get it." She dumps her milkshake out too. Either her appetite is gone or she doesn't want me to steal it to replace the one she threw out. "You're too good to hang out with me again. I'm your last freaking resort and you can do better now, so to hell with me, right?" She sticks her tongue out at me and stomps away toward the stairs.

"Lise." I reach out to grab her arm and she pushes my hand away.

"Go away," she snarls. "If you want another milkshake you can forget it." She runs up the stairs and slams her bedroom door. That fails to satisfy, so she slams it again for good measure.

"Um." I look over at Willa, who doesn't seem entirely surprised by Elise's tantrum.

"She's been a little high-strung this morning," Willa says. "Worried about you." Well, now I feel like an ass.

"I'll be right back."

She nods. "I'll be down here."

↔

At first glance, Elise's bedroom is empty. But I know my dork of a little sister. I go over to her 'cupboard under the stairs' (the closet) and open her hidey-hole.

"Your glasses are going to fog up." They always do when she wears them and cries at the same time. But she does it anyway, because the glasses comfort her. She squeezes Hedwig closer to her chest and tells me to go away.

"Scoot over."

I pull the string on the bare bulb that lights her closet and step in beside her. It's a tight squeeze, sitting next to her on the floor. We fit much better into cubbies like this when we were kids.

"I'm sorry."

"You're like a crappy foul-weather friend," she whines. She has a point. I came to rely on her company when I was sick. And now that I'm getting better… well, I suppose things will go back to the way they were before I was ill, when our lives were more separate. We don't have a lot in common, really.

Elise climbs onto my lap. "That was, like, the *one* good thing about you having cancer—you weren't too cool to hang out with me anymore."

"Lise, you have your own friends." I tuck her little head under my chin and she wraps her arms around my neck. The frame of her glasses pokes my chest. "Is this because I went to Ottawa?"

Elise shrugs. She sniffs back snot and I scan the closet floor for a stray sock to blow her nose on.

"I know this will probably go to your head, but you are sort of cool—for a big brother, anyway."

"Careful, the closet door is narrow."

She laughs weakly. "I just liked being the only one who knew that, y'know?" She lifts her head and looks up at me through those foggy glasses. No wonder she's the favorite kid; she's adorable without even trying.

"Well, that," she says, laying her head back down, "and I also liked getting to hear all your little secrets."

I groan and try to shift her off my lap. Elise whimpers like a puppy and locks her arms around my neck.

"Let go. The confidence has gone to your head."

"Nuh-uh."

"Uh-huh."

"Nuh-uh."

"Lise."

"Jem," she mimics my tone.

"As much as you benefit from my loneliness, there is a very real person waiting downstairs."

"Ugh. Fine." Elise lets go and crawls off my lap. She opens the closet door and shuffles out into the room on all fours. "Go have your stupid friends."

"Nuh-uh." I grab her around the waist and haul her to her feet. She squeals loudly. "You're along for the ride."

"I don't need a pity invite."

"It's more of a hostage situation." I turn her around and throw her over my shoulder like I used to, even though she feels way too heavy now and my shoulders are sore from last night. She struggles a little for the sake of her image, but lets me carry her back downstairs. I set her down in the kitchen and Elise's eyes go wide behind her round glasses.

There's a reason I keep Willa around. In the five minutes we were gone, she went through the cupboards and found bowls, baking sheets, and the ingredients for what I'm guessing will be cookies.

"Oatmeal raisin or pecan chocolate?" she asks.

Elise pushes her glasses farther up her nose and swallows. "Uh, pecan chocolate, please."

It wasn't what I had in mind, but an afternoon baking with my sister and Willa is still a pretty good way to end the weekend. It makes Elise happy, at least, and I'm totally her favorite brother right now.

I'll have to find a way to rub that in Eric's face tonight…

Monday

I fall asleep in Social Studies. I don't even realize that I've dozed off with my head in my hand until my chin slips over the edge of my palm and I head-butt Willa in the shoulder.

"Dude," she scolds me, and pushes me back to my half of the worktable.

"Sorry."

Willa looks at me shrewdly, and very deliberately pokes my shoulder where she pushed me. I wince and slap her hand away.

"Why are you so tender?"

"I bruise easily, okay? Quit poking me."

Willa pulls my cuff back a few inches, enough to expose the bruises that I've managed to keep hidden from Mom and Elise. She asks if I walked into a pole.

"Several, actually," I answer stiffly. It's none of her business.

Willa shakes her head and turns back to her book. I roll my sleeve back down, tugging it so far that it almost covers my hand completely.

Willa hands me a mint.

"It was just a small mosh pit, and I was only on the edge."

She snorts like my explanation is funny. "Totally not what I was thinking."

"What were you thinking?"

"Rough sex," she quips. "Either that or a fight with a five-year-old." It takes a few seconds for me to realize that she insulted me with that last part, because I'm hung up on the idea of Willa *thinking of me having sex.* I thought she thought I was a complete write-off—some sort of closet case or asexual.

Well, she pictured you naked and didn't gag. Good sign?

> *She was probably joking, you idiot.*

It doesn't matter if she was—you can't deliver, remember?

I knew that stunt with Ava was going to come back to haunt me. I feel my face go hot with the residual shame of Sunday morning. Why the hell did I say yes to her when I knew better?

"You've got a dirty mind, Kirk."

"It makes life interesting," she answers simply, as though we're talking about the merits of powdered versus liquid dish soap.

"You find my sex life interesting?"

"Do you have one?"

I hate it when she wins.

After class, Mrs. Hudson calls Willa and I up to her desk. She has the latest component of our term project in her hands, and I don't think she intends to compliment it.

"I think you two have gotten off track a little bit," she says. "This is a very good project you've designed, but it's starting to look like a science experiment."

"Uh...yeah." Should we make art out of soil contamination?

"This is supposed to be a Social Studies project. You should be taking your chosen issue and relating it to the concerns of the community—to people. Stating the facts isn't enough. What I expect for your paper and presentation is an opinion about the issue and a possible solution to the problem."

I take the assignment back with a sigh. "We'll rework it."

"Can we change topics?" Willa interjects. How nice of her to speak for both of us. I have no interest in changing topics after we've done part of the work on this one.

Mrs. Hudson hesitates. "What did you have in mind?"

"Give us until tomorrow to submit an alternate proposal. If it's no good, we'll revamp the pollution project."

She'd better not expect me to do any more work than I have already if she's determined to go back to square one.

⦿

Willa comes over after dinner with a small stack of typed pages in her hand. It's our revamped project proposal. I grab my backpack and suggest that we take our work up to the library. It isn't until we're sitting across from each other at the worktable that I see Willa's new proposal. The title makes me choke: *The Effects of Critical Illness on Individuals and Families.*

"No."

"It's the only subject we both know inside out."

"Absolutely not."

"We have easy access to interview subjects."

"Did you not hear me?"

Willa gives me a snarky look. "What's your problem?"

"My problem is that I don't need the whole class to know my business."

"They stare because they're curious. Take that way, and they'll just be assholes who gawk," Willa says levelly.

"We're not doing this."

"We both know that I'll be doing most of the work, and this is a topic I'd like to pursue."

I tear her proposal in half. She can just print another one, but ripping the project sends an appropriate message.

Willa leans forward on her elbows and speaks with a condescending smile. "You know Harper, you aren't the center of the universe. Neither are you the only one who has personal experience that might come in handy for this project. Get over it. It sucks, but if we can exploit the shit things we've gone through for this stupid project, it means we can stop mucking about with soil samples."

She isn't going to back down on this. I almost suggest that we do separate projects, but that would mean a lot more work and a failing grade for me. I pick up the torn title page instead and amend the topic: *The Effects of Critical Illness on ~~Individuals and~~ Families.*

"We're just focusing on you."

"What about your family?"

"I'd rather not include them."

"Give them the option, at least."

"No."

"Why not?"

"Because it's painful."

Willa just shakes her head and collects the pieces of the proposal. "I'll redraft the outline. See you at school tomorrow." She grabs her backpack and heads for the door. I don't go after her. I don't want to fight about this.

Willa: April 23 to 28

Tuesday

I'm going to miss moments like this when I graduate high school. Paige is putting her plan to make Chris jealous into action by flirting with Joe right in front of him at lunch. Moore is embarrassingly happy with the attention, but Chris takes it in stride. He turns to me and starts a game of hot hands.

I suck at this game, but it's probably karma's way of getting me back for encouraging Paige in the first place. Chris goes easy on me, flirting just a little to put it back in Paige's face. All of this is a wasted effort. They'll be back to making out in the halls again by the final bell.

It's around the time that Joe begins to tell Paige the specs of his new guitar amp that Paige seems to realize this was a bad idea. Chris whacks the back of my hands again, but he holds on this time, laughing at my ineptitude. I never realized what small hands he has. He has fingers like a hobbit.

Chris rubs his thumbs along the backs of my hands. Touchy. Feely. Completely gross.

"Got a job lined up for the summer yet?" he asks.

"Not yet."

"My parents are hiring for the summer soon. You should apply." Chris's parents own a bed and breakfast on the outskirts of town. It's popular for outdoor weddings because they have a large, well-maintained Victorian garden. Working with Chris doesn't entirely appeal to me, but it's better than flipping burgers.

"Okay." My willingness makes Chris smile. "I'll stop by and drop off an application."

We're watching a movie today in Social Studies about the juvenile justice system. I zone out and doodle on the sole of my shoe. The movie limits the amount of in-class conversation that Mrs. Hudson is willing to tolerate. A paper plane note flies past the screen every two minutes.

Jem sends a plane twelve inches to the right, directly into my hair. It says: *You know Elwood's going to rape you in the guest room.*

It is absolutely none of his business where I work. Jem has been petty and snippy about Elwood before, sometimes with good reason, but this is a new low.

I write back, *You can't rape the willing,* and slide the paper his way. Jem glares at the note for a good long time before crushing it in his fist. Part of me fears for Chris's tires.

As we get ready to leave at the end of the hour, Jem slips a second note into my sweater pocket. I read it before the start of my next class, but almost wish I hadn't.

I made a dinner reservation. Saturday, 7 pm. I'll pick you up.

That bastard even drew a smiley face underneath. And under that: *P.S. Elwood's a tool.*

Mature as ever, I see.

Wednesday

Mrs. Hudson returns the new project proposal. She's green-lighted it, so now all we have to do is play catch-up with our research, not that it will be hard. Jem refuses to speak to me for the rest of the lesson.

Thursday

I consider telling Jem that Mrs. Elwood called me back the same day I submitted an application and offered me a part-time job (probably with Chris's influence). But I know it would bother him, so I don't say anything. Of course, I didn't count on Chris cheerfully informing me over lunch that he'll be training me at my first shift on Monday. Jem looks pretty annoyed.

"The front desk is pretty simple," Chris says. "The hard work is maintenance and cleaning." He starts to tell me about the reception bookings they have this summer, but I'm only half-listening. My attention is divided between Chris and the thoughtful, troubled way Jem runs his fingers across the side of his jaw. I'd bet my car he's working on something snarky to say.

Chris notices my preoccupation and beats Jem to the punch.

"Miss a spot shaving?"

Jem and I both pause and Hannah chokes on her orange juice. Jem upends Chris's lunch tray all over his lap, pushes his chair back, and walks away. I consider leaving with him, but he probably wants to be alone.

"Crap, this is a new shirt," Chris complains.

"You'll survive."

Jem doesn't show up to Social Studies. That doesn't surprise me. I don't see him for the rest of the day, and he doesn't call for music before bed. I send a short *Goodnight* text that goes unanswered.

Chris's remark must have put quite a dent in Jem's ego. I'm hardly innocent of the same crime—I called him Uncle Fester when I barely knew him, but at least I was provoked. Chris had no reason to say anything to Jem.

I start to count backwards on my fingers, adding up the time I've known Jem against the forty-nine days he had officially been in remission when I asked. It took Tessa nearly six weeks to start regrowing actual hair after her last round of chemo. It was thin and fell out easily, and had the texture of newborn hair. I would never ask Jem, of course, because he's so sensitive about his hair, but I do wonder how much longer until he ditches the hats altogether.

I pick up my phone and text Jem again, even though he didn't reply to my last. *You still awake?*

It takes Jem five minutes to answer: *Maybe.*

Every barrier has its version of 'open sesame.' I reply: *Elwood's a tool.*

I'm awake.

I call him and he answers with a droll, "Did I miss anything in Soc?"

"Not really. I don't want to talk about school."

"Okay…?"

"Did you shave your head before chemo?"

I can hear him lick his lips on the other end of the line. "I don't want to talk about that."

"I still have the razor I shaved my sister's head with."

"Oh."

"I cut her hair off with the kitchen scissors and then shaved the rest. I was so worried I was going to cut her by accident."

"Did you?"

"No. I went slow. It took me more than an hour to do the job."

"Why are you telling me this?"

"Elwood is an idiot. Don't listen to him. Don't let him make you feel inferior."

Jem doesn't say anything. The silence stretches on, so I make it easy and let him off the hook.

"Goodnight, Jem."

"G'night."

Friday

I open my locker at lunchtime and a note falls out at me. It's from Jem.

Meet me at the picnic tables.

I swing by the cafeteria to buy food and then head out to the picnic tables. Jem is already there when I arrive, sitting on the tabletop with his feet resting on the bench. I toss him a carton of milk and climb up beside him.

"You're not hiding out here, are you?"

"No." Jem shakes his head and folds open the milk spout. "I just wanted you all to myself, is all."

I give him a sideways look and he stares right back, completely unapologetic.

"Are we still on for tomorrow?" he asks.

Ugh, I had almost blocked out all knowledge of his dinner plans. "I told you I don't do dinner dates."

"And that prohibits you from going out to grab a bite with a friend?" I mull that one over and he nudges my shoulder with his. "Come on, Kirk. I think we both need a night out of Smiths Falls."

"Out of Smiths Falls?"

"The place I had in mind is in Ottawa."

"That far?"

"It's only an hour away, as long as traffic isn't bad."

"I still don't think—"

Jem lays a finger over my lips, cutting me off. "Please don't make me kidnap you."

"Can't we do something else?"

"What if I said I was really excited to try this restaurant?"

"I'd say you're a liar."

Jem laughs. "We're still going." My protest has been overruled.

He takes his iPod out of his jacket pocket and hands me an earphone. He chooses "Love of the Loveless" by the Eels. These uncomplicated moments with Jem are rare, just sitting on the table with music and food and no real need for conversation. We coast through a few songs before "Electro-Shock Blues" comes on. Jem and I share a sideways look, and he changes the track to "P.S. You Rock My World."

I'm starting to like these wordless conversations.

I swing by the stationary store after school to pick up a poster board and sup-plies for Jem and I to make AV crap for the Soc project. I call Jem to ask if we need anything else before I leave the store.

"What color poster did you get?"

"White."

"Did you get anything to decorate it?"

"Black Sharpies."

"This is going to be the most boring poster ever."

"I know."

"I like it. It denotes a suitable lack of effort."

"Fantastic." I hang up on him and head to the checkout counter. On my way I pass the office equipment aisle and an open bin catches my eye. It's full of rubber finger caps, the kind that make page flipping easier and prevent paper cuts. I pick one up and try it on. It gives me an idea.

Jem hears my shoddy muffler and appears in the front door as soon as I exit my car. "I didn't know you were coming over."

"I can't stay." I mount the front steps and hand him the poster board and Sharpies. "The Crappiest Poster Ever is your job, okay?" This is the kind of contribution Jem can stand; one that doesn't make him confront any of his demons.

"I'll put the bare minimum amount of effort into it," he promises.

"I got these for you, too." I take the plastic bag of finger caps from my pocket and hand it over. "For music." I head back to my car before he can open the bag and make things uncomfortable. "G'night, Harper."

I get a phone call at eleven o'clock at night, long past the time when Jem usually calls. I'm tempted to just let it ring and fall back to sleep, but he'd give me a hard time about it in the morning.

"Hello?" My eyes refuse to stay open.

"Hey."

"It's late."

"I'm sorry."

"Why'd you call?"

"Just listen, okay?"

There's a rustle as Jem moves the phone, and after a few seconds I hear the opening strains of a classical nocturne. He's playing. The melody is slow and mournful, but I feel warm listening to it, because it means he has his cello back. He can play his music without pain.

After a few minutes the song is interrupted by Ivy's gentle voice. "It's late, honey. Why don't you finish practicing tomorrow and get some sleep?"

"I will," he promises, and there's silence until his bedroom door closes. Jem picks up the phone. "You still there?"

"Still here."

"Sorry. Mom wants me to go to bed."

"Tomorrow's another day," I agree. It was nice to hear Jem play, but I'm eager to get back to sleep.

"I'm rusty, but…" I can hear him smiling. This is good for him. A musician needs music.

"It was beautiful, Jem."

"Thanks for the rubber caps."

"You're welcome. Now go to bed, it's late."

"Good night, Willa."

Saturday

I make supper for Frank at five o'clock, but I don't eat anything. I don't want to spoil my appetite, and the reservation is at seven. I tell Frank about my plans to go out with a friend so he won't assume I'm up to no good.

"Aren't you gonna eat first?"

"We'll grab a bite while we're out."

I leave Frank to devour his tacos and go upstairs to get ready for an evening out. Unfortunately, that means shedding my weekend getup of torn jeans and old plaid shirts. I strip out of my comfy clothes and open my closet. I'm lost.

What the hell does one wear on a non-date? I have a feeling that jeans and a tee won't cut it, but the thought of having to get dressed up creeps me out. Skirts are quickly ruled out. The chenille sweater I wear on holidays is too good. Plain tees and band shirts aren't good enough. My button-front blouse is linty. Eventually I compromise: dark jeans on the bottom and a black sweater on top; the perfect balance of 'I'm going out' and 'I don't care.' I don't usually wear makeup, and since this really isn't a date, I decide not to bother now. I leave my hair down and pass on any form of jewelry. I grab my plainest pair of grey gloves. I do one better than runners, though: black flats, both understated and good enough to go with the sweater.

Then I realize I've spent twenty whole minutes fretting over what to wear to see Jem, and I want to hit something.

Frank doesn't quite know how to read my appearance when I go downstairs. I don't look like I'm going out on a date, precisely, but I don't look like I'm just going to school, either.

"Who are you going to be with, again?" he asks.

It's useless to lie to him in such a small town. "Jem Harper."

My answer irritates Frank. "You're going out with that kid?"

"We're just hanging out together."

"Alone?"

"Just us two, yeah."

"Are you sure that's a good idea?" Frank narrows his eyes at me. He's a hard man to read, but I see the worry under his ambiguously slanted brows.

"We're friends."

"Will, I know you've had a rough time these last couple years, and I don't have anything against you being nice to the Harper kid, but you have to be careful."

"I am." I consider telling Frank how often Jem and I meet at each others' houses when he's on a long shift and that we don't just do Soc homework, but I don't want to give my brother a stroke. He worries enough about me.

The doorbell rings. I head to the front hall and quickly grab my jacket and purse. Frank follows me warily, as though he's preparing to send me off to my death.

I open the door and Jem smiles at me nervously.

"Hi. Let's go." I put a hand on his arm and practically shove him down the front steps. I want to get out of here before Frank gets the idea to lecture us, or to threaten Jem with the treat-my-sister-right-or-else speech.

Frank comes out onto the porch and Jem says, "Nice seeing you," over his shoulder as we walk away. Frank doesn't say anything. He just folds his arms and glowers at us across the driveway.

Jem seems to find my behavior funny. He smirks at me and follows me around to the passenger side of the car. "You look really nice," he says softly. If he said it at normal volume I'd think he was just paying me a generic compliment—an obligatory social nicety—but his voice was so quiet that only I could hear, and the implications of that make me antsy.

"So do you." He looks good in a dress shirt, or maybe it's just the way this shirt actually fits him. He swims in the sweaters and long-sleeved tees he wears on a daily basis.

Jem smiles at the compliment and turns to open the car door for me.

"You know this isn't a real date, right?"

"I know." His smile wavers a little. "I'll drive you home whenever you like."

I get into the car. I wonder if he opened the door for me to prove to Frank that I'm not going out with some jerk, or because he's trying to get something out of me. He holds open a few doors, does the gentlemanly thing in public, and in return my hand goes down his pants by the end of the night. Thus altruism dies with a groan and a sticky mess.

It takes thirty long seconds for Jem to get in the car and pull away from my glaring brother on the porch. As eager as I was to get away, once alone in the car with Jem, I start to get nervous. What did I get myself into?

"What are you expecting tonight?"

My question puzzles him. "A fun night out, where I—hopefully—don't get sick during." We come to the stop sign at the end of my street and he looks over at me with furrowed brows. "What are you expecting?"

"I don't know." I really don't. Confusion is starting to become my natural state around Jem.

The drive to Ottawa doesn't feel as long as it usually does. Jem keeps the conversation going, chattering in a nervous way until we're on the highway, and then he begins to relax a little.

"Are you going to tell me where we're going?"

"No. I like surprises."

"But you already know."

"I enjoy *giving* surprises." He looks over at me and smiles. "I hope you're hungry."

Suddenly the sheer lunacy of going to dinner with Jem hits me, and I laugh. What the hell am I doing here? I don't do normal, pedestrian things like dinner dates. As little face-time as I can get with a guy while still satisfying us both is my preferred MO—it's clean, it's uncomplicated, and I don't miss him when he's gone.

"What's the joke?"

"You wouldn't get it."

It's nearly dark by the time we get to Ottawa. Jem takes us through an old, hilly neighborhood not far from the busy Rideau Street area, and parks along the street near a convenience store. He says this is the closest parking to where we're headed.

"Ready?"

We have to walk about a block through tidy streets—Jem says he used to live around here—before rounding the corner toward a sidewalk-side plaza with a food co-op and a New Age bookstore. Jem points out the third storefront as our destination.

I can't help but chuckle when I see the sign. *The Circle: Lounge and Gastropub.* Underneath the main shingle is a poster with a guarantee of 'the finest vegan cuisine in Ottawa.' I wonder if they have much competition for that title.

"It was your idea," Jem says with a smirk. He has a point, and a damn good idea it was. He'll have more of a selection here than he would on the average restaurant menu.

Inside, The Circle feels a lot like a living room. Tables of varying sizes and shapes share the U-shaped dining space with couches and easy chairs. Bookshelves line the walls and there is a tea and dessert bar on the left wall. In the centre of the restaurant, a wide-beamed staircase leads up to an open loft and further dining space. No two pieces of furniture are the same, so the seating is just as eclectic as the books on the shelves. Slow music plays at low volume, emphasizing the easygoing atmosphere of the restaurant.

"For two?" a passing waitress asks.

"Please." Jem gives her his name to cross off the reservation list.

"Sit wherever you feel most comfortable." She continues on to serve other patrons, and Jem gestures that I should select our seats.

I choose the back corner. It's quieter than the front of the restaurant or the area near the serving bar, and close to the bathrooms. Jem takes the seat nearest the wall and I move my chair to sit beside him instead of across.

"Would you rather have this seat?"

"No." I shake my head. "I just like to people-watch." True enough, but I also don't like the face-to-face setup; it feels too much like a date, which this isn't.

The waitress comes by with two menus and a pitcher of water. She looks sort of badass, with a labret in her lip and dreads knotted into a bun. I like her immediately because she looks without staring.

I give a little sigh of relief when I open the menu and see that the general ingredients of each dish are listed. That'll make it easier for Jem to order. I find myself scanning the list of options for something he can eat before I consider my own selection.

Jem frowns at the menu like it's written in Swahili.

"The unbeef stew looks good."

He looks up and I point to the item on his menu. It's not so different from the soups I've made for him recently, except that it contains tofu and a little more spice than I would venture to use.

"It does look good." He gives me a grateful little smile and clears his throat. "What are you getting?"

I order the veggie potpie with a side of chickpea salad. Jem orders the unbeef stew and decides to stick with water for a beverage, so I order a glass of soymilk that I can trade with him if the stew is too spicy.

This is a neat little place Jem chose. I would come here for the books alone. They're eclectic and some of them are meant to be signed by diners, like a guest-book. I reach around Jem's head and pluck a copy of *Jane Eyre* off the shelf. It's a well-kept second edition, printed in London. I wonder how it ended up in a vegan lounge in Ottawa.

"Have you read it?" he asks.

"A time or two." Gross understatement. "I own two copies—I loaned one to Tessa and she killed it."

Jem smirks. "How do you kill a book?"

"You read it to death—until the pages are loose and the glue on the spine is crumbling and the covers are bent and the corners are dog-eared. I still have the beat up copy, but it's so fragile it's practically unreadable. I had to buy a new one."

"She must have really liked that book." He takes the restaurant's copy out of my hand and skims through it. The pages smell old and the cloth cover is discolored with light damage.

"She wasn't much of a reader, but she did like the Brontës."

"Doesn't it bug you to volunteer at the hospital?" Jem asks suddenly. "It must remind you of…" He leaves the sentence hanging. He can't describe what he means, and there's no need to.

"No. It's…comforting."

If Jem had eyebrows, one would be raised right now.

"After awhile it feels…like only the people there get it. Everyone is dealing with tough shit—the nurses who care but are tough as nails, the patients, the families…. It's the only place where I really fit in anymore."

"You fit in well at school."

"I lie through my teeth at school."

Jem smirks at me. "I figured."

⚮

The unbeef stew has chunks of potato, tofu and vegetable floating in the broth. Jem doesn't attempt these at first, playing it safe with spoonfuls of broth. I've eaten with him every day at school for over a month now, but when it's just the two of us it's different. I try not to eat too fast so he won't feel rushed.

"How's your potpie?"

It's surprisingly tasty for a vegan dish. The filling is creamy and the crust is flaky without being dry. The chickpea salad is equally delicious, served with garlic bread for dipping. I offer Jem a taste of the latter, but it's too sweet for his liking.

"Must be the relish."

"Well, damn," he says.

"What?"

"I always liked relish on hotdogs."

"You might again, eventually."

He shrugs like he doesn't hold out much hope, and I make a mental note to hunt down a recipe for mild relish.

Jem spears a chunk of tofu with his fork. "Should I?"

What am I, the food whisperer?

"Chew it slowly." He's used to soft and pureed foods. He'll have to chew long and carefully to avoid upsetting his stomach.

At first I think it's the tofu that gives Jem a hard time, the way he makes that face, but the potatoes and carrots present the same difficulty. The stew is almost room temperature now because of his slow pace, so heat shouldn't be an issue.

"Are you okay?"

"Yeah." Jem winces. "It's just tough to hold it on my tongue for so long."

"Too spicy?"

"No." He shakes his head. "Just…a lot of flavor."

I offer him my soymilk to take the edge off. From the outside we must look like an old couple, chewing long and slow, with up to a minute between bites. Jem's bites become smaller and smaller as he attempts to compensate for the strong flavor and the amount of time he has to chew. His pace slows to a crawl and I can see he's struggling to work up the nerve to take each small bite.

I squeeze the hand that holds his spoon. "You don't have to finish it."

"I just need a break." He sets his spoon down and turns his attention to me. "Tell me something."

"What?"

"Anything. Where did you work when you lived in St. John's?"

"I had a part-time gig at this little shop called Independent Music." Jem's eyes light up like I've just revealed some wonderful secret. "We sold CDs and vinyl on the first floor, and the second floor was for instruments and recording equipment—microphones, speakers, and the like. A lot of the regular customers would give the employees free tickets to their shows. The boss called it 'market research' to get all the staff to go."

"And why the hell did you leave?" Independent Music was the perfect job. Jem would have loved it, too.

"Family troubles, mostly. My parents were on the verge of kicking me out, but Frank took me in."

"Why'd they want to kick you out? You seem pretty responsible."

I casually wave away the subject. "Call it a persistent difference of opinion and one major attitude problem." And that's all he needs to know.

I steal a piece of potato from Jem's bowl and he pretends to scowl at me. "What about you?"

"What about me?"

"Any fascinating student jobs?"

Jem shakes his head. "I temped one summer as a filing clerk for the architecture firm my mom used to work for."

"In between stints at music camp?"

Jem's eyes narrow. "Yes," he answers carefully. "It's not as dorky as you think."

"You don't know what I think."

"Enlighten me."

"Try to eat more and I'll tell you." I nod to his bowl. Jem grudgingly breaks off a piece of carrot with his spoon and begins to chew at a glacial pace.

"In my experience, the band kids are a pretty wild bunch. Their travelling competitions sound like one long party."

Jem points out that he wasn't a band kid. "Music camp is more politics than party. It's extremely competitive."

"Art is vanity."

He smirks wryly at that.

"So how many people wanted to strangle you when you won that competition to play with the orchestra?"

Jem's cheeks turn pink. I don't understand his sense of embarrassment—it's an accomplishment to be proud of, not to hide.

"Well," he says slowly. "About five wanted to strangle me—the five that were also in the running for the top spot. And then there were another four cellists who didn't qualify to begin with, but who still would have enjoyed dislocating my fingers one by one."

"But they all smiled and congratulated you, didn't they?"

"That's the culture of performers for you."

"I used to tap dance," I volunteer. Jem seems to be struggling not to laugh. "Really?"

"Yeah, but I sucked."

This time he does laugh. "Is that why you don't dance in public anymore?"

"I dance in public. I'm just picky about where and with whom."

"Bit of a snob, are you?" he teases.

"We all have our weaknesses." I steal a carrot out of his bowl. "I make bad decisions. You throw up."

"I haven't all week."

I give him the eye. "What, you think you're better than me now?" He snort-laughs at that. I better not ever crack a joke while he's drinking. The results would be disastrous.

"It's good to hear you're feeling better." I nudge him under the table with my foot. Jem nudges me back.

The waitress comes by to clear away my empty plate. She asks if Jem is finished, even though his bowl still has plenty of food in it. He admits he's eaten all he can and the waitress offers dessert menus. Neither of us are hungry enough to eat more.

"Do you drink coffee?" Jem asks. His tone makes me think that he wants me to say yes so we can stay here longer. This is sort of a record for us in terms of comfortable conversation.

"Two mint teas, please," I tell the server. She leaves with the order and Jem quietly tells me that he really isn't up to eating or drinking anything else.

"I don't expect you to finish it. A mouthful or two is enough—it cleanses the pallet. How's your stomach?"

"Fine. Full."

"A little mint tea helps digestion."

We're both too wussy to drink the tea steaming hot, anyway. We end up staying at The Circle for another hour, waiting for the tea to cool and sipping slowly. There are no lulls or gaps in conversation—everything and nothing is a suitable topic, from his favorite haunts in Ottawa to what I miss about St. John's, and what we'd each choose if we could have a superpower.

"Telekinesis," Jem declares without hesitation.

"You're a control freak, aren't you?"

"Whatever," he says with a laugh. "What about you?"

"Invisibility."

Jem nods. "Sounds like you."

"And you say you don't get me."

"I don't."

"Liar."

⊷

The drive home feels even shorter than the drive to Ottawa. Jem even walks me to the door at the end of the night. Non-date or not, that's a new thing for me.

"Thanks for coming out with me," Jem says. "I had fun."

"I did too." My simple admission makes him beam. "This was...nice. Not at all what I was expecting."

"What were you expecting?" He slips his hands into his pockets. I look him up and down, trying to find the right words to explain what I had in mind before we went out. He dressed nicely, made an actual dinner reservation, treated me politely and asked me about myself; all new things for me, but none of them wholly unpleasant.

I shrug. "I don't know. That it would blow up in our faces and make school awkward. Or that we would just piss each other off and I'd have to find a place to bury you in pieces."

Jem chuckles at that. He gets my humor.

"Thanks. This was…different."

"Better than the hypothetical?"

"Much."

Jem smiles and I half-turn to put my key in the door. I wonder if I should invite him in. I usually don't tell guys where I live, never mind bring them home, but this technically wasn't a date and it's not as though Jem hasn't been inside my house before.

Warm fingers touch the underside of my chin, turning my head gently. When my face comes around he's right there, closer than I expected and leaning down to my level. He kisses me, and it is the strangest sensation I've felt in a long time. He uses so little pressure that the warmth of his skin is more noticeable than his lips. It's a chaste kiss, but he lingers over it; not long enough to be gross, but enough to give the impression that he enjoys it.

When Jem pulls away he doesn't go far. Our foreheads are practically touching, and the hand he used to turn my face toward him is still resting on the side of my neck. With anyone else I would find such a hand placement intensely uncomfortable, but now it's…oddly tolerable.

"Willa?"

I don't know what I'm supposed to say. Or do I return the gesture? Some reaction is due, obviously, I just don't know what.

"Um." I close my eyes, trying to pick one thought from among the dozen ideas swarming around my head. Jem takes my closed eyes as an invitation and leans in to kiss me again.

There's heat behind it this time. I don't know if it's him leaning in or me leaning back, but soon my shoulders come up against the front door. Jem sighs against me and brushes his thumb along my jaw in a slow, appreciative way, as though he's studying me. His right hand finds mine and laces our fingers together. My other hand drops my keys. Aw hell, this actually feels good.

And that's when it hits me that I'm kissing Jem Harper pressed up against the door of my brother's house. It's like looking down on myself from above, watching this moment, and wondering where the real me went. Pushed up against the door? What is this, some crappy rom-com?

I wrap my arms around his neck and push him right back. Jem's hands go to my waist as though he's trying to catch me, and we take two steps back—far enough for his hips to come up against the porch rail. His hands fist around the sides of my sweater, pulling me closer. I expect him to grab my ass, but he doesn't. I could get used to this whole gentleman thing.

I'm not sure if it's the drugs in him or what, but his kisses leave a strange heat behind on my skin when he moves his lips. He sort of pecks when he kisses, closing his lips around mine, drawing his lower lip across my mouth with just a hint of suction before pulling away, tight-lipped, and coming back for another.

I take his lower lip between mine before he can pull away and suck on it gently.

He gives a soft sigh and grabs me tighter.

I slowly unwind my arms from around his neck, coming down around his shoulders to his front. Suddenly Jem breaks away and yanks my right hand off his chest.

"What?"

He doesn't immediately answer. His lips are a little swollen and he's out of breath. I get it before he has to explain: my hand came close to touching his central line.

"Did I hurt you?"

"No." Jem looks at me searchingly, waiting, no doubt, for disgust or hesitancy. I twist my hand out of his grip and place it on his waist instead of his chest.

"Maybe we should stop," he says.

"You want to?"

Jem hesitates over that one, biting his lower lip. He wants to keep going, even if he thinks he should stop. I regret touching his chest now. I shouldn't have spooked him like that.

"Or we could stop talking and continue," I offer. And for the first time since I've known Jem, he doesn't argue with my suggestion.

⮵

Frank is still up when I get inside. He looks me up and down with a suspicious eye and asks how my evening went.

"It was nice. We went to a vegan place in Ottawa."

"*Vegan?*" My meat-eating, fish-catching, deer-hunting brother makes the term 'vegan' sound like a horrible swear word. "Are you turning vegan?" I can see he's worried what my cooking would turn into if I did decide to change my diet.

"No, I was just trying something new."

Frank grunts in a gesture of both suspicion and acceptance, and asks if I'm in for the night. I tell him that I am and excuse myself to take a shower.

I study myself in the mirror while the water heats up. My lips are a little red, but not enough to explain the strange tingling sensation. It's lessened since I stopped kissing Jem, but still noticeable. It doesn't taste like morphine, which feels sort of numbing. He has long since finished chemo, so it shouldn't burn. I don't know his other drugs well enough to speculate about them. Those meds are probably for his transplant, and I have no experience in that area.

I step into the shower and stand with my face directly under the spray, holding my breath until I can't anymore. The water isn't even that warm yet, but my skin feels hot and sticky, the way it used to after spending time outdoors in summer. I'm too pale to feel so sun-soaked.

I try to imagine what school will be like on Monday, but I can't. Before we said goodbye, Jem said he wanted to make plans again. I should have said no, but instead I said I knew a place where we could go on Wednesday. It's a little place that Frank used to take me when I was a kid, but I should have thought things through before I invited Jem there—before I invited him to think that we're somehow dating.

I'm still drying off when my phone rings and Jem smirks up at me from the screen.

"Did you forget something?"

"No." I can hear him smiling. "I just wanted to say goodnight."

I thought we said goodnight on the porch? "Oh. Goodnight then."

"I had fun tonight."

"I'm glad."

"Did you?"

"Yeah, I did." As weird as it was, no single moment stands out as painful or unpleasant—even if I am panicking a little about seeing him at school on Monday.

"Can I take you out again sometime?"

"We already made plans for Wednesday."

"Yeah, but I mean—"

"Jem," I tell him firmly, "you're doing that thing where you try to monopolize me."

"Sorry. Wednesday."

"Sleep well."

"You too."

I hang up and set my phone aside. I can't decide if Jem is cute or just desperately needy. Most people wait longer than thirty minutes to call back after a date. Er, a non-date.

I go to turn out the lights and catch a glimpse of myself in the mirror above my dresser. My face is red. Shit. I flick the light off so I don't have to look at myself and crawl under the covers.

I have a feeling that space is going to become an issue between Jem and me, but it doesn't worry me as much as it used to. We've negotiated this already. We'll deal when it comes up again. Two months ago I would never have thought this of him, but I actually enjoy his company when he loses the sarcastic veneer of bullshit and bitterness. He's most beautiful when he allows himself to be.

Sunday

When I go downstairs for breakfast, I find Frank at the dining room table. I guess he's skipping a Sunday with Doug for once. He gestures to a pot on the stove and says there's oatmeal if I want it, but upon inspection it just looks like a clump of burnt oats. I can see why he ordered so much pizza before I moved in.

"Uh, thanks, but I'll just have cereal."

"Something wrong with my cooking?"

"No, not at all. I just, you know, want to live."

I pour myself a bowl of cereal while Frank stubbornly persists in eating his burnt oats.

"I talked to Mom last night," Frank announces as I reach for the milk.

I look up so fast that I bang my head on the lip of the freezer.

"Easy, kid."

"What did you talk to Mom about?"

Frank pulls out the dining chair next to him, inviting me to sit. I stand there with the milk carton in my hand and wait for him to get to the point.

"Will, what would you think of maybe finding someone to talk to while you're here?"

"No."

"Mom thinks—"

"Mom agreed to ship me off to Smiths Falls so I could get a clean break. No more doctors, no more meds, no more group sessions—no more screwing up my life."

"Yes, she did agree with that," Frank answers mildly. "But you're breaking your half of the bargain."

"How? My grades are good, I'm starting a new job tomorrow, I volunteer—my life here is about as vanilla as it gets."

Frank sighs. "You're putting yourself back to square one, getting close to the Harper boy. You wanted a clean break, so don't put yourself in a position to get hurt. No one wants to see you suffer like that again."

"Are you telling me not to hang out with Jem anymore?" I can hardly avoid seeing him, us being project partners and all, but if Frank was bound and determined he could put a real damper on the time I spend with Jem outside of school.

"It's great that you're being nice to him, but leave it at that. You're a smart girl—I want you to think long and hard about what would happen if he got sick again. Don't be getting attached to people who can hurt you so bad."

Too late.

"I'll think about it."

I put the milk back in the fridge and leave without eating breakfast. I just want to go to the hospital, even though I'll be early for my volunteer shift. I need to be in a familiar place and to keep my hands busy, because I really don't want to think about it like I told Frank I would.

I can't picture Jem's absence. I could picture Tessa's before she died; where the hole in my life would be. It turned out bigger than I imagined, but at least I could see it coming. I can't imagine my life in Smiths Falls without Jem. He's too ingrained in my routine. When the hell did I allow that to happen?

The text I receive mid-morning confirms it: *My place or yours today? We can cook here if you like.*

It's practically a given that we use our free time to do things together. He even knows what I would most like to be doing right now. Damn it.

I reply: *I'm volunteering today.*

After?

I need to think.

I should at least try to think it through, for Frank's sake. I don't want to worry him, and as much as it displeases me, he has a point. I consider calling Mom when I break for lunch, but I already know what she would say. She's one to put faith in professional help, and I'm sick of that scene.

I slouch lower in the cafeteria chair and turn my iPod on to drown out the noise of plates and utensils clinking. Frank may have a point, in theory—*if* Jem should get sick again, *if* I get attached enough to be hurt by him. But thinking of last night, I can't put a bad label on Jem. He treated me better than any other guy ever has. I enjoyed being with him. I liked kissing him, even if it did feel a little weird.

I try to imagine distancing myself from Jem again. The first time I was fueled by resentment and fear, and that made it easier to stick to it. Cold hard calculation is a flimsier reason to inflict such pain on both of us, especially after I promised not to cut him out again.

The idea of life without him around bothers me much more than it rightfully should. He pops up in my thoughts for the rest of the day at times when I least expect it. I haven't even spoken to him today, and by the end of my shift I feel like I've spent the whole day in his company.

Part of me wants to go over to the Harper house, but the other part of me knows better than to give my parents more ammo. Before I even leave the hospital I lay down across the seat in my car and call Hannah. She's a good listener and insightful without being nosey.

Mrs. Trilby passes the phone off to Hannah, who sounds like she's in a good mood. Maybe something happened with Brian.

"What are you up to?" I ask.

"Not much. Gardening with my dad."

"You want to go do something?" It's a ridiculous request. It's four o'clock on a Sunday; everything is about to close. There's nowhere for us to go.

"What did you have in mind?"

"I don't care. I just need to get out of my head. I've been thinking in circles all day."

"Oh. Okay. Something heavy on your mind?"

Only about a hundred and thirty pounds' worth; not terribly heavy.

"Nah, it's just a riddle I can't solve, is all."

"Can I hear it?"

"The riddle is a person."

Hannah hums softly. "And you can't get this person out of your head?"

"No, I can. Just not for long."

"Sounds like you're interested."

"So how's Brian?"

Hannah giggles—and she's not the giggling type. I can practically hear her blushing over the phone.

"I asked him to the grad dance. Got tired of waiting." She giggles again. That must mean things went well.

"Tell me everything."

⌁

I get home feeling pleasantly numb. Hearing all about Hannah's happiness did wonders for my uneasiness over the Jem question. But now that I'm alone, the vicious cycle of dead-end thoughts starts again. Hannah said I sounded 'interested.' Am I? I ask that question to the mirror and watch my reflection respond to that thought. This doesn't feel like a crush. I'm not tripping over myself. I don't go out of my way to see Jem. I do, however, put more effort into cooking for him than I do for anyone else. I think about him entirely too much when he isn't around. I let myself get too relaxed when I'm in his company—he slowly pulls all my secrets out of me.

I think a bumbling, obsessive crush might actually be the better alternative.

Jem: April 29 to May 3

Saturday

The house is quiet when I get home. The living space is dark and empty, and sounds of life on the second floor are minimal. Just two months ago Mom waited up for me, eager to hear if I was getting a social life. I suppose I should be glad that it's old news now, but part of me is itching to tell someone how wonderful my night was.

I go upstairs and fall down on my bed, grinning from ear to ear. The whole thing went better than I imagined. I didn't have to talk to Willa's brother and justify why she was going out with Cancer Boy. Conversation in the car was easy and relaxed, and Willa seemed to enjoy her meal even though it was vegan. I ate real food without getting sick. And kissing her…

I roll onto my back and take out my phone. I want to hear her voice one more time before I go to bed. Willa answers on the third ring.

"Did you forget something?" she asks.

"No. I just wanted to say goodnight." And to be the last thing on her mind before she falls asleep, like she's always the last thing on mine.

"Oh. Goodnight then."

"I had fun tonight."

"I'm glad."

"Did you?" I know I'm being greedy, but I want to hear her say it again.

"Yeah, I did."

"Can I take you out again sometime?"

"We already made plans for Wednesday."

"Yeah, but I mean—"

"Jem," she says firmly, "you're doing that thing where you try to monopolize me."

Shit. She's right. "Sorry. Wednesday."

"Sleep well."

"You too."

Willa hangs up and I lay back, cruising on the high of a great night. If this ever wears off (and I doubt it will), I have anticipation for Wednesday to tide me over.

A series of sharp knocks on my bedroom door interrupts my musings, and I reluctantly leave the bed to answer it. Elise stands on the other side of the threshold, bouncing on the balls of her feet.

"When did you get home?" she demands. She looks me up and down and notices the phone in my hand. "How'd it go?"

"Fine."

She somehow reads into my monotone, monosyllabic answer and squeals shrilly. Elise throws her arms around my waist, ignoring my protests and complaints of suffocation.

I dislodge her arms and she jumps up and down, flapping her hands. "Ohmigod, ohmigod, ohmigod. Um…yay?"

I can't help but laugh. She's more flustered about the whole thing than I am. "Tell me everything!"

I wouldn't know where to start. I don't think I could describe half of it…at least not without sounding like a romantic sap, anyway.

"I'll tell you tomorrow."

She's a little disappointed, but seems to understand that I'm not ready to divulge details. "Promise?"

"Yeah."

Elise walks back down the hall to her room, pausing halfway to do a series of little hops and squeal with delight. Good to know I have her rooting for me.

Sunday

I wake up sore and sallow with a grin on my face. Last night's high has carried over to today, and nothing can sour my bad mood. Not the handful of pills before breakfast, nor the flimsy packaging on waterproof patches, nor the fact that Eric seems to have used most of the hot water—nothing. I kissed Willa and didn't get punched in the face for it. She liked it. She didn't want to stop. And best of all: she agreed to go out again.

As I get dressed I toss around the idea of calling Willa before I head over to her house. We've been just dropping by each other's homes for weeks, but I don't want to push my luck. I've got a good thing going with her now and I don't want to screw it up.

I pause with Willa's number half-dialed. How am I supposed to act around her now? Should I say something? Give her a kiss when I say hello? Wait for her to make the first move?

I need to exploit my sister's girly intuition. I head down the hall to Elise's bedroom and knock on the door. She doesn't answer, but that's to be expected before noon on a Sunday. I open the door and step in quietly.

Elise doesn't sleep like a normal person. She nests. All her bedding is clustered in the center of her mattress, and therein somewhere she lies and sleeps.

"Elise?"

I reach under the edge of the mass, find what feels like an ankle, and pull. Elise slides out from under the blankets like a baby giraffe falling pathetically from its mother's womb. She blinks at the light and flinches away.

"Wake up."

"Go away," she whines. Elise turns and tries to crawl back into her nest. I grab the back of her pajama shirt to keep her close.

"I need your help."

"Don't care."

"Elise."

"Nothing is urgent enough to wake me up at the ass crack of dawn like this."

"It's ten-thirty."

Elise huffs and stops struggling. She goes limp, splay-limbed at the foot of the bed. "Fine. Bring me coffee and I'll help you."

"You're going to be short forever, the way you drink that stuff."

"Don't care. Worth it. Coffee. *Now.*"

I go downstairs and retrieve Elise's mug from the cupboard. It's the one she uses every morning, with a big looped handle and a pink E on the side. It's also about the size of a cereal bowl. Elise likes her coffee hot, black, and in quantities large enough to send a horse into cardiac arrest.

When I enter Elise's room again she's reburied herself in her nest of bedding. I pull back two of the blankets and a little hand slips through the folds to smack me away.

"I brought your coffee."

"I changed my mind. Come back in six hours."

"Lise."

She grunts from somewhere in the mound of blanket.

"I kissed Willa last night."

At first I think she's gone back to sleep and didn't hear me, but then her skinny hand pops out again and makes a grabbing motion.

"Alright, give me that coffee."

Elise sits on her bed looking very much like a zombie while I pace back and forth, outlining my questions. The more questions I voice the faster they seem to multiply. It's like having a freaking hydra in my head. Elise keeps her face in her mug, drinking steadily, and only stops to ask the odd question about what happened last night.

"Give me your phone," she says when I pause for breath. I hand it over and she mutters, "What am I going to do with you?"

"What's that supposed to mean?"

"You worry like a five-year-old girl but have the common sense of a guy. You're hopeless." Elise starts typing on my phone.

"What are you texting?"

Elise turns the phone around and holds it up. *My place or yours today? We can cook here if you like.*

It's perfect—exactly what Willa would want to hear, in a way that's not likely to set her off. Now why the hell couldn't I have thought of that?

"Because you have a crush on her, genius," Elise says. "It's supposed to make you stupid."

"Did you just call me stupid?" I try to swipe her coffee and she hisses at me like a cat.

My phone buzzes with Willa's answering text and Elise retreats into her nest of blanket, hogging the phone so she can read the message first.

"Give me that."

"You're not gonna like it."

"*Give it.*"

Elise passes my phone out from under her blanket. The text reads: *I'm volunteering today.*

I send back: *After?*

I need to think.

I hand the phone back to Elise. "Translate to guy-speak."

Elise merely glances at the text before tossing my phone back to me. "She needs to think."

"Really? Thank you, I couldn't have worked *that* out for myself."

Elise sticks her tongue out at me and takes another swig of coffee. "She's probably panicking a little."

"What do—"

"You do nothing."

"But—"

"She's a big girl. Let her think it out on her own. If she feels pressured she'll push you away."

"But—"

"Jem," Elise rests her fingertip on my nose. "Zen, okay? There's nothing you can do but wait. Let the mountain come to Mohamed, or whatever that saying is."

"The mountain *doesn't* come, Miss Brilliant."

"Fine then, you can be the mountain." She hands me her empty coffee cup. "Is that all?"

"But what if—"

"Ugh, shut up already," she whines. "You've done what you can. The ball's still in her court—just wait for her to send it back, okay?"

Elise burrows back into her tangle of blankets and pillows. I have a feeling I'm not going to get any further help out of her at the moment. Neither of us are morning people, but she's an extreme case.

"See you in six hours."

Elise's reply is muffled by her nest, but it doesn't sound kind. I leave her to rest, but not five minutes later Eric, who *is* a morning person, starts blasting music in the next room. It's his workout playlist. She's never going to be able to sleep through that.

I go downstairs for breakfast, compulsively checking my phone every five minutes, and come back upstairs to find Elise in my bed. She chose to transplant her nest to a quieter room instead of getting up.

"How the hell can you sleep with a gallon of coffee in you?"

"Bugger off," she slurs.

"No, it's my room and I'm bored." I don't remember what I did with weekends before Willa. I guess I wasted time with Elise, but that doesn't seem to be an option at the moment.

"You're bored?" she says incredulously. "You have two hands and a penis. This shouldn't be a difficult equation."

I turn around to leave. She can be a really lippy little monster when she's tired.

"Don't drool on my pillow."

"Too late."

⌖

Mom emerges from her office around two-thirty, eager-eyed and buzzing with energy. Work must be going well. She sees me folding clothes out of the dryer and says, "It's so nice that you're getting your energy back." She gives me a squeeze and a kiss on the cheek.

"I'm spring cleaning my office. Want to help?"

Spring cleaning Mom's office is like purging a bleached forest. She gets rid of all her drafts and incomplete sketches, fills two boxes with recycling, and finds about a hundred things she thought were lost. These newly found items tend to sidetrack her a lot. Eventually she forgets spring cleaning altogether and hunches over her drafting table, muttering something about girders.

I make myself at home in the corner with her shredder. It was my favorite non-toy when I was a kid, and still doesn't fail to amuse. I'm feeding pages through one at a time for the fun of it when Elise walks by the office door carrying a toy baton. She sees me looking and puts a finger to her lips.

"What?" I mouth. Elise points behind her and continues on to the end of the hall. I lean out the door to see what she was pointing at. Eric is asleep on the couch with the TV on.

Elise props the side door open with her old baton. She's got running shoes and a jacket on—Eric is about to get his comeuppance for waking her up this morning.

I look over my shoulder at Mom. She's still absorbed in her girders. Elise tiptoes down the hall, trying not to let her rubber soles squeak on the floor, and leans over Eric. She gets in real close and blows softly on his face. The breeze is just enough to disturb Eric. He wrinkles his nose in his sleep and swats a hand across his cheek. Elise keeps at it until he opens his eyes, and then she lurches into action.

"Facepalm!"

She brings her palm down on his forehead with a crack and runs like hell. The side door is the closest, so she sprints down the hallway. The door is already open—all she has to do is grab the baton on her way past and run as fast as she can for cover in woods behind our house.

"Shit." Eric rolls off the couch with a hand to his head, stumbling a little. He starts after Elise and I switch off the shredder.

It takes very precise timing, but I manage to throw Mom's swivel chair out into the hall at the exact moment Eric runs past. The collision in such a narrow hall sends him head over heels in the most impressive acrobatic display I've seen in a long time. He and the chair tumble to the floor with a crash and a few loud obscenities. Mom doesn't even look up.

"Turn that TV down," she says.

I dash out of the office and run in the opposite direction from Elise, toward the front door. Eric can only chase one of us. It seems like a great idea until I catch up to Elise in the driveway. She doubled-back around the house.

"What the hell are you doing?" I grab her by the back of her jacket and stuff her into the narrow space between the wall of the garage and the garbage cans. I hear the side door slam behind Eric and I take off toward the screen of trees. At least I know he's out for Elise's blood first, since he used the side door.

I'm at a disadvantage in the forest around our home. Eric is an avid hiker who knows the landmarks well, and I haven't been outdoors much since we moved here. I follow the grade of the land down toward the ravine and sit down in a little niche on the riverbank. The curve of the bank hides me well enough, and I need to rest after that run. Soon enough I'm going to regret not bringing a jacket.

The forest is peaceful, but I have a hard time appreciating it. The calls of birds make me jump and the way the branches rustle in the breeze makes me think I hear Eric coming to kick my ass. By the time I hear footsteps they're too close for me to make another run for it. I press my back further into the niche, hoping to hide.

Elise jumps off the bank and lands in front of me. The suddenness of her appearance startles me and I bump my head on an exposed root.

"Ow!"

"Shhh!" Elise puts a hand over my mouth. She's got a wicked grin on. "Have you seen Eric?"

"No."

Elise reaches into her pocket and pulls out Mom's car keys and Eric's wallet. "Want to go for ice cream?"

⚬

Elise gets a triple-scoop cone of chocolate, cotton candy and peanut butter ripple. What the hell, Eric's paying, right? I get plain vanilla and we take our cones back out to the car.

"Here's to a good last meal," Elise toasts. We 'clink' cones. It might very well be our last meal. I don't know what Eric will do to us for revenge, but I'm sure it will be memorable.

"Where'd you get the idea to do that, anyway?"

"Oh, I've been scheming over that one for awhile," she says. "I just needed the perfect opportunity." She smiles proudly and takes a big bite of ice cream.

Elise doesn't fully grasp the point of ice cream cones. She bites with her lips instead of licking them. I'm glad she's so inept, because that's one less way for her to flirt with that jock she's crushing on.

It's not safe to return to the house yet, so we discuss where to go next. Elise votes for the beach.

"Do you want to drive?" The roads are pretty quiet in Smiths Falls on a Sunday. Elise won't be eligible to renew her G1 license for another eight months, but I think she can handle a short drive to the beach. It's partly my fault that she lost her license, anyway.

"Really?"

"Yeah." I get out of the car and we switch sides. Elise has to adjust the driver's seat all the way forward to reach the pedals. I quiz her on all the signals before we even shift out of park, and it takes some fiddling with the mirrors before they're at the right angle for her.

"Okay, back out—*slowly*."

We make it out of the parking lot without incident. Elise is a little jerky on the brake, but she does okay. I coach her along the quietest route toward the beach road, down suburban streets and well-worn gravel roads. She stays almost fifteen km/h below the speed limit the whole way at my insistence, and I can tell it annoys her.

"I *can* drive the actual limit, you know."

"Not until you're legal to drive, you can't."

The parking lot at the beach is empty when we arrive. It's not exactly a nice day for swimming.

"I miss driving," she says as we get out of the car.

"That's what worries me."

I don't have a jacket, so I open the trunk and take out the emergency blanket Mom keeps there in case of breakdown during the winter. I fold it in half and wrap it around my shoulders for the walk down the beach.

Elise runs ahead a little bit, splashing in the shallow puddles that form in the dunes. Whenever she finds a flat rock she runs up to the surf to skip it. Her all-time record is eight skips on a single throw.

She throws another and we count the skips out loud, cheering it on. Only six this time. Elise starts hunting for another flat rock.

My phone buzzes in my pocket. Willa's volunteer shift must be over. I open my inbox to find: *Stay out of my thoughts, damn it. Do you have any idea how annoying it is to have you pop up in my head all day?*

Uh, and that's my fault? My first instinct is to do the polite thing and apologize, even though I have no control over the situation. Elise sees me looking at my phone and comes bounding over for a look.

"Aw, she's thinking about you," she coos. She got that out of Willa's scathing message?

Elise takes my phone and types a reply.

Sorry, but I like it in here. You'll just have to deal with it ;)

"Who the hell taught you how to flirt?"

Elise hands back my phone as she considers my question. "Prime time TV and Emily, I think."

Thank God she didn't say Ava.

My phone vibrates with Willa's reply and Elise practically tackles me in her eagerness to read it.

Don't answer this call. Let it go to voicemail.

My phone starts ringing a second later. Both Elise and I stand there and stare at the phone between us, like its ringing is somehow unusual or puzzling. It comes to the end of its ring cycle and a few minutes later I receive a voicemail alert.

"She left you a long message," Elise says.

Despite the blanket, I'm getting cold. I pocket my phone and we head back to the car, back to the house. We're barely out of the parking lot before Elise asks if she can listen to Willa's voicemail.

"No."

"You're going to show it to me anyway so I can make sense of it for you," she argues. She has a point, but I want to listen to it alone first.

"Please?"

"Fine, but if I tell you to shut it off, you shut it off, no questions asked."

"Deal."

Elise accesses my inbox while I drive and sets it to speakerphone so we can both hear.

"You have one unheard voice message…"

There's a click, followed by a blip of white noise, and then "One Step Closer" by Linkin Park starts blasting through my cell speaker. Elise looks from the phone to me and back again, questioning.

"Is this some sort of joke?"

No, this is Willa. This is Willa freaking out, just like Elise said she would.

The ball was in her court…

We listen as the song plays out in all is excruciating misery, waiting to see if Willa left a real message at the end of the track. She didn't. She hung up just before the last notes of the song.

"I don't think she's panicking," Elise says thoughtfully.

"You don't?"

"No. See at first I thought she was taking her time to consider, to mull things over, because of the whole cancer thing. And you're kind of an asshole, but this…"

"What?"

"This is her own personal junk. Hmmm." Elise taps my phone against her chin, pondering her hypothesis. She doesn't say anything for a whole minute and it's driving me insane.

"You can't just say shit like that and not follow it up with anything."

"Well, I don't know." Elise shrugs. "I don't think anyone can be so angry without first being angry at themselves. If she hates you she must hate herself way more."

"What are you, Gandhi?"

Elise sighs and sets my phone down in the cup holder. "Fine," she agrees with an Indian accent. "Ignore what I said. But if I'm right you owe me."

I wait a few hours to let Willa cool off. By eight o'clock I think it's safe to say she has probably vented into her cutting boards and saucepans and may even be in a talking mood.

I call her house line and Frank answers. He passes the phone off to his sister with a clipped, "The Harper boy's calling for you."

Willa's 'hello' is terse.

"Can you talk?" This isn't the kind of conversation most people want to have with the family lurking over their shoulder. Willa tells me to hang on, and for a few moments all I hear is footsteps and the quiet click of a door closing.

"Now I can. Did you get my message?"

"Is this what you normally do after a date goes well?"

"I'm certifiably nuts, you know."

"I believe it."

There's an awkward pause where she doesn't respond, and I don't know what else to say.

"Did you find something to do with your day?" she says.

"Yeah. Elise and I did some stuff."

"That's nice." It's an uncaring, trite answer. I feel like I'm talking to a distant relative to whom I have little to say.

"Why did you send me that song?"

"It seemed like an effective way to communicate my mindset."

"If you want me to leave you alone, just say it. Don't hide behind music and call that communication."

"Did I say I wanted you to leave me alone?"

"You didn't say anything."

"Well I don't want you to."

"Oh, thanks, *now* I understand."

"Harper," she says like she's clinging to her last shred of patience. "I'm really awful at describing how fucked up I am. You scare me. *I* scare me. I don't know what the fuck to do with you." She blows out a heavy sigh that echoes across the line.

"What do you want to do with me?"

"I don't know."

"But you do know that you want to send me cryptic messages with angry music and avoid me whenever something changes about our friendship."

"It's kind of my thing."

I want to kick something. "You're insane."

"I told you."

I consider ending the call, just hanging up and letting her sift through her thoughts a little more, but she interrupts me. "It's all screwed up," she says. "Something just works when I'm around you. And when I fight it, it *still fucking works.*"

"Is that so horrible?"

Willa makes a frustrated sound in her throat. "I hate you."

It's hard to believe that this is the same girl who invited me to keep kissing her on the porch last night. It must be absolute hell inside her head.

"Do you ever feel anything besides hate?" I ask.

It takes her a second to answer. "Yes," Willa says curtly. "Apathy." She hangs up on me. Wily bitch.

I call her right back and Willa answers on the first ring. "You know, when someone hangs up on you, it's because they don't want to talk to you anymore." The words sound vaguely familiar.

"Well too fucking bad. We're going to talk about this. You can't just avoid me whenever the hell you feel like it. You're making this more difficult than it has to be."

"No, Jem, it really is that difficult."

"Chicken."

"Shut up."

"No. I'm going to back you into a corner like you do me and hope you smarten up."

Willa huffs. "What do you want? Some touchy, feely, stream-of-consciousness monologue?"

"I want to know why you're on the edge and about the break." I will make her dissect that song line by line if that's what it takes to get to the root of the matter.

"Because you'll kill me if I don't kill you first."

Jesus Christ, not this again. This chick is obsessed with proverbial murder.

"You don't mean that."

"You have no idea," she whispers.

"I said I wouldn't suck you dry."

"And I actually believe you." Willa snorts as though she thinks she's an idiot to take me at my word.

"So why—"

"Let me sleep on it."

"You're just going to keep panicking until you deal with this."

"You want me to deal with it right this second?" she says like she's answering a challenge. She's absolutely wicked when she's in a stubborn mood. "Here's dealing with it: I swore off a lot of shit when I moved here, and that included guys. You're the first guy whose last name I knew *before* I kissed him. You're the first one I've even thought about when you're not around. You do not bode well for my attempt at self-improvement and I'm losing the capacity to give a shit about that."

This is the first time Willa has ever volunteered information about her regular day-to-day life in St. John's, and I don't know what to make of it.

"How come you never talk about Newfoundland?" I ask. "You talk about your family there, but…"

"Why the hell would I want to revisit that place, even to talk about it?"

"So that other people can know you."

"I am not the place I come from, regardless of what went on there."

"*Who* you come from doesn't sound so fulfilling."

"What the fuck do you know?"

"Nothing. You won't tell me."

"I will. Someday. And then you can hate me, too."

"Stop hating yourself."

"Stop punishing yourself for having cancer," she retorts.

I open my mouth to rejoin but nothing comes out. I have absolutely nothing to say to that. I don't even know if she's right or wrong.

Finally I say, "No I don't." Even I'm not convinced by that denial.

"Yes you do," Willa argues tiredly. "You do it all the time. You walk around acting like you're so damn unworthy of whatever nice thing people do for you at school. You get all pissy whenever Elise attempts to have her own life, even though you readily ditch her to go live your own, and then you spew guilt all over the place trying to make it up to her."

"Elise has nothing to do with—"

"Yes she does. You punish yourself with guilt that you needed to use her to achieve your own health."

I sit there with the phone pressed to my ear, gaping. Her forwardness doesn't surprise me—when has she ever held back on the snark?—it's the fact that she's right.

"That's between me and Elise." I intended to say it firmly, but the words come out meek and muted.

"Fine."

"But you do hate yourself."

"That's between me and myself."

I hate how she can twist words like that.

"I'm coming over."

"What?"

"I'll be there in twenty." I hang up before she can argue and head downstairs to borrow Mom's car.

Nine o'clock isn't exactly a typical hour for a social visit. Frank looks at me like I should know better when he answers the door.

"Something I can help you with?"

"May I please come in and speak to Willa?"

Frank looks as if he's about to say no and perhaps give me a stern lecture.

"Let him in."

"Will, it's a school night."

"He won't be long."

Frank grudgingly steps aside and lets me over the threshold. Willa stands above us, halfway down the stairs. She has that apathetic look in her eye; the one that makes me feel like she can see right through me.

Willa gestures with a nod. "Come up."

Willa closes her bedroom door behind us and invites me to sit wherever. I stand.

"I'm not leaving until you talk," I tell her gently.

"About what?"

"You know what."

Willa grimaces and folds her arms over her chest. She leans back against her door and gnaws on the inside of her cheek.

"Relax, you're not on trial for murder."

"Shut up," she snaps. "Don't fucking belittle me."

My first impulse is to return her sudden aggression with more of the same, but I've learned what taking her bait leads to. She always wins. She always finds a way. So I don't play along.

"What spooked you this time?" It's a simple question and hard to avoid, stated plainly like that.

"You did."

"How?"

"You just did."

"Are you sure it was me?" I went out of my way to treat her well last night. I let her have her space today when she asked for it. It was a gamble to kiss her, but she gave every impression that she liked it.

Willa huffs. "No."

"If I told you to say what was on your mind, would you?" I add a sarcastic tilt of the eyebrow. My tone irritates her and she latches onto the bait.

"I might actually like you," she retorts. "There. Fucking happy?"

Uh...ecstatic.

I start to smile and then scale it back. I don't want her to think I'm somehow amused by her confession.

"That's what's got you all riled up?"

"Yeah." She frowns bitterly and bites her cheek again. It's like she's mad at

262

herself for feeling something beyond hate and apathy—or for blurting it out like that.

Or because she knows it's a bad idea.

You knew it was a long shot she'd ever want you.

Last night on the porch was a fluke.

Can't blame her for not wanting you. You don't even want you.

"I can see how that might be…upsetting."

Willa's gaze snaps up from the floor to meet mine and her eyes flash with that familiar anger.

"I mean, I get it. I know I'm not…a desirable option." I shrug lamely. "And you didn't know me before I got sick…or maybe that's a good thing."

Willa takes her weight off the door and drops her arms. Her hands curl into fists and she actually trembles while snarling at me, "That is the stupidest fucking thing I've ever heard."

"No it's not. I was different before—"

"Shut up."

She leaves the door and marches over to her dresser. Willa reaches into the back of her top drawer and pulls out a crumpled pack of cigarettes. "Don't tell Frank," she says as she opens the window to vent the smoke.

"You're going to stand there and smoke in front of a cancer patient?"

Willa lights up without hesitation. She's done this before.

"You know, just because you have cancer all through you doesn't mean you quit craving these." She holds up the lit cigarette. "I used to drive Tessa to the store to buy smokes. Mom and Dad wouldn't anymore, but it calmed her. It calms me."

"You helped her buy cigarettes when she had cancer? Isn't that a little irresponsible?"

"You say that like you don't know what desperation feels like. I'm sure you've asked your family for all kinds of shit."

I hate it when she's completely right about me without knowing a single detail. They've all made sacrifices for me, but none of them are angry like Willa. None of them had their investment go bust like she did.

"This was her last pack. She never finished it." Willa holds open the box top and counts the remaining cigarettes. "About a week after she died, I smoked so many I made myself puke."

"So why'd you do it?"

"It's a hell of a way to remind yourself that you're still breathing."

I scrub my hands over my face, trying to find a scrap of reason to hold on to. It's like talking in circles with her. Any attempt to direct the conversation just gets me more lost.

"I wish I'd known you before all this stuff happened to you." She looked like such a happy kid in the pictures I've seen. She was probably a really sweet girl once.

Willa stubs out the remains of her cigarette and tosses the butt out the window. "And would you know me as you are now," she asks levelly, "or as the guy you were before cancer?"

It's a trick question. I'm sure of it.

"Before. We could have been normal friends." Now all I do is make her angry and miserable.

"Bullshit. I would have hated you before."

I'm pretty sure she hates you now, too.

"You don't know that. You didn't meet me until I was half-dead," I snap.

"And the other you was better?"

"Yes." He was whole.

"Well what the *fuck*," she shouts, "was so special about him that he's worth hanging onto? He didn't survive this, so why are you still kicking at his corpse and yelling at him to wake up?"

Willa's bedroom door opens and Frank steps in. "What's all the yelling about?"

Willa hangs her head, shaking it slightly. "Nothing. Absolutely nothing."

"Why does it smell like smoke in here?" Frank eyes his sister and points a commanding finger at her. "You said you were going to stop this crap, Will."

"I am." She reaches back to shut the window. "That was my last one." There's half a pack left in her back pocket.

Frank turns to me. "I think you should go. That's quite enough excitement for one night." I bet he thinks I'm a bad influence. Like I'd encourage her to inhale carcinogens after all I've been through. I wouldn't wish that kind of hell on anybody—not even Elwood, and that's saying something.

My phone buzzes in my pocket during the drive home. I immediately pull over, hoping it's Willa and that we can finally get to the bottom of this. But it's not Willa. It's a text message from Elise: *Got a bad feeling. Prepping mango shakes in advance.*

I lean forward and thump my head against the steering wheel. Damn it all to hell.

Monday

Willa doesn't look entirely pleased to find me at her locker when she arrives at school, but she doesn't look angry either. She wears an expression I've never seen before—is it nerves?

"Good morning." I speak softly, as though she's an unfamiliar animal I'm trying not to spook.

"G'morning."

"Are we still on for Wednesday?"

She considers that for a moment. "Yeah," she says. "We are."

"About last night…"

"I'm sorry Frank kicked you out."

"Don't worry about it." I bury my hands in my pockets. "You really should stop hating yourself so much, though."

"Haven't you ever made a mistake you can hardly stand to live with?"

Her question blindsides me with its strangeness. It's an oddly personal question for Willa. I stand there mulling that over for a few seconds before it occurs to me that it was a genuine question and Willa expects an answer. I don't have one.

"What was yours?" I ask. She wouldn't have said that unless she had a regrettable mistake on her mind.

Willa closes her locker and says she has to get to class.

I can't ask Willa what her mistake was. She's already dodged the question once, and if I keep picking at it she'll snap. I just need a bit of patience—she'll tell me eventually. It might be years from now, but that's fine; I intend to keep her around for a while.

I slide a note her way in Soc: *Want to come over for dinner tonight?*

Can't. I have my first shift 4-8.

Fuck Chris Elwood straight to hell. I hope his asshole is as wide as Texas by the time Satan gets bored with him.

Willa passes me another note. It's directions for Wednesday. It is sort of comforting to think that Willa is going to spend time with Elwood because she has to. She spends time with me because she *wants* to. Hard to believe, I know, but I'm glad nonetheless.

I slide another note her way: *Bring pepper spray to work.*

You worry too much.

I prefer to believe that paranoia is just a healthy understanding of the nature of the universe, thank you very much.

I spend the bulk of my afternoon with my cello. It's still a far cry from the marathon practice sessions I used to do regularly before I got sick, but it's progress. I practice until my knuckles bleed and show up to dinner with Band-Aids all over my hands.

"Oh, honey, take more breaks next time," Mom says when she sees all the bandages. I agree to make her feel better, and when supper is over I retire to my room for a nap. It's more tiring than it looks to play cello for three hours straight.

I wake up feeling utterly content, even before I open my eyes. I smile and sigh, and then I realize that my pillow is breathing. I open my eyes to find my cheek resting against the curve between Willa's ribs and hip. When did she get here? My arm has made its way around her waist, holding her close. She has her iPod in her right hand and the other resting against my back.

"Are you awake for real this time?" she asks.

Oh God. What does that mean? I look up at her where she leans against the headboard and blink the sleep away from my eyes.

"Was I awake before?"

"When you rolled over to put your head there you very distinctly said 'pizza.'" She chuckles while my face goes red. She hasn't told me to move yet. Should I?

"Do you need anything? Water?"

Sometimes it's bloody inconvenient how well she knows my needs—like when I would rather let those needs go hang just to keep her close.

"It can wait."

"Don't suffer," she says, and slips away from me. I resist the urge to grab the hem of her shirt and pull her back to me, but this bed feels empty when she's gone. I pick up her iPod in her absence and select her playlists. What else has Miss Enigmatic been listening to this week?

I stare at the little screen, perplexed. Her playlists are all titled with guys' names: Gary, Chris, Luke, Jem, Cody, Joey, Brian, and Frank. The one titled 'Mom' stands out. Frank is obviously her brother. I know who Luke and Chris are, but not why they have playlists named after them. And Cody? Cody the twit who asked Willa to the grad dance? Joey is Joey Moore, the guitar-playing kid she sits with at lunch. I'm not sure who Brian and Gary could be. At the bottom of the list she has a file labeled *St. John's*. I open it and find a cluster of three more playlists: Steve, Candice, and Darryn.

I go back to the main list and select the playlist she has named after me. A lot of the track titles I recognize from our bedtime music exchanges. Some I don't know. Few of them are happy songs, though. Just for comparison's sake, I look at Chris and Luke's playlists. The songs in Chris's are all over the map, but Luke has a lot of top forties.

Willa comes back with a cup of water and I return to the main playlist page.

"The hell, Kirk?" I hold up the iPod and she accepts it curiously.

"What? I organize my songs by who they remind me of."

"Who's Gary?"

"My dad."

"Why do you have a playlist named after Cody?"

"He made quite an impression."

God damn it.

Willa pokes my lip. "Don't pout."

I gently bite her finger, holding it between my teeth while she tries to pull away. It makes her smile.

"Quit trying to eat me and drink your water."

I let her go and thank her for the drink. Willa settles in while I sip it. She lays down next to me this time instead of sitting against the headboard.

"How was your first shift?" I set the glass aside and roll back to her.

Willa shrugs. "The job is pretty straightforward. Mrs. Elwood is nice. Chris is…"

"Chris."

"Yeah."

She doesn't say anything about the hand I rest across her stomach.

"Did you come over here right after?"

"Yeah."

"I'm sorry I wasn't awake to greet you."

"It's alright. I like watching you sleep."

I sit up on my elbow so I can see her face better. "Did I really say 'pizza'?"

"Yeah. You must have heard me giggle, too, because you followed that up with 'Olives. Don't let that fucker have any.'" She giggles again and I lower myself down from my elbow, lying much closer to her this time.

"I must have been talking about Eric. He hates olives."

"Is that so?"

I give Willa a squeeze. "Thanks for coming over. You really do cheer me up."

Willa knits her fingers with the ones I have wrapped around her side. "I had a motive, you know."

"Hmmm?"

Please let it be a good one.

"I'm a little embarrassed about how I freaked out on Sunday. It wasn't you—something my brother said made me think, and I psyched myself out. I shouldn't have taken it all out on you."

I give her hand a friendly squeeze. "Thanks."

"I'm sorry I shouted at you. And about the phone message. And hanging up on you. And the smoking. Fucking-A, why the hell are you still friends with me?"

That makes me snort. "You have a certain charm, believe it or not. That, and you feed me."

"Seriously, though, I am sorry for all that."

"Apology accepted."

Willa rubs her thumb along my palm, careful of the bandages. She doesn't ask what happened but wants to know if it hurts.

"Not much. It's just small cuts."

"You have beautiful fingers," she says. Her voice is far away, like she's talking to herself.

"Did you mean it when you said you liked me?"

"Yeah." The corner of her mouth twitches up in an approximation of a smile. "I guess I do."

"I guess I like you too." I give her another squeeze. "Do you want to may-be…?"

"What?"

"I dunno. Date?"

"You mean, do the couple thing?"

"Yeah."

"Like, call each other boyfriend/girlfriend and stuff?"

"The two generally go hand in hand, yes." I wonder too late if that was a bad choice of phrase.

Willa wrinkles her nose. "How about we agree just to see each other?"

It's difficult not to let my disappointment show. I try to appreciate her reluctance, but the result is still the same. Her acceptance comes twinned with rejection, and as good as the former feels, the latter stings in sensitive spots.

"That's all you want right now?"

"Yeah." Willa sighs with what sounds like regret.

"Don't promise me anything."

"I don't want to promise you nothing, either." She turns her head to look at me. "I do like you. I'm just not good at this stuff."

I tighten my fingers around her side. "We'll go slow, if that's what you want."

"What I want and what I can stand aren't always the same thing."

I have no idea what she means by that, and I have a feeling she wouldn't explain even if I asked.

"So…seeing each other?"

"Agreed."

I lean over to kiss her and Willa dips her head to the side, giving me easier access to her mouth. It feels good to know that she enjoys kissing me. She even wraps an arm around my side, mirroring the way I hold her. I move in to deepen the kiss and she pulls away.

"Too much."

"Sorry."

"Not your fault." She gives me another peck on the lips and then rolls away to sit up. "I should go."

"Are you sure?"

"Yeah." She straightens her shirt around her torso and picks up her bag. I get out of bed to walk her to the door and she grimaces like she finds this painful.

"You're not running away, are you?"

"Only a little," she says quietly. Willa reaches for the doorknob and I grab her arm.

"So stay."

"It's almost nine. It's a school night."

"You're rationalizing."

"And it's working."

I fold her into a hug and she sighs softly. She won't give up on leaving, but that doesn't mean I'm going to let her go without a proper goodbye.

"I'll walk you out."

Elise yells, "Bye Willa!" as we cross the front room. Mom calls out a farewell from the kitchen.

"I'll see you at school tomorrow." I open the door for her as she shrugs into her jacket.

"Yeah, school."

Willa grabs me by the front of my shirt as she steps through the door and tows me out with her. The door is barely closed behind us before she pushes me up against the wall and kisses me. And it is an entirely different kind of kiss from the one she pulled away from upstairs—it's rough and deep enough to drown in. Her hands are everywhere, grabbing at my sides and shoulders like she can't get close enough. I understand the feeling perfectly and pull her just as close. God, she feels good.

Willa pulls away just a suddenly as she jumped me. "I'm sorry," she breathes.

"For what?" I would be embarrassed by my breathless state, but I can't find the will to care just now.

Willa wipes her lips on the back of her hand. "That I'm so fucked up." She turns around and dashes down the front steps. I watch her drive away while I collect my breath. She waves from the end of the driveway.

Holy shit.

I turn to go back inside with a smile on my face. When I open the front door, a flashbulb promptly blinds me.

"Ha!" Elise cheers, and pulls the Polaroid out of the dispenser. "Your face was perfect."

"What the hell do you think you're doing?"

Elise makes kissy noises at me and fans herself with the Polaroid. God damn it. Elise turns on her heel and skips down the hall toward the kitchen.

"Mom! Guess what Jem just did!"

Hell no.

I race after Elise and clamp a hand over her big fat mouth. My other arm locks around her waist, holding her while she struggles.

"What?" Mom asks.

"Nothing!"

She comes to the kitchen door to investigate the scuffling sounds and finds me holding Elise hostage. Great. I hardly look innocent now.

"What's going on?"

Elise tries to say, "He kissed Willa," but the words are unintelligible from behind my hand.

"Let her go, Jem."

No sooner have I released Elise than the words explode from her mouth.

"When?"

"On the porch, just now."

"With Willa?"

"That's what I said."

"I can hear you, you know," I snap at them.

Mom and Elise both look up as though they're surprised to find me here.

"I didn't know you were dating," Mom says. A smile slowly creeps onto her face. She likes Willa, probably because she hardly knows her.

"We're not. It's complicated."

"These things have a way of working themselves out." Mom pats my cheek. "It's about time good things started coming your way."

Elise smugly inspects her newly developed Polaroid. I try to snatch it from her and she shoves it down her bra. God damn it.

Tuesday

I pack up my homework and a magazine for the long wait at the clinic. Part of me wishes that Willa was volunteering tonight so there would be a chance that we'd run into each other. Or better yet, that she would choose to visit and keep me company during the session.

I wonder what she's doing tonight...

Elise flings my door open without knocking and says, "Does this top work with these shoes?" Ugh, why couldn't she have picked Eric to single out as her pseudo-sister?

"I don't know. They're both...nice?"

"I'll wear my purple sweater instead." She turns to go and I call her back.

"Where are you going?"

"To the movies with some friends." Her answer makes me suspicious. Why didn't she just say Carey?

"Who?"

"Kipp and Nina and one of their friends."

"Like a double date?"

"No, their friend is a girl."

"You're sure he doesn't still think you're a lesbian, right?"

Elise rolls her eyes at me.

"You should quit chasing him, Lise," I tell her seriously. "You know it's not a good situation—he's dating someone else *and* leaving Smiths Falls in a few months for college. You're setting yourself up for pain."

"I'm not 'chasing him' anymore," Elise says indignantly. "We're friends. That's it."

"And you're okay with that?"

She smiles and nods. "Yeah. A lot can happen when you're away at college." She winks. She isn't 'just friends' with him, she's biding her time.

"I think you're going to be stuck standing around waiting until he's married to this chick with the 2.5 kids and the picket fence."

"A lot can happen in a few years—to both of us."

I hate it when her bad ideas are logically sound.

"Be careful."

"I will." She drums a quick beat on my doorframe and spins away with a little hop. "Besides, you know how good I am at bouncing back."

That she is, quite unfortunately—it gives her zero motivation to stop dropping her own heart off high places. The day will come, though, when she falls too hard to bounce. I'm dreading it.

Wednesday

I go out onto the porch to wait for Willa after school. It's a gorgeous day out. The sun is shining and it's so warm that I probably won't need my sweater the whole time we're out. Slung over my shoulder is a messenger bag full of Willa's suggestions: two Jell-O cups, a spoon, and enough medication to tide me over for at least six hours. When she told me that last one I was excited that she wanted so much time with me today.

Willa's car rumbles up the driveway at three-thirty sharp. She's got the windows rolled down and a smile on her face.

"Is it as good as St. John's?" I ask her as I climb into the passenger seat. Willa leans out her window and pretends to consider the sun.

"It's a tie." She waves to Mom in the front window and backs out of the driveway.

"So where are we going?"

"It's a surprise."

Willa is in her scruffy weekend outfit, so we're probably not going out in public. She told me to wear old clothes and beat up shoes, too.

Willa sighs and adjusts her sunglasses on her nose. "Days like this, I miss my other wheels. I had to leave Kyla in St. John's to move here."

"You named your car Kyla?"

"So? I bet you've named your dick," she says. "And Kyla's a bike."

I snort. "I guess this rusty shitbox is a step up from peddle-power in Newfoundland weather."

"A *motorbike*. And summers there are nice. Winter doesn't last forever."

I try to picture Willa on a motorbike. It looks something like Audrey Hepburn in *Roman Holiday*. "So what, you had some cute little moped?"

"No," she says with disgust. "She's a red Harley Davidson Xr1200 Sportster. Tessa left it to me in her will."

"And your parents let you keep it?" Most parents have better priorities set for their children, like not getting smeared across the highway.

"They wanted me to sell it, but I refused."

I try to picture Willa on a proper motorcycle, cruising down the highway with her hair a mess behind her. I mean, come on, how many teenage girls drive motorcycles as their primary means of transportation? I imagine her pulling into the school parking lot every day; guys were probably drooling over her bike, if not her.

"You know, you're kind of a badass," I tell her.

Willa scoffs. "Please, if I had balls they'd be bigger than yours."

Willa turns off the pavement and onto a secluded dirt road. We creep along that for a while until the road abruptly ends, and for some reason Willa decides that this would be a good time to get out of the car.

"Did you take the wrong road?"

"No." She grabs an overstuffed backpack out of the trunk. "We're going to hike a ways. I've got water. I assume you brought your Jell-O."

"Yeah, but…"

"We won't walk far." She squeezes my elbow. "And we've got all afternoon. We can go as slow as you want."

⊕

Our timing is perfect—sort of. By four it's still warm enough that the worst of the bugs have retreated, and Willa and I pass through the woods relatively unmolested. Within ten minutes of hiking I take my jacket off and tie it around my waist. I hesitate to do it, but eventually I push my long sleeves up too. Willa has already seen and touched my arms. She knows what they look like.

Willa calls a break after half an hour and fishes two water bottles out of her backpack.

"Are you doing okay?" she asks as I sip. Her fingers wrap gently around my free wrist. I would think she was just being nice and maybe even a little flirty to touch me like that, but I know it's really a subtle way of feeling my pulse.

I lift my hand and rest two fingers against her neck. "I'm fine." Her heart is racing. But she's not even winded. What the—?

Willa smirks and takes my hand off her neck. She doesn't let go, though. She keeps a loose hold on my fingers and starts walking again.

I adjust my hand to hold hers properly.

Willa measures our trek in half-hours, though that's no way to track distance. The longer we walk, the slower my pace becomes. It's hot and I wish I hadn't worn a black wool hat.

Willa notices that I'm struggling and puts an arm around my back, lending me her shoulder. I would be embarrassed if this wasn't a great opportunity to put my arm around her. I indulge my imagination in the idea of the two of us as a real couple, out for a leisurely hike…and getting touchy. Variations of this scenario occupied my thoughts before Willa picked me up today. I even patched my Hickman up in case things got…interesting.

Willa steers us over to a fallen log and makes me sit down.

"Is it the heat?" she says. She crouches in front of me and opens her backpack to dig for more water.

"Among other things."

"Anything I can do?"

"Just give me a few minutes."

Willa asks if I have an undershirt beneath my tee. I tell her I'm not going to take my shirt off.

"Well the wool hat can't be helping. Leave it off for a while."

"No."

"It's not like—"

"*No.*"

Willa swallows whatever she was about to say. "Walk behind me," she suggests quietly. "I won't look."

"Please stop."

Willa sits back on her bottom and hangs her forearms over bent knees. "Okay. Your call."

We stay by the log for fifteen minutes—long enough for me to eat a Jell-O cup to keep my sugars up. Willa sips at her water bottle, saying nothing. I take one of the hands that hangs over her knee and she doesn't pull away.

"How far are we from where we're going?"

"Not far now. Maybe another twenty minutes at our slowest pace."

I wonder if she knows how much it means that she said 'our' slowest pace, not mine.

"That far?"

"Don't quit on me now, Harper," she teases.

"I won't." I squeeze her hand and she actually smiles. I didn't know she had it in her to be this welcoming. This…happy.

I lean in to kiss her and she pulls away slightly. I'm left hanging there, bent over and lips parted for a kiss that isn't coming.

"I'm doing the best I can," she says. At least her tone is apologetic. I still feel like an idiot.

I sit back up and clear my throat. "Sorry. I should have, uh…"

"Kept walking? Yeah, good idea." Willa stands abruptly and shoulders her backpack.

So much for that.

But she still lets me hold her hand.

"Almost there."

Somewhere nearby I can hear a creek. "Where are we going?"

"You'll see."

The trees break off suddenly, opening into sloping beach beside the creek. It's sudden appearance surprises me and Willa's hand slips from mine as she continues walking.

"Frank used to take me here when I was little. There used to be trees all the way up to the bend," she points to where the creek winds away from sight, "but there was a fire here a few years ago—lightning strike on a pine. So now it's all sand and dirt."

I look around at the gap in the trees, at the dark brown sand and river-smoothed pebbles. It's beautiful, but I can't shake the thought that this place is one giant scar.

Willa stops and turns to me with a curious expression. "You coming? I brought us a little picnic."

⌒

It's amazing how much Willa managed to fit in her backpack. An old bed sheet is our picnic blanket. To drink she brought two bottles of orange and mint iced tea, and the 'food' fits in three thermoses. Willa laughs at my enthusiasm as I open each one and smell the contents. One is vegetable soup, the second is the sweet milkshake she left in my fridge on Elise's birthday, and the third smells like raspberries.

"Appetizer, entrée and dessert," she says proudly.

"This is great. So what are you eating?"

Willa nudges my shoulder. "You're going to learn to share."

I shake my head and reach for a spoon. "No way. I flunked that shit in pre-school and it's too late to learn now."

Willa takes the cup lids from each thermos and pours one-third helpings out for herself. I can't eat as much as she's left me in the thermoses. I tell her so and she tells me to just shut up and eat. The soups and shakes aren't a smooth puree. Willa left chunks in these. She trusts me to handle solids now.

We eat slowly, languidly, talking about school and family and crap TV. She's easily amused by stories about Elise and Eric. I tell her about the time Elise crawled into the dishwasher as a toddler, just to explore, and the spring-lock door shut behind her. We didn't find her for a whole hour.

"Was she scared?"

"She didn't want to come out when we did find her."

Then there was the time Eric and I found a dead raccoon in the backyard and carried it inside, swinging it around by the tail.

"I once gave a cat a haircut," Willa volunteers.

"Was your mom mad?"

She smirks. "It wasn't our cat." She tells me the story as she packs up the empty thermoses—how she lured the cat onto her lap with leftover bacon bits and proceeded to cut big patches of hair off its back with her mom's pruning

274

sheers.

"It seemed like a good idea at the time. I was only five."

Willa puts the thermoses away and zips up her backpack. I don't want to leave yet. I lay back on the blanket and fold my hands behind my head.

"This would be a great spot to stargaze."

"You're into that?"

Actually I think it's dorky and cheesy, but it also has the potential to be a romantic activity. I tug gently on Willa's shirtsleeve to get her to lay down next to me.

"We should come here at night sometime."

"Maybe this summer."

I can hear the real meaning underneath the words: *When you're well enough to do it.*

"During the grad dance."

"What?"

"We said we'd make plans the night of the grad dance, remember? Let's come here."

"Thanks."

"Sure."

"No, I mean, thanks for not trying to talk me into going to grad with you instead, since we're...seeing each other now."

I've never been one for school dances. I wouldn't want to attend prom, but if Willa did, I'm sure I could muster the enthusiasm to go with her.

"I won't be graduating this year." I think it's obvious by this point, but it still warrants saying.

"Me neither," Willa says. That surprises me. She's a good student. How can she be short on credits?

Willa looks over at me and sits up on her elbow. "You have a beetle on your hat." She pinches it between her thumb and forefinger and lifts it away. Its little legs flail in the air until she sets it down beyond the edge of the blanket. Cool a girl who isn't totally freaked out by bugs.

Willa brushes the spot on my hat, dislodging a few blades of grass from the black wool. She smirks.

"You know, before I knew your real hair color I pictured you with black hair, like Elise and Eric." It's both pleasing and disheartening to know that she pictured me as being healthy. Pleasing because I'm flattered she cares so much, and disheartening because the mental picture is probably a lot nicer than the reality of my appearance.

I shake my head. "No. I got all the recessive genes. Eric used to tell people that I was adopted."

"It must have been hard on your parents when you were born a ginger," she teases me. "But at least they had Eric—one normal child." She laughs and I tell her that Eric can hardly be considered normal.

"He's obnoxious at best."

"And what are you?"

"Charming?" I roll onto my side and put an arm over her waist. "Interesting? Witty?"

"You're an idiot."

Willa rolls over too—away from me. For a moment I think she's turning cold, but then she takes my wrist and adjusts my arm around her waist. She scoots back until we're practically spooning. I have to say, snuggling in the open feels damn good. It absolutely tickles me to think of all the guys who only wish they could do this with her.

"Do you think you'll ever want to make it official?"

"Make what official?"

"You know, do the whole boyfriend/girlfriend thing with me."

"I've never had an exclusive boyfriend," she muses aloud. I don't know whose benefit she's saying that for.

I fiddle with one of the buttons on her shirt. "I wouldn't be enough for you?"

She deserves someone who doesn't exist in pieces. I wouldn't be anyone's first pick, least of all hers. She can do better than me and she knows it.

"I didn't say that. I just said exclusivity would be a new thing for me."

"Is there someone else?"

"Not necessarily."

"If I wasn't sick...?"

"Don't." Willa rolls over slowly and sits up on her elbow, studying me. "I care a lot less about the fact that you had cancer than you probably think."

"You should care—"

Willa lays her finger over my lips, cutting me off. "Don't project your self-loathing onto me. I wouldn't have called you beautiful if I didn't mean it."

I take her hand away from my mouth. "This isn't some...I don't know, fetish, is it? You're always saying how beautiful your sister was when she went bald. Are you just, like...*into* cancer patients or something?"

Willa smirks. She gives a short, unintentional snort, which breaks into a full-blown laugh. I feel ridiculous.

"I'm into you," she says. "But you're not just a cancer patient. And no, it's not a bald fetish. Empowered people are beautiful."

"I'm not *empowered*." I'm totally pathetic.

"You're stronger than I'll ever be. You're close to your demons, and that's a hard thing to find in a person, especially at our age." Willa leans forward on her elbow and kisses me softly. When she starts to pull away I lean in for more.

Willa puts a hand on my collarbone to keep me back. "But I still intend to kill you."

I roll my eyes. "Enough with that, okay?"

"Nope."

"Well then get on with it so I can kiss you again."

276

Willa has a little chuckle at that. "I am killing you," she announces with a kind smile. "You're bleeding to death and you don't even realize it."

I can't tell if she's joking or speaking in metaphors or just delusional, but her words take me back to a cold, frightening place. I really did come close to bleeding to death—twice.

"That's not funny."

"Wasn't meant to be." Willa's hand leaves my collarbone to stroke my cheek. "Where did you go just now? You looked scared."

"Nowhere."

"Whatever."

"Tell me what you meant by that."

"Tell me what kind of cancer you had," she returns. It's a guaranteed stalemate of things neither of us wants to tell.

"I told you it doesn't matter. I don't have it any more."

"It could still kill you faster than I ever could."

I move her hand away from me. "You're a little messed up, you know." Who says shit like that to someone so lately in remission?

"Yes." Willa stands up and shakes her limbs out, dislodging stray blades of grass. "You want to know how messed up?" she says as she stretches her arms over her head.

"Probably not."

She chuckles darkly. "Trust's a scary thing like that. Not to have it and want it drives you crazy. To have it and not want it will cost you."

I'm not entirely sure I understand what she means. I sit up on my elbows and study her face. She looks so relaxed.

"Do you trust me?" she asks.

"Maybe."

"I know you want me to trust you. The surprises. All this give-and-take philosophy. The one-on-one time at lunch, and making me talk to you when I get my head all caught up in thinking." She shakes her head and smiles. "You sure you want all that? I've got weighty baggage."

"I do too."

"But you don't trust me with it."

Willa crouches down to be eye-level with me again. She grabs me by the side of the neck and holds my head against hers, cheek-to-cheek and temple-to-temple. I put my hand around the side of her neck and hold her just as close.

"What's your deepest, darkest secret?" she whispers.

That I prayed for Elise to die.

I can't tell Willa that. I can't tell anyone that. But I know the secret she really wants to hear—the one she's been asking about for months. I angle my head just slightly to whisper directly into her ear.

"Acute myeloid leukemia."

"Damn," she says lowly. "That was my second guess." The fact that she had a list is annoying as all hell.

Her turn to put herself out there. "What's your secret?"

Willa presses her lips against the spot in front of my ear. "I killed Tessa."

Willa: May 3 to 7

Wednesday

I pull back from our mutual headlock to find Jem wide-eyed and confused. "Don't tell me you thought you were the only one who had dark shit hidden away?"

"You mean you…?" He leaves he question hanging and cocks his head, gaping at me. Then he starts to pull away. "You helped her OD?"

"Yes."

Jem shakes his head stubbornly. "Bullshit. You'd be in jail now if that were true."

"You have to get caught to get punished."

"You fucking *lied about it too?*"

I wonder if he can hear how loud his voice is. Jem stands up and walks around aimlessly, rubbing the back of his neck.

"I don't understand."

"She asked me for help. You ought to know how little privacy the sick have—I hoarded the spare pills in my room. There was medication all over the house. Every second day I stole one of her painkillers out of the bottle. I had a little bundle of them in one of her antique handkerchiefs, tucked under my bed."

Jem starts to slowly shake his head like he knows where this is going.

"We talked about it a lot beforehand. Mom and Dad didn't want to talk about the possibility that she could die, but some things *have* to be said. I used to drive her to appointments whenever she was fighting with our parents and didn't want them around."

Jem is still pacing restlessly. I throw a dirt clod at him. "Will you stand still and listen?"

"What if I don't want to?"

"You think I care what you want? You think *anybody* cares what other people want in this world?"

Jem gives me a dirty look. "If she *wanted* to die peacefully she should have gone to a hospice, not home. Haven't you ever heard of snowing a patient?"

"It wasn't my idea," I tell him through clenched teeth. "You think I had a vote in this shit? I was sixteen, for fuck's sake."

"Old enough to know better."

I smile to keep from biting the inside of my cheek. "You know you've considered a contingency plan too. And if Elise was the sick one, you'd have done the same as me had she asked. Tessa had lymphoma, and then it showed up in her liver and small intestine. Would you have taken those odds?"

Jem stares at me blankly for a few seconds. He turns away very carefully with a pinched look on his face and holds up a hand as if to say 'quiet.' Jem vomits on the tall grass. I get up and pass him a bottle of water.

"Don't fucking say anything," he tells me. He rinses his mouth and asks me to go back to the blanket. I just sit there and wait, watching him stand with his hands on his knees, slowly getting a grip on himself.

When Jem finally stands upright his attitude toward me has gone from hostile to cold. "Did she die quickly? Peacefully? Was she even conscious?"

"Do you really want to hear this?"

"Answer the fucking question."

I blow out my frustration on a long breath and consider refusing to say any more. I want to say it, though. This is the first time I've admitted the true events out loud. My parents always suspected, of course, but I always denied everything.

"Right before dinnertime she started bleeding in her gut. Mom was in the room with her—there was blood and diarrhea all over the bed." Jem looks a little green at that and swallows with difficulty. "I stopped making dinner and helped carry her to the bathroom while Mom stripped the bed. Put her in the bath. Washed her."

Jem very carefully sits down on the beach. He looks a little clammy, but he's still too upset to even share a picnic blanket with me.

"After I got her clean her stomach was still upset, so I put her on the toilet. She asked for the pills. Mom was going to insist that she go back to the hospital because of the bleeding. Tessa didn't want to go back. She was ready to be done."

Jem is slowly shaking his head again.

"I gave her the bundle of pills and took another bottle out of the bathroom cabinet. There was enough between the two. I gave her water. Helped her swallow. She was in pain and shaking too badly to hold her own cup or put the pills on her tongue."

Jem hangs his head in his hands. He knows exactly the kind of pain I'm talking about.

"Tessa didn't want me to watch, and she was worried about me getting in trouble. She told me to go back to the kitchen as soon as we said goodbye. It would look like she died from the bleeding.

"So I left her there. Mom tried to go into the bathroom and I said, 'Give her a little dignity,' and suggested calling her doctor."

Jem finally interrupts. "You could have let your mother say goodbye."

"If she wanted to she could have said it any time in the last year, or when Tessa refused treatment."

"You're cruel," Jem murmurs.

"I know. I warned you."

We're silent for a time, and when I tug gently on Jem's shirtsleeve he startles badly. "Look." I peel off my left glove. The people who have seen my bare hands are few and far between. I've kept them covered in public for years now.

"What did you do?" Jem whispers—disgusted or awed, I can't tell. The deep, thick scar on my hand runs from the area between my thumb and forefinger, down the back of my hand and around the side of my wrist. It was a nasty wound to begin with, and infection made the scarring worse. A thin, secondary scar runs parallel to it, where doctors had to cut me open to clear out the necrotic tissue. I came within an inch of losing my left thumb.

"I went back to the kitchen. Back to making dinner." I mime holding a knife and carrot in my hands, chopping neatly. "I was distracted already, and when Tessa hit the floor Mom freaked out. She let out this shriek.... The knife slipped and I sliced my hand wide open."

At the time I hadn't even noticed the bleeding. All that mattered was Mom's frantic pounding on the locked bathroom door. Dad kicked the door in, and the force of it gave my dead sister a nasty head wound. If she hadn't already been lifeless on the floor, that blow would have ended it for her.

I put my glove back on but Jem continues to stare at my left hand. "Any deeper and I would have lost the thumb."

He looks up at my face with a probing stare. "How the hell did they not catch you? There must have been a shit-ton of pills in her stomach."

"They only did a partial autopsy. The big concern was whether the head wound was a sign of foul play. Everything else just looked like a death from cancer—not worth the time and money to investigate. Besides, she hadn't eaten in days because of the pain, and an IV kept her hydrated, so no one expected to find anything in her stomach."

"You should have let her die naturally."

"I did what she wanted."

"You should have said no." Jem's voice is steadily rising in volume. Shock and disgust are beginning to lapse into anger. "You don't take advantage of someone in a vulnerable moment and make a permanent decision like that."

"It was her decision."

"You still should have said no."

I stand up and gather the blanket into my backpack. I don't need a lecture from Jem. "We're not having this conversation. I took enough shit from my parents; I don't need it from you too."

"So your parents do know?"

"Mom suspects. I was the last one with Tessa, and the empty pill bottle was still out on the counter. She couldn't prove that Tessa hadn't opened it herself, though." I shoulder my backpack. "She didn't turn me in. Maybe losing one daughter was enough."

When I walk away I don't care if Jem follows me. He can find his own way home if he doesn't move his ass back to the car fast enough. I'm almost disappointed when he catches up to me, but then he has to grab my wrist and yank my left glove off. He turns my wrist as though he's inspecting a dead animal.

I try to pull my hand back and he says, "If there was any justice you would have lost the thumb."

I slap him across the face with my mutilated hand without pausing to think. Jem reels a bit, though I didn't hit him very hard.

"You are an asshole," I tell him slowly. "I accepted all your bullshit and baggage when everyone else just wanted to ignore you. Some fucking friend you are to not even *try* to do the same for me."

"I've bent over backwards to accept your bullshit," he yells back. "But this takes the fucking cake, Kirk."

"Fuck you."

"What do you want me to say?" he demands. "'Great job, you killed a sick, helpless woman. It all makes sense now.' Come on!"

"You've got a lot of nerve to think that I expect congratulations for killing her."

"Well what do you want?"

"I want you to fucking listen! God damn, Harper, I wasn't always a heartless shrew."

He snorts incredulously. Asshole.

"I regretted it immediately, alright? I should have found a way let her go more peacefully, or stayed with her. I should have told Mom and Dad what we were up to." I throw my hands up. "That's some heavy shit to deal with when you're sixteen."

"I'm sorry you're a lousy murderer," he says condescendingly.

I wish I hadn't told him. I walk away, angry at myself and at him. My self-directed anger is nothing new, but the anger I feel for Jem is of a different breed. I accepted him and his demons before I knew what they were, and as soon as I share mine, he insults me and passes judgment.

"If it makes you feel any better, the whole experience wrecked me," I tell him bitterly.

"Why would that make me feel better?"

I shrug. "Justice. I didn't get off scot-free, even though I did keep my thumb." I don't know why I bother, but I flex my hand in demonstration. My thumb joint doesn't move like it should. "I can't grip stuff properly anymore."

"What a fucking tragedy."

"I got in trouble a lot after Tessa died; racked up a few citations in a couple of months and ended up with some community service and probation."

"Some justice," Jem scoffs. "You fuck up that hard and you get a few weeks of picking up garbage along the highway? That's bullshit."

"She died in August and I got a psych detainment just before Christmas."

Jem gives me a look that I've seen a hundred times before—like I have a second head or a bomb under my shirt. "A psych detainment?"

"I tried to kill myself."

Jem doesn't say a word.

"I missed Tessa's funeral because I needed surgery to repair the ligaments in my hand, and I missed Christmas because I was in a mental hospital."

"You think she would have wanted you there?" he says sourly. How good of him to consider that this isn't easy for me to talk about.

"I don't know." I resolve not to let him make me cry. "I know you don't care, but those three weeks in the psych ward were where a lot of my issues began."

"Uh, I think they began before that," he says dryly. "That's how you landed in a psych ward in the first place."

"What the fuck do you know?"

"Did your parents kick you out when you turned eighteen? Is that why you're living with Frank?"

"I left voluntarily."

Jem snorts derisively and looks the other way. "Do you have any more water?" he asks moodily.

"Piss off."

"Seriously, I need to take my meds."

I laugh humorlessly. "You want my help to take pills? That's rich."

Jem grabs my arm and makes me stop. He glares at me and reaches into his messenger bag, pulling out bottles of pills. He shoves these into my hands and pulls out more. There are nine bottles in all. I don't recognize the names on half the labels. I'm guessing those are transplant-related.

"I'm just gonna dump my baggage on you all at once whether you like it or not," he snaps. "There. You want to help me sort through dosages? Listen to every fucking thing about what each drug does to me? Let's see if you can get it right this time or if you kill someone else, you reckless bitch."

I take a deep breath through my nose and try to respond civilly. "I get it. I'll shut up. Forget I ever trusted you." I dump the pills against his chest. He catches some and others drop to the ground.

"Willa!" he calls after me as I march away. I don't stop. Jem frantically packs up his bottles and jogs after me. The short distance is enough to wind him.

"Just let me take a bottle." He grabs my backpack and I throw him off.

"No. You don't treat me like that and then ask me for favors."

"*Please.*"

"Why should I?"

"Because," he yells, out of patience, "it fucking hurts!"

That brings me up short. I stop and study him. Underneath his frustration and anger there is a definite look of pain. I should have noticed it, but I was too distracted and angry at him to see properly.

"All the walking, the stress, it adds up. I need to take—"

I swing my backpack off my shoulders before he can finish and take out the only bottle of fluid left. It's just a few swallows of orange mint tea; not enough to take nine bottles' worth of pills with, but enough to take his Oxy.

"We'll stop for more water at the gas station along the way, and you can take the rest," I tell him.

"Don't do me any favors," he says bitterly, and throws back three pills in one swallow to save fluid. He makes a face as they get stuck at the back of his throat and wastes more tea trying to get them down.

"Plug your nose," I say tiredly. "It makes the pills go down with less water."

Jem gives me that snarky look again. "Did you pinch her nose? Or did you learn that taking sedatives from a Dixie cup in the nuthouse?"

"Yeah, actually, I did." I snatch the empty bottle back from him. I walk away and it takes Jem a second to follow.

"How long were you in the psych ward?"

"Three weeks. I had to detox and do some therapy before they'd let me be an outpatient."

"Detox. You were drugging yourself up too?"

This time I refrain from hitting him.

"It's a convenient way to avoid living with yourself. It was mostly pot, anyway. The stuff I had to wean off of was antidepressants. I'd been referred to this grief counselor and the dosage was never quite right."

"Are you still on antidepressants?"

"I got off them last year."

"What about therapy?"

"After I was released I was put into this group therapy program at the rec center. It was the only one my parents' insurance would cover."

"Did it work?"

"No. It made things worse. I started hanging out with the bad influences from Group, and it all went downhill from there. My school's guidance counselor liked the idea of sending me to a reform school but my parents didn't— they think reform schools have nothing but fuck ups and criminals. I'd just learn new tricks and more bad habits. Dad wanted to ship me off to military school."

"So you could learn to be even colder?"

I'm cold for a reason, damn it. It's not easy to live with this shit.

"Given the choice, I'd take the reform school. I've spent enough time around junkies and thieves to know how to screw with their heads. It's always the same game with them."

"You're talking about the kids from group therapy?"

"Nah, they're just garden-variety fuck ups. Kids with daddy issues and anger management problems. I meant the people I met in the psych ward while I was on suicide watch." I can't help but smile grimly at the memory, even though I never tried to talk to any of these people again. "Cliques form on the ward," I tell him. "It's the prison mentality. You've got to group together in there or you go really fucking nuts. It was four of us—a schizo, two addicts, and me."

"Quite the prison gang," Jem remarks drolly.

"I beat the shit out of one," I tell him. "That's sort of how we met. She called me Kevorkian and I hit her with my lunch tray."

"Jesus, Willa."

"Yeah, that didn't exactly bode well for me. I'd just gotten out of detox and they put me in solitary for two days to cool off. But when I was allowed back into the common area, her and me became friends. Sort of. There's only so much they can do as friends. Junkies will do and say anything if they think they can score from it."

"You sold her your meds, didn't you?"

"Laura was only pleasant when she was docile, yes." I look over at Jem to find him shaking his head. It's bad enough that I have to deal with Mom and Dad's disappointment without Jem heaping his onto the pile.

"She was there to detox, but she'd take anything. I'd slip her my Lithium when I could. That stuff is hard on the gut."

"So even when you were on antidepressants you weren't really taking them."

"Not all the time. But not all of them worked out so hot when I did take them, either." I don't elaborate and Jem prompts me to continue. "Well it was Zoloft for the first few months, up until I landed in the psych ward, but that made me a little...intense."

"Did you hit multiple people with lunch trays?"

"No, but I had these paranoid spells where I'd get all worked up and angry. So I detoxed and then they put me on Lithium, but that made me hallucinate. I left the hospital with a prescription for Prozac. It killed my appetite and I dropped twenty pounds, so they switched me to Cymbalta. That drug worked for shit, so Elavil came next." I look over at Jem. He's frowning thoughtfully at my list of drugs.

"Remember how I said I threw a brick through the kitchen window?"

"Yeah..."

"I wasn't entirely honest. It wasn't my parents' kitchen window. It was the kitchen window in the fifth-floor apartment of an abandoned walkup. I broke it because the frame was stuck and the window wouldn't open. I was going to jump."

He murmurs, "Jesus, Willa."

"I didn't do it. Clearly."

"The meds made you suicidal?"

"That's what I told the doctors. They scaled things back with my meds after that."

"What do you mean 'that's what you told them?'" Jem demands. "What really happened?"

"I felt like shit. My sister was dead and I'd killed her; everyone at school thought I was a fucking psychopath; and my only human contact was with parents who could hardly stand to look at me. Eternal silence seemed like a good decision at the time."

"So why'd you stop?" Jem asks quietly. "Why didn't you jump?"

I kick a rock off the path. "Same reason you didn't take your mom's sleeping pills. There's something, deep down, that can't support that kind of self-destruction." I nudge Jem with my elbow. "That's how I knew you'd never come to an attempt; I've been there. I know what the edge looks like and it leaves a stain on a person."

"Kirk?" Jem says softly.

"What?"

When he speaks again his voice is quiet and bitter, not kind like I expected. "That's a really stupid reason to want to kill yourself. You have no idea what real suffering feels like."

It hurts me more than anything has in a very long time to learn that Jem Harper isn't the person I thought he was. But I really shouldn't have trusted him to begin with.

⌘

I take Jem back to his house, but when I stop the car he doesn't get out immediately. He just sits there for a few seconds with this deeply thoughtful look on his face, and then it suddenly occurs to him that the car is no longer moving.

"I'll see you tomorrow."

"Yeah." He says it in a distant way, like he didn't really listen to what I said. Jem gets out of the car without looking at me and slams the door behind him. I'd almost forgotten what a permanent goodbye sounds like.

Frank notices that something is amiss when I get home. He keeps asking questions and I tell him to piss off.

"Are you in some kind of trouble?" The question grates on my nerves because I used to get that one from Dad all the time. When I made up my mind to clean up my act at Thanksgiving, no one believed I would do it, even after I did. There were too many hatchets buried in shallow graves to let bygones be bygones.

There were always things we couldn't fix, no matter how much we tried as a family. It was Dad who took me to a grief counselor the week after Tessa died. The counselor was an okay guy. Had a gentle voice and his office smelled nice, but talk therapy didn't work its magic on me. There were things I couldn't say—that I'd killed her, for one, and that I hoped my hand would never heal as a form of bizarre penance, for another. On came the antidepressants, which didn't work any better than talk, but that was my own fault. Those drugs aren't meant to be taken with other substances, and by that time I was already involved with the wrong crowd. It occurred to me the day after Tessa died, when I woke up and realized that I didn't have anyone to call: I had no friends. My leisure hours had been spent hanging out with my sister or holed up in hospital waiting rooms. I'd lived in Newfoundland for over a year and hadn't made a single friend. No one knows what to say to the girl whose only hobby is caring for a dying sister, anyway.

So I made some friends. I made the friends who knew about pain and could teach me how to get blitzed out of my fucking mind. I can't say it felt good. It felt like nothing, and the nothingness was pleasant compared to the agony of conscious awareness. Dad caught me. It wasn't hard. I wasn't trying to hide my stash of drugs by that time.

It was then that I decided not to let other peoples' emotions weigh on me. Dad's disappointment was too much to bear, otherwise. He'd been driving me to counseling and paying for prescriptions I wasn't interested in taking seriously. I got clean. For two weeks.

Turns out the antidepressants were better when I was drugged up on other shit too. I'd been clean exactly a week when things started to get strange.

They say depression is like all the color being sucked out of life. That's not quite it. It's a lack of process. Every action ends halfway. Every train of thought fails to come to fruition. Nothing comes full circle; has its place; carries much meaning.

It was the longest day of the year when I went up to the fifth floor the empty apartment building near my house. It was slated for demolition anyway; no one would care about a broken window or blood on the pavement.

I honestly don't remember getting caught. I don't even remember being on the window ledge, except for the sensation of wind on my face. I remember nothing except being in the back of a police car and the familiar ride back to the hospital. I had a date with a psychiatric detainment.

I was hospitalized for three weeks with other teens, until they were sure that I was no longer a danger to myself. I still didn't like the antidepressants, and after a week I started tonguing them and selling the pills to an addict down the hall. She could get me what I really wanted: peace and quiet. Laura would cause trouble—some ruckus in the communal lounge, usually—and we would all get sent to our rooms until things settled down. I relished the undisturbed time, lying on my bed and feeling nothing but my own breath and the texture of institution-quality sheets.

When I got out, I actually missed the hospital. At least there I had privacy for fifteen minutes at a time. At home, not a second was my own. My parents drove me to and from school. When I insisted on riding Tessa's bike, they would follow me to make sure I took no detours. I wasn't allowed to shut my bedroom door or have visitors beyond the living room—not that any came. Caring for my wayward ass became a full time job, one that burnt my mother out within six months. She knew what I had done to her firstborn. Couldn't prove it, but she had a feeling. It haunted her that I would never admit to assisting Tessa. There was no point talking about it.

While Mom and Dad thought they were monitoring me, I was really getting into a whole new set of problems. The Group I was enrolled in for therapy was just as much about giving them a break as it was about my sanity. Mondays the Group did community service—worked at soup kitchens and such—and on Wednesdays we did therapy. Fridays were activity night, when we would play sports and games at the recreation center. It sounds peachy, but to get into the program you either have to be at-risk or damn closed to it. I was playing tetherball every week with the same kinds of screw-ups and delinquents that had steered me wrong in the first place.

Let's just say that what my parents don't know constitutes sufficient reason to kick me out of the house. They didn't, to their credit; they generously sent me to live with Frank. After three months of behaving, I could feel myself starting to slip again, and I looked around and realized that I'd wasted three years of my life on nothing more than self-destruction. So I made promises, and I gambled that distance from my situation in St. John's would help me keep them.

I always was a fuck up.

The look of disgust and annoyance that Jem gave me on the drive home keeps coming back to me. "How could you fuck up that badly?" he said. "That many times, too. You couldn't have left it at one mistake?"

Thursday

I don't see Jem when I get to school, which is weird because he usually gets here before I do and hangs around my locker. But what else could I expect? I see him at lunch when he comes into the cafeteria, and try to keep a neutral expression. He looks the other way and goes to sit with Elise and her friends. Shit.

Cody pulls my attention back to my surroundings by offering me a coupon for a one-month subscription to World of Warcraft.

"I thought you were into Starcraft?"

"Only sometimes," he says. "WoW fills in the rest of the week. You should join. We need reliable people for raids and—"

Please shoot me now.

Soc is no better. Jem tosses the joint assignment across the table instead of passing it properly and is incapable of discussing it without sarcasm.

"Stop being such a moody little bitch," I tell him lowly. "If you have something to say to me, just say it."

"What is there to say?" He turns back to the textbook with a disgusted sneer.

"I hate you."

"I don't care."

↔

I sit in the driveway with my engine shut off, not quite sure of how I got home. That's a bad sign. I haven't had walking blackouts since I was cycling off Zoloft. Maybe I should carpool to school tomorrow…

I get out of my car and very deliberately walk to the front door, trying hard to keep track of everything around me. Frank isn't home yet, and the last thing I want right now is solitude. Even sitting next to him on the couch, watching TV and saying nothing would be better than being alone.

288

It sucks that the first person I've ever trusted with the whole story just crapped out on me. I knew he would probably hate me for it, but it's Jem. I thought he'd have his tantrum and then demand we work things out, like he always does. But no. I'm too messed up for the friendless kid with cancer. I wonder if he'll tell anybody, and if they'll believe him if he does. I never told any of my schoolmates in St. John's the whole story, or those fucks in Group or even my shrinks. I thought Jem would get it because he is equally fucked up, albeit in a different way.

What a letdown.

I'm staring at the fridge, trying to figure out what to make for dinner without actually thinking, when the phone rings. Maybe it's him. I snatch the handset off the wall.

"Hello?"

"You sound excited," Luke says, chuckling warmly. "What's going on?"

"Nothing. Just making dinner."

"Come here after," he says. "We haven't hung out all week."

"You know what?"

"What?"

"That sounds pretty freaking fantastic. I've had a shit week."

I don't even bother to eat before I go over to the Thorpe house. Luke is waiting on the porch for me when I get there. He picks me up in a hug and asks what would make me feel better.

"A distraction. Anything."

"It's a nice day for a hike," he offers. He doesn't have to say anything else to sell me on the idea. I enjoy these tranquil places out in the wilderness. Luke and I spend the evening exploring the rocks around his camping cave. We find birds' nests in the crags and pass a family of sleeping raccoons. The runt of the litter is awake and blinks at us with something like bewilderment.

Eventually, the worries of my day slip away and I'm lightened by easy pleasures and good company.

When we get tired of walking we head back to the cave to sit on the rocks. Luke puts his hands on my waist and boosts me up.

"You're like a little doll," he says. "You weigh next to nothing." When he climbs up next to me he puts an arm around my back. "What was so hard this week?"

Luke touches my hair, combing his fingers through it. I consider telling him what really happened, but I couldn't do that without telling him about my sister. I don't think I ever will tell him that particular part of my history. That would complicate things, and Luke is a very simple sort of friend. He knows the new Willa—the one who isn't a fuckup.

"Just…a little drama with a friend."

"Girl drama?" Luke guesses.

"No, just some stuff with my project partner." That's the only way to describe our relationship now—just two students assigned to work together for an hour a day.

Luke squeezes me gently. I lay my head on his shoulder because it feels good, and he kisses my hair.

"You've got to stop that, you know."

"What?"

"All this affection. Our families are going to start thinking that there's something going on between us."

"Would that be so bad?"

"Them thinking it? Or something going on?"

"The second one." He tries to kiss me and I turn my head so he gets my cheek.

"We're friends. That's it. We talked about this."

"Is it the age difference? You know that technically we're only a year and four months apart. It's not much—"

"I don't date."

"What, never?" He laughs softly, like he just heard a joke

"Isn't it enough to just be my friend?" I can't help sighing. I'll have few friends left if Jem tells people about me.

"It is," Luke assures me. He hugs me closer and adds, "For now."

"No." I pull away. "There's never going to be any more."

"You say that now, but—"

"I say it because I mean it. I'll always mean it. You're like my brother, okay? Just drop it."

His eyes are tight and his lipse tense. I expect him to snap at me, but he responds with eerie calm instead. "You're upset."

Luke smoothes my hair. Is he saying that to discredit my refusal?

"Let's talk about something else."

"I'm gonna go home." I stand up and walk away.

"Willa!" Luke calls after me. I don't stop or turn back. Luke jogs after me and grabs my arm. "You want to go back to the house? To the beach? What will make you feel better?"

I think Luke is the only person left who would actually ask me that question.

"Got any weed?"

⊷

I step out of my car, disappointed and sober, to find Elise on my porch. She sits on the stoop, tapping her hands on her knees. Her bike lies on its side on the front lawn.

"Are you okay?" she says, pointing to my neck. Turns out that Luke is mind-numbingly straightedge when it comes to substances, but he was willing to help me take my mind of reality in the back seat of the car for an hour. If he left a hickey, I'll kill him.

"Bug bite."

"Oh."

"So what are you doing here?" I reach into my purse for my house key. Elise grabs me by the back of my jacket and makes me face her. She looks so perplexed.

"I was worried about you. Jem's being more of a jerk than usual. I thought maybe you guys had a fight, but he's not saying anything."

"And you care because…?"

"Because you're good for him. If you had a fight or whatever, I'm sure it can be resolved."

I can't withhold a skeptical snort. "I doubt it."

"Try, please," she says in a plying voice. She has no right to ask me that, ignorant as she is of the details. He cut me out, not the other way around. He was the one who insisted that I don't know what real suffering is.

"You want to carry some peace-making message to him?"

"If it'll help," she agrees.

"Okay. Tell him he's an absolute bastard—a scrawny, ugly, bald motherfucker who is going to die cold and alone. He'll know what it means." I step inside and slam the front door behind me.

It takes a long, hot shower to get rid of the scent of Luke and pine. I still feel slightly dirty afterwards. Frank left some takeout in the fridge for me, but I can't choke down more than a few bites. It's about half-past when my phone buzzes with a new text message.

Was it absolutely necessary to make my sister cry?

I reply: *Tell her to keep her nose out of it, then.*

It's none of Elise's business what goes on between Jem and I. It's not her responsibility to fight his battles for him, either, or to negotiate peace as if we're kindergartners fighting over a toy.

I don't hear from anyone until late that night, when I get another text from Jem.

I told her about you.

The five short words make my blood run cold. I'm done. Life as I know it in Smiths Falls is over. I should never have trusted him.

I send: *You don't deserve friends.*

I drop my pillow over my head and try not to scream. This is how it starts. It might take a day or two, but soon everyone will know. I'll have to explain, and no one will accept—if they even let me explain to begin with. It'll be a lonely two months until school is out, and then an even lonelier summer. My catch-up semesters will be quiet ones. I'll be the outcast and he'll be back to normal by then—he'll have a voice and friends and not a shred of pity for me.

I might as well just give up now and move back to St. John's.

He sends me: *I can't believe I ever liked you.*

It's not necessary to tell me what a monster I am.

I've been vilified by everyone I know already. I got the message, loud and clear, that I'm a bad person. The fact that I tried to be better by moving to Smiths Falls is irrelevant.

Ask Hudson to assign you a new partner tomorrow, I tell him. *Don't put yourself through the trouble of having to acknowledge me.*

He replies: *I'll do that.*

And there it is. All alone. Again.

Friday

I don't go to school. I can't take it. I tell Frank I have a migraine and he obliges me by calling the school to justify my absence. At first I think he actually believes me, because I spend the day in bed, drifting between sleeping and waking. I have no appetite. The light hurts my head. I can't say for sure where it hurts.

In the afternoon Frank offers to take me to see a doctor, but I'm not fooled. He doesn't mean he'll take me to the family doctor for a checkup and some painkillers, because he doesn't believe my migraine excuse. He means he'll take me to a shrink to find out if this is an encore performance of clinical depression.

"I told you not to hang out with that kid," he says when I refuse. "I warned you, and now look at yourself. It's just like before—"

"I was overmedicated," I say loudly. "Not that you'd know; you weren't there. It had nothing to do with Tessa or with *anything,* and this has nothing to do with Jem."

"Don't take that tone with me. Doug said you told Luke you'd had a bad week—normal people don't get so blue they can't get out of bed after a bad week."

He doesn't know the kind of bad week I've had. Two days and I actually miss Jem's snark. His negativity took the edge off my misanthropy.

"You and Doug gossip like sixteen-year-old girls," I complain. I throw off my blanket and get out of bed. "There, I'm up. You happy?"

"Fine, I'm happy," Frank retorts. "Do something with your afternoon."

"I'm going out."

"Oh no you're not."

"You just told me to do something."

"Around the house! Take it easy for the day!"

"You don't even know where I'm going." Neither do I, but that's beside the point. I grab a pair of shoes off my floor and my keys off the dresser. Frank follows me all the way to the front door, arguing with me to stay indoors and take a day to rest.

I have no idea where I'm going, unwashed and dressed in sweats. I end up parked in front of Tim Hortons, watching the other cars go by. I have no energy, so I recline the driver's seat and stare at the ceiling. It's almost four—the Group session at the rec center in St. John's is just about to start. Dollars to donuts, Ray is still there and hating every minute of it.

I suppose that's something I could do here, if word gets around that I'm a homicidal maniac: find a group therapy resource (it would appease Frank) and get my human contact from the screwballs there. I would probably have to drive to a larger town like Ottawa or Brockville to find a youth group, but beggars can't be choosers. Then I wonder if I really want to get involved with more people like Steve, and the idea loses its appeal.

I get home just after sunset. Frank grills me about where I've been. He doesn't buy that I've been sitting in my car in a parking lot all afternoon, doing nothing.

"You could have sat around and done nothing here," he says. "You didn't have to worry me."

"No one asked you to worry." I open the fridge and look for something to eat, even though I'm not hungry.

"I'm your brother. It's in the job description." Frank offers to make me something to eat, but I don't feel like eating burnt food tonight. I just pour myself a bowl of cereal and sit there with a blank look, chewing it slowly. It tastes like sand.

As soon as Frank leaves the kitchen, I check the call history on the phone. He called Mom not a full hour ago. Any day now they're going to gang up on me; I know it.

✧

I stare at my computer screen, baffled by the e-card my mother sent me. We're long past the ability to communicate effectively about serious matters and emotions, so instead I get an email with I a silly picture of a kitten in a cowboy hat telling me to cheer up. The image of the kitten blinks its big blue eyes and stiffly wags its tail. I think I might vomit.

The need to erase the kitten sends me on a deleting binge. I purge my inbox, scrapping all the correspondence (what little there is) from people back home. I haven't gone out of my way to get in touch with anyone from St. John's since I moved here. A few people sent emails asking where I was—those were the people who I didn't care enough about to say goodbye to before I left the province. I'm in the process of deleting those when I come across the last email I received from Steve.

I didn't say goodbye to him in person, either. I couldn't stand to. I sent him an email after I was already settled in Smiths Falls, making it clear that I wasn't coming back to St. John's or to Group. His reply was short and smarmy, just like him: *That's a shame. I'll miss you, Baby Girl. Stay strong.*

Steve always was a nervy fucker. It was a real shit thing to call me Baby Girl after two years. You could always tell which of the girls in Group he was fucking at any given time by the condescending nickname he bestowed on us all. I think it was how he kept from calling each of us by the wrong name at an inopportune moment. I never outright told him to piss off when he said it, but I would always tell him that he wasn't my dad. Steve would just laugh it off and say 'Thank God.' He didn't mean it in an advantageous way, either. He meant that in a, 'you're so screwed up I'm glad you're not my kid' kind of way.

As I delete the email I say a little prayer to whoever's listening that he breaks both arms simultaneously.

Saturday

Vacuuming the carpets on all four floors of the Elwood Arms B&B makes the morning go by at a reasonable pace. It keeps my hands busy and I'm so focused on getting everything perfectly clean that I don't have time to dwell on Jem—much. When I'm done vacuuming I spend two hours washing and pressing sheets.

"Come out front for a while," Chris says when he sees me folding sheets. I try to decline, but he insists. When we get to the counter I find out he just wanted help sorting through credit receipts by date. It's a boring task, but it keeps both hands and mind busy, so I do it without complaint.

"How come you weren't at school yesterday?"

"Food poisoning."

He expresses his sympathy and says he's glad I felt well enough to come in today. "Work is pretty boring when you're the only one here."

"I'm gonna go make up the beds."

I take the basket of clean sheets up to the second floor. There are nine suites in the house, each with a queen bed or larger. I bend down to pick up the first sheets off the basket and Chris puts his hand on my back. I jump at the sensation—I didn't realize he followed me from the lobby.

"Easy," he tells me with a smile. "Didn't mean to scare you." His hand is still on my back. "Let me help you with that." Chris goes to take the fitted sheet from me, deliberately touching my hand in the process.

"Have you slept with Paige yet?"

My question surprises him. "What?"

"Have you slept with her yet?"

Chris gives me this uneasy look, as though he isn't sure if I'm playing a joke on him or not. I take the sheet from him and throw it across the bare mattress.

"All this on-again-off-again, fighting in public, making each other jealous, making out in the hallway…is she so back-and-forth and spiteful because she gave you something she wishes she hadn't?"

Chris does one hell of a goldfish impersonation. "That's, uh…private."

He hasn't slept with her.

Chris smiles awkwardly and gestures to the door. "I'll leave you to it." He heads back to the front counter. I almost wish Jem were here just so I could say, *See? I don't need pepper spray to get Elwood to leave me alone. A sharp tongue does the trick.*

⌖

Mom calls that night under the pretense of catching up with me. I know she just wants to make sure I'm not causing more trouble. She keeps me on the phone for an hour, talking about work and the neighbors and Newfoundland weather. She asks me about school and work, and I give her the highlights. Mom surprises me by remembering most of my new friends' names.

"What about Jem?" she asks. "You haven't mentioned him yet." I bet she was waiting for me to say something about Jem; to prove whether Frank was right or wrong about what a bad idea it is for me to hang out with him.

"We haven't spoken much this week."

"Why not?"

My first instinct is to lie, because that's what I always do when uncomfortable questions arise, but this is my Mom. She already knows who I am at my worst.

"I told him about St. John's."

Mom is silent for three whole seconds. The tension is simply delicious.

"What exactly do you mean by that?" she asks slowly. She sounds like a counselor trying to talk someone down from their ledge.

"I told him about Tessa, and the psych detainment, and the group therapy. And about getting messed up on antidepressants and planning to kill myself. Not the whole story, exactly."

"And why would you do a thing like that?"

"I don't know. I trusted him."

"You wanted a clean break," she says. "You had one there. You haven't known him that long and you trusted him with damaging information."

"I'll handle it."

"Willa, you didn't handle it well last time."

"This is different."

"How?"

I take a deep breath through my nose, but it does nothing to help my patience. "Shortage of tall buildings?"

"Put Frank on the phone."

I hand the phone over to Frank and disappear to the second floor. I don't want to hear what they have to say about me. As I sit there doing nothing my phone buzzes. Guess who has to make my bad day even worse?

Do you still have my Nightdodger CD?

You're not getting that back. I'll keep it just to spite him.

Jem replies: *Bring it to school tomorrow.*

Make me.

I knew it was going to cost me to be Jem's friend. Why shouldn't I get a free

CD out of the deal? In exchange for two paranoid parents, an overprotective brother, one dead heart, months of soup, my reputation and my sanity, of course.

You're being a child,

You're being a prick.

From what I can hear of Frank's half of the phone conversation, he and Mom are getting upset. I turn on my iPod and crank the volume to block them out.

The first track is from *Spirited.* Stupid Shuffle.

Frank hangs up the phone with a slam. I cringe. He's probably going to storm up here next and give me hell. I curl up on my side facing the wall and drop my pillow over my head. It's cowardly, but I can't deal with this crap right now.

My door opens without a warning knock.

"You awake?" he barks at me.

"Maybe."

"I'm going down to Doug's. I'll be back in an hour." He says the last part with emphasis, as if he's warning me not to try anything because he'll be back in time to catch me.

"Fine."

I don't breathe easy until he's gone. Frank was a hell of a lot easier to live with before I knew Jem.

Sunday

"Frank?" I knock on my brother's bedroom door. He doesn't answer, so I knock again. When I open his door I find his bed undisturbed. Upon inspection, his toothbrush is dry and his toiletries untouched. He didn't come home last night.

I'm not exactly worried. Likely he had a beer at Doug's, and then another, and then a few more, and decided to spend the night. Frank isn't a heavy drinker, but when he's stressed he's been known to binge a little. He and I have that in common. I suppose I should feel guilty for being the cause of his stress, but apathy is about all I can manage right now.

When Frank does come home he's going to be sore at me and hung over to boot. I decide having hangover-friendly food waiting for him might help my case. It's time for an old stand-by: Oma's chicken soup. Simple, easy, and comforting. The pot will need tending to over a period of hours, but for the most part it just has to sit and shiver.

I set an alarm to remind me to add more water later, and go lay down on the couch. I turn the TV on, but that's just for show. Soon I'm more asleep than awake.

It's almost eleven when I hear the back door open. Frank is home. I throw off my blanket and scramble to my feet, eager to make an impression of usefulness. If he catches me lazing around he'll get on my case about depression again. I hurry into the kitchen to offer him a cup of soup.

It's not Frank at the back door.

Jem stands there with his hands in his pockets, looking uncomfortable.

"I destroyed your CD. You can fuck off now."

The corner of his mouth twitches. "That's a shame. I was gonna let you keep it." I suppose it's good that I was lying, then.

"Um, can we talk?" he says.

"I thought we'd already said it all." I go over to the stove to stir the soup.

Jem tells me it smells good, as though trite compliments will make me more amenable to conversation. I ignore him, but he steps further into my house and touches the back of my sweatshirt.

"You don't look well."

"Neither do you."

He drops his hand. I've hurt his feelings—again. I can't justify why I still care about that.

I look over my shoulder at him, with his pursed lips and slanted brows as he struggles to think of the right thing to say. The blood vessels in the corners of his eyes are a little inflamed. How sad is it that I notice such a subtle difference?

"You need carrots. And protein. What the hell have you been doing with yourself?" I tiredly reach down a bowl from the cupboard and retrieve a ladle from the drawer. I give Jem a bowl of hot broth with as many carrots as I can scoop out.

"You don't have to—"

"Eat," I tell him. "I'm not giving it to you to be friendly, so don't waste your time feeling guilty. Just eat it."

"I want to talk to you."

I hand Jem a spoon. "Talking doesn't work out so hot for us. Just eat." I gesture to the table and offer him a seat.

"I said stuff I shouldn't have."

"No shit. Let's not beat a dead horse by discussing it, okay?"

"I came here to apologize. Some of those things I said...I really didn't mean them."

I drop the ladle into the sink with a clatter. "Well that's the kicker, isn't it? Which words *did* you mean?"

Jem starts to squirm. "I was mad, okay?"

"Don't get defensive. I know you were upset. There's only one thing you said that I really care about anyway."

That makes Jem distinctly nervous.

"You know the one."

"Maybe I did mean it," he says quietly. "I'm not sure."

I point to the door. "Get out of my house."

He doesn't move.

"I didn't mean that you haven't suffered," he says quickly. "But...it's different.

You haven't lived in fear for your own life. You wouldn't think like that—you wouldn't take your life so lightly—if you had, I mean…uh…" He fiddles with the edge of his pocket. He does that when he's flustered. Bites his nails, too.

"Is that what you came over here to say?"

"I came to say a lot of things."

I point to the table yet again. "Eat first." I turn to head down the hall and Jem calls me back.

"Willa?"

"I'm just going to get dressed. Eat your damn soup already."

I would be irritated that Jem's presence necessitates changing out of sweats, but I've been wearing these since yesterday.

When I come back downstairs Jem's bowl is empty. I put on the kettle for mint tea, because if he ate that fast he probably didn't chew properly. Jem still looks hungry—he's eyeing the pot on the stove—so I fill his bowl up again and he smiles shyly.

"Thanks. I wasn't sure if I should just take seconds without asking."

I toss him a yogurt pop for dessert. It's a simple gesture, but it gives him cause to stop and study me.

"Are we okay now?"

I sigh. "We're talking again."

Jem: May 3 to 7

Wednesday

I march through the front hall, straight upstairs to my room. Mom hears me come home and calls out an offer for reheated soup. I decline, and the words come out sharper than I intended. I'm still on edge. I'm still pissed off. I still want to take Willa by the shoulders and shake some sense into her.

Knowing she'd come so close to throwing her life away over fixable problems makes me so deeply angry, I don't even know how to articulate. Her problems had workable solutions—solutions that didn't involve putting her body through hell on a gamble. She didn't have to go up to the top floor of a building and jump.

Unless she was lying, and it really was the meds acting for her. I wouldn't put it past Willa to lie about that; she doesn't like to feel weak or out of control. I end up Googling her list of drugs. I almost feel guilty about doing it, but then I think of how she's probably running a search on AML, and decide *Fuck it*. Looking at the info for her latest drug, Elavil, I wonder if she lied about being med-free, too. Apparently it can cause irritability, hostility, and impulsivity. Sounds like someone I know.

I need to get out of here. Maybe 'here' isn't really a place; maybe it's my own head I need to get out of, but I go downstairs and ask to borrow the car anyway.

"Where are you going?"

I have absolutely no idea. But I can't tell Mom that. "I want to see if the clinic can take a walk-in; get my treatment over this week." It's a good enough reason for her, so she lets me take the car.

I have every intention of trying to find a calming place—maybe the park?—or perhaps just a place where I can vent and rage without being heard. But I don't end up anywhere near the park. I miss the turnoff and end up near the hospital, even though it was supposed to be a cover story. Maybe I should see if the clinic can take a walk-in. But then I think of having to sit still for three hours at a time like this, and I know I wouldn't be able to stand it.

I'm about to pass the hospital entrance when I spot a car parked in the north corner of the lot. It's a lime green Volkswagen beetle—it stands out without trying. The sight of it brings nothing but dread. I pull in and park the car.

⬦

The nurse at triage in Pediatrics is Laura. She smiles when she sees me and even remembers my name, even though I haven't been here for a few months.

"I thought I told you not to come back here?" she jokes.

"Just visiting."

Laura hands me the clipboard to sign in as a visitor and gives me one of the guest badges. She asks me who I'm here to see.

"Meira."

"Room 303."

Is it by nostalgia or chance that she's still in the same room?

The door of room 303 is ajar when I approach. I poke my head in and smell the stale odors of sanitizer and vomit. She's back for more napalm.

"Can I come in?"

"Whatever." She's got the curtain drawn around the bed. I step over to her side of it and try not to look surprised that she's much worse than I anticipated. Meira was never a sizable person in the time I knew her. She was already on the ward when I got here, and she left just before I went into isolation. Last fall she was small and thin, but now she's absolutely emaciated. Her skin is faintly yellow and her eyes are bloodshot.

"Take that off," she says, and reaches a boney arm up to snatch my hat. "It's like wearing a burqa in a strip club." Meira isn't the vain type. She wears her scars with a sense of morbid pride.

"What happened to never coming back here?" I pull up the visitor's chair and sit beside her.

"I'd be home if I could be."

"Same diagnosis?" Last time Meira graced this ward with her scathing presence, she was being treated for masses in her upper intestine and stomach. Meira starts to shake her head and then thinks better of it. She must be fresh off a treatment.

"Stomach's clear. It's just my liver and pancreas that are boned." She says it so casually. I can feel my face go pale. She's got a double-stamped death warrant.

"Are you here for maintenance chemo?" The likelihood of surviving either of those cancers, never mind both, is slim. Chances are she's here to keep the problem from growing too big too fast, and thereby buy herself a little time.

"What are you here for?"

"To visit you."

"That's sweet." She says it with a wry smile. Meira doesn't do 'sweet.' Her pretty face and short stature belie an acerbic wit and cruel sense of justice. Meira doesn't take anybody's bullshit, a trait that has made her infamous on the ward.

She and I used to hang out with the other teens in the common lounge at the end of the hall. It's a room with couches, tables, a TV and glass walls all around. Through the one wall we could see into the pediatric psychiatry department, right next to the ward specifically for kids with eating disorders. I don't know why they thought putting the cancer kids and the anorexics together was a good idea, but we were stuck with them. We all hated them, but Meira took it more personally than most.

Our lounge shared a corner with their therapy room. Every day we would see the counselors file in the patients, and they would sit around the table before perfectly measured, nutritionist-designed meals. And they wouldn't eat. They'd sit there as a group and read the ingredients on every fucking item out loud, going through little mantras about how it was good for them to consume X amount of vitamin C and so many grams of carbohydrates, while ten feet away, a dozen or more of us were willing but unable to eat the same things.

All they had to do was eat, and they'd live. They didn't need strong drugs and harsh medicines, or surgeries or radiation treatments that burn the skin, or whole new organs—they just needed to fucking swallow.

Meira snapped one day in October when one of the girls burst into tears over a cup of applesauce. Meira was in rough shape at the time, but she still felt it was worth it to haul her wrecked body and IV pole all the way around to the other side of the wing, into the room where lunch was being eaten. We all just stared, too stunned to believe that she'd actually mess with these people.

"No one invited me," she said, playing on her sweet appearance. Meira welcomed herself to a seat and said, "You're not gonna eat that?" She snatched the tray from the crying girl and began to eat, making all kinds of appreciative sounds and remarks about how good it tasted.

After that Meira was confined to her room. She set six kids a few months back in treatment and spent the rest of the afternoon throwing up applesauce, but she refused to apologize.

"You gonna come to my funeral?" Meira asks. She says it like she's inviting me to her birthday party.

"Sure."

"I get discharged in two days if all goes well. I'm going casket shopping."

"Are you scared?" She seems to be at peace with the fact that she's going to die. Maybe she's known for a while now and has already crawled through the five steps to acceptance. I never could get there, even when the odds were stacked against me. I only got as far as bargaining.

"Yeah," Meira admits. "But it's sort of…easy. I don't have to worry about the future. I don't have to stress over picking a college or save for retirement…. I can do what I want. I'll miss out on a lot of stuff, and sometimes that really pisses me off, but this whole dying thing is sort of liberating."

I'm not sure if I should believe her. Meira tends to deadpan a lot, even when she's being ironic or sarcastic, so it's hard to tell.

I blurt out, "My friend just told me she tried to commit suicide," and immediately feel like a jerk for saying it. Meira doesn't need to hear about my issues when she's drowning in her own.

"Did she have a good reason?"

"No."

"Well that's a kick in the teeth." Meira pats my hand. "Try not to hold it against her. Not everyone knows what life is worth."

"I'll try." Will I? Or am I agreeing with Meira because I feel guilty that she's dying?

Gillian, the redheaded nurse who corks on her break, comes in with an IV bag in her hands. Meira smiles like it's Christmas and Gillian tells her it's the good stuff. She takes an empty bag off the pole and hangs the new one—it's morphine.

"Can you make it a fast drip?"

⟳

I hang around the hospital until Meira's medication makes her fall asleep, and then I slip my hat back on and make a quiet exit. The next time I see her, she probably won't be breathing.

It takes me ages to fall asleep, and when I do I have nightmares. I see Elise, weak and pale and shriveled, like something out of a concentration camp. 'Sorry,' she says, 'It's you or me.' She presses a withered hand to my chest. Her little shove topples me over, back over the edge of a very tall building, and I jolt awake with the sensation of falling.

"Shit..." I get out of bed to splash cold water on my face. I haven't had pulling-the-plug dreams since I last checked out of the hospital. Fuck Willa for disturbing my sleep like that. Fuck her for killing a woman who could have died with a little dignity.

As I wipe my face I consider the frightening idea that Willa might have been mentally unsound before the shrinks ever got to her. Maybe that's why she decided to go out of her way to make sure Thomasina died—Willa said she asked her to hoard pills, but what if that was a lie? Maybe that poor woman was abused in her most vulnerable state, and no one came in time to save her from her insane sister.

Of course, even more disturbing is the idea that Willa killed Thomasina with an entirely clear head; that she had it in her to be so cruel and cold and calculating, slipping pills into Thomasina's mouth one by one and forcing her to swallow. Not everyone has it in them to end a love one's suffering. Willa did. So what kind of person does that make her?

I feel like I didn't even know her before now. All the nice things she did, all the encouragement she gave me, was just cover for the twisted creature underneath. Her blunt way of speaking, her refusal to take anybody's bullshit—those are things she probably picked up during her time amongst the rough crowds of the mental hospital and therapy group. That's not the real her; it's who she became when she killed her own sister.

Who she was before that doesn't really matter. If Willa was ever a nice person, that girl died with Thomasina.

Before I fall asleep, I consider the third disturbing thought of the night: maybe she really should have jumped.

Thursday

My bad night of sleep makes me dozy all through my morning classes. I can hardly stand to keep my head up, much less pay attention. I fully intend to crash in the nurse's office at lunch, after I get something to eat.

It's out of habit that I notice where Willa is sitting. She looks up at me and offers a pained sort of smile. I turn away and head for Elise's table. I can't even look at her.

"Are you okay?" Elise asks me. A few months ago it wasn't weird for me to give up eating after only half a Jell-O cup, but now my lack of appetite is notable.

I can feel Willa's eyes boring into the back of my head. It makes my skin crawl.

"Will you leave me alone?" I grouch. Elise lets me be—after stealing the remainder of my Jell-O.

Social Studies is hell. I can't look at Willa without feeling the intense urge to yell at her, so I don't. Civility is a challenge. I carelessly pass the assignment form to her and Willa rounds on me.

"Stop being such a moody little bitch," she says seriously. "If you have something to say to me, just say it."

"What is there to say?" There are no words for how completely repulsed I am by her behavior—the parts I can riddle out, anyway. I'm still convinced she's a liar and I have no interest in talking to her anymore. I turn back to my work, away from Willa.

"I hate you," she whispers. How very much like her.

"I don't care."

↦

After dinner, Mom and I spend some time cooking. We do four kinds of soup so we can freeze the leftovers and I have food for a week. I try to ignore the fact that the recipes are all written in Willa's slanted, messy penmanship. Eric keeps coming through the kitchen to steal pieces of chopped vegetables off the cutting boards.

Mom and I chat a little about her work, but when it comes time to tell her about how my day went, we hit a stall. She senses that I'm not in much of a talking mood and starts singing lowly. If it weren't for her extensive knowledge of Alison Krauss music, it would be easy to forget that she grew up in Saskatchewan.

"Sing with me."

The side door flies open with such force that it bangs back on its hinges and slams shut. Elise storms in, red-faced and tear-stained. She's sobbing like Dumbledore died all over again.

"What's wrong, honey?"

Elise blows right past Mom to throw her arms around my waist. She clings to me and cries loudly. All attempts to extract information from her are useless; she's crying too hard to speak clearly. Mom and I share perplexed looks over her head.

"That boy?" Mom mouths. I shrug. "Did you and Carey have a fight, sweetie?" Mom says. She rubs soothing circles across Elise's shoulders. Elise just shakes her head no, she didn't fight with her friend, but that's all she can communicate.

"Come on." I shift her so she's clinging to me sideways and walk her upstairs with an arm around her shoulders. I take her to the bathroom to splash cold water on her face. Her tears don't really stop, but she's able to catch a breath with her head between her knees and a cool cloth on the back of her neck.

"What happened?"

Elise pants a little, trying to find her shaky voice. "I w-went to talk to W-Willa—"

Oh fucking hell.

"I thought maybe you guys had a fight, and"—she interrupts herself to wipe her drippy nose— "that you'd make up if you just…I dunno, talked?"

"Why would you try to interfere?"

Elise sniffles. "Because the two of you fight over the stupidest stuff."

"What did she say?" Wrong question. Elise's face crumples into a look of anguish and a fresh wave of sobs makes her impossible to understand. Holding her doesn't seem to help. I keep wiping her cheeks with my thumbs, but it's like sandbagging in a monsoon.

"What did she say, Lise?"

Elise shakes her head. "I'm not gonna repeat it."

"That bad?" Elise nods and tucks her head under my chin. "Do you want your toy wand?" Dumb little things like that always make her feel better.

"Yeah, so I can stab her with it."

"What did she say? Tell me."

Elise firmly shakes her head. "It was mean. Very mean."

I keep trying to badger the story out of her, but she won't budge. Eventually her tears run out of steam and she starts to collect herself. I give her a minute alone in the bathroom to wash up—and give myself an opportunity to text Willa.

Was it really necessary to make my sister cry?

It's going to take one hell of a reason to keep me from keying her car tomorrow.

Willa replies: *Tell her to keep her nose out of it, then.*

Bitch. She has no right to be mean to Elise; my sister didn't do anything to her.

Elise comes out of the bathroom and crawls onto her bed. She sits facing me, crosses her legs, and hugs a pillow to her chest. "What," she says seriously, "did the two of you do to each other?"

"Never mind."

"I do mind. Nobody says hurtful stuff like that without a good cause. What happened?"

"Willa's got...secrets."

"We all do. What's that got to do with you?"

"She told them to me, that's what."

Elise narrows her eyes at me. "And what did you do?"

It's a very long story and not at all easy to tell. Elise interrupts frequently, asking questions and making me repeat myself. She wants to know my exact words, my exact inflection, Willa's tone of reply and the details of body language, like the conversation was a play and she's dissecting it in drama class. She starts to cry again at the rough parts, and then practically jumps down my throat when I try to stop telling the story.

"Tell me the *whole thing*, Jem," she says through her teeth.

"You'll just get upset."

"I'm already upset. Tell me what you said!"

Elise's eyes are still red and puffy at the end of the story, but she's no longer crying. She hugs her pillow tighter against her front, looking off into space with a deeply thoughtful expression.

"I get it," she says quietly.

"I always knew there was something off about her, but I didn't think she was actually insane."

"Not that." Elise shakes her head. "I mean why she did it. Everything else—the series of bad decisions, I mean—started when her sister died. It's...it's the consequences, sort of; not the root of he problem."

"When she *killed* her sister," I correct her. "The difference is subtle, but meaningful."

"No, she *helped* her sister to die. I understand why," Elise insists. "If it's all the same, if her sister was going to die anyway, Willa did it out of love. The sister didn't have to suffer any more. She could have hung around in pain for weeks."

"You're missing the point. It's illegal to help someone commit suicide. She had no idea what she was doing—just gave her sister a fistful of pills. You don't know that it was painless and peaceful."

Elise leans over to kiss my shoulder. "I would have done it for you," she murmurs. "Legal or not."

"What?" I push her away so I can read her face. She's being completely serious.

"If you were going to die I wouldn't want you to suffer." Her lower lip trembles. "If we could say goodbye and I could help it end quickly, well, I think that's a better way to go than just waiting for the inevitable." Her voice cracks a little on the end. "It's not cruelty—that's love."

"If you love someone you don't make their last moments about fear and let them die alone," I argue quietly. I can't believe we're having this conversation. I've gone out of my way for months not to talk to Elise about dying, and here it sounds like she thought the whole thing through when I wasn't looking.

"I don't think it matters," she says. "Once you're dead, you don't much care about any of that. And the people who keep on living get to do it with the knowledge that they did what they could." She sniffs back snot. "There's nothing graceful about dying, anyway." Willa said that once. "We prolong lives so much longer than we should in hospitals."

I can't believe I'm hearing this shit. I get off her bed and head for the door.

"Thank God you're not my next-of-kin."

The slam of the door behind me doesn't do enough to distance me from that conversation. She would have accelerated my demise, if it had been up to her. And all I thought about for her was a quick and natural death.

Mom hears my loud exit from Elise's bedroom and comes to the upper hall to investigate.

"Is she okay?"

"She's fucked." I slam my bedroom door behind me and lock it.

I take a shower to calm my nerves, but it doesn't help. When I get out I find a note from Elise slipped under my door: *I'm sorry.*

I can't deal with this shit right now.

I need to talk to someone who gets it, which immediately rules out all of my Ottawa friends. I thought Elise would understand my position, having gone through my illness alongside me, but that turned out to be a fucking catastrophe. The only person who can stand to talk to me about the fucked up shit in my life is…Willa.

As I hang my bathrobe back in the closet—the guy in the mirror looks hideous and pinched—I consider all the awkward ways that telling Elise is going to come back to bite me in the ass. I shouldn't have said anything. I should have brushed her off, like she did when I asked her what Willa said.

If Willa hadn't made her cry none of this would have happened.

I grab my phone off the dresser and send a short text: *I told her about you.* Before I can tell the rest of the story—that Elise actually agrees with her messed up, borderline homicidal method—Willa replies with: *You don't deserve friends.*

So that's what she thinks of me, is it? I may be standoffish and grouchy, but I'm not inherently a bad person. I don't deliberately harm the people I love.

I can't believe I ever liked you.

It's not necessary to tell me what a monster I am.

I don't think I could. There's no word for what I think of her.

Ask Hudson to assign you a new lab partner tomorrow, she texts. *Don't put yourself through the trouble of having to acknowledge me.*

For once, I'm glad she's shutting down and pushing me away. It spares me the trouble of having to make peace with her.

I'll do that.

I toss my phone aside and flop back on my bed with an angry sigh. It's not cold in here, but the air pricks at my bare skin. I should stop wallowing, get up and put clothes on. But I don't. I lay there and stew in anger.

I only relent and sit up when my teeth begin to chatter. The guy in the closet mirror is watching me again, studying me where I sit on the corner of the bed. Jesus, he's gross. I want to tell him to fucking eat something and hasn't he ever heard of a tan? He's like an androgynous alien, boney and hairless with a machine sprouting out of his chest.

I shut the closet door on him. But then I'm left alone with myself, cold and naked.

As I put on clothes, systematically covering up the disgustingly pale flesh and jutting bones, I find some relief in Willa's confession. Now that we're no longer involved, my inadequacy doesn't matter.

If only I could get her out of my fucking head.

Friday

Elise doesn't say anything to me over breakfast. Or in the car. Or when I sit down with her clique at lunch. I chance a look over at Willa's usual table, but she isn't there. Weird. As I cross the parking lot to get to the portables I notice that her rusty Toyota isn't here, either. She's absent. Willa is never absent.

Maybe she's sick.

> *She was fine yesterday.*

Maybe she transferred out.

That bothers me far more than it should.

I didn't get to say goodbye.

> *Are you sure you want to?*

I want some closure, at least. I want her to apologize to Elise. I want to part ways with the knowledge that she's going to a place that will be able to deal with her problems.

Willa's absence distracts the hell out of me all through Social Studies. Maybe I could talk to Paige Holbrook or Hannah Trilby—Willa might have mentioned to her other friends if she was planning to leave school.

Her other *friends?*

> *Slip of the tongue.*

I take stock of the parking lot once more as I head to English for my last class of the day. Her car still isn't here. It's stupid, but I head for the nurse's office instead of my English class. I've never come here as a visitor. The nurse looks up at me from her desk and asks if I'm not feeling well.

"No, I'm fine. Has Willa Kirk been in here today?"

The nurse finds my question surprising. "No, she hasn't."

"Great."

I leave the main office to…stand in the parking lot. Where was I going?

My phone is in my hand and I'm dialing her home number. Hopefully she's just sick and stayed home to rest.

Hopefully? What do you care?

Frank answers the phone with a gruff hello. I ask if Willa is available to come to the phone and he asks to know who is calling.

"It's Jem Harper."

"Aren't you supposed to be in school?"

"Yes, sir, I am."

"Well then would you like to explain why you're obviously not in class, calling my sister in the middle of the afternoon?"

"I...uh, I noticed Willa was absent from our Soc class. I wanted to know if she needed me to bring anything she might need. Homework, things in her locker..."

"Get to class," he says. "And leave Willa alone, while you're at it. She's had enough trouble." He hangs up on me.

I have this rotten feeling of dread in my gut. *She's had enough trouble.* Maybe her brother or parents pulled her out of school without warning her—a reform school might be in the cards after all.

One of the hall monitors sees me standing in the middle of the parking lot. He comes out of the building and calls out to me, "Do you have a pass?"

She's gone and you're never going to see her again.

I turn and vomit between the cars. My head is spinning. The only thing that keeps me upright is the hand I have braced on the trunk of the nearest car.

"Hey!" The hall monitor approaches me and lays a tentative hand on my back. It's such a light touch, as though he's afraid I'll break. Willa never once touched me like that.

"You all right?" Before I can answer he announces that he's going to walk me to the nurse's office. Stupid, overeager freshman.

Then I realize the tire I threw up on belongs to Chris Elwood's car, and I feel a little bit better.

Saturday

The sun is high in the east by the time I roll out of bed and walk, still more asleep than awake, to the bathroom to take a shower. I strip with my brain on autopilot and cover my central line just as steam begins to rise from behind the curtain.

As I doze under the warm spray, coherent thoughts begin to circulate. They're timid and fragmented at first: *I'm hungry. The chord progression needs work. Where'd I put my iPod? It's Saturday—what time is it? Late enough to go over to—*

That's a sobering thought. No more Saturdays at the Kirk house. Not that I want to go over there, but...what the hell will I do with my time?

Having no friends turns out to be really good for the homework situation.

I bet that's why dorks are all so studious; not by choice, but by virtue of bore-dom. I knock out all my assignments by noon and have nothing left to do. There's nothing on TV. It's too rainy to go for a walk. There's nothing to do in Smiths Falls. Mom and Dad are out of the house, shopping for shrubs to plant by the porch. Elise won't talk to me and Eric is at work. And I can't stop think-ing about Willa. Every hour it gets harder to resist the urge to call her. For all I know she could already be on a campus where students wear wristband tracking devices and lockdown is the norm.

I don't really care about her. I just want to know what's going on.

Riiiight.

    Shut up.

I call Ava. I need a dose of her twisted reality to take the edge off mine.

"What do you want, bitch?" Ava's crass greeting makes me feel a little bit better. I ask her if she's busy and she says she's setting up for a band practice.

"Why are you calling?"

"Boredom." It's a synonym for loneliness in my case. Ava sees right through me and asks if I've got nothing better to do.

"Pretty much."

"How's that girl you've been chasing?"

"Uh, I don't want to talk about it."

"What, is she dating some shaved gorilla now? Doesn't know what she's miss-ing out on with you?"

"It's not like that."

"What's it like?"

"Never mind."

"You sound sexually frustrated. Your voice goes up an octave like that when you're horny." She laughs at me. "Is your girl a tease?"

"No." Maybe. Or maybe I just have an overactive imagination. But it's hard to picture her in a nice way now. All that comes to mind are fistfuls of pills and the ragged scar on her hand.

Ava can tell I'm not being truthful. "Rub one out. Ease the tension."

"Ava."

"Oh, right." Her tone dips from lighthearted to flat and sarcastic. "Is that what happened? Did you get her into bed and then disappoint her?" Damn it. I thought it had been long enough—Ava's attention span is a short one—and that she wouldn't be sore about our abortive screw anymore. I guess not.

"I'm sorry."

"Don't worry about it."

"No, really, I'm sorry. I shouldn't have done that. I knew you didn't."

"Why did you do it?" she says shrewdly.

"Why did you?" I'm used to that trick causing the end of a conversation, the way it does with Willa. Just ask her something she doesn't want to tell, and the whole discussion shuts down. I'm so used to it that I'm caught off guard when

Ava actually answers the question.

"I felt bad for you." I don't need to hear that. "Your turn."

I swallow, considering how I can lie plausibly about this. I can't.

"I...sort of, um...I liked the feeling of being wanted."

"Was the, uh, *problem* really because of the cancer?" Ava asks. I can't help but smile. She's not trying to give me a hard time; it's just that her pride is wounded. I know a thing or two about that, but she doesn't deserve to second-guess herself.

"Ava, we both know you're the sexiest chick to ever attach an amp to a violin."

"Flatterer."

"Fine, whatever, but it ups my street cred to say I banged you, so don't go telling people otherwise." That makes her laugh and she calls me a lying cocksucker. I'm officially forgiven. I let the tension out of my shoulders and crawl onto the bed, relaxing against the pillows for a comfortable and hopefully time-consuming conversation with my foul-mouthed friend.

"Come on now, how's your girl?" she asks.

"I don't want to talk about it." And Willa certainly isn't mine in any sense of the term.

"Did you give up on her already?"

"It's not like that."

Ava scoffs. "You want to explain it in a way that doesn't make you look like a gaping vagina? Because you were already behaving like a pussy about her before, and this sounds worse."

"I was not."

"Yes, you were. Massive vag. And not even the good kind with a wax job and a hood piercing—I mean a had-six-kids bat cave kind of vagina."

"Ava."

"Spill. What happened?"

"Nothing."

"You were freaking depressed over her just a few weeks ago. What, did your 'crush' burn out?"

"Something like that."

"Bullshit. It wasn't just a crush."

"Yes it was." I can't let Ava think she's right. She never can resist the urge to say 'I told you so' when opportunity presents itself.

"Did you finish that song for her?"

I sigh. "Yeah."

Ava crows. "I knew you were writing one! Did she like it?"

"I didn't give it to her."

"Why not?"

"It's complicated."

"She's-screwing-someone-else complicated, or she-plays-for-the-other-team complicated?" Figures; those are the only two obstacles Ava has ever encountered in her romantic life. Except for that awkward non-screw with me, of course.

"In a we're-not-even-friends-anymore kind of way."

That takes Ava aback. "Why not?" she demands.

"She's not who I thought she was."

"Well…so what? You knew she wasn't perfect, and you still had it bad for her. It's not like you're so perfect—you play *Mozart*, for crying out loud."

"I can't explain it. Just take my word for it, okay?"

"Jem," Ava says seriously. "You were happy when you talked about her. Your whole face lit up. You were the old you again. It's stupid to throw away the things that make you feel that way."

"She doesn't make me feel happy."

"Liar."

"She makes me feel…exposed."

Ava laughs, low and sultry. In the background I hear the feedback of an amp being plugged in. "Same thing sometimes, isn't it?"

This is making me uncomfortable—cue subject change. "Are you still cheating with that cellist?"

"Jem." Ava's tone is light, but there's a no-bullshit business about it. "I'm going to break this down for you, because the powers that be gave you a cock instead of a clue, and you're a chronic fuckup when it comes to women: you still like her. Don't tell me you don't. You tolerated five whole minutes of conversation about her and just now tried to change the subject. So whatever the reason is that you're not friends with her anymore, *fix* it."

"Or what?" The attempt at false bravado sounded better in my head.

"Don't get me wrong, I still love you bitch, but you could do with a little happiness."

I groan. "The cellist, Ava?"

"Demon in the sack. Phil doesn't know—too busy sucking endangered seal dick to notice. Now back to you: start working on fixing your shit. Get that smile back. Oh, and find a way to empty your balls. Celibacy doesn't agree with you."

"Shut up."

"You're grouchy when you're horny."

"Let go of the idea of Willa and I—drop it right now 'cause it's never going to happen." It hurts to say that out loud, but it's probably true.

"Ah, she has a name," Ava coos. "At least talk to her, okay? Never burn a bridge."

I sigh and Ava scolds me for being pessimistic. "Don't be a twat."

"You're a twat."

"No, I *have* a twat. And if you want me to keep quiet about that time with my twat and your dick, you'll smarten up and fly right."

"You can be a real bitch, you know."

"Bitch, please, you love me."

"Don't get cocky."

She laughs at me and says she has to go. "Gotta make real music. You know what that is, you classical dork?"

"Does it sound like an elephant being raped? Cause your last song—"

"Twat." Ava blows a raspberry into her phone. "Okay, really, I have to go. Love you, bitch."

"Ditto. Whore."

Ava hangs up, and I'm back to being bored. I play my cello for a little while, but once again it fails to satisfy. How is it possible that every separation from Willa messes up the most basic things in my life—my family, my music, my sleep? She's like a virus.

You miss her.

I don't even want to look at her.

Yeah, 'cause that's why you got all shell-shocked by her absence yesterday.

Call her.

No.

You know you want to talk to her.

On some level I do miss talking to Willa. But what is there to talk about now? We can't just go back to discussing music and Soc homework after…after what was said. The only thing left to say is…well, I'm not sure what, exactly, but I want to diffuse the tension. I'm tired of feeling it weigh on me.

This doesn't strike me as the kind of conversation that should be had over the phone. I need to find a way to talk to her in private, face-to-face. But she probably doesn't want to see me.

So I text her: *Do you have my Nightdodger CD?*

I know she has it. I loaned it to her a week before our hike. Retrieving it will give me an excuse to go over to her house and see her. We can sit down and hash this out. I have a feeling it'll take a while.

She replies: *You're not getting that back.*

Spiteful as ever, I see.

You're being a child.

She replies: *You're being a prick.*

This chick is driving me crazy.

Mom and Dad return from their gardening trip, damp with rain and seemingly optimistic about their plans for the area around the front porch. Mom sees me sitting up with my cello and smiles.

"What are you playing?"

"Just puttering around." I raise my bow and start playing her favorite song. I want to project a sense of normalcy to mask the fact that Elise and I still aren't speaking and I'm having problems of my own. The music does comfort her; she hums along with it as she heads to the kitchen. It's one of those simple, gentle melodies that make great love songs. This one has no lyrics, but it sounds loving nonetheless.

When the song ends I look up and see Mom and Dad slow-dancing in the kitchen. At least somebody's happy.

Sunday

I step out of the shower, still annoyed that it's morning already, and turn on the bathroom light. It takes me a few bleary seconds to notice the message written in the steam on the mirror: *Clear the air.* There's a milkshake sitting on the counter. How the hell did Elise get in here without me noticing?

I still drink the milkshake. Her loopy words on the mirror feel like more of a demand than a suggestion. I dry off, get dressed, and go downstairs to meet her. Dad is at the stove, trying and failing to flip-toss a pancake. It falls to the floor and Eric shouts, "Five second rule!" Mom is engrossed in the Sunday morning crossword, and Elise is nursing a giant cup of coffee with her knees pulled up. I walk around behind her chair and wrap an arm around her shoulders. She grunts tiredly as I kiss the top of her head.

"I'm sorry," I whisper. Elise reaches a hand back to pat me on the head. I love that apologies can be this simple with her. "Thanks for the milkshake."

"Sure."

I pull my chair out and Elise says, "So how's Willa?" She says it lightly, but I can hear the agenda in her tone. Mom looks up from the crossword with a smile. She's just as interested in my response as Elise is.

"Invite her over now," Dad says before I can answer. "I can make more batter." I think he just wants an excuse to practice his flip-toss some more. Even if Willa and I were on good terms, it would be hard to sell her on the idea of pancakes fresh off the floor.

Elise gives me a pointed look and it dawns on me that the message in the mirror wasn't solely about her. I have to end the situation with Willa.

"Actually, I was going to go over there." I ask Mom if I can borrow her car.

Elise elbows me playfully.

"No, you can't come."

"Why not?" she pretends to pout. She knows perfectly well why not. "I like Willa. She's a good friend." The last two words bear a special emphasis, making it clear whom she's still rooting for, if I still had any doubts.

"Forget it, Lise."

❧

I park down the street from the Kirk house and sit there for about five minutes, giving myself a pep talk. Just go in, tie off the loose ends, say goodbye and pretend that I never knew Willa Kirk.

I don't want to get out of the car. If I do that I will put in motion the end of my only friendship in this tiny, boring town. But is it a friendship worth keeping? I was vulnerable like Thomasina not so long ago. Willa probably would have treated me with the same lack of respect and compassion, and that knowledge is deeply disturbing.

When I finally do approach the house, I'm relieved to find that her brother's car isn't in the driveway. I'm not his favorite person, and it bodes well for me that he isn't around to shut down this conversation with Willa before it can even start.

I go up to the front door to knock and I catch a glimpse of Willa through the front window. She's laying on the couch, sleeping. Should I wake her? I go to ring the doorbell, but then I hesitate. Maybe I should come back later. I shouldn't wake her up… Or I could wake her up with something nicer than a doorbell.

I try the handle. It's locked. Same with the side door off the garage. I go around to the back door. It, at least, is open. I let myself in as quietly as possible, but Willa wakes up anyway. She comes into the kitchen and stops dead when she sees me standing there.

Willa looks like hell. She has dark circles under her eyes and her clothes seem to hang on her like a scarecrow without stuffing. Her hair is limp. Her face is pale. She looks…sick.

"I destroyed your CD. You can fuck off now." Not exactly the welcome I was hoping for, but it'll do.

"That's a shame. I was gonna let you keep it." It's just a CD—a small price to pay for ending this with as few complications as possible. Willa doesn't seem to care. Her face is completely blank.

"Um, can we talk?"

"I thought we'd already said it all." She turns away from me and goes to the stove. I've upset her already, if she's turning to cooking, or maybe she was still upset before I walked in.

"Smells good." It smells like a holiday meal; like warm meat and vegetables and sweet, juicy gravy. It seems indecent to be hungry when I came here to cut ties, but I can't help it.

Willa doesn't answer me. I tug gently on the back of her sweater, hoping she'll at least face me, but she doesn't.

"You don't look well." She looks sore and pathetic. I'd give her a hug but she'd probably punch me for trying.

You'd do what now?

Nothing. It was just an errant thought.

"Neither do you," she says dryly. I let go of her sweater. I should probably go; she doesn't want to listen to me.

You're giving up already?

It's not the right time.

I don't believe you.

Willa finally looks over her shoulder at me. Her eyes narrow and she frowns.

"You need carrots. And protein. What the hell have you been doing with yourself?"

She turns to open the cupboard and I almost smile. She wouldn't want to feed me if she hated me entirely, right? Maybe we can talk this out like human beings and not have it turn into a fight. And that soup smells fantastic. Willa carefully scoops some out for me—heavy on the carrots—but her eyes are still sad. Normally they spark when she doles out the results of a successful recipe.

I start to wonder if she's giving me food because she feels obligated. I don't want to owe her anything. "You don't have to—"

"Eat," she interrupts. "I'm not giving it to you to be friendly, so don't waste your time feeling guilty. Just eat it." I would, but she's killing my appetite. If she's not being friendly, than what is it that motivates her? Pity? Guilt? Duty? Maybe I underestimated her sincerity when she said I didn't deserve friends.

"I want to talk to you."

Willa hands me a spoon. "Talking doesn't work out so hot for us. Just eat." She's not going to let down her dismissive attitude. I'll just have to work around it, or I'll never get the opportunity to say what I want to say.

"I said stuff I shouldn't have."

Willa dismisses me again: "No shit. Let's not beat a dead horse by discussing it, okay?" No dice. I came here to clear the air, not to mooch soup and sit in silence.

Elise did a more than adequate job of pointing out my screw-ups during my explanation of Wednesday. I have a feeling that Willa will be more amenable to discussion if I take responsibility for my wrongdoings first, so I open with: "I came here to apologize. Some of those things I said..." Should I insult myself or just keep it simple? "I really didn't mean them."

Willa throws the spoon into the sink. Shit. I should have insulted myself.

"Well that's the kicker, isn't it? Which words *did* you mean?"

Nothing sucks worse than the moment in an argument when you realize that you might have brought a knife to a gunfight. I know I said some rude things to her, but I couldn't possibly recount them all. I was angry—I wasn't thinking through what I said. It was impulsive and heated. She probably remembers every nasty word to hold over my head, and I only remember the highlights.

"I was mad, okay?"

"Don't get defensive," she tells me flatly. "I know you were upset. There's only one thing you said that I really care about anyway."

My stomach drops. I know exactly what she's talking about.

"Maybe I didn't mean it. I'm not sure."

Willa points to the back door. "Get out of my house." I'd better fix this quickly, before she shoves me out the door.

"I didn't mean you haven't suffered. But...it's different. You haven't lived in fear of your own life. You wouldn't think like that—you wouldn't take your life so lightly—if you had, I mean…um…" How do I explain that the fight to live is more difficult than the decision to die?

And you would know…?

Look at Meira.

"Is that what you came over here to say?" she asks.

"I came over to say a lot of things." If she'll let me.

Willa sighs and points to the dining table. "Eat first." She turns away and pads down the hall. I'm not done talking to her yet.

"Willa?"

"I'm just getting dressed. Eat your damn soup already." That last sentence gives me hope. She said it without heat, just her usual foul mouth. Her tone was almost fond, like the way she speaks when she tells me to shut the hell up for annoying her. And Good Lord, this soup is good… I'm plowing through it like it's the last food on earth when my phone vibrates in my pocket. It's a text message from Ava: *Have you fixed your shit yet? Got a gig coming up. Want you to bring W.*

Her enthusiasm is depressing.

Fixing it. Ending it. When's the gig?

Ending? You are a fucking dipshit.

She punctuates that text with several aggressive emoticons.

Get over yourself and be happy, damn it.

I'm at her house right now. Not a happy place. I hit 'send' and look around the kitchen. I'm not sure how truthful that text was. This kitchen is the site of a lot of stuff between Willa and I—soups and fights and bargaining, harsh words and gentle touches. I don't want to give all that up just yet, but I can't stand to let the reality of Willa's mistakes slide by. I can't condone what she did. I can't see how we would make our way to being friends again, whether or not I want to be. I sort of hope this whole closure thing takes all afternoon, knowing it'll be the last time I really talk to her.

I hear Willa's footsteps on the stairs and I pocket my phone. The rest of my soup is gone in two big bites before she can even walk the length of the hall.

I'm not exactly sure why Willa 'got dressed.' She just seems to have traded grey sweatpants and a pajama top for black sweatpants and a hoodie. But her hair seems to be combed, and she generally looks a little better than she did five minutes ago.

She takes one look at me and plugs in the electric kettle. Tea? Willa picks up my bowl and ladles more soup out for me.

"Thanks. I wasn't sure if I should just take seconds without asking." I'm barely back in her good graces, best not to push just yet.

Willa sets the bowl in front of me and then opens the freezer. She tosses me a strawberry yogurt pop. She knows I love these. She wouldn't give it to me if she was only feeding me out of pity or guilt, would she?

"Are we okay now?" I expected to have to work to set the stage for a civilized conversation.

Willa looks at me with that deeply penetrating expression. "We're talking again."

"About that…"

"Say it. Don't dawdle."

"We have things to discuss."

"You didn't get it all out on Wednesday?" She gives me that look that makes me feel totally exposed without saying a word. I apologize for the way I interrogated her on the hike, and she agrees to sit down at the table with me. Willa pulls her hood up and folds her arms as if she's cold.

I can't cut her down when she already looks so downtrodden and vulnerable. It's like wringing a kitten's neck. I lick my lips, stalling. It didn't used to be this hard to just *talk* to her.

So talk.

"Tell me about the psych ward."

"What's there to tell?"

"I don't know. I've never been in one."

Willa sighs resignedly. "Take a prison mentality, since most people who wind up in psych wards don't do so voluntarily, and throw in the fact that half the people there live in an alternate reality, a third are going through hell trying to detox, and the rest are starving to death, and you have a psych ward. Questions?"

"What group were you in?"

"I was in detox at first, but when I acted out they'd give me sedatives, so sometimes I fit in the 'alternate reality' group. I could come back to the rational surface when I skipped a dose, though."

"You mean when you passed off your meds to a recovering addict?"

Willa rolls her eyes. "I get it. I'm Satan. Are you done now?"

"I didn't say that."

"Your tone did."

"I didn't mean it that way."

"Then what did you mean?"

"I was trying to clarify the situation. You said you gave your meds to a junkie."

"And that makes me a horrible person."

"I didn't say that!" I don't really care about the addict. I don't think it was Willa's most admirable moment, but it's small change compared to killing her sister.

"I gave her my Ambien because she bothered me, alright? People get in your face if they know you have a prescription for something good. Giving her my Ambien got her out of my face, and in return she did stuff for me."

"What kind of stuff?"

"Prison mentality, remember? You have to have a group of people you rely on to keep the cage from overshadowing the wide world beyond. Sometimes she'd give me extra food, or access to a newspaper, or cause a scene so the rest of us could get a few minutes without the orderlies breathing down our necks."

"The staff must have known she was stoned."

"Of course they did. They just had a hard time tracing her sources. She'd take anything, so they knew by her behavior—calm one day and buzzing the next—that she had a couple people to pump drugs from. Antipsychotics made her into a total nightmare."

"You still shouldn't have given your pills to her."

Willa snorts. "It was either that or get in a fight with her. There are no heroes in hell. You just get by as well as you can, and that's it."

"You're rationalizing."

Willa steals a cold carrot out of my bowl. "Alright, smartass. Let's say I tell you that you shouldn't have taken all those chemotherapy treatments. Sure, it made you cancer-free, but look at all the shit it cost you along the way. Would you throw your hands up and admit I'm right? Or would you defend your decision to live in pieces instead of die whole? We're all just getting by with the options available to us. Get off your high horse."

"That is complete bullshit," I tell her. "You made a choice to do what you did. I didn't just decide one day to have cancer."

Willa just shakes her head. "You don't get it. All the things you loved, the things that cancer cost you—do you think that loss would have been any less significant if it had come from a bad decision instead of random accident? Would it have made you feel *empowered* to throw it all away on purpose? Or would it haunt you that the responsibility was yours to bear?" She snatches my bowl away and gets up to dump the dregs of soup in the sink.

"You told me my feelings mattered when I agreed not to cut you out," she says. "So quit belittling me."

I hate it when she's right. "I'm sorry." The apology doesn't do much good. She's on a roll now.

"You bitch, piss and moan constantly that you're so fucking hard-done-by. Imagine how awful you'd feel if you were actually at fault for the bad things that have happened to you."

"What do you want me to say? That you've got the harder life?" That makes her pause. Willa stands there in the middle of the kitchen with her mouth hanging open. I've stunned her speechless.

"You...are so fucking dense," she says quietly, as though she can't quite believe it. "This isn't a contest. I don't want to one-up you. I want to *matter* to you."

"You think you don't matter to me?" What planet is she on? I wouldn't be here if she didn't matter to me, even against my better judgment. I wouldn't be driving myself insane trying to come to terms with her messed up past and frustrating personality. I wouldn't be so thoroughly distracted by her absence from school. I would have walked away from her without a backward glance and been glad to be rid of her—yet here I am.

"Forget it," Willa says. She nods to the back door and tells me I can go now. I look at her, standing with her arms folded and the shades drawn over her eyes.

She's cold and closed in, retreating instead of continuing the fight.

"We're not done talking."

"Yes, we are."

"Will you drop the frigid bitch act for a minute? I know you're human underneath. I am trying to understand the shit-ton of stuff you dumped on me last week, okay? I'm *trying*—and you haven't always done that for me, so don't act like I owe you anything. But I can only muster up so much compassion for—"

"Shut up," she interrupts me. "I don't want your fucking compassion. I trusted you to at least treat me with civility, and you called me a nutcase and said that my pain was insignificant. Now how the fuck does that compare to me refusing to attend the pity party you've been throwing yourself for *months*?"

She shouts the last part, so the silence that follows is like thick fog. It chokes the room and amplifies the distance between us, even though Willa is only a few feet away from me, fuming by the counter.

Her anger doesn't frighten me the way it used to. This is Willa. When things get rough she shuts down and blocks people out. When that fails she gets angry, pushing away instead of merely obstructing. And when that doesn't work…she cracks.

I say, "Regardless"—her eyes narrow at me—"we're still not done talking."

Willa's bedroom is more of a mess than usual. I suppose it's to be expected. Willa herself is more of a mess than usual. She picks up a CD case off her shelf and hands it to me.

"No, keep it, really."

"This doesn't mean I forgive you."

"Ditto."

Willa sits down heavily on the edge of the bed. She's got an odd sense of peace—or perhaps defeat—about her, and I don't know how long it will last. She might give anger another try if I give her an excuse.

"You took the rest of your meds when you got home?" She draws my memory back to Wednesday, to trying to take three pills at once without enough fluid to wash them down. Gag.

"Yeah."

"Were you hurting before you said anything about it?"

"Just a dull ache," I tell her quietly.

Willa nods sadly. When she speaks her voice is soft and mournful. "I shouldn't have made you hike like that. I should have waited to take you there."

I can't help but find that amusing. "Kirk, it would have hurt with or without the hike. I've got joint pain from—" I hesitate. I'm in the habit of avoiding this subject; I don't know how to talk about it. So I leave the sentence hanging and shrug. "You probably already Googled it."

"I didn't."

Well, now I feel like a jerk for researching her medications.

"Really?"

"I told you, I care far less about your cancer than you think I do." Willa sighs like she's exhausted. I take a seat next to her on the edge of the bed and she doesn't stop me.

My phone vibrates again. The buzzing sounds louder than it actually is in the silence of Willa's bedroom.

"Excuse me."

I check my phone, expecting another angry text from Ava, but it's a message from Elise: *I put your backpack on the back seat.* My mind immediately goes to medication. Is there something I forgot to take today? Something I didn't bring with me that Elise thought I would be gone long enough to need?

"Uh...give me a minute."

Willa doesn't say anything. She just stares straight ahead with that dead look in her eye and gives no indication that she heard me. I leave her like that and go out to the car to retrieve my backpack.

The backpack is empty of school stuff, but there is a book. I recognize the black cover without having to open it. It's the photo album that usually sits on my third shelf. What the hell is it doing here?

Elise's loopy handwriting is on a sticky note on the cover: *Please don't screw this up.*

I call Elise from the driveway. She skips the hello and asks if Willa and I have made up yet.

"Why the hell did you put this in my bag?"

"I thought you might need it."

"Why?"

"I thought she'd be...curious. You said you asked her questions, but she didn't ask you any. Willa must wonder. And didn't she show you her pictures?"

"This isn't a tit-for-tat situation."

"She's your friend."

"Lise, I'm not sure what you were expecting, but I'm not here to make up with her. I'm here to get a clean break."

I move the phone away from my ear to spare myself from her squawk of indignation. "But it's *Willa.*"

"This doesn't concern you."

"You're not going to get a clean break," she says moodily. That little snot.

"Goodbye, Elise." I hang up on her and silence the ringer so she can't bother me by repeatedly trying to call back.

Shit.

I lock the car without putting the album back. Should I show it to Willa? Do I owe her an explanation when I plan to cut ties? Is it fair to share all this stuff and then never speak again?

I turn the album over and find another of Elise's cheeky little surprises: she taped a recent Polaroid of me to the back cover. It's the snapshot she took after I came in from kissing Willa on the porch, right before Elise ratted me out to Mom.

That's the smile Ava was talking about.

I look stupidly happy in the photo. It's an image of a simpler time, before Willa's baggage parked itself between us, revealing her to be something much more sinister than just an angry teenage girl.

She can deal with your baggage.

> *My baggage doesn't include killing someone.*

Compared to her you look normal.

> *All the more reason to end it.*

But what are you without her?

I look back to the Kirk house. I could just get in the car and drive away right now. Willa probably wouldn't miss me. She's just as upset with me as I am with her, and she's practically in a walking coma—I bet she hasn't even realized I've left the room yet.

A week ago that would have worried you.

> *I don't care anymore.*

Sure.

> *I don't.*

So drive away.

> *We're not done talking yet.*

You just can't stand to leave.

❧

Willa has moved all of two feet in the ten minutes I was away. She lies on her bed with her pillow resting squarely over her face. Blocking out the world, or a half-baked attempt to suffocate herself?

I lift the pillow off her face and Willa lazily opens her eyes. "I thought you left."

"I just went down to the car."

Willa sits up as though the movement is a great challenge and swings her legs out of bed. "Don't let me keep you if you have some place to be," she says.

"I don't," I assure her. "We're not done yet." I sit next to her on the bed. "We still have to go to school and have class together. It'll be awkward and unproductive unless we, uh…reach an understanding."

Willa sighs and nods. "I'll leave you alone if you leave me."

"That's not what I meant." I shouldn't speak so impulsively. As soon as the words are out, I wish I could take them back.

So what did you mean, smartass?

Willa asks the same question in fewer words.

"Um…I don't think we should totally ignore each other."

Willa looks over at me with dead eyes and a smirk. "Right. I forgot the part where you continue to use me until you can make other friends."

"No, it's not like that."

"Don't tell me you still want to be friends?"

"No, I don't." I'm too disappointed in her to manage that. "But…I'm not ready to just cut you out completely."

"What if I'm ready to cut you out?" She's giving me that sideways look that could mean anything, and it's difficult not to show the effect her question has on me. She's good at cutting people out cold turkey; it sucked last time she did it to me. I shouldn't care about that anymore, but I do, and the wound is fresher than I'd care to admit.

"Are you?"

"No." She shakes her head. "I still think well of you, for the most part. You're the one who thinks I'm a monster."

Do I think that?

"You think I'm a self-pitying fathead."

"Only sometimes. Most of the time you're pretty cool. You've grown on me." Willa offers up a weak smile. It's sad to watch her meager attempt to seem happy. She knows it's not working, so she relaxes her mouth back into an apathetic frown and clears her throat.

"Did you forget your meds?" She points to the backpack near my foot.

"No. Um…" I open the bag take out a black photo album. It's… a peace offering? A way of settling a debt?

"I still owe you, for showing me yours…" Willa stares at the book and makes no move to take it from me.

"Show me."

"Uh…" I was sort of banking on her looking through it herself. I don't want to have to discuss it. If she asked questions I would answer them, but I don't want to do show-and-tell. I can't.

"Are you just doing this because I showed you mine?"

"Yeah, speaking of, did you have braces? Because your teeth were really messed up as a kid."

Willa gives me a dry look. "Don't try to change the subject."

"Fine, I owe you. Here." I try to hand her the book.

"You don't owe me your history, and I don't want it if that's the only reason you're offering."

"Will you just take the book?" I extend the album to her again.

"No."

"Why can't you just cooperate?"

"Because you obviously want me to." She smirks without humor. "You think showing me this stuff will really make you feel better about the situation?"

"Maybe?" It's one less loose end if we even the score. We'll fully know each other's pasts, insofar as we can, and the decision to cut ties will be informed and equitable.

"Show me, Jem."

I don't have the guts to show her. If she left it up to me, I would never open the cover. I need her to take it and turn the pages and really look and see, the way she made me see Thomasina.

Maybe if I talk long enough, explaining the album without really showing her, she'll get impatient and take it from me.

"You already know I had a transplant. Elise was the donor. She and I are a match, but Eric and I aren't, and he felt sort of…left out. He, um…well, he had a harder time with me being sick than Elise did. But he had this idea—he took pictures. I hated him for it at the time, but he said that at some point down the road I was going to have a rough day and I could look at these pictures to put a *real* bad day in perspective."

I hand her the album. She doesn't take it.

"If you don't trust me enough to show me, you shouldn't have brought it here."

I hate it when she's right.

Bite the bullet.

I balance the book on its spine and let it fall open. We're starting from the middle of the book, then, at the shots Eric took around Christmastime. The shots on this particular page are of Elise and I. We're lying side by side in the same hospital bed, even though that's against the rules. We're both wearing red and green toques and Elise has a surgical mask over her nose and mouth. Eric drew a smile on her mask for the photo and put an ornament on my IV pole.

"That was a week or so after they let me out of isolation, from the transplant."

"It looks like Elise bounced back pretty well."

I swallow and refrain from answering. Just a few weeks before that photo was taken, Elise suffered life-threatening complications. My baby sister almost died trying to save me. I couldn't even visit her; my immune system was too diminished. I relied on Polaroids from Eric as proof that she was still alive and on the mend. Maybe 'relied' isn't the right word—I practically demanded photo updates several times a day. I had to burn those pictures, afterwards. I couldn't stand to look at them.

Willa flips back to the beginning of the book and new set of photos. I still had hair when Eric began taking pictures. In these I'm curled up in the fetal position, green in the face and sweating from the pain. Mom is holding a cold cloth against my neck. I remember that photo. I puked all over myself just a few minutes after it was taken.

Willa flips the page, to the pictures of Elise and I after she knit me that first hat. I look morose underneath my affected smile as she perches with her chin on my shoulder, next to her new creation. The next photos are of my second round of chemo, where I had to have injections put directly into my spine. Willa pauses on those for a long time.

"It didn't hurt," I say. "They numbed me. I just had a bit of a headache after."

She touches my dad's image in the photo. He was with me for that treatment. While I was curled up for a jab in the spine he sat facing me and we talked about music. I remember asking him if he'd ever done an injection like that on a patient. He said he had, and he looked so uncomfortable that I quickly changed the subject.

"Were they drawing fluid or injecting you?"

"Injecting."

"And Elise gave you marrow? Or was it something to do with your kidneys?"

"Marrow." I snort at the memory. "You want to know something? We had the transplant scheduled for early October. I had chemo and full-body radiation to prepare for it; ended up feeling like shit. And then she got an ear infection. We had to put off the transplant until she was well again. I went through hell for a procedure that got delayed."

Willa chuckles with dark amusement. "Is that irony? Or just bad luck?"

"Bad luck, but it could have been worse. My good luck was that she was a match and willing to donate."

Willa flips a few more pages. She remarks that Eric isn't in any of these photos.

"He was behind the camera." I skim ahead a few pages to the solitary photo of Eric in the whole album. It was taken by accident, and his face is only visible in the corner of the frame because the lens was pointing toward a mirror. Eric had a rare serious expression on at the time.

Willa studies that frame for a long time. "How'd he handle it?"

"Eric..." How do I describe my brother's reaction? "He was angry at first. He took off to Ottawa and stayed with Celeste's family for a few days. When he came back he was sort of resentful—sometimes of me, or our parents, or because we were all pretty much helpless." I shrug. "He came around during my second round of chemo. I had all kinds of bleeding problems at the time—nosebleeds so bad they required a trip to the ER, bruises all over, you name it. I couldn't clot properly and I had low iron so I was weak all the time. Most days I couldn't even walk down the stairs or cross the room without feeling tired. So... he carried me. I'd put an arm over his shoulders and shuffle along beside him. On Mom's birthday I was too weak and dizzy to do stairs, so he picked me up and brought me down to the kitchen so we could celebrate as a family."

"That's really nice of him."

I smile for effect and tell her I agree. It's convenient to leave out the part of that story where I passed out at the breakfast table, landed on my nose hard enough to make it bleed, and ruined Mom's birthday with a trip to the ER.

Willa continues to flip pages, studying the Polaroids with a look of frank interest. She snorts at the picture of Elise with her hand stuck in the second floor vending machine. "Her pretzels got caught."

When Willa gets to the picture of Mom hugging one of the doctors she pauses. Eric took this picture while standing behind the doctor, so all that's visible is Mom's face over his shoulder and her arms around the doctor's neck. She's grinning and crying all at once in this picture.

"Good news," Willa notes. I tell her that that was the day Elise's tests came back with a positive match for donation. Willa actually smiles.

I take the book from her then and close it. Might as well end on a happy note, and I know that most of the other pictures in that book are sad ones. I put the album in my bag and Willa quietly offers not to talk about her sister with me anymore.

"It upsets you, and we can't really relate on that subject anyway."

I want to say yes. "Are you sure?"

"I'm not used to talking about her. I don't know how to do it in a non-creepy way."

"You talked to your shrinks about her."

"I lied," she whispers. "All the time. I lied in Group, too, but everybody did. I never told anybody the real thing. I would just make up stories until they were satisfied that I'd said enough."

"Why would you do that? They were there to help you."

Willa raises her chin a little. "I didn't trust them not to judge me for it. Come on, sixteen-year-old kid kills her sister—everyone has an opinion about it. So I told them what they wanted to hear and nothing else."

She didn't say it outright, but her accusation swims just under the surface: *I didn't trust them not to judge me for it.* She trusted me with her secrets, and I judged her for them.

"I shouldn't have snapped on you. If I had walked away and cooled off—"

"Jem," Willa interrupts. "I didn't expect you to be happy about it."

"I know, but I shouldn't have said that stuff you. I meant some of the things I said, but it was still rude to say them."

Willa rolls her eyes at me and flops back on the bed. She curls away from me, facing the wall with her knees drawn up. "Don't you ever get tired of feeling guilty?" she says. "I'll forgive you for what you said because I'm tired of feeling awful about it, just like I'm tired of talking about my sister. I shouldn't have told you about it. The whole point of moving back to Smiths Falls was so that my mistake would no longer define me to others. It was stupid to tell you, really."

Willa doesn't move when I lay a hand on her back. It's a strange thing, looking at her in this position. It's usually the other way around. I rub small circles between her shoulder blades and she doesn't tell me to stop.

You can't do stuff like that and expect a clean break.

My hand stays. It just feels right.

You're an idiot.

"Why'd you do it?"

"Tell you?"

"Kill her."

"Don't ask me that. Mom used to ask me that."

"Was it mercy or resentment?" I want to know if Elise is right—if she did it out of some twisted form of love, or out of selfish desire to end the nightmare.

"I don't remember," Willa murmurs.

"Okay. Now tell me the truth."

"You wouldn't believe me."

"You don't trust me."

Would you if you were her?

Willa rolls over to face me. That deadly calm look comes over her face. Willa looks like that when she's on the verge of shutting down.

"She wanted to die at home. She said there was no need to sign a DNR because no one was going to dare call an ambulance if something happened to her at home. She and Mom had a huge fight over it.

"Tessa quit her Oxy—refused pain relief for weeks. She knew her body would give out faster if she was allowed to feel the strain, and she didn't want to hang around too long. Death was inevitable, but that made it imminent."

Willa pauses, and I'm not sure if I'm supposed to say something. But she just takes a few seconds to collect herself. When she speaks again her voice isn't as flat and smooth as before.

"She had all kinds of surgeries. By the end she couldn't eat or drink anymore, except what they could give her intravenously. They wanted to give her a trach and ventilator too, but she said no. It was all crap to prolong a painful life. She didn't want to live like that."

I open my mouth to argue—just because Thomasina wanted something at one point in time doesn't mean she wanted the same thing when it came down to the moment of suicide. Maybe she underestimated the pain and would have liked to die with dignity, under proper sedation, in the hands of trained professionals; not naked on the bathroom floor, shitting blood and afraid of her family's intervention.

Willa claps a hand over my mouth before I can say any of that.

"She wanted to die. She saw the opportunity and I helped her take it. Mom actually blamed herself before she blamed me. She thought if she had just gone into the bathroom to check on her…"

"Did she ever forgive you?"

"We don't talk about it." Willa sits back against the wall. "We used to get into screaming matches because I wouldn't admit what I'd done. Owning up to it meant legal trouble. But she knew. I didn't tell her why I did it. I didn't want her to feel like my bad decision was any reflection on her bad decisions—she wanted the ventilator for Tessa." Willa shrugs. "Forgiveness is sort of irrelevant, all things considered. Can't bring back the dead."

Willa looks away from me. She stares at the floor with utter apathy. Shut down again. She can't feel broken if she doesn't feel anything.

How could I have known Willa and not realized she was carrying all this around? How could she have kept this from so many different people—her counselors and parents and friends? From me?

"I'm sorry," I tell her quietly, "that I freaked. I should have heard you out. I should have really listened."

Willa still doesn't look at me. "I don't blame you." The words are so quiet I almost miss them. "I've never told anyone before," she continues equally quietly. "I didn't know how to say it. I didn't know how to help you see..." She cuts herself off with a painful gulp. Her cheeks turn warm and her eyes are glassy under her lowered lids. "It's funny, but I never *really* believed that she was going to die until I saw her lying there."

It's painful to watch her *not* cry, holding in sobs between shaky breaths. I put a tentative arm around her shoulders and Willa slowly leans toward me, like a tall tree falling. She sniffles a little between deep, calming breaths, unwilling to fall to pieces.

"So why'd you tell me?" I ask lowly.

It takes Willa a few seconds to answer. She draws a few shaky breaths, testing the smoothness of her voice. "Because we liked each other. I didn't know where it was going. We might have learned to love each other. You can't love someone if you don't really know them. And if you can't love them at their darkest moments...you just can't love them, period." Willa swipes the cuff of her sleeve across her eyes, mopping away tears before they have the chance to escape her lids.

"You think we could have had that?" The images, the lunatic fantasies, of Willa as my girlfriend seem so far away. They star a girl who was merely bereaved, not shattered and abandoned and technically a criminal. I don't know what to do with this new Willa.

"Doesn't matter." She shakes her head. "Everything's different now."

"Friends?" I offer. "I didn't ask Hudson to switch us. We're still project partners. But..." I don't want her to slip out of my life completely. It's boring and lonely without her. She's become a part of my life in Smiths Falls. I sort of need her, and I'd like to think she needs me, whether she'd admit it or not.

"Let's start over," Willa says. "Back to just...whatever we were before."

I lay my cheek atop her head and squeeze her to my side. "Okay. We'll be... well, we'll try again."

Willa sighs. "I'm tired."

"Do you want me to go?"

Please say no.

Willa shakes her head. We sit there for a little while, saying nothing. I move my hand slowly against her arm, rubbing a small length in what I hope is a comforting manner. Eventually Willa sits up without a word and turns away from me to lay down. She faces the wall again and pulls her knees up. It feels like she's pulling away.

"Are you sure you don't want me to go?"

Willa tucks her pillow under her chin and murmurs, "Please stay." It's unbelievable that two little words should give me such a sense of relief. But I don't question it now, because it feels good and Willa looks…well, she looks like she needs something.

You? Please.

Yeah, me.

There are no words left and so much yet to say. I take her iPod off the nightstand and lay down behind her. She's so small, curled up as she is. I nestle my front against her back and fit a bud into her ear.

"Can I pick?" she says quietly, and holds out her hand for the iPod. I pass it to her and Willa chooses "Iris" by the Goo Goo Dolls. It's gentle and passionate—the very reason I chose this song for our bedtime exchange a few weeks ago. It's a tone that Willa needs right now, but I don't think that's what she had in mind when she chose it. The chorus seems more poignant than ever.

I wrap an arm around her middle and hold her close. Willa adjusts her position slightly, straightening her back so it's easy to spoon her. The bridge of my nose rests against the curve at the back of her skull, breathing in the scent of her hair. I used to imagine this—cuddling with Willa in her narrow bed. I never imagined it quite under these circumstances.

"Iris" comes to a close, and it's my turn to pick. I scroll through Willa's list of songs, looking for her Great Big Sea collection. We need something upbeat, something to remind us of how our weird friendship began, and I have a particular song in mind: "Bad As I Am." Willa is mildly amused by this selection. She can't help but tap her toe to the beat.

When it's her turn to pick she takes us back down again with "Mad World" sung by Gary Jules. I hold Willa a little tighter, stroking circles on her wrists. It's a simple piano melody and the words are slow and measured, like something in a dream. The lyrics could have been written about Willa.

"You dream about dying?" I whisper.

"You do too." It's not a question. I both love and hate how she just knows me like that.

"Never of cancer," I tell her.

"Of course not. That's too obvious." She sighs. "You always die by falling."

"How'd you know?"

Willa shrugs. There's a sort of finality to it, like she isn't going to tell me now or ever. "I always lay down alone, like a wild animal in the woods, and it all just slips away."

"Willa…was it really the meds?" I hope she'll know what I mean without me having to really say it. I don't like to think of her trying to kill herself.

Willa shrugs. "You can't tell that you're fucked in the head when you're fucked in the head."

"Was that the only time you thought of...?"

"No." Willa turns down the volume on her iPod so we can hear each other better. "And yes. I experimented with cutting, but that didn't last long. I just wanted to try it 'cause some of the other kids in Group were doing it."

"You harmed yourself to fit in?"

"I wanted to see if it was really a satisfying release. They were just little nicks. I used the blade from a pencil sharpener—can't do much damage with that. It didn't make me feel any different, so I stopped."

Willa turns the volume back up, ending this line of conversation. The song finishes and she passes the iPod over her shoulder to me.

I want to suggest "Jumper" by Third Eye Blind. "Too much?" I ask.

Willa rolls her eyes and mutters something that I probably don't want to hear. The only word I catch is 'dumbass.' I opt for "Lightning Crashes" by Live instead.

"I'm kind of glad I told you when I did," Willa says suddenly. "It saved us a lot of wasted effort."

"What?"

"The way you reacted, the way we can barely be friends now—it just proves that we didn't feel that strongly about each other. A crush crumbles easily like that."

"I don't *not* like you."

"I don't not like you either." Willa looks over her shoulder at me. "But an 'us' wouldn't work. There's no trust. We can barely manage respect."

I want to say 'give it time,' but I don't want to make a promise that I might not be able to keep.

"Did you think about an 'us,' before?"

"I wondered."

"About what?"

"A lot of things," she answers vaguely. "It doesn't matter now. The failure of it all hinges on the fact that, once again, I am my mistake. I can't undo that; just have to live with it."

If I didn't know her, I might have missed the undertone of pain in her voice. It saddens me to know she thinks of herself that way, bogged down and isolated by guilt.

I tighten my arm around her middle, holding her securely. "You're not your mistake."

"But you still don't forgive me."

"No, I don't." I don't think I can. It will color how I look at Willa from now on, but...I'm not done looking at her.

"That's okay," she says softly. "You're not alone."

It's a strange sort of truce, this. We don't hate each other. We don't exactly like each other. We're friends in the most intimate sense of the word. We've apologized, but not forgiven. We've trusted and sacrificed for a payoff that isn't clear yet. It feels…right. I'm content with the arrangement. I ask Willa if she is and she answers in a tone of surprise: "Yeah. I am." Her warm little hand laces its fingers with mine. "This was really…honest."

"That's new for us."

Willa snorts with wry amusement. She takes the iPod and announces that we need something relaxing. "Something that sounds like a lullaby."

"Are you sleepy?"

"I'm coasting." She puts on "Possibility" by Sierra Noble and tells me it's her go-to on nights she can't sleep. My go-to on sleepless nights is the sound of Willa's voice. I don't tell her that.

Willa falls asleep first. I stay awake to watch her, enjoying the slow cadence of her breathing and the simple fact that she's comfortable enough to fall asleep next to me. I can't stay awake for long, though. It's the first peaceful sleep I've had all week.

✧

A hand on my shoulder roughly tugs me back to consciousness. Frank Kirk has quite a firm grip. My eyelids flutter and he turns my shoulder so I'm lying on my back. He looks pissed off, but I guess I would be too if I found some guy in my sister's bed.

"What are you doing here?"

The sound and movement makes Willa stir.

"I, uh…"

"Downstairs."

I don't hesitate to obey. I know the man has at least two firearms in the house and I'm already on his shit list.

Willa's bedroom door shuts behind me. I head for the stairs, but I can still hear the conversation through the door.

"What's this all about?"

I feel bad that Willa is the one being grilled for something we share equal responsibility for. I stop to listen on the upper landing, but I can't hear Willa's reply.

"You don't *know?*" His tone pisses me off, even if he is her guardian. He asks her if 'things' are 'serious' with 'that boy.' Whatever the hell that means, in the most condescending terms.

Willa answers no and Frank demands to know why I was in her bedroom.

"We were just hanging out. We fell asleep."

He tells her not to piss on his head and tell him it's raining. "You were just hanging out, all wrapped around each other, and fell asleep?"

"Stranger things have happened." Maybe I should reopen the question of Willa's sanity if she's willing to be cheeky at a time like this.

"You're grounded."

330

Willa laughs—actually laughs out loud—and says that grounding is moot in a sleepy town like Smiths Falls. She should have kept her mouth shut, because the next thing she loses are her phone privileges for talking back.

"So where were you last night?" What a strange question to ask. Her tone is light and genuinely interested, like she's not in the middle of being punished.

"You're going to sit up here and think about what you've done," Frank says. Willa's bedroom door opens and I hurry down the stairs.

"What are you still doing here?" he calls after me. "Go home."

I head out the door as quickly as I can. I check my watch and realize that Willa and I were asleep for over an hour.

As I dig through my pockets for the car keys I realize I left my backpack with the photo album upstairs on Willa's floor. Shit. She'll have time to go through the whole thing now, when I'm not around to influence her impressions with an explanation of each photo. It's a hundred page record of what a pathetic, sick bastard I am.

I stop on the sidewalk and consider going back to the house. What's worse, interacting with Willa's pissed off brother or permitting her open access to my photos?

A paper airplane to the side of the head interrupts the formation of my mental pros and cons list. I look over to see Willa leaning out her bedroom window. She points to the paper airplane on the lawn and I bend to pick it up.

Sorry. He's not usually rude. He fears history will repeat itself.

I cross the lawn to stand under her bedroom window. "Can I have my album back?"

Willa disappears inside for a moment and comes back with my bag. She drops it carefully out the window and it doesn't take much to notice the weight difference. She took the photo album out.

"Give it back."

"I'll give it to you at school tomorrow." Willa withdraws her head and shoulders from the window.

"Just throw it down."

"I'll trade you." Willa leaves the window, and when she comes back she throws a smaller blue book down to me. "See you at school." She closes the window, ending all communication until eight o'clock tomorrow. Her mouthing off means I can't call her and I don't have her email address to bother her in cyberspace.

I look down at what she gave me in place of my photo album: a blue canvas book with *Journal* embossed in silver italics across the front. Willa handed over her diary? She doesn't strike me as the diary-writing type. It could be considered rude to read this right in front of her window—she could be watching—but I still flip it open to the first page.

Another surprise. Instead of Willa's drunk-toddler scrawl, the page lines are filled with very neat cursive. The flyleaf says: *This book belongs to T. Kirk. If found,*

please return to...
    This could be interesting.

Willa: May 8 to 12

Monday

I get called down to the main office just before lunch. I trudge over and present my pink slip of summons to the secretary.

"They're waiting for you. Third door on the left." She points down the hall, past the principal's office where other administrative offices are kept. I head to the third door and find *S. Neil – Guidance Counselor* written on the nameplate. I bet this has something to do with the courses I requested for next year—or rather, didn't request. The registration form is still buried in my locker somewhere. I sort of forgot it in the midst of…stuff.

I knock and Mr. Neil calls me in. I step around the door to find that I'm not the only guest in this crowded little office. Frank is waiting for me too, and the top of Mr. Neil's desk is covered in brochures for counseling programs in our area.

"Have a seat, Wilhelmina." Mr. Neil gestures to the only vacant chair in the room. I don't bother to correct him about my name. This will all be over faster if I don't give attitude. Just let them shepherd me into whatever youth group will best satisfy their anxiety, bullshit my way through the system, and come out the other side having lost only a few hours in therapy and gained some freedom.

"How are you feeling today, Wilhelmina?" I know the trick he's using. It's the same one that police use to negotiate with hostage takers and people threatening suicide—call the person by his or her name as much as possible to show that complete attention is focused on the person and his or her issues. I hate it.

"Hungry."

Mr. Neil chuckles at my little 'joke.' "I meant emotionally. How are you coping with school?"

"It's alright." I glance at Frank out of the corner of my eye. He doesn't look happy. Did he expect me to walk in here and pour my soul out to a guy who looks like he should be breaking eggs on the floor of the Quick Stop?

"Have you made friends since moving here?"

"Yep."

"Good friends?"

"Very good." They treat me like any other girl, and Jem and I are giving acquaintanceship another try. That's about as good as can be expected on all fronts, given the circumstances.

"Your guardian and I were having a discussion before you came in."

Does he think I'm so stupid I can't figure that out?

"We think you could benefit from participating in some form of counseling, given your history."

Given my history. I wonder how much Frank told him. He must be here on his lunch break—he probably wants to wrap this up quickly so he can get back to the hospital.

"And how long will I have to behave myself before everyone stops looking at me like I'm a problem to be fixed?"

They stare at me.

"I've been off meds for over a year. I've been behaving for six months. Does this pigeonhole have an exit?"

"No one is suggesting that you need to be fixed," Mr. Neil says gently. "Counseling isn't a punishment. We wouldn't suggest it unless we thought it would help you."

I hate the way he uses 'we,' as if he cared about me before my case was brought to his attention, or as though he'll care after I leave this office. It makes Frank, my parents, and the school seem like a united front that I can't possibly stand up to by myself.

"Whatever you want."

Because the reality is that I can't stand up to them alone.

By the time I get to the cafeteria, the lunch line has died down. I grab something to eat and head for the usual table, which is crowded and noisy. There's only one chair left available, between Joe Moore and Jem, who has graciously decided to sit here again. There's a hierarchy to the seating arrangement. The only person willing to sit next to Jem is Hannah. Joe got the adjacent seat because he isn't popular enough to merit a better place in the pecking order.

"Where were you?" Jem asks. Hannah leans forward to look past him and asks me if everything is okay.

"Just a problem with my electives."

Hannah asks what I'm taking next year. It would be great if I had an actual answer.

"Uh…Art, and…Physics."

Jem blurts out: "But you suck at both."

"Dude."

"I've seen your stick figures. They look like shit."

"I bet you'd be really good at abstract art," Hannah says in an attempt to smooth over Jem's jackassery. I'm not that fussed. This is just normal Jem.

"I can finger paint." I flip the bird at Jem and he casually steals the juice box off my tray.

"The art teacher's ridiculously mellow, anyway," he says as he unwraps the straw. "You've got to *try* to fail that class. You're boned for Physics, though."

"Some of us actually study for our classes."

Jem gives me a look of obvious condescension. "Willa, you're a woman; you can't do math."

I snatch the juice box back and leave him with the straw. Hannah looks like she might be genuinely offended.

"No secret what you're taking next year—the same courses you'll fail this year." I hold the juice box out of reach as he makes another grab for it.

"Music and Geography."

I slap Jem's hand for getting too close to my box.

"Do you want mine?" Hannah offers Jem her unopened apple juice, probably just to get us to stop horsing around at the table.

Jem looks at her as though he can't understand why she would offer and says, "No, I'm not thirsty. I just enjoy harassment."

I snatch my straw out of his fist while he's distracted with Hannah, so he steals my pudding in retaliation.

A look of understanding suddenly comes across Hannah's face, and she smiles. "You guys are cute."

Everything comes to an immediate grinding, screeching halt. Jem and I both freeze. He drops my pudding back on the tray like it's hot and gets up from the table. Hannah casts a worried glance after him as he walks away, but I don't turn to look.

"Should I not have said anything?"

"Don't worry about it." I'll try not to hold the awkwardness against her. She can't have known. I never told her any of it.

⌣

I leave Hannah and the others outside the cafeteria and head for my locker. Jem appears at my shoulder out of nowhere and says, "Are you really taking Art?" I startle and he chuckles at me.

"No, I'm not taking Art."

"What are you taking?"

"I never handed in a form." I turn away from him to open my locker, but he just leans against the locker beside mine and continues talking face to face.

"Sorry I just took off like that."

I play dumb. "You left?"

Jem lightly smacks my shoulder and tells me to be serious for a minute. "I didn't mean to be rude."

"You weren't."

"Did you tell anyone about that dinner in Ottawa?" He doesn't want anyone to think we're dating.

"No. Did you?"

"No one in Smiths Falls."

I pause with my hand on my Soc textbook. "What the hell does that mean?"

"I mentioned it to a friend back in Ottawa. No big deal."

I shut my locker and tell him that he'd better grab his stuff for class. The bell is due to ring in two minutes.

"Can I have my album back?"

"No." I walk away.

"Why not?" he calls after me.

"I'm not done with it yet."

⟿

Jem's strategy for getting his photos back faster is to tell me about how it's so not worth the time to look at them. He pursues this oh-so-convincing line of reasoning all through class, even though I give him every indication that I'm not listening and not about to give that book back any time soon.

We bump foreheads over the assignment sheet and Jem accuses me of doing it on purpose.

"Let me see." I put a hand to his forehead, pretending to inspect the non-existent lump. Jem lets me because he's an attention whore. I flick the spot where I bumped him and steal the assignment.

"Ow," he complains.

"Whiner."

Jem elbows me. He's not that irritated; he's still smiling. When I look up from the assignment sheet I find he's stolen my notebook and answers.

"Dude."

"What?" He's got his smartass grin on, the lopsided one that makes him squint. His new eyelashes are just long enough to touch when he does it.

I snatch my notebook from under his elbow and tell him to go to hell.

"I'm taking you with me."

"I'm driving."

"The hell you are."

⟿

I warm up a piece of leftover chicken when I get home from work and take it straight upstairs to work on my new pet project. I've only got so much time before Jem stops asking for his photos back and demands them instead, so I have to make the most of my access to that book.

Eric is a very thorough photojournalist. The pictures in this album—most of them Polaroids—have a definite sense of narrative. He likes the candid shot. He captures people in their thoughtful moments.

The story opens with a photo of a sickly, but much healthier Jem sitting in a recliner in the hospital with his dad beside him. The setup of the room is familiar: he's at the beginning of a chemo treatment. Jem looks straight into the camera, glaring at his brother for taking pictures. Dr. Harper looks similarly annoyed, but his posture and forehead reveal anxiety.

Flip the page ahead in time by only a day or two, and the recliner is gone. Jem is in a bed, green in the face and sick as a dog. The only good Ivy can do for him is to bathe his face and neck with a cool cloth.

Elise plays cards with a petite bald girl. Ivy falls asleep on a waiting room couch. Whole chunks of hair are left behind on the pillow. About the same time that a bald spot develops on the back of his head, the first hat appears in the album. It's the same color as his hair.

The narrative moves to the Harper house. Jem, laid up on the couch. Elise, poised in front of a blender with a scheming smile on her face. Her hair was so long—straight down to her waist and black as a crow. One of the pictures was taken through the gap in the bathroom door. Jem is visible in the mirror, setting up swabs and a syringe at the counter. He looks pissed off and his lip is curled back as though he was about to shout at Eric when the shutter closed.

His weight loss isn't really noticeable until twenty pages in, during what appears to be his second round of chemo. His cheeks are a little thinner and his shoulders have a habitual hunch. In one of the pictures he's in what looks like a lounge, watching TV and quietly ignoring his companion while she vomits into an emesis basin beside him. There's a sweet picture of him and Elise, both sleeping. He's curled up in bed and she's in the chair beside. Their hands rest loosely intertwined on the edge of the mattress.

From there, Eric chose to take pictures of all the nursing staff, like yearbook photos. On the white strip of each Polaroid he wrote their names and one memorable thing about each of them.

Laura, likes watermelon. Maggie the Trekkie. JoAnne, brings in cookies. Kim, reads good books.

When the yearbook catalogue is over, the narrative resumes at home. Jem is bent over a sink with a blood drenched towel against his nose while Dr. Harper tries his best to help. Eric included a companion shot of Jem's bed. Presumably the nosebleed started in his sleep, because his sheets and pillow are soaked with blood.

The snapshots move to the hospital for a while. There's a nice shot of Elise sitting on her dad's lap, proudly holding out her arms to be photographed. She's got a band-aid and cotton ball on each elbow, and one higher on her shoulder. Maybe she was preparing to donate marrow, or at least being tested as a potential match.

Frank knocks on my door and I close the album as quickly as possible. I answer the door and tell him there are leftovers in the fridge; I'm not cooking tonight. Frank doesn't say anything, but he awkwardly hands me a pamphlet for a youth group in Perth: *Companions in Christ: the Healing Power of God.* It's held in the community hall of a church.

"We're not Catholic. We're not even religious."

Frank clears his throat. "I know, but it's the closest one. If not that, you'll be going to Ottawa." He takes the pamphlet from me and opens it. "They meet on Sundays after services. You'd only have to go one day a week. It shouldn't affect your school."

"It's not the whole day is it?" I skim the brochure, but it's vague about how long sessions last. At least the program in St. John's never kept us past the two-hour mark.

"I want you to go."

And I want to make him happy. "I will."

Tuesday

Chris and Paige have broken up again. What is that, three times this month? Paige spends the majority of lunch hour crying over what a jerk Chris is while Diane and Hannah try to comfort her. I stay out of it to keep myself from laughing—Paige is mainly aggrieved by this breakup because it means she has no one to go to prom with.

"Prom is a whole month away. You'll find someone to go with," Hannah consoles. Diane very helpfully points out that Paige's dress is returnable, like there isn't much hope of finding a date now.

"Why don't you just go stag?" The three of them look at me as if I'm a weirdo for suggesting it.

"Maybe Cody will go with you," Diane says. Paige starts crying all over again.

⌁

I burn my wrist while frying beer batter fish for dinner and exclaim, "Jesus friggin' Christ," without thinking. Frank tells me I better start learning to curb that kind of language. "What if something like that slips out on Sunday?" He gives me a hard look. He's right.

Frank offers to drive me to the session this weekend.

"I said I'd go, and I will."

"I didn't mean you wouldn't," he argues. "I just thought you might like some support or something."

Does driving count as support?

I shrug. "If you really want to."

Upstairs, I continue my study of The Narrative of Jem Harper's Cancer, as I've come to think of it. I flip to where I left off, with the pictures of Elise donating blood. Jem doesn't look much better for having received it. He's got cotton plugs in both nostrils and bruising around his eyes.

Not long after that I come across the photo of Ivy getting the good news about Elise's donor status. She looks so relieved and overjoyed. On the opposite page there's a shot of Dr. Harper squeezing his little girl in a bear hug, as if he's proud of her for having the right genes.

Flip once, and Jem looks less than happy. He's on a bed with his knees pulled up and his head in his hands, hunched up as though the news was bad. There's no follow-up photo; nothing with his facial expression, or any clue as to why he would have been sad instead of happy. The pictures resume with him in a procedure room, lying on a table for radiation treatment. In subsequent photos the burns are visible on his neck and face. He went through another round of chemo, in the recliner this time; Ivy cuddled him.

The next ten pages of photos aren't very focused. They were taken through the window of an isolation room, so all I can see of Jem and the staff is a vague outline above the glare. He's always lying down. His IV pole is always holding three or more bags of fluid. In the few shots where he's close enough to the camera to be seen clearly, the rash on his hands is dark purple and bandaged in places. There are sores around his mouth and across his cheeks, too.

The marrow worked, but it was clearly a hell of a fight.

Wednesday

Jem slides a note my way in Social Studies. *Do you have any plans for tonight?*

I write *No* and slide the page back to him. Technically I'm grounded, but I can tell Frank that I got called in to work.

Jem slides it back. *Do something with me tonight?*

What?

Surprise.

I look over at him and he offers a shy smile. Do acquaintances do surprises? I don't even particularly like surprises.

We'll stay in Smiths Falls this time?

Yes.

I agree to his surprise. I have nothing better to do. As we pack up at the end of class Jem says, "I'll pick you up."

"When?"

"Five-thirty." He leaves before I can ask anything else. I suppose I should count myself lucky that he didn't ask about the photo album again.

Jem shifts the car into park and I ask him if he's serious. I figured he was taking me to his house to hang out, but we're at the hospital instead. He gives me this sweet smile that I just know is a precursor to one of his attempts at persuasion.

"I was hoping you'd agree to keep me company."

"So why didn't you just ask that?"

"I didn't think you would." Jem points out that the public library is only a few blocks from the hospital. I can go there and get a ride home from him later if I decide not to keep him company.

"Just ask next time," I tell him as I step out of the car. "There are worse things than being told no."

⁓

The nurse in the Dialysis Clinic is a very petite Asian woman with butterflies on her scrub shirt. She doesn't say much, other than to give her patient orders: "Lift your arm. We'll take your blood pressure standing now." Jem seems very conscious of the fact that I'm watching. He won't look at me. When the nurse asks him to open his shirt so she can access his Hickman, I see the worried look on his face and duck behind the curtain before he has to ask.

Nurse Butterfly works fast. It only takes her half an hour to set up all the tubing and program the machine. When I return to the cubicle, the machine is humming softly and Jem is lounging with a surgical drape over one shoulder.

"Is that for my benefit?" I point to the drape. "I don't think it's gross. It's not the first Hickman I've seen."

Jem ignores my question completely and offers me an orange from his backpack. Before I can say yes he tosses me one anyway. It's a fat navel orange, soft and juicy. I pull back the peel and cleave off a piece for each of us. Jem just sucks on his, extracting the juice and taking as little of the pulp as possible. He can't eat much during dialysis without getting sick, so he leaves most of the orange to me.

"Are you in a talking mood?" he asks. What kind of question is that?

"Uh…"

Jem reaches over to his backpack on the side table and pulls out Tessa's journal, the one I gave him on Sunday. The edges of about a hundred Post-It notes poke out around the pages, and I can't help but laugh.

"If only you read your English homework so thoroughly."

I move to take the journal and Jem withdraws it from my reach. He opens it to the first Post-It note with the seriousness of a lawyer and asks, "Who is Pat?" He makes it sound like he's asking for a murder confession.

"Her high school sweetheart." Tessa kept a diary very sporadically. That one journal lasted her nearly twenty years. The earliest entries were made before I was even born.

"He's not in here much."

"They didn't date for very long."

Jem flips to his next Post-It. "What language is that?" He turns the book around to show me.

"Dutch. Our Oma is from Soest." There are occasional chunks of the journal written in Dutch. Oma tried long and hard to teach her grandkids her language—none of our nursery rhymes and Christmas carols were English—but I never caught on. Tessa was always good at that kind of thing, though.

"Do you know it?"

"I can understand it better than I can speak it." I hold out a hand for the book and he gives it to me this time. I can understand one word in three, so I piece together the sentences as best I can. It's a description of 'the baby,' dated January 18th.

"My parents took their sweet time naming me." Jem finds that funny. I ask him if his parents inflicted him with an outdated name to honor someone. His cheeks turn a little bit pink.

"Irrelevant."

"Whatever, *Jeremiah*."

He snatches the journal back and turns to the next Post-It. "Why does she use gardenia as an adjective?"

If one thing is clear about Tessa's journal, it's that she didn't write it for others to read. She's got her own shorthand and acronyms and she leaves out the obvious details simply because they're obvious. Like the line: *Saw that movie I've been wanting to see. Satisfying ending. Good music.* And that's it. She knows what she's referring to. What does it matter that no one else does? It's her diary. Jem seems to have picked out every one of Tessa's gaps and inconsistencies and he questions them relentlessly.

"Was she flighty?" he asks.

"She was very picky about what was worthy of her attention." Tessa was obsessed with motorcycles and good TV, but couldn't have cared less about books. She referred to our local newspaper as The Horseshit Gazette and believed that people who talk to their pets in public are deeply unhappy and unwilling to admit it.

"Who's Henrie?"

"My mom." Jem's eyes widen at my answer and he remarks on how much scathing commentary there is on my mom in the journal.

"They didn't really get along," I tell him. "Mom is the easily distracted type. Tessa appreciated a clear sense of direction."

"Did they fight a lot?"

"Sometimes. They didn't talk for a few years because everything led to a disagreement."

"Sucks." Jem flips to his next Post-It and turns the page around to face me. "Why? Just why?"

Tessa also liked to occasionally amuse herself by sketching little cartoons. The one in question is of a Betty Boop-like pinup girl in a negligee that, for all intents and purposes, is see-through.

"What?" It's a private journal, after all.

"I kept count," Jem says. He skims a few pages and pinches a chunk of the binding between two fingers. The chunk represents the space of about five years. "She had six boyfriends that I can count."

"I wouldn't call them boyfriends."

Jem stares at me with unabashed surprise. It's clear from the diary that my sister had an active sex life, but that doesn't paint a complete picture of her relationships.

"What? She was in her twenties. She wasn't looking to settle down."

"And you knew what she was doing?"

"Well not the mechanics of it. I was only a kid. But I met some of her guys. They were nice people."

"What, she just casually introduced you to her fuck-friends?"

I laugh without meaning to. "It's not like sex is bad. It's natural. So she was getting laid, big deal. She was beautiful."

"Yeah, but…gross."

"Your family doesn't talk about sex? We used to talk about it all the time."

"In *detail*?"

"She didn't go out of her way to tell me, but if I asked a question she'd give me a full and honest answer." I had a lot of questions around the time the school board decided to supply my class with inadequate and confusing sex ed. I asked Mom and she panicked a little bit at my abrupt inquiry. She tried to convince me that sex is magical and beautiful and that flowers were somehow involved, and that only people who are really in love do it. So I went to Tessa to see what it was *really* all about, and she gave me the insert-tab-A-into-slot-B info. No flowers, just skin. She made it sound like something a person would actually engage in willingly. We didn't get into Tessa's views on sexual politics until a few months before she died, sitting at her kitchen table with coffee that neither of us drank. I'd casually used the word 'slut' in conversation and she told me to watch my tongue. "Men think they own sex," she said. "They demand that a woman be sexy, but condemn her for having sex." She made a sound of disgust in the back of her throat and blew on her steaming coffee. "But worst of all," she said, "are the women who condemn other women for the same reason."

The drape over Jem's shoulder starts to slide down as he flips pages. I move it higher and Jem practically slaps my hand away.

"Sorry. Reflex." He looks so embarrassed over such a small thing.

"Don't worry about it." The words don't really mean anything. He's going to worry about it anyway. He's flustered and awkward and fidgeting with the drape.

"I didn't see anything."

"Okay."

"I didn't."

He looks at me and for a moment I think he's going to say something, but then he turns back to the book and asks me what 'pasen' means.

"Easter eggs."

❧

It's nine-thirty by the time we leave the Dialysis Clinic. Jem asks if we can make a quick detour on our way out and we end up in Pediatrics. Maybe he's feeling nostalgic.

Jem approaches the nurse at triage and she reminds him that visiting hours are over.

"I know. I just wanted to see if Meira was discharged yet."

"Yeah, she was."

Jem smiles without happiness and says that's great news. The nurse doesn't look happy. We turn to go and she calls out, "Jem…" That's a loaded tone. There's something she wants to say, but probably can't because of confidentiality law. She settles for trying to communicate with a pressing look, and Jem frowns.

I can't stand the tension. "Was she discharged via the morgue?"

Jem flinches, but the nurse lets out a sigh. "No." The unspoken part of her sentence rings loud and clear: *Not yet.*

It's a quiet ride down in the elevator. Jem doesn't say anything as we leave the hospital and cross the lot to his car. I ask him who Meira is and he says, "Just this girl I know."

"Does she have leukemia too?"

Jem doesn't answer right away. We get in the car but he doesn't start the engine. He just sits there and blows out a long sigh.

"No. It's all through her gut. It's in her liver and pancreas now."

She's doomed. Once it's in the liver, it's over in the blink of an eye. Jem knows this, and it upsets him.

"Were you guys a thing? A little romance on the ward?" I smile to show that I'm joking, but I'm not good at making light.

"No. It's not like that." Jem looks over at me with a drawn expression. "She's only sixteen. She's barely old enough to drive and she's going to die."

I reach over and take his hand. His skin is cold, but not unpleasantly so. Jem blows out another sigh and looks out the window, trying to maintain composure. He starts the engine and says we should get going. I turn the car off.

Jem gives me a *what the hell?* look. I take him by the shoulder of his shirt and pull him toward me, into the hug he obviously needs but won't ask for. His arms readily wind around my ribs and hold me in a vice grip. His head rests on my shoulder.

"Do you really want to go home?"

Jem shakes his head mournfully. He tightens the hug even further, but I resist the urge to complain about lack of airflow. He needs this.

I scan the dashboard as best I can without moving away from him. It takes me a while, but eventually I find the button I'm looking for. I hold it down and the sunroof begins to slide back.

Jem lifts his head to see what's going on.

"Why are you opening that?"

"The stars are out. We'll sit here till you're ready." I feel around the side of my seat for a lever or button to move the backrest.

"It's under the seat," he tells me, and shifts his own seat back. It's like watching the night sky on a TV through the square in the ceiling. The stars are out as much as they ever are in spring. Wisps of cloud continually swirl across the sky, blocking some stars and letting others shine through.

"I'll give your album back tomorrow."

"Thanks," he says dully. "You can take your journal back."

I'll grab it from him later, when he drops me off at home.

He asks me why I gave it to him.

"So you'd let me keep the album a little while longer."

"But why her diary?"

"It seemed fair. We traded personal records."

"But when I read it—"

I reach over and lay a hand on his shoulder. "Jem, there's no moral to the story. It's a diary, not a fairytale. You can't read too much into it."

"I thought you wanted me to know something about her."

I shrug. "I didn't know what you'd do with it."

"So it was just collateral? You didn't care if I read it?"

"Pretty much. It's sweet that you did read it, though."

"You looked through my photos."

"Yeah." I look at him out the corner of my eye. "Why were you sad when Elise's donor results came back?"

"I wasn't sad," he answers in the same muted tone. His words come slowly. "I was overwhelmed." He swallows and it sounds loud in the quiet of the car. "I cried like a fucking baby."

I roll onto my side. Never mind the night sky, I want to watch him. Jem knows I'm doing it, but he doesn't even glance at me. He looks straight ahead through the sunroof with a passive but unhappy look on his face.

Jem's hand leaves his side and reaches across the gap between our seats. He grabs the first thing he can find on me—my jacket collar—and pulls. His scrawny arms are stronger than they look. He tows me forward until my head is practically level with his shoulder.

"Jem…?"

He folds me into a hug and sighs mournfully. "How are you the only one who gets it?" he murmurs. "I don't understand you. How is it you understand me?"

"You understand me better than you think you do."

"No, I don't. I don't get you at all." He sounds genuinely troubled by this.

"I wouldn't like you if you didn't." I try to lift my head but Jem holds me fast. "Or are you talking about what I did to my sister?"

"All of it."

"You're never going to understand all of it. I don't, and I live with myself."

"But—"

"Hey." I pat his shoulder. "You've given me things I didn't even know I needed, okay? Give yourself a little more credit. You're a good friend."

His arms tighten a little further around me. It's difficult in this position, but I try to hug him back just as hard. I think Jem secretly enjoys a good squeeze.

"I should take you home," he murmurs. It is almost ten o'clock on a school night.

"Where the hell did the evening go?"

Jem loosens his arms but doesn't push me back to my own chair. "I'm sorry I wasted your time tonight."

"I didn't mean it like that. Time flies when you're having fun."

"You had fun?"

"Yeah."

"In a dialysis clinic?"

"Yeah."

"With me?"

"Yes, you were there."

Jem gives me a sideways look and shakes his head. "You're so weird."

He sits up then, shifting his backrest up to driving position, and I move back to the passenger seat. We turn on the radio for the drive home to fill the silence. There's nothing much to say, now.

I switch it off when he turns onto my street. One last opportunity to ask a question, while he's still in the mood to answer them.

"You spent Christmas in the hospital?"

"Yeah. I was discharged just before New Year's." He pulls up in front of my house and parks along the curb. "It freaked my dad out that I was so sick around Christmas."

"Why?"

"He works in medicine. He's seen a lot of sick people and old people hang on for just one last family holiday and then give up."

"He thought you would?"

Jem doesn't answer that. "You know, it was only a day before you moved here that I got the okay to stop wearing a mask in public."

"Did you write 'fuck you all' on the front of it?"

Jem chuckles a little. "I should have."

I get out of the car while we're still on a happy note. He thanks me for coming with him and I thank him for caring enough. "See you at school."

"Yeah."

I step out of the car and he calls my name before I can shut the door.

"What?" I lean down to look at him. He's got this puzzled expression, as though he's not sure how to phrase what he wants to say.

"What's the playlist for tonight?"

I smile, because he still wants to exchange music even after we've spent the whole afternoon together.

"'Call and Answer,' Barenaked Ladies."

Jem smirks. "'Hurts So Good,' Mellencamp."

"'You Let Me Down,' Joel Plaskett."

"'I Go Blind,' 54-40."

"Goodnight, Jem."

"Goodnight."

⌖

Frank is in the kitchen when I go inside, making a bag of microwave popcorn. He asks me how work went and I tell him it was fine.

"Someone left a message for you." He nods to the phone. I dial into the answering machine and wait for the tone.

The message begins: "Hi, um, I got this number from Elise, so if you don't know who Elise Harper is just hang up and ignore this message."

Silence.

"Still there? 'Kay, well my dumbfuck friend—you probably call him Jem or some other civilized variant—hasn't been returning my messages, so I don't know if he screwed things up with you or not—and he's a total idiot if he did; you sound like a cool chick—but anyway I wanted to invite you to a show in Ottawa. It's this gig at a place called The Plains; couple bands performing and shit. Let me know if you want to come and I'll get you in, no cover. I'm…*curious* about you."

Holy crap, rambler. I don't trust the way she says 'curious.' What did Jem tell her?

"Oh, my name's Ava. Should have mentioned that. Call me back whenever, and if you're still talking to Jem, tell that little bitch that even brain damaged monkeys can answer a text message."

The machine beeps and the message comes to a stop. I think I might like Ava.

Thursday

Grounding really is a useless punishment, especially in Smiths Falls and especially when it doesn't apply to my friends in Port Elmsley. Frank thinks nothing of letting me go visit Luke. I have a feeling he's only going to enforce my sentence if he thinks I'm setting myself up for a relapse into sheer idiocy.

We end up on the floor of Luke's garage with a bucket and sponges, washing second-hand windowpanes.

"I kind of want to set a deadline for this," Luke says. "Time-to-beat, kind of thing."

"Let's aim for Victoria Day."

Talk turns to summer plans. Luke wants to save up for a car, but is also considering a motorcycle.

"I miss my bike."

Luke chuckles. "I thought your parents were happy you aren't riding that thing anymore."

My dad in particular has a strong dislike of motorcycles. He doesn't like risks. That's why he's always lived in small towns, works a nine-to-five gig that depresses him, does the same thing every weekend and always orders the same food at his favorite restaurant. He's a creature of controlled habit. It's obvious where Frank gets his personality from, and he's no fan of my bike either.

"They've already shipped me out of the province. What more can they do?"

"You know, before you moved here, Frank told my brother you had turned into a pretty wild chick. I thought Frank was full of it, but now I'm starting to see what he means."

"Don't look too closely. You'll spot horns."

When I get back to decent cell reception on the drive home, my phone goes haywire on the dashboard with alerts for missed calls and texts. I pull over to answer it, just in case it's an emergency, and find they're from Jem.

I guess you're volunteering tonight, if you're cell's off, is the most recent text. Before that he sent *Call me, please,* and *You didn't give back my album.*

Crap. I forgot it. The album is still sitting in my desk drawer, under a box of tampons to keep Frank from snooping.

I leave my car running in the driveway and dash inside to get the book. It's not a broken promise if I give it to him today. I slip it into my backpack as I head back downstairs and Frank asks where I'm going at nine o'clock at night.

"Gotta return a library book. It's overdue."

He lets me go without a word, and it makes me wonder. I pause on the threshold and call into the living room, "I made a study date after school tomorrow."

"Yeah?"

"Yeah, for Social Studies."

Frank comes to the hall with a disgruntled expression on his face. "And you can't get your work done in class hours? You have spend extra time and make an appointment with that kid?"

I give him a tight smile and start to close the door behind me. "I won't be gone long."

Turns out I'm not really grounded. I'm just not allowed to see Jem.

When I get to the Harper house, Elise answers the door. She's wearing a Belleville Quidditch Tournament 2008 t-shirt and pajama pants. I expect her to turn me away at the door, given how I spoke to her last time we met, but she holds out her arms for a hug.

"Uh...okay." I give her the hug and apologize for making her cry.

"You were mad at him, not me, right?" she says

"Yeah."

"Then we're cool. Just remind me to never piss you off." She turns with a giggle and tows me inside by the hand.

"I came to give Jem's photos back."

"Oh, great," she chirps. "He's asleep already, but I'll make sure he knows you dropped it off." She rocks back on her heels and asks if I want hot cocoa.

"Nah, I don't want to keep you up."

Elise rolls her eyes, "It's nine-thirty," and goes to the kitchen to turn on the stove. Elise shows promise as a food scientist. She figured out Jem's favorite milkshakes, and she has a very precise method for mixing the chocolate powder and milk so it doesn't turn out chunky or flaky. My mug is human sized. Hers looks like something out of Brobdignag. I set the photo album on the kitchen island.

"I think it's really cool what you did, shaving your head and all."

Elise beams. "Thanks. I raised nearly eight thousand to do it," she says proudly. "I didn't tell Jem I was doing it beforehand. It was a surprise."

She takes my hand again and pulls me away from the kitchen, up the stairs to her room. Her little legs have to scurry to set a brisk walking pace.

Walking into Elise's bedroom is like walking into an art gallery. Every single inch of the walls and most of the ceiling is papered with posters. They're squished so close together that none of the wall is visible in between. Most of them are pictures of *Harry Potter* characters, but Justin Bieber has his section of wall space, right next to Paramore. Too bad her brother's musical taste hasn't rubbed off on her. I'd gladly put a stamp of approval on her Jagged Little Pill poster, though.

Elise skips over to her bookshelf and comes back with an orange vinyl photo album. She proudly shows me the photos of the event where she shaved her head. She did it in what looks like a high school auditorium, up on stage with hundreds of people watching.

"It was a contest," she said. "Eric and I organized it at our old high school. We figured the people who actually knew Jem would be inclined to donate more. The two people who donated the most got to cut my hair."

The photos show Elise's balding occurring in two stages: first, a girl cut off her long ponytail. There's a shot of her holding it up proudly. Then, a guy used to electric razor to shave the rest clean off. The whole thing got people really pumped, from the look of it. In one photo she's posing, sans hair, next to a giant get well card with about a thousand signatures on it.

"Mom and Dad didn't know we were doing it, either," she says. "We told them we were visiting Celeste."

There's a nice shot of her and Eric in the car, relishing the scheme and their success.

"What did they think?"

"They were shocked." Elise absentmindedly touches her hair. "But they were really proud of us."

"Jem must have been, too."

"Not right away."

Elise flips ahead to the page she wants. It's a picture of her and Jem in what looks like a hospital lounge. Jem was sitting in a green recliner with an IV pole parked next to him. Elise was on the armrest with an arm around her brother's neck, posing for the picture. She was completely bald, except for a faint shadow across her skin that hinted at hair beginning to grow. Elise had a grin on, but Jem's face was totally blank.

"He didn't like it that I did that."

"Why not?"

"I think he really liked my long hair and how girly it made me." Elise shrugs. "He used the word 'ruined,' if I remember right." Elise flips the page to the next photo. This one was taken from behind the recliner and to the left, and it doesn't look like Elise or Jem knew the picture was being taken. Not much of them is visible, but Elise is on his lap instead of on the armrest and their arms are wrapped around each other's shoulders.

"He was pretty upset, actually. We thought Mom and Eric were gone at that point."

We both look up at the click of a door opening down the hall. It's at the far end, near the library. Elise shelves her album just as Jem comes within view of her bedroom door, bleary eyed and shuffling his feet.

"I thought you were asleep?" she says.

Jem ignores her question and speaks to me: "I heard your car outside. I thought you'd come up."

"I didn't want to disturb you."

"She brought your photos back." Elise steps forward and gives her brother a hug. "You look tired."

I say, "I should go." Jem doesn't need to be kept up by a late-night visitor. Elise gently tugs at his waist, trying to coax him back to his room.

"No, stay," he says to me. If I still had any doubt, the worried look on Elise's face tells me that staying isn't a good idea. I put a hand on the back of Jem's shoulder and gently usher him along the hall, back to his room.

"Okay, but not long."

Jem's shoulders sink a little, but he doesn't complain. Elise bullies him back into bed and graciously leaves us alone to say goodnight.

"What's the playlist for tonight?"

"Whatever helps you fall asleep fastest." I switch off the bedside lamp and Jem sighs in the darkness.

"I tried calling you."

"I know."

"Were you volunteering?"

"I was in Port Elmsley. Crappy cell reception."

"Oh." He doesn't sound happy. "Did you have fun?"

"I did. Luke's thinking of buying a motorcycle."

"Show me a picture of your bike sometime," he says. "I don't believe you drive a Harley." My eyes are beginning to adjust to the dark. I can just make out his teasing smile.

"Fine, I'll show you."

The back of Jem's hand brushes my leg as he feels for my hand in the dark. "Will you stay a while? I'm not tired, really."

I laugh and tell him he's a bad liar.

"Come on, Kirk."

I let go his hand and walk around to the other side of the bed. He falls asleep faster if he's being touched, anyway. I sit on the edge of the mattress and rub circles between his shoulder blades.

Jem sighs. "Do you want music?"

"No," I say softly. "Just sleep."

It takes only a few minutes for his breathing to slow with slumber. I keep my hand on him a while longer, until he starts to make that snuffling sound. It's not quite a snore, that snuffling. Jem just twitches his nose in his sleep.

I circle the bed to collect my backpack off the floor. My eyes have fully adjusted to the dark now, and I can see the innocent expression he lets show in sleep. His lips are slightly parted and I can hear the breath sliding over his teeth.

I consider taking his hat off for him, but he's touchy about keeping it on, so I leave it. Then I think of how if I'd met the healthy Jem Harper, we probably wouldn't be as close as we are. He wouldn't have given me the time of day, and I would have thought he wasn't worth my attention. I certainly wouldn't have ever gone to dinner with him, kissed him, or told him about my long series of life-altering mistakes. This is a strange thing we've got going on, he and I.

I kind of miss kissing him. His enthusiasm was flattering, and it never felt like a means to an end. And he had such soft lips.

Those lips close now as he swallows in his sleep. I have a guilty thought: that it would be nice to kiss him again; but I refrain. We're in friendship limbo—lips are off limits. But he's asleep. He would never know.

Very softly, I kiss Jem's relaxed lips. His skin is warm with sleep, and even though he's too far under to respond, it feels nice. I pull away carefully, wary of waking him, but then his mouth twitches.

Jem smiles in his sleep.

Friday

It's a nice day out, sunny and warm enough to skip wearing a sweater. I head out to Port Elmsley and find that Luke is a little more enthusiastic about the weather. He's mowing the lawn in shorts with his shirt off, like it's August already. He waves when I pull in and something about his eager grin makes me nervous. Then I get the sinking feeling that he's trying to impress me.

I get out of my car and he powers down the mower. Luke tries to give me a hug but I take a step back and gesture to the house. "Is it cool if I hang out inside until you're done? Is your dad home?"

"Sure, if you want. Dad's not home, though."

I can't help but appraise Luke. He's still got some of that adolescent gangliness, but mostly he's long bones and subtle muscle. It's odd—he has absolutely no hair on his chest, not even below his navel or around his nipples. Then I start wondering if he's vain enough to shave it like a swimmer or model, or if it's just genetic.

Suddenly I wonder what Jem looks like under his shirt. I bet he doesn't have hair (at the moment) either.

Luke catches me looking and smirks. "See something you like?"

"You just remind me of someone I know."

He doesn't like the sound of that. "Yeah? Who?"

"Doesn't matter."

Luke pokes my cheek and chuckles. "You're blushing." I am not God damn it...

"You got a crush I don't know about?"

"If you don't know about it, there's a reason." I don't feel comfortable hanging around the Thorpe house if it's just the two of us, but I can't put my finger on why. Luke and I have hung out before when no one else is around, but now I've got a bad feeling. I make my excuses to get back to Smiths Falls—I have plans; homework; anything. I just don't want to be around Luke when he's half naked and clearly trying to tempt me. Maybe that's the feeling in my gut—guilt about my promise to Mom that I'd behave myself.

I park in front of the house, get out of my car, and stand there leaning against the door. I don't want to go in yet. I can see the flicker on the living room window that means Frank has the TV on already. He'll ask me how Luke is and I'll have to make something up. All that stretches in front of me is an evening of cooking dinner and doing homework.

My phone vibrates in my pocket and even if it's Paige calling to complain about Chris, I'll take it. But it's not a call, it's a text message from Jem.

Bored. Wuu2?

Absolutely nothing.

Would your brother kill me if I came over?

Yeah, Frank probably would. But then he'd feel bad about it, because of the whole cancer thing.

Meet me at the park?

20 mins.

I get back in my car, smirking at the absurdity of it all.

351

We're not doing this right. I don't think we were this friendly before we were friends.

His answering text makes me smile: *Shut up, I miss you.* He could have said he was bored or had nothing better to do, or wanted a favor from me, but he didn't. He misses me.

And *that* freaks me out.

Jem: May 12 to 19

Friday

I get to the park before Willa. It's just a square plot of land next to the library with a swing set and a sandbox. I take a seat on the bench across from the swings to wait. It's almost dinner hour, so the park is empty of children. I watch the swings swaying on their chains and wonder if Willa would ever let me do something storybook stupid like push her on them. Probably not. That's not what barely-friends do, anyway.

I'm startled out of my imagination by the thump of Willa's foot landing next to me on the bench. She climbs over the backrest instead of just walking around it.

"Do I have to teach you how to use a bench?"

Willa gives me a dry look and says, "Are you sure you're qualified? You can barely drive standard, can you really handle a bench?"

"I can too drive standard."

"Don't think I didn't notice how the shifter grinded after you drove my car."

"You're so full of shit."

Willa takes a piece of gum out of her pocket and puts it in her mouth. I thank her for offering me some and she says, "Open your mouth." I'm not dumb enough to fall for that one. Eric spit his gum into my mouth when I was ten, and once is enough.

Willa offers me a hard mint instead. I smile. It's a little bit flattering that she carries these around in her pockets for me.

I bet she carried them for Thomasina too, before she killed her.

"So, you were bored?" she says.

"Shitless."

"My brother is sending me to group therapy."

"Damn," I say, because she sounds unhappy about it. But really I'm thinking that it's probably a good thing for her to get some help.

"It gets worse."

"What?" More antidepressants? Suicide watch?

"It's held in a church." She makes a noise of disgust and rolls her eyes. I take it she's not religious. The subject has never come up, but I don't want to make any assumptions.

"Do you pray?"

Does she think she's going to hell for killing Thomasina?

Willa looks at me with an expression of gentle scolding. "That's an extremely personal question, Jem." If I didn't already know she was serious, her use of my first name would have done it.

"Is the subject of religion altogether off limits?" Because I'm curious now, damn it.

353

"I hear your mom and brother go to church."

"You heard? You were just randomly talking about my family?"

"Small towns." She smiles. "Makes you miss the privacy of the city, doesn't it?"

"Ironic, isn't it, that the more surrounded we are by people, the more isolated we become."

"That's not irony, that's human nature. We're hard-wired not to be able to visualize any group of humans greater than the size of the natural herd."

Are we hard-wired to put each other out of our misery, too?

"You sound incredibly pretentious when you channel Darwin."

"Shut up or I'll help you de-evolve." Willa pushes herself off the bench and goes over to the swings. For a moment I think that I might actually get to push her on a swing, but she stands on the seat instead of sitting and pulls on the chains, rocking the swing side-to-side instead of back-and-forth.

"We had swings like this at the park by my house in St. John's," she says. "But they weren't used much. Teenagers used to wind them up around the top bar until they were unreachable."

I stand in front of her with my hands in her pockets, watching her rock.

"Is that why you don't know how to use it properly?"

"I loved doing this when I was a kid." She pulls harder on the left chain, widening her arc. "I would pretend I was a surfer. Then I saw the ocean and tried it. The whole thing is grossly overrated."

"Do you want a push?"

Willa gives me a look that reads, 'What do you think?' That's a no. I grab the chains and halt her motion.

"What the hell?"

I climb on with her and she makes a little squeak of surprise as the swing tips with my added weight. I'm slightly heavier than she is, and the swing lists to my side so she has to lean back to keep from falling into me.

"Lower your hands on the chain," she says with a laugh. "Your center of gravity is too high." I slide my hands down half a foot and our balance evens out a little more.

"Happy?"

Willa shifts her right foot forward and pulls her left one back, deliberately jolting the seat so I have to scramble to readjust. I jolt her right back but she bends her knees to stay on. She gives the left chain a tug, and we're both destabilized by the side-to-side rock. An equally hard tug on both chains stops the rock and shakes the seat.

Willa is laughing. She loves this. I lower my hands on the chains and bend my knees, angling the seat so far that she gives another squeak of surprise. Her feet are practically on the edge, trying to stay balanced. Her arms shake with the effort of trying to hold herself up on flimsy chains. If she let go right now she would fall forward on me.

I hold it for a few seconds, and then let up. The swing moves back and forth with proper balance while Willa catches her breath.

"You are such a shit."

"You enjoyed that." She did. She's still smiling. Willa just rolls her eyes at me. Standing upright and balanced like this, our fronts are almost touching. She's right there, and it occurs to me that I could just bend down and kiss her right now.

What?

 Nothing.

That's what I thought.

 Maybe just her cheek…

Willa steps off the swing and adjusts her sweater around her shoulders.

"Come with me on Sunday?"

"What?" I step off the swing.

"Frank wants to drive me. I'm not looking forward a long, silent car ride with him on top of therapy. Please come with me."

"You want, like, moral support or something?"

You should support her getting help.

 It won't change anything.

She'll be happier.

 And what'll I be?

Willa gives me the eye and says, "You're pretty screwed up yourself. You might fit in to Group better than you'd think."

"I'm not going to gush to a bunch of strangers."

"Pfft. Neither am I."

If she's going to lie again what's the point?

 Help her. Encourage her. She did it for you.

"One condition."

"What?"

"You come with me to dialysis again."

"That's it?"

"You come to my unpleasant stuff, I'll go to yours."

Willa considers that for a moment before holding out her hand. "Deal." We shake on it. Her blue glove feels soft against my palm.

"Let's walk," she says. We head down the sidewalk with no specified destination in mind, in the direction of what constitutes 'downtown' Smiths Falls. Almost every business is already closing up for the night.

"You really like working for Chris's family?"

"It's a paycheck. Better than bagging groceries."

I tell her my sister is thinking of doing just that and Willa tells me to offer Elise her condolences.

"So has Elwood molested you in the back room yet?"

Willa laughs out loud, and I get the sense that I'm missing part of the joke.

"Other way around," she says. I'm definitely missing part of the joke, but I play along and smile anyway.

"What happened?"

Willa shakes her head. I can't help but wonder if she did fool around with him, and the thought disgusts me. Why would she even joke about it? Does she like him? Unlikely, considering how often she speaks condescendingly of him. But she talks to me that way too… and she liked me. Has she moved on to Chris I-don't-know-basic-anatomy Elwood?

You say 'moved on' like there was something to move from.

There was.

Well, that was quick of her.

Maybe she's only fooling around with him because we went nowhere.

Right. Because Chris Elwood is an obvious second choice to Cancer Boy.

I'm beginning to think she just felt sorry for me and mistook it for affection.

"Didn't he and Paige break up?"

"Again."

"Was it because of something you did?" I give her a sideways look and Willa rolls her eyes.

"Calling me a home-wrecker now? I didn't do anything with Chris. If Paige isn't just talking out her ass, he's not worth it." She makes an obvious hand gesture. So she just casually talked to Paige about the size of Chris's dick?

"Is that what girls talk about in the locker room?"

"No, we compare breast size and help each other shower." She elbows me teasingly. I elbow her back. "Change of subject," she announces. "I got an interesting call earlier this week."

"Yeah?"

"Ava said to tell you to answer her messages. Been dodging an old friend from Ottawa?"

Oh shit. How did Ava get Willa's number?

"You talked to Ava?"

"She left a message. She's quite charming."

"What did she say?"

"Well," Willa begins dramatically. "She called you a dumbfuck and invited me to a show in Ottawa."

"No."

"What do you mean 'no'? You are a dumbfuck."

"You're not going."

"I hadn't decided," she replies stiffly. I put a hand on her arm and try to make her see reason.

"It's a metal band. You don't even listen to metal."

"Alright, now I just want to go because you don't want me to."

"Willa."

"Are you going?"

I wasn't planning on it. "Yes. We'd have to put up with each other all night and—"

"Good. We can carpool." Damn it all to hell.

"You're being deliberately difficult."

"Duh."

Goddamn it, she drives me crazy. She can't just trust me when I say it's not a good idea and do what she's told?

"You're not gonna try and act like my dad all night, are you?" she says.

"Blow me."

Willa stops on the sidewalk and drops to her knees. Sweet Jesus. She looks up at me expectantly, challenging. "Well? Whip it out, Harper."

Part of me wants to do it, just to be a smartass and call her bluff. But the saner half of me thinks this is a horrible idea. So I stand there.

After a few seconds of nothing, Willa stands up and smirks smugly. "That tiny, is it?"

Crap, there is absolutely no good comeback to that. What am I supposed to say? *Actually, it's so massive that were I to bludgeon you across the face with it, you would lose teeth.* Right, that'll go over well.

I stand there for a few seconds after she walks away, working on that whole inner peace thing so I'm not tempted to strangle her.

I wonder if she'd be any good at—

     Shut the hell up.

I follow Willa. She doesn't slow down to wait for me. When I catch up with her I throw my arms around her shoulders in a restraining bear hug and make her promise to be careful if I agree to go to Ottawa with her.

"Fine."

"Good."

"You can let go now."

"Nah." She annoys me, I annoy her. That's just how this works. Willa turns her head to look up at me over her shoulder.

"Ava knows we're not...right?" The gap in her sentence is loud.

"Did she say something?"

"Does she think that?"

"I'll talk to her."

"Okay. Thanks. 'Cause this isn't a date."

"Clearly."

"Good."

"Good."

I resist the sudden urge to kiss her temple. How can she annoy me this bad and still be so appealing?

"What's that look?"

"What look?"

"That look you just had."

"No idea what you're talking about." I let her out of my arms. She's about to round on me when I change the subject, "So what time is this sob-fest on Sunday?"

Willa huffs. "We leave at eight." I regret my deal with her already. Who wants to get up early on the weekend?

Saturday

I wake up from a nap to find that it's two o'clock. My phone is still in my hand and the alert for a new message is flashing. I tried to call Willa all morning and texted when she didn't answer. All her replies were vague and deferential.

Later.

Not now.

Can't talk atm.

Her latest message isn't any more comforting: *Crazy busy. Having fun.* And my mood takes a nosedive. She's having fun, is she? And it was too much trouble to invite me along?

I get out of bed and shuffle downstairs. Eric has the afternoon off work. Maybe I can talk him into a few rounds of Call of Duty. At the very least I think I can get Elise to hang out with me.

I enter the kitchen to find that the house is a lot more crowded than I first suspected. Elise is at the island counter with Willa, who is teaching my sister how to carve a chicken. The bird smells fantastic and is roasted to that perfectly golden color. At the table, Eric sits with Elise's jackass crush and his really hot girlfriend. The girlfriend's name escapes me, but she's telling Eric a story about a great Mexican restaurant in Kanata.

Elise takes her freshly carved, extremely juicy slices of hot chicken and pre-pares sandwiches for everyone. Willa sets a small morsel of dark meat aside and puts the rest of the chicken carcass in a large pot. I think she's going to make soup from that. The prospect of fresh chicken soup excites me, but then I re-member that it takes hours to make, and everyone is just sitting down to lunch now.

I walk around the island and congratulate Elise on the chicken. "Did Willa show you how to do that?"

"Yup." Elise nods vigorously. "Trussed it and everything." She carries plates over to Eric and her guests—hot chicken sandwiches on rye with cheese, lettuce and tomato. God, I wish I could eat that.

I approach Willa at the stove where she's loosening as much meat as she can off the bones with her fingers. "Hey."

"Sleep well?"

"I didn't know you were coming over."

Willa winks. "I was down here the whole time, you hermit." Behind me, Eric makes an inarticulate sound of pleasure and says that Elise's sandwiches are awesome. Damn it.

I lean in to speak quietly, "Did you make anything I can eat?" It's cool if she didn't; I have leftover soup in the fridge and yogurt too.

"Of course I did."

Willa opens the fridge and takes out a cereal bowl with a layer of cling wrap on top. I don't recognize the contents, but it's pretty chunky. Willa gets two plates down from the cupboard and reaches past me to grab a foil-wrapped package from the side counter. The foil package turns out to be a round loaf of very pale bread. It's still warm. Willa cuts off four slices and sets them up to make sandwiches.

"What's in that?" I ask when she uncovers the cereal bowl.

"Mostly chickpeas, with some carrots and other things." Then she does something very strange—she takes off her gloves. Willa takes the small amount of dark meat she set aside from the chicken and begins to shred it between her fingertips. She drops it in with the chickpea mess and mixes the whole thing together with a fork. A serving of chickpea salad goes onto each of the plates, and she closes it to make sandwiches. Willa cuts the crusts off one.

She can see I'm worried.

"It's rice bread; very easy on the stomach. I made it this morning," she says. "You've handled chickpeas before, and you're okay with semi-solids now. And the chicken is in small chunks. Chew it slowly."

She picks up her sandwich and takes a bite. "Let me know if I made the relish mild enough."

"What?"

"I made extra-mild relish to go with the chickpeas."

She made relish? What is she, eighty? Willa smiles and tells me she left a jar of it in the fridge, in case I like it. I can't believe she remembered. I only mentioned relish in passing, weeks ago.

I pick up one half of my crustless sandwich and inspect it. It looks reasonably edible, except that it's solid. I hate getting sick, but it's even worse in front of company, and there are three guests in the house.

Willa picks up our plates and carries them into the living room, away from the others. How did she know?

She sets the food down on the coffee table and takes another bite of her sandwich.

"Just try it," she says. "If you don't like it, don't swallow."

I suck it up and try a small bite. The bread is soft and bland, which is perfect for me. The chickpeas fall apart easily as I chew, and I don't even notice the shreds of chicken. I can see the relish in the mix—little flecks of orange and green—but its taste is nothing more than a sweet kick to balance the richness of the chickpeas. I can chew it thoroughly without being overwhelmed by the taste.

"It's good." Willa beams at the compliment. I hear an unfamiliar laugh in the kitchen that must be from Elise's crush, but it doesn't bother me so much at the moment. I keep enjoying my sandwich—the simple fact that I can eat a sand-wich again, and that it sits comfortably in my stomach without making me sick. It takes me thirty minutes to eat it at my slow pace, but at the end I'm pretty damn proud of myself.

"Thank you."

"I'll leave you the rest of the rice loaf. It makes pretty good toast. There's some low-sugar jam in the fridge with the relish."

"When did you make all this?"

Willa shrugs. "When I had the time." She stacks our empty plates and says, "I was going to give them to you Wednesday before last, but…I sort of blew it."

"Oh."

She shrugs again. "You have it now."

Willa looks uncomfortable with this line of conversation. It makes her vul-nerable. So I take a turn, because I owe her: "I'm weaning off Oxy." My stom-ach is feeling better, but it's a tough process. I haven't even told my siblings. I don't want to worry them, in case I have to go back on the drug.

"You're ready for that?"

"We'll see."

Willa nods understandingly. She gets it. She always gets it. "Let me know if you need anything."

"I've been trying that, uh, heartbeat thing…to fall asleep."

"Is the pain worse then?"

"At the end of the day. And when I first wake up. Lying still for so long…"

Willa nods, but I'm not sure she's really listening. She's got that very thought-ful expression in place. The fingers on her right hand absentmindedly trace the long scar on the back of her left. Maybe it's a sign of trust that she's kept her gloves off around me for the better part of an hour.

"Have you tried rosemary tea?" she says.

"What?"

"It's good for joint pain and circulation."

"Did you make that for…her? When she wouldn't take painkillers?"

Willa nods. "Lots and lots of tea. My Oma knows a lot about herbals." She stands up suddenly to clear away the plates. "I'll write down how to make it. Maybe your mom will help you with it."

She leaves before I can say anything else. I sigh and wait a few seconds before getting up to follow. Willa must have told some wild lies to her old therapists, because even a touch of the truth is enough to upset her. Tomorrow is going to be…interesting.

Sunday

Mom drops me off at the Kirk house bright and early. Frank is polite, if not exactly friendly, and I have a feeling he would be a lot less welcoming if my mom wasn't with me. Willa is wearing a skirt 'because it's church.' She looks pretty but miserable, and Frank is wearing a nice jacket, which makes me think that the skirt wasn't her idea.

We take Frank's car to Perth. It's a long drive and we don't even have the benefit of music to make it go by faster, since conversation is out of the question. Frank keeps the tuner on the local news and traffic station the whole time.

I can't wait to get out of the car when we get to St. Paul's church. It's an older church, built from chunky gray stones. A steeple stands at the head of the nave, and the heavy wooden doors are open to welcome parishioners. Then I see the sign beside the door welcoming us on behalf of the Catholic Diocese of Perth.

"I didn't know you were Catholic," I whisper to Willa.

"We're not," she answers without bothering to lower her voice. "Mom is, sort of, but Frank and I are heathens."

I've only been to a Catholic church once before, when Morgan and Ava had their confirmation ceremony and invited a few friends to the party. Every church is different, but the bones are much the same: the columns, the elaborate altarpiece, the stained glass windows and carvings of saints along the walls. As we enter the foyer the lady ahead of us dips her fingers in a bowl of water and makes the shape of a cross in front of her chest. Frank doesn't imitate the gesture on his way past the water bowl, but Willa shrugs and gives it a try.

We find a pew and Frank takes a moment to inspect the kneeler curiously. I guess it's been awhile since he was in a church.

I'm not sure what to expect. In the back of my head I think of when the pope's funeral was broadcast on TV, and there were a lot of old white guys in robes burning incense and wearing funny hats while chanting. I wonder if there will be any of that here.

As it happens, there is. The organ in the balcony starts up with an opening hymn and a guy dressed in black comes down the aisle swinging a thurible. The smoke smells nice at first, until it's *everywhere*, and then it's suffocating. He's followed by four altar servers and a priest in a green robe, carrying a fat bible.

There's a lot of ritual at the front before we're allowed to sit down. It seems pompous and excessive, and when it's all done they *still* keep us on our feet. The opening prayer is in Latin. Why did I agree to come to this?

Within twenty minutes, I'm glad I wasn't born into a Catholic family. There's a lot of singing, chanting, repeat-after-me, hand gestures, and we move so often you'd think the priest was trying to keep us awake by force. Stand, sit, kneel, stand, kneel again! We're told to 'give each other a sign of peace,' whatever that means, and Willa gets a weird look for giving an old lady the live-long-and-prosper sign.

The three of us stay in the pew while the rest of the crowd lines up for communion. I'm pretty sure you have to be a member to receive it, which disqualifies our little group.

"How much longer, do you think?" I whisper. Willa can only shrug. Thankfully it isn't too much longer. We kneel, then sit, then kneel one more time, and then we stand and sing one last hymn while the priest and his entourage file out the back. I'm happy to be free until I realize I'm not—therapy starts now.

↭

The 'youth group' as it is so wittingly called, is held in the parish hall next to the main church. It's a rectangular building that looks like a bare reception room, the kind that businesses rent out for weddings and occasions. There are about twelve folding chairs arranged in a circle. The group leader, a guy in his mid-twenties, sits across from the door with a few pamphlets and a bible in his lap. I hope he doesn't quote from that too much. Willa and I take seats a few spaces away from him, but not directly across. If we're in his direct line of sight he might pick on us to *share*.

Willa scoots her chair so close to mine we're practically touching. The other kids give us weird looks for it, but Willa pretends not to notice.

The group leader, Arthur, welcomes us all and starts the meeting off with a prayer "that we learn to accept ourselves and others and to become better people in Christ." This whole thing sounds wildly optimistic.

"Let's all introduce ourselves," he says, and we go around the circle. I feel like I'm in kindergarten.

"It's nice to have new faces here," Arthur says to Willa and me.

"Oh, I'm not really *here*," I tell him. "I'm just supporting her." I point to Willa and she elbows me.

"He is not."

Arthur smiles and kindly ignores this irregularity. "What brings you here today?"

Willa and I stare at each other with a mutual expression of *You go first*. Neither one of us speaks, and after the silence gets awkward the girl across from me asks, "How long have you been in treatment?"

I wonder if I could get away with punching a troubled Christian girl in the face, because I sure as hell want to. My illness is none of her business. I stand up to leave and Willa grabs my arm. She pulls me back down to the chair so hard I almost fall into her lap.

"He's in remission," she says stiffly. "And I watched my sister die at home." That's a nice, tidy way to abbreviate assisted suicide into something people can stand to listen to. She gives Arthur a hard look and he moves on to the other group members.

One of them is a recovering user. He makes himself seem pretty badass, but then it turns out he just liked to smoke a joint or two on the weekends before he saw the light, and who hasn't gone through that phase?

One of the girls is here as part of bereavement counseling. She lost her brother in a drunk driving accident. The boy beside her as bullying issues, and no wonder, because he's got 'victim' written all over him. The guy next to me introduces himself like he's at an AA meeting, except he just says, "It's been thirty-four days," without specifying what he's free of.

"I think he's lying," another boy pipes up. Arthur gives the kid the eye and says we don't belittle our fellows here.

Willa leans past me to ask AA Boy what he's thirty-four days clean of, and this stellar specimen of human intelligence replies that he's overcoming a crippling addiction to pornography.

Willa gives him the look I so desperately want to. "Really? Isn't watching that stuff just a regular hobby for teenage boys?"

Arthur chimes in with some points about how pornography and the viewing thereof violates the temple of the body. He even pulls out a few bible passages to support his argument.

"So, what are you into?" Willa asks. "Solo? Doubles? Fetish? Gay? And isn't it a damn shame that RedTube put up a pay wall?"

Arthur cuts Willa off before she can say more. "Let's not discuss this in any further detail. We're all very proud of Greg for overcoming his addiction."

"Yeah, overcoming," Willa whispers. "Coming over and over and over…" I try not to laugh so Arthur won't call on me, but he does anyway.

"I suppose congratulations are in order," he says. "Remission. That's a big step."

And you, my dear sir, are a joke.

"Yeah."

"May I ask what type of cancer you had?"

"No."

My abruptness doesn't bother him. Arthur's voice goes all gentle and he asks, "So what brings you here today?" Willa did, but apparently that's not a legitimate answer. Willa notices my hesitation and slips her little hand into mine.

"Bereavement," she says.

Arthur turns to her. "For your sister?"

"Not me." Willa nods to me. "Him. It's like that line from Arnold, 'Wandering between two worlds, one dead, The other powerless to be born, With nowhere yet to rest my head, Like these, on earth I wait forlorn.'" Clearly the quotation of a work non-biblical throws Arthur. "The old him is dead. The new one is in transition. Grief is involved."

Arthur turns his benevolent gaze on me. "Jem, would you say that's a fair assessment?"

Yes, but that doesn't give her the right to answer for me.

"She blames herself for her sister's death." None of them know she really killed Thomasina, but that's beside the point.

Arthur seems mildly amused by the way Willa and I contribute each other's issues to the group instead of just dealing with our own shit.

"Clearly the two of you are very close. It's obvious you have a real connection." His eyes flit to where our joined hands rest on my knee. Willa and I don't say anything.

"How long have the two of you been friends?"

We both have to pause to think about that. The answer feels ridiculous: "Three months." The short length of time surprises Arthur, too.

"Well, it's clearly quite a bond." He asks some more questions about Willa, some of which she answers herself, but I end up fielding all the personal ones. Willa deals in facts: it's been more than two years since Thomasina died. She had lymphoma that spread to her liver and intestines. She died of internal bleeding. The emotional shit—that Willa and Thomasina were close, that she still carries a lot of guilt and self-loathing, are things she doesn't want to talk about, so I do, because this is stuff that Arthur needs to know if he's going to help her.

"Is there anything you'd like to share, Willa?" Arthur offers.

She declines, and the floor goes to the girl whose brother died. She's clearly been here before. She's good at the personal sharing thing—has a whole monologue of her feelings prepared.

My ass is numb from sitting by the time we break. The session ends with another prayer, and we're all free to go. Most of the group hangs back, waiting to talk to Arthur one-on-one or to say goodbye to other group members. Willa and I just leave, back to the main church building to find Frank.

The sanctuary has emptied out. It's just a long, tall hallway with colored patterns on the floor from the stained glass. I'm looking around for Frank when Willa suddenly grabs my elbow and pulls me through the door on our left.

The space beyond the door is dark and cramped. We're in a confessional. Willa wraps her arms around my middle and squeezes, hard.

"Thanks for coming."

I hug her back. The top of Willa's head fits right under my chin.

"You're welcome." Her hair is so soft. "You had to pull me in here to tell me that?"

Willa shrugs. "I didn't want Frank to catch me *touching* you, heaven forbid."

I snort and point out that if her brother sees us leaving a confessional together, he's probably going to think we were making out in here.

We could...

Because talking about her dead sister would definitely put her in the mood, idiot.

Willa lets go of the hug and steps out of the confessional. I follow her into the aisle to continue our search for Frank. He's not in either of the side of the chancel or in the little side chapel dedicated to St. Paul. We don't find him until we pass by the parish office, and Willa spots him through the window in the door. He's in conversation with the priest and looks very troubled.

"Shit," Willa mutters. Her shoulders sink and she turns away. It doesn't take much to figure out that she's the cause of her brother's worries.

Willa marches away from the office, out the nearest door that leads away from the parking lot. I'm not sure she wants company right now, but I follow her anyway. We're barely ten feet beyond the side door when she stops dead and stares at the cemetery behind the church.

"I didn't know they had a labyrinth." She points to the center of the cemetery, to a paved space surrounded by shrubs and four benches. It looks like a place where people can congregate before and after burials.

"A what?"

Willa takes the gravel path up through the cemetery, right to the edge of the paved platform. It's red paving stone inlaid with grey to form the shape of a circular line pattern with a flower in the center.

"They put a maze in a graveyard?"

"It's not a maze, there's only one path." Willa points out the solitary route through the symbol. "You're supposed to walk it and meditate."

"You've done it?"

"I've seen it done. Discovery Channel."

"You want to try it?"

Willa walks around the edge of the platform to the spot where the circle opens to let people in. She pauses at the entrance for a moment and then steps onto the platform. It's by impulse that I reach out and grab her hand, and she doesn't seem to register it—she just pulls me along with her, onto the narrow path that winds back and forth on itself. The path takes us around the center of the pattern, around the flower, back and forth, back and forth. The outside of the circle seems wide and remote, like we're so far from the goal on the fringes of the path. I keep looking down, tracing how far we've come and how far we're going. Willa doesn't look the same way. Her head is bowed and her eyes unfocused, tracking the space immediately in front of her and nothing more. She doesn't look at the distance, at the forward and backward motion of it all. Her pace slows to a crawl. I walk close behind her. Willa still has one of my hands in hers. I rest the other on her waist, moving forward with her.

Every step forward is a step back, the way the path winds back on itself over and over. It's like walking through a mind full of indecision. When she stops, I don't immediately realize why, and then I notice the scalloped tiles. We're at the end, which isn't really the end. The center of the circle is a spot big enough for three or more people to stand. The hand I rested on her hip slips around her front in a gentle hug. She lets me hold her, and it feels good.

"What now?"

Willa sighs. "We go back." She turns to face me with a strange smile. "You lead."

The fact that the returning path is the same but opposite throws me off the whole meditation thing. It's harder to lead than it is to follow. I reach a hand back to where I can feel Willa walking behind me, but she doesn't take it. She puts her little hands on my shoulder blades. It's a gesture that's both comforting and encouraging.

I feel her forehead come to rest against my back.

"Are you ever afraid to touch me?" I murmur. I know it's not easy for her to look at me sometimes, even though she does it anyway. Her touch, though, makes her more unique than she must realize.

"Never." I can't feel her forehead against me anymore. Her hands move down from my shoulders, running slowly to the small of my back and returning to their original spot. Her fingers trace the backs of my shoulders, down my arms, and in between my fingers. We end the walk hand in hand.

Kiss her.

"How do you feel?" I look up to find Arthur sitting on one of the benches around the platform, watching us with a smile. "It's very centering, isn't it?"

How long has he been sitting there?

"Yeah," Willa says. "It is."

Arthur gives us this cheeky grin and says he should have known we'd walk it together. "Friendship is a blessing. A bond like yours is an uncommon gift from God. I'm glad you seem to treasure it."

What are we supposed to say to that?

Monday

Four. Fucking four. Four fucking opportunities to kiss her this fucking weekend and I didn't take a single fucking one. But why the fuck should I have?

No, I'm not stressed. Why do you ask?

"This is nice," I tell her. "Uncomplicated."

Willa throws a potato chip a few feet from the picnic table, just to see what happens. A seagull snaps it up and waddles off with the chip clasped in its beak.

Willa's got her blank look on, but that doesn't mean she doesn't know what I'm talking about.

"Yeah, uncomplicated…" She puts a chip in her mouth and chews slowly. "We should take bets on how soon karma is going to screw it all up again."

I scowl. Pessimism is my job, damn it.

The bell rings and Willa stands up to go back inside for Social Studies. I don't immediately follow, and she actually stands and waits.

"Dipshit," she says when I take too long, "that was the bell." I get up and we trudge back to the main building, taking our sweet time about it.

"What does your brother think of your filthy mouth?"

"Hates it." Willa crumples her empty chip bag. "I had to watch my language around the Jesus freaks yesterday. It sucked."

I tell her she can pay me back for having to endure that Group session this Thursday at five-thirty.

"Bring your album," she says. "We can dissect your life this time."

Hell no.

Tuesday

Fuck you, Oxy.

The hot water on my shoulders feels nice. It soothes the worst of the joint pain and relaxes me. I don't want to get out of the shower. I know it will start to hurt again once the warmth is gone. I'm used to a dull ache, but weaning off the painkillers has just made me more aware of the soreness.

I come out of the bathroom to find a steaming mug of tea on my dresser. Thank you, Mom. I'm slowly getting dressed, muttering "fuck Oxy" under my breath at every painful step, when Dad knocks on my door and asks if I need help.

"A little stiffness is to be expected," he says as he helps me on with my shirt. My shoulders are too stiff to lift my arms over my head.

"Don't tell Lise and Eric, okay?"

He's reluctant to agree, but he does promise not to say anything until I decide to tell them myself. I don't want to worry them. They've gone through enough because of me.

Wednesday

I wish my sister was a lesbian. Maybe then I wouldn't have to stand here and listen to this ignoramus talk about Radiohead like they're the best band in the world. Eric is running late, and unfortunately he has the keys, so Elise and I are stuck waiting by the car for him. That's when Mr. I-Have-A-Hard-On-For-Radiohead came up and started talking to her. Apparently, Elise's favorite band is suddenly Radiohead too. What a coincidence.

"I liked you better before you sold your soul for tail," I tell her as we drive away. She turns around in the front seat and asks, "Have you kissed Willa again yet?" She smirks wickedly and I know she's got some evil plan to use her ill-gotten Polaroid against me. I give her the finger and Eric chimes in with surprise, "You kissed Willa?"

"On the porch," Elise answers.

"Wow." Eric shrugs with his eyebrows. "I thought she had standards."

"Shut up."

Thursday

I pick Willa up at five, as per our agreement. As we pull away from her house she reaches into the backseat and picks up my backpack.

"What are you doing?"

Willa unabashedly rifles through my stuff. "We need to make a quick stop first," she announces.

"What?"

"You were supposed to bring the album, remember?" I was hoping she had forgotten about that.

"We don't have time to go back to my house."

"That's okay," she says. "Let me take your car after we get to the hospital. I'll get the album from your house and come back to meet you." Because I'm just going to let her poke around my bedroom when I'm not there. Even if Mom or Elise was with her, they would still give her too much information.

"Next time, okay?"

The Dialysis Clinic is on the second floor of the hospital, next to the fracture clinic. Willa keeps her hood up as we walk to the elevators, trying not to be seen and roped into volunteering by any of the people in green vests. She relaxes when we get in the elevator, but hunches up again as we cross the second floor to the clinic.

"Hey," Willa says. She gently tugs the side of my jacket to get my attention. "I'm gonna go to the washroom first. I'll meet you in there."

"Sure."

It's not until I'm taking my jacket off for treatment that I realize it doesn't feel right. One of the pockets is empty. Willa stole my keys.

She's gone for thirty minutes; long enough that I'm already hooked up to the dialyzer and mad as hell when she gets back. And she doesn't just have the photo album with her. She's got the album, a shoebox, and a black note-calendar in her backpack.

"Did you raid my entire room?"

"Yeah. Jeez, you keep a lot of porn," she says. I do not, and her sarcasm isn't improving my mood.

I hold out my hand for the keys and she drops them in my palm without apology.

"I could have reported the car stolen, you know."

"So why didn't you?"

"You're in enough trouble."

"How kind of you." She smirks. "On to business." Willa unlocks the brakes on the side table and brings it in front of my recliner. She pulls her chair up to the other side, like she's a cop about to interrogate a suspect. Her evidence comes out piece by piece: the album, the calendar, and the shoebox. The opens the book covers first.

"Help me understand this timeline," she says. "The calendar doesn't start until your first round of chemo. When were you diagnosed?"

"July second." Barely a week after we moved here. Mom took me to the doctor to get antibiotics for a persistent, fatiguing bug, but things didn't go as planned.

Willa skims Mom's medical notes on each page of the calendar. She knows what most of them mean, which is sort of sad, but it's also nice because it means she has fewer questions. Most of them revolve around the calendar and the album together. If there is a significant event on the calendar but no corresponding photos in the album, she questions it relentlessly. When did I become unable to digest solid foods? Was I able to go to school in between treatments, or was I kept in isolation because of flu season?

"Why do you want to know all this?" It's moot to tell her these inconsequential details. It has no bearing on the here and now.

"I'm trying to figure it out," she says.

"Figure what out?"

She lifts her gaze from the calendar and looks me straight in the eye. "At what point you died." She's good at that—at knocking the breath out of me with five little words.

"Something in you *did* die," she insists. Willa takes a Polaroid from the first page of the album out of its sleeve and sets it on the table, and then places a much later photo beside it.

"It's not even the same person." She points between the two photos. In one I still look human, sitting for my first treatment and masking my fear with anger. In the other I'm stripped apart and I don't have the energy to be angry anymore. I'm just weak and vulnerable and alien.

Willa puts the photos back in their places. "I'll probably kill you, you know."

Is there anything left to kill? Or is she hoping I'll ask her to hand over an entire bottle of pills?

Willa closes the books and turns to the shoebox. Why did she have to bring that?

"I found this on your shelf," she says. Willa sets aside the lid and peers at the contents. It's just a collection of junk—old hospital bracelets and a broken keychain and some stray photos from before. Willa picks up one of the bracelets and smiles. "We have the same blood type."

"Fascinating."

She rolls her eyes at my sarcasm.

"How could your parents give you such a normal middle name after *Jeremiah?*"

"Shut up."

She smiles at me and taps the yellow strip on the bracelet. "You were a fall risk?"

"I was weak."

She puts the bracelet aside and starts flipping through the loose photos. They're pictures that have been given to me from friends over the years. Willa stops on the one that Emily took last June, right before I moved away and my biggest problem was that I was pissed off about moving to middle-of-nowhere Smiths Falls. The piano and my cello had already been moved to the new house along with most of the furniture, so my usual method of venting frustration was out. Elise got tired of me moping around and bugged me to take her to the beach at Gatineau Park. A few friends came along. In the photo I'm giving Elise a piggyback ride and she's got her hand stretched out to pass a water bottle to Morgan.

"You look happy," she says. I was, sort of. It was a good day when that was taken. Mostly. I can't help but remember what a whiney little bitch I was that morning, ignorant of the fact that my life was beyond wonderful. I'd never even considered that I would get sick. That kind of thing happened to other people, not to me. I'd never been so lonely I felt hollow. I'd never hated to look at myself. I'd never traded insults with someone I could barely stand just because it felt better than being invisible.

Willa looks at the photo so intently. I wish she wouldn't. I looked human in that picture—just an average teenage boy, walking on the beach with friends. I am never going to look like that again.

"I was already sick when that was taken."

She looks up at me as though she was just a million miles away. I point to the bottom of the photo, where a smattering of bruises showed around my knees and calves. Just little marks, so innocuous on their own, but hinting at something deadly and destructive under my skin.

I try to take the picture from her and Willa holds it out of my reach. She gives me a stern look, like she thinks I've got some nerve to try to take it from her. Willa sits back in her chair, out of my reach, and studies it some more.

"I might need to be *alone* with this photo."

I realize that my mouth is hanging open when Willa leans forward and makes a jerking motion in front of my lips. I shut my mouth and grab her hand to make her stop. She did *not* just say that.

"You're a little red," Willa says with concern. And how am I *supposed* to react to a girl telling me that she wants to masturbate to a photo of me in a bathing suit? Jesus…

Willa slips the photo into her back pocket—oh God—and turns back to the shoebox. Would it be cheeky or just plain perverted to ask for something of hers in return?

Willa picks a folded white laminate sheet out of the box. She unfolds it and finds my well-worn speech card. For a long time she just stares at it without saying anything.

"Was it the vomiting that made it hard to talk?" she asks quietly. "All that acid?"

"No."

"Radiation?" she guesses. I nod. She smiles softly and traces the most worn-out box on the whole card, the one that says *I need a hug*. "We had one of these for Tessa, too," she says. "She couldn't talk long because she couldn't get a good breath once her liver swelled up. Too much pressure on her diaphragm. Sometimes her mouth was tender so she couldn't even mouth silently to us, so we had hand taps to communicate." She pokes my palm in demonstration, tapping out a pattern like Morse code.

"Did she say much?" It seems tragic, having to tap such personal requests for help into someone's palm. Willa picks up my hand where it rests on the arm of the recliner and makes me point my index and middle fingers, like a peace sign. I bend my fingers down at the knuckle and Willa does the same before joining our fingers like gear cogs.

"That's how we said 'I love you.' It's actually the Sign for 'puzzle.'" Willa looks up with a strange smile. "Like a perfect fit."

⌖

It's late when I get home; even though my body is tired, my mind is wide-awake, thinking of Willa's questions and the things she told me. We made plans to carpool to Ava's show tomorrow. I don't know what story she's going to tell her family to get them to let her go, but knowing Willa, I'm sure it'll be a masterpiece of fiction.

As I hang up my jacket I hear rustling in the pocket. I reach inside to find that Willa has put her sly fingers to work again. I pull out the photo of me at the beach, the one she slipped into her back pocket earlier like she wanted to take it home. She gave it back.

She was just teasing me. Of course she doesn't want...

Shit.

Thank God I didn't make an ass of myself by asking for something of hers.

Friday

Eric will take any excuse to get out of Smiths Falls for the weekend. He agrees to drive Willa and me to Ottawa and plans to crash at Celeste's place that night. It takes about five seconds for Elise to start whining about being left out of the road trip.

"Can I come?"

"No."

"Why not?"

"Because there's no way in hell I'm taking you to The Plains."

She lobbies Eric next, but he's not interested in bringing her to Celeste's house. Elise's energy could never be contained in the museum the Harcourts call a home. The results would be disastrous.

Elise makes a point of stomping around in a foul mood and blaming us for dooming her to a weekend in Smiths Falls. But she comes around. She even packs us snacks for the road.

⌖

When we pull up in front of Ava's house, she's visible in the front window, yelling so loudly I can hear her from the car. She's arguing with her brother about waffles, as far as I can tell.

Willa smiles and says, "She's exactly like I pictured her."

Ava answers the door while yelling at her brother to take the dildo out of his ass, it's choking out the single surviving neuron in him. Then she turns to me and says, "Holy shit, you brought her."

"Not by choice."

"Isn't he a stick in the mud?" Ava says to Willa, and folds her into a hug like they're old friends.

I'm glad that I'm the de facto DD tonight. If I'm sober I can keep a better eye on Willa. Ava tells her that her bedroom is the third door down the hall, and that she can store her backpack in there. Willa is gone for all of three seconds before Ava turns to me and mouths, "Holy shit!"

"What?" I whisper back, when I really should be telling her to keep her mouth shut.

"How have you not tapped that yet?"

"Will you shut up?"

"If you're not going to, I will."

"She's straight."

"You've asked?"

No. "Yeah." I'm pretty sure.

"Every girl is straight until she's not. Or until she's had a few." Ava winks. God no.

"Don't you dare."

"Why not? You're done with her."

Willa comes back from the bedroom and Ava nonchalantly wraps an arm around her waist. Neither of them has any idea what they're in for.

"Let's get you a drink," Ava says, and steers Willa away to the kitchen.

"Be gentle with her," I call after them.

"Piss off, Jem," Willa scolds me.

Ava laughs. "That's the spirit!"

❧

Ava likes Willa. She *really* likes Willa. Ava has a type, and this wouldn't bother me precisely—Willa is a big girl, perfectly capable of turning away unwanted attention—except for the fact that Willa seems to like Ava too. I can't tell if she's tolerating Ava's flirting out of politeness or if her interest is genuine.

"How long have you two known each other?"

"Three years," Ava says. We're sitting around her kitchen table while the others do a little pre-drinking and eat junk food. Ava casually lifts her feet and rests them on Willa's lap, like they're intimate friends. Willa doesn't push her away.

"Ava's a dyke." Might as well be up front about it.

She laughs at me. "Only sometimes. I keep trying to convince him to try queer," she points at me, "but he won't do it."

372

"Can't be room for much else with that stick up his ass."

Did Willa just insult me?

"Oh, *the stick*," Ava groans dramatically. "He's better when he's a little tipsy." She winks at Willa. "He's a handsy drunk."

"I am not."

"You should have seen him the first time he got wasted," Ava tells Willa with a giggle. "It was at our friend's birthday party. He got shitfaced and insisted on cuddling with the cat all evening." The two of them have a good laugh at my expense. It would be easier to get back at Ava if she had any sense of shame whatsoever.

She finishes her beer and gets up to stand behind Willa's chair. "Can I do your hair?" She's already got her fingers all through it, giving Willa a sensual scalp massage. Willa smiles and tells her to do whatever she wants.

God, I hate Ava. She's such a talented slut.

If I were a smoker, I'd be sucking them back right now. I lean against the car door, fidgeting as I wait for the girls. The three of us are taking Ava's Gremlin. The others are carpooling with Emily in the minivan, and we'll meet up in the parking lot. The plan for the evening is a poor distraction from the slowly-but-surely-driving-me-insane fact that Ava and Willa are getting changed in the same room right now. For all I know Ava could already be—

Don't even think it.

I breathe a huge sigh of relief when the girls come out of the house. They don't look like they've been screwing around. Ava is in a suitably slutty outfit for the stage, carrying her violin case. Beside her, Willa looks like the portrait of conservative ideals. She's not wearing a skirt, which relieves me from the worry that Ava will try to get a hand up there. She's wearing heels, but they're not that high. Ava's top is barely worthy of the name, but Willa's is…huh.

Tits.

> *Be cool.*

Tits. Willa's tits.

> *Moron.*

God bless cleavage.

> *She'll catch you staring.*

"Harper."

"Nothing."

The girls give me a weird look. Ava is the first one to dismiss my awkward outburst. She tosses me the keys and climbs into the car. Willa is nursing a smirk.

Damn it all to hell.

◇

Ava's band doesn't go on till one. We arrive at eleven and she uses her connections to get us in through the stage entrance. We don't even get carded, and the only weird look I get from the guy who lets us in has nothing to do with my age.

"I think you'll like this place," Ava says to Willa, and links their arms.

Ava buys Willa a drink, and Willa lets her. Ava gets four of her favorite lemon drops and makes Willa do one shot with her. I expect her to wince—those things are disgustingly sour—but Willa downs it without trouble and moves on to whisky.

"I figured you for a rum and coke kind of girl."

Willa looks at me as though she just remembered that I'm here too. "If you can't drink the hard stuff without sugaring it up, you shouldn't be drinking."

"Amen." Ava clinks her shot with Willa's glass before tipping it back. I don't think she was really listening to what Willa said, because when she's done with her lemon drops—sugared up liquor—she orders a Mike's Hard Raspberry.

"I like sweet things," she says to Willa, and brushes her hair behind her ear. I have a strange urge to snap Ava's wrist. The urge only becomes stronger when Willa angles her body toward Ava, away from me, and says she likes things that hurt going down.

Ava chuckles lowly. "I heard you were a tough one." Her hand slips around the side of Willa's waist, lightly fisting her top. "That shirt really does look good on you."

Of course it does, she's not wearing anything underneath.

Ava leans in a little more, putting her body so close to Willa's it's a wonder she doesn't just grab her by the vag and save time. She leans in for a kiss and Willa turns her face away from Ava to sip her drink.

"You like to dance?" Willa asks.

"Mmm-hmm."

"I hate it."

Ava laughs and tugs at Willa's hand. "Let's see if we can't change your mind."

Willa doesn't even put up much of a struggle. She goes to the dance floor with Ava, abandoning me at the bar without so much as a glance. I buy a bottle of water and go to find Morgan. Hopefully she'll have found a booth where I can lurk and spy on Willa.

You forgot your creepy trench coat at home.

Shut up.

Morgan does have a booth, and with her are two people I vaguely recognize from high school. They're a little giddy because it's their first time out in Hull since they turned eighteen. Morgan reminds me of their names and we do the obligatory social niceties. I have no interest in conversation, and the three of them quickly realize it. I'm largely left to my own devices—watching the dance floor like a stalker—while they chatter.

Ava is a fucking whore. Great musician, fond friend, but a fucking whore—one that is currently grinding on my thoroughly straight friend whom she knows I have a thing for. So what if Willa and I didn't go anywhere? It's the principle of the thing! You don't hook up with your friends' hang-ups.

Willa doesn't really know how to dance. She mirrors Ava's motions, grinding back and forth with her and exchanging hand placements – a grip on the neck, on the hip, *on her ass for Christ's sake.*

"Jem. Jem!" Morgan flicks a bottle cap at my face.

"What?" The word comes out harsher than I intended. Morgan nods to the object of my focus: Ava, half naked and practically wrapped around Willa.

"Are you sure you should be letting her do that?" Morgan asks. "You know Ava doesn't do commitment. If your friend gets attached—"

"She's not into girls."

Morgan raises an eyebrow and looks over at Willa. "Uh, you sure?"

Yes, God damn it.

Morgan snorts as Ava sticks her tongue down Willa's throat. Willa doesn't pull away. She doesn't even wince. She just tilts her head to that perfectly accessible angle, closes her eyes, and relaxes into the embrace.

I feel cold. She likes it. And her hand is on Ava's neck…where she used to rest her hand on me. Ava's hands are around the back of Willa's hips, under her shirt, touching skin I never got to touch.

"Hey," Morgan calls my attention back to the table. She sets a shot glass full of amber liquor in front of me. "I know you're not supposed to, but in extenuating circumstances…"

It's beyond tempting to drink, but it won't solve anything. I don't need to be sick as well as fucking dead inside.

I look back to the dance floor, but Willa and Ava are gone. I turn all the way around in my seat, being wildly obvious in my attempt to locate them. Morgan gestures to the stage door, tucked in the corner behind one of the massive speakers. Oh hell. Why would Willa go off with her alone?

I leave the booth and wade through the crowd to the other side of the hall. Security is shit here, and I walk right through the unmarked stage door without anyone noticing. Backstage, it's all smoke and gloom. The band on stage is using a fog machine and the wings are choked with vapor. Beyond that, where the stairs lead down to the rooms below stage, the smoke from cigarettes and other pleasures hangs heavy in the air. I know where Ava will be—where she always stages her trysts—so I head straight down without bothering to check the wings.

There are six rooms under the stage: an electrical room and storage closet, three dressing rooms, an equipment closet, and a bathroom. One of the dressing rooms is open and Ava's drummer is smoking like a murder suspect.

"Have you seen Ava?"

He looks at me with a hard eye and says, "Don't tell me she's fucking *you* now." Shit, so she's already screwed and tossed this drummer. He'll quit the band within the month.

"No." Tried and failed that. I leave him to make love to his ashtray and head down to the smaller dressing rooms at the end of the hall. The one on the left is occupied by a sleeping piece of jailbait, probably waiting for the band on stage to come back so she can glom onto their five minutes of fame. I try not to wake her as I leave. The other dressing room is empty.

I check the bathroom, but it's empty too. The electrical room is locked for safety reasons. The only room left is the equipment closet where they keep spare chairs and microphone stands and crates of liquor. The light is on when I open the door, but it looks empty too.

Then I hear whispers.

"This isn't half bad."

"It's cheap, but I like it."

I look around I stack of chairs, into the far corner of the room where crates of vodka are piled high. The girls are slouched on the floor, passing a small joint back and forth. Ava does most of the smoking, but it makes me wonder if Willa is only into girls when she's less than sober.

Ava leans over to kiss Willa and she turns her head. "You only get one."

Ava still tries to touch her, to get a hand inside Willa's shirt or down her pants. Willa passively accepts it for the most part, but she won't kiss Ava or even look at her.

I shouldn't be watching his. I feel sick.

"Touch me," Ava whispers.

"Why the fuck would I do that?"

Ava isn't deterred. She's palming Willa's tit like she owns her. I can't take another second of it. I turn to go.

◆

"Did you find her?" Morgan asks. I pick up my bottle of water and try to drink, but the fluid gets stuck in my throat and I cough. I don't have to say anything. The look on my face says it all. Morgan offers me another shot.

"No."

It's twenty long minutes before Willa reappears at the stage door. It's after midnight; Ava and her band have to start preparing for their set. She didn't even do Willa the courtesy of walking her back upstairs after taking advantage.

Willa's hair hangs over her face. I can't read her expression. She heads across the dance floor, toward the center of the mob and the mosh pit at the front. She's trying to get lost in the crowd.

I get up before I lose sight of her altogether and weave through the press of bodies. Willa bumps up against my front before she realizes it's me, and then she looks up at me with the deadest eyes I've ever seen on a living person. My hand fists the front of her shirt. It's loud and hot and crowded and I don't know which to do first—comfort Willa or crack Ava's fucking skull.

"I need a little air," I say. "Come with me?"

She touches my neck. I foolishly dare to hope that it's affection, but her fingers still on my pulse point. She thinks I need air because I'm lightheaded. Her kindness has everything to do with me being sick.

"Okay."

We grab our jackets from backstage and go out to the alley. The pavement is wet, but the rain has stopped for the moment. I lean back against the brick and Willa amuses herself by kicking stray pebbles into the nearby sewer grate.

"Having a good time?"

Willa nods and kicks another stone. Her pupils are still a little narrow, but she seems fairly sober.

"So, you like Ava?"

"She's okay. She's funny."

"Was she telling you some good jokes backstage?"

Willa smirks at me, but her eyes are still dead. She doesn't seem upset that she got caught. I'm not even sure if she's sorry that she did it—she shuts down like this when she feels anything in abundance, be it good or bad.

She's single, dipshit. She can fool around if she wants to.

"I've heard better." Willa says. "The tongue ring adds a nice touch, though."

I resist the impulse to add *I know*.

"Do you play both sides?"

"Not really." She shakes her head. "I just sort of...go with it. She gave me what I wanted, so..."

"What if she did something you didn't want to do?"

Willa shrugs. "I wouldn't let her." Something in my question makes her even more distant. What is she thinking? What did I remind her of?

"Hey." I reach out and touch her jacket. "Come here." I pull her in and she leans against me in a one-armed hug. She's slightly damp from exertion and she smells like the inside of the bar. Her hair smells like weed.

"I shouldn't have let you go off with her."

Willa pulls away from me. "You don't protect me." Her words sound like both a declaration and an accusation. I want to protect her. She needs it, even though it might pain her to admit such a weakness.

"Are you okay?" I ask.

"I'm fine." I can tell she's going to stick to her story no matter how hard I push, so I let it be.

"I've been thinking."

"Uh-oh."

"Hey."

Willa taps my forehead and tells me not to blow a fuse. I grab her hand and hold it.

"I've been working on this whole forgiveness thing. Trying to wrap my head around it." She needs to know that she has someone in her corner—that I'm trying to stop judging her, trying to understand her. And that I won't let her go off with someone I *know* is bad news ever again.

Willa's face goes blank. She steps away from me and takes her hand back. "Forgiving me for my sister, you mean?"

I nod.

"That's a venture you'd best stop before you start," she says. "You'll get no-where."

"Just because you didn't…"

"Fuck off."

"I don't want to hate you." I should be mad at her right now. Two weeks ago she was kissing me. This week she's screwing around with my friend in the basement of a rotting concert hall. I should be royally pissed off that I meant so little to her, but I'm not. I'm…hurt. And I think she is too.

"That's not the same as forgiving me. You don't have to do that. I wouldn't blame you if you never did."

I put my hands on her shoulders and she tenses like she thinks I'm going to hurt her. I wouldn't. I simply pull her close enough to speak into her ear.

"I still like you."

Willa doesn't say anything back. No argument, no agreement, no disagreement or affirmation…just silence.

"I hate it that Ava was all over you, and that she took you backstage alone. It was driving me fucking crazy earlier knowing that she was watching you get dressed."

"*Helped me* get dressed," Willa corrects me. My hands tighten around the shoulders of her jacket.

"Were you going to let her get you drunk?"

Willa doesn't answer. Is that a guilty silence? The unpleasant thought creeps into my brain: that Willa might have done all this on purpose, knowing it would bother me. She only met Ava a few hours ago, and it's a pretty low thing to screw the friend of an ex.

"Are you screwing around with my friend to piss me off?"

Willa tries to pull away. "Because it's all about you, Harper."

"Answer the question. Are you trying to make me jealous?"

Willa blinks at me like I'm not speaking English. "Jealous of what?"

"I still like you." She must have known; God…

"So?"

That's all she has to say? I tell her I like her and she says *so?*

Willa shrugs my hands off her shoulders. "Don't you dare."

"What?"

"You're gonna complicate this. Isn't it enough that we're talking? That we're friendly? It's okay that you still resent me for what I did, everyone does, but don't twist that around and try to make something out of it. It's not gonna work."

I let her go. "Forget I said anything." She takes a step back from me. "You're clearly over…whatever we did. Go tongue-fuck Ava a little more. Put your face between her fucking legs; I don't care anymore."

Willa blows out a long breath. "I've been stealing kisses from you while you sleep."

A fuse blows. There's nothing but white noise in my head, trying to connect two impossible thoughts in a way that makes sense. Stealing kisses. From me. Even though she said *so?* and nothing else.

When it all comes back into focus, I realize that I've been staring into space like a fucking imbecile for an awkward length of time.

Willa turns to go back inside. I try to tell her to stay but all that comes out is an incoherent and very undignified squeak. If she notices, she ignores me. The fireproof door shuts behind her with a heavy thud.

"Fuck!"

Sure, now you can talk.

Do I go after her? What do I say?

I open the door and rush into the dim, foggy space between the door and the stage. I'm short exactly one plan and rational thought is a stretch at the moment—I just have to find her.

God has a sense of humor. I run smack into Ava on the stairs.

"Have you seen Willa?"

"Uh…"

"Since you toyed with her," I clarify. Ava points to the stage door over her shoulder, and I leave without another word. I know where Ava lives. I'll deliver hell on her doorstep later.

I burst through the stage door, only to run into a wall of bodies. It's almost one o'clock and The Plains is at capacity. The dance floor is packed and the people in the booths and at the bar are crammed in cheek to jowl. I press through the crowd, using my unhealthy weight to my advantage as I slip through the cracks. I wish Willa was taller. I can't see her anywhere.

The churning motion of the crowd shifts as the band's last song winds down. Their set is done. Some people head to the bar, cutting me off, and the rest stand in groups waiting for the next set to start. It's hard to weave through a stagnant crowd, but that makes it easier to spot the girl I'm looking for. I take a step toward her just as the lights go up again and Ava draws her bow across the strings, teasing the audience with a blast of sound. The responding noise level from the crowd is almost as deafening.

Ava chuckles into the mic. "This one is for everyone who's got the balls to go after what they want." The drummer breaks into a relentless rhythm, and the chaos begins. It's beautiful.

So is she. I grab Willa by her nearest arm and pull her against me. She looks genuinely frightened. Why?

Even with my mouth next to her ear, I have to yell to be heard over the music. "Why the hell didn't you wake me up?"

Willa shrugs helplessly. "We're fucked up, Jem." Yeah, granted, but every couple needs their thing.

I bend down and give her a fully conscious, articulately sensory, much desired kiss. It's a brutal sort of relief to do this with her, because I'm barely satisfied before I want more.

Willa is a very giving woman.

Willa: May 20 to 25

Saturday

I wake up on the couch with the sun shining in my eyes. I roll to avoid it and find Ava passed out in the recliner. I didn't even hear her come home. She stayed at the bar later than everybody else and was supposed to get a ride home from a band mate.

I get up and cover Ava with a blanket. It's seven-thirty and the house is still quiet. I head to the bathroom and hear snores from the other two rooms. Everyone else is still asleep.

Jem slept in Ava's room last night. I poke my head in on the way back from the bathroom, just to check on him. We didn't say much last night. There wasn't much to say, and I didn't know how much he knew about Ava and me. We stayed with the crowd where it was too loud to talk, but he was greedy for small touches and signs of affection. After the show things kept coming up—finding the people we went there with, talking Kyle out of that one last vodka shooter, making sure he got home in one piece…

Jem is still out cold. He's in his usual sleeping position: curled up on his side with his chin tucked to his chest. He still has his hat on, which fails to surprise. Jem doesn't like to show his scars, and in a house full of people it's hard to hide. I crouch beside the bed to touch those pouted lips and he stirs.

Jem takes a sleepy swipe at me and grabs the front of my t-shirt. "The hell?" he mumbles. His eyelids flutter as he tries to wake up. "You're supposed to wake me up for this stuff."

"I did."

Jem tugs harder on my shirt, pulling me closer. I slip under the quilt with him and he wraps an arm around me with a sigh. For the next half hour, I'm his human teddy bear.

I make myself some toast with jam for breakfast. I need something sweet to kill the taste of stale whisky on my tongue. As I wait for the bread to pop up I think about the contents of the fridge. The only thing in it that's safe for Jem to eat is yogurt, but I don't want to just write him off with a crappy, boring breakfast if there's something I can throw together.

I sit down at the kitchen table, wishing I'd brought some honey or rice bread for the road. As I brood and chew, I feel an arm wrap around the front of my shoulders in a hug. It's not Jem—her hair tickles my neck and she smells like the bar.

"Aren't you an early riser," she says sweetly, and kisses the back of my head.

Why the fuck is she still touching me? I told her last night that I wasn't in that basement to do anything but inhale.

"Oh, I'm just full of tricks," I tell her dully. I don't want to tell her off when I'm a guest in her house, but if I bore her she may lose interest and leave me alone.

Ava chuckles and nuzzles the back of my head. "So I've heard." What did she hear?

"Want me to show you how to make a newspaper into a weapon?" How's that for a trick? Maybe I'll demonstrate how to draw blood and break bone with it, too—she can be the dummy.

Ava laughs and heads to the fridge. She says she doesn't think it's possible to make a newspaper dangerous. I resist the urge to look for one to prove her wrong.

I get up to wash my plate without a word while Ava pours a bowl of cereal. I'm wrist-deep in suds when she comes to stand behind me, hugging me and resting her chin on my shoulder.

I want to elbow her in the gut.

"Do you not grasp the concept of being used for weed and nothing else?"

Ava sighs in my ear and pets my hair. "Do you like him?"

Now I really want to hit her.

"He's not ready for anything serious, you know," she whispers. "So much of him has changed, he's not ready for…intimate relationships."

In my short eighteen years, I've met a lot of people who were full of shit. People who, by all rights, should have had it coming out their ears—who I should have been able to smell a mile away. But Ava's insightful pile of bullshit makes me wonder if she even knows Jem. I bet he's never told her a secret. I bet she's never been allowed to witness a weak moment.

My hand stills on the dish sponge. "What do you see when you look at him?"

"Oh, he's still in there," she assures me. "But he's…different."

No. He's dead.

"Ava?"

"Yeah?"

"Get off me before I shank you with a butter knife."

She chuckles as if I'm joking and kisses me on the cheek before departing with her cereal. I rinse my dish and put it in the drying rack, eager to go get dressed, to get out of her company for five minutes. When I turn around Jem is standing right there, leaning against the kitchen wall with his arms folded. He doesn't look happy.

"What time do you want to get out of here?" he asks.

I shrug and tell him it's up to him. Jem gives Ava a scathing look—which she misses—and says the sooner the better.

"I'll get dressed."

I head down the hall to the bedrooms and Jem follows me. I assume he's going to get changed too, but before I get to Ava's bedroom door he grabs me by my upper arms and holds my back against his front.

"Don't listen to a word she said," he says in my ear. "She's…"

"Full of shit, I know."

Jem blows an angry sigh out through his nose.

"How long were you standing there?"

He ignores my question. "What do *you* see when you look at me?"

I roll my eyes. "Do I really have to tell you again?" His grip loosens a little and I walk away from him, into the bedroom. I lock the door behind me. I just want five minutes of peace to get dressed.

He knows what I see. I've been telling him for months. He just never listens.

⟁

I sit up front with Eric on the ride home. I figured it would be less awkward this way, and Jem has the whole back seat to lay down if he feels tired.

There isn't much conversation on the way home. Jem constantly has his phone in his hand, texting. When I look back at him in the mirror he's sometimes pensive, other times pissed off, and just before he conks out with his head against the window he looks sad.

We stop for gas in Kemptville. Eric sends me inside for snack food while he fills the tank and Jem sleeps on. When I come back to the car I set the food up front and climb into the back with Jem. It's not good for his neck to be slumped over like that.

Very carefully, I unwrap the seatbelt from across his chest and loosen the band across his hips. He's still not that heavy, and it only takes a slight pull to get him to lean toward me. I make a pillow on my lap from my folded jacket, and Jem snuggles in without ever really waking.

His phone buzzes on the seat and I pick it up to switch it off. Then I get a devilish little thought: perhaps I should record an annoying ringtone for him, like he did for me.

I have no idea how his phone works. I scroll through the menu, looking for a settings or voice recorder option. His text message inbox has a lot of unread texts in it. It keeps flashing red, begging for attention. I open the inbox to get the alert to stop flashing.

All his most recent messages are from Ava. Judging by the way his face looked an hour ago, this probably isn't a pleasant conversation. I open the earliest message, just to see.

Relax, we hardly even did anything.

I get the feeling she's talking about me, and the next message confirms it: *Just a little making out. She wasn't even that into it.*

I can count on one hand the number of times I've actually wanted to be physically close to someone in that capacity. I didn't want Ava. I just wanted…a decent joint.

Don't give me that shit, you said you were done with her.

I still can't believe he's not.

Last time we talked you were planning to stop being friends with her.

I think back to Ava's phone message. She sounded like she thought Jem and I were no longer on speaking terms, and that she was extending the olive branch to me in spite of that. I wonder if it says something about Jem's relationship with Ava that he tells her about his anger but not his happiness.

Her next message is a little mean: *Well did you really think you'd get anywhere?*

I stop reading and shut off his phone. What does Ava know?

Eric drops me off at home and I very carefully slide my legs from under Jem's head, trying not to wake him. He sleeps like a bear in January. I thank Eric for the ride and he tells me to come around again soon.

"Mom misses you."

I promise to come tomorrow, maybe after I'm done pretending for the people at Group. As they pull away I take out my phone and send a text to Jem. He'll get it when he wakes up.

I'm sorry I didn't say no to her.

Frank is out when I get home. He left a note on the counter about going to Port Elmsley to help Doug fix a wiring problem. The note doesn't say when he'll be home, but that doesn't surprise me. Home improvement projects have a way of getting out of hand, and even if they do finish today, Frank will probably stay for a beer and an hour or two of Sports Center. At least, that's how Frank will explain it when he gets home.

I unpack last night's clothes and take advantage of having the house to myself. I send Mom an email with the week's news, playing up the part about how therapy was so incredibly life changing and I can't wait to go back and work through some of these issues. Let her have a little hope.

Frank doesn't come home for lunch, and I don't know if he'll be here for dinner, either. But I feel like cooking, so I start preparing zucchini fritters. I'm shredding the zucchini when my phone vibrates.

I walked in when Ava asked you if you liked me.

So Jem saw her wrapped around me. He heard her say that he's not worth having a relationship with. No one needs to hear that. It hurts like hell to be told that, no matter how many times it's said.

I didn't answer her because it's none of her business. I do like you.

Thanks.

Maybe he was better off not answering that message, if that's what he's going to say. He'd have thrown an insecure shit-fit last night if I'd said 'thanks' to his admission.

Jem texts me: *I'm trying, okay? I want to make peace with what you did.*

You're an idiot.

He doesn't have to forgive me in order to be civil to me. As far as I'm concerned, even trying to make peace with my past is a waste of effort.

Optimists usually are. That's why I'm a pessimist.

I almost smile. *Never change*, I tell him. That dork sends me a smiley face in reply. He's got a sentimental streak and it's disturbingly adorable. I set my phone aside and heat the oil for the fritters. I almost have the entire batch fried and ready before my phone moves again.

Can we 'see each other' again?

I stare at the screen for so long I forget the pan on the stove and two of the fritters burn.

"Shit!" I throw the fritters in the sink and take the pan off heat. The fritters are so burnt they're unsalvageable. I scoop them into the garbage can and turn back to Jem's message.

How do I answer it?

We need to talk about this.

Okay.

Can I come by tonight?

Not tonight. I don't feel well. Maybe tomorrow, okay?

Do you need anything? As long as I'm cooking, I could make something for Jem and take it over to his house later.

Rest. Tomorrow, okay?

Maybe I should be grateful for the delay, because I don't know what the hell I'm going to say to him.

Sunday

I love Mrs. Elwood. She calls early in the morning and gets me out of group therapy by asking me to cover a shift. Frank isn't happy about me missing a session, but I point out that I need the money for college (yeah right) and he grudgingly agrees to let me skip a week of therapy. I think he just doesn't want to sit through mass again. I text Jem to let him know about the change of plans, but he doesn't reply. He probably just read the message and rolled back over to sleep.

I have the opening shift at the B&B with Chris. The house is quiet for the first hour while we wait for guests to come down to breakfast, so I busy myself with sweeping the floor. Chris gets the task of setting up the dining room and back patio for the meal.

I feel bad about the way I talked to him last week, when it was just the two of us working. I took my problems out on him and aside from a tendency to flirt, he's a pretty good friend.

"Hey, Chris."

He looks up from the sideboard buffet. "Yeah?"

"You want to do something sometime?"

Chris smiles. "Like what?"

"I don't know. Maybe we could get a group together to go to the movies?"

"What do you want to see? I'd love to go with you." I don't miss the fact that his wording leaves out any suggestion that this will be a group outing. I suggest a slapstick comedy and tell him I'll invite Brian and Hannah, and he can invite who he wants.

Chris shrugs. "We could just go the four of us. That's almost a full car. Double dates are fun, but any more than that is a crowd."

I should have known he would assume. "Oh, this isn't a date," I tell him as politely as I can. "Come on, Paige is my friend. What would she think of me if I asked you out so soon after you two broke up, huh?"

Thank God they break up every other week.

Chris agrees, but I can see he isn't thrilled. He's just telling me what I want to hear. I can't hold that against him. I know what it feels like to spin lies because the truth isn't fit to swallow.

I leave the B&B at five, ready to head home for dinner. I wonder what Jem is doing—a persistent thought that has an obnoxious tendency to intrude on my brain—and remember our promise to meet and...talk.

I sit in my car and call him, wondering what I'm going to say when we sit down to discuss where we stand.

Jem answers the phone sounding completely exhausted. "Hey Willa."

"Are you okay?"

"Fine. What's up?"

"I just got off."

"You *what?*"

"Easy, pervert. I just got off *work*. Can I come over so we can talk about... yeah?"

"Um, now isn't a good time," he says awkwardly. "Can we postpone again?"

"You're not stalling, are you?" I tease him. He chuckles and assures me he isn't.

"I'm just not feeling well enough for company." Jem apologizes and promises that tomorrow night we'll set time aside to sit down and talk about...stuff.

"Tomorrow, then." I intend to hang up, but then he asks me if I've heard Bad Religion's new album.

"Don't tell me you have it?" That bastard. We talk about it for an hour, dissecting every song—he plays them one by one into his cell mic. Jem's favorite track is "The Devil in Stitches." I like "Turn Your Back On Me."

"You're going to make me a copy, right?"

"Consider it done," he agrees.

"I knew I kept you around for a reason."

He laughs and I look at the clock. Shit. It's almost six. I've been laying across the front seat for too long, chatting the evening away. I say goodbye to Jem and he tells me that I don't have to come with him to dialysis this week, since we didn't go to my therapy together.

"Pull your head out of your ass," I tell him. "I'm coming with you."

I call Frank as I drive home to ask if I should pick up takeout on the way. He's already eaten leftovers, and apparently there aren't any zucchini fritters left. That was quick.

I tell him not to expect me home till late and take the road to Port Elmsley instead.

⌘

Mr. Thorpe is out when I arrive. It's just Luke and his sister Briana, who is holed up in her room, blasting metal.

"She's been in a pissy mood lately," Luke says, and apologizes for the way the walls shake. "Are you hungry?"

Luke makes spaghetti. He boils the whole package of noodles, which could regularly serve a family of four. Luke eats about three helpings alone. His idea of an appropriate portion for me is enough pasta to make me feel stuffed and dozy.

"Leave the dishes," he says. "We'll do them later." We kick back on the couch and try to decide between Asian-language cartoons on channel three and competitive pole vaulting on channel nine. Luke says we might be able to pick up an English cartoon network if we adjust the rabbit ears, but neither of us wants to get up to do it. We're full and sluggish, so we make do with foreign cartoons. It doesn't even matter that Briana's music drowns out most of the sound.

Luke starts making up lines for the characters, talking over the noise and being silly about it. He makes me giggle and we start to recreate the whole plotline of the episode: the girl with pink hair is a government agent, spying on the guy with white hair who is actually a rogue alien who just likes to probe people and has lost all interest in his species' mission to conquer earth. The little girl with black hair is his accomplice and is actually a robot controlled by a tiny fellow alien, M.I.B.-style.

"What about the guy with the glasses?"

"Oh, he'll be dead by the first commercial break."

When the cartoon ends we give championship pole-vaulting a try. Without humor to stimulate me and with a full belly to make me sleepy, I quickly start to doze. The last thing I remember is the relentless thundering of Briana's music in the background of my consciousness, and when I wake up I'm no longer on the couch. I'm in Luke's bed, tucked in with the quilt up to my chest.

It's been years since someone carried me to bed. I stretch my legs with a sigh and something touches the back of my head. Luke pets my hair and asks if I'm awake.

"No. Go away."

He chuckles as if I'm joking and lays down next to me. Next thing I know, I'm being spooned and his hair is soft against my cheek when he kisses my temple. God damn it, I thought I explained that this shit is off limits.

"Luke."

"Mmmh?" He runs his hand down the curve of my ribs and hip. His lips are at my shoulder and he's close enough to my back that I can feel his misplaced excitement. I bet he was waiting for me to wake up. Pervert.

"We talked about this."

"Give me a chance." He rolls me with a hand on my shoulder and before I can tell him to fuck off straight to hell, he's got his mouth on mine, pressing our lips together in what I think is an attempt to be passionate. It's not, it's just pathetic. Luke lays his weight in top of me, pressing his cock up against my thigh. I really have to stop fooling around with virgins; they just don't get it. Absolutely no subtlety.

I reach down and grab him, hard. The first time he tried this bullshit, I didn't say anything. But since then I've told him no more. If he's going to seriously try this with me, I'm going to hurt him and I won't feel bad about it.

Turns out Luke likes a rough hand. He wraps his fingers around mine and makes me grip him even harder. Fucking hell. I twist a little and he snatches my hand away with a soft exclamation.

Luke pins that hand near my head and begins to leave big wet kisses down my neck. It's like something out of a bad movie. He rolls his hips against my front, humping me through our clothes, and moans into my neck like a fat man with a hot pie. His other hand slips between my legs, rubbing me through my jeans. Jesus Christ, he's going to try that again, is he?

"Stop that."

"Is this better?" He moves his hand in circles instead. I can't wait until this country declares open season on idiots.

"What do you think?"

Luke gets a hand under me and squeezes my ass. I try to kick him, but I can't reach much with my hips pinned down. He thinks I'm leaning into him and starts to kiss me with more 'passion.' He gets a hand up my shirt and I swear, if he starts fumbling with my bra I'm going to lose my shit completely.

Luke lifts himself up on his elbows and looks down at me with a weird expression. "I don't have a condom."

I put my hand on his shoulders and shove, hard enough that he falls off the edge of the bed with a crash.

"Who the fuck said you would need one?" I tug my shirt back into place and get out of bed. "I told you no more of this shit," I yell at him as I storm out into the hall. I need to get out of here. I shove my feet into shoes and grab my purse off the counter. Briana's music comes to an abrupt stop.

"Willa, wait!"

"Fuck off, Luke."

"Why do you keep turning me down? I've treated you a lot nicer than your other 'boyfriends,'" he demands rudely. What does he know about me and my sex life? At least the others *asked* before they touched me.

"My boyfriends are none of your business, jackass. I keep turning you down because *I don't want you.*" I feel like throwing something, but I suppress the urge and head for the door.

"I know why your parents sent you here."

I stop with one foot out the door. "What?"

"I know about your sister. And the shit you did after. No wonder your parents shipped you off to live with your brother. I bet they were sick of the drama."

I let the screen door close. "You don't talk about my sister."

"I overheard our brothers talking. Frank told Doug what you did to Tessa."

"You know fuck-all, you little shit."

"Do your parents not want you to date because of the shit people you got involved with back home? I think they'd be over the fucking moon if you dated someone normal—someone they know isn't insane."

"Are you trying to talk me into dating you?" I can't believe his sheer idiocy. "I'm seeing someone, you arrogant prick."

Luke gives me a skeptical look. "Oh yeah? Who?"

It's more of a lie than truth, but I can't let him think he has an opening. "Jem Harper."

Luke stares at me for a few seconds, and then bursts out laughing like I'm a joke. "Jem *Harper?* The guy with cancer? Whoa, shit, you are nuts."

"Shut your fucking mouth, Luke."

"And what happens when he croaks? Are you going to completely lose your shit again and hurt Frank?"

I really fucking hate Luke Thorpe right now. To insult Jem is one thing—Jem never did anything to him—but to suggest that I'd hurt my family on purpose is crossing a line.

"Jem's not dying," I answer through my teeth. "He's in remission. And you could go out tonight and get hit by a car—and the way you're going, it'll probably be *my* car."

Luke sneers at the threat.

"You say shit about me and Frank again, you're going to regret it."

I give him the finger and turn to go.

"Are you gonna kill Harper too?" Luke calls after me. I don't want to stop, but God fucking damn him for saying that to me. I turn and Luke's got this bitter sneer in place.

"Forget it. You're not worth it. I *know* what you did to her."

I drop my purse on the porch and reenter the house. Luke folds his arms as I step up to him, looking down on me with disgust and arrogance. That little shit.

I take a swing at his jaw. My whole weight is behind it, and the arc is long enough that he can see it coming—and he doesn't even move. My first two knuckles connect with his jaw and his neck twists to the side. What kind of idiot doesn't block or duck?

He expects it when I wind up for the second punch, and he lunges at me. Luke shoves me into the banister. He's got his hands around my elbows, pinning my body to the edge of the wood. I'm not above sacking him. My only education is in how to fight dirty. Luke's not a fighter, and he leaves his legs wide open for my knee to come up and bruise his balls. He might have the advantage of height and weight, but I've got experience and I know how to capitalize on his pain.

Luke lurches and gags as I lower my knee. His grip loosens enough that I can get my arms free, and I shove him back as hard as I can. My leg wraps around the back of his calf, tripping him.

Luke hits the floor like a sack of potatoes. The adrenaline has deafened me and all I can see is his smug face twisted up in pain. I take advantage of his prone position by sitting on his chest with my knees pinning his elbows down. I knew I loved his stupid haircut for a reason—it gives me something to grab as I pull his face in toward every punch. He gets two across the cheekbone and one across the jaw, hard enough to bust his lip open. My hand is going to hurt like hell when this is over, but right now I can't even feel it. I wind up my other arm to strike the opposite side of his face, but Luke gathers himself enough to flex his arms and throw me off.

As I fall on my back to his left I strike out with my foot and manage to land one last kick to the jaw. Luke is up and on me in a second, equally fuelled by adrenaline. He goes for the kill shot. His hand wraps around my neck, squeezing me. He's got me held at arms length, beyond the reach of my fists, and his leg pins mine down. He thinks he has the upper hand. Stupid boy.

I slip my thumb between his palm and my neck, gripping his wrist. My other hand grabs the back of his elbow. I twist his wrist back on itself and push his elbow joint in the wrong direction. His shoulder naturally rolls with it and he cries out in pain before his face even hits the tile floor. I roll on top of him and put a knee in his back.

An arm bar hurts like hell, even relaxed. Luke struggles, kicking his legs and flexing his shoulder. I just push harder. One quick move and I could snap his fucking elbow.

Not bad for a little girl.

Luke has the nerve to ask for mercy. What does he think this is? High school wrestling? There's no tapping out in this match.

"Shut up," I bark at him. I replace the hand on his elbow with my other knee and he cries out in protest. My free hand grabs him by the hair, jerking his head back. His eyes are already bruising and he's got blood running down from his split lip.

"Yeah," I snarl at him, "I killed Tessa. So *what the fuck* do you think I'd do to you?"

I throw his arm away and he whimpers in pain. Fucking pathetic. I take one last kick to the ribs as I walk away.

It's not until I bend to pick up my purse that I realize Briana is watching from the top of the stairs. "Go help your brother clean up," I tell her, and slam the front door behind me.

Monday

It's nice to know that my left hand still good for throwing punches. I wear gloves with long fingers to hide my bruised knuckles. The first two knuckles on both hands are a little swollen and the tops of my fingers are purple. The marks are satisfying, because they're the only ones on me and I know Luke looks a hell of a lot worse. He didn't even make a mark on my neck when he choked me; his grip was too brief.

I can see Jem a few hundred yards ahead of me as I head toward the school. He's the only one in the crowd wearing a hat in May. He's a little hunched to-day, which could mean anything from pain to tiredness to a particularly cranky mood. Given his new drug regimen, I'm going to bet on pain.

I catch up with Jem at his locker a few minutes later. He looks miserable, slowly turning the dial on his lock. For a moment he just stands there, and then he angles his shoulders, trying to get his backpack to just slide off him.

I come up behind Jem and take the weight of the backpack, easing it off him as gently as I can. His joints must be killing him.

Jem looks at me with a forlorn expression. "Thanks."

"That bad?" I hang up his backpack and he nods.

"I'm only taking half my regular dose, and only half as often."

"Withdrawal symptoms?" I ask lowly. Jem shrugs. Some things are too per-sonal to talk about.

"Nothing I can't hide," he says. It annoys me a little that he's hiding his dis-comfort to keep others from worrying. But he's done it before, and I know how hard it is to talk him out of these asinine ideas.

I hand him a mint and head off to class.

Jem doesn't show up to lunch, which annoys me even more because it means he feels worse than he's letting on. I take some of my frustration out on my lunch—enough that Hannah notices that I'm eating more aggressively than usual.

"Just trying to eat quickly. I've got stuff to do."

"Studying?"

"Something like that."

When I get to the nurse's office, I find her gone. The staff are on lunch break too. I peek behind the curtain at the twin cots and find Jem laying on his side, looking like death warmed over.

"Nothing you can't hide, eh?" I tuck the blanket tighter around his shoulders and sit by him, keeping him company and rubbing his back. The pain in his joints is no better or worse than usual, but his stomach is easily upset. He's afraid to eat anything because it will make him sick, and prolonged hunger makes him lightheaded and cold.

"Is it nausea?"

Jem turns red in the face. "No," he mumbles. One of the more uncomfortable side effects of opiates is constipation. Now that he's on a lower dose, his digestive tract has to reconfigure the whole food processing situation.

I go back to the cafeteria and buy him a fruit juice. He can drink, at least, and he needs the sugars.

"Does Elise know I'm in here?" Jem asks as he sips.

"Probably." Elise is highly attuned to her brother. "I bet she just thinks you're a little tired, though."

"Thanks for your help. I'll pay you back for the juice."

"Damn right you will."

Jem chuckles at my tone and drinks more of his juice. He has to sit up a little to do it because I didn't bring him a straw. He doesn't need to be sucking air back right now. The gas would just be harder on his gut.

"Come here." Jem holds out an arm to me, inviting me to sit next to him against the headboard. I scoot over to join him and he wraps an arm around my shoulders.

"What happened to your hand?" He picks up my right hand and pulls my glove off to look at the bruises.

"I beat the shit out of a my friend."

Jem's eyes widen. He pushes both my sleeves up to my elbows, looking for hidden bruises. I tell him I'm fine but he insists on checking.

"Who were you fighting with?"

"Luke. You've met him."

"That kid?" His voice pitches up. "He's got at least thirty pounds on you, Willa."

"More like forty."

"Please tell me it was play fighting." Jem still inspects my head and neck for hidden bruises. He wouldn't believe me if I told him that Luke didn't land a single blow.

"No."

Jem glares at me. I feel like a little kid in trouble. "What were you fighting about?"

"He was talking shit about my sister. And you."

Jem swallows. "What about it?" He puts my glove back on, hiding the bruises.

"That I was an idiot to get close to you. And he knows what I did to her—he acted like I should be grateful that he wants anything to do with me."

Jem murmurs my name and kisses my hair, like I'm a child telling a parent about a nightmare. The arm around my shoulders squeezes me tighter and he tells me that I'm better off without Luke.

"I might not be able to go with you on Thursday after all. Once Frank finds out I'm going to be grounded till Christmas."

"Even though Luke started it?"

"I threw the first punch. And I almost broke his arm." Jem looks so surprised that I can't help but laugh. "I also threatened to run him over with my car."

"Jesus, Willa."

"You'd do the same if someone said shit about your family. He said I was crazy to hang out with you because you could die tomorrow and I'd go insane again."

Jem wraps his other arm around me in a soothing hug. "Now, when you say you *almost* broke his arm…"

"I definitely sprained his wrist."

"Good girl." Jem kisses my head again. He says he's sorry I hurt my hand and thanks me for sticking up for him.

"Jem?"

"Yeah?"

"You're an idiot."

He laughs. I think he's the only one who can take my insults in stride. 'Go to hell' is a nice euphemism for 'I love you,' but so few people understand that.

Jem's nose brushes lightly across my cheek. It's like he's asking for a kiss.

"We still need to have that talk."

He sighs like I've just told him to go clean his room. "We only have twenty minutes left before class. We won't have time to finish talking about this if we start now."

"Fine. Tonight?"

"I have a doctor's appointment."

"Honestly? Or are you stalling again?"

"You think I'd lie?" he says with a smirk. "Really, I do. Cancer is one of those things that you have to check up on from time to time."

"Are you worried?"

"No. I'm feeling better." He smiles as if to prove it. It's total bullshit. He's blown me off for days because he's been feeling so poorly. I refrain from pointing out that feeling lightheaded and shitting his guts out are hardly big improvements on his physical condition. He probably already knows, whether or not he wants to admit it.

"Fine. Tomorrow."

Jem finishes his juice and lays down to rest before the bell rings. I lay down with him, lending Jem a little bit of warmth. The blanket on the cot is pretty threadbare.

"I'll try to make it through Soc," he promises as he lays his head on my shoulder. His arm is around my middle, mooching warmth.

"If you can't, I'll walk you back here."

"Thanks," he murmurs. His cheek feels so cold against my collarbone. He needs to eat something, soon. I consider swinging by the cafeteria one more time before class. He can sip another bottle of juice during the lecture. Jem shivers slightly and I rub circles on his back, trying to warm him up. If he stays here instead of going to Soc, he might as well steal the blanket off the other cot, too.

Jem lifts his head and looks up at me. His expression is troubled. I adjust the blanket to warm him further but he leans away from it—toward me.

Jem kisses me very softly, just like the first time on the porch. We were supposed to talk about this first...

The door of the nurse's office opens and Jem takes his sweet time pulling away. I have to put a hand on his shoulder and push him back, and by that time it's too late. The other student in the door is watching us with red cheeks.

"Um...is the nurse here?" she squeaks. I don't know this girl, but I've seen her before. She's a freshman, skinny and still suffering through the first awkward stage of puberty.

"She'll be back soon." I get off the cot and swat Jem away when he reaches to take my hand. "Are you sick?"

She bursts into tears. How do I know it's a Monday? I guide her to a chair and make her take deep breaths. She looks perfectly healthy to me. The nurse's office is pretty sparse, but all the basic equipment is here. I ask if she came here for an icepack or bandage and she just sniffles and shakes her head.

"Do you need anything before the nurse gets back? Water, maybe?" I pass her the Kleenex box to wipe her nose.

She takes out a sheet of notepaper and writes the problem down, too embarrassed to just say it. I go to the supply cabinet and dig through the drawers of gauze and towels. The school must keep some feminine supplies around...

The only pad I find is thick enough to soak up the entire yearly rainfall of the British Isles. I can't believe any woman could bleed enough to need this and still survive. I give it to the freshman and she takes it into the washroom, still sniffling.

"She okay?" Jem asks from behind the room divider.

"Shut up, Jem."

She calls through the door, "I have a question." She wants to know where she's supposed to stick the adhesive tabs on the sides. I can't believe that's an actual question and want to tell her to take a wild guess, but that would be mean. I answer her question and Jem snickers behind the divider. Jackass.

The girl emerges a few minutes later looking flustered. I have to assure her that the giant pad isn't visible through her jeans to get her to calm down, and send her away with the rest of the Kleenex box. Poor kid.

Jem gets up and shuffles around to the other side of the divider, weary but smiling. We have to leave for class soon.

"Do you think she'll tell anyone what she saw?" He nods to the cot behind him.

"No. Then she'd have to explain what she was doing in the nurse's office to begin with."

He nods, satisfied that I'm probably right. The freshman will be too embarrassed to admit that she was ever in here, let alone that she saw anything. "We'll talk," he says. "Promise. Tomorrow."

"I believe you."

⌁

I finish my homework when I get home, and when I head downstairs to make dinner I find company in the house. Luke is at the kitchen table, sporting a black eye, a fat lip, a tensor support, and talking to Frank like everything is just fine and dandy. They're discussing plans for an overnight fishing trip with Doug and Mr. Thorpe.

"Hey Willa," Luke says. He sounds so cheerful, as though I didn't beat the living shit out of him last night.

"What happened to your face?" I challenge him.

"Boys being boys," Frank says with a smirk. Luke has already lied to him.

"Do you not know how to block a punch?"

Luke gives me a look that tells me not to push my luck. I suppose he thinks I owe him now, since he lied to my brother and covered my ass. No harm in being delusional.

I fry up some fish for supper. It makes Frank happy, and after the dishes are done I don't linger. I don't want to give Luke any opportunities, so I head out. It's as good a night as any to volunteer at the hospital.

⌁

"Pick up, it's me."

I lift my head and look at the clock. It's one o'clock in the morning and I really have to change that ringtone. I actually mean it this time.

I pick up the phone. "Mmmph?"

"Help me."

I'm wide-awake and sitting up with one foot on the floor before I realize I've moved. "What's wrong?"

"It's not working." The pain in Jem's voice is so palpable it gives me chills.

"What's not working?" My bare feet hit the carpet. There are jeans on the back of my desk chair.

"Heartbeat," he answers shortly. Oh God, he's hurting.

"Take another dose." He still has an open prescription for OxyContin. He can take as many as he needs until he's ready to be off painkillers, which he obviously isn't. The zipper on this sweater is stuck.

395

"Can't. Not till five."

"Take it. You're in pain—you need it."

"I'd have to wean off it again." Jem blows out a sigh that breaks with a wince of pain. I've had this conversation before.

My keys bite into the skin of my bare hand.

"Then you'll wean off them again. You need it now. Take it." Before I lose my mind, please.

"Please, just help me. I don't want to take—"

"I can't help you." I want to. "There's no shame in it." My voice cracks as I repeat myself. "You need…you need to take another dose, okay?"

"Willa…" I shut the car door and Jem's breathing changes. "Don't come over."

"I'm not." What a ridiculous thing to say. Then I realize that I'm sitting in my car, in the driveway, and Frank's bedroom light just came on. I even have one hand poised above the ignition slot.

I drop my keys on the passenger seat. "Just take your medicine, okay?"

"Please, just…talk. I don't know. Keep my mind off it. *Please.*"

It hurts more to cry quietly than it does to sob, but I don't want him to hear me. I think he does anyway. "Um…" I've got nothing else, so I sing. It's an old Dutch lullaby, one that Oma sang to me when I was a kid and needed soothing. I don't know what the words mean and I can't remember the third verse so I repeat the second, voice wobbling with emotion until I run out of verses.

Frank opens the car door and demands to know what the hell I'm doing. I push his hand away.

"Are you crying?"

"I'm sorry," Jem says.

"Take another dose."

"Just a few more hours."

I can't fucking stand it. I hang up on him and dial his house number. It's Ivy that picks up. She sounds worried by the lateness of my call.

"Jem needs another dose. Force him if you have to." I hang up on her too, drop my head against the steering wheel, and fall thoroughly to pieces.

Tuesday

Jem isn't at school today. I find myself thankful for that. If he's not here it means he's at home resting, and I don't have to look at him and think of last night. He's so stubborn, just like Tessa was. I used to slip small amounts of powdered painkillers into her food on the worst days, but most of the time she caught me. She could tell when she started to get high and I would get scolded.

Tessa was stoned—not my fault—when the hospital's social worker first brought up the DNR paperwork. Tessa couldn't have located her feet at that point. Mom was still convinced that Tessa was going to live, but my sister just chuckled and said she didn't want machines doing her living for her. "I'd much rather you just held a pillow over my head," she said. And thus began another fight.

Holding a pillow over her head probably would have been a cleaner way to go.

I'm in a lousy mood when lunch rolls around. I arrive at the table and everyone suddenly stops talking. The hell? Diane has a mean smirk on and looks away from me with a snicker.

"What? Do I have ink on my face?" I was chewing on my pen in class...

Paige makes a very conspicuous change of subject, leaving me to wonder what they were saying about me. I have this paranoid feeling that Luke might have said something, but how would the rumor have gotten around my school? Luke doesn't even go here.

I tell myself to stop being a twit and put the whole thing out of my mind. Whatever Diane is smirking about, it probably isn't worthy of my attention.

I drive over to Jem's house after school with a feeling of dread. What if he's still in pain? I don't want to make him feel bad about calling me last night, but he must know that it hurt me to listen to him in agony. We'll have to talk about that. We need to find a balance...before he sucks me dry. And before I let him.

Ivy welcomes me into her home with a hug. "He was asking for you earlier," she says of Jem. There are no pencils in her hair. She must not be getting much work done, taking care of her son all day.

"He was?"

"Thank you for calling me last night. Jem wouldn't have said anything. He's back on a full dose," she assures me. "It's made him a little loopy after weaning off. I wouldn't take anything he says seriously. He probably won't remember the conversation in a few hours."

"Is he still hurting?"

"No," she says gently but firmly. Ivy puts an arm around my shoulders and walks upstairs with me. It's nice to have someone to make these marches with. Mom and I never even held hands on our way in and out of the hospital. Even before Tessa died, opinion divided us. I put an arm around Ivy's waist, enjoying the companionship.

We stop outside Jem's door and Ivy nods to the library. "I'll be down the hall if you need anything."

"Thanks."

I expect Jem's room to be dark, but the drapes are wide open to let the light in. He's laying in bed with his flannels on, tucked in and dozy. His eyes open when I come around to the side of the bed, but he looks dazed and distant.

"Hey."

"I am so sorry," he murmurs. Jem reaches out a hand to take mine and misses.

He has poor depth perception right now. I give him my hand and he squeezes my fingers.

"I upset you."

"Yeah." I sit down on the edge of the bed. It's a struggle for him to look up at me. His eyes don't want to stay open and his pupils are really narrow. He's high as a kite.

"When did you get here?" he says curiously.

"Just now."

"Did I call you last night? Or the night before?"

"Last night."

"I shouldn't have called you." Jem bends forward, lifting his head off his pillow to lay in my lap instead. "You're a good friend," he says drowsily, and pats my knee.

In the back of my mind I'm scolding myself for wanting to laugh at him right now. Snarky Jem Harper, talking like a sentimental drunk.

I don't need to tell him about how bad it hurt that he refused to take his pills, or that he kept me up all night worrying. Jem doesn't need that right now—if he can even comprehend it in this state. The guy just needs a hug and a blanket.

I help him put his head back on the pillow and lay down beside him on the comforter. Jem immediately rolls to lay his head on my shoulder.

"It's okay that you called me."

His eyes remain closed, but he smiles like an angel. I hold him for a little while, listening to him breathe. I only know he's awake because he doesn't make that snuffling sound once.

"You're soft," he mumbles.

"Thank you."

Jem tilts his head to look at my face, and for some reason he's surprised. "Willa." Who did he think I was?"

"Jem."

His arm slides up my front until his hand latches on to my collar. "Are you mad at me?"

I press my lips together to hide my smirk. I don't want to laugh at a serious question. He's already forgotten that we just discussed this.

"Yeah, Jem. Livid. Really, horribly mad at you."

"No, no, no…" He takes my face between his hands, trying to be serious while I'm trying not to laugh. "Don't be mad. 'Kay? Don't. Just…knock it off." I think he's lost his train of thought already. His eyes have that passive, drugged up expression.

"Okay. But what will I do with all this cat food?"

"Um…" His hands relax on my face and he looks away, seriously considering the problem of all the non-existent cat food.

"Give it to the pigeons."

"Oh yeah? Pigeons?"

"They'll eat anything." He reaches up to nest his hand in my hair with a sigh of contentment. "Shitty, bastard pigeons…"

I laugh and Jem whines in the back of his throat. "Stop wiggling," he scolds me.

"I like you when you're stoned."

"I'm not stoned."

"No?"

"No. Just…tired."

I pet his head and tell him to sleep if he wants to.

"What time is it?"

If I tell him he'll just ask again in five minutes, so I keep it vague. "Afternoon. Nap time."

"I don't have my shoes."

"Where are you going?"

"I think I left them at the…thing…"

I pat Jem on the back. "Don't worry about it. We'll find your shoes later."

"What do I need shoes for?"

"Napping."

His brow crinkles over closed eyes. "That's not right…"

I smile and kiss his forehead. "Go to sleep, Jem."

Jem's sleep is never deep or whole. He drifts between dozing and waking, unable to fully enter either state. He's too drugged up to be conscious, but too well rested to slip into sleep. He lies still for periods of time, sometimes thirty minutes or more, until I'm almost sure he's asleep. But he always comes back to the surface, asking what time it is or prompting for help with some ridiculous worry: "I think I left the book in the sink." I enjoy these silly conversations and am guilty of goading him on once he gets rolling.

"Pickles," he murmurs as I massage lotion into his dry hands.

"You like pickles?"

"No. They're bitter," he says grumpily. His head lolls back on the pillow, eyes half-open. "Always complaining about something…"

I laugh so hard I snort and Jem mimics me. Cheeky bastard. He snorts so hard he gives himself hiccups, and still has them twenty minutes later when Elise comes home from a friend's house and climbs onto the bed for a visit. Jem lays on his side to face her while she chatters softly, telling him about her day in a gentle, indulgent voice. She knows he's not able to keep up with the conversation, but a nice voice can be soothing. He interrupts every so often with soft remarks of, "Willa was here," and "Where did Willa go? Is she coming back?" He's so dazed he manages to lose track of the fact that I'm sitting right behind him the whole time, rubbing his back. Still, it pleases me to be able to reach over and take his hand when he asks after me. My 'sudden' presence is enough to make him smile and sigh.

It takes so little to make Jem happy.

When Elise leaves to go do homework, Ivy comes in to give him his next dose of medicine. I expect Jem to get even loopier as a fresh dose of Oxy settles in his system, but he becomes sluggish instead. His words are slow and slightly slurred. I sit at the end of the bed and give him a foot rub while we discuss streetlamps (they have eyes, don't you know). It only takes a few minutes for Jem to lose the thread of the conversation. We drift into comfortable silence.

"Breakeven," he says.

"What's that?"

"The Script."

I have no idea what he's talking about until he says, "Play it." His iPod isn't in the nightstand drawer. I look to his laptop and turn the volume up on the speakers. He has a lot of songs by The Script, it turns out.

The opening guitar riff of "Breakeven" is gentle and melodic. Jem sighs at the sound and relaxes against his pillow. I turn back to the bed, back to Jem's ticklish feet. I like this song. It's very…Jem. It's also very like him to remember the title and artist of a particular song at a time when he can't name which way is up. The chorus is powerful. His chest rises with each crescendo, like he's breathing in the music, nourished on its power.

Jem's eyes are closed by the end of the song, so I lean over and switch off the music before the next track can start. I don't want to disturb his rest.

"Willa," he whispers.

"Yes?"

His voice is so quiet I can only make out his words by watching his lips move. "I need you."

I scoot farther up the bed to be closer to him. "What do you need?"

Jem's fingers clumsily tangle with the front of my shirt. "I want you."

I pet his head. "You are so high."

"I'm serious." He blinks a few times, attempting to focus. I can see that it takes a great amount of effort just to look straight ahead. "I like you. I'm alive when I'm with you."

"We're not talking about this until you're sober and coherent."

"But…" He tugs on the front of my shirt, pulling me closer to him. I think he's just confused and wants a hug, not *me* in any serious way. So I give him a hug, but he tries for a kiss.

"Not right now, okay?"

"I can pretend to be asleep," he says sweetly. It's a genuine offer, befuddled as he is, and I can't help but chuckle.

"I like you," he insists.

"I believe you."

"Willa?"

"Yeah?"

"I think I'm gonna throw up."

Holding his head over the basin while he pukes, I can't help but think: this is exactly how we first met. Green Jell-O included.

Thursday

So much for that freshman not saying anything.

As far as I can tell, the game of telephone has spun the story like this: Jem and I kissed in the nurse's office. Jem and I made out in the nurse's office. Jem and I got to second base in the nurse's office and are secretly dating. One rumor in particular—that he's relapsed and I fooled around with him out of pity before he dies—I think must have been started by a malicious bitch indeed. Diane Garth comes to mind.

As I head to History I hear a cluster of freshmen whispering loudly: "But he's bald! Gross!"

Up ahead I see Elise scurrying through the crowd, weaving between taller, larger people. She's headed for me. Christ, she's probably going to chew me out if she thinks the latter rumor is true.

Elise throws her arms around my waist in an enthusiastic hug. "Ohmigod, ohmigod, ohmigod," she squeals. Not exactly the reaction I was anticipating, unless she's trying to kill me with kindness.

Elise lets go and punches my shoulder. That's more like it.

"Why didn't you tell me you were dating my brother?" she hisses. "Why didn't *he* tell me? I get left out of everything."

Elise is quick to forgive this imagined exclusion. She links her arm with mine and makes me walk with her.

"How long has it been going on? Since that night on the porch? I bet it was." Now I know which of many false tales she's heard.

"We aren't together."

"But I heard—"

"Nothing happened."

To my horror she pulls out a cell phone and starts texting.

"What are you doing?"

"Telling Carey she's full of it." Elise's phone pings as the message sends. She pockets her phone and links her arm up with mine again. "So do you like my brother?"

I can hear her phone vibrating from here. News travels fast.

"It's complicated."

"Promise you'll tell me first when you start dating?" Elise puts on big doe-eyes. She looks just like Jem when she does that, except he puts a little more effort into the pout.

"Don't you mean *if* we start dating?"

"Nope."

I don't even bother to go home after school. I drive directly to the Harper house. It's time to stop putting off this little chat, especially now that people think there's more to me and Jem than we've discussed. My immediate to-do list has shortened to two items; to hell with everything else:

1. Sort out stuff with Jem.
2. Sort out the rest of my screwed-up life.

I think I can probably knock number one off the list this afternoon. The second one might take a decade or five.

Eric lets me into the house with a grin and calls out to the rest of the family that "the chef is here."

"Sorry, I'm not here to cook."

"Aren't you?"

"Sorry."

"How hard would I have to twist your arm to get another sandwich?"

I chuckle, but a muted voice from the living room cuts in before I can answer: "Leave her alone, man."

Eric holds a hand out, inviting me into the living room. I find Jem sitting in the recliner under a blanket, eating a bowl of Jell-O. He looks more focused than yesterday, but his face is still sallow.

I take a seat on the couch and he offers me a drink.

"No, thank you."

"Are you hungry?"

"We need to talk."

Jem swallows and nods. He sets his half-empty bowl of Jell-O on the side table. "Here, or upstairs?"

"Are you well enough to move upstairs?"

Jem gives me an approximation of his cocky smirk. "I'm sick, not crippled." He sets aside his blanket and stands up. I follow him up the stairs, keeping to his slow pace so he won't feel pressured to overexert himself. His socks shuffle across the rug and his pajamas hang on him in an unhealthy way. I touch his back without thinking, trying to locate the man within the scarecrow. Jem looks back at my hand and gives a small smile.

We don't go to Jem's bedroom. We go to the library instead, where we can both sit in chairs and pretend this is a civilized discussion. We take the two squashy chairs in the reading nook. Jem looks cold already, so before we start talking I head down the hall and come back with a blanket for him.

"Thanks," he says as I tuck the bottom edge under his feet. I want to tickle his toes, but he would probably kick me.

"How long were you here last night?" he asks. Can't blame him for not re-membering clearly.

"A few hours. Maybe four or five."

"That long?"

I would have stayed the night if I thought he needed me.

"You were saying funny things."

Jem sighs ruefully. "Did I say anything embarrassing?"

"Oh, plenty." I smile as he buries his head in his hands with a groan. "I liked 'Breakeven,' though. High Jem has great taste in music."

"I played 'Breakeven'?"

"You told me to put it on, yeah."

Jem's face turns the exact shade of a ripe tomato. "Oh Christ…" he mutters.

"What? It's a great song. It really calmed you down last night."

Jem rubs the back of his neck, fidgeting uncomfortably. "When we got home from Ottawa…I played that song for about an hour straight," he admits. "I was thinking about you…and Ava."

"I'm sorry." I think that's my third apology. Pity words don't erase actions. This isn't where I wanted to begin our conversation about 'seeing each other,' but that night in Ottawa has to come up at some point, so we might as well get it out of the way early.

Jem looks me in the eye. "Did it hurt you to go with her?"

I was hurting before she got anywhere near me.

"Yes."

There's a look in his eyes that says *good*. I deserve that. "It hurt me to watch you go."

"I'm sorry." That's four.

"Can I say something?"

"Of course."

"But you have to promise not to get angry or snippy."

My eyes narrow. I hate being asked to promise stuff like that. Why do people always make others swear not to get mad right before saying something that would rightfully piss anybody off?

"You're doing it already," he says.

I take a deep breath and try to dispel my irritation.

"About Ava…" He stops himself and takes a long pause to think. I tell him not to blow a fuse and he tells me not to joke. "This is serious."

"So get on with it."

Jem looks across at me and swallows before speaking. "I wanted you to want me," he whispers. "Not her." Jem rubs the back of his neck, uncomfortable again. I am such a shit.

"I'm sorry." Five. He doesn't respond. "It's getting easier, I think," I tell him. "Being vulnerable." A few weeks ago he wouldn't even tell me what kind of cancer he had. It's not much of a compliment, but it's the best I can do towards an apology for my own lousy ability to bare myself in conversations like these.

"Well it isn't. You could meet me halfway, you know."

"Trying." And failing, with a triple encore.

Jem purses his lips and sighs. "Anything you want to say?"

I hope he already knows this, but it still warrants saying. "I didn't want her."

Jem can't look me in the eye. "After we agreed to start over…it was like you gave up. Like you'd never even wanted me. I thought you'd confused liking me with…something else. Like being friends was an easy way out."

There's a pain behind my ribs that I used to kill with cigarettes and other such poisons.

"You didn't want me," I point out. "What did it matter if I wanted you?"

"Some people fight for what they want," he says quietly.

"Fighting is just the first step to getting beaten down."

Jem looks up at me with pain in his eyes. "You're damaged, Kirk."

"Look who's talking."

"I hate what you did…but I can't shake the fact that you…" He trails off, biting his lip. He can't think without fidgeting. "I feel *good* when I'm with you. I feel like me, and whole." His cheeks turn pinker with every word. "I want you to feel that way about me."

He looks away again, unable to meet my eye.

"You think I tell my darkest secrets to people I don't feel myself around?" I ask. "This is the whole me, Jem. It's ugly."

He shakes his head. Who is he to tell me who I am?

I meet him halfway to full exposure: "I do stupid, painful shit because it's better than sitting around, feeling like hell over what I've done—to Tessa, to you…. I hit my friend in the face because he insulted you. I went off with Ava because she was a temporary distraction from you. I make you food because it's just easier than telling you what I think."

"Feel," he mutters. The interruption throws me off my train of thought.

"What?"

"What you *feel*," he corrects me. "You said *think*."

"What's the difference?" I blow out a sigh and he shrugs.

"Everything." He sounds so blasé. "What *do* you feel?"

I have a strange urge to lie. "Nothing."

"Sorry, I'm not yet fluent in Willa-ese." Is he teasing me? "What does 'nothing' mean in English?"

"Don't make me say this shit. You know I don't do *feelings*."

The corner of Jem's mouth twitches in a sad smile. He reaches across the short gap between our chairs with his first two fingers extended. They nudge my hand where it rests on the arm of the chair, weaving between my fingers.

I love you.

I can't for the life of me remember why I thought it was a good idea to show him that gesture.

"Be with me."

"This isn't going to work."

"Pessimism is my job," he tries to joke, but it falls flat. "*Try.*"

"Why bother?"

"Because it's painful not to."

That pain behind my ribs rears its ugly head again. My first urge is still, and probably always will be, to kill it with smoke.

"I need to think about it."

Thursday

So knocking number one off my to-do list didn't work out so hot. But that doesn't mean I can't take a stab at number two: sorting out the rest of my life. Luke falls under that category, and he's as good a place as any to start. I owe him apology for what I did to his face and wrist. I'm also owed an apology, for what he said. We need to settle up.

I arrive at the Thorpe house to find Luke in the kitchen, cooking fries in hot oil. It's spilling everywhere and the kitchen smells like grease. Complaining about the smell is Briana, who occupies the chair closest to the kitchen door. She's polishing spoons. I guess this is her folks' idea of keeping her busy and out of trouble.

Luke looks up when I walk in and nods. "Hey."

"You got a second to talk?"

"*Talk*?" Briana interrupts. She looks at me over her shoulder. "Have you learned how to use your words like a big girl?"

I ignore her and look to Luke for an answer.

"Sure." He sets his spatula down and leans back against the counter, arms folded and hard-faced. I suppose not many happy-go-lucky smiles have come across his busted mouth lately.

"I came here to apologize."

"Okay."

"And to set some limits—about what it's not okay to say about my family."

"What about her family?" Briana cuts in.

I tell her, "You have no lines in this play."

"Nothing," Luke says, staring me straight in the eye. "She's just a selfish bitch who hurts her family as often as she can manage."

Fuck him.

"I'm sure your mother would be proud to hear you talk like that." Mrs. Thorpe has been dead for more than twelve years, and my words finally seem to get to him. The belligerent expression fades from Luke's eyes, but he still doesn't look away.

"I heard your parents shipped you off to live with Frank 'cause she couldn't stand you anymore," Briana says to me. Luke has been running his mouth.

"And your dad'll do the same to you if you keep it up." I nod to her hands, holding the spoon and rag. It's pretty toasty in this house to be wearing long sleeves. "If you meant it you would have cut up the wrist, not across it."

"Fuck you." Briana scoffs. She glares at me over her shoulder as if it's my fault for seeing through her. I'm not picking a fight with this wounded girl. I didn't come here for that. I walk around the table and stand between her chair and Luke, blocking her out of this conversation. I'm shit at apologizing anyway and I don't want to prolong this.

"I'm sorry I roughed you up so bad." Luke's eyes are still bruised and there's a mark on his jaw where I punched him. His wrist has faded welts around the bone, but at least he's not wearing his tensor support anymore.

"You hear that? The dumb bitch is sorry," Briana snarks.

"Interrupt me one more time; I dare you." I give her a hard look and she wrinkles her nose at me. Briana doesn't say anything. I turn back to Luke, prepared to finish my apology, when she speaks up from behind me.

"*Bitch.*"

That is fucking *it*. I turn to her and snap, "You think acting out will make people give a shit about you? If you mattered at all they would already care."

Briana stands up and squares her shoulders like she's going to hit me. Luke quickly jumps up to put himself between us. "Hey!" He puts his hands on Briana's arms, holding her back. I'm not sure if he's trying to stop the fight or protect Briana, but either way, it feels good to be feared.

"I don't understand why he fucking likes you," she spits at me. Briana throws Luke's arms off and storms out the door, muttering curses as she goes.

"That was low, Willa," Luke tells me sternly. What do I say to that?

"I have a temper."

"You're disgusting." Now there's a phrase that never tires with use.

"Likewise, Luke." I turn to go. "Sorry about your face."

"I meant it," he calls after me.

"So did I."

↩

Jem can sense that something is off with me when I meet him at the clinic for his dialysis session. "My life has no shortage of people who piss me off," I say.

"Who pissed you off today?"

"Luke."

"You did almost break his arm." Jem looks like he's trying not to smile when he says that.

"That's not all I did," I tell him that I called a troubled fourteen-year-old girl a worthless attention seeker and told her to give up and accept obscurity.

"What is your issue with keeping your damn mouth shut?"

"It has these hinges on the sides, you see." I open and close my jaw, demonstrating. Jem calls me a smartass and I tell him it takes one to know one.

"Have you thought about…?" he hints.

"Still working on that," I tell him. "Be patient."

"I can be patient," Jem assures me. "Kind of. I'll try really hard."

That makes me laugh. "What does 'trying hard' look like for a lazy bastard?"

"You're right, I give up—have you thought about it yet? Huh? Have you?

What are you thinking? Tell me."

"Oh shut up." I try to embrace the fact that I like it when Jem makes me smile during a lousy time.

Jem takes my hand and holds it on the armrest of the clinic recliner. "Take your time, Willa," he tells me seriously. "It's not like I'm going anywhere."

Jem: May 26 to 29

Friday

It's depressing, seeing the little green pill in my morning handful of 'candy.' Two weeks ago I thought I would be done with this crap forever. It sticks in the back of my throat as I swallow. I manage to wash it down, but the image of the little green pill—of the bottle on the bathroom counter—sticks to my ego. I'm too screwed up to go without painkillers.

They said the joint pain would fade within a year, probably less. I'm still waiting on that.

I give the bright side the benefit of the doubt as I get dressed. There are a few things to look forward to today: two days worth of missed assignments and lecture notes; eating yogurt for lunch, because my stomach is still weak from the fluctuating opiate doses; having to justify yet another absence to the school secretary, who shows pity all too readily. In fact, today would be entirely crap if not for the fact that I'm going to see Willa. I send her a text as I look through my drawer for my blue shirt—the one she likes because it actually fits.

You're lending me your Soc notes.

Her answer makes me smile: *Make me.*

I find Willa in the parking lot before school. She's standing by her car, digging through that black hole of a backpack. She's so absorbed in her search that she doesn't hear me come up behind her. I put a finger to her back like a gun and say, "Give me your Soc notebook and no one gets hurt."

I expect a snarky remark, but she just hands her notebook over her shoulder. "Just a heads up," Willa says as she zips her backpack. "That freshman blabbed."

"What?"

"There are a few rumors drifting around. Nothing major."

"What rumors?"

Willa shrugs and looks away. Now is a really lousy time to be evasive. I should smack her over the head with her notebook.

"That we made out, and that we're secretly dating because you're dying and I pity you."

I shouldn't be surprised, given the general level of intellect at this school, but what the hell?

"Have you said anything?"

"No."

"So, what? We ignore it?" I don't want to. I want the rumor to be true—the part about dating her, anyway. If everyone thinks I got a piece, but only out of pity, her pack of dumbass admirers might redouble their efforts in an attempt to show her a better time than Cancer Boy ever could.

"I think that would be best." Willa turns to go inside and I grab her sleeve. I'm not done with her yet. I've got one more burning question before she walks away and we pretend to be nothing more than friends.

I pull her in close enough to speak lowly in her ear. The words won't come. I don't know how to ask this, or if I really want to hear the answer.

"Um…"

Willa sighs. "No, I don't pity you." Thank God she can read my mind.

"Have you thought about…?"

"It won't last." So she keeps saying.

"That's not a no."

Willa arches an eyebrow at me. "And that's a technicality." She turns to walk away. I follow her, and Willa actually adjusts her pace to walk with me. For once she isn't pulling away. Cue the choir of angels.

I slip my hand into hers as we enter the main building. Her fingers don't grip me back and she's got a worried look on her face.

"You didn't say no," I remind her.

Willa's fingers curl around mine one by one. She hasn't actually said it, but the willingness of her touch, the display of affection in a very public school hallway, is better than hearing her say yes. Her hand is my proof that she does care. Willa does want me.

⮑

Whoever said schadenfreude is wrong obviously never met Chris Elwood. He looks like he's just dying to say something, the way he eyes Willa and I. She brought me a thermos of soup today, and Chris can tell from the way we eat one-handed with angled arms that we're holding hands under the table.

Would it be rude of me to shout, "HA!" at him across the table? Probably? Well damn.

Paige keeps eyeing Willa with looks ranging from curiosity to shrewdness. I bet she's going to corner Willa the first chance she gets and make her spill about dating Cancer Boy.

"Come over tonight," I say to her.

Willa spares me a glance. "Fine."

Fine? Just fine? Not 'I'd love to' or 'sounds good'? *Anything* to make it sound like she isn't agreeing out of pity for a poor sick freak like me?

Chris leans over and asks Willa if they're still on for tomorrow night. What's tomorrow night? I give Willa a questioning look, but she ignores me to invite Brian and Hannah along. It's a group outing to the movies.

I squeeze Willa's hand to remind her that I'm *right here* and she has the audacity to turn to me and say, "What?"

"You could invite me, you know." I try not to sound like a bratty child, but it's tough.

"Isn't it implied that you're coming?"

We're automatic dates now? I actually like the sound of that... Plus it makes Elwood the fifth wheel. I am so there.

"What time?"

⌁

I think Eric is bugging the crap out of Willa, but she hasn't told him off yet. He hovers around the kitchen island, watching intently and trying not to drool while Willa shows Elise how to test the readiness of pork chops. Elise loves the attention, and she loves learning to cook.

"So where'd you learn how to do this stuff?" she asks as Willa slides the chops back into the oven.

"My grandma loves to cook too. I had to learn—my mom's idea of a balanced meal is frozen pizza."

Elise tells Willa about the time Mom tried to make cornbread using blue corn. The result was grey squares of starch that tasted like sandpaper and felt even worse going down.

Eric presses his face to the oven window, watching the meat. "Are they done yet?"

Elise rattails him with a dishcloth and tells him to get away from the oven. On the stove, pots of sweet potato and green beans bubble away. Willa is making fresh apple compote—whatever the hell that is—for the pork. Eric keeps trying to taste it. Finally Elise slaps his hand and tells him to go set the table.

"Do you really think the way to a man's heart is through his stomach?" she says as Willa drains the sweet potatoes. So that's why my sister wants to learn to cook, and why that Latham jerk was here last weekend for fresh chicken sandwiches.

"Depends on the man," Willa says.

"It does not," I interject. Elise doesn't need any ideas about wooing that jackass with food. Willa looks over at me with a raised eyebrow. Crap. Food was the first thing that made me warm to her.

Elise puts her scrawny arm to work mashing the sweet potatoes while Willa glazes the green beans. Elise complains that all the steam is making her hair gel lose its hold. "It's at such an awkward length right now," she complains.

Sorry, sis.

Willa smiles at Elise's hair woes and says it probably doesn't help that her hair never lies flat.

"Ugh, I know."

"Mine doesn't either," I remind her. She's not alone with her wild hair.

Willa pauses with her hand on the blender and smiles at me. "Doesn't? Present tense?"

"Never mind."

"Can I see?"

"No." She lets it go, but Elise can't resist making a crack at my expense.

"He's prone to wicked hat head, you know."

Saturday

I head over to the Kirk house late in the morning. I have no plans for today, except to spend it in Willa's company.

She's gonna get sick of you, the way you're always showing up.

Never.

I let myself in and all I can hear is "I'm Gonna Be" by The Proclaimers blasting in the living room. Willa is in the kitchen, mopping the floor and singing along with such enthusiasm that I know she doesn't think she has an audience. No one sings with that much gusto in public unless they're drunk. I stand in the hall and observe her, enjoying the show even though I know she's going to give me hell when she finds out I was watching the whole time.

It's when she starts playing air guitar with the mop that I can't help but laugh, and she catches me. She looks absolutely horrified, which only makes the situation funnier.

"Encore!"

Willa marches up to me. For a second I worry that she's going to break the mop handle over my head and beat me to death with the pieces, but she just hands it to me with narrowed eyes and tells me to pitch in.

"Do I have to sing along?" I tease her.

Willa pretends to punch me in slow motion. I lean into it for the sake of the joke and she opens her hand to touch my face at the last second. She strokes my jaw in a subtle, welcoming way.

"You mop. I'll clean windows."

I want to touch her through that baggy flannel shirt.

"Sure."

"I made myself a chore list for before we go out," she says as she heads to the kitchen. She reaches under the sink for the bottle of Windex and oh that ass...

"Brian is driving. Is that cool with you?"

"Of course." Going out tonight wouldn't be my first choice of activity, but I can fake enthusiasm if she really wants to go. If it were just a double date with Hannah and Brian, and Willa and I had some clear label on whatever it is we're doing, I'd enjoy it more.

"We don't have to go." I give her a (hopefully) persuasive smile. "We could stay in and rent something to watch."

Willa hums noncommittally. "I owe Chris some friend time."

She owes that douche nozzle what?

"Don't give me that look."

"What look?"

"It's that look that dogs give their owners before they leave the house. You don't have to come tonight if you don't want to."

"I do want to," I assure her. I push the mop across the kitchen tiles as she wipes the windows. "So…are you wearing that?"

Willa looks down at her torn black jeans and hand-me-down flannel. "Are you serious?"

"You look comfy."

"I look homeless."

I set the mop against the counter and show her how huggable flannel is. Willa doesn't pull away, either. She wraps her arms loosely around my neck and rests her head on my shoulder while I trace the shape of her ribcage.

"Where's your brother?" I murmur.

Willa sighs. "No, I will not screw you while he's out."

"I didn't mean it like that." I rub her back through the flannel, trying to console her. How could she have such a cheap thought? Would she expect that kind of behavior from me?

"So he's not home?"

"Why?"

"Because I'd rather not get the living shit beaten out of me for kissing you."

"You haven't kissed me."

"I want to." I press her weight against the counter and cup the back of her head where it rests on my shoulder. I use it to guide her face up to an angle where I can touch her lips. Willa kisses with her eyes open. It's weird, but I try not to mind it. It's like she doesn't want to stop looking at me. And watching the way her face changes, the way she responds to each kiss with more than just her lips, I wonder what I missed with other girls while my eyes were closed. Did their eyes turn dark like Willa's? Did their cheeks turn pink and warm? Did they negotiate with their eyes as well as their lips, demanding, teasing, asking for a different pace, goading and hinting at ideas?

It takes forever for her to let me get away with a little bit of tongue. She opens up to it slowly, parting to allow just enough exploration to drive me insane. And then she draws my tongue past her teeth and sucks gently. The sensation makes my face warm and my chest tight with the added effort it takes to breathe. I draw my tongue back, taking her lip with it, and return the favor. Her fingers tighten around my shoulders.

"Be with me."

"Still thinking about it."

"Willa—"

The damn phone rings. I expect her to let it ring through to voicemail, but she slips away from me to answer it. I'm left hanging with my hands on the counter, listening to the conversation that is more important than making out with me.

"Hello?"

Please let it be a telemarketer.

It's not, because Willa doesn't immediately hang up. She's silent, but I can hear the faint sounds of the caller speaking.

"Haven't you learned not to piss me off, Luke?" I look over my shoulder at her. She looks calm enough, but her voice is hard and her tongue is sharp. I wouldn't piss her off right now.

I take the handset from her. "Don't call here again." I slam the phone down and pull Willa into a hug. "You should have let it ring."

"You should let go." She shrugs my arms off and goes back to her paper towels and Windex.

"Are you really thinking about it? Or are you just saying that to put off rejecting me?"

"The floor isn't going to mop itself."

"Willa."

"I am thinking," she insists. "Be patient. This pros and cons list could take awhile."

"Don't rationalize it. Just do what you want to do."

"I want to think it over. Get mopping."

"In a second." I take her shoulder and turn her away from the window. "Let me try convincing you again."

For an undecided person, Willa sure kisses with enthusiasm. The bottle of Windex hits the counter with a thud and her arms wrap around my neck. She's quick to let my tongue in this time. I generally prefer gentle kisses, but I'm really starting to like the way she sucks and nibbles at my lips and tongue. It's like passion without force, and I try to return the favor. Willa snickers suddenly.

"What?" It's probably not the wisest decision on my part to keep kissing her when I expect an answer, but I can't leave her mouth alone.

"I was just imagining," she says between kisses, "what my brother would say"—I cut her off as my teeth close gently around her lower lip—"if he found a hickey on me." She chuckles.

"You want one?"

"No, I'd rather live to see nineteen." She lets go of my shoulders and hops up on the counter. Sitting like that, we're nearly equal height. Willa grabs the sides of my neck and pulls me in for another kiss. My hands trail up her denim-covered thighs, around the back of her hips. I just barely refrain from squeezing her ass—I don't want to push my luck. She scoots so far forward that she could easily wrap her legs around me...

"Why the hell are you still thinking?" I murmur against her lips.

Willa ignores my question. Her thumbs trace the curve of my collarbone, as if she just knows where I most like to be touched. My fingers grasp at her soft back—no bra, again—pulling her closer.

Then I feel the tips of her fingers slide under the back of my hat, and I tweak.

I pull away and take a big step back, tugging the edge of my toque back down. Willa remains on the counter for a second, breathless and hands outstretched. Then she closes her reddened lips and lowers her hands with a sigh.

"That's why, Jem. Because you're dead. You think of yourself as the Jem who moved here from Ottawa, and you can't stand it when that illusion is broken."

What do I say to that?

Willa slips down from the counter and reaches for the mop. "Sooner or later you have to start living with yourself. It sucks, but it's the only way to live."

I feel sick all of a sudden. Willa gives me a look of concern and offers me her bed to lay down in. As I trudge up the stairs, still breathless and a little shaken, I consider that she might be right about our potential as a couple.

That doesn't stop me from wanting her, though.

❧

Willa keeps the music down while I rest. I wish she wouldn't. It might help me relax. At the moment all I have are the distant sounds of her cleaning house, and it makes me feel far away. Her sheets smell nice though. Not as nice as Willa, but still pretty awesome.

Willa's room is the only part of the house that looks lived in, but not much can be inferred from the objects she leaves out in the open. It's generic stuff that everyone has—unsorted laundry, a hairbrush, some books and a pair of shoes. I open the drawer of her nightstand to see what she's *really* like in private.

You can learn a lot about a person by what they keep in their nightstand drawers. What objects and sentimental things can they not stand to be far from in their most vulnerable hours of sleep? Are they practical or cluttered? In Willa's nightstand I find a second-generation iPod with no headphones, a blister pack of what I'm assuming is birth control with none of the pills missing, and a roll of receipts held together with an elastic band. What a suspicious lack of crap. She must hide her meaningful things elsewhere, if she has any.

Willa comes in just in time to catch me with my hand in the drawer. She stands there and stares while I quietly push it closed.

"Sorry. I was looking for a mint." That's believable, right?

Willa shakes her head. "I hate it that your bad habits are also mine."

"What?"

"I snooped through your drawers while you were napping."

Suddenly drawer-poking is offensive when someone else does it. I wonder what she saw in there. Why can't I remember what I keep in my nightstand? I had the thing open just this morning.

"Find anything good?"

Willa just shrugs. Damn it.

❧

The carpool to the theater is crowded, but I don't mind. I get to have Willa's thigh and shoulder pressed up against me the whole way, and hold her hand on my knee. Up front, Brian and Hannah hold hands on the center console. Chris, slouched in his seat, looks thoroughly put out.

I don't let go of Willa's hand during the walk across the parking lot, or while we wait in the theater lobby. The other three go to the concession stand for popcorn and drinks, but Willa and I hang back. She insists she doesn't want a snack.

"You're not abstaining from popcorn just because I can't have any, are you?"

"My, my, you think highly of yourself." She swats my arm. "I don't like popcorn when it's cheap, never mind five bucks a bag."

"What do you mean you don't like popcorn?"

"I just don't."

"Mutant."

Chris comes back from the concession stand with a drink and Twizzlers. He asks Willa again if she doesn't want anything.

"I'm good."

I like the way Chris keeps looking at our joined hands, so obviously bothered by it. It feels good to finally pay him back for being a complete dick to me. Revenge on Elwood is an ongoing process—as being a dick always is with him.

Willa notices Chris's preoccupation too, and she lets go of my hand. She actually apologizes for making him feel like a fifth wheel.

"I heard you guys were a thing," he says.

Willa is embarrassingly quick to correct him. "We're not." Excuse me while I go hang myself...

Chris turns his attention to me with badly feigned concern. "I heard you were sick again."

"I'm not."

"Really? You look a little fevered." My face is red from anger and embarrassment; trust Chris to capitalize on that for a joke.

"Are you?" Willa presses the back of her fingers to my neck. I slap her hand away and instantly feel like a jerk for snapping on her. She looks at me like she wants to tell me off. I've proven her right again, being oversensitive about my appearance. But in my defense, Elwood has been a dick to me before. It's hard not to rise to his bait.

Hannah and Brian return from the concession stand.

"Are we seeing this movie or not?" I turn to go, ignoring the perplexed looks from Hannah and Brian. I want to backhand the smirk right off Elwood's face.

⚘

I hate Chris Elwood. He offers Willa a Twizzler during the previews and watches all too closely as her mouth moves along its length, slipping inch by inch into her moist mouth. I want to reach out and take her hand, or lean over and give her a kiss—anything to throw Chris off his agenda—but she doesn't think too highly of me right now. She thinks I'm dead inside and delusional to boot. And to her credit, she's right. Maybe we're better off as friends now. Later, a few months from now when I look human again, it might work; when I have something more to offer her than this washed-up carcass.

The lights go down for the start of the film. Willa has the worst taste in movies. It's a goofball comedy, full of obvious jokes and juvenile pop culture references. A couple is making out in the back row—loudly, I might add. I miss that.

Willa laughs at a ridiculously overdramatic golf cart stunt. Her hand finds mine in the dark and holds on securely, without hesitation.

Take that, Elwood.

Sunday

Waking up at seven on a weekend sucks balls. It sucks even more after a lousy night of sleep—Ava woke me up with six drunken apology texts. I try my best to sleepwalk through showering and dressing, and drag my tired ass downstairs to find food. Everyone else is still asleep—even Mom. I suck back some juice and yogurt to tide me over, and as I brush my teeth I conclude that I am going to sleep all the way to church.

It's just Willa and me today. Frank has already given up on going to church, and his sister doesn't need to be escorted to and from therapy like a kindergartener.

Willa looks just as tired as I feel when she picks me up. She's got a tall thermos of coffee with her and says, "If I fall asleep at the wheel, punch me." Comforting.

Willa and I don't go to mass. We stop at a diner in Perth for breakfast. Willa orders waffles and I nurse a tall glass of milk. I think the waitress imagines she's being subtle, the way she doesn't look at me while delivering the food, yet stares at me from behind the counter. I watch Willa drown her waffles in syrup, totally unfazed by Shirley the waitress's curious gaze.

"Do you mind being stared at when you're with me?"

"No." She licks syrup off her thumb. "Better you get stared at than me."

"Gee, thanks."

"You're welcome." She gives me the strawberry garnish on her plate as a peace offering and digs into her soggy waffles. "Does it bother you to be stared at?"

"Duh." I wouldn't have brought it up if I was okay with being gawked at.

Willa looks over at the waitress, who promptly averts her eyes and busies herself wiping mugs. Every few seconds I can see her peering at me under her lashes.

"Watch and learn." Willa raises her hand and waves the waitress over. Shirley grabs a pitcher of orange juice and makes her way to our booth, thinking Willa wants a refill.

"More?" she offers.

"No, thank you. I just had a question about the diner."

"Yes?"

"Does it improve your tips to stare at the customers like sideshow freaks?"

Shirley turns red in the face and mumbles, "I'm sorry." She scurries away, through the kitchen door and out of sight. We don't see her for the rest of the meal, and Willa pays the bill for her waffles with exact change.

❧

The church hall seems even plainer than last time we were here. Willa and I walk in hand in hand, and once again she scoots her chair closer to mine. The porn addict sits down on her other side and offers her a smile.

"I don't like RedTube much either," he whispers before Arthur calls the meeting to order. Arthur opens the session with the Serenity Prayer:

God, grant us the
Serenity to accept things we cannot change,
Courage to change the things we can, and the
Wisdom to know the difference
Patience for the things that take time
Appreciation for all that we have, and
Tolerance for those with different struggles
Freedom to live beyond the limitations of our past ways, the
Ability to feel your love for us and our love for each other and the
Strength to get up and try again even when we feel it is hopeless.

That's Eric's favorite prayer. Don't ask me how I know this. Arthur makes a point of welcoming me and Willa back to group, since we missed last week's session.

"Tell us about your week," he says. He doesn't address either Willa or me specifically, since we end up speaking for each other anyway.

"She's being indecisive."

"He hates the way he looks."

"It's only temporary," another girl chimes in. "Hair grows back." She speaks to me with a gentle expression in her eyes, but it's still Willa who replies.

"But he'll never look the same as he did before he got sick," she says. "He's a walking contradiction. He hates the fact that he's invisible, but he hates when people notice him because the looks remind him that he's not well."

My hand barely moves—just the slightest twitch of the pinkie—but she sees it and understands. Willa gives me her hand to hold.

"Appearance is a big part of who we are," Arthur says. "But it's not all of who we are. The beauty of the human spirit shows in the things we do, not the way we look."

I expect him to bust out a quote from scripture, but he spares us. He speaks to the group as a whole. "Each of us here has personal struggles with self-esteem, don't we?" He makes my problem sound like the worries of a tweenage girl.

Willa leans over to whisper in my ear, "You're beautiful." Her obvious secretiveness makes Arthur turn his attention from me to her. He asks Willa if she has a difficult decision looming.

"Not so difficult," I say. Or at least that's what I think.

"Would you like to share it with the group? Get an outside perspective?" he says directly to Willa. She doesn't even look at him. She just shakes her head and says she's praying on it.

"Are you really?" I say.

Willa looks at me sideways. She's got the shades drawn over her eyes, showing no emotion. "Yes."

"Talking to God helps," Arthur encourages her. "He has a way of helping us through difficult decisions."

"I don't talk to God," Willa says. "I talk to the dead."

"You lost your sister, yes?"

"Among others. There was a friend..." She shrugs. "I don't know when he died, but he didn't have long to live when I last saw him."

She never told me about that.

Arthur encourages her to pray directly to God, or at least to a saint, and then moves on to another group member. I wonder if I should be worried that Willa is talking to Thomasina in her head. For one, it's a little crazy. For another, she's said a few times that Thomasina wouldn't have liked me. These imaginary conversations do not bode well for me.

I don't say much for the rest of the group session. AA Boy is only six days porn-free this time. Willa claps inappropriately. Next to me, the kid with bullying issues bursts into tears during his turn, which is uncomfortable as all hell to watch. Arthur hands a box of tissues to Pothead and tells him to pass it down the circle to my neighbor. I hold out my hand to take the box, but it stops with Willa. She holds it up and raises an eyebrow at Arthur. "Really? This is the best you can offer?"

She gets out of her seat and gives the perpetual victim a hug. If there's one thing Willa understands, it's ostracism. The kid looks so relieved to receive a shred of commiseration that I can't stand to look at him and have to turn away.

Two of the other girls get up and join the hug. I don't know that it's helping, because his sniffling turns into full-blown sobs; or maybe that's what catharsis sounds like.

"Now, now, don't crowd him," Arthur says. "Give Michael some room to speak."

Willa is a little busy, so I answer for her. "Arthur, shut the fuck up."

↭

After group, Willa walks Michael to his car. He's not such a bad guy, it turns out. I leave to use the bathroom before the long drive home, and when I come back out Willa is nowhere to be found. Her car is still here, so at least I know she didn't leave without me.

I try the parish hall, but the doors are already locked. I check the church, but the pews seem to be empty and so is the side chapel. I knock on the door to the ladies washroom, but there's no answer and when I open the door a crack I can see that the lights are off. I try calling her cell but she doesn't answer.

"Fine, be difficult."

I find Willa down in the cemetery, sitting on the flower in the center of the labyrinth. She's fascinated with that thing. Her legs are crossed and her elbows rest on her knees, holding up her chin. She's a million miles away. I cross the stones to crouch down in front of her.

"Hey."

"You cheated," she says of my stroll across the labyrinth.

"Are you okay?"

"I didn't want to let him drive away," she admits. "People like him end up on the six o'clock news for killing themselves."

"He won't," I try to reassure her. "He's going to be fine. He had a good day in group."

"And he'll have a shit Monday at school."

"You can't worry about everyone, you know. You'll stretch yourself too thin."

Willa doesn't say anything. I take her hands from under her chin and pull her up. I lead, she follows, out of the labyrinth, properly—together.

↭

I thumb the children's missal as I sit in the empty pew, waiting for Willa. She's giving confession a try. It wasn't her idea, which might screw up the whole spirit-of-contrition thing, but I think it could be good for her to unload to an anonymous stranger.

In the back of the missal I find a list of the Ten Commandments. No wonder Willa has been in the confessional so long. Thou shall not kill. Broken. Honor thy mother and thy father. Broken. Thou shall not commit adultery. Grey area, but only because she isn't technically married. Thou shall not steal. Way broken. Thou shall not bear false witness. Broken. As far as I know she's an atheist, so there goes 'Thou shall not worship any other God but Me.' Likewise for thou shall keep the Sabbath day holy and thou shall not take the Lord's name in vain.

419

Eight out of ten Commandments broken. This could take awhile. I wonder if she covets shit...

"Jem." I look up to find Arthur standing at the end of the pew, arms laden with hymnals left at the back of the church. "Waiting for confession?" he asks. He's being extremely polite, considering I told him to shut the fuck up not a full hour ago. I guess he's turning the other cheek.

"Willa's worried." Even outside of Group, I can't stand to tell him about myself.

"Oh?"

"About Michael, harming himself."

"Michael has been doing better lately," Arthur tries to assure me. Because people who are of sound nervous constitution burst into tears in front of a group of strangers. "Six months ago I might have thought that of him, but he's made quite a bit of progress."

I'm still betting on Willa's gut feeling. She's been there; she knows what drives a person to his or her own personal ledge. I tell Arthur about Willa's botched attempt.

"It's touching, the way you both take care of each other," he says. "But you both need to learn to speak for yourselves in Group. Self-expression is an important part of healing and growing as a person. Will you encourage Willa to bring up her issues on her own?"

"Will you at least start trying with people like Michael? When you suspected six months ago did you get him on suicide watch?"

Arthur stares at me for a few seconds. He promises he'll call that poor kid's family to discuss the problem, in exchange for my promise to speak about my own junk in Group. He walks away to the parish office, tottering behind his stack of hymnals. If Arthur is full of shit, he's good at hiding it.

You did the right thing.

What if that kid wasn't really going to hurt himself?

What if he was?

You'd resent him.

Would not.

You resented her for trying to jump.

I shake away thoughts of Willa in the same state as Michael. I can't think of her like that. It makes me so intensely uncomfortable that I can't breathe.

It seems like an hour has gone by before Willa opens the confessional door and steps out. She looks bewildered and little sad.

"Can I borrow that?" She takes the missal and flips through until she finds the page with the Our Father prayer printed on it. Willa sits down on my lap with it and sighs.

"Apparently I need to recite this ten times and everything will be better."

I take the book from her, closing my fingers around her little hands. "No one ever taught you how to pray, did they?" I already know the answer. She described herself as a heathen two weeks ago. Religion wasn't part of her up-bringing.

"It doesn't make everything all better," I tell her quietly. "It centers you." Even still, she recites the Our Father ten times. I say it with her, and it reminds me of monks of various religions, chanting to focus their attention on the divine.

"I don't feel any better."

"I'm sorry."

"You really think you want me?" She sets the missal in the slot for hymn-books.

"Yeah, I do." I brush a lock of hair behind her ear. Willa has her problems, but for all her flaws she's still a good person, even when she doesn't mean to be. She would comfort a total stranger if they needed it. She would stay up all night with me, riding out the pain. The food she makes, and lending me her notes… Before I even liked her on the most basic level, she was good for me, refusing to put up with my bad moods.

"I think I want you too," she says quietly. I can't help but smile. "One condition, though?"

"What's that?"

"I'm not dating the old Jem," she says firmly.

"I'm trying." Only not really. I think Willa knows I'm lying. She slips her hand into mine.

"You've got to let me be with the new you. I don't like Old Jem. That guy's a prick." Her smirk is infectious.

"Okay." She bends her neck for a chaste kiss—we are in a church—and she still tastes like maple syrup from breakfast.

I could fall uncontrollably in love with you.

"Come on." Willa gets off my lap and offers me a hand up. "Lets get out of here."

⌇

Willa fits in seamlessly with my family. I resented that when she cut me out because her absence was everywhere, but now I love it, because her presence fills a gap I never really noticed. I love the way she talks to my mother with such patience, not seeming to mind that Mom can't stay on one topic for long and the conversation always comes back to architecture eventually. Mom doesn't think anything weird of the arm I keep wrapped around Willa as we sit on the couch, but when Dad comes in from the yard he does a double take. He actually stops mid-sentence and gapes at us.

"Yes?" Mom prompts when he doesn't finish.

"Er, have you seen the rake?"

"I might have." She gets up and goes to the garage to help him look. The minute they leave I capitalize on their absence, turning Willa's chin up for another kiss. We keep it simple and tongue-free, just in case my parents come back suddenly. It's hard to deny that we've been making out if our lips are swollen and wet.

Suddenly I feel a breeze on my cheek. I open my eyes and find Elise standing behind the couch, hands and chin resting on the backrest. She's got an impish grin on and looks from Willa to me with eager eyes.

"Whatcha doing?"

What the hell does it look like?

"'When,' Elise," Willa answers. My sister squeals and throws her arms around Willa's neck.

"Don't strangle her."

"Finally!" Elise sings, and skips away flapping her hands excitedly. I apologize to Willa about my sister's behavior, but she waves it away.

"As long as Eric doesn't react the same way."

My brother already likes Willa—he's tasted her food—and doesn't say much when he finds out that she and I are a couple. He just tells us not to violate any of the downstairs furniture and asks if Willa is staying for dinner.

"Sure. I'll make chicken pot pie."

Eric turns to me. "Marry her."

⌖

You'd think our parents don't feed Eric, the way he eats. The chicken potpie (made with Elise's gleeful assistance and Mom's thank-God-I-don't-have-to-cook support) gets devoured quickly. There are no leftovers and Dad jokes that we should have rationed such good food. I can see Eric eyeing the sweet potato soup made just for me and I shift my bowl away from him.

After dinner I take Willa upstairs, away from the hubbub of family life. I know she enjoys being in such an active home, but for the moment I want her all to myself.

Willa makes herself comfortable against the headboard with her knees pulled up. If I lay down so soon after a good meal I'll fall asleep, so I sit in the desk chair instead and prop my feet up on the edge of the bed. I try to play footsies with her and she calls me a romantic dork.

"You're not changing your mind about us already, are you?" I say it teasingly, but I do worry about that. Willa could decide that she doesn't want to be with Cancer Boy, and I wouldn't be able to find fault with that reasoning. I know what a pain in the ass I am to deal with.

"Are you?" she challenges.

"No. But if you decide you can't put up with me..."

Willa rolls her eyes. "You still think you're special for having baggage?"

"Whatever." I hate admitting that she's right. "So we're really doing this?"

"So it would appear."

"How are we going to tell your brother?" Frank probably won't like it. He may even come down hard on Willa because of it. But she and I owe him that little bit of honesty, and there's always the remote chance that Frank will be okay with it.

Somewhere in hell, a snowball is laughing at me.

"We don't have to tell him."

"We should be honest. You live with him, after all."

Willa shrugs it off. "If he's not going to introduce me to his boyfriend, I don't owe him the same."

"What?"

"Never mind."

We'll come back to that issue later. Right now I want to do right by Willa's guardian.

"It'll be no different than introducing me to your parents."

"I haven't introduced *friends* to my parents in years, never mind boyfriends."

"You've had several?" It's a complicated sort of question. I can't hold it against her—I've probably had as many girlfriends since the beginning of high school as she's had boyfriends. But there's the fact that she might have expectations of what a relationship is like, or leftover baggage from some jerk that didn't do right by her, and that can complicate the present.

"Just three," she answers quietly. "Maybe only two, if you want to get technical."

"Who was the sort-of-boyfriend?"

Willa looks at me with a sarcastic tilt of her eyebrows. "What, you want his name?" I give her the you-know-what-I-mean look and she relents. "He ran the Group I used to go to in St. John's."

"Like, he led it?"

"Yeah."

Old enough to be a counselor, but not-quite-dating Willa. It doesn't take much to figure out what was probably going on: some jackass counselor taking advantage of the people who came to him for help. She can't call him a boyfriend, but that doesn't mean they didn't do things.

"Did you sleep with him?" Immediately after the words are out I feel like a complete ass for saying them. I try to take them back, to apologize, but Willa doesn't seem so offended by the question.

"Yes. I slept with the others, too, in case you're wondering."

"I wasn't."

"Sure."

Willa smirks. "What about your girlfriends?"

"What about them?"

"Which one took your cherry?"

I consider how to answer that, but my red ears beat me to it.

"Still a virgin, huh?" Willa snickers at my embarrassment and I hurry to correct her.

"Technically."

"What's technically?"

"We played put-the-tip-in a few times, but it hurt her so we didn't…"

Willa nods. She's got her sense of amusement under control now. "Was she an everything-but kind of girl?"

Yes.

"Neither of us was ready to be doing…that. We just got carried away a few times."

"You never know where you might end up," she says philosophically. I get up from my chair and sit next to her on the bed. Willa unbends her knees and rests her feet in my lap.

"Can I ask about your first time?"

"My first time what?"

"Sex."

"Define sex."

I stare at her for a few seconds before I realize that it's a serious question. She sees my delayed thought process and makes a suggestive hand motion.

"Yeah."

"That was with one of the other people from Group. He was an anger management case."

I worry that he hurt her.

"He was hearing impaired. People had bullied him and he was a really angry guy as a result. Picked a lot of fights."

"And he was one of your boyfriends?"

Willa nods. "Ray. It was interesting. He could only hear loud noises so the whole thing was very…tactile."

I hate to picture Willa with another guy. But even worse than that mental image is the idea that she goes for guys with physical problems. One boyfriend with a hearing problem, another recovering from cancer…

"And your other boyfriend?"

Willa shrugs. "Just a guy I worked with at the music store. He was older than me. We were on-again off-again for awhile." She rolls her eyes at some memory. "He liked to collect things. His place was full of useless shit. He had a whole shelf of shrunken heads and he was really into the idea of a zombie apocalypse." I can't help but picture the stereotypical pierced, tattooed freak that would be into crap like that. Surely Willa could have done better than *that* guy.

She can do better than you too, idiot.

"Willa?"

"Yeah?"

"Did you report your counselor?"

She shakes her head. "No one would have believed me."

"Of course they would have." I reach out to touch her face, fixed into immobility because of this personal subject. Willa doesn't react to the thumb I brush across her cheekbone.

"He got into counseling because he was a heavy drinker in college. Got behind the wheel wasted one night and ended up in a bad accident. His shtick was motivating kids not to end up like him. He had a whole speech laid out, about how being a paraplegic was the best thing that ever happened to him because it led him to help screwed up kids."

Willa throws her hands up. "He was a good guy. Active in the community, went to church. People thought the sun shone out his ass. If I told people about him they'd think, 'What? Steve?' and he could refute my claim easily. He's paralyzed—people look at guys in wheelchairs and think 'oh, he's harmless.' Like he couldn't possibly want sex, let alone have it, so what could he do to me?"

I see her point. I know firsthand how people look through those with physical problems, like we're ghosts or witless children. But that means I also disagree with her, because I know just how much someone in that position can do to take advantage, and it's no more or less than an able-bodied guy.

"He touched you."

"I never said no."

"Did you say yes?"

"Sometimes," she admits. "It felt good. Distracting." The corner of her mouth turns up in a sarcastic smirk. "Are you sure you still want me?"

"It's not you that bothers me."

"It's them?"

I nod.

"None of them raped me, Jem. What happened was my responsibility, too."

"Do you want me to hold it against you?"

"People generally do."

"Does your mom know?"

"That her daughter is a slut? She doesn't know the details, but she's neither blind nor an idiot, so I'm sure she does." Willa shrugs. "Doesn't matter. She resents me anyway."

I sigh. "You know, most people, when they realize they've dug themselves into a hole—they let go of the damn shovel."

"But I'm almost to China," she says with a fake pout.

"You think your parents *want* to resent you?"

Willa sits up and smiles without humor. "I moved here for a clean break—and to get away from my mom. Do you know how awful it feels to sit across the dinner table from someone who is clearly thinking *You killed my daughter*?"

I don't know how to answer that, so I don't, and she continues. "You're a bit of a dreamer, I know, thinking you can forgive me, but she won't."

"I don't think you'd know what to do with yourself if you were forgiven." The words hang there for a beat, and then Willa smirks.

"That's the difference between me and you: I don't dream of impossible things."

Monday

I wake up to find Elise tickling my ear. I swat her hand away and roll over, hoping that she'll leave me alone to sleep some more. My alarm goes off and I smack it so hard the clock falls off the nightstand.

"Oh, good, you're awake."

"No I'm not."

"Can you bring Willa home for dinner tonight?" she asks.

"She was just here last night."

"So?"

"So she has a life, Lise. She might have to work tonight."

Elise pouts. "I like having her around. You're less of a grump when she's here." Elise kisses my forehead and hops off my bed. "At least invite her, okay?" she says as she leaves my room.

I force myself out of bed and into the shower. The warm water on my skin is the only consolation I get for climbing out of bed so freaking early. As I lather up, my penis begins its usual morning tease. It's been happening for a few weeks now, on and off: the beginnings of an erection, which, if encouraged, completely vanishes. My dick is like a damned gopher, poking its head up and withdrawing at the first sign of attention. Not that the attention feels that good. The touches that used to excite me barely do anything anymore.

I lather up my thighs and crotch first, knowing that even the casual brushing against a washcloth is enough to kill my boner. But today it doesn't. It twitches and hardens further until I've got a promising semi.

I don't know what I'm expecting, but I take a few casual strokes anyway. My usual grip feels too gentle to be pleasurable, but anything tighter almost hurts. I lean against the shower wall and experiment a little, varying strokes and grip. All of it feels foreign and mediocre compared to my pre-cancer activities. The only good thing I get out of it is the pride of knowing that I can still get it up—under the right circumstances. I don't even come close to a climax, but I decide that's probably for the best. My last one hurt like hell.

By the time I step out of the shower, my erection has wilted completely. As I towel off I still feel little tremors in my thighs and stomach, the last evidence of arousal. It doesn't seem right that my knees should shake like that when I didn't even get off, and I resent the way I have to sit down to put my feet through my underwear without falling over. Inconveniences like this should come with a screaming orgasm, damn it.

I stand up to get the rest of my clothes, and a sudden pain between my hips brings me to my knees. It's like being kicked in the balls, the way the pain radiates up my abdomen and makes me want to gag. My thighs tremor under my weight, and when I roll onto my side, holding my sore middle, I notice an unpleasant feeling of wetness.

My last shred of dignity is killed by the possibility that I might have pissed myself too. I worry that something might be wrong with my kidneys. The pain, this sudden accident…

I crawl to the bathroom to inspect the damage, not daring to try to stand on shaky legs. My boxers aren't as wet as I first thought they were, and the wetness isn't pee. It's semen, smeared all over my crotch and thigh. I ejaculated—without a hard-on, without stimulation, without pleasure. God damn, it hurt. I can't decide which is worse: pissing my pants at eighteen, or jizzing in my shorts like a twelve-year-old.

I use the bathroom counter to pull myself to my feet and grab a washcloth to clean myself. That skinny weirdo stares back at me in the mirror.

You are such a freak.

I know.

Willa: May 29 to 31

Monday

Three days of avoiding Paige's prying questions and my streak goes bust. She corners me in Math during a work period with demands to know *everything* about Jem and me. When it started, how it started, what if he gets sick again? Is it weird that he is still pretty ill? Is he a good kisser? Have we done anything romantic? We discussed exes and my parental issues—oh so romantic. Paige even asks how we're going to celebrate our one-week anniversary.

"Uh, I don't do milestones." And our one-week anniversary would fall on a therapy day. We'd spend it with Arthur and the other screwballs. I try to joke about that with Jem when I see him at lunch, and to my horror, he takes it seriously.

"We could do something after."

"Did you miss the point of that story? Who the hell celebrates a one-week anniversary?"

Jem does that really annoying thing where he blatantly ignores me. "We could go to The Circle again."

"But—"

"I bet they have a good lunch menu too."

"Jem."

"Or it might be nice enough that we could do some kind of picnic at the beach."

"Jem—"

"Or would you rather have dinner together?"

I take a calming breath. "If I agree to any of the above will you stop listing stuff and get off this idea?"

Jem grins impishly. "Sure."

"I vote lunch at The Circle."

"Excellent choice." He cups my chin and plants a soft kiss on my forehead. I might have underestimated the breadth of his romantic streak.

When I get to the cafeteria I take one look at the table, at Paige's eager look and the way she fidgets in her seat, and I know she's thought of more questions to ask—in the presence of all our other friends who really should mind their own damn business. I buy my food and take it out of the cafeteria, begging an excess of homework that I need to finish. I end up on the picnic table, sitting on the top and resting my feet on the bench, watching the seagulls. Jem eventually ends up with me. He's a little sore that I didn't tell him about eating outdoors.

"Are you trying to avoid me?"

"Not you—Paige and her Inquisition." I pat the tabletop beside me but he doesn't sit there. Jem sits between my knees, resting his elbows over my legs. Within minutes he's a million miles away, thinking of music. I watch the fingers on his left hand move unconsciously over invisible strings while his right wrist twitches and his toe keeps time on the pavement. I want to hear what he's playing. His fingers are so agile, but I can tell by the way he moves his fourth finger that the dry skin and scars around that knuckle make it difficult to move. Regardless, he still plays beautifully.

My hands move from the slope of his shoulders, down his arms to weave between those long fingers. "I want to hear you play," I whisper in his ear. Jem smiles.

"I'm not that good anymore, you know. I'm out of practice and my dexterity is crap."

"You play beautifully and you know it."

"I'll show you a recording sometime," he says. "You can compare before and after." I don't know why he imagines I would want to do that. I suppose because he's constantly mourning the difference, but I have no interest in the before.

"You shouldn't hate your body," I murmur in his ear. Jem looks at me out of the corner of his eye.

"Wouldn't you hate this body?"

"I dig this body." I wrap my arms around his chest. Our fingers are still intertwined, so his arms come with me, hugging himself. It's a damn shame that he hates his own skin. I reckon he just doesn't know what to do with it anymore. He's grown so used to his body being the source of pain and discomfort that he's forgotten that it can also be the site of pleasure and contentment.

"Wait till your body betrays you," he says quietly. "You'll get old. You'll break down too."

"Come over tonight."

Jem nods. He's got his thinking face on—the one that makes him look like he's contemplating the fastest way to kill a goldfish with a screwdriver.

"I'll make soup." That gets a smile out of him.

"What kind?"

"What kind would you like?"

"Um…" He licks his lips, considering the possibilities with obvious excitement. "Carrot? No—chickpea. Wait…maybe that one with broccoli…or beans. No—peas."

He's so adorable I can't help but smile. "You can get back to me on that."

"Can I say all of the above?"

I kiss the back of his head. "Why not?"

❧

The soup turns out to be a stew of sorts, using some every vegetable in the fridge, chicken stock, and a scoop of honey. Jem asks me to leave chunks as I set up to run it through the blender. I think someone's proud of his ability to handle solid foods.

He takes our bowls into the living room while I move a load of laundry from the washer to the dryer, and when I get back to the living room I find that Jem has finished his bowl and started on mine.

"You're supposed to eat slowly."

"But it's good," he answers with his mouth full.

"If you throw it up I'm not making more." Jem grudgingly slows down, complaining for form's sake, and I let him have my portion. A toasted Eggo can be my snack.

We watch crap TV, lounging on Frank's couch and saying little. Jem leaves an entire couch cushion between us, and I don't know what to make of that. Maybe he's trying to maintain a respectful distance, after what happened the last time Frank came home and found him here. I want to test that hypothesis, so I scoot closer to him. Jem doesn't look up from the TV, but he puts an arm around me.

When the timer on the dryer buzzes he almost jumps out of his skin.

"Sorry, it's just the dryer."

"Yeah? Do you need help folding?"

I don't think I've ever heard a guy sound so eager to do laundry before. But if he wants to help, I'm not going to say no.

I bring the clothes into the living room and we start folding on the coffee table. Jem tactfully avoids touching any of the underwear and sticks to folding shirts and pants. I like watching him do these homey, domestic things. I can watch his face and see his thoughts drift, and there is always something undeniably sexy about a guy who does housework without complaining.

"Thanks."

"Don't mention it. I like doing laundry." Jem presses a hand towel to his face and inhales deeply. "You use Ultra?"

"You can tell just by smelling it?"

Jem's ears turn pink, but he smirks. "I really like doing laundry. It smells so nice and it's relaxing."

I take one of the bath towels and throw it over his head, blanketing him in the scents of Gain and Ultra. He laughs and leans back on the couch, pressing it tighter around his nose and sighing dramatically. He just lounges there for a few minutes, enjoying the warm towel.

"Are you going to help fold or what?" I say eventually.

"I'm not home."

"Jem."

"Leave a message."

I lift up the edge of the towel and find him smirking at me.

"Damn it, she found me."

He looks so sweet, wrapped up and warm. So I slide under the towel with him for a kiss. And by a kiss, I mean Jem grabs me in such a way that I couldn't leave the towel fort if I wanted to. He kisses me slowly. He doesn't push for depth or tongue, which is a nice change. He does let me nibble at his lip, though. I shift to sit on his lap when we pause for a breather. It's hot under the towel but he won't let me push it off.

"Can I ask you something?" he says between leaving little kisses on my cheeks.

"What?"

"Do I smell okay?"

I sniff his underarm. "Your deodorant's working."

"That's not what I meant, but thanks."

"What did you mean?"

Jem shrugs like it's no big deal, but then proceeds to get all embarrassed and fidgety. I lean in so he can whisper it in my ear instead of having to say it to my face.

"When Emily visited she noticed I smelled…off. It bothered her."

I move my face away from his cheek to smell the crook of his neck. He has always smelled the same to me, so I really have nothing to compare to, but he doesn't smell bad. He smells like clean skin and unperfumed soap and that unique scent that is simply Jem. Mingled with that is a faintly medicinal scent that could be skin cream, but more likely it's his medications making themselves known.

"I like the way you smell."

Jem finally pushes back the towel and wraps his arms comfortably around me. "You smell nice too. Like lavender and fear."

"Oh shut up." My hands run languidly from his shoulders to his hips, simply feeling him. I know Jem likes attentive touches like these. His ribs aren't as distinctly felt as when I first met him.

"How much do you weigh now?"

Jem blushes. "About one-thirty."

I feel bad that my curiosity has made him self-conscious again.

"Thank you for feeding me."

"You're welcome." I stroke a stretch of his newly filled out waist. "One-thirty, hmm? Soft enough to cushion me if I decide to jump you."

Jem smiles. "Yes, there is that." He gives me a kiss.

"I'll keep that in mind."

He has such a devious little smile when he's anticipating something he wants. His fingers flex around my sides, holding me tighter.

"I wonder if you'll seem pudgy when you're back to normal weight. I've only known you to be very thin."

Jem quirks a finely haired eyebrow at me. "Pudgy?"

"Pudgy." I pinch his cheek to piss him off. Jem mock-glares at me and says that the term 'pudgy' is only to be applied to small children and animals.

"Does that mean I can still call you pudgy when you act like a brat?"

Jem growls with frustration. "Will you get off pudgy and jump me already?"

"Right now?"

"Yes."

"Right this minute?"

"Yes!"

I oblige by diving at him. Jem tips back on the couch with me sitting over him. I like the way he pecks when he kisses. The soft suction feels nice, like he's trying to pull me into his mouth, while at the same time pressing his tongue into mine. This feels...innocent. That's new for me. I lower my weight against his front and his arms wrap around my back. "Pudgy, she says," he mutters against my lips. I can hear Jem rolling his eyes.

"So what"—kiss—"do I"—kiss—"call you if"—long kiss to shut me up—"you do pudge-up?"

Jem huffs. "You really want to talk about this right now?"

"Only because it bothers you." I poke the tip of his nose. "It doesn't really matter; I'm only joking. You're sexy no matter what you weigh." Jem's face turns sad. He pets my hair and kisses my cheek softly.

"If I do gain too much I want you to lie to me exactly like that."

I smack his hand away. "I'm not lying."

"Can we not talk about this?"

"Are you always this bad at taking compliments?"

He pouts. Damn it.

"Don't you dare."

Jem starts with the low whine in the back of his throat that reminds me of injured puppies. I can't hear that and not want to cuddle his manipulative ass. I drop my head to his shoulder with a groan and Jem winds his arms around me with a smug smile.

"You're not allowed to do that ever again."

"I'll consider it." Jem nudges my cheek with his nose. "Kiss me."

"No."

"I'll do it again."

"Dick." He ignores my insult and hums pleasantly against my lips. I express my irritation by skimping on enthusiasm, but Jem seems to enjoy the challenge of slowly but surely getting me to kiss him back, with tongue. His fingers slip under my t-shirt at the small of my back, teasing the skin.

"You're so soft," he murmurs.

The front door opens, quickly followed by the rug-stomp of work boots. Jem and I both freeze, knowing we're caught. My brother can see right into the living room from the foyer. Frank just stands in the threshold with his hand on the doorknob, staring at us. I can't decide which is more worrisome: that the gun cabinet is unlocked and a mere ten seconds away, or that the vein in his temple looks ready to burst.

"Uh, hi Frank."

"You'd better be doing CPR," he says.

"It's not what it looks like."

"Right. You tripped and he fell."

Let's hope that vein holds up. "We're dating."

Frank doesn't say anything. He stares at the two of us for a long time, and when he speaks again his voice is quiet. "I think it's time for you to leave."

Jem gets up to go. We don't chance a kiss goodbye, but he squeezes my hand with affection. Jem even apologizes to Frank on his way past.

The door closes and I try not to think about the fact that I am in such deep trouble. Frank can smell fear. I try to stand up and he tells me to sit down.

"We're talking about this." Frank sits in the easy chair across from the couch, but he's too restless to stay sitting, so he stands up and paces the room with his hands on his hips.

"You said you weren't going to date anymore," he says. "That was part of your idea of a clean break—no more smoking, no more drugs, no more motorcycles, no more bad influence friends, and no more boys."

Should I tell him that I have almost all those things here?

"You're digging yourself into a hole, Willa. It's one thing to get involved with a boy when you're still…figuring things out. But *that* boy—"

"He has a name."

Frank sighs. "Harper—"

"It's Jem, Frank."

The vein twitches at me. "Jem isn't good for you. It hurt you so bad when Tessa passed away"—when I helped her kill herself—"and even if he stays in remission, you don't need to be dealing with his problems on top of your own."

"And what do I need?"

"You need to focus on your schoolwork."

"I'm getting A's and B's in all my classes. I haven't cut class since I've been here."

"Why do you feel the need to date? Your life is orderly here without all the… *drama* of dating."

Oh, the reasons…

"Is it Jem you don't like, or me dating in general?"

Frank hesitates, a sure sign of a lie. "Like I said, schoolwork—"

"What about Chris Elwood?"

"What about him?"

"Or Luke. Would we be having this conversation if I was dating Luke instead of Jem?"

"Luke's a nice kid." I knew it. "If you wanted to date someone who is *good for you*, and you had a nice, respectful and *slow* relationship, I could maybe be okay with it."

"So what did Luke tell you when he explained the black eyes?"

The frown slips from Frank's face into the calculating expression of a big brother. I've as good as told him that I was involved, and he knows I've got a history of solving problems with a well-aimed punch.

"He said some of the boys were wrestling and it got out of hand."

"And how does it get out of hand so bad that he ends up with two black eyes and a sprained wrist? Did you see the bruise under his jaw, too? And I can tell you his ribs were probably purple."

Frank cuts to the chase. "What did you see, Willa?"

Poor Frank. He wants to cling to the idea that I was a witness instead of a participant.

"I saw him put his hand down my pants and proposition me for unprotected sex." And the vein goes wild. "He seems to be under the impression that I should be grateful for the attention, since I'm a murderer and nobody wants me, right?" I give Frank a hard smile. "But where would he have heard about that, hmm?"

My brother has his thinking cap on. I can see it. "No one else was home..."

"Well then Luke has some sick intuition."

I get off the couch while Frank puzzles over the facts. "Jem doesn't do that kind of shit to me. Stop looking at him as a problem and notice that he's good for me."

I head into the kitchen to start dinner. A sense of normalcy might help Frank's blood pressure. "Oh, and if you decide to report me for assault—"

The front door slams. Did he leave? I go to the front window in time to see Frank peel out of the driveway. He takes a left, toward the highway and Port Elmsley.

This isn't going to be pretty.

⌖

The glare of headlights on the front window wakes me up. I sit up on the couch and look to the clock on the ancient VCR. It's after midnight. Frank has been gone for six hours. He comes in, looking haggard and pissed off, and hangs up his jacket without a word.

"Frank?"

Frank turns to head upstairs, but he spares me a short explanation as he goes: "Luke denied the whole thing." That bastard. "The bruise on his jaw is still fading. It came from a low angle—from a shorter person. Luke's friends are tall boys."

Frank pauses on the stairs and looks at me over his shoulder. He knows the bruise came from my strike.

"If he touches you again you have my full permission to hit him."

I love my brother.

"Are you okay?"

Frank pauses and gives me a strange look. "Yeah, I'm good."

"What did Doug say?"

Frank just rubs his hand restlessly over his mouth and doesn't answer my

434

question. "Don't think this gets you off the hook about dating that Harper kid," he says.

"You can't dictate who I date."

Frank steps off the stairs and stands in the doorway, haggard and hands open in pleading. "What am I supposed to tell Mom and Dad? I'm supposed to be taking care of you and you go and date a cancer patient."

"Don't tell them anything. That's worked well for both of us over the years."

Frank's eyes narrow. "Nice try."

"Is the issue really that he's a cancer patient? You know he's in remission."

"Yes, that's the issue. Remission today isn't any guarantee about tomorrow, Will. Furthermore, I don't need to come home and find you two making out on my couch."

"It offends your fag sensibilities to see a guy getting some action from a girl, huh?"

One look at Frank's face, and I regret making that comment while sitting down. It's been a long day, and he's in the perfect position to descend and beat the living shit out of me. And from the look of him, he wants to. Frank is red all the way down his neck. His thin lips are pressed together so tightly that his long, slow breath whistles through his nose.

"Don't use that word in my house," he says quietly.

I get off the couch and head for the stairs. "I knew it."

"Shut up."

"I don't care who you fuck, just don't give me shit about Jem."

"I will give you shit, because this is my house and you are a guest here. I could have let Mom and Dad toss you out on your ass when you turned eighteen, but I did you a favor."

I turn on the third stair to face him. "So do Mom and Dad know you're queer?" Frank's tense silence answers my question. "They probably already know by now anyway. You're kind of obvious."

I turn to go and Frank calls me back. "Get your ass back here, we're not finished yet."

"We are." I keep walking up.

"You're not dating that boy!" he yells after me.

"I won't tell Mom and Dad if you won't."

"That does *not* fly, Will." I can hear his work boots on the stairs behind me. "I'm a grown man, not some teenage delinquent."

"A grown man who can't admit to mommy that he likes to suck cock." I slam my bedroom door behind me, and surprisingly, Frank doesn't try to open it. I stand there listening to him fume out in the hallway, and after a few minutes of murmured curses he heads back downstairs.

It doesn't take long for me to regret picking that fight. I should have pretended to value Frank's input on my love life and carried on with my own business behind his back. And the stupid thing is, I'm not even that mad at him. He was kind of good to me tonight, but I had to make a big deal out of his prejudice against Jem.

I give Frank an hour to cool down and then go downstairs. Frank is sitting at the dining table, shirt undone, with a beer in his hand and two empties nearby. He gives me a look I've seen on Dad so many times: wounded disappointment.

"I'm sorry."

Frank just shakes his head. I clear away the empty bottles and take a seat across the tiny table.

"I only said that stuff because I knew it would bother you. I didn't mean any of it."

"You're too old to be running your mouth like that."

"I know. I'm sorry." My brother doesn't accept the apology, but that's understandable. "You and Doug are together?"

Frank manages a sad smile that slowly turns into a grimace. "For a while now."

"How long?"

He rolls his shoulders uncomfortably. "Since high school."

"That long? You know if Doug was a chick Mom would be on you to get married by now."

Frank sort of chuckles at that. "It's simpler when no one knows. People can't interfere with a relationship they don't know exists."

"Privacy's a nice luxury," I agree. I nod to the couch and promise that Jem and I won't screw around in the living room. "We'll keep that stuff upstairs."

Frank groans and scrubs both hands over his face. "Why couldn't you have let me believe that you're still a virgin? For Christ's sake, you're my baby sister."

"Please; you knew."

"Why can't you at least date someone…" Frank tries and fails to find the appropriate word.

"Why can't you date girls?"

"Don't."

"You give me a hard time about dating Jem and I'll give you a hard time about Doug."

Frank just looks away and sips the last of his beer. He's cutting his losses—for now. I have a feeling that this is an argument we're going to have many times over.

"What the hell happened with Luke?" Frank says suddenly. "He's a good kid. He's fond of you. A little young, maybe, but no life-threatening illnesses."

I snort at Frank's sales pitch. "I gave him that fat black eye, remember?"

"You said no more fighting."

"He started it."

"Luke started a fight with a girl." Frank's incredulity doesn't surprise me. "He probably just came on too strong. He's sixteen, he doesn't know these subtleties. You could have let him down gently instead of picking a fight."

"That's bullshit. Luke started it when he humped my leg, stuck his hand down my pants, and offered to fuck me bareback. The black eye was the only mark that was *visible*."

Frank looks a little sick. "Did he hit you back?"

"Tried to choke me. I didn't let him."

Frank blows out a long breath. "Briana's not the only kid that's in trouble."

"Luke hides it well." I know Luke's motive, even if it disgusts me. He was trying to replace sex with intimacy, the kind he doesn't get at home with his mother gone and his dad so busy with Briana. Luke was just trying to fill a void that he didn't want anyone to know existed. I know the feeling, and I know how it feels to use people to fill the gaps. I'm not interested in being used anymore.

"He gets by on charm, you know. Acts all nice to get close to people, and then takes advantage."

"He's not that kind of kid," Frank argues.

I shake my head. "You don't know who people really are until you've seen them at their worst and weakest."

Frank and I share a look across the table. At his worst he's a coward, and I'm a murderer.

Tuesday

I haven't heard from Jem since he was asked to leave, and if I know Jem, I know he's worrying. When I wake up I send him a text: *You awake?*

It takes less than a minute to get a response. "Pick up, it's me." Jem skips the hello and opens with a frantic, "I'm so sorry. Are you okay?"

"I'm fine."

"Did he give you a lot of trouble? I shouldn't have—"

"It's fine. He's not keen on you, but I diverted that conversation. I told him about beating the shit out of Luke."

Jem swears softly. "What happened?"

"He didn't even yell at me. He went to Port Elmsley for a few hours and when he got back he said I could hit Luke again if there's a next time." I chuckle at the absurdity of those words. There's a lot Frank can't protect me from, but when he can he spares no effort. I can appreciate that as long as Frank can be convinced that Jem isn't bad for me.

"We should talk to him," Jem says. "About us."

"Sure."

"I mean it. Soon."

"Let me soften him up with a nice meal first."

"Tonight?"

"Maybe. We'll play it by ear."

Frank beats me and Jem to the punch when it comes to discussion. I come downstairs for breakfast to find him waiting for me, and he's clearly been thinking quite a bit.

"There are gonna be rules," he says firmly.

"Good morning to you too."

"One: he's not allowed in your room."

I head for the coffee maker. It's too early to do this without a stimulant.

"Two: you have an eleven o'clock curfew."

I suppress the urge to groan. My curfew was fluid before I was dating Jem, as long as Frank knew where I was.

"Three: your grades better not suffer."

"Do you want some oatmeal?"

Frank barely loses steam. "Yes. Four: no *romance* around the house." That makes me snort. I ask what falls under the category of romance, just to make him say it. Frank gets all flustered and says, "You know…kissing, cuddling… CPR."

I laugh and he barks at me to be serious.

"Sure."

"Good." Frank clears his throat. "As long as we're on the same page."

"Jem thinks you hate him, you know."

Frank makes this awkward motion that is somewhere in between a nod and a shrug. "I don't dislike him," he says vaguely.

"Fair enough." If only he'd met my other boyfriends—then he'd be welcoming Jem with open arms.

❧

Diane is more of a bitch than usual today. She's bent on sharing her misery with everyone else, and has come to school with the plague. Or at least it sounds like it, the way she sniffles and coughs all through lunch. She can't take a hint, either, and whenever someone inches their chair and food away from her colony of bacteria, she adjusts her chair to be part of the group again.

"Will you cover your damn mouth?"

Diane glares at me through puffy eyes. Screw it; she already hates me so I'm not fussed with being nice to her. And she is disgusting—we're trying to eat here, and her cold has relegated Jem to the distant end of the table, as far away from her as possible because the last thing he needs right now is an infection.

"Maybe you should go home," Paige says in that 'friendly' voice that borders on bossy.

"I'm fine."

"Your nose is running." Cody points. We're treated the squelching sound of snot as she blows her nose at the table. She sets the used tissue on her lunch tray, right next to her peas.

Her passive-aggressive stunt doesn't last much longer, though. Mrs. Hudson takes one look at Diane when she walks into Social Studies and tells her to go home. Thank God.

⊖

Frank calls to tell me he'll be working late tonight. "You call and tell me if you're going anywhere," he says sternly. He means if I'm going to see Jem.

"I have to work tonight." I conveniently forget to mention that Jem is here at the house with me, hanging out before I go to work at five. I tell Frank that there are leftover fish and scalloped potatoes in the fridge, and spend five minutes convincing him that reheating it in the oven is better than the microwave. He thinks mushiness is a fair price to pay for quick food. Men.

When I go upstairs, I find Jem studying my bookshelf, reading the backs of novels and judging the covers. I collect books like he collects music.

"See anything that interests you?"

Jem shakes his head, and I'm not surprised. He's more interested in concrete sciences than he is in literature and art.

He asks if he can have a picture of me. What a strange question.

"Like, you want to take one?" Most people wouldn't ask. They'd just whip out their cell phone and snap a few shots in the spirit of self-entitlement.

Jem shakes his head; he doesn't want to take a photo. He wants to know if I brought any pictures here from St. John's, family photos and the like.

I take my photo album out of my closet and hand it over. "Take what you want." Mom has all the negatives saved, anyway.

Jem looks through that damn album for a whole hour, even though it's only thirty pages thick. He doesn't ask questions either, which is very un-Jem. He ends up taking two photos to keep. One was taken by Mom as I was waiting to pull out of the driveway for school. I'm looking to the side, watching for traffic, but my face is obscured by my helmet. I think Jem just likes the image of me on a motorcycle.

The other picture was taken a year ago, at the rec center. I was sitting on the floor of the gymnasium, eating a cupcake. We had snacks for Parents' Day at Group. Steve is visible behind me in the photo, but his face is out of frame. His service dog, a black lab that always had a soft spot for me, rests his chin on my shoulder and eyes my cupcake.

I'm not sure why Jem chose that photo. I didn't think he would want evidence of my long and convoluted history with therapy groups, or of Steve. I don't want to ask him about his reasoning.

I expected him to get weird after I told him about the guys I dated in St. John's. I thought that little tale would be the final straw for Jem, since assisted suicide and emotional ineptitude didn't do the trick. But he's still here, reaching for my hand and fishing for kisses. There are times, though, when I swear he's thinking about it. I keep waiting for him to change his mind and pull the rug out from under my feet. I suppose I should just enjoy him while the moment lasts.

⊸

I wonder if it's by design or accident that Chris and I always have matching shifts. At least he isn't in a talkative mood tonight. We spend the early part of our shift cleaning the suites of today's check-outs, and every time I look over, I see him texting. It's not until the end of the night that I learn that he's trying to secure a prom date, now that he and Paige aren't an item anymore.

"Anyone I know?"

"Heidi Hallonquist."

I vaguely remember the name. I'm pretty sure she's on the track team or the field hockey team or something... I hope Heidi doesn't own a car, because Paige is probably going to key it when she finds out she can't crawl back to Chris as a last-ditch prom date.

"Have you gone in with anyone to pool the cost of a limo?" he asks.

"I'm not going to prom."

"Harper isn't taking you?"

"Nope."

Chris gives me a sympathetic smile. "You can come with the group if you want. We wouldn't make you feel like an extra wheel."

"Thanks, but Jem and I have other plans."

"Oh yeah? What are you doing?" His tone is a little nosey.

I shrug. "Oh, I'm sure it'll be a blur of illicit drug use and wild sex." I smile and Chris laughs weakly. Are my jokes really that off the mark? At least Jem thinks I'm funny.

It's nine o'clock when I get off work. Jem will probably be in bed soon, but Elise has been bugging me for company. I call her to let her know I'll be stopping by and when I pull into the driveway twenty minutes later, she runs up to give me a hug.

"What do you think it means when a guy says you're really funny?" she asks with her arms wrapped around my middle.

"Uh, I think that means he listens to you long enough to grasp the punchline." I pat her shoulder. "Who told you that?"

Elise sighs and launches into the whole story. She's still googly-eyed over that basketball player.

"Can you tell I'm wearing a push-up bra?"

I've never been in the big sister role, so I don't know how these conversations are supposed to go, but nevertheless I take the invitation to inspect her tits. Elise is petite in every way imaginable, but her sprightly bearing makes her seem bigger and brighter than she really is. Elise is actually quite pretty.

"It looks good." I don't know what else to say so I offer her a high-five. Is that appropriate?

Elise has some serious things she wants to talk about once we get upstairs, out of range of her parents and brothers. She has to go to prom because she's on the events committee that organizes the evening, and she wants to know if it would be inappropriate to ask what's-his-name for a dance, or if that would be a slight on his girlfriend. I wouldn't know. I don't do school dances.

"It sucks so bad," she says with a pout. "He's working away from Smiths Falls for the summer and he's going to university after that, so the end of the school year is the last time I'll see him."

"There's some time, then."

"Twenty-seven days," she answers precisely.

"You can keep in touch. I'm sure he'll come home for visits."

"Yeah, to see his family and his *girlfriend*."

"He'll make time for friends too. You'll see him again."

"Not nearly enough." She huffs and flops down on her bed like a starfish. "If we still lived in Ottawa I could still see him on weekends and stuff."

"Elise?"

"Yeah?"

"Does this guy know you like him?" My guess would be yes. She's not exactly subtle.

Elise shrugs. "Who knows? He thinks I'm *funny*."

"Funny can be good."

"As friends."

"Does his girlfriend make him laugh?"

Elise has to think on that. "Sometimes." She pulls a pillow over her face to muffle a frustrated groan. "Why can't I just get over him already?"

"That's what this summer is for. To get over him and maybe have a dumb fling."

"I wish he was my dumb fling..." Jesus Christ. Too bad she's not a few years older, so she could numb some of this angst with tequila. But she's got one thing going for her as a teenage girl: she's allowed to cry it out.

"Where's he working this summer?"

"Camp Concord. He's a counselor."

"Why don't you apply? You're good at social planning and having fun; I bet you'd be great at the job."

Elise shakes her head. "It's two hours away."

"That's not so far."

"I don't want to leave."

"Have you never been away from home before?"

"I have, yeah. But if Jem gets sick again..." She closes her eyes and swallows her thoughts. "I need to stay nearby. He's still so fragile."

I hadn't doubted her before, but hearing Elise talk about it—about giving bits and pieces of her body to Jem—only reinforces the dedication she has to her brother. I knew Jem was a protective older brother, but I hadn't considered Elise a protective younger sister until now. Even if she could donate nothing for him physically, she would want to be near him while he's sick.

"What would Jem think of you working at that camp?"

Elise rolls her eyes. "He'd break my legs to keep me from going. He doesn't like Kipp."

"Why not?"

"Kipp's too old for me. And too attached. Among other reasons."

"What reasons?"

Elise shrugs. "Brother reasons." Now I'm curious. "Jem's probably asleep by now," she says. "But if you're quiet you can see him before you leave."

I poke my head into Jem's room as quietly as I can. The light is on, but Elise was right, he is asleep. He's sprawled across the foot of his bed, out cold, with a copy of *The Scarlet Letter* under his limp hand. He can't bear to stay awake through his English homework. Absolutely no appreciation for classic literature.

I take the book away gently and start to remove his watch. I don't want to wake him up, but I can tuck him in sideways like I did the night of Elise's birthday party. When I push back his sleeve to expose his watch, I feel a faint tickle on my fingertips. The hair on his arms has really started to grow back.

I lean in to look and see the fine, red-brown hairs on his forearm. In the right light I would miss them entirely, they're so short. I'm close enough that Jem can feel my breath on his wrist and his fingers twitch. I back off, but he groans in his sleep and rolls over to stretch, coming slowly to the surface. He turns to the side and buries his face in the coverlet—and lets out the loudest fart I have ever heard I my entire life.

I don't know if it's the shock of it, or perhaps a childish urge to giggle at bodily functions, but I collapse into hysterical laughter on his floor. I laugh so hard that I can't breathe and my eyes start to water, 'cause it's just so damn funny. I hope none of the other Harpers hear me, because I don't know how I would explain what has me in stitches. How can someone so thin contain so much hot air?

My laughter makes Jem look up with surprise, and his expression quickly shifts from disorientation to a look of horror. That fart was deliberate—he thought he was alone.

And that just makes it that much funnier. I'm going to suffocate from laughing and it's all his fault.

Jem mumbles 'excuse me' as his face turns bright red. I don't think common courtesy can cover this one. I vainly try to wipe my streaming eyes as laughter bubbles up through my throat in short pants.

"Christ, boy, did you shit yourself?"

I don't think it's possible for his face to get any redder. He offers me a tissue to wipe my eyes and says, "Please don't die laughing."

"If I do, make sure my tombstone blames you." He lets me giggle for a few more minutes before telling me to knock it off. There's a time limit on laughter, apparently. I flop down on his bed in a breathless heap and try to keep a straight face when I ask him how his night went.

"Fine." Embarrassment has made him terse. I poke the corner of his mouth and tell him to cheer up.

"Do you need to wipe?"

"Shut up."

"Nah."

"Don't tell Eric about this. I'll never hear the end of it."

"Sure." I lean in to kiss his frowning lips. I skipped that step in the wake of my hysterical giggle fit. Jem doesn't have much enthusiasm for it, and I can tell by the way he wraps his arms around me that he's gearing up to sulk.

"Thanks. I needed a good laugh."

"Because I'm a joke."

"Don't put words in my mouth."

He nestles his face in my neck and inhales. "You know," he says to my collarbone, "just when I didn't think I could be more repulsive to a girl..."

I smack him lightly on the ribs. "You're not repulsive." Jem's ego is a fragile one. I gentle him with soft touches and whispers in his ears—that I love his hands, and his eyes, and the way he holds me. Let him feel valued. He accepts little kisses on his jaw with closed eyes. When he sighs his breath smells like red Jell-O, and when I use my hands on his shoulders to gently push him back down to the bed, he pulls me with him. Jem can't stand much distance—but distance is relative.

I'm still not used to the way he doesn't immediately reach for my ass as I straddle his hips. His hands manage to move from my thighs to my waist without touching the stuff in between—I'd study physics just to find out how the hell he does it—and once there his hands stick to my sides and back. This gentleman thing is nice, but I can see myself getting bored of it.

Jem wants slow kisses tonight, long and deep and tender. I oblige, taking my time over his mouth. Sucking his lower lip, stroking his tongue...

The hand that rests high on my ribs inches its way to my side, like he's thinking about copping a feel but hesitant to do it. I spare him the internal debate and move his hand myself.

"You're okay with this?" he murmurs against my lips. I don't roll my eyes, but it's a near thing.

"No, I made you grab my tit by accident."

"Check." He leans up to meet my lips and gives my chest a gentle palm massage. His hand is shaking.

"Are you okay?"

"Yeah." He smiles against my lips. "It's been awhile. I want to treat you right."

"Likewise." Jem's other hand moves under the back of my shirt, along my skin. "Feeling deprived?"

"Happy," he murmurs. I kiss his neck, which he really seems to like, and he even lets me nibble his earlobes. It's my hands he has a hard time with. While his continue their languid circuit between my chest and back, tracing bare pieces of skin and circling my nipples with his thumbs, mine keep getting bumped away. At first it's casual—his hand slowly moves mine away from his ribs to rest on his shoulder. Then his elbow keeps me from getting too friendly with his waist, and when I move to touch the skin above his collar he shifts his shoulders away from me.

"Jem." I grab both his wrists and hold them together between us. "This isn't going to work."

His face slips into such a wounded, frightened expression. I guess I should have phrased that better.

"I'm not just going to sit here like a blow up doll and let you grope me. You have to let me touch you too."

"Oh. Um." He swallows so nervously you'd think I'd just asked him to nail his own ear to the wall. "I'm sorry. Maybe we should stop for awhile." He slips his wrists out of my hands and rolls away, ready to leave the bed. I wrap an arm around his waist before he can stand up and pull him back against me.

"I'm not saying right this minute, but at some point you will have to let me touch you." I plant a kiss on the back of his neck.

"I know, but...not now."

"Soon?"

"When I'm well again."

"That long?"

Jem blows out a deep breath through his nose. "I'm sorry."

"Does it factor in that I think you're sexy, even when you're like this?"

"I'm not."

"Well who the hell gave you a vote?"

Jem snorts softly. He's not ready to smile, but he's more willing to listen. He folds his arms over the one I have wrapped around his waist. "Can we just...?"

"Mmh?"

"Can we just cuddle for awhile? No more...stuff." He turns to look at me over his shoulder and I kiss his cheek.

"Okay."

He comes back to bed, but I can see that he's miles away. Jem lays on his back and holds me close against his shoulder with our legs overlapping. He stares at the ceiling.

"What are you thinking about?"

"How much longer." He sounds like he's regretting his self-imposed rule to wait already. That's the problem with abstinence: it has the lifespan of a house-fly.

I move my hand up from his waist to touch his cheek, but he catches me halfway and puts my hand back where it was. I made the same mistake I did that time on Frank's porch—I brushed my hand along his chest instead of lifting my arm up. My hand was too close to his central line for comfort.

I take Jem's hand and lay it on top of mine.

"Give me a tour."

"What?"

I move us so our hands are hovering just over his chest. "Show me where it is. Show me how not to hurt you."

Jem moves our hands away. "It'll be gone soon."

"How soon?" We don't talk about his treatment or prognosis. I don't know if he's close to completing treatment, or if he will ever be without need of it. He seems to be optimistic, but he could just be saying that as a way to forestall teaching me about his body. Or maybe it's denial.

Jem tips his chin to whisper in my ear. "*Please*," he says earnestly. "Just be patient with me." His hand fists the front of my shirt. I hate it when he begs. It's so hard not to give in.

I have to sit up on my elbow to reach his ear and whisper back. "Please trust me to love you enough."

Jem buries his face in my neck. We don't say anything, but I can feel the tension in his shoulders and in the hand that grips my side. I try to be soothing, rubbing his back and humming to ease the silence. By the time we say goodbye for the evening, he seems much more at peace, but I know it's only a temporary truce.

Elise won't let me leave without a hug and promise to visit again soon. Jem follows me out onto the porch to say goodbye in privacy, without his sister bouncing in the background.

"Soon," he promises.

"Sure." I give him a kiss and turn to go, but he grabs me back.

"It's not trust," he says in my ear. "I trust you…" He kisses my temple. "Do you love me enough to wait?"

If I thought he needed it I'd give him forever. But I don't think anything of the sort.

"Give me an inch."

"Don't take ten."

"I thought you trusted me?"

Jem folds me into a hug. "I do." He doesn't bother to hide it when he smells my hair and sighs on the scent. "I love you."

I like it that there's nothing left to say. No plans to make, no assurances required by jealousy, no soppy goodbye. Just a kiss and a 'sleep well,' and I'm off into the night.

Jem texts me tonight's playlist: *"Awake My Soul," Mumford & Sons.*

Wednesday

Hollywood is full of it. In movies, things are magically supposed to change after people say 'I love you,' but in reality nothing does. Thank God, because I'm not sure I'm qualified to deal with happiness. Jem doesn't seem to feel weird about it, either. There's no need to say it at every opportunity or write each other mushy love notes. We're just coasting.

I'm fairly certain that I like it.

The girls are discussing summer fashions over lunch. Apparently pastel blue is popular at the moment. I can't believe anybody actually cares about this crap.

"So what's with the gloves, anyway?"

I look up from my lunch to find Diane giving me a probing look across the table. She glances from my sea foam green gloves to my face and back again.

I tell her, "I like them."

"No, really. Your wardrobe is so emo. You never wear any color."

Today's outfit is pretty standard: gunmetal grey tee, black jeans, and a black hoodie. Everything I own is black and grey, except for my gloves and socks.

"You're supposed to wear black when someone close to you dies."

I get falsely sympathetic eyes from Paige. I'm pretty sure Jem just rolled his.

"Oh, right, your sister was sick," Diane says. "*That's* why you moved to New Brunswick."

"Newfoundland."

"Whatever, same difference."

Jem is shaking his head at Diane like he thinks she's an idiot. She is, but it's rude to say so. I nudge his foot under the table.

"So what happened to her?"

"She died, obviously."

"What did she have?"

"Cancer."

Diane wrinkles her nose in an affected wince of sadness. "That's what happens to smokers."

"Want to know what happens to people who don't know when to shut up?"

The feet of Jem's chair scrape against the floor as he leans away from the table, holding his stomach. He makes a sound of discomfort and everyone looks at him like he's a bomb without a timer. Christ, what now?

Jem claims to be feeling unwell. "Walk with me to the nurse?"

I take what's left of my lunch out of the cafeteria and dutifully walk with him. It means I'll have to put off teaching Diane a lesson in manners, but she'll be rude again in the future. I can be patient.

As soon as we're beyond the cafeteria doors, Jem straightens up and walks like everything is just fine.

"You shouldn't have to listen to that shit," he says. "Who cares what Diane thinks of anything?"

He faked a stomachache to give me an excuse to leave?

"Were you trying to protect me there?" That is both bizarre and completely unnecessary.

Jem smirks and takes my carton of milk out of my hand. "You looked like you were about to punch Diane in the face." He's not far off the mark; I was considering stabbing her hand with my fork.

"You don't need to do that."

Jem shrugs. "I'd do it again. Your mourning is none of her business."

I take my milk back. The bastard drank the last of it. "Dude."

"Want to go throw rocks at seagulls?"

Jem: June 1 to 4

Thursday

Willa and I play checkers in the clinic. She's really horrible at games of strategy, but I shouldn't be surprised. I've seen her fail hard at tic-tac-toe.

"Will you stop being so damn smug?" she snaps when she's down to three pieces.

"This is smug?"

Willa gives me the finger and makes her move. Now she's down to two pieces.

"You ass."

I could be nice to her, but... "We should talk about plans for Sunday."

Willa narrows her eyes at me. She knows I'm trying to annoy her. "What about it?" she says through her teeth.

"We're doing lunch at The Circle?"

Willa stares at me like she can't wait to get to the point. "Anything else, Captain of the Bloody Obvious?" I don't think it fazes Willa that the only thing separating us from the other people in the Dialysis Clinic is a thin curtain. They can totally hear her filthy mouth.

"What would you like to do after? We could see a movie."

"I want to hike the creek again," she says. I wasn't expecting that. She's fought the whole notion of arbitrary anniversaries until this point; I didn't expect her to suggest plans.

"The same one as last time?"

"Yeah."

"Why?"

"It's our place."

I can sort of see her perspective, wanting to return to the place where we first shared our secrets...where I said horrible things about her and she slapped me. Or maybe not.

"Are you sure?"

"We'll bring enough water this time," she promises.

"Alright." I reach for her hand. "Thank you. It's a date."

"One other thing."

"What?"

"My brother wants you to come over for dinner tomorrow night."

"Are you serious?"

"I promise he won't do any permanent damage. He might harass you a little, but he respects people who hold their ground."

"Gee, thanks for that pearl of wisdom."

"Don't be difficult."

"I know you are but what am I?"

Willa huffs and rolls her eyes. "I'm dating a third grader."

I love pissing her off.
Friday

My day has not officially begun until I get a hug from Willa. I find her in the parking lot—not so difficult, since I'm pretty sure her rattling muffler can be heard in Winnipeg—and get my morning hug. Willa has been surprisingly amenable to affection since we started dating, holding my hand and reciprocating hugs and kisses, but sometimes I wonder if she really wants to or if she does it to appease me. She doesn't seem any happier or angrier than normal, just more demonstrative.

I mention that she's been more open and affectionate lately as I kiss her good morning—a knot of freshman are openly staring. To hell with them. Willa shrugs and pinches my earlobe.

"You're not something I need to hide from anymore." The way her tone pitches up at the end makes it almost a question. I grin from ear to ear. She considers my arms a safe place. No more hiding her true self, no more defensive anger over shit that doesn't matter. We're finally on the same team. I have her trust and honesty, and those are a rare gift from Willa.

"Don't let it go to your head." She pokes the corner of my grinning mouth.

"Too late."

I know there is plenty that she still hides from, but I still feel good about this small change in her. She hasn't been open with anyone else since Thomasina. It's progress.

⊷

Cody has Diane's cold now. Despite the fact that she should probably be in quarantine, she has decided to come to school again. I wonder if she's even taking cold medicine, or if she's playing up her symptoms on purpose to get sympathy and attention. Cody, at least, has a reason to be at school with a cold. He has a test he can't miss, but he keeps a careful distance from everyone at lunch and at least he is taking something for the coughing.

Diane takes the empty chair beside Willa. I expect her to ask Diane to move or to get up and switch seats, but instead Willa puts her foot on the edge of Diane's chair and physically pushes it about two feet to the left.

"Hey!"

"You're invading my bubble."

Whatever witty riposte Diane has in store is cut off by a massive sneeze that she barely bothers to cover.

"You're phlegming all over the table!"

"No one needs to catch your cold before grad," Paige interjects. Diane narrows her eyes and asks in a spiteful tone if Paige has found anyone to go with yet. She hasn't, and it's a sensitive subject with her, so Hannah does the gracious thing and interrupts the tension. While the chatter turns to movies, I study Willa. I promised her we'd make plans to avoid the grad dance. I'll have to think of something special to do with her that night.

❧

I'm due to arrive at the Kirk house at five o'clock for supper. I wear a nice shirt, but nix the idea of a tie. I don't want to look like a kiss-ass. I ask Mom to give me a ride, mostly because I want to exploit her gentle presence to keep Frank Kirk from shooting me on sight.

"You seem nervous," she says as we turn onto the Kirks' street. I've met girl-friends' parents before, but this is different. Frank already has a grudge against me and I know he's suspicious of me as a cancer patient, like I might unintentionally hurt his sister with my health problems. I already have, so in a way he's right. He just doesn't know it yet.

"Not nervous, just terribly alert."

Mom even offers to walk me to the door. Luckily it's Willa that answers. She gives Mom a hug and extends the dinner invitation to her as well.

"Thank you, but I have to get back." She gives me a hug goodbye and I almost wish she would stay.

"Is your brother in a good mood?" I whisper to Willa as I hug her hello. She just shrugs. Helpful as ever, I see.

Frank is in the kitchen, sitting at the table and nursing a beer. He asks me if I want one, which seems like a pretty obvious trick question.

"No thank you, sir." The man looks at me like I'm a strange, wild animal in his house that he isn't sure how to deal with—whack it over the head with a baseball bat, or keep a door open and hope it leaves on its own? He sits there and stares at me while I make myself useful to Willa however I can, stirring pots, setting the table. She's making beer batter fish and home cut fries for her brother, and barley with vegetables for me. She serves herself an equal portion of both my food and Frank's, like she's trying to be impartial.

Frank looks from the bowl of barley to me and something clicks behind his eyes.

"Is that some vegan…stuff?" he asks. Something tells me he had a different word than 'stuff' in mind.

"No, Frank, it's just barley," Willa said.

"Barley?"

"You're drinking it," she says before he can complain, and points to his beer. Frank doesn't say anything, but he doesn't look happy.

I like the barley dish, almost as much as I like the fact that Willa made solid food for me tonight. Eating soup in front of her brother, who already doesn't like me because of my illness, wouldn't do me any favors. The barley is bland and easy to chew, mixed with small slices of boiled celery, carrot and chickpeas.

I detect a hint of lemon and ginger in the dressing.

"So, Jem, how are your parents?" And thus the inquisition begins.

"They're doing well. My mom is working on plans to expand a school in Ottawa."

"That must keep her busy."

"It does." She's been singing in her office a lot, so that's a good sign.

"And your dad?"

"Same as always. He likes working in Smiths Falls better than Ottawa—fewer violent injuries in the ER." The crime rate in Smiths Falls is boringly low. The worst Dad sees are domestic and workplace accidents, and maybe the odd car crash.

"I there's a nasty flu going around," Frank says. "But I suppose that's not something a surgeon would see much of."

Willa rolls her eyes and says, "This bitch at school has it and is determined to infect us all."

Frank casually scolds her for foul language and then asks me if I'm feeling all right.

"I'm fine. Better every day." And I actually mean it this time.

Frank nods thoughtfully as he chews. "So…what are the odds of you getting sick again?"

He flinches as Willa kicks him under the table.

"Jesus, Frank."

"I don't know, sir. I don't look at the stats. That's just a quick way to drive yourself insane. Knowing the national average won't predict an individual patient's future." That's what Dad always says. I'm pretty sure he looks at the stats.

Willa's toes rub mine under the table. It's like she's apologizing for the awkwardness. I rub her right back.

"But if you did get sick again," Frank persists, "it would be harder to beat it twice?"

No sense in lying to him. "Yes."

Frank gives his sister a hard look. Willa picks up his beer and drains the remaining two inches before pushing away from the table. "Excuse me, I'll just go beat my head against a wall."

"Willie, come finish your supper."

"I'm not hungry." She goes to the kitchen and starts filling the sink to wash dishes. I start to stand up, to go join her or talk her back to the table, but Frank stops me. "Jem."

I sit back down for a moment.

"It's nothing against you personally. I think you're a decent guy. But I don't think you're good for her, and you both need to face that reality." He nods to the kitchen door and his sister.

"Respectfully, sir, I disagree." I take my plate and hers and clear them away. Let him eat his dinner alone.

I find Willa vigorously scrubbing a frying pan, taking out her frustration on the Teflon. The pan is scratched to shit because her brother can't be trusted in the kitchen. I set our plates beside the sink and wrap my arms around her.

"Are you okay?" I whisper into her hair.

"He promised he would behave," she says stiffly.

"It's no big deal."

"It is a big deal."

"Let it go." I rub her arms and shoulders, trying to calm her.

"I'm sorry."

"Don't be. I expected worse."

"You shouldn't *expect* to be treated like shit."

Frank comes in from the dining room, carrying his empty plate and scowling. "Rule number four," he says. Whatever that means.

"Frank," Willa says, "go watch TV."

Saturday

I get up at a reasonable hour for a Saturday and enjoy a shower. As I get dressed I hear Elise playing music down the hall. She's blasting Wheatus in her room. I thought I hid that CD from her months ago.

She starts belting the lyrics to "Teenage Dirtbag." Ugh, how is it even possible that we share DNA?

I barge into her room without knocking and march over to her CD player. "Hey!" she protests as I eject the disk.

"As your brother it's my job to protect you from epically shitty music." I open the window and fling the CD out like a Frisbee.

"Jem!" And now my eardrums are bleeding. Elise punches me in the shoulder and races downstairs to retrieve her CD from the lawn, yelling "Mooooom!" all the way.

"You'll thank me when you're older!" I yell out the window at her. Elise picks up her CD and gives me the finger. I send it right back at her.

Elise stomps inside and appeals to the parental court for justice due to the microscopic scratch on her shitty CD. It doesn't go precisely as she thought it would: Dad takes one look at the name on the disk and says, "You *paid* for this?"

"Dad!"

"Have a pancake."

⠿

Elise comforts herself with a *Harry Potter* marathon, including the DVD extras. Eric sits down next to her to offer comfort, but when he hears about what happened he just laughs. That puts Elise in an even worse mood. She hears the doorbell ring when Willa arrives, and tries to mar my happy moment by practically shouting the dialogue along with the actors.

"Morning." I lean in for a kiss as Elise declaims along with Mrs. Weasley's Howler. Willa looks to the living room and raises an eyebrow questioningly.

"She's having a rough day." I put an arm around Willa and usher her upstairs.

"Something about that guy?" Willa asks lowly as we cross the upper landing.

"What has she told you?" If he did anything to her, I will break him.

Willa shrugs. "Nothing. She's been trying to get over her crush." I automatically grin at the news.

I take Willa into my bedroom. Maybe we can create a playlist together for once instead of over the phone.

Willa locks the door behind us. What for?

"I like those jeans," she says. They're the one pair that fit me.

Willa casually squeezes my right cheek and gives my butt an appreciative pat.

I realize my mouth is open when she makes a jerking motion in front of my lips. I'm just surprised, is all. I'm not used to being... attractive. She touches me so casually, as though there's nothing complicated or different about grabbing my ass.

I grab hers right back.

"I've been waiting for you to do that."

She has?

I slip my hand into her back pocket. Willa's arm wraps around my neck as she reaches up for a kiss. The hand in her pocket flexes as she begins to walk me backwards. My knees touch the foot of the bed and we fall back on it together. Willa is careful to break her fall with her arms so as not to hurt me.

"I like your shirt."

It would look better on the floor.

"Always the tits with you, isn't it?" Like she's complaining. "Will you take off your hat?"

I refuse to let her kill this moment. "Nope."

"It's t-shirt weather and you're wearing wool."

"Actually, I think it's alpaca. You'd have to ask Elise."

"Alpaca is wool."

"Nuh-uh."

She opens her mouth to argue so I pull her down for a kiss. It's my favorite way to interrupt her. Willa tries to talk anyway.

"You really"—kiss—"won't"—kiss—"take—"

"No, it stays. I keep my hat on, you keep your pants on."

"And what if I don't want to keep my pants on?" She gives me a wicked smirk. Willa loves to call my bluff.

"Well then too damn bad."

"Where are your parents?" she whispers.

"Uh, Dad's at the hospital. Mom's in her office." I can see where she's going with this. "Eric's just down the hall, in the library. Close enough to hear."

"We'll have to be quiet, then." She dips her neck into mine and I can't think straight when she kisses me like that. Some magnetic force attaches my hand to her boob. She's wearing a thin cotton bra—no wire, and I can feel *everything* through it.

"Did you ever think about this, before?" I ask. My voice might be a little husky. Might.

Willa just chuckles. Her teeth close around my earlobe and I melt. My thumb makes its way to the little valley between her breasts, and I feel a ridge of plastic. She's wearing a front-clasp bra.

Sweet baby Jesus, yes!

You're not going to do anything with it, genius.

"Did you ever picture *me* naked?" she murmurs with a smile. I freeze for a second. Not because I don't want to admit that I did—do—picture her naked, fondly and frequently, but because I think her tone just implied that she thinks of me in the same manner. I bet she imagines something better than the reality; more weight, fewer scars, hair in all the appropriate places…

"You look guilty," she observes.

"Uh…"

Willa giggles and kisses my cheek. "What? You got some weird fantasy?"

"No." Bending her over in the bathtub. Over the desk. In my desk chair. Against the door. On the couch. On the rug. On her knees in front of my piano bench… "Nothing unusual."

You forgot 'in the car.'

Willa rolls onto her side next to me and props her head up on her elbow. Her other hand stays wrapped around my middle, idly stroking my side. "Tell me."

"Uh…"

She whispers in my ear, "What do you think about when you're *alone?*" Does it get her off to hear this? Does Willa like dirty talk?

"Um…" I'm just full of eloquent answers today. The honest answer to her question is 'how much I know it's going to hurt should I manage to come,' but that's not sexy. I should lie, if only for form's sake.

"I think about you."

"What am I doing?" Her breath is hot on my neck. The magnets in her nipples tug at my hand again. Willa only encourages me to touch.

"You're on your knees."

She chuckles. "And where's my mouth?"

Screaming for more.

"You're facing away from me."

"And what are you doing?"

I swallow. I don't want to set up the expectation that I will be able to follow through on this fantasy in the near future, because I won't.

"I'm…"

"Do you want to show me?" Her hand migrates from my waist to my crotch.

Unlike Ava, she doesn't bother to feel around. She goes right for the goods and strokes me through my jeans. Hello, marshmallow dick.

I pull her hand away. "I don't want you to touch me there."

Willa looks more than a little confused.

"I'm sorry. I shouldn't have played along—I teased you."

Willa's eyes travel southward and I bend my knees up to make it look like I'm hiding a boner. She isn't fooled.

"You're not into it?"

"I am, really." It's Ava all over again, only this time I don't want to push Willa away and shut her out while I lick my wounds. "It's complicated."

Willa raises an eyebrow. She sits up, and just the smallest signal of her pulling away makes me panic a little. I pull her back down and she lands on me awkwardly. I kiss her desperately and squeeze her ass to prove that yes, I am into her.

Stay with me; stay with me...

I can tell she's confused, but she still kisses me back. At first she doesn't know what to do with my sudden aggression, since our kisses are usually slow and gentle, but then she picks it up and matches me stroke for stroke. I get her bra undone through her shirt—I love front clasps—and Willa grabs my hand away.

"Jem." I am in such trouble. "Fair is fair. You don't get to touch me if I can't touch you."

"I *do* want you," I try to impress on her.

"But you don't want me to touch you."

"In certain places," I agree lamely. Willa stares at me for a few seconds. There's understanding in her eyes, and that's the only reason her silence doesn't scare the shit out of me.

"Is it a kidney thing?" she asks.

"What?"

"Why you don't want to be touched there." She signals to my crotch with her eyes. "I don't know much about kidney problems. Is, uh, incontinence an issue?"

I can't decide whether I should throw myself out the window or stick my head in the oven. I've sabotaged myself again, somehow managing to turn a hot makeout session into a conversation about whether I piss myself involuntarily.

What is wrong with Willa that she looks so damn understanding? What if I said yes, I do pee my pants and wear an adult diaper? There is something seriously wrong with her if she would stick by a guy like that.

She takes my hand and I don't want her to think I'm *that* guy. I end up telling her the whole sordid story. I tell her that if I get hard it's almost always by accident, and I don't stay that way long enough to finish. There's no intensity of feeling down there. When I do finish, it feels like I've been kicked in the balls; just painful ejaculation with no orgasm to make it worthwhile.

Willa listens to the whole thing patiently. When I run out of words she cups my jaw in her hand and tries to kiss me. I don't want to be kissed; I've never felt less sexy than I do right now, and I don't want her to try to 'fix' my problem the way Ava did.

"How long has this been going on?" she asks.

"Since winter."

"No wonder you're so grouchy," she says. "Months without an orgasm. I'd be climbing the walls."

"Not funny."

"Put on a t-shirt."

"What?"

"Short sleeves. I want to show you something."

"I'm not in the mood."

"Humor me, please." She smiles so sweetly, but I just can't do it. I close my eyes and rest my forehead on hers with a sigh.

"*Please*, Willa, let it go."

She wraps her arms around me tightly, drawing me into my favorite kind of hug. Willa holds onto me like she wants nothing more than to be as close to me as possible. She's not overly gentle with me; I'm her boyfriend, not a piece of glass.

"Can you feel your heart beating?"

I sigh, happy and grateful. Willa always knows how to center me.

"Yes."

"Feel it in your wrists?"

"Yes." My wrists are pressed against her shoulder blades, holding onto her just as hard as she is to me.

"In your elbows?"

"Mmmh."

"In your ears?"

She keeps going, whispering places and breathing softly against my neck until I'm so relaxed I'm almost asleep. She rubs my back and tells me she loves me, and I barely have the will to care when I feel her pushing my sleeve up.

"Feel your heartbeat here," she says, and plants a long, wet kiss on my inner elbow. She lifts her lips away and licks me softly, dragging her tongue up the center of my elbow. The skin there is so thin I bet she can feel my pulse with her lips, and I, in turn, can feel every bit of her lips in acute detail. She slowly repeats the movement on my other elbow. A sigh escapes me as her fingers trace the backs of my knees.

"How do you feel?" she whispers as she lowers her face to my arm again. Willa trails slow kisses up the inside of my arm from my elbow, lingering over the sensitive skin. Her hands are under my hips, lightly tracing the indentations at the back of my hipbones. I couldn't possibly feel calmer and my skin feels warm and tingly.

"Beautiful," I murmur, because for the first time in a long time, it's true. I won't mean it twenty minutes from now, but I try not to think about that. I nest my hands in her soft curls.

"Your heart is beating faster." She's right. I'm relaxed, but my heart is double-timing it, pounding in all the places Willa made me feel—my elbows and knees and neck. I have a sudden craving to have my throat touched, and pull Willa away from my arms to attend to the skin there.

She trails her tongue from the hollow of my collarbone to the tip of my chin. Sweet bliss. My hands and breath tremble as she traces the underside of my jaw with her lips, laving at my earlobes.

"Jem?" she whispers with her teeth around my earlobe.

"Mmh?"

"Where do you feel your heart beating?"

"Everywhere."

"Everywhere?"

I nod dumbly and try to recapture her lips for another kiss. My skin feels hot and swollen, like a ripe berry about to burst. I feel so blissfully alive and I don't want her to stop touching me.

"Jem?"

"What?"

"You realize you're hard, right?"

No one has ever had to point that out to me before. I look down, flabbergasted, to find her quite correct. It's not exactly a steel rod, but it's the first promising erection I've had all month.

"Do you want to do something about it?"

Yes.

> *No.*

Maybe.

> *Why the hell are you leaving this up to me?*

"It's going to hurt."

"Do you get any pleasure out of being touched? Or is it all pain?" Willa kisses my neck and I shiver. It's an odd sensation, like the ghost of what being touched used to feel like.

"It doesn't feel bad until the end. It's just…frustrating. I don't get anywhere." Willa's hand makes its way to my inner thigh. "Shall I?"

"No."

"Do you want to do it yourself?"

"No. Just kiss me, okay?" I pull her face to mine, trying to resurrect the good thing we had going before my cock had to get in the way with its dirty tease. Willa opens her mouth to my tongue. We play in her mouth for a while, licking and sucking on each other's lips. Then she has to thrust her tongue into my mouth, goading me on. Willa wants to tongue-fuck.

Her arms tighten around my back and she shifts her legs, tangling them with mine. My yet-to-disappear hard-on is sandwiched against her front. I try to ignore it and pour what I can into our kiss. Willa loves it. She opens up to it. She moans into my mouth and part of me wishes she would wriggle just a little bit, putting friction elsewhere. But I know that's a bad idea.

I put an inch or two of distance between our lower halves and Willa breaks the kiss.

"Did I hurt you?"

"No."

"Oh." Willa grabs my waist and thrusts her hips against mine. The small relief of that brief action is enough to make me grunt and thrust back just as hard.

Bad idea.

Very bad idea.

You're not going to want to stop until it's too late.

Willa smiles at my obvious pleasure and adjusts her hips to give me a better angle to grind against.

I pull away. Fucking hell, I can't do this.

I roll onto my back, out of her reach, and try to catch my breath. Willa wants to know if she hurt me. Like all that matters is whether or not I find this physically painful.

"You weren't just…*trying* to get me hard the whole time, were you? Just to prove you could or something?" I don't want sex with her to be an ego trip. I want her to want me—not to prove that she can get me to work right.

"No." Her tone makes me want to believe her. "There's such a thing as phantom orgasm, you know." Her fingers close gently around my exposed elbow. "It's gentler, but…powerful. I thought if you couldn't have a real one you might be able to have something else. You were shivering—I thought that was it. But then he clued in." She gestures to my crotch with her eyes. I'm still hard. Another minute or two without stimulation and it'll wilt, just like it always does. My body's not big on satisfaction these days.

"Did it feel good?"

Yes.

"I don't know." I sigh. "It's not worth the pain."

"What happens when you stop just before the pain comes?"

"I don't. It sneaks up on me and then it's too late."

A thoughtful crease appears on Willa's forehead. "Before you got sick, could you tell when you were about to come?"

"Yeah, of course."

"But you can't now?"

"No. There's no orgasm, just sudden pain and sometimes jizz. Okay? Leave it alone."

She doesn't. "Where is the pain?" Her hand settles over my navel, stroking little swirls against my shirt.

"Here." I trace a line from my balls up to my abs. The pain always feels like being sacked, the way my gut tightens and makes me want to gag.

"That's not so surprising," Willa says.

"What?" I'm actually worried for the guys she dated before me if she thinks an agonizing orgasm is normal. Willa rolls her eyes and accuses me of not paying attention in sex ed.

"Ejaculation is muscular. Orgasm is a nervous function." Her hand strays to my crotch, palming my erection, which has decided not to fade after all. I brush her hand away and she pushes me right back.

"You can have an orgasm without ejaculating, you know." Willa carefully slips her thigh between my legs and rocks against me gently to keep me hard. "It takes a lot of muscle strength or the absence of a reflex—but it's possible." She leans in to kiss me and I realize that I'm panting. This is so embarrassing—I should be pushing her off...

"I don't feel anything good, you know. Touching it might keep me hard, but I'm not going to get off. It doesn't feel...like anything."

Please let her quit now.

"If it didn't feel like anything you'd be numb," she says, still rocking. "Treatment has changed things, but you're not dead down there. What does it really feel like?"

Stop panting, damn it.

"Like...not enough." She applies more pressure and I angle my hips away from her with a yelp. "Too much."

"What about my hand?"

"No."

"My mouth?"

Mine falls open. Willa's hand leaves my shoulder and starts to unfasten my pants.

"Please, it's gonna hurt." I grab her hand to make her stop.

"I won't try to make you come," she promises quietly. "I just want to understand what feels good and what doesn't. You can tell me to stop—just let me start, okay?"

Her hand wiggles free of mine and lowers my zipper the rest of the way. Willa removes her right glove and her hand slips inside, through the gap in my underwear. I jump when her fingers touch my bare skin. "This doesn't do it for you?" Her hand slides ever so gently along my penis. She doesn't try to remove it from my pants, and for that I'm thankful.

"You might as well be touching my arm."

Willa chooses to take that as a hint and leans in to kiss my inner elbows again. It's a little sad that that touch feels better than her hand on my dick. Her fingers tease their way from base to tip, exploring my shape. She smirks against my arm between kisses. "You're uncut?"

"Don't tell me *that's* your turn off." Of all the things about me...

"No." Willa gives me a kiss and then moves to my neck, kissing and licking the spots I like best. "Touch me," she whispers. I stroke her through her shirt, teasing her nipples. Maybe I can turn the focus of this on her and she'll forget about giving me a handjob.

Willa's hand slips out my fly. Thank you, Jesus. I grab at her sides and clothes and kiss her roughly, trying to be a distraction. I think it's working. Her hands stay planted on the mattress for support and she whimpers when I suck her lower lip. Distraction accomplished.

My dick is throbbing at the loss of attention. The erection will fade, but that doesn't help at the moment, because my natural urge is to find some sort of friction.

Willa leans more of her weight on me to deepen the kiss and I can't help it—I lift my hips to meet hers, pressing my groin against her.

Willa takes this opportunity to tug my pants down over my raised hips. The waistband gets as far as the top of my thighs before I break away and reach down to stop her.

"No." She won't let my pull my pants back up. I try to cover myself with my shirt but she pushes my hands away. She's sitting on my knees in such a way that I can't leave the bed or draw my legs up for cover.

"Willa…"

"Jem."

I drop my head back to the pillow and close my eyes. I should have stopped this sooner. I hate this nakedness that has nothing to do with my body. I want her to stop touching me and just hold me before I fall the fuck apart.

"I want you to stop."

"Okay." Willa leans forward and wraps her arms around my shoulders. Her head comes to rest on my shoulder, her hot breath on my neck. I try to shimmy my jeans back up and Willa tells me to stop.

"Take a second." Her fingers gently clasp my wrist. "Listen."

I actually pause for five seconds, listening to the silence. "What?"

"If the sky had fallen we'd have heard it by now." She smirks. "I'm not running away, Jem. I don't think you're ugly. I want you."

"Don't look at me." The words come out in a cracked whisper.

"Look at me," she says. "Give me one minute, that's all I want."

"What, exactly…?"

Willa scoots down so she's kneeling over my knees instead of my hips. She looks so calm, so determined. My shirt is still covering the essential bits, but Willa slowly moves it away. I can hardly stand to watch.

"I love you." Her fingers weave between mine. She gives me a tender smile. And then her head dips.

"Wait—wai—!" Willa's mouth comes down around me and my fingers squeeze hers. *Fuck.* Her first pass is a gentle one to moisten my skin. I feel the sweat break out on the back of my neck as she lowers her mouth for the second time. Jesus Christ. I've gotten head before, but this feels…different. Less sensitive in some parts, and more sensitive in others. The slow caresses of her tongue make me whimper.

"Hmm?"

"Good," I agree breathlessly. "Gentle."

I should really stop this.

    You should.

Yeah.

    You're not going to.

Nope.

Willa's hands leave mine to touch me elsewhere and I fist the blanket for lack of a handhold. My skin has that hot, ripe-berry feel again; that high of hypersensitivity, the acute awareness of every movement and the corresponding sensations each elicits; the little flicks that her tongue laves against the most sensitive part of me, bringing just enough pleasure to drive me insane, but not nearly enough to make me come. And I'm fine with that, because for the first time in forever, it feels *good*.

Willa has to hold my hips down with her forearms to keep me from bucking. In my defense, it's been awhile...and she's incredible. Her mouth is gentle and pliable enough to give me stimulation, but not firm enough to cause discomfort—the perfect balance that my hand can no longer achieve. She spares no effort: the warm wetness, the slick sounds, her teasing tongue... I press my teeth together and seal my lips to keep from screaming.

I find her hand where it rests below my navel and grab on. I want to praise her, to thank her, but if I try to speak right now I'll just end up moaning loudly for the whole house to hear. I squeeze her fingers, trying to convey all this, and she squeezes me back. Willa understands.

There's a feeling I haven't had in awhile: a distinct build. Willa must know it, because she increases the gentle pressure of her mouth. Willa has to lay her whole arm across the front of my hips to keep me still. I want to thrust so badly. I want to scream. I want to come but I can't—I know it's going to hurt.

"Stop."

She keeps right on going. Her hand and mouth work together, driving me along a collision course toward orgasm.

"Willa—"

She moves just as the first sensation of climax blurs my vision and reduces the world to white noise. Every muscle, every nerve ending, is focused on the pulsing at my groin and the sweet, empowering pleasure of a long-overdue orgasm. Part of me waits for the pain, but it never comes. The rest of me is awed that I could forget what this feels like, because it's much better than I remembered—until I black out. It's just for a moment, but when I open my eyes again I feel dizzy and displaced.

I think my skin did burst. I don't feel like a ripe berry anymore. I feel like goo. Like splattered pulp. I'm in shreds and my heart is pounding. I can't breathe. Maybe because it's the first one in a long time, my orgasm doesn't fade immediately. It lingers long after I'm finished coming, and when Willa touches me to clean off my stomach my skin is on fire.

"You're shaking," she says. Willa's face swims in my line of vision. My ears are ringing.

"I know." No wonder.

She touches me once and I pull back, startled by the sensation. I turn away from her and swing my legs over the side of the bed. Head rush. I try to stand up too fast and end up stumbling into the bedside table. That's going to bruise.

My nerves are tweaking and I'm going to be sick. I hurry to the bathroom, lock the door, and promptly vomit. I haven't eaten enough, and very little comes back up before I start chucking bile. It's nerves—I can't get a good breath and my limbs are shaking. When the urge to puke passes, I lean back on my haunches and realize my pants are still around my thighs. Thin strings of semen have run down from my stomach into my lap. I get up on shaky legs and grab a washcloth.

I splash my face with cold water first and rinse the taste of puke out of my mouth, and then I start to clean the mess down below. It's much thinner than I remember it. Fucking chemo. I hope Willa is okay—she didn't swallow, but she shouldn't be ingesting any amount of my drug-laced body fluids.

Willa knocks on the bathroom door. "Jem?"

"I'm fine." I sound like a twelve-year-old boy caught with his dick in his hand.

"I didn't ask, 'cause I know you're not." Damn it. "Do you need anything?"

"No. I'll be out in a minute." I hear her step away from the door and the sound of her sitting down on the bed. I should have told her to go home and I'd see her tomorrow, even though that's terribly rude. I don't want to go out and face her.

I look up at the mirror while I re-wet the washcloth, and wish I hadn't. That's the view Willa had of me. Those hipbones sticking out. The scanty, pathetic pubic hairs. I instinctively cup my hand over my junk, as though I can protect my body from my own thoughts. I can still feel her spit on my penis.

I think she likes your cock. What other girl shows that much enthusiasm with a dick in her mouth?

    Don't think about her like that, you sick fuck.

Maybe she'll want to do it again sometime.

    Not for a while.

You won't last 'a while.' She's too good at it.

    Not until I look human again.

You think she'll wait on you that long?

I need to get Willa out of here. It's got to be the rudest thing I've ever thought of doing: *Thanks for the blowjob, would you mind taking off now? I'm too busy hiding in the bathroom like a wimp to even kiss you goodbye.*

Maybe I don't need her to leave. Maybe I just need her to be farther away than just on the other side of the door. I pull my pants back up and unlock the bathroom door.

"Willa?"

"Yes?"

"Maybe you should go downstairs and watch TV with Elise. I'm gonna be awhile."

"Are you okay?"

"Yeah, yeah. I just want to take a shower."

Suddenly she's right on the other side of the door, looking through the gap at me with naked eyes. "Can I join you?"

"No!" I answer way too fast. Willa slips past the gap in the door and shuts it behind her.

"I'm sorry. I just—"

"Shush." She locks the bathroom door and pulls her shirt over her head. I just stand there like a stunned little boy while she undresses in front of me, right down to the skin. Her skin is like opals: fair with flushes of color underneath the surface. She stands there for a few seconds, watching me watch her, and then switches off the light.

There's very little light coming from under the door, and there are no windows in this bathroom. I can't see a thing.

Willa finds my hands in the dark. "These are yours now." She laces her fingers with mine. "I won't look at anything you don't want me to, okay? You control where these go." Her fingers squeeze me and every single fiber of my being thinks this is a bad idea.

Her hand leaves mine and a moment later I hear the splash of water in the shower.

"Come on." Willa takes the hem of my shirt and starts to lift it over my head. She even knows how to handle removing the shirt so as not to catch it on the caps or tubing that hang out of my chest. Fuck. I help her undress me, but make no move to remove any of my own clothing. I can't seem to move. My limbs feel like lead and my stomach is in knots. I don't enjoy feeling exposed like this, but there's nothing to see—I can only feel her next to me—and I can't find my voice to protest.

"You're shaking."

I don't have anything to say to that. She steps away a little and I hear the swish of her long hair as she ties it back.

"You'll have to take off your hat."

No, and you can't make me.

Willa senses my hesitation. She reaches out experimentally and finds my jaw. "I won't look there," she says. "I won't look higher than your eyes." Her fingers trace the bone ridges around my sockets. "Or past your ears." She softly pinches my lobes.

My hat is the only piece of clothing I remove myself. I push it back with trembling hands and leave it on the counter.

And then I can't feel her next to me. "Willa?"

"Here." She's about to step into the shower. I hear the sound of the curtain rings moving against the bar.

"Give me a second."

"Take your time."

It's a little sad that I've done this so many times that I can do it in the dark now: place a patch over my Hickman to keep the water off it. My hands are still shaky, but I manage just fine. And then there's nothing to do but shower.

I stand outside the tub for a good thirty seconds before Willa reaches around the edge of the curtain and tells me to take her hand.

The second the skin of our palms connects, I want to pull away. I'm not ready to be physically bare in front of her, even in the dark. I feel weak and ashamed and I want to run out of the bathroom and leave this behind.

Her gentle hand pulls me into the tub. Willa is screwing with my inner compass. I'm afraid of her, but she's the only thing that can comfort me right now. I would push her away, but then I wouldn't be able to fall into her arms and block out the world.

Neither of us makes any attempt to really shower. We stand under the spray, close enough to feel the droplets bounce off each other and the animal scent of warm breath between us.

"Where do you want my hands?"

I'm tempted to tell her to keep them to herself, but I know that's not what she wants to hear. I reach out slowly and find her arms, and then her wrists. Her hands hang there, relaxed and pliable as she waits for my instructions.

I can't do it. I don't want her to touch my naked body. I don't want to be 'seen' in this way. The raw exposure of it overwhelms me, and my throat burns with the threat of tears. All that keeps her from seeing everything I'm ashamed of is the darkness and a few inches of space. She's so close, and she knows so much already. To press her body against mine would be to know more, and yet she's still willing to give me control and space.

I press the backs of her little hands against my mouth. It's all the intimacy I can afford to allow her—as if this wasn't already the most intimate moment of my life. The shower spray disguises the few tears that escape.

"Jem?"

If I answer her I'll end up in pieces like a nervous wreck.

"I can leave if you want."

Please don't leave me alone right now.

She feels me shake my head with the hands I still hold against my face. Even in the dark, it's obvious how close to the edge of composure I am. I am so... *fucking*...scared. Willa goes up on her toes to kiss the backs of my hands and then says, "I want to show you something."

Slowly, like she's trying not to spook me, she pulls our hands away from me and puts them on her. My hand comes to rest on her abdomen.

"Feel that?" She traces my finger along a ridge of smooth scar tissue, almost four inches long. "I had appendicitis."

My hand gets brushed along her hip as she turns away from me, and then she's redirecting my hand to her lower back. There are more scars here, scattered like pockmarks.

"I broke a jug and slipped and fell on the shards. Fourteen stitches in all."

She repeats this recital elsewhere, calmly and patiently. In the darkness, she acquaints me with each and every one of her flaws. Not for one moment do I get the sense that she expects recompense.

"Where do you want my hands?" she says when she has run out scars. I find her wrists again in the dark. This woman will never know her own capacity to move me.

I place her hands on my waist. I know she can feel the way my hipbones jut out for lack of body fat, but that seems less important now. Willa won't judge me.

I need to give her something, but the words won't come. I make do with a hand on her chest, slowly tracing the shape of a heart over her breast.

"I love you too."

I bite down on my lip to the point of pain, trying to hold myself together. My head dips forward until it rests against Willa's, and I wrap my hands around her neck and collarbone. She's so small, so warm. I want to tell her how profound this really is, but I can't; maybe she already knows.

I hold onto her under the spray for a long time. True to her word, she never moves her hands. I can't thank her enough for that.

"Willa…"

"Shush."

"You're beautiful."

She goes up on her toes to kiss my trembling lips. "If I tell you the same, will you promise to believe me?"

I bite down on my lip again and shake my head. Whatever delusions of my adequacy she might have, they're borne of ignorance. She didn't know me before. She doesn't know what a shell I am of my former self. I'm ugly compared to him, the person I was a lifetime ago.

"One day you will," she says with muted confidence. The water is starting to go cold, so she shuts it off. Willa gives me one last kiss and tells me to wait here.

I start to panic again as she steps out of the shower. Is she going to turn the light on? I hear her get a towel out of the cupboard and gather up her clothes off the floor. The light comes on, and a second later the door closes.

It's with trepidation that I peek around the shower curtain. Willa is gone, but I can hear her getting dressed in my bedroom. She must have turned on the light just as she stepped out. She was being generous with my privacy.

I know almost instinctively that I will never be able to repay her for today. I'm not sure I want to. Feeling that exposed, that emotionally raw… maybe this is one of those once-in-a-lifetime things, because I don't think I could go through it again. Not even for Willa.

And yet, I'm glad I had it with her. I couldn't have had this with anyone else.

↪

I take my time getting dressed. Physically I'm no different, but parts unseen are raw and worked over. I turn to sweats for comfort and my softest hat. As I look through my closet for a shirt I hesitate. Willa asked me to wear a t-shirt earlier, and I denied her. It seems silly now to have tried to hide my arms, having just shared something so intimate with her. I fish a t-shirt out of my drawer and put it on.

It's been so long since I've worn short sleeves that it looks a little strange to me. I stand in the mirror for a minute, studying the way my arms look, pale as they are. My new hairs are short and soft, hardly visible unless you look closely, but knowing Willa, she'll probably notice.

Elise still has her *Harry Potter* marathon going in the front room. I poke my head in, but Willa isn't with her. I find her in the living room, lounging on the couch with her feet up and a folio of sheet music on her lap. She skims the pages, even though she can't read music. Maybe I'll play for her, later. She smiles when she sees me coming and holds her arms out. Her fingers make little grabbing motions like she can't wait to touch me, and she isn't wearing her gloves.

"Hi." I lean over her for a kiss. Her hands go right to my arms, reveling in the bare skin.

"I'm sorry I was stubborn about it, earlier."

"You're beautiful." She grins and pecks my lips. I sit against the armrest of the couch and Willa shifts to sit between my legs. Her back rests comfortably against my front and I wrap my arms around her. I should have been able to give her this upstairs. Orgasms and cuddles are like Oreos and milk—they just go together.

"Thank you," I murmur.

"I meant to ask, did it hurt?"

"No," I whisper. "You were very gentle. It felt…amazing." I kiss her ear and I can hear her smile.

"Try that when you're on your own."

"What? Blowing myself?"

Willa giggles. "I guess you were too distracted to notice my hand." Without further preamble she turns around and shoves her hand between my legs, pressing firmly on the stretch of skin behind my balls. "It gives your muscles less room to move, and less opportunity to ejaculate the wrong way." She kisses my cheek. "It would hurt here, right?" Her fingers trace the line from my groin to my abs, and I nod. "It's muscular. Months of resting and no sex—ejaculation involves muscle contraction, you know. You've got to keep it in shape or it strains."

"How do you know this?"

"My pervert counselor. Learned all kids of cool stuff about muscles and reflexes." Willa smiles apologetically. "I had one hand here, too." She puts the heel of her hand at the base of my abs, right below the spot that usually tightens and hurts when I come. "Support the muscles properly until you're back in shape. Try leaning on a pillow or something."

I take her hands—the small hands that never hesitate to touch me and never hurt me. I kiss Willa's forehead and tuck her head under my chin. I think about how Ava reacted, how my body would freak out most girls, and know this could have gone horribly. I want to thank Willa for being so understanding and even a little bit pushy, but I don't know how to say it without sounding corny.

"You're about to ruin the moment, aren't you?" she says with a cheeky smile.

"I'll try to control myself." I reach for the folio of sheet music she had earlier. "Come on. Let's play."

Sunday

Arthur is even more of a goofball today than he normally is. He wants to talk about mothers. Something about honoring the Virgin Mary.

"Let's discuss the significance of mothers to our lives. It doesn't have to be a biological mother; maybe just someone in your life who is a mother figure."

No one really knows what to say to that, which shows how hopeless Arthur is as a group leader. The girl whose brother died in a drunk driving accident says that her mother has been severely depressed ever since. The porn addict's mom made him come here because Jesus cries every time he rubs one out while watching free amateur video of shaved pussy.

"She escaped her mother," I say of Willa.

"He's afraid of hurting his."

Arthur is in the middle of scolding us for not speaking about our own issues when Michael chimes in: "I think my mom is disappointed with me." I'll have to remember to thank him for changing the subject.

Willa and I take off as soon as Group ends. No labyrinth today—we have other places to be, and an arbitrary anniversary to celebrate. We take off to The Circle for lunch. The restaurant looks even better in the light of day, with the early afternoon sun shining through the tall front windows. Some of the panes are made of stained glass—they throw rainbows on the bookshelves.

Willa and I sit at our usual table—yes, we can have a usual table after only eating here once—and she scoots her chair to the side again. I was so nervous last time I brought her here. It wasn't a date, but I wanted to show her a good time. I wanted to make her smile and hear all about her life, even the mundane details, and I wanted to do corny date things like play footsies with her. Anything to make her see me as a real guy.

I start making up for that night by looping our ankles together under the table. Our joined hands rest on the edge of the placemat. Willa suggests the tofu spring rolls and I whisper that she looks beautiful. I should have told her that on the night of our non-date too, but I didn't want to push my luck.

The waitress comes by to take our orders. Spring rolls for Willa, split pea soup for me.

"Happy anniversary."

Willa obligingly clinks her water glass with mine. "Are you one of those people that needs an occasion to be happy?" she asks.

"No. Just you."

"You're such a sap."

I lift our joined hands and kiss the back of hers. "What do you want to do on the hike today?"

"Anything we want."

I like the sound of that.

⌀

We stop at the grocery store to pick up bottled water and snack food for the hike, and then we're off along the highway. Willa even lets me drive. It's warm enough that we can roll the windows down. I keep one hand on the wheel and rest the other on her denim-covered thigh. Willa is in her weekend outfit, regardless of the fact that we were just in church. I love seeing her in loose plaid and faded black jeans.

Willa's hand mirrors mine on my thigh. Her fingertips trace little patterns around the inner seam, teasing me.

"That tickles." I pull off onto the narrow road, into the bush.

"Does it?"

Once we're under the cover of trees, out of sight of the road, Willa leans over and starts to undo my pants.

"What are you doing?" I reach down to stop her. She leans down and plants a row of kisses on my thigh, leading up to—

"No, Willa."

"Would you rather wait until we're parked?"

Maybe?

"Why is it suddenly always sex with you?" The words sound like more of an accusation than I meant them to, and just like that, her dead look is back. Willa takes her hands off me, sits up, and stares straight ahead out the windshield. Her face is like stone.

I shift into park at the end of the road and shut off the engine.

"No more hiding, remember?" I put a hand under her chin to turn her toward me and she slaps it away with a sudden violence. In a blur she's out of the car and the rusted door slams behind her. Shit.

I follow her out of the car. "Willa." She's pacing around the narrow dirt road, looking pissed off and running her hands along her scalp. "Can we talk about this?"

"Are you mad that I pushed you?" she demands.

"No, but—"

"Or is this more of your stupid clinging to the guy you were before cancer?"

"Willa." I approach her carefully and lay my hands on her shoulders, trying to contain her. I might regret that in a moment. "I'm not blaming you for anything. But it feels like all you want is sex, and I *need* to move slower than that."

She has such a strange expression. It's like she's sorry and confused all at once. "Emotional cripple, remember?" she says, pointing to herself. "I don't know how to have a relationship without sex. God, I am fucked up." She shrugs my hands off her shoulders and paces some more. I don't want her to beat herself up; not when we came here to have a good time.

"We match then, don't we?" I don't think she's ready to joke, but she hums in acknowledgement.

"I'll stop pushing." She stops pacing for a split second and I jump on the opportunity to gather her into a hug.

"Thank you. For being patient." I kiss her forehead and she rolls her eyes.

"I'm not that patient. I just don't want to be the same fuckup on a loop."

"You're not."

"Are we going to hike or what?"

⌁

I still need to take breaks along the hike, but the route to the creek doesn't take us nearly as long as it did last time. The quality of those breaks is nicer, too. One pause to cozy up to Willa on a log, another to make out against a tree…. We hold hands most of the way and conversation consists mostly of music.

The tall grass along the edge of the burnt-out beach is fully green now. The milk thistle buds are starting to open, coating the bank in fluff. I pick a clover flower and tuck it behind her ear. Willa calls me a dork and sticks it in the fold of my hat instead.

We set up camp on a high point on the beach. We lay and rest for a little while, drinking to stay hydrated and snacking on fruit.

"I want to explore a little," Willa says. We follow the creek a bit farther away from the road. It's narrows to a little stream between the rocks and trees, but in one place a small waterfall has formed. The space below it has been eroded into a deep pool of dark water, and the shallow, pebbly stream resumes at its other side.

"I wonder how deep it is." Willa throws a pebble in and we watch it sink. The bottom of the pool is invisible.

"Deep enough," she says, and kicks off her shoes.

"What are you doing?"

Willa sheds her clothes, right down to her bra and panties, and cannonballs into the pool. I take a step back to avoid the splash. Willa resurfaces with a whoop.

"Is it cold?"

"That's why I jumped in all at once." Willa swims over to the edge below my feet and hooks her fingers over the rock. "I know you can't swim right now," she gestures to her chest, "but will you dip your feet in?"

I kick my shoes off, shed my socks and roll the hems of my pants up to my knees. Two days ago I wouldn't have even considered showing Willa my pale, bare legs, but today I try to be okay with it. I sit on the rock ledge and dip my feet in.

"Shit, it's freezing."

"Whiner." Her hands run up and down my calves under the water, helping my skin adjust to the temperature. She tickles my feet and I flick water in her face.

"Do you like swimming?" she asks as she does a quick lap of the pool to warm up. Without her hands on my legs, little silver bubbles begin to appear close to my skin. I look like a glowing alien.

"It's more Elise's thing, but I like it." I like watching Willa do it in the cold water, in her green bra and panties. If only they were white and the water made them see-through. The temperature has made her nipples obvious, at least.

"I have eyes, you know."

"Those are nice too," I agree without looking up. Willa flicks water at my face. "Out of curiosity, how are you planning to dry off?" We didn't bring a towel with us. I don't like the thought of her being uncomfortable.

Willa shrugs. "Sunbathe."

Thank you, Jesus.

She swims for another quarter hour before the water gets uncomfortably cold and she concedes to get out. This might be my favorite part: watching her walk around practically naked in our private slice of paradise. She wrings the water out of her bra without removing it and I think I saw a bit of nipple there.

"You remember the rule about staring?"

"What?" Oh, right: if I stare I have to touch, or it's teasing. I wouldn't want to tease her…

Her skin is cold and moist and I bet she'd warm up faster if we cuddled. I offer and Willa smiles. "I'd like that." The droplets on her skin are mostly dry by the time we set up out picnic blanket on the sand. Willa puts on her big plaid shirt and slips her bra off from underneath. I'm a little disappointed that I don't get to cuddle with mostly-naked Willa, but Willa wearing only drenched panties and a loose flannel shirt is nice too. We lay facing on our sides and tangle limbs. Her damp head fits below my chin.

"You know, you could push a little," I hint.

You're going to regret saying that the next time she tries to take your clothes off.

Willa chuckles. "I think you're still a little too high maintenance for wilderness sex." That's an interesting way of phrasing it. My body isn't screwed up, it's 'high maintenance.'

"You're such a tease." I snap the waistband of her wet panties and she squeaks.

"If I wanted to tease you, you'd know it."

"Oh yeah? How?"

Willa lifts her head from under my chin to look me in the eye. "If I wanted to push you I'd have jumped in the water naked."

Why did I ask her not to push, again?

Because any normal guy's dick would be twitching right now. What's yours up to?

"We really have to come back here sometime." My enthusiasm amuses her. She indulges me a little, and we make out under the warm sun with her still half-naked and wrapped around me. I get three of the buttons on her shirt open before she notices, and when she does she just shrugs and goes back to kissing me. I love Willa's tits. Perfectly palm sized, with the softness and texture of a ripe peach, only I bet her skin tastes sweeter.

I might have accidentally said that out loud.

"What?"

"Uh…your tits are like peaches?"

Willa doesn't even blink. "Okay. Your balls are like lychee nuts."

"What?"

Willa goes back to kissing me without bothering to answer. What the hell is a lychee nut? I'm not sure if she just insulted or complimented me. I take Willa's face between my hands to stop the kiss and make her tell me.

"It's a pink fruit about the size of a walnut. It's got wrinkly skin and bitter white pulp inside." How far did she think this analogy through?

"You're a little strange."

"Yup." She separates herself from me and reaches for her jeans.

"Drop 'em."

Willa ignores me and stands up. She shimmies out of her underwear—damn those shirttails for hiding all the good stuff—and steps into her pants.

"Let's go explore a little more." She holds a hand out to me.

"I can make out with you again later, right?"

Willa rolls her eyes. "Why do you ask such obvious questions?"

I follow her with a gleeful smile. I do like the image of her bra and panties left alone on the blanket as we walk away. I like Willa in comfy, touchable clothes… with nothing underneath.

I might need to go slow with her, but I sure as hell don't want to.

Willa: June 4 to 6

Sunday

Jem follows me around the edge of the beach, exploring the treed areas closest to the grassland. The spaces between the trees are mostly clear, but by high summer this will all be filled with ferns and underbrush. Jem keeps a hand on my waist, comfortably tracing my hipbone through my shirt. I can feel him watching me while we explore the woods.

Whenever I look at him he's got a hungry look on his face. It's not a possessive expression, but one of clear longing. I've never seen that before. Steve looked at me as parts of a whole. Ray's looks clearly read *mine*. From the others there were suspicious looks, indifferent looks. If they wanted me it was for fifteen minutes at a time and no talking.

"What are you thinking about?" I ask.

"Summer." His answer surprises me. I was expecting something like 'your tits' or 'things I'm going to do to you when we get home.'

"Summer?"

"This summer." Jem wraps his arms around me and gently pushes my back up against a spruce trunk. "Time with you…and bikini season." He chuckles at his own joke. I didn't know Smiths Falls had a bikini season. "And actually going swimming with you," he adds quietly. His smile is hesitant but real.

"Oh yes? Any word on when you're losing the hardware?"

"I'll let you know."

"You're not going to wear that hat all summer, are you?"

Jem smirks. "No. Not this hat, specifically. I've got a collection that I rotate daily." I really should give the sarcastic bastard a smack, but all I manage is a kiss instead. Being around him screws with my natural impulses like that.

"Take it off," I encourage him.

"Later."

"There's no one around. Just you and me." I'm not wearing my gloves, but that does nothing to encourage Jem. He doesn't see a parallel between our masks.

Jem shakes his head. "Not yet." It's not an argument worth having, so I let it go.

We return to our blanket when the afternoon sun makes us lazy and warm. Jem is quick to fall asleep after all the hiking, and I amuse myself by tickling his ear with a long blade of grass. It makes him snort in his sleep, but he doesn't even wake up a little bit until I've tickled him a dozen times.

"Mm'zit?" he mumbles. I have no idea what that means.

"What's that?"

Jem rolls over with a sigh and puts an arm around me. "Soft," he mumbles. Apparently my boobs make a good pillow. I rub his back and pet the slope of his neck. He's so warm and alive. I think about peeling back his hat for a peek, since he sleeps so soundly and probably wouldn't notice, but that would devalue the gesture when he does decide to trust me with that part of himself. I let it be.

"I'll try not to screw it up with you," I whisper.

This is a new thing for me, to be with a guy and not screw him in place of conversation—to actually know his full name and have met his family and shared in his hobbies. Steve waited just long enough for me to trust him—or at least he thought I did. Creating pretty fictions for people isn't so hard, as long as you commit to the lie. We were quite a pair—a liar and a snake.

He asked me about gardening, like he was just making pleasant conversation. I didn't like gardening, but I'd grown up around a woman who did. I knew enough to talk with him about it. He said he was thinking of putting some 'color' in front of his house and invited me to go to the plant nursery with him that weekend to choose trays of cheap annuals.

And back at his house, with dirt on my knees from planting, he sat me on his lap and kissed me. I didn't *not* like it, and by that point everything I did was just another part of the grand lie. I came back every weekend—to water the plants, ostensibly; it's not easy to wheel on grass, you know.

I was numb enough that it didn't shock me when he progressed from kissing to touching, and from touching to taking clothes off. The man was good with his hands, and my hormones were definitely not on my side.

"You can touch me back, you know," he said with an indulgent smile, like I was naïve and cute for not trying to reciprocate freely. I wasn't keen on touching his dick, but it turned out he didn't have that sort of thing in mind. His erogenous zones were displaced by injury—he wanted me to kiss his arms and chest and neck. Nails on his biceps drove him insane. That was the reason Steve only went for younger girls—women his own age weren't interested in a relationship without 'real' sex. Young virgins, on the other hand…

We'd been at this little ritual of 'watering the flowers' for a few months when Steve pushed me back against the edge of the dining room table and made me sit on top. It was the perfect height and angle to expose me to a guy in a chair. I was used to hands touching me, but I wasn't expecting his mouth. And I liked it.

I didn't bother to water the plants the following week. We went straight to the bed and stayed there for three hours, because that's how slow and methodical sex was with his body. He touched everything. He showed me how a guy comes without an erection. He shocked me out of my numbness for five minutes at a time, and made me feel too stupid with pleasure to care that if I wasn't numb, life was agony.

I remember looking at his legs that day, really looking, as we lay there after. No touching. No talking. No cuddling. It was the first time I'd seen all of him bare, and I was fascinated by the way his well-muscled torso gave way to thin, immobile legs.

"I'm used to it," he interrupted my musing. "Everyone's normal is someone else's weird." I remembered that lesson well. It was the only honest thing Steve ever said, to the best of my knowledge.

Ray was equally full of shit. We never had great communication, what with the language barrier and all, and it was a relationship based mostly on hate sex. His hate for the world, mine for myself. The most we ever did was meet each other halfway. He read my lips and I deciphered his awkward speech. My ASL vocabulary never grew beyond the essentials: *I want to fuck; Don't bullshit me; Strip; Condom; Fuck off and die.* My lack of signs was fine by him—he didn't want me for conversation. We'd just screw on the spare mattress in his parents' basement when they weren't home. It was different than it had been with Steve. There was a dick involved, for one. The lights had to stay on, for another. The whole thing was very tactile. Touches took the place of words. Ray liked me to face away from him when we fucked. He didn't like the dead look in my eyes.

That look scares Jem too. I can see it in his face, and every time his fear almost moves me.

Things are going to be different with Jem. Because I want them to be, and because he's different than the others. He's decent. He has a heart that hasn't been rendered incapable of love.

I pet his sun-flushed cheek and murmur, "When are you going realize you're too good for me?" I'm counting on it that he will. He thinks I'm the one who's settling, but that's just the trauma talking. At any given moment there are two people living in Jem's body: the boy who's still dying of cancer, and the man with a big heart who's been to hell and back. One of them is living on borrowed time.

I wake up after the sun has moved below the treetops, still cuddling with Jem. I can hear him murmuring, but the tall grass rustles in the breeze and I can't make out every word. I only catch a few: love, Soc, summer. His lips are so close to my collarbone that I can feel it when he speaks. Jem twists a lock of my hair around his finger.

"How long was I out?" I roll toward him and stretch. Jem opens his arms to catch me. I'd nuzzle into his chest, but he would probably freak out.

"Not long."

I stretch my back and give him a kiss. The afternoon in the wilderness has been fun, but I think it's time we did other things. I suggest driving back to Smiths Falls for a meal with his family.

"My parents notice when you're not around," he says as we fold up the blanket. "It's like you've always been there—now your absence is the noteworthy thing." He chuckles.

"Are you sure it's me they notice? Or do you make it obvious by turning into a grumpy bastard when I'm not around to spoil you with kisses?"

"Spoil me?"

"Yes."

"Well you're not doing a very good job." He brings the corners of the blanket up to my chest to fold and leans in for a kiss.

"You only get one."

"Oh." He deliberately pouts. "Maybe I'll save it for later, then."

I kiss him. Manipulative bastard.

As I pull on to the highway I suggest Jem call his mom to let her know that we'll both be there for supper. He rolls his eyes from where he lounges in the passenger seat and points out that there won't be any dinner unless we make it ourselves.

"What the hell did you guys eat before I started coming over?"

"Frozen veggies and hamburger helper," he says with complete seriousness.

"You poor, deprived child."

Jem laughs and relents, agreeing that I do spoil him. Eric too, apparently, since he's been complaining whenever someone else takes the last of the left-over 'Willa food.'

"Elise can cook."

"That's a recent development," he grumbles. Jem's phone rings. He checks the caller ID and answers the call without hesitation. "Hi Mom."

Ivy's voice is just an indistinct buzz to my ears. A crease appears between Jem's eyebrows.

"I'm fine. What's wrong?"

There are three long minutes where he just listens with that thoughtful expression in place, and then he tells her that he's almost home. "Bye. Love you." He ends the call and slumps forward, scrubbing his hands over his face.

He's quiet for a long time, and then all of a sudden he exclaims, "Shit!" like he forgot his keys or something. "Shit. Fuck!" He punches the dash and the glove compartment pops open. Jem slams it shut with another 'fuck.' "God fucking damn it!" he yells with real force. Last time I heard someone yell like that, it was a bike messenger giving a reckless driver a piece of his mind.

"Jesus Christ, what's the matter with you?" He sounded fine on the phone, and I've never known Jem to be so angry with his mother.

Jem looks at me like he just remembered that he isn't alone, and this isn't a private tantrum. "Meira died." After all that yelling his speaking voice sounds quiet.

"Who's Meira?" And why is she worth yelling about while I'm trying to drive?

"You remember that time we went down to Pediatrics after dialysis?"

"Uh-huh." I'd forgotten the girl's name, but I remember that she was dying at the time.

"She died this morning." His voice cracks on the word 'died,' and he curses under his breath again. I don't tell him I'm sorry, because I know from experience that it means jack shit to hear people say that, so I agree with him: "Fuck."

"I know." Jem tilts his head back and sighs. He's quiet again for a little while, but as we turn onto his street he mutters another curse word under his breath. "She would have been seventeen next week."

I don't bother to ask if they were close or if they spent much time together outside the hospital. What happened on the ward probably matters more. They're like soldiers who've shared a tour of duty; it doesn't matter if they see each other after, because the bond is already forged.

"When is her funeral?"

"Tuesday."

"Do you want me to go with you?"

Jem shrugs. I look over to find his face oddly blank. Is it shock? Disbelief? Or conscious numbness? I know better than I'd care to admit what each of those feels like, but I can't do much besides hold his hand on the seat between us while I drive home.

Elise comes out of the house when I turn into the driveway. She runs up to Jem's side of the car and barely lets him out before she throws her arms around him. She offers soup as comfort food and Jem says he isn't hungry.

I'm not sure if I should leave or come inside. Jem is too distracted for a proper goodbye, and I wonder if I should just slink away quietly and talk to him later, after he's sorted through some of the emotion with his family. Then I notice Eric watching me from the front window, eyeing the way I stand apart from the grieving group. He inclines his head a little, inviting me inside.

The Harper kitchen has the feel of a funeral parlor. Jem is still quiet, and Ivy chatters nervously to fill the silence. Elise is full of hugs for her brother, but like me, Eric hangs back. Ivy tells us all the details—that Meira died this morning of multi-system organ failure. That's the piece of information that finally breaks Jem's blank façade, and he storms away with a sound of disgust. He rushes up the stairs and slams his bedroom door.

"Let him be for awhile," Ivy says to no one in particular. I take it as a hint and say my goodbyes. I go home, make Frank some supper, and wait for Jem to call. He doesn't, and I don't blame him.

Monday

It's just after midnight when the ringing of my phone wakes me. I roll over and feel around for my phone. The caller ID is for the Harper house. I try not to fault Jem for staying awake so late with his grief.

"Hello?"

"Hi, Willa?" It's not Jem. For a moment I'm confused.

"Eric?"

"Yeah. I got your number from Elise's phone."

"Why are you calling so late?" I expect to hear horrible news. No early morning phone calls have ever been for a good cause. I sit up against the pillows and try to wake myself up enough for this.

"Has Jem said anything to you?"

"Not since I left this afternoon."

"He's been acting…strange."

"Strange how?"

"Not talking. Or really doing anything, actually. He just sort of drifts around. You can tell he's thinking, but he doesn't seem upset, and his friend just died." There's a blustery echo over the line as Eric sighs into the phone. "You think he'd… I don't know, be angry or sad or something. He just slammed that one door and that was it."

It would creep Eric out that another person fails to express emotion. He lives out loud and expects others to do the same.

"He'll get there."

"If he says anything—"

"I'll let you know." I like Eric a little more, now. He's a good older brother. "Are you okay?"

"Fine."

"You sure?"

"She was *Elise's age*," he says quietly, and blows out another breath. "That could have been Jem."

"Don't grieve something you haven't lost," I tell him. "Elise and Jem are fine."

"Elise told me you saw the photos," he says. "You're crazy to want to join this circus."

"I've been crazy for a long time."

There's an awkward silence where neither of us knows what to say. Eventually Eric apologizes for calling so late. "I'll let you sleep."

"You should too."

He doesn't say he will one way or the other. "Good night."

"G'night."

↩

Paige finally found a date for the grad dance. She's taking some junior from the track team because her options among the seniors have been exhausted and apparently this guy is fairly good looking. That's all it takes to qualify with Paige. But if she's happy, I'm happy, even if it means she's more chatty than usual at lunch. It's mostly girls at the table today, since Cody is still sick and Joe has come down with the flu too. Diane is over her cold, which means she is no longer the center of attention, and that fact grates on her while the rest of the girls discuss prom.

"I don't know why you're so interested," she says to me in her usual tone of condescension. "You're not even going."

"I'm not sure why you *are* going, except to punish everyone else."

Diane glares at me like she's trying to melt my face off with sheer force of will. Paige feigns obliviousness rather than feed Diane's ill temper, and asks me if I think it's cheesy for prom dates to match clothing.

Uh, always. "It depends."

"My dress is mauve. I could probably find a matching tie for him."

"Trying to make the poor guy look whipped?" I give her a wink to show I'm (sort of) joking.

"Maybe a complementary color," she says thoughtfully. "I placed the corsage order in white—that goes with everything."

I nod along while she lists ideas for how she's going to do her hair. Apparently up-dos are overdone, and she's determined to be different. I am so bored of prom and it hasn't even happened yet.

"Or you could put it up to be ironic."

"What?"

I hate having to explain jokes. "Nothing. You should wear your hair down."

Paige seems to realize that I'm losing interest in the subject. "So how are things with you and Jem?" she asks. Whatever I say, I'm sure she's going to relate it back to her own interests.

"It's good. We haven't killed each other yet."

Paige laughs as though she isn't sure if I'm joking. Or maybe relating Jem to death makes her uncomfortable because he looks so ill.

"Isn't it a little...*weird*, though?" she asks lowly. I'm pretty sure everyone at the table still heard her.

"Why would it be weird?"

"I dunno." Paige shrugs. "I mean, when you're kissing him, isn't it odd to... well you can't, like, run your hands through his hair or anything, you know?" Figures she would care about that instead of something genuinely important, like the possibility of relapse and death.

I just chuckle. "Yes, Paige, I do know. That's a small sacrifice to make."

"But, like, isn't it weird that he's bald and stuff?"

"Not really. I've never actually seen his head. He keeps his hat on all the time."

"*All* the time? Like, he never takes it off in front of you?"

"Nope."

Paige's questions suddenly desist, and I look over my shoulder to see Jem enter the cafeteria. Paige is good at timing her gossip. I wonder if she's ever been caught by her subject.

Jem looks like he hasn't slept and his dog ran away from home. He's fifteen minutes late for lunch, but he doesn't have any food with him and he doesn't buy any. All he has is the half-empty water bottle that he used to take his noon medication. It's as if a little cloud of gloom follows him to the table.

Jem leans around to kiss my cheek before taking the empty seat between Elwood and me. I give him a hug and he whispers in my ear that he's fine, even though I didn't ask—a sure sign that he's not. Today was practically guaranteed to be a lousy day for him, what with the death of his friend, but he doesn't have to hide it.

Chris leans forward to talk to me around Jem. "Really, Willa, never?"

I give Chris my best shut-up-or-I'll-bury-you look. He's tried to joke with or about Jem before, but now is not the moment for a jab in good fun. Paige looks away, trying not to involve herself.

"What never?" Jem asks me. He's trying to be personable and participate in the conversation, but I can tell that it costs him a great amount of effort. He's in a fragile mood and doesn't need to know that people were gossiping about him.

"I was predicting that Elwood would never get laid."

Jem snorts with amusement and Chris scowls. Maybe I should have just dismissed the whole thing instead of being a smartass. I'll have to be nice to Chris at work tonight to make up for it.

Chris reaches up. By the time I realize that he's making a move to pull Jem's hat off, it's too late to get out of the way. Jem shifts his chair sharply towards mine to avoid Chris's hand and I get bumper-carred onto the floor. Jem stands up so fast our chairs fall like dominos and hit me in the shoulder. There's the crack of bone-on-bone and Paige shrieks. I push the fallen chair away in time to see Elwood hit the floor face first.

"Hey!" The lunch monitors descend on our table like flies to a corpse. Chris's face is bleeding. I think that asshat might actually be crying. Jesus Christ, Jem actually hit him.

"Get to the office," the monitor barks at Jem. One of the lunch monitors grabs his arm, even though he gave no indication that he was going to make a break for it. They help Chris up and practically carry him out of the lunchroom. The twit clutches his split lip like it's a damn war wound.

Hannah kindly helps me off the floor and asks if I'm hurt.

"I'm fine." Diane is shaking her head in disgust, but everyone else at the table looks unaccountably excited. Lunchroom fights aren't that common here.

"Holy shit," Paige hisses. "He's not like that around you, is he, Willa?"

"What?"

She lowers her voice and asks me very seriously if Jem has ever tried to hit me. For a second I think she's hoping I'll say yes to further the dramatic intrigue. The question takes me so off guard that I laugh, which freaks her out.

"I have to go." There are too many people here and I can't think straight. On my way to my car I pass by the front office. I see Elise through the glass wall, arguing with the secretary. I guess she's demanding information, and not having much luck at it.

⟴

Jem's parents are quick to ground him. They've barely set that punishment when they make an exception to it. He's not going anywhere, but they won't stop me from coming over. Elise calls me after school to tell me this and rant about injustice.

"He was provoked, so they only suspended him for three days instead of four."

"What about Chris?"

"Technically he didn't do anything except try to humiliate Jem, so he got off with a detention for provoking another student. It's so unfair." I can't agree with her. I would have probably set the same punishments if I'd been an objective third party. And besides, a three-day suspension looks a hell of a lot better on his permanent record than an assault charge.

"How is he now?"

Elise sighs into the phone. "He's locked in his room, blasting music." I can hear it in the background but I can't tell what song or even what band it is.

"He's not playing Tchaikovsky, is he?" An alarming number of the tracks in Jem's 'To Hell With Everything' playlist are by that composer.

"It sounds like Radiohead from here—I'm on the *porch*. He has such bad taste in music." Elise sighs again like her brother's musical preferences are a personal hardship. "So when are you coming over?"

♲

Elise wasn't kidding when she said Jem was blasting music. It's so loud I can hear every word of "Creep" from the front yard. When I go upstairs I find Dr. Harper and Eric trying to dismantle the handle on his door.

"He locked it." Eric has to yell his explanation over the music. He stops taking the door apart to let me knock and tell Jem that it's me through the door, but I don't think he can hear me. So I take an egg around back and throw it at his window. That gets his attention. Ivy isn't too pleased, though.

"So, I guess the silver lining in this is that you get a long weekend?" I say when he lets me into his room. Jem just sits down heavily on the closest piece of furniture—his desk chair—and shakes his head. "Don't try to cheer me up."

"Okay." I step around Jem and take a seat on his desk. I rest my feet on either side of his legs, just on the edges of the chair. He takes this odd pose as an excuse to wrap his arms around my hips and burrow his face into my stomach.

"It was kind of my fault, you know," I say.

"What?" He looks up at me but keeps his pale cheek pressed to my body.

"Remember when you came in for lunch and Chris asked me, 'really, never?' He said that because a minute earlier Paige was asking about us."

He gives me a look like he can't see where I'm going with this.

"She asked if I thought it was weird, about your hair and stuff. I said I'd never seen you without your hat on, and that's where Chris got the idea to…" I gesture to his hat.

"To try to rip it off me?"

"Yeah."

Jem bows his head back against my front. "It's not your fault. Elwood has been a dick to me before."

"He has?"

He nods against me. I put my arms around him and rub the stretch of back between his shoulder blades.

"Last fall, I was out of the hospital but still highly susceptible to infection. I'd missed a lot of school, so I needed to go. But I was in such rough shape I had to wear one of those blue surgical masks around people." Jem snorts self-deprecatingly at the memory. "You remember how Michael Jackson used to walk around in those masks sometimes? Elwood started a joke that I was hiding a botched nose job."

"No one would be dumb enough to buy that."

"They didn't *believe* it, they just thought the notion was funny. It was one big joke."

"Could have been worse, I guess." I stroke the nape of his neck. "Remember when Britney Spears shaved her head? You could have got saddled with that comparison."

"Not funny, Willa."

"Well when it comes down to it, it's just Chris Elwood, and who the hell gives a shit about him anyway?" The corner of his mouth twitches up in a sort of smile. It always does cheer him up to listen to me bash Elwood.

"I still feel bad, though. I shouldn't have been talking about our business with Paige. Elwood would have never got the idea."

"Why was Paige asking?"

"She wanted to know if I feel deprived because I can't run my hands through your hair," I say with a laugh. It's such a frivolous notion. Only someone like Paige would take it so seriously.

"Do you?"

"No."

"It's growing back," he says shyly.

"Can I see?" I know he's going to say no, but I guess I'm a sucker for rejection.

"Does it bug you that I insist on keeping my hat on around you?"

"No. It makes you comfortable. You don't have to take it off."

"What did Paige think when you'd told her you'd never seen me without it?"

I shrug. "I don't know. I think she was surprised that I've never seen your head."

Jem reaches up and grabs the top of his toque. He pulls it off slowly, staring at the ground, and sets the hat on his knee. "Now you have."

At first it's shocking. The pale skin of his forehead just keeps going where I'm used to seeing the color and texture of a toque. I can see the bones of his skull and the veins beneath the skin. He doesn't have a defined hairline yet, but what hair he does have exists in patches. The hairs are matted by his hat and stick to his head, a quarter of an inch long and spaced randomly. They're baby fine and deep red, like the color of sweet potato skin.

"Huh." I pull off a glove and run my hand over the smooth skin, feeling the slight tickle of his fine hairs.

"What do you think?" His eyes are still on the floor and his tone is laced with something resembling dread.

"Do you really want to know?"

For a split second his face shows absolute pain, and then goes stony blank as he pulls his hat back on. Jem buries his face in my front and wraps his arms tight around my hips and waist.

"You don't have to stay if you don't want to," he says softly. That almost makes me laugh. How could I leave, held in a vice grip like this? Or maybe he means that I should leave him altogether.

"You can't get rid of me that easily." I pet the wool around his scalp. When I push his hat back again, Jem flinches and presses his face tighter against my front, hiding.

"Do you really want to know?" I ask again.

Jem shakes his head. The hairs under my hand feel as fine as a newborn's. I pet his head against the grain and the slightly damp strands stick up like feathers. I shape a little Mohawk with what's there and giggle at my fun.

"Don't laugh at me."

"I'm not. Let me have my fun, damn it." I bend my face down to the top of his head and nuzzle him. His hair tickles my lips and nose. "You feel like a kitten."

Jem snorts. "A freaking kitten."

"Was it always this dark?" I remember it being brighter red in the picture downstairs, but it could have been the lighting.

"Yeah."

I slide my butt off the edge of the desk and step down onto the floor. Jem lets go immediately, like I'm trying to leave. I'm only moving from the desk to sit on his lap facing him. I fold him into another hug and he rests his head on my shoulder with a sigh.

"I know you don't really want to know, but I think this change in you is beautiful. You're really getting better."

"It's gross," he whispers.

"It's cute." I like the feel of his hair, all soft and fluffy with newness. I run my hand over the bare patch at his crown and find that it isn't actually bald—the hair there is just shorter than the rest and very pale blond. It's the first growth. Those hairs will fall out eventually and grow back in with color. The other bald patch—which really is a bald patch—is behind his left ear. I wonder if that's a radiation burn or just a cluster of follicles that are slow to wake up.

"Maybe Paige was right," I say as I play with his wisps. "This is pretty fun."

"Oh shut up," he scolds me softly.

"Will you leave the hat off more often?"

"Not here," he says, and shifts his shoulders uncomfortably. "It upsets Mom. And I don't want *anyone* else to see." His own admission troubles him and he frowns. "I'm sorry."

"It's fine." I give him a kiss. "It'll be our thing."

The bedroom door opens suddenly and Dr. Harper walks in, already speaking. He stops mid-sentence and stares at us while we stare back, each of us dumbfounded and unsure of what to do or say. Can we write this compromising position off as he-tripped-and-I-fell?

Finally, without saying anything, Dr. Harper turns and closes the door behind him.

"Crap," Jem mutters. He pulls away a little and reaches for his hat. "We should go downstairs."

"I didn't get you in more trouble, did I?"

"No, I think it just surprised him. He's used to this kind of thing from Eric, not from me." Jem smiles shyly at that, and takes my hand for the walk downstairs.

⌣

"Do you want food?" I ask. It's only four-thirty and I don't have to be at work until six. Jem accepts and Elise scurries in from the living room. "Me too?" she pleads.

Jem goes to his cello, which is a much healthier method for venting, and Elise and I start peeling apples from the bag in the fridge. We're making applesauce—with a side of frozen yogurt, if the mood strikes. I use honey instead of sugar for Jem's sake, and try to teach Elise how to taste-test over heat without being a wimp about the temperature.

"Roll it on your tongue."

"That just burns more of the tongue," she whines.

"Wuss." Her brothers must have conditioned her to that word, because she takes it as a challenge and tastes the next stage of the sauce without even making a face.

"Good girl."

As soon as the smell of cooking apples becomes obvious, Eric appears. He tells us it smells good and hovers obnoxiously close to the stove, trying to sneak a taste.

"Go away," Elise shoos him. "We'll call you when it's ready." The idea bulb flashes over Eric's face and he announces that he's running out to the store to buy Oreos. Apparently they go with applesauce.

The food conversation draws Jem away from the front room, probably out of paranoia that Eric will hog whatever Elise and I make. He wraps his arms

483

around my waist from behind and asks what's on the menu.

"Applesauce." I take a potato masher out of the drawer and start pulverizing the cooked apple chunks.

"Applesauce?" I can't quite measure his tone. I look over my shoulder in time to see him swallow and clamp a hand around his mouth and nose. He bolts down the hall toward the downstairs bathroom.

"Shit." I cover the pot with a lid and open the kitchen window to vent the smell of cooked apples. I didn't know it would nauseate him.

"Aw, crap," Elise mutters, and smacks her palm to her forehead. "Applesauce." She looks genuinely worried.

"What's with applesauce?"

"There was a...thing, with Meira and applesauce. I'd forgot all about it." Elise looks over her shoulder toward the bathroom. "Otherwise I'd have suggested something else."

I sigh and pull out the kettle to start mint tea for when Jem gets out of the bathroom. I owe him an apology and something to settle his stomach.

"He was like that even before he got sick, you know," Elise says quietly.

"What?"

"Anything big put his gut in knots. He used to be sick to his stomach before every music recital, even though once he was on stage everything went beautifully." I'm not sure why, but his insecurity is almost endearing.

"I'll finish the sauce for Eric," Elise says. "You'll keep Jem occupied?"

"Of course."

When Jem comes out of the bathroom he's startled to see me on the other side of the hall, waiting for him. "How long were you standing there?"

"Only a moment." I hold out the mug of mint tea. "For your stomach. It's lukewarm." I only wish I had a bit of ginger syrup to add to it.

Jem accepts the mug and shifts uncomfortably. "I didn't mean to be rude. I'm sure the applesauce is really good."

"I didn't mean to make you sick."

"It's not your fault."

"I'll come to the funeral tomorrow, alright?"

Jem sighs and folds me into a hug. He buries his face in my hair and takes a steadying breath. "Please keep that promise."

"Of course I will." Someday I will need something from him, and I have no right to ask unless I'm there when he needs me. "You could have asked."

"You didn't know her." Jem's finger winds a lock of my hair behind my head.

"Funerals aren't for the dead."

Jem snorts like my remark is somehow funny. "What was your sister's like?" he whispers. No one has ever asked me that before, and I don't have an answer because I didn't attend the funeral. But I don't want to think about my own woes at the moment.

"Come on." I pull back from the hug and take Jem's hand. "I'll tell you some other day. Enough sadness. Time for music."

⸎

Work is a little bit tense. I'm delegated the task of manning the front desk to-night while Chris handles the back room tasks—washing dishes, mopping the kitchen floor, etc. All in the interest of hiding his freshly swollen lip, of course. His parents wouldn't let him off work for the night. I think they just wanted to punish him for picking on the kid with cancer.

"How was detention?" I ask.

Chris has a hard time frowning with a busted lip, so he narrows his eyes and curtly replies, "Fine."

I eye his lip and tell him, "It probably wouldn't have swollen up so bad if you hadn't broken the fall with your face."

"Thanks," he says dryly, and turns around to mop the pantry. "Tell Harper to learn to take a joke."

Because shame is simply hilarious.

⸎

Frank is still awake when I get home, sitting in front of the evening news. He asks me how work was and then starts to complain about too much *sun* in the five-day weather forecast, for crying out loud.

Frank has been around more often lately, and I think boredom is wearing on him. There was no get-together with Doug this weekend. He hasn't been down to Doug's place once, and I haven't heard them talking on the phone either. I guess it's awkward since he confronted Luke about coming on to me. I've screwed up someone else's life all over again.

I wonder if Doug said Frank was unwelcome, or if he's staying away of his own volition. Maybe he doesn't know how to handle the tension, or maybe he's got some misguided notion of solidarity with me, victim girl.

Regardless, his constant presence is driving me crazy. My brother is easiest to live with when he's never home.

"So, since it's going to be a nice weekend," I hint, "got a hike planned?"

Frank just grunts noncommittally. That's a no. I'll have to make plans to stay out of his way this weekend.

"I'm going to bed."

"G'night."

Then I remember that I meant to ask him something. I stop on the lowest stair and turn back to the living room. "I'm signing out of my afternoon classes tomorrow. Just letting you know."

"What for?"

"Personal reasons."

485

"What for?" Frank repeats in a slower voice, like I'm an idiot.

"A funeral."

The way Frank looks at me, I'm sure he's going to say no. "Whose?" he asks.

"Her name's Meira." I tell him that I knew her from my volunteer work at the hospital, since Frank is hostile to all things associated with Jem.

"I don't think you should miss school."

"This is important to me."

"So is your education."

I smile. "Dude, I don't need your permission to leave school."

Frank grumbles under his breath, which is the closest thing I'm going to get to agreement.

"Do you miss him? Is that why you're grumpy?"

Frank gives me a crusty look. "Get some sleep, Will."

Tuesday

It's not so hard to find something appropriate to wear to the funeral. My closet is wall-to-wall black and grey. Today is different, though, because I walk out of the house without a pair of gloves on. It feels strange and I debate he decision all the way to my car, but by the time I pull onto the road I've decided that there's no going back. Call it a misguided show of solidarity.

I get questions about the deep scar on my hand all day, but it isn't until lunch hour that Elwood sees the mark. He gives me a probing look and asks how I hurt my hand.

I extend my left hand toward him with only one finger raised. "None of your business. Just thought I'd show it off before you decided my gloves needed to be ripped off of me."

Elwood looks like he wants to choke me. "It was a joke."

"And it was as funny as cancer," I agree.

Elise is going to Meira's funeral, but Eric declines. Mrs. Harper picks me and Elise up from school after lunch. I lean across the back seat to hug Jem and find that he smells strongly of mint. I don't want to know what his stomach has been up to today.

"You okay?" I ask. He looks like he hasn't slept well.

"Sit in the middle seat?" he whispers. I buckle into that narrow space that can hardly be called a seat so that we can be close. Jem lays his head against mine and I encourage him to sleep a little on the drive.

"I'm not tired," he lies.

"Suit yourself." I take his hand off my knee and try to relax him with a massage. It worked when he was upset about Emily's visit. The tension gradually leaves him as I work my thumbs along his palm and stroke the sensitive skin between each finger. I try to avoid tugging on the scars around his knuckles as I rotate his fingers, which seem so long compared to mine. He has the nails of a cellist.

Jem leans on me more and I look up, expecting to find him angling in for a kiss, but he isn't. He feels heavier only because he's inert with sleep. Ivy looks at us in the rearview and smiles privately.

"He didn't sleep well last night."

"Nightmares," Elise adds.

I hate to wake him up when we get to the church, but attending his friend's funeral is important to him.

"Do you think this is a bad idea?" he says quietly as we head toward the church.

"Why would it be?"

"Her family." He swallows nervously. "We were in treatment together. She died…and I didn't." He's worried they'll resent him for surviving. I squeeze his hand and tell him not to worry.

"It'll mean something that you came to pay your respects."

Meira's visitation and funeral are being held back-to-back at the Lutheran church. She's laid out at the front of the altar, surrounded by flower arrangements, with mourners filing past her family on their way to pay their last respects. The four of us join the line to offer condolences to Meira's family. Her mom knows all the Harpers by name and thanks them for coming. The boy next to her, young enough to be Meira's brother, doesn't say anything. He looks as though he'd rather be anywhere else.

I don't know what I was expecting, but the name 'Meira' sounds so traditional that it doesn't seem to fit the girl in the casket—which is crimson red and lined with black satin. She's so small she could pass for twelve years old. I can see the embalmer used dye to make her skin look less yellow, but the effect isn't that obvious and she looks really pretty, for a dead girl. She's sort of goth, with black liner around her lids and deep purple lipstick.

"She hated wigs," Jem mutters, looking at the blonde curls they've put on her.

"She seems kind of badass." That makes Jem smile.

"You have no idea."

I always thought cremation was weird, but I still think burial is weirder. I researched it when I looked up corpse disposal after Tessa died—the body is sliced strategically to drain the blood; a giant spike with a vacuum hose attached is used to suck the semi-digested food and fluid out of the abdomen; the mouth is flushed out before being glued shut, and then embalming starts. The formaldehyde comes in a range of colors that the mortician can select to hide the graying flesh and make each individual skin tone look 'natural.' In preserving a corpse for however short a time, they have to practically mutilate it and then hide the fact that it was ever touched.

Meira's fingernails are painted black, probably to hide the jaundiced look of them. I touch her hand and Jem gasps at me like I've done something blasphemous.

"What?"

He just turns away and goes to find a seat in the pews. I guess he's a little weird about death, for understandable reasons.

The funeral mass starts promptly at one. And it is *weird*. Meira recorded a farewell video before she died, and they play it on a projector screen near the pulpit in place of a eulogy. She has a very dry sense of humor, and I start to regret that I never met her while she was alive. Elise and Ivy both tear up, and I'm surprised that Jem isn't more emotional. He looks very beaten down, like a tired man at the end of his rope, and I remember what that feels like, when it's all just too damn sad to cry.

Meira is buried in the cemetery behind the church after the service. The funeral directors have covered the pile of displaced with dirt with Astroturf, as if that'll soften the blow. Meira's red casket is even more vibrant under the grey sky and amid the sea of black clothing. The minister does his ashes-to-ashes bit, and she's lowered into the ground.

Elise points out her headstone. Under Meira's name and dates are the words: *In a hundred years, they'll say she could have been cured.* I wonder what Meira's mom thought of her daughter's headstone design.

It's morbid, but I wonder what mine will say.

⚘

Ivy says she'll take me back to school to get my car from the parking lot, and invites me to drive back to their house for a visit. I ask Jem if he's up for company, because he doesn't look like he is.

"No." Jem shakes his head. "I'm tired. My head is starting to hurt. I'm just going to nap the rest of the afternoon."

"Okay." I let him rest his head on my lap for the drive back to the school. Maybe his three-day suspension is a blessing in disguise. It gives him time to deal with his problems and get some proper rest.

"Hey," I whisper to him. Jem turns his head on my lap to look up at me. "'A Million Dollars,' Joel Plaskett."

Jem takes the back of my hand and kisses my knuckles. His eyes close with a contented sigh. "Thanks," he murmurs so quietly I can barely hear. "You're exactly what I need, right when I need it." It's only when he has to let go of my hand that he notices. "You're not wearing gloves."

Jem: June 6 to 7

Tuesday

What the hell does one wear to a funeral in the middle of the day? I hate wearing ties, but a dress shirt seems appropriate, given the circumstances. I wear my black toque out of respect. What am I going to say to Meira's mother?

I'm sorry she was so unlucky.

I need to see Willa. It's irrational, but she soothes me better than music. I have a whole hour to wait before Mom and I pick her and Elise up from school, and I can barely stand it. Eric has declined to go to the funeral, even though it means an afternoon free of classes. Eric is weird about funerals—my fault.

Mom pokes her head into my room. "Did you eat yet?"

"Yeah." I didn't. I tried to eat a Jell-O cup and my stomach wouldn't let me.

I hope it's not an open casket. I hate open casket funerals. I don't want to have to look at Meira like that.

Mom steps into the room and begins to pick at my black button down. She tells me to tuck it in more so it won't look so baggy. This shirt hangs on me horribly.

"I'll change." I have a black sweater I can wear instead. Mom leaves and I shed my shirt. The black sweater was a gift from Elise—obviously, because there's no way I would ever buy a turtleneck of my own free will. I hate turtlenecks, something I conveniently remember just as I pull it over my head. Putting these things on stirs some latent memory of being squeezed through a vagina. Once was enough.

"Won't you be too warm?" Mom asks when I come downstairs.

"When am I ever too warm these days?" If everyone is comfortable with the temperature, chances are I'll be complaining of cold.

"Come on." She wraps an arm around my waist as we head out to the car. "You look very nice."

"You too." I give her a sideways squeeze. She's done a good job of keeping it together today, but I heard her crying last night when she couldn't sleep. I know she's thinking about how easily it could have been me in Meira's position.

I thought about that when I was at my sickest—what it would do to my family if I died. Some days that was all that kept me going, knowing that it would hurt them if I quit. I don't want to imagine what Meira's family is going through right now, because it's too easy to imagine my parents and Elise and Eric going through the same agony. What am I going to say when I see them?

I'm sorry there was no miracle for her.

☙

We pick up Elise and Willa at the school, and my nerves settle for thirty blissful minutes while I have Willa close to me. I doze off by accident and she wakes me up in the parking lot of the church with a kiss.

I don't want to go inside. It was a bad idea to come.

"Come on." Willa takes my hand and leads me out of the car. I shouldn't have slept on the way here. I haven't thought of anything to say yet.

I look around the parking lot and see another family I recognize, heading toward the church. It's Mrs. Sumner and her two boys. I met her daughter, Rachel, on the ward. I wonder if she's still there, or maybe she recovered, or maybe she's dead, too, and I just didn't hear about it.

These people won't want to see me. I'll remind them of what their kids went through and what could have happened if cancer hadn't killed them.

"Do you think this is a bad idea?" I ask Willa, wanting more than anything for her to talk me out of it.

"Why would it be?"

"Her family. We were in treatment together. She died…and I didn't."

Willa squeezes my hand and gives me an understanding smile. "It'll mean something that you came to pay your respects."

I think I'm squeezing her hand too tightly, but she doesn't complain. I hold onto it for dear life and try to breathe. This is the right thing to do—to pay my respects to Meira. But funerals aren't for the dead.

It helps that Willa is so calm. She walks into the church with confidence and holds me in place when I want to bolt. Then I remember that this must be hard for her too. She's dealt with death, and if her consistently black wardrobe is any indication, she's still in mourning. I try to refocus.

Mom goes up to Meira's family first and shakes her mother's hand.

"Ivy. Elise." I'm surprised she still remembers their names. "Thank you for coming."

"I'm sorry for your loss."

Is that all I have to say? Or should I say something…more? I shake her mother's trembling hand and murmur, "I'm sorry."

"I'm glad you're well," she says, and I'm surprised by her sincerity. I thought she would hate the sight of me.

We move out of the way to let the next mourners greet the family and make our way up the aisle to approach Meira's body. Evidence of Meira's personality is all over the church, from the purple calla lily arrangements to the color of the casket. She clearly had this well planned.

At first I think it can't be Meira, with the makeup and the blonde curls. That girl looks beautiful, and I'm used to seeing Meira at her physical worst.

"She hated wigs." I wonder if it was Meira's or her mom's idea to bury her with china doll hair. The wig fits well, so maybe she bought it while she was still alive and asked to be made presentable for the visitation.

"She seems kind of badass," Willa says. That's one way to describe her, and

I can't help but smile.

"You have no idea."

It's her stillness that makes her so strange. There's a complete absence of small movements—the rise and fall of breath, the subtle twitches of skin and pulse. She's not Meira, the person; she's Meira, the thing.

Willa reaches out and touches her hand. Jesus Christ. Just imagining the cold, lifeless feel of her skin makes mine crawl, and I have to look away. Willa takes a minute to follow me to the pew. I don't want to look over my shoulder and see her hand lingering on Meira's dead one. It's creepy, and part of me is unreasonably upset that Willa would even think to do that. She has no right to touch the body of someone she never even met.

The opening hymn is "How Great Thou Art," which seems distinctly un-Meira. Maybe the minister wouldn't let anything other than traditional hymns be played for the service. The minister gets up and welcomes everyone to the church, and announces that Meira will be saying her own parting words.

I reach over to take Willa's hand, wondering too late if it's the same hand she used to touch Meira.

The video eulogy is beyond uncomfortable. The girl lying up at the front of the room, inanimate and cold, speaks on a projector screen. She never lost her wicked sense of humor, right till the end. "Don't spend too much time mourning, okay?" she says. "I *know* you have better things to do, like salivate over the next Apple product release." Typical Meira. This was clearly filmed just a short time before her death. Signs of liver failure are obvious. Her pupils are unfocused by painkillers and even though she was sitting up and at home, she had a nasal cannula fitted under her nose. Occasionally there are short blips in the film that suggest it had to be shot as a series of several takes, giving her time to rest in between. Meira thanks everyone who helped her in some way when she was sick—her nurses and doctors and the friends who stuck by her through the shit times.

"Don't waste your life. You never know when, or by whom, it could be changed forever or snatched away." She deadpans after that punch to the gut, and after a long pause she winks. The video cuts out, and it's over. After a short blessing, the pallbearers get up from the pew to take her out to the cemetery. Meira is carried out to the warbling tune of "Make Me A Channel of Your Peace." Either she designed the music program for her funeral during a sudden fit of repentance, or she was trying to be ironic.

I drift out to the cemetery, caught up in the flow of the crowd and towed along by Willa and Elise. My sister leans on my arm, crying softly. Willa holds my hand, and therefore holds me together, observing everything and everyone with her keen eye. I wonder what she's thinking.

"Ashes to ashes, and dust to dust." The minister sprinkles dirt and holy water on the casket. Meira's family place white roses atop the scarlet wood, and then the funeral director lowers her down.

"Look," Elise whispers, and points to the headstone. *In a hundred years, they'll say she could have been cured.* Lord, I hope so. I wish it could have come in time for her.

⌁

I try to nap when I get home, tired as I am, but I can't sleep. I feel restless and slightly exposed, like I've forgotten to do something important but can't remember what it is. I play Willa's music suggestion and it relaxes me some, but I still can't fall asleep, and the minute I know class lets out I send her a text.

Can't sleep. Need music ideas.

Don't sleep, she sends back. *Your head's too full. Get up and do something to tire yourself out.*

Great load of help she is.

Sweatpants on, Jell-O out, TV on. Watching TV can be tiring, right? At least it'll keep me out of my allegedly full head. Elise comes home and curls up under the couch blanket with me to watch a *Band of Brothers* marathon. Elise is totally the wrong person to watch this with, but at the moment I really don't care. After squealing "Ohmigod Ross!" when Captain Sobel comes on screen, I'm implored upon to close caption the entire episode for her.

"Who's that?" She asks that question every time a guy in uniform comes on screen. Apparently she can't keep track of faces.

"I don't get it." She says that a lot, along with other inane questions. "Is this set in World War I or II? So they're in the Air Force? Why are they jumping out of planes if they aren't in the Air Force?" Elise sticks it out for two episodes before her ADHD gets the best of her and she quits. I spread out into her body-warmed part of the couch after she leaves, and not long after Mom reminds me to take my meds. My head hurts, so I put off weaning and take a full dose of Oxy. Turns out this show is even better when I'm high.

Two episodes go by before the buzz wears off and I trust myself to stand up. I get up for another cup of Jell-O, only to find Elise in the kitchen with the cupboard open, trying to reach a box of crackers down from the top shelf. There's a logical flaw in her methodology, however, because the shelf is about seven feet off the ground and Elise isn't even five feet tall—and she's jumping up and down, trying to reach the crackers. I refuse to believe that I share DNA with a creature too dumb to use a step stool.

I reach up and grab the crackers.

"Thanks," she says, and quits hopping. I put the box on top of the fridge instead and walk away.

"Jem!" She pouts. "You're a jerk." Elise goes up on her toes, trying to reach the box. Her little hand barely grazes the top of the freezer.

"You're right, I'm sorry." I push the box farther back from the edge.

Elise slaps my arm and declares a moratorium on milkshakes.

"I'm motivating you to grow," I argue.

She climbs onto the counter—using her head for the first time today—and goes for the crackers.

"Mom! Elise has her feet on the counter!"

"Jem's being mean to me!" Elise counters.

The office door opens and Mom pokes her head out. There are four pencils in her hair—not a good sign. "Is anybody bleeding?" she asks gravely.

"No."

"Good." She shuts her office door firmly. Best tread lightly until she starts singing at work again.

⇜

I try to nap again after dinner, hoping a stomach full of soup will help me sleep. It doesn't. My brain won't shut up and that niggling feeling is back. I run through mental lists, looking for something I may have forgotten. Medication? Homework? Promises?

Elise comes into my room and crawls onto the bed. She fits herself in close behind me, trying to spoon with her much smaller body. It feels comfortable to have someone else close by, and the way she gently strokes my upper arm for warmth. I get the feeling that she's lulling me into a false sense of security before exacting her revenge for the cracker incident.

"You okay?" I hedge. I shouldn't assume the worst of my sister. Maybe she needs to talk. About life, or about Meira and death.

"Fine," she murmurs. "I just don't want you to have more nightmares." She hugs me and I mutter an apology for picking on her shortness.

"Just wait until I hit my growth spurt," she says indignantly. I stifle a yawn and she encourages me to sleep. "I'll stay while you do."

I want to tell her not to bother, but Elise might have a point—some company would be nice, if I'm going to dream about Meira, cold and still and underground. It pinches the ol' ego some, needing another person to fall asleep. Maybe I'm just one big lump of need. What have I given back to anyone lately?

"Do you need anything?" I ask Elise. She hums and pretends to ponder.

"A fake ID?" She's trying to get on my nerves.

"Fat load of good it'd do you. You couldn't pass for nineteen at a hundred yards on a dark night."

"Still."

"You don't need a fake ID. You're a good girl." Who will never get as wasted as her bad-influence older brothers or let any guy touch her below the neck.

"You have one," she says slyly.

"Why were you going through my wallet?"

"You don't keep it in your wallet."

Damn it.

So I change the subject. "I can't sleep."

Elise hums a little, testing out melodies in her throat. Mom comes in to check on me and finds us curled together. Lucky for me, she doesn't tell Elise to leave me alone.

"Do you guys remember taking naps together when you were little?" she says. I don't know why she asks such questions; as if Elise or I could possibly remember anything that happened to us when we were toddlers.

"No, Mom."

"Terrible Twos," she says with a serious nod. "You guys wouldn't go down for a nap unless I tucked you in together, and there'd always be a fight over whose blankie was whose. Ten minutes later you'd be snuggling like best buddies."

I vaguely remember that. Elise was terribly jealous of my Batman blanket.

Mom gives us kisses and says she'll be just down the hall, researching in the library. Elise's breath is soft on the back of my neck, and there's something about being held that makes it easier to slip into sleep.

Elise's theory about company as the cure for nightmares goes bust. My first awareness of the dream is a bed I didn't fall asleep in, with the creepy hospital smell and guardrails on both sides of the mattress. The room's familiar lack of color and natural light make me feel cold and exposed. I'm tied down with tubes and wires that burrow under my skin, choking me, tethering me. I try to push them away and end up even more hopelessly tangled. Somewhere out of sight machines—the anchors of the tubes that tie me down—whir and beep and wheeze in gruesome compensation for my broken body.

I try to push some of the tubes away and they burrow deeper into my skin like live snakes.

"You shouldn't do that."

I look up to find Meira at the end of the hospital bed. She leans over the footboard and smirks at me with her black-painted lips. Her gothic eyes leer at me.

"That's all that's keeping you alive." She points to the tubes, and her hand is all bones. She's wasting away in front of me.

"You're living on poison." Meira laughs at me. "Which poison is gonna kill you first, huh?"

She crawls onto the bed, wading through the sea of tubes and heedlessly stepping on my limbs. I'm invisible between the weight of the machines that simultaneously live for and kill me.

"Don't even bother breathing." She steals the nasal cannula from under my nose. Other tubes replace it, gagging me. Meira reaches for the port in my chest.

"No!"

Meira tears it out at the root and I jerk awake with the cold taste of fear in my mouth. Elise has her arms around me, frantically murmuring, "It was only a dream. It wasn't real."

It felt real. My hands are shaking and I think that whimpering, gasping sound is coming from me. I roll away from Elise and pull my shirt up. For once I'm happy to see and touch the central line in my chest.

"Lower your head," Elise says. "You've got to calm down." She makes me kneel forward and put my head down. I try to breathe evenly with her, but I have no control. My body is in the hands of someone else; someone who wants to fuck with me—God or Meira or someone else, but not me.

Elise gets off the bed and when I call her back to me my voice breaks on a sob. I can't be alone right now.

"Mom!" Elise calls, and wraps her arms around me. "It's okay," she says. "I'm not going anywhere."

Too many times I've done this—buried my face against my sister and cried like a fucking baby. Mom's arms wrap around me from behind, encircling both Elise and I.

"What's the matter?" she murmurs in her gentle, mothering tone; the one she used when we came to her with cuts and scrapes as kids.

"Bad dream," Elise says.

Mom kisses my head and shoulders. "You're safe, hon."

It could have just as easily been me.

⌖

Insomnia keeps both me and Mom awake well into the night. We can't sleep for the same reasons, but we don't talk about them. We sit in the kitchen with green tea and talk about inconsequential stuff like school and work.

"Willa does well in school, right?" Mom asks.

"Mid-to-high range marks," I agree.

"Does she want to be a chef?" she says with a knowing smile. The passion Willa has for food is obvious even to the casual observer. There's real love in it, for the craft and for the people she feeds.

"I'm so happy she got you to eat soup," Mom says, and squeezes my hand.

"She used to cook for her sister, you know."

"Oh?" I fill Mom in on the story of Thomasina, how I'm not the first cancer patient Willa has been close to. I leave out the part about assisted suicide, the psych detainment and the suicide attempt, because that's stuff Mom doesn't need to know. She has worried enough for one lifetime, and I want her to think well of Willa.

"She's a very strong young woman," Mom says lowly. Her eyes are fixed on something distant as she traces the lip of her mug. "I had wondered."

"About what?"

"Most teenage girls are shallow," she says, and takes a sip of tea. "I wondered why she was so at ease with the fact that you're still recovering."

I want to tell Mom that she's more than at ease. Willa thinks I'm beautiful.

Isn't that something?

Dude, there's a whole herd of flying pigs out back.

The clock on the stove beeps at midnight and Mom says, "You should try to get some rest, sweetie."

I shake my head. I'm too scared to fall asleep again, knowing that haunted dreams will ruin a perfectly peaceful night.

"Do you want some warm milk?" she offers. "A sleeping pill?"

"No, thanks." I tried one of her pills before, out of curiosity. The sudden, overpowering crash reminded me of the health lecture on date rape drugs. I'm not keen to repeat that experience.

"I'll walk you upstairs." She puts an arm around my shoulders and steers me out of the kitchen. I don't have a choice in the matter.

Twice during the night I wake up with the feeling of eyes on me. I want to roll over and tell Mom to take her own advice and swallow a sedative, or apologize for upsetting her, but I do neither. I lay there and pretend to sleep until I slip under again, and when I wake for the third time with vague shadows of inde-cipherable nightmares still clinging to my lids, I'm alone. I hope Dad is taking care of her.

Wednesday

Day three of my suspension. I get to go back to school tomorrow and see Willa. That seems so far away right now, since time has a way of crawling when I wake up with a splitting headache. Several nights of lousy sleep are catching up with me in full force. I roll over and dig through my nightstand drawer for a spare bottle of Oxy—that's right, I have 'spare' narcotics. I try to swallow the pill but it sticks in my throat. My tongue is a little swollen and it hurts to swallow.

"Crap." That voice is too high to be mine. I poke around under my jaw and find my lymph nodes without effort. They're swollen. I'm sick.

"Shit, shit, shit." I get out of bed and tell myself that the achiness is no worse than it is on a normal day. I try to swallow more water and it only makes the pain in my throat worse. According to the clock it's seven a.m. My family is just waking up, but I don't have anywhere to be; if my headache hadn't woken me I'd have slept in till ten.

I head down the hall to Mom and Dad's room. Mom is in the shower, but luckily Dad is available. He looks up from buttoning his shirt and asks if I'm okay.

"My throat hurts." It's scary how fast he goes into doctor mode. He loses the expression of a concerned parent and adopts the look of a calculating clinician as he feels under my jaw and makes me show him the back of my throat.

"My head hurts, too."

He sits me down on the bed and takes my temperature. It's only half a degree above normal.

"That's promising," he says. "Your immune system is weaker than normal, but your fever is so low that I think you'll be okay. No need to worry." So why does he sound worried? "Have some orange juice and rest, okay? Call me if your symptoms change." He thinks it's probably viral, but if things get worse he'll take me to the clinic to get tested and pumped full of antibiotics. There's something to look forward to.

I head downstairs to find sick-food at Dad's suggestion. There are oranges in the fruit bowl, but I'm reluctant to eat them. When I reach for the orange juice as a gentler substitute, I find an empty carton in the fridge. Fuck you, Eric.

I go back to the oranges and consider making my own juice, but the result will probably have more acid than the store-bought stuff and will burn my tender throat. I'm already prone to mouth sores from high-acid foods, and having a swollen throat on top of that just adds insult to injury.

I grab the phone off the wall as Elise shuffles into the kitchen for coffee. If there's a way I can get vitamin C without hurting myself, Willa will probably have an idea.

"Hello?"

"Hey, it's me."

"What are you doing up this early? You get to sleep in."

"I'm sick."

There's a pause, and then Willa spits "Fuck," into the phone. "Do you think anyone would care if I murdered Diane in broad daylight?"

"Maybe."

"I'm tempted."

"I need to eat something with vitamin C."

"Oranges," she replies immediately.

"Oranges and I don't get along."

"Is it a heartburn problem?"

"Mouth sores."

"Do you have carrots in the fridge?" It's safe to say we do. Mom has been buying the five-pound bags at the grocery store ever since Willa got me hooked on vegetable soup.

Willa tells me to take out a pen and paper. She relays a recipe for carrot and orange soup over the phone. The way she uses vague terms of measurement makes it obvious that she's reciting the recipe from memory. Maybe it was a favorite of Thomasina's—or maybe 'a handful' of orange juice is an actual unit of measurement.

Willa makes me recite the recipe back to her to make sure I got it all.

"You can eat it cold, if your throat is too sore for hot foods."

"Thanks."

"Feel better, okay?"

"I'll try."

"Love you."

"Love you too."

She says she has to leave for school.

"Hey, Willa?"

"Yeah?"

"'Everything' by Morissette."

Willa chuckles shrewdly. "As in *Alanis* Morissette?"

"Maybe."

"I didn't figure you for a fan of angry-chick music."

"I'm not, Elise is."

"Sure."

"I'm serious."

"Enjoy your soup."

"Willa—"

She hangs up on me with a laugh. Cheeky imp.

Elise reaches across the counter and snatches up the recipe for soup. "What are we making?" She kindly helps me prepare the pot and ingredients. And by 'help' I mean she lets me sit down and juice oranges while she does the rest. Eric comes downstairs for breakfast, acting way too chipper for such an early hour, and asks what we're making. I'm still pissed at him for taking the last of the orange juice.

"I hope you shart in a socially devastating situation."

Elise's hysterical giggle is somewhere between a squawk and a snort.

"What's up his ass?" Eric asks her.

"He's crabby 'cause he has a cold." The words are barely out of her mouth before Mom comes downstairs and descends upon me, feeling my forehead for fever and making me show her my inflamed throat. She suggests that everyone wear mouth and nose masks around the house until I kick the infection, since I'm so fragile. I tell her that's not necessary—and completely humiliating—but my siblings support the idea. Fucking traitors.

Despite the aching in my throat and head, I try to make the most of a day in bed by catching up on my assigned reading. I'm three chapters behind schedule on *The Scarlet Letter*. That said, I really hate English. They make us read these classic novels as though anything in them is relevant to modern life. Like any of us need to know how to go about shaming and punishing an adulterer—Jerry Springer does that for us.

I stop to look at my bookmark a lot. I use Willa's photos for that purpose, mostly to motivate me to at least open the book once in a while. I love the one of her on her bike. I only wish I could see her face in that one. It makes me wonder if I'll ever see her ride that bike in real life, and I kind of like her reckless side. It makes her interesting.

Willa's other photo is in my nightstand drawer, tucked away and looked at only when I'm having an off moment. The snapshot was taken at her Group session, at a time when she was just as damaged as I am—and she got through it, is getting through it, in her weird way. If she can bounce back, I can too.

Sometimes I look at it and think about the faceless man sitting behind her in the wheelchair, and I tell myself that no one is ever going to hurt her like that again. Willa would probably call that stupid over-protectiveness; she doesn't like to admit that she's capable of feeling hurt. I know just how strongly she can feel—I've seen it, and the photo in my drawer is a private reminder to myself not to hurt her with the failures of my own stupid body.

Between looking at her photo and the medications settling in my system, I read about four pages of *The Scarlet Letter* before I pass out again. Screw it, I'll just watch the movie adaptation.

᳖

Dad calls from work at noon to check up on me. My symptoms haven't changed—still got a raging headache and sore throat. The fact that my nose isn't stuffed up seems to concern him. He promises to bring a swab kit home from work to sample the mucus at the back of my throat. Goodie.

"Have you been eating?"

"Soup," I tell him.

"How's your stomach?"

My headache and Oxy have a playdate right now, so my stomach is pretty pissed off at me. I've been working on the milkshake Elise left in the fridge for the past hour.

"It's fine."

"And your temperature?" He insists on waiting on the line while I take my temperature. It's one degree above normal. Dad goes through so many questions I wonder if he's working from a list, asking if I've cleaned my central line today and did the skin around the port show signs of inflammation or infection; have I noticed any bruising on my body; am I resting continuously or in short blocks?

"You're doing better than I expected," he says, and asks me to put Mom on the phone. While they talk I head upstairs to take a shower, because I lied to Dad when I said there was no bruising—I really don't know if there is or not. I'm still wearing the same pajamas I slept in last night and haven't bothered to look at my skin all morning.

Upstairs, with my bedroom door securely locked, I strip down and stand in front of the closet mirror, inspecting myself for marks. The air feels cold on my bare skin, but I persevere. I still can't look at my face in the mirror without cringing, but the reasons have changed—with the weight gain it's becoming easier to see the old me in him. It's like watching Frankenstein's Creature take shape, cobbled together of disjointed parts to make a hideous whole.

I take a shower with the water turned on too hot, trying to relax my aching muscles. The pleasure of it is cut short after only five minutes as the inescapable weight of cancer-fatigue creeps up my legs and spine, making the sluggishness of a head cold seem like a day at Disneyland. It's been nearly seven months— five or less of these miserable bastards to go, if the doctors are right and I really will adapt to the transplant. Somehow, I doubt it.

The walk from the bathroom to my bed is roughly ten feet. It might as well be ten miles, the way my feet drag and my shoulders want to collapse. I fall back onto the bed after a brutal trudge and consider just napping in my bathrobe. I lay there for a few minutes, too tired to even move the blankets over my body, before it becomes clear that the cotton bathrobe isn't going to keep me warm enough for comfort. And the dresser is a whole five feet away.

I reach over to the nightstand and pick up my phone. Thank God Eric doesn't have to work today. I call him and the phone rings just across the hall.

"What's wrong?" is his answer. He knows I wouldn't call him from one room away without a good reason.

"I need help." The words are barely out of my mouth before the doorknob rattles.

"Your door is locked."

"I'll open it." Might as well climb Everest while I'm at it. It takes me awhile just to get up off the bed, and the walk to the door is painstaking. Every muscle in my body is demanding that I quit. I unlock the door and Eric doesn't wait to push it open.

"What's the matter?" He can see I'm ready to drop and puts an arm around my ribs, lending me a shoulder and practically dragging me back to bed.

"Fatigue," I tell him.

"Should I call Dad?"

I feel bad for worrying him like this. Maybe it's the fact that he's wearing one of those stupid blue masks around me, but his eyes are even more piercing than usual.

"No, it's not the virus. Just regular transplant shit."

Eric squeezes my shoulder—ow—and sighs. "Let's get you dressed." My brother treats me well; I barely have to move as he helps me into pajamas and tucks me into bed. He even offers to set up a laptop on the nightstand so I can watch a movie while I rest.

"Thanks, but I'll just sleep it off." I feel bad that he's so good to me. Eric is normally an open book, but his face goes blank whenever he helps me with something personal or medical. Sometimes his eyes tighten when he looks at me and I know he's hiding disgust. I don't want to bother him more than is necessary.

"I'll let Mom know you're up here," he says. Eric goes to shut the blind and I ask him not to. I like the sunlight on my bed. It keeps me warm.

"Sure. Sleep well." He puts my cell phone on my pillow, just in case, and leaves me to rest.

"Thanks, bro."

⟜

When I wake up my head feels like a bowling ball and it is fucking *arctic* in here. I reach out a hand to grab my meds off the nightstand and why are they so far away? Come here. Come *here*, damn it. Misbehaving fucking pills.

My head feels like a bowling ball about to explode under pressure. I can't keep my eyes open. The light burns and what time is it? Waking or sleeping? School or weekend? I reach out a hand and the pills don't come any closer. Is that my hand? It can't be, it's too small.

Why is there no water? I had a glass of water. Eyes aren't open, that's why. Open them and it burns and my head feels like a bowling ball about to explode under the pressure of Niagara fucking Falls. So cold...wet. I had a glass of water. Why is there no water?

Sound hurts everything, even the places that shouldn't even have nerve endings. There's pressure in my chest, but not nearly as much as in my bowling-ball-bomb-under-the-falls skull. Open my eyes and light sears straight through my brain.

Cover my head. That hand is moist. It's heavy. Get it off the head, before it explodes and takes your hand with it. I knew a guy, once...

"Jem?"

Like it's that easy to trick me into opening my eyes. Keep them closed. Where's the water?

Blinding pain and arctic fucking cold. I have no head.

Metal on my tongue. Not this again. How many days this time? How much poison? No water, never mind, I'll just throw it up. Am I going to throw up? Is that why I can't breathe? Chest—stomach—chest?—where's the pain? Which of my overlapping aches spells trouble?

Drip, drip, drip down the back of my throat. My tongue is dry. My nose is bleeding backwards.

"Mom!" Sound shatters every nerve and how can my nose bleed when I don't have a head? Am I asleep? I can't taste the blood; my tongue is too dry. Water. Eyes open...

The shadow that blocks the sun can't see the blood. It's going to overflow my mouth. My swollen, dry tongue will choke it. The hand moves to make her understand—it didn't get blown off.

Drip. Drip. Look at it—it's right there. Blood. Blood. How much more chemo? Doesn't matter. Gonna bleed to death.

The shadow moves and the light blinds. Grab. Don't leave. It's soft and my head is going to explode again. Shattered in the cold.

501

"Willa." She knows about suffering. She'll see it going drip drip drip down my throat. Did she make me bleed?

"She's here." The shadow is lying. I know it like I know there's supposed to be water. Water and Niagara Falls and I knew a guy...

Elise: June 7 to 10

Wednesday the 7th of June. Windy.

We only crave
Peace
When we don't have it.
When it's shattered by the
Chaos
Of that thing called
Life.

Dad's Beatles compendium makes good homework music. I round off my English homework as John tells me to give peace a chance, and I close my books with a satisfied sigh.

I head down the hall to Jem's room, even if only to watch him sleep. He's been doing pretty well with his cold so far, even though his immune system is weak. There's nothing to be done for a virus except what Tylenol and orange juice can accomplish.

I find Jem curled up under his blanket like a mole in a hole. He coughs and I offer to get him some water as I circle the bed to face him.

Jem looks like death warmed over. Mom was just in here an hour ago. Why didn't she do something for him? He's shivering so badly that his teeth chatter and his skin is moist and clammy. He coughs again and won't open his eyes when I tell him to.

"You feel really warm." I go through his bathroom cabinet to find the thermometer and try to take his temperature. He keeps talking, saying "Poison, poison," and won't take the thermometer in his mouth. I have to hold his jaw like a dog's and support the thermometer under his tongue myself. He's burning up.

"Mom!"

When I push back Jem's blanket I find his pajamas and sheets soaked with sweat. Mom comes in, followed closely by Dad and Eric, and I can see by the look on her face that this isn't the way she left Jem an hour ago. His fever must have spiked rapidly.

I show Mom the thermometer. Jem is still muttering to himself, saying nonsensical things. His fever is so high that he's delirious.

"Stay with him." Mom takes me by the shoulders and stands me directly beside Jem while she runs to the kitchen. She comes back with a plastic bag and starts to collect his medication bottles to bring to the hospital. She'll need the obscenely huge binder with all his recent medical records, too.

Dad does a quick series of examinations: temperature, pulse, sweat pattern, eye clarity, and then announces that he's going to start the car and bring it around to the front door.

Eric dumps out Jem's backpack on the desk and starts to gather the comfort things he'll need if he's admitted to the hospital: pajamas, underwear, toothbrush…

Jem grabs the front of my t-shirt and twists. The heat of his fever has cracked the normally dry skin around his knuckles, and I get a few drops of blood on me. I can't understand much of what Jem says, but he's pretty insistent about his nonsense.

Eric tries to wrap him in a blanket for the trip to the hospital, but Jem's slow thrashing and his stubborn clinging to the front of my t-shirt make it difficult. He starts saying Willa's name in varying tones—first questioning, then with relief, and again with a sense of fearful urgency. Assuring him that she's right here is the only way to get him to stop wriggling, though he doesn't let go of my shirt. I have to pry his hand away one finger at a time so Eric can carry him downstairs. My temporary absence distresses him and he begins to whimper for me in between coughs. He asks Eric if I'm awake yet.

He's downright delirious—he thinks I'm still in the hospital.

"I'm right here," I tell him. It takes him all of about thirty seconds to forget and start asking again.

I open the rear door of Mom's car and crawl in first. Eric carefully sets Jem on the back seat and I hold him upright while we adjust the blanket and his position. His coughs are shallow and he's whimpering like he's in pain.

Mom takes the passenger seat and Dad drives. How many times are we going to have to make this drive to the hospital, four of us panicking while the fifth flirts with disaster?

⌘

Dad's job at the hospital helps with admission in the ER. He's a trauma surgeon; he works with these nurses and doctors every day. The RN that admits Jem knows my brother by sight. She's admitted him before, but he's usually a little more conscious.

There are no beds immediately available, so they park the hospital wheelchair we brought him in with at triage and take his blood pressure and temperature. The nurse has to lift his head for him and hold his jaw to keep the thermometer in place.

Mom, Eric, and I get pushed out into the waiting room, but not before the nurse announces to the on-call doctor that Jem's fever is at thirty-eight-point-six degrees. That's not so bad, if I put it in perspective. I was pushing forty degrees last winter before I lost consciousness. But I wasn't a cancer patient.

Dad insists on staying with Jem at triage, but can't do much about the nurses who direct the rest of the family into the waiting area.

This is the part I hate. These rooms, with their rows of chairs and outdated magazines and large clocks on the wall, are the home of helpless desperation.

This past year I have spent far too much time sitting in these rooms, feeling useless, waiting to hear news about my brother. Why can't *Obliviate* work in real life?

Mom starts to cry and Eric folds her into a hug.

"I'm going to go get coffee."

✧

The hospital cafeteria has a limited menu at this time of night. All the dinner items are long sold out. I pour myself a large Styrofoam cup of coffee and grab a seat near the window. I don't want to go back to the waiting room yet, even though I know that in five minutes, the possibility of missing important news will drive me back to Mom and Eric.

Coffee is my good luck charm. Whenever I have to wait for news like this, I have a cuppa and take an extra Ritalin to balance the jolt. It sounds stupid, but it's a ritual that has, thus far, yielded pretty good results. I think I had an entire pot to myself when I was waiting to hear if I was a suitable donor for Jem. I had unbelievably good luck that day.

I finish one cup and buy another. I use the last of my spare change on the coffee and a blueberry scone for Eric. I take it back to the waiting room to find that nothing has changed.

"How much have you had?" Eric nods to my coffee cup as I hand him the scone.

"One and a half."

"Should you be having caffeine right now?" He nods to the double doors that separate the waiting area from the emergency room.

"Damn," I mutter, and hand the cup to him to finish it. If the doctors tap me for a donation, Jem is going to get quite a jolt off it. Elise Juice comes laced with Ritalin and caffeine, on tap and a perfect thirty-seven degrees.

"Have you eaten?" Eric holds out the scone to me. I take a bite and give the rest back to him. "You're one tough chick, you know that?" he says to me, and then eats the remainder of the scone in one bite. This is harder on him than it is on me, I think. I'm not entirely helpless. I can keep myself healthy, in ready shape to be a harvest zone for spare parts. I'm tough enough to keep taking it—the healthy lifestyle, the threat of being sliced open, the pain and infections, etc. It's easier to focus and do that than it is to sit here, doing nothing. Jem and I are bonded by the shared medical consequences of his diagnosis. And Eric... he's the solid foundation of this family that we all take for granted far too often.

"Thanks, bro."

He gives me a dollar and tells me to go buy some orange juice. Eric is my homeboy. Jem is my hero.

Thursday the 8th of June. Sunny.

Thousands of droplets
Hit the windows every minute
But the only ones I hear are the
Drip
Drip
Drip
Of the IV

The ride to school doesn't feel complete without Jem stretched out across the back seat. I miss his snoring and brooding and complaining. When we pull into the parking lot I see Willa leave her car to come join us. She doesn't know what happened to Jem yet.

Eric and I turn to each other and extend fists. We Rock-Paper-Scissors for who has to tell her. Eric loses.

When Willa approaches the car he starts off by giving her a hug. Way to tip her off to bad news, bro.

"I guess he's still feeling sick?" she says.

"We had to take him to the hospital last night. His fever spiked."

There's something comforting about the fact that Willa doesn't immediately panic.

"Did they admit him?"

"He spent the night."

"I guess it's not just a cold, then?"

Eric shrugs. "Jem's fragile."

"Should I try to visit?"

Eric shakes his head, trying to be casual about it. "They're trying to limit his exposure to people while he's sick. And it's not that bad. He'll probably be home late today or maybe tomorrow." That's a lie; we don't know when Jem is coming home. His condition still isn't much improved, apart from the fever. He's developed a cough and can barely speak, his voice is so hoarse.

"You'll keep me posted?"

"Of course." Eric gives Willa another awkward hug and holy crap, what is that mark on her hand? She leaves to go inside with her head down.

I round on Eric once she's out of earshot. "Why did you say that? He won't be home today," I hiss. Eric doesn't even look at me. He's watching Willa's back with an uncharacteristically thoughtful expression.

"I didn't want to scare her, or for her to change her mind about him."

"Willa wouldn't do that."

Eric just shrugs. He doesn't trust Willa to stay, because he wouldn't if he had any choice in the matter.

Eric drives me over to the hospital during lunch period. I want to visit Jem. I wanted to see him last night, but the staff didn't think it was a good idea to let visitors in so late. Unfortunately, Mom and Dad agreed, and I've had to wait patiently for the past twelve hours. I do not cope well with patience.

Eric declines to join me.

"What's he going to think if you don't come?"

"I'll see him later."

"But—"

"Go on, Lise, you're wasting lunch hour. I'll wait in the parking lot." When I persist he claims to have a test this afternoon that he needs to study for. He even has his Chemistry text with him as evidence. I quit busting his balls about it, even though I don't believe him. Eric never studies—he's one of those people who can do well without having to try too hard. This test, if there is indeed a test, is just a convenient excuse to avoid visiting Jem.

I sign in as a visitor and dutifully sanitize my hands and don a mask. Standard operating procedure. I actually kind of like the packaged smell of these masks, now.

As I head down the ward I see Mom in room 204, speaking quietly with another mother. The other woman is crying and Mom is holding her hand. Must be a new patient on the ward; a new family to commiserate with. If Mom is there it must mean that Jem's sleeping, so I enter his room as quietly as possible.

I find Jem asleep, half on his side and breathing loudly. One of his feet pokes out from under the blanket. I cover it and pull a chair up beside him. It makes me feel better just being close to him. I can relax knowing that he's relatively okay (read: breathing).

He doesn't wake up when I set my notebook on the edge of his mattress and use it as a desk. I feel like writing, surrounded by the silence of this room—with the rain pounding on the window and my brother's raspy breathing and the sounds of the equipment and noises of the hospital. Silence is relative.

Jem can sleep through anything. Always could. I tuck my hand into his curved one. He still feels unnaturally warm.

When I was little I had the sense that Jem somehow belonged to me. That he was *mine* to follow and observe and idolize. I followed him everywhere. I wanted to do what he did. I would practically fawn over him whether he paid me any attention or not. I was in my glory during the moments when my hero would allow me to be his sidekick, if only for an hour or two, and sometimes, when no one was watching, he would even condescend to play Barbies with me. I craved validation from my second brother like no one else. Even when he became a teenager and was too cool to hang out with his little sister, I wanted his attention. I should have minded that he blew me off over and over again like he was too cool for me, but I didn't really. I *wanted* him to be that cool. I wanted other people to admire him the way I did. I would do anything to gain a moment of his notice, even when he was totally self-absorbed in what clothes he wore or the stupid things he did to impress girls who would never appreciate him properly.

As terrifying as his illness is, I don't have to look hard to find the silver lining. Cancer allowed us to reconnect. He had time for me again, as long as I had patience for his moods, and I was pleased to find that we hadn't grown so far apart. Everything I'd idolized about Jem as a kid is still true. He is thoughtful and tough as nails and in need of quiet reassurance—he just expresses himself differently now.

Eric is unchanging, and I like that about him, maybe because we're nothing alike. He's steady; he likes to stay the course he's chosen. Jem is frustratingly fluid, overly sensitive and has a bad habit of overreacting. He doesn't make it easy to justify my favoritism.

Hurry up and wait
For a sign that will be
Missed.
Watch the line, the
Numbers, the
Beat
Of the meaningless pattern
That means everything.

"Read it to me?" he rasps. I look up to find Jem awake. I can only tell he's conscious because of his breathing. He can't open his eyes because they're crusted shut.

I set my pencil down and go get a warm cloth to wipe his eyes clean. Jem murmurs 'thanks' as I soak his lids and brush away the gunk. When he opens his eyes they're bloodshot and glazed.

Jem reaches for my notebook to read my scribblings. I usually don't let anyone read my poems, not even Mom, but Jem is a special case and he knows it.

"I'll read it." I set aside the cloth and recite the poem. It bothers him. He thinks he's making me worry, as if watching his heart monitor could become an unhealthy obsession. Eric and I call it 'hospital TV.'

"How come you never write about Eric?"

I shrug. "Eric isn't subtle. You're a pattern. Like music. I can make poetry out of that." I tear the page out of my notebook and leave it on the side table for him.

"What else have you written lately?"

I offer to write something about Willa. It's a diversion I know will pique his interest, because I don't want to give my brother an honest answer. The truth is that I haven't written very much of anything in weeks that isn't about Kipp. It would bother Jem if he knew. He doesn't like Kipp—or maybe he just doesn't like it that I've found another boy to adore; like I've outgrown my need for my hero.

The orderly comes by with a meal tray for Jem. He doesn't have much appetite, but I help him eat the fruit cup and juice box. He leaves the chicken and peas untouched, not that I blame him. It looks like a frozen TV dinner.

"I'm cold," he complains quietly. I offer to get him another blanket, but he asks for a hug instead. I scoot my chair as close to the bed as I can and he shifts his weight to the edge of the mattress. His forehead comes to rest against my neck and his thin arm wraps around me. I hold him as best I can, rubbing his back to warm him up. Maybe he wasn't talking about physical warmth when he said he was cold....

"I hate being here," he whispers.

"You'll be home soon." That doesn't cheer him up much. I hold him and rub his back and tell him little things about my day. He never would have listened to me ramble like this before he got sick, but now my normalcy is comforting.

"Your favorite nurse is making rounds," I offer. Jem doesn't react. He's too busy having a blue moment. Not long after we're joined by said nurse—a petite ball of energy with *Snow White* scrubs and Cheshire Cat stickers on her shoes.

"Hey Kim."

"Is he awake?" She nods at Jem.

"Yeah. Bad day."

"I'm right here," he mutters into my neck.

"Still coughing?" Kim makes Jem roll over so she can listen to his breathing. He's not in a friendly mood today, but I know he likes Kim best. Jem doesn't click with many people (surprise), but she's the only nurse that he doesn't complain about. The others all either smell funny, talk too much, have cold hands, are too rough, or don't have enough enthusiasm.

"Nice scrubs." He sounds sarcastic, but she takes it in stride.

"Are you Sneezy?"

"No. Coughy."

"I'd say Grumpy." She places her stethoscope and makes him cough. "Like you mean it."

He hacks away for a few minutes. Jem sounds like a chain smoker. It's as if something is trying to crawl back up his throat as noisily as possible.

"You're sounding better," she says cheerfully. Really? That's *better*? "How's your appetite?"

"Fine."

"He ate a fruit cup," I volunteer. Jem lazily smacks my arm for presuming to speak for him.

"Can I go home yet?"

"Soon, probably. Your fever is coming down steadily. I'll come check you again later." She squeezes his shoulder with a reassuring smile and turns to go, on to the next patient. My time here is up as well. Dad comes in as I go out. He's on his lunch break too.

"What's the news?" Jem asks him.

"None. Just came to see how you are." Dad always gets tense around Jem when he's in the hospital—Dad's hospital, where he spends about eighty percent of his waking hours and should feel right at home.

"I'm sick," Jem says, in the spirit of pointing out the obvious. There's an awkward moment while Dad fishes around for something to say. I see him eyeing the half-eaten meal tray like he's going to comment on it, and I know Jem's short temper won't bear that right now.

"I'm gonna head out, Dad."

"Oh?"

I nod and give him a hug goodbye. He grabs my hand as I let go of the hug and says, "I'll walk you out."

A minute and a half is usually how long his visits with Jem last before one of them gets upset.

⌘

I spend the evening getting things ready for when Jem is discharged. The spare bedroom is closest to Mom's office, where she could keep an eye on him while she works. I think about making up that room for him, but then he wouldn't have a private bathroom, and he really needs that.

I pull the sheets off his bed and wash them, and then set about sterilizing the bathroom surfaces. Eric comes in while I'm elbow-deep in bleach and feels the need to remark on the smell. I tell him to take the sheets out of the dryer.

I have little rituals that keep me sane whenever Jem is really sick. After I make the bed and stock the fridge with Jell-O, I take his black photo album into my room. Eric originally took these pictures for Jem's benefit, but I've gotten something out of them, too.

Jem keeps facedown the pictures he can neither bear to look at nor get rid of. Some of these are my favorites. One is of Mom asleep across four waiting room chairs. She looks uncomfortable and completely exhausted. I can see why that shot bothers Jem; he's very sensitive to others' pain, and wouldn't want Mom to suffer unnecessarily on his account.

My favorite picture isn't even properly arranged in the book. It's taped facedown to the flyleaf at the back cover. Eric wrote the date on the white tab of the Polaroid. This one was taken twelve days after I went into the hospital to be a donor.

The day of the harvest procedure couldn't have come fast enough for my liking. I went through testing with Eric to find out if either of us were a match, and when my results came back positive I would have let them harvest that day,

510

if they could. But there was waiting to do; I had to have surplus stem cells in my blood, and Jem had to be in a temporary state of remission for this thing to work, so on came the radiation and chemo.

To prepare my body for the harvest, I had a series of injections over several days so that the stem cells could be sifted directly from my blood. A few needles is nothing, and I foolishly went into it feeling cocky and self-righteously proud of what I was doing for my brother. I have thoroughly learned my lesson on the subject of pride, because instead of being a walk in the park, I had the week from hell.

My body didn't react so well to the injections. It was like having the flu—my muscles and bones ached. I could barely eat without my stomach getting upset. When I did manage to fall asleep, I woke up drenched in sweat.

I didn't complain, though, because that would have been totally selfish and wimpy. Jem was in the middle of much harsher treatments, and had been feeling a lot worse than me for months. I could stand a little discomfort without making a fuss. I don't think I fooled anybody, though. The whole family knew I was miserable.

The cells were collected over four sessions. I was told I'd just have to sit there for few hours while a machine did the blood filtering. What I *wasn't* told was that my small veins—what isn't small about me?—weren't sturdy enough for the procedure. I had to have a catheter inserted into a larger vein at my neck, which was about as pleasant as you can imagine.

I didn't complain, but I was secretly counting down the hours during that last apheresis treatment. I smiled for the Polaroid shots that Eric was taking to keep Jem informed. He was bored that day and I was agitated, so we played with that camera for a long time, taking crack photos for fun. We accidentally got a snapshot of the exact moment my chest started hurting and I couldn't get a breath. My left lung collapsed—yet another complication in a parade of total crap. The pain and shortness of breath made me lose consciousness, which I think was a good thing, because when I woke up I had a chest tube hanging out of my side. And up till that point, I'd thought the hardware in my neck was gross. This was just plain creepy, and on top of that, it hurt like hell.

I couldn't leave the hospital, and the boredom nearly drove me insane. I couldn't even get out of bed with that awful tube sticking out of me. The only thing I could do was lay there and wait for the hellish dressing changes. I might have complained, just a little.

Jem needed Mom, so by default I had Dad spending time with me in that stuffy hospital room. I always thought Jem was being too hard on Dad whenever he went into 'doctor mode,' but I began to see what my brother was talking about. Dad is insufferable when he's talking about drainage and oxygen saturation, and touching my shoulder like I'm a stranger.

Dad couldn't be with me all the time, though. He still had shifts to work, so Eric stayed with me when neither of our parents could be there. Eric was there when things started getting weird. I felt like I was dreaming and regular events were happening out of order. Things Eric said made no sense and every time a nurse came to my bed I couldn't understand what she was doing, even though they were basic tasks I'd seen done before.

Bacteria had gotten in around that *thing* in my neck. I'd developed sepsis, and the early symptoms looked like a regular response to the pain in my chest, so they didn't catch it right away. I was pretty disoriented by the time treatment began, so in essence I missed the whole thing. They sedated me and put a tube down my throat to supply oxygen. A lot of liquids got pushed through that *thing*, until my lungs filled up with fluid and it was hard to breathe. In Eric's photos I look totally swollen and red, like a pig with a blotchy sunburn.

But like I said, I missed all that. The following week I left the hospital with IV antibiotics, and I got over it with very few lasting scars. The little marks on my chest and neck are nothing; it's the scars in my head that annoy me. Sepsis caused capillary leakage in my brain, which in turn caused seizures. I've only had two more since leaving the hospital, but every time I seize I have to restart the waiting period to get my driver's license back.

I'm at peace with the whole thing now, because it was all worth it for Jem's survival, but at the time I was feeling pretty sorry for myself. As I was leaving the hospital in my borrowed wheelchair, Mom took me by the ICU to see Jem. We couldn't go in, of course, but there are windows around all of the isolation rooms. Jem had been in one of these for weeks because he had no immune system left.

It didn't occur to me until later that Mom and the nurses must have arranged this in advance. Jem was sitting near the window, waiting for me. The nurse, all gowned up in sterile gear to protect my brother, stood behind him like a sentinel the whole time with her hands resting on the handles of the wheelchair she'd used to move him.

It was sort of like communicating with a prison inmate, but without the phone. We both pressed a hand to the glass, lining our fingers up. He mouthed, 'Are you okay?' to me and I nodded before asking him the same question. 'Yes,' he mouthed. 'Thank you.'

He didn't look okay. His eyes were slightly glassy; he was pale and when his mouth moved I could see angry red blisters on the inside of his lips. The skin on his hands and arms had a strange rash. It seemed that in an attempt to make him healthy, both of us had become sicker.

'I'm okay. Healing.' I pulled back my collar to show him the tidy dressing on my neck, and then I uncovered the one on my side where the tube had been. Jem looked at me with worry and pressed both hands up against the glass, like he was trying to reach me.

'I'm sorry.'

'I'm okay.'

He kept repeating it: 'I'm sorry, I'm so sorry...' He started to cry and the nurse's hands closed around his upper arms. She pulled him back into his seat and began to wheel him away.

My reaction was purely impulsive. I slammed both fists against the glass and shouted, 'Hey!' at her. Mom grabbed my wrists to keep me from doing it twice. 'We're in a hospital,' she reminded me sternly. I tried to stand up, to get a better look at my brother—he was arguing with the nurse—and Mom sat me right back down. 'Neither of you should be overexcited right now.'

'Let me talk to him.'

'He's upset, we need to let him rest.'

I pressed my hands and face up against the glass, too stubborn to let Mom take me away until we absolutely had to leave. Whatever Jem said to the nurse worked, and she let him come back to the window. We must have looked like quite the pair, sick as dogs with our hands and faces pressed close to the glass in this strange approximation of a hug. He cried and I wheezed, and when Eric came up from the parking garage to see what was taking us so long, he snapped a Polaroid. Much later, Mom said it was one of the nicest things she'd ever seen, the way Jem and I cared for each other like that.

I grab a pen and compose impulsively on the flyleaf where he keeps that picture:

You are so inconvenient to my existence
That I can't even stand to look at you
I look at myself in the mirror
And you stare back.
You are me and I am you
This inconvenient mutual existence
One living, the other dying
You subsume my existence
And I let you
'Cause I love you

Friday, the 9th of June. Foggy.

I put in my money
To buy nuts with honey.
Damn vending machine ate my dollar.

It's just me and Eric for dinner tonight. Dad is at work and Mom is with Jem. There were a lot of nights like this last fall, when Eric and I ate alone with the unspoken knowledge of why our family was half-missing.

We eat in front of the TV. I know Eric visited Jem today, but he hasn't offered and details and I don't want to pry. Eric doesn't like talking about sad things.

His phone rings during a commercial and he leaves the room to answer it.

Why? He usually only does that when Celeste calls. She has her own ringtone so we all know when it's her. As if anyone believes they're still just friends.

Eric comes back to the living room and says he's going out for a while. "Where?"

"Just a get-together at one of the other player's houses." Eric's whole social life is sports. I wonder if Kipp will be there, if it's a party attended by jocks, but I don't want to ask. Eric would rip on me for it, not let me go with him, and probably tell Kipp that I asked. Humiliation with a side order of fries.

With Eric out for the night and me all alone, I cozy up in sweats and park myself in front of the computer. Time to creep a certain someone's Facebook page.

A little box pops up in the corner of my screen with a chat alert. It's him. *Him*. Any attention from him turns me into a puddle of goo. And it feels so nice to be goo. I'd never have imagined it would, but it does. I just have to be careful of sewer grates.

S'up?

That's about as verbose as it gets with Kipp. He's a man of few words, but he gets his point across.

I type back: *Nothing. Sitting at home.* And I tap my foot impatiently for the whole five seconds it takes him to answer. I wonder if he's going to the same get-together as Eric...

You should come out tonight.

Damn it. The one night he invites me out, and I don't have a ride. And Mom and Dad aren't around to ask permission. I shouldn't just go out and not tell them. And the thought of leaving makes me nervous. What if I can't be reached in an emergency? The little voice in my head argues with me to just take my cell phone and go out, but I still worry. Anything could go wrong with that plan— bad reception, too much distance between wherever I am and the hospital, unreliable means of transportation... Now if Apparition was real, this wouldn't be a problem, dang it.

I can't. My brother is in the hospital. I need to stay by the phone.
Ok.

That's it? Did he even want to see me tonight? It stings that he so readily lets go of the idea of making plans. A minute later he signs off without saying goodbye.

I ought to hex that jerk.

I go downstairs, scoop myself a big bowl of chocolate ice cream—not as good for heartache as conventional wisdom purports, but comforting nonetheless—and eat it alone in the dark kitchen. I even take the time to sculpt a little castle in my ice cream before it melts into a sopping mess. The hum of the refrigerator keeps me company. I bet this is how James felt when Lily—

The doorbell rings. What the heck is that about? No one visits us, and certainly not past dinner hour. Maybe it's Willa, come for company and news.

I pick up my bowl and carry it with me to the front door. It's habit; I've learned to never leave delicious food unattended in this house, and nothing is going to part me from my ice cold comfort right now.

I open the door and *crap*, it's him. And I'm standing here in my pajamas, ice cream in hand, hair uncombed, and ready to freaking die.

"Hey," he says like nothing is wrong. "You busy?" He freaking knows I'm not.

Kipp holds up a plastic shopping bag and steps in. I forgot to invite him in the middle of my mental meltdown.

"Um, no, not busy," I mumble belatedly as I shut the door.

"Mind if I keep you company?"

How sweet of him to ask. "I don't mind. You sure you want to?"

"Yeah." He reaches into the shopping bag and pulls out a package of microwave popcorn, a pack of Twizzlers, and two DVDs.

And I freaking melt. Totally goo. No bones left. Mush to the core. He is too flipping perfect to even be talking to me.

"Your pick," he says, and hands over the DVDs. He brought *Wall-E* and *Finding Nemo*. Somebody likes cartoons.

...Me. And him. And isn't that awesome?

"I'm in the mood for robots," I say. "I'll just go change first..."

"Nah," he says. "You look comfy."

I'm wearing pink fuzzy slippers, Jem's sweatshirt, and baggy flannel pants that I stole from Eric after he put holes in both knees. Comfy might be an understatement. I look like I'm preparing for hibernation.

He leads the way to the living room, since I'm incapable of being a good hostess. I turn on the TV and crack open the DVD case.

The disk inside isn't *Wall-E*. It's a white and red one called *Young People Fucking*. Ohmigod. Should I say anything, or should I just put it on?

I put it on. I'm curious. Yes, *curious*.

Kipp leaves to put the popcorn in the microwave and I put the TV on mute. Can't let the main menu track give away my little switch, can I?

"Shall I start it?" I call to him.

"Go ahead."

The movie opens with two people arguing on a couch. It's pretty well lit, for porn. Not that I'd know, or anything. It's not like I have two older brothers who *never* clear their browser history or create strong passwords for their computers.

The couple on screen kisses. A subtitle at the bottom declares them "The Friends." Please God, let that be a sign.

Kipp comes back with popcorn. He stops dead behind the couch and stares at the screen like he's never seen a TV before. And then he goes beet red. He is so freaking cute when he blushes.

"Uh...was that in the wrong case?"

"Yeah. But it's cool." I pat the couch next to me. "So where'd you find this one?"

Kipp scratches the back of his neck uncomfortably. "It was at TIFF."

An educated taste in smut, I see. Kipp offers to put on *Finding Nemo* instead.

I try to make a joke of it: "Are you saying that because you think I'm too young for anything above PG?"

"Uh, no." Kipp looks over his shoulders like he's wary of being watched. "Is anyone else home?"

"No." Hint?

"I don't think your parents would thank me for bringing a movie like this into their house."

"They won't be home till late, and I'm not all that impressionable, I promise." A little voice in the back of my head keeps telling me not to stare at his mouth. I should really listen to that. I should…

I should have put on a horror movie. That would give me an excuse to cozy up to him…for comfort.

A woman moans and gasps on screen as the camera pans up her legs and torso. She's getting fingered on the couch. "Think she's faking?" I say, trying to ease the tension and Kipp's embarrassment. For a shy guy, this must be doubly awkward. He chuckles at my question and agrees with me.

"She's putting on a show."

"You know what faking sounds like?" Eric must be rubbing off on me. I don't normally make crude jokes like that.

Kipp gives me a look. "No," he says defensively. There's a moment where I wonder if I've really offended him, but then he laughs at himself.

"Trying to embarrass me, Shrimpy?" Not even my brothers can get away with calling me stuff like that. But he can.

"Is it working?"

He throws a kernel of popcorn at me and I lean over to catch it with my mouth. He throws another to see if the last one was a fluke, and then another. I just keep catching them. Kipp makes a crack about me having a talented mouth, and it's my turn to blush.

"Too bad I don't have someone to appreciate it properly." I'll blame that one on Eric's influence too.

"Don't rush it," Kipp says. "Stay unattached as long as possible."

"Says the guy in a serious relationship."

"You're still pretty young."

"And apparently I look like a lesbian."

"For the hundredth time, it was an accident!"

I laugh at his indignation and elbow him teasingly.

"I didn't say you were wrong. For all you know I could be plotting to steal your girlfriend away from you."

"I'd like to see you try."

"We should put money on this." We spend the next ten minutes arguing what counts as a 'loss' in this wager, and who should have to pay whom in what event. If I steal Nina away, shouldn't I have to pay up to compensate him for the loss of his girlfriend? If I can't steal her, have I lost the bet and therefore have to pay? He manages to twist the scenario in so many different ways, all of which end with me paying him.

"You should be in law school." I elbow him and mutter 'jerk' loud enough for him to hear.

"I'm probably not doing a good job of keeping you company," he apologizes. Kipp mutes the TV. "Do you want to talk?" He sounds like he expects me to say 'yes' and get all weepy—catharsis on demand. I turn sideways on the couch to face him and ask how job training is going. He's been driving up to Camp Concord on weekends all month, doing things like brushing up on First Aid and basic Sign Language to communicate with the hearing impaired campers. This is his first weekend off all month. I bet Nina is working tonight; otherwise he'd have never had the time to hang out with me.

"It's going okay." He shows me how to sign my name. I like the feeling of his fingers on mine, guiding me where to place my thumb to make an 'E.' I like how obvious the letters are; the signs look exactly like they're written. He puts up with my questioning about how to spell other names and words. I just don't want him to stop touching me, even if it is just my hand.

"I wish I'd known this last year. There were weeks when my brother was in isolation and we could only mime through the hospital windows. Specific signals would have been great."

"You were his donor, right?" Kipp asks seriously. "That time you were out of school for three weeks?"

"You remember that?" I thought he didn't even know my name until this semester. Kipp shrugs and smiles apologetically.

"Your family isn't from here. New people don't come around that often. It makes you interesting by default." And new people don't often provide such great gossip fodder, like having an ill son.

"I gave him marrow, yeah." I nod. "But I had some complications. I wasn't supposed to be out of school for three weeks. More like two or three days."

"But you're okay now?" How sweet of him to ask.

I smile. "I got a gym exemption for this year because of it. That's an awesome silver lining." That, and Jem's survival.

Kipp smirks. "You don't like sports?"

"Sure I do. I'm just picky. I was on the swim team when I lived in Ottawa."

"Were you any good?"

"Yup." Not to brag, or anything.

"We should go to the lake when it's warm." I might be hallucinating this. "Maybe later this weekend, if the weather is nice. Oh," his brow furrows, "maybe not this weekend, with your brother being…"

I wave away the awkwardness. "We've got this summer." And I will hold him to the promise of swimming, even if we have to go with a group of people. I wouldn't mind that, as long as it involves wetness and bathing suits…

Eric comes home and I quickly pause the movie. Luckily we're not in the middle of an incriminating scene—the image on the screen is of two heads. Eric looks from us to the screen and back again.

"What are you guys doing?"

"Just watching a movie."

"What movie?"

"It was at the Toronto International Film Fest—"

"Pass." He turns to go, but then stops to remind me not to stay up too late. His tone makes it sound like he's really telling our guest to leave.

"The movie is almost over."

"Does Mom know you have a company?"

"Eric, you're adopted, nobody loves you." I get a smack upside the head for that one and a cheery reminder to brush before bed. "You sound like Dad."

"Eat your vegetables, you'll get scurvy!" Eric says with a laugh, and finally, mercifully, leaves us alone.

"Sorry about him."

Kipp looks at me with a quizzical expression. "I'm adopted."

Oh *fuck*.

He laughs. "I'm just kidding. The look on your face was priceless." Merlin's beard, he scared the crap out of me.

"I should probably go." Kipp stops the movie and gets up to retrieve the DVD.

"Are you sure?"

"It's late."

"Okay." I try not to sound disappointed. "Thanks for keeping me company."

"It was, uh…interesting." His ears turn a little bit pink as he puts the disk back in the wrong case and packs up his stuff from the coffee table. We clean up the refuse from our snacks and I walk him to the door.

"Good luck with work," I tell him. "Say hi to Nina."

"Thanks."

I can't believe I'm saying this, but… "Is the camp still hiring?" I hope he'll say 'no' just as much as I want to hear 'yes.' A 'no' would spare me the indecision and guilt of spending a summer away from my brother.

Kipp thinks on that for a moment. "Cooks and stuff, probably. I know they've hired all their counselors, but they might need more support staff. You're a good cook." He smiles at me and my heart squeezes. Compliments from him are like candy, and that smile…

"See ya, Shrimpy." Kipp musses my hair and heads out the door. I need to find a nickname for him.

Saturday the 10th of June. Cloudy.

At breakfast, Dad announces that Jem is being discharged today. He says it like Jem is a new baby brother we're expecting to bring home from the hospital—someone we've never met before, alien and fragile but also very special. What a load of crap. I avert my eyes and stare into my coffee mug, but Eric gives Dad a look that reads *We know the drill,* and Dad retreats into a tone of detached professionalism.

"Let's keep it down so your mother can sleep," he says. "She was up most of the night." Just like every night. For a guy who deals with catastrophic injuries on a daily basis, Dad is useless when it comes to saying the right thing.

The morning seems long, waiting for Jem to come home. I call Willa to let her know that he'll be out of the hospital, even if he isn't up to having visitors, because I know she's been worrying. And because time is crawling, I keep her on the phone for almost an hour until she absolutely has to leave for work.

"Keep me posted, okay?" she says.

"I will. He'll probably call you himself once he gets his voice back."

"Right. Because Jem is a patient person."

I have to say, she knows my brother well.

I stay home while Eric goes to the hospital with Mom and Dad to pick Jem up. I can set things up while they're gone—warming his pillowcases in the dryer, digging the humidifier out of the linen closet, filling a hot water bottle...

I go out to the porch when I hear the car pull in to the driveway. I expect them to get out right away, but Dad opens the rear door and has to help Jem up. He sways a little and has to lean on Dad's shoulder. I thought he was well enough to come home. What are they doing discharging him when he's too sick to even stand up?

Getting Jem inside and situated is a long ordeal. While Mom tucks him in, Dad removes medication bottles from Jem's backpack and sets them up along the nightstand. There seem to be a lot more bottles than he left with.

"Are you hungry?" Mom asks. Jem shakes his head. Dad starts portioning out pills and Mom leaves to get a glass of water to wash it all down.

"I'll make you as many milkshakes as you want," I tell him.

Jem smiles. "Thanks." His voice is high and hoarse. It takes a few minutes to get all the medication he needs into him, and then Dad sets the cup of water aside and tells him to rest.

"Come on, sweetheart," Mom says to me, and holds out her hand. I start to move away and Jem grabs the back of my t-shirt.

"Uh...I'll follow you down," I tell Mom and Dad.

They look from Jem to me with concern. "Is there something you need?" Dad asks.

"Elise," Jem says, and leaves it at that. They share one of those parental looks that make me believe in telepathy, because they somehow come to an agreement without saying a word, and give us a moment of privacy.

"Not too long," Mom says, and shuts the door behind them.

As soon as they're gone Jem reaches up and pulls my mask off.

"What's the matter?"

"Has Willa…?"

"She called. She's been worried about you. I told her you were coming home, and I'd let her know when you were up to having visitors."

The tenderest smile I have ever seen crosses his face when I say that she phoned in his absence.

"Will you call her?" His voice cracks on the second word and the rest of his sentence is barely a whisper.

"You're not up to having a phone conversation right now." I hate telling him no, but it's for his own good.

Jem clears his throat and tries to speak again. "Invite her here."

"Are you sure you want to see her now?"

"Yes."

He looks like absolute hell. His lips are dry and cracked from harsh breathing; he's pale and the bags under his eyes haven't been so dark since last winter. Does my vain brother really want to be seen like this?

"I'll call her." I shouldn't, but I know Willa is good for him in her own way.

Jem's face stretches into a beatific smile. "Thank you." He reaches for my hand as I adjust the edge of his hat and squeezes it. "You're so good to me. Thank you, for everything. You're so special to me."

What the heck is that about? It's been four hours since his last painkiller, not counting the one he took five minutes ago, so I can't write that last statement off as loopiness. Jem never says sentimental stuff like that. He laughs at me when I say it.

"I'm gonna go call her now."

He softly calls, "I love you, Lise," after me as I leave. I shut the bedroom door behind me as worry writhes in my gut like a live snake. If I didn't know any better, I'd think he was saying goodbye.

Eric: June 8 to 10

Today

I sit in my car outside the entrance to the Rideau Trail, too tired to hike. But I wouldn't want to be anywhere else.

I only started coming to the trails here after Jem got sick. It's remote and peaceful, and if I want to I can sit and think, or hurl rocks at trees and scream at the top of my lungs. Celeste has even met me here a few times, when things were really rough. She told me that I shouldn't feel ashamed of being angry with God. Understanding words, especially from an atheist.

I'm not angry with God anymore. I'm disappointed.

My phone buzzes in my pocket. I have to get back. My turn at the hospital starts in two hours. I need time to go home and take a shower and pull myself together before going to be with Jem.

I answer the call as I pull out of the parking lot. "Yeah?"

It's Mom. "Take your time getting over here, okay? I'm going to stay a bit later tonight."

I don't think she's slept for more than an hour at a time these past two days. She's going to burn out, like she did when both Jem and Elise were in the hospital together.

"You need to get out of there for a bit, Mom. Sleep in a real bed, not a crappy plastic chair."

"You know I won't sleep."

"Try. You're no good to us if you're exhausted."

I don't go home. I go straight to the hospital, even though my turn doesn't start for another hour. Mom needs to go take care of herself.

I have a little ritual I do whenever I go see Jem in the hospital. On my way down the ward to his room, I recite the Serenity Prayer in my head. It's familiar and simple, and calms the nerves, because it's hard to see him so ill. I never get over the shock of it.

When I step past the curtain that divides Jem's bed from the rest of the room, he's facing away from me. Mom is holding an emesis basin under his chin as he coughs up bloody phlegm.

I used to wonder if all this wouldn't have happened if I'd been nicer to him; if I'd shared my toys more as a kid, or if I hadn't told him that Santa isn't real, or if I hadn't made sport of him so often. Maybe it's payback for that time I snuck a cigarette behind the garage, or cheated on a test. But I know it's not. There's no reason to it all. So I gave up wondering.

"Here, bro." I help him rinse the taste of phlegm out of his mouth while Mom empties the emesis basin. There are bruises on his throat. From coughing so hard? Is that where the blood in the phlegm is from, or are his lungs bleeding slowly? I ask and he simply touches his throat. He's too sore to talk.

I make a mental note to bring his phrase card next time I come here. He's in no shape to be miming his needs.

"You should go," I tell Mom. "Recharge and come back tonight."

She hums and haws, reluctant to leave, until Jem rolls his eyes tiredly and points to the door.

"Honey, don't feel you have to send me away," she says.

He jabs a finger at the door.

I hand her the keys to the car. She takes her sweet time leaving, waiting for Jem to change his mind and tell her to stay, or to medically require her presence, but he doesn't. So she kisses him goodbye, grabs her bag, and leaves.

No sooner as the door closed behind her than an epic coughing fit explodes from his chest. He must have been holding that in the whole time she was dawdling.

There's more blood in his phlegm. His eyes are bloodshot from the pressure of coughing for so long. They're glassy with fever and watery with infection. He doesn't look like he's really here, but I know he is.

"Fuck," he mouths, and slumps back against the pillow. It's a wonder that such a thin person can have so much mucus inside him. I adjust the oxygen tube under Jem's nose and his eyes flutter and close.

"Can't catch a break, huh?"

He shakes his head. He drinks a little more water to soothe his throat, and after awhile I help him out of bed and across the short stretch of tile between the bed and the washroom. They're hydrating him with intravenous saline. That stuff makes a person piss like mad, and of course Jem is too proud to just use the plastic urinal by his bed.

"Look at the bright side," I tell him as I tuck him back into bed. The short trip to the bathroom and back has winded him, even with extra oxygen. "If your kidneys still worked completely, you'd be getting up a lot more often."

Jem smirks and gives me the finger. Atta'boy.

The Next Day

As I heat frozen pasta up in the microwave, I wish I could invite Willa over to cook. It would give Elise something to do, helping with the meal, and we could have something real to eat. And Willa is good at being…normal. But I can't invite her over because she would ask questions about Jem, and I don't feel like talking about it.

Elise doesn't ask about Jem, thank God. I know she knows I was at the hospital today. She saw me leave the house. She doesn't need to worry. She doesn't need to know that Jem passed out on the bathroom floor this afternoon and pissed himself, and that there was blood in his urine. They think he was bleeding lightly before he fell—that he ruptured a vessel around his own kidney by coughing too hard. Poor kid.

And I feel like shit because I shouldn't have left him alone when he was ready to faint. But short of standing over him while he took a piss, what could I have done?

They'll make him stay in bed and use a plastic urinal or bedpan now. He hates that. As long as he doesn't fall again, I don't care what he wants. He's lucky he didn't hit his head on the side of the sink when he passed out.

Maybe I'll go over to the hospital again tonight. Give Mom a break so she can go eat dinner, and I can check on Jem. My cell rings in the middle of dinner and I take it into the other room to keep from disturbing Elise while she watches TV. It's just the bank calling to offer their balance protection program on my account, but it's an excuse.

When I come back into the living room I tell Elise I'm going out.

"Where?"

"Just a get-together at one of the other player's houses." Keep it vague. Elise nods, but she seems a little put out at being left alone. I'd take her with me, but then she'd know I'm lying and seeing Jem would worry her.

"Bye, Lise."

"Drive safe."

❧

Jem is asleep when I get to the hospital. Mom and Dad are conversing quietly with a doctor by the door. I try not to hear whatever news it is and focus on Jem. His breathing sounds marginally better than it did this afternoon.

Then I notice there's a small splash of blood on the corner of his speech card that Mom forgot to wipe off, and I wonder if he's really getting better. We beat this, damn it. Cancer didn't kill him, and he was getting so much better. He can't die of the common cold now and ruin it all.

Jem cracks an eyelid at me.

"Winning or losing?" I ask. He mouths 'winning,' but I'm not sure if he's just telling me what I want to hear.

Jem taps his ear and points to our parents. He's telling me to listen, as if he knows I'm purposely blocking out their conversation.

They're talking about bringing him home. To recover, or to die? I can't tell. But Jem always said he didn't want to burden anyone by dying at home for sentiment's sake.

I vividly remember the day Jem asked me to bring him a notebook and a pen at the hospital, because that simple request lead to so many harder ones. He had his composition books at the hospital to work on creating music when he couldn't actually play, but he wanted regular notepad paper and a pen. A pencil wouldn't cut it anymore.

I think he got the idea from his roommate Evan, or at the very least the information, because when I brought the paper and pen to him that evening he told me to shut the door, and then promptly proceeded to dump a ton of bricks on my chest. He wanted me to help him plan his own funeral.

I hadn't cried in front of anyone since he got sick, but that just about snapped me. Seventeen years old, and he wanted to plan his funeral.

"I asked you for a reason," he said when I tried to back down. "It would upset Mom and Dad, and Elise would throw a fit." He was right about that. Elise was putting herself through hell at the time, trying to get ready to make her marrow donation. There was a chance that the transplant wouldn't work, though, or that the pretreatment would kill Jem before the transplant could even be done. He wanted to be prepared for that eventuality.

I still don't really understand the concept of planning one's own funeral. You can't really 'attend' it, after all. He said he wanted to take the burden of planning off of Mom and Dad, but I think planning a funeral gives people something to do in the wake of loss. It keeps them busy for a little while.

Jem knew how to do it properly, too, which makes me think that he talked to someone about it. He had to have a witness to his living will and funeral plans. It had to be hand-written, in ink, and we both had to sign it. If he wanted to make changes, he had to cross out the words and initial beside the change. He had clearly put some thought into this before I showed up—from what music to play to what readings Dad would like best to hear. He wanted a closed casket, because 'gawking at a corpse is weird' and said to bury him in something he might actually *wear*. 'It's my own funeral, fuck if I'm wearing a tie.' I brought up the funeral of a kid we went to school with in Ottawa, killed by a drunk driver, whose casket had been white and mourners had been invited to sign it like a yearbook. Jem wasn't keen on that idea. 'It's a fucking funeral, not homecoming.'

It was at that point I realized I would probably have to get up and say something at his funeral. I'm not eloquent by any means, but who on God's green earth has the right words to say in front of a crowd when their little brother dies at seventeen? That he lived a good life? That he's partying up with Jesus now? At least he isn't in pain anymore?

Jem can deal with a lot of shit, but sappy eulogies were his limit. "None of that garbage," he said. 'I don't care that we're Anglican, we're doing this Catholic style: the priest does his bit and everyone else can bugger off.'

'What if someone wants to say something?'

'They can do it at the visitation. Fuck up the sound check, not the concert.'

He was even less willing to negotiate on the subject of music. Jem knew what he wanted and what he didn't, and what he did not want were hokey hymns. His list of songs included Chopin's "Nocturne in C Sharp Minor," Tracy Chapman's "Change," and Mom's favorite: "I'll Fly Away" by Alison Krauss. Always the thoughtful one in the family, Jem.

'Don't you dare let them play cheesy shit like 'Amazing Grace."

'What's wrong with 'Amazing Grace'?'

'I don't know how people got the impression that it's good for funerals. It was written by a slave trader.'

'Really?'

'Don't play it.'

I still think it's good for funerals. It's a nice song about how we all sin, we all die, and some find their way back to God.

The curtain moves aside and Mom and Dad come up to the bedside. "Good news, sweetie," Mom says. "Your fever has been coming down steadily. You'll be able to come home soon."

"When?"

Mom's answer is vague—a day or two, depending on how fast the blood in his phlegm disappears. I ask Dad if they'll really send Jem home when he's so weak, but Dad says now that the fever is almost gone it's all right. The mucus is the body's natural way of expelling the last of the virus and defending against new germs in the meantime.

"A few more days will also help to make sure his kidneys can take the hit," Dad adds in the same pitch. I hope they can, because if Jem needs spare parts from Elise there's a chance she'll have more complications. I can't stand it again. All the bad stuff happened to her on my watch—the collapsed lung, the seizures. I don't care that it wasn't technically my fault; watching her gasping for breath, turning blue right before my eyes, marks the worst moment of my life. And after her fight with sepsis, she was such a shell. We all thought the oxygen deprivation and seizure had caused brain damage. I almost thought it would be better if she didn't come home after that. I didn't want my vibrant, wonderful little sister to be reduced to the level of an infant.

I did a lot of bargaining with God.

"They'll keep him for the weekend at least, right?" I ask Dad. The longer they keep Jem in good care, the better chance both he and Elise have.

"They won't send him home before he's ready," Dad assures me. What a convenient way to sidestep my question.

It's Morning

They really are discharging Jem. Apparently his fever is pretty much gone, and apart from a tendency to cough up phlegm, Jem is ready to go home to recover. I don't like it. I think they should keep him for at least another day, until he's a little stronger. I argue this with Dad over breakfast, but all he can say is that it's not his decision. "You know Jem hates the hospital," he tries to reason. And I hate the dentist, but I still go when I need to.

"They need the bed," he says when he gets tired of arguing with me.

"*Jem* needs that bed."

Dad gives me a testy look. "Trust me. It won't be easy, but he's strong enough to come home, okay? Enough."

Mom insists on driving over to the hospital early, even though Jem isn't being discharged until at least two o'clock. He missed his dialysis appointment this week, so he's hooked up to a dialyzer now, and the plan is to discharge him when that treatment is done. Mom is the first one off the elevator when the doors open, but Dad and I follow at a more reluctant pace.

Dad hates seeing Jem in the hospital. The only way he can deal with it and not lose his mind is to treat him like a patient, and that's a sure way to test Jem's temper.

A nurse is with him when we walk in, taking his blood pressure. She has him in a good mood and that's better than I could have ever asked for.

The dialyzer takes up quite a bit of room beside the bed, so I make myself comfortable against the far wall with as much distance between me and that creepy thing as possible. It turns my stomach a little, watching the blood flow through the tubing and get spun around like the feed on a cassette tape. Jem catches me looking at it before I have time to hide my disgust, and his mood takes a nosedive.

I don't even want to be here. I only came because Dad asked for my help.

Mom pets Jem's head and kisses his cheek. She tells him about shopping for fresh fruit with Elise to make milkshakes for him. Jem tries to show enthusiasm, but it obviously costs him a lot of effort.

It takes another half hour to finish his dialysis treatment, and then another forty minutes to get him ready to leave and complete the discharge paperwork. He's at the tipping point between sick enough to need care and not sick enough to merit a bed in the hospital. I try to keep it in perspective, because all of his symptoms will look worse in the atmosphere of the hospital. It's not that bad that he's still so achy and stiff that he needs my help to put his clothes on—that's just a regular flu symptom. So he coughs a little—he'll be okay soon.

"What are you looking at?" he snarls at me. We glare at each other for a few seconds before my inevitable win comes: Jem has to break the stare to cough, and I chuckle.

"Score."

"Shut up."

Dad comes back in with the discharge paperwork tucked under his arm. "Don't antagonize your brother." I'm not sure whom he's talking to. "You ready to go?" he asks Jem. Dad doesn't seem bothered by the lack of response; he's just eager to get home.

Mom brings the car around the door of the hospital while Dad and I wait with Jem inside the vestibule. The wide hospital wheelchair makes my brother look even thinner. He's well bundled in a thick fleece blanket, but he's still shivering slightly. It's a damp day and that makes his breathing worse.

As Dad and I help Jem into the car, I silently hope whoever gets my brother's newly vacant bed desperately needs it, because otherwise I'm really going to resent this whole situation. He's still so weak and sluggish that he can barely buckle his seatbelt.

"Just sleep, honey," Mom tells him. "It'll be a quick ride home."

As we pull out of the parking lot, Mom drives so slowly you'd think she was a first time parent with a newborn in the car. Jem leans a little closer to me in the back seat and asks how warm it is outside. "It's pretty warm." The rest of us are wearing t-shirts, but he's bundled up and cold. I put an arm around him to warm up and feel his cheek. It's clammy.

"He's a little warm. Maybe we should take him back to the hospital," I tell Dad.

"I don't want to be in that fucking hospital," Jem mutters. "I'm fine." I think the wad of phlegm he proceeds to hork up would beg to differ.

⌖

When we pull up to the house Elise comes out onto the porch, eager to be part of the action. I think it disappoints her to see that Jem is still so sick, even though he's home.

Dad and I each lend him a shoulder for the long, slow walk inside—because Jem does insist on walking, even though it's no great difficulty to carry him. The distance is about twenty feet between the car and the living room, and by the time we get to the couch Jem has to sit down. He can't get a breath.

"You shouldn't stay down here," Mom says. "You should be in a proper bed. You need your rest."

Jem complains for the sake of his image, but doesn't put up much of a fight as I lift him and carry him upstairs to his room. Mom and Elise tuck him into freshly washed sheets that he can't smell and prop him up on pillows to ease his breathing.

Dad starts measuring out pills from the bottles on the nightstand. Mom goes to get a glass of water, and I leave to move the car into the garage. The only one who doesn't move is Elise. She sits cross-legged on the bed beside Jem, watching him like a loyal dog.

Moving the car is too short a task, and I dread having to go back inside. It's tense like this when he's ill at home. We all walk on eggshells, waiting for the other shoe to drop.

I close the garage door and call Celeste. She asks if I'm still at the hospital and I tell her we just got home.

"How are things?"

"No worse than usual." That's not saying much.

"How are you holding up?"

"Surviving." It's a mark of how well she knows me that Celeste doesn't ask if I want to talk about it. If I wanted to, I would.

"My phone is always on me. Call whenever you need to, okay?"

"I will."

"We'll work out a visit when things settle down again."

"Alright."

"Should I let you get back? Or do you want to shoot the shit and pretend?"

"I just wanted to touch base." Celeste has a way of centering me. I like the normalcy of her—absolutely nothing changed when I moved away.

"I'll let you go then."

"'Kay."

"Love you."

"Love you too." We say goodbye and I pocket my phone. I have to get back inside. There's so little I can do for my brother, and it would be a horrible thing to be AWOL when he really does need something from me.

I enter the kitchen to find Elise sitting at the island with the phone in front of her. Mom stands nearby, listening with a stony expression. The call is on speakerphone and Elise puts a finger to her lips when she sees me. I listen to the voice and recognize it as Willa's. I don't think she knows she's on speaker.

"I get off work at three. I can come straight after," she says.

Elise is inviting her over? Jem just got settled.

"That works," Elise agrees. "See you then." She hangs up the phone and I turn to Mom.

"You think he's up to having visitors so soon?"

Both Elise and Mom shake their heads.

"Jem insisted," Elise says. "We can make sure she doesn't stay long. A bit of company might make him feel better."

Mom sighs resignedly and admits that Willa does know how to behave around sick people. "I think we can trust her not to disturb him."

It's only forty-five minutes until Willa is due to arrive. I ask Jem if he wants to take a shower. Three days of nothing but sponge baths haven't done him any favors. Jem agrees and I ask Dad for help. An extra set of hands is necessary to help Jem out of his pajamas. We strip him on the edge of the bed and wrap a bathrobe around his skinny shoulders.

While Jem brushes his teeth, struggling not to cough for two whole minutes, Dad does all the work of covering up the central line in his chest. I'm glad he knows how, because I wouldn't know what to do with it. I run the water hot at first to warm the bathroom and the surface of the tub, and then dial it back to a comfortable temperature.

Dad reaches out to help Jem off with his bathrobe, and Jem asks him if he wouldn't mind leaving.

"Are you sure?"

"I'll be all right. Eric's here." It's a non-answer; one that gives Dad cause to cast suspicious looks between us. Likely there's something that Jem wants to say to me in private, and I'm not sure I want to hear it.

"If you need anything I'll be down the hall." Dad leaves and Jem sort of sighs. Maybe it's not a sigh. Maybe he's gasping for breath.

"What was that about?"

"I can't deal with him in doctor mode," Jem says. He looks to the shower and changes the subject. "Is the water running warm yet?"

I help him out of his bathrobe and lend him my shoulder for the short walk between counter and tub. A small part of me feels bad about this; he has to sacrifice so much dignity just to take a shower. But the better part of me just wants to help my brother and not be ashamed by it.

Jem's knees shake with standing. He holds onto the towel rack with his free hand and tries to step into the tub. He can barely lift his foot half the distance he needs to clear the lip. His shin bumps softly against the side of the tub and he tries again.

"Here." I lift Jem up and sit him down on the floor of the bath. He can't possibly stand for an entire shower. I detach the showerhead and run the water over him to warm up.

"You don't mind doing this, do you?"

"Of course not." I give him the showerhead to hold and stand up to reach the soap off the shelf. He just has to sit there, warming himself with the water, while I wash his back and neck and head. I would say his hair, but it's hardly worth the name. The sparse strands look like a fourteen-year-old's first mustache, in between the bald spots. A few of those hairs get washed down the drain as I rinse him off.

He has to wash his own chest—he knows how not to disturb his Hickman. I help him wash his arms and legs and feet.

"Help me up slowly?" he says when he's ready to get out of the tub. I get three towels ready. One I drape over the toilet and the other I wrap around his shoulders while he's still in the tub. Moving him causes a head rush and Jem throws his arm out like he's going to fall.

"I've got you." I set him down on the toilet and wrap that towel around his hips.

"My fuckin' head…" he mutters.

"Relax." I use the third towel to dry him off while he tries not to shiver. I try to do the job as fast as possible, but there's no keeping Jem warm in this state. I ease him into his bathrobe and walk him back to bed.

He's too dizzy to sit up alone, so Jem lays down while I collect pajamas and socks from his drawers.

"I forget what it's like," he says. "Being healthy."

"This is just a minor setback."

"I feel like shit."

I set the clothes down on the bed and give him what Elise calls my Big Brother Glare. "Are you going to let Willa see you feeling sorry for yourself?"

That shuts him up.

Willa: June 8 to 10

Thursday

One short conversation has completely changed the tone of my day. School is something that happens far away. It's a familiar feeling—this invisible, airless chamber that separates me from the throngs of other students. I felt it when Tessa was dying, when I couldn't find anything funny or pleasurable and everyone else's life seemed to be so simple and perfect. After that, I felt nothing for a long time.

Now, I'm stuck with the knowledge that Jem has an infection serious enough to merit a night in the hospital. I think Eric was full of shit when he said Jem would be home so soon. The hospital wouldn't take a patient so lately in remission and send him back home the very next day.

Up ahead I see Diane, gesturing widely as she complains to Paige about something inconsequential. I have no intention of approaching her, but my feet steer me that way and I walk through the hallway crowd, right up to Diane. I get so close that she has to take a step back.

"Hi Willa," Paige says, right before she gets it that I'm in no mood for pleasantries. Diane wrinkles her nose at me. She takes one step and her back comes up against the bank of lockers.

"You're standing too close," she says in that annoying soprano voice.

"Shut up, whore."

She gasps indignantly.

"Next time you get sick, cover your fucking mouth when you cough." I reach up and close a hand around her mouth and jaw. She tries to dodge my hand and I press her head back against the lockers. "Or better yet, cover your nose too." My other hand covers her nostrils. Diane starts to struggle. "Until you fucking suffocate and relieve us of your presence, you dumb bitch."

I let her go, and a small part of me enjoys the look of fear in her eyes. If there's anything I miss about my life in St. John's, it's that people automatically knew not to fuck with me.

I walk away, and not twenty minutes later a hall monitor summons me to the front office. Diane squealed. I miss out on first period, sitting in the vice principal's office while Diane sobs out her overdramatic rendition of events. I deny everything. There are no marks on her; she can't prove a damn thing.

"Other people saw!" Diane protests shrilly. Paige is called down to the office to corroborate. She doesn't seem to remember a thing either.

I don't know if it's fear of me or deep dislike of Diane that motivates Paige, but I owe her for this.

Elise and Eric aren't at lunch. I don't usually sit with either of them, but I notice their absence in the cafeteria. It scares me. Did something happen to Jem, bad enough that they had to leave school?

I go out to my car to make a phone call. Elise's cell doesn't even ring. The call goes straight to an automated message from the phone company that says the number is unavailable. She has her phone turned off—she's at the hospital.

I drift through the remainder of my classes like a living ghost. It's strange how easily that mode of being comes back to me after all this time. When my mind isn't blank with incomprehensible fear of the future and indifference to the present, it's winding in circles, and it always comes back to the sneaking suspicion that Eric told me half-truths this morning. What if it's not just an infection? What if he relapsed and doesn't want me to know?

Six months to rebuild my life in Smiths Falls, and for all that, it's flimsy and completely out of my control.

Frank is still at work when I get home, and the silence of the house seems oppressive. I sit down in front of the TV with the intention of turning it on, but I don't. I sit there and stare at the box, wondering what Jem is doing right now.

There's a knock at the front door. I grudgingly get up to answer it, and when I open the door I very nearly slam it closed again. It's Luke, and he doesn't look friendly. He looks tough—the happy-go-lucky kid is gone from his eyes. He holds himself in front of me with something resembling respect, and nods hello.

I lock the screen door. He could still get through it if he really wanted to, but some semblance of a barrier makes me feel better.

"Willa." Luke shifts his eyes awkwardly and says, "Can we talk?"

"Okay."

"Can we go for a walk?"

"I'm not going anywhere with you."

Luke's nostrils flare, but he doesn't lose his temper this time. "That's fair, I guess."

"What did my brother say to you? He hasn't been down to Doug's place since." Every time I'm home, Frank is unfailingly parked in front of the TV or puttering around the garage. The man needs a hobby and a break from the loneliness.

Luke shrugs dismissively. "He said a lot of things."

"He told me you denied everything."

"Would you admit to being beaten up by a girl?"

"I think you just didn't want to own up to calling me a murderer." I start to shut the door.

"I'm sorry, okay?"

I want to laugh at the absurdity of such a question. "No, not okay. Not okay at all, Luke."

"I was upset."

"Still not okay."

"I like you."

"You thought I was an easy lay."

"I was hurt by what you said."

"Good."

My belligerence finally starts to get to him, and he snaps, "I'm trying to apologize here."

"And I'm treating you the same way you treated me when I tried to mend things."

Luke leans his arm on the doorframe. It's a position of proximity and dominance that I'm not sure I like. "Can we make it okay so our brothers can be on good terms again? Doug's been in a nonstop bad mood since they fought."

"So they did fight. You want to tell me what else was said?"

Luke fidgets. He's not willing to own up to any more of his less-than-admirable behavior.

"If things are okay between us, it'll be okay between them too," he reasons sternly.

"It was *okay* when we weren't talking."

"We're practically family."

I bury my face in my hands and groan. I just want this conversation to end. "Fine. We'll be civil. But this is never going to be *okay*."

"You'll never forgive me?" he asks flatly. "Even though you know what it's like to make a mistake."

I just shake my head and reach for the door. "Luke, the day I forgive myself for that mistake is the day I forgive you for using it against me." He grabs the screen door handle and tries to jiggle it before I can shut him out. "Don't hold your breath."

Friday

After school, I put in a call to Mom because I haven't checked in with her for a few weeks. At first it's nice. Since she quit her second therapist and started going to a third, her method of dealing with all that resentment toward me is to act like nothing happened. She talks to me like I'm a kid away at boarding school—how are my classes, my friends, my job. She tries to talk about boys as though our last phone call didn't involve a fight over Jem, who she carefully refrains from mentioning. I don't bring him up either. She'd sense my weakness for him, and then she'd worry.

"Are you still going to counseling?" she finally asks.

"Every week."

"Do you feel comfortable there?"

The group leader is a twit whose main qualification seems to be a bible study certificate; I spend more time worrying about the other group members than I do my own problems; it's yet another of my life's activities that involves Jem; it depresses me that I don't know how to pray.

"I'm learning a lot about myself." Or, rather, who I want to be.

When I come downstairs I find that someone besides Frank is here. Luke is in the kitchen, leaning against the counter and shifting his eyes like a criminal.

"Who the hell let you in?"

"Your brother's out back. He doesn't know I'm here. The door was open." He gestures to the front hall.

"What the hell were you thinking, coming here?"

"That I owe you. Big."

Shoot me. I want to scream but it comes out as a sigh. "Get in the fucking car."

"What?"

I grab my keys off the counter and give Luke the eye. "You heard me."

⟜

"Do you remember your mom?" I take the road into town. It's late in the afternoon, but we might make it in time to catch the last of the lunch special at Frank's favorite diner. I need to be normal for five minutes, and to get out of my head. But if I get out, I might never get back in.

Luke gives me a curious look. I give him a stiff glare in return. If he knows all my issues, his are fair game too.

"Sort of."

"Does Briana?"

"I don't think so." Luke reaches over to turn on the radio, but not before murmuring, "I can't remember how she smelled."

⟜

We miss the lunch special. The fact that I find this disappointing shows just how close I am to becoming unhinged. I wonder if that's better or worse than being numb.

"What happened to your hand?" Luke asks as we peruse the dinner menu. I've lost count of how many people have asked me that since I ditched the gloves.

"Mauled by a tiger."

The waitress comes to take our orders, and when she's gone Luke feels the need to break the silence. "So why aren't you with Harper right now?" he asks. "The two of you still together?" Luke's tone is complex—like he doesn't want to know the answer, but knows exactly what answer he does want to hear.

"He's in the hospital." I don't want to look at Luke's face and see *I told you so* written all over it. "Don't tell Frank."

"Why aren't you there with him?" Luke asks with genuine curiosity. "He's your…. You should be there."

"He's immunocompromised. They're limiting his visitors to reduce his risk of further infection."

"I don't want to pry, but is his cancer back?"

"No."

Luke closes his menu and stares at me. I can feel his eyes on the top of my head. "Do you want me to go with you to the hospital?"

"Is that your idea of making things up to me?"

Luke tries to take my hand and I withdraw it. He sighs like my noncompliance bothers him. "It's what a friend would do."

"We're not friends."

"What are we?"

"We're in it for our brothers." And that's all this is, now.

When Luke and I get back to the house, Frank has the garage door open, puttering around as usual. He looks surprised, and then suspicious, as Luke and I both step out of the car.

"Where were you two?" he asks.

"We had lunch."

Frank's eyes shift between us, trying to riddle it out. There isn't much to infer from our silence or posture, but he seems to sense that we're back on speaking terms. Neither of us has a black eye, at least.

"Everything's good, I trust?"

"Fine." I excuse myself to 'do homework' while Frank and Luke make conversation. I hear Luke invite Frank out to Port Elmsley in the near future, and sigh with relief. That'll make Frank happy, and it'll give me some solitude around the house.

I start preparing dinner for him—ham sandwiches and salad—and do another neurotic message check on my phone. Nothing. I text Elise for an update but she doesn't get back to me.

"Frank! Food!"

Luke doesn't stay—claims he has to get back, and we part with a civil goodbye. Frank asks if we're okay now.

"We're talking." That's more than I want to give him, but it's what I have to give to make my brother happy. He tucks in to his sandwich and devours half of it before he looks up again.

"How come Jem isn't around?" Frank may not like Jem or my relationship with him, but as a creature of habit Frank has become accustomed to visits, particularly around the weekend. If Jem isn't here, I'm usually at his house.

"He's having some testing done." It's a fairly benign lie, and one that covers my ass should Frank learn that Jem spent part of the weekend in the hospital.

"Is he alright?" Frank asks suspiciously.

I nod. "Just a routine checkup. Cancer's one of those diseases you have to follow up on occasionally." I get an eye roll from Frank for stating the obvious. He senses my fickle mood and lets me be without further prodding. I don't leave the kitchen until bedtime. By the time I retire there is no less than five days' worth of food in the freezer (Frank is pleased) and I feel marginally better. I fall asleep knowing that feeling won't last.

Saturday

Elise calls me during breakfast to chat. Jem is coming home today. She doesn't let slip many details about his physical condition, but mentions that he won't be up for having guests right away.

"I understand." I don't like it, but the best thing I can give him right now is the privacy to rest and heal.

I change the subject. "Have you applied for work at that camp yet?" I know Elise wants to, even though she doesn't think she should. She admits to having printed an application off the camp website, but she hasn't filled it out or sent it in.

"You should."

"Mmm. I need to be here."

I have to let the call end to go to work, but not before I extract a promise from Elise that she'll call to let me know how Jem is doing.

"I'll tell him you said hello."

"Tell him he's my favorite asshole, okay? He'll know what it means."

Elise snorts into the phone. "Now I know how you put up with him. Two peas in a screwed up pod."

That sounds about right.

↔

Work drags. It's a busy day at the B&B because the dining room and garden have been booked for a Christening reception. My mind is elsewhere and each plate of food I bring to the buffet, each batch of lemonade I squeeze for the garden party, gets me one step closer to the end of my shift. Every time I go into the pantry I surreptitiously check my phone for messages. Still nothing from Elise. It's early, yet. Jem isn't due to be discharged until this afternoon.

It's odd, missing him and not knowing when I'll see him again. I've never missed anyone who wasn't family before. With every other guy I dated, I couldn't have cared less where he was or what he was doing when we weren't directly interacting. This absence from Jem makes me feel strange. I get the sense that if I could hear him or touch him, everything would settle back into its proper place, even though I know that such an idea is beyond naïve.

Mrs. Elwood can tell I'm a little distracted. She keeps me in the kitchen after noon, because how badly can I screw up washing dishes?

"Willa." I jump as Mrs. Elwood speaks right over my shoulder. I quickly try to figure out what I'm in trouble for—did I space out? Forget to shut off the tap?

"Sorry."

Mrs. Elwood gives me a quizzical look. "Phone's for you." I slip away to the laundry room and pick up the line there.

"Hello?"

"Hi Willa." Elise sounds cautiously optimistic. "Just calling to let you know that Jem's home safe." The news doesn't give me the relief I thought it would. He's still sick, just in a different location, and I still have to keep my distance so he can recover.

"Oh. Good."

"He was asking for you."

"Let him know I miss him and I'll see him soon."

"Um, Mom said it's cool of you come over later. For a short visit, anyway. It might cheer him up." Now I wish it were a slow day at the B&B so I could blow off the last half hour of my shift to go see him.

"I get off work at three. I can come straight after."

"That works," Elise agrees. "See you then."

I didn't think it was possible, but time crawls even slower.

I drive directly to the Harpers' house after work, buzzing with nervous excitement the whole time. I'm relieved that I get to see Jem again so soon, but I know it won't be pretty. He wasn't in the hospital for nothing.

When I pull into the driveway, Dr. Harper steps out onto the front porch and waves at me. I half expect him to turn me away at the door—his wife made a mistake; Jem really isn't well enough for company yet.

"How are you, Willa?" he asks as I climb the front steps. I follow along with this exchange of pleasantries, and then he invites me into the front room. "I want to talk to you."

We sit across from each other on the couch and loveseat. The way he leans forward with his elbows on his knees and speaks carefully, softly, reminds me of the way doctors explain prognoses to next-of-kin. He tells me what to expect from Jem—his level of energy, his symptoms, and how long I'll be able to stay. He tells me that Jem's kidney is bruised and still may bleed slightly, so I shouldn't hug him too hard. I'll have to wear a mask around him, both to keep him safe from my germs and keep me from catching his, and wash my hands thoroughly.

"When will he be back to school?"

"When he's up to it. I don't know when that will be."

Elise, hovering restlessly during the conversation, interrupts to ask if her dad is done reading the riot act. She takes his stern look as a yes and grabs my hand. I get tugged off the couch and into the kitchen to wash up and don a mask, and then Elise hurries me up the stairs to see Jem.

"Calm, Elise," Dr. Harper warns her. "Don't unsettle him."

"We won't!"

Elise knocks on Jem's bedroom door, but doesn't wait for a response before pushing it open and stepping inside. "Willa's here!" she announces in a sing-song voice. Her mood almost irks me, because I can't find it within myself to show so much cheer.

I didn't think it would be this hard, seeing him, but he has the telltale signs of a lung problem and it brings back memories I wish I didn't have. His lips are white and cracked, and I can hear his breathing from across the room. He has a weary look in his eye that is either exhaustion or slight oxygen deprivation.

Jem holds out his arms and I gather him up in a hug. I push his hat back because I want to feel that little bit of softness. His fingers tug at my sleeves and dig into my arms as I kiss his temple and whisper in his ear. "I missed you."

"Take that off." His voice is hoarse. Jem tugs my mask off and I indulge him with a kiss on the corner of his mouth before putting it back on. I promised his dad I would wear it.

It hurts Jem to talk, so we don't. We touch and nuzzle, reacquainting ourselves with the scent and shape of each other. His collarbone seems to stick out more than it did last week. It feels like he's lost weight, and his hands and the tip of his nose are cold. I hold his hands to my neck for warmth. He uses the hold on me to pull me in closer until I'm cuddled against his shoulder.

We entirely forget the fact that we're not alone at this reunion until Elise's feet shift softly against the floor. She looks a little shocked, and maybe even guilty at intruding, as she backs out of the room.

"I'll uh, go now."

Jem smiles at me as she shuts the door. "Good," he whispers. "I want you all to myself."

"Hush." It obviously pains him to talk. It sounds like his throat is swollen and he has patchy bruises around his neck. When he breathes there's a nasty sucking sound that I know all too well. There's a plastic bowl set on his bedside table, presumably for this exact purpose. I grab it and a tissue and tell him, "Arms up and cough." He looks at me like I just told him to pick up dog poop with his bare hand.

"Give me a minute?" he says. He's making small gasps—reflexive coughs that he's trying to suppress. He takes the bowl and glances at the door.

"I've seen you puke at least five different colors and you want privacy for this?" I put an arm around Jem's back and help him sit up a little farther. It only takes two cupped thumps on the back before the reflex to cough overpowers his self consciousness, and the wet gob that caught in his throat comes up to say hello.

"Rinse." I hand him water to cleanse his mouth and take the bowl away to dispose of the mess.

"You're not a nurse," he scolds me softly when I return from the washroom. "Come cuddle." Jem just wants to be held. We negotiate a comfortable position that keeps him propped up and comfortable, with room for him to turn away and cough when he feels the need. He rests his head back on my shoulder, half-sitting, half-spooning, and dozes languidly.

I track the rise and fall of each fragile breath. Old habit has come back in full force, waiting for a hitch or a sign of distress. I have to keep reminding myself that Jem's situation is different; he's on the mend, not terminally ill. He's home, and he's healing. His hands grip my little ones with living connection. So close and warm, I slip into that comfortable state of relaxation between sleeping and waking, only to be woken a short time later by the pounding in my chest. Something is wrong, and I know it even in my sleep.

Jem isn't breathing.

Jem: June 10 to 11

Saturday

I've never slept so well or so deeply. I wake up with a soft set of lips pressed to mine, but not my girlfriend's—my dad's. I choke back the stale air he forces into my lungs, coughing painfully. The center of my chest is on fire.

"Jem?" He calls my name over and over again. Dad leans over and shines a pocket flashlight in my eyes. Thank you, I need to be blind on top of everything else.

He makes me squeeze his hands and tell him the date. I'm on the floor next to my bed and cold without a blanket. I need my blanket. Willa kneels opposite my dad with one hand on my wrist and the other on the phone.

"I got through." She passes the phone over to Dad, who says he needs an ambulance at our address.

"I'm fine."

He ignores me and starts rattling off the details of my condition. That can't be right. Willa's fingers adjust position on my wrist, looking for a better pulse point.

Dad hangs up the phone and Willa says that my fingers are turning blue. They are not. It's really bright in here…

Suddenly I'm lurched upwards so Dad can set a pillow under my shoulders. He asks if I can breathe. Of course I can. He asks me again, and again, and calls my name.

"I said yes." All I can manage is a whisper.

"You didn't say anything."

My head is splitting and my chest is heavy. It feels like I have to cough, but when I try barely anything happens. It's like pushing against a solid concrete barrier. Willa's hand leaves my wrist and a moment later I feel her tugging at my sock. "His feet are blue too."

Both their hands are on me then, taking my socks off and pushing my pajamas up my calves. Their hands press along my legs and feet, looking for pulse points.

"Just a few more minutes," Dad says to me. There's a hysterical edge to his voice that unsettles me. If the doctor is worried, I know it's bad. His fingers rest on my neck while Willa's resume their place at my wrist. I close my eyes and listen to them compare counts on my heart rate.

I think I fall asleep, because the next thing I'm aware of is the smooth feel of sterile gloves against my skin. A plastic oxygen mask is fitted over my mouth and nose, and when I open my eyes a man I've never seen before is leaning over me.

"He's been in and out of consciousness," Dad says. No I wasn't. I was sleeping.

539

I can't see Willa anywhere. The EMT attaches a blood pressure cuff to my arm while his partner—a petite blond woman—asks me questions to check my level of consciousness. She presses a digital thermometer into my ear and announces that I'm running a fever. Again? Fuck me.

I close my eyes as they lift me onto a stretcher. The familiar straps close around my body. I watch languidly as the door and then the hall and stairs pass by, but I still don't see Willa. I see Elise and Eric, both their faces strained with worry. I want to tell them not to be upset, but my body just wants to sleep.

The EMT asks Dad if he's riding along with me. He says he will. Where's Willa? She was just here a few minutes ago...

As I'm lifted into the back of the ambulance I see her standing next to Elise. Her face is pale and blank, like a ghost. She's still here. She didn't leave.

As Dad climbs in beside me Willa steps closer and raises a hand to wave. That's when I see the blood. It's all over her cheek and neck, running down her jaw. I try to point, to tell her she's bleeding.

"Willa."

"It's okay," she tells me. The whole collar of her shirt is red. Jesus Christ, what's wrong with her?

"Will—"

The doors close, cutting me off. I try to tell Dad that she was bleeding, but he doesn't get it. He just keeps reassuring me that everything is okay. That's not the point. I'm talking about *her*.

"BP's dropping."

I think I'll sleep.

Whenever

My mouth is dry. How's that for a coherent thought? My chest hurts like hell and my head is pounding so hard I don't even want to open my eyes. I'm cold, and I can tell by the smell that I'm in the hospital. I'm not in my own clothes, either, and the oxygen tube under my nose has dried out my airway.

I mumble 'water' and a moment later someone fits a straw between my lips. The water is warm but I don't care.

"How you feeling?" It's Elise's voice, but the hand that squeezes mine feels like it belongs to Mom. That writer's bump is hard to mistake.

I grunt at them and Elise offers more water. "The lights are dimmed. Open your eyes?" she says hopefully. All they want is signs of life, so I crack an eyelid for them.

"You were in and out, yesterday. How are you feeling now?"

"Just kill me."

Elise knows I'm not serious, just cranky, but she pouts anyway and whines my name.

"You'd get to see if Thestrals are real after all," I croak. For a second she looks genuinely tempted. Uh-oh.

Mom nudges Elise and tells her to go inform Dad and Eric that I'm awake. I tell her not to bother, I'm going right back to sleep. Mom nods to the door anyway and pets my head as Elise leaves. She sound of the door closing makes my ears ring.

"Just sleep," she says.

"W'time is it?"

"Twelve."

"At night?"

"No, noon. It's Sunday, sweetie." I cough and she makes me take another sip of water. Mom tells me my fever is back and that the infection in my lungs has developed into pneumonia. I burst a blood vessel in my throat, so I should be on alert for any more signs of pain or bleeding.

"What'd the doctor say?"

"You're going to be fine." Mom doesn't usually bullshit me like that. Either she doesn't know the prognosis yet or I'm so well and truly screwed that she doesn't want to admit it. She adjusts my blanket around me for warmth and I wish I was at home, in my own bed, under my own blankets, and preferably with a certain someone to cuddle with.

My memory of last seeing her is vague. She was holding me, I think…and bleeding?

"Is Willa okay?"

"She's fine. Eric drove her to work today." Mom rubs my back and the gentle vibration makes me want to cough. I resist the urge, knowing it will hurt. "She spent the night."

"At our house?"

"In the waiting room."

I close my eyes and I can feel my pulse in my temples. I can't believe she stayed, knowing that she probably wouldn't be allowed to see me. She probably got very little sleep, and crappy sleep at that, before going to work. Why would she go to work? She should have gone home to sleep…or stayed with me. I wish she had.

"She'll come again?" I don't know why I'm asking Mom. It's not like the woman has a crystal ball.

"Yes, sweetie," Mom assures me anyway. I'll take what I can get.

I think I'll sleep.

When I wake up I can hear Dad behind me, talking lowly to someone whose voice I don't recognize. They're talking about urine—output and protein content and traces of blood. So I try to doze off again, because I don't need the humiliation of listening to people talk about my piss, and I don't need to be reminded that I have a hard rubber tube in my dick.

The heart monitor gives away my waking state. Dad puts a hand on my shoulder and asks if I'm okay.

"What time is it?"

"Two."

Is it so hard to specify morning or afternoon?

"Can I get some painkillers?"

"What hurts?"

Everything. "My head."

Dr. Harper uses his connections to get the medication order through quickly, and I get to crash on heavy painkillers. Now I can block out his unpleasant doctor conversations without even trying.

When is she going to get here?

And I sleep.

Willa: June 10 to 13

Saturday

A nurse gives me an oversized scrub shirt to wear in place of my bloodied one. She stays with me while I wash the blood off my face and neck over the designated sink, and I try not to be too disgusted with the smell of hospital soap.

"Any word on why he was coughing blood?" I ask as I dry my face. I don't think Jem was even conscious when he started coughing red.

"I don't know the details. He isn't my patient," the nurse says, and escorts me back to the waiting room. One of Dr. Harper's colleagues was good enough to see me. Some of Jem's blood landed in my mouth, so he gave me a prescription for antibiotics and an order to stay away from Jem until it becomes clear I haven't caught whatever infection he has.

I should really just go home, but instead I end up spending the night in the waiting room. I don't know how *not* to be here.

"What happened to your hand?" Elise asks in the wee hours of the morning, tracing her thumb along my scar. We're sharing the narrow couch, spooned together but failing to sleep.

"I was startled and the knife I was holding slipped." That's the most she'll ever know of it, anyway.

Sunday

I get a ride home from Eric after work. My car is still in their driveway. I don't want to, but I go home first. I spend about five minutes there—just long enough to brush my teeth and change out of the clothes I've been wearing since Saturday, and then I take off to the hospital.

I ride the elevator to the third floor with a guy carrying a flower arrangement. The plastic decoration in the bouquet says *Congratulations* and he has one of those foil balloons that says *It's a boy!* It's hard to believe people come to hospitals for happy reasons, but there you have it.

I took my temperature before coming and know that I'm not showing any symptoms of infection, but I won't risk it. I take one of the masks from the nurses' station, even though Jem will foolishly insist I take it off, and a pair of blue gloves. When I enter his room Ivy is sitting by the bed and Jem is asleep.

"He's breathing better," she tells me quietly. "His fever's coming down."

I can't get too close to Jem, so I sit in the spare chair across the room. Ivy and I talk quietly for a few minutes. So far the pneumonia has only affected the upper lobes of his lungs, so they're trying to treat him before it can spread to the lower lobes.

Dr. Harper joins us after a few minutes. He's in scrubs, but he's missing his white coat and ID badge, as though he just finished a shift.

"Dr. Burke wants to talk to us," he says to Ivy. "Is he sleeping soundly?"

Ivy nods and Dr. Harper begins to check Jem's monitors and IV drip, like an obsessive compulsive going through a ritual. It must be worse to watch Jem go through this knowing every little thing that can possibly go wrong.

Ivy excuses herself to use the washroom before meeting with Dr. Burke.

"I'm taking her to eat something, after," Dr. Harper says to me when she's out of the room. "She hasn't been eating right. Will you be okay alone with Jem for a little while?"

"Take all the time you need."

Ivy brings a three-inch binder with her to meet Dr. Burke. I'd bet my left boob that it contains Jem's medical records for the last six months alone. She kisses his forehead softly before departing and Jem doesn't even stir.

We're alone, and this feels very familiar. The heart monitor's periodic beeps, the whirring of the IV pump, the rasp of unhealthy breathing. If I closed my eyes I could well be back in St. John's, three years past. Even the blue blanket is the same.

A thin nurse with dyed red hair pushes back the curtain around the bed and comes up to the side table with a plastic kit in her hand. She says hello to me quietly and calls Jem's name, but he's thoroughly unconscious. Her task still has to be done, though, and she pulls back his blanket and hospital gown to clean his Hickman.

It's amazing what Jem can sleep through. Either he's really drugged up or exhausted, because he doesn't seem to register the removal of the adhesive patch, or the open air that makes goose bumps rise on his skin. What finally does make him flinch is the cold swab around the catheter entry point. His eyelids flutter, but he quickly realizes what's going on and relaxes. Maintaining the machinery in his chest is nothing new and exciting.

"It's good that he sleeps so soundly," the nurse says as she flushes the catheter. I just nod, not really in the mood to make conversation. The nurse tidies up her contaminated surfaces and snaps off her gloves.

"I'll cover him back up," I say before she moves to do it. She nods before moving on to the next task on her busy shift.

I take Jem's wrist and gingerly guide his hand through the arm of his gown. He makes a plaintive noise in his throat as I move him, so I leave the tie behind his neck undone. I don't want to bother him any more than necessary.

"Just sleep," I tell him, and kiss his forehead.

"Eh?" Jem reluctantly opens his eyes and gets this look of outright panic when he sees me. "Where's Mom?"

"She and your dad went to go talk to Dr. Burke."

"How long have you been here?"

"Ten minutes?"

"Did you see…?"

"Yes."

Jem turns his face away from me to cough. His whole frame shakes with the force of the fit.

"I didn't want you to see that," he says when he regains his breath. I offer him water for his throat and he has to suck on the straw in quick bursts between shallow breaths.

"Oh hush, you're beautiful."

Jem closes his eyes and winces. He's reached his limit, and he's starting to shiver. I pull the blanket back up and tuck it around him.

"Please leave," he says softly.

"I can't. I promised your parents I'd stay with you till they get back from dinner."

"I don't need a babysitter."

"I'll let you stay up late and watch cartoons." The joke falls flat; Jem isn't in the mood for humor.

"Please, Willa."

I sit back down in the visitor's chair and scoot closer to the bedside, even though I know I should leave space. "I don't find it gross." I take his hand and he squeezes me back. "I don't care that you've got hardware in your chest. You're still sexy. You're still my favorite."

"Please don't try to justify it."

"Okay. But I did promise your parents I'd stay. They won't be gone long. They're meeting with Dr. Burke and then grabbing something to eat."

Jem's only response is to turn his face back up to the ceiling and close his eyes.

"Is Dr. Burke the guy taking care of you here?"

"He's my hematologist," Jem says simply. "The guy taking four vials of blood a day since I've been here."

"They're worried about relapse?"

"I don't know." He sighs. What he means is that he doesn't want to think about it. "I was waiting for you to come today."

"Yeah?"

Jem nods. "You should have gone home last night."

"I felt better here." I wouldn't have been able to sleep at home, anyway, and if something happened to him I might get the chance to say goodbye.

Jem tugs on my hand. "Can you just...?"

"What?"

He sighs. "Hold me?"

The request makes me wince. "I can't."

Jem looks like a puppy that's just been kicked. "Please?"

"I'm not even supposed to be touching you right now." I squeeze his hand. "I shouldn't even visit yet, really. Yesterday when you coughed some fluid went into my mouth and I'm supposed to keep my distance until I'm sure I didn't catch the same infection."

I trace little circles on his wrist with my gloved hand instead, trying to offer some small comfort.

"I'm sorry," Jem murmurs.

I shake my head. "You were unconscious; couldn't help it."

"It was blood, wasn't it?"

"Yes."

"I thought you were bleeding."

"No big deal if I do."

Jem slowly rolls onto his side, coughing slightly with the change in position, and draws his knees up for warmth. I help arrange the blankets over his body and tuck him in as best I can without getting too close. He's laying on the absolute edge of the mattress, as close to me as possible without actually touching.

"I'm scared," he whispers.

"I'm with you," I whisper back, because nothing is more meaningless than 'It's going to be fine.' I'm not going anywhere, no matter how bad things get; once I commit I can't flake.

"Thanks for being with me," he murmurs. I smile and pet his warm cheek.

"Where else would I be?"

⌖

The Harpers return an hour later, somewhat recharged and fed. Ivy settles in like she plans to stay late or even spend the night. Visiting hours are almost over, so Dr. Harper offers to walk me to my car.

As we pass through the automatic doors he slyly mentions that the meeting with Jem's doctors went well. "Their primary concern is treating the pneumonia," he says. I read between the lines and take that to mean Jem hasn't relapsed. Cancer would trump pneumonia, right? Dr. Harper says Jem will be kept as an inpatient for a few more days, at least. He talks about bruised kidneys and forcing the phlegm out of Jem's lungs at regular intervals. He tells me how fragile Jem is, even though he seems to be getting better. These things feel so routine to me that it isn't until we're halfway to my car that I realize he's testing my mettle—whether I can stand Jem's baggage, or at least refrain from making him feel ashamed of it.

"I'll be back tomorrow," I assure him. Dr. Harper gives me an appraising look, probably trying to decide if I sound disgusted.

"You're good for him, you know," he says. "You cheer Jem up."

"I try."

"He needs that sense of normalcy."

I stop with my hand on the door of my car. "You know he's really hard on himself for not being normal, right?"

Dr. Harper nods. "When he was an inpatient on the ward and had friends there it was easier. But now he feels those differences strongly."

"Tell him he looks good more often," I encourage. "He needs to hear it until he believes it." Because he's going to, damn it.

↭

When I get home, Frank is waiting for me. He has coffee and cookies on the kitchen table, which makes me think this is an intervention. He even looks a little bit like Dad, except this time there's pastry instead of drug paraphernalia on the table.

"Have a cookie. We need to talk."

I trudge to the table and take a token bite out of one of the cookies. I don't have an appetite when I know I'm about to get in trouble. I do, however, take a few sips of coffee. I'm sleep deprived and that might impair my ability to argue.

"Where were you last night?"

"At the hospital with the Harpers."

"All night?"

"All night."

"You should have called."

"I'm sorry."

Frank gives a frustrated shake of the head and sips his over-sugared coffee. "How's Jem?" he hedges.

Semi-lucid. Coughing up phlegm. Running a fever. Beautiful when partially clothed.

"He's fine."

"There was an ambulance called to his house yesterday." Such things don't escape notice in a small town, let alone a paramedic's attention.

"He wasn't quite ready to come home from the hospital yet, so they took him back."

"In a speeding ambulance?"

"He has a lung infection."

Frank gives me a pressing look. He knows I'm not telling the whole story and wants me to cut the bullshit, or else.

"It's pneumonia. They're keeping him as an inpatient for a few more days."

"Are you okay with this?" What a strange question. It's not like my permission matters in this affair.

"Uh, of course?"

"I suppose this means you'll be at the hospital a lot."

"Yeah." That's a given.

"And you're going to be...okay?"

"I won't unplug anything, if that's what you mean."

Frank gives me a withering look. "I'm trusting you with this," he says seriously, "because I know he's important to you. And you're stubborn. But mostly because he's important to you—and I need to know that you're not going to become…*troubled* over seeing him…like that."

I can't guarantee that it won't upset me if Jem takes a bad turn, but at the moment I'm comforted by the knowledge that he's in the care of professionals and that his condition is treatable. I'm holding out on faith that I won't have to watch him die. I simply can't contemplate going through that again.

"I won't."

"Just don't be spending all your time there. You've got homework."

I take another bite of my cookie. "So how's Doug?"

Monday

Paige passes me a note in Math class. She's been very friendly since she lied to bail me out of trouble on Friday, and now seems to be the moment to repay the favor. The note says:

I tried to call you yesterday.

Apparently I'm already late in repaying this favor. I write back, *I was at the hospital with Jem. No cell phones allowed.*

Is he dying? Are you okay?

It's nice of her to ask, though *is he dying* looks odd in her tidy purple penmanship.

I slide the note back to her with a firm *No.*

↶

I find out what Paige wants after class, when she asks me to take a walk with her before we go to the cafeteria. We end up sitting in my car, and it takes Paige a few false starts to tell me what she needs.

"I know what you're going to say," she says.

"Then let's assume I've already said it."

"I wouldn't ask, but my aunt works at the drugstore."

Now that she's mentioned a location, I can see where this is going. "You want condoms? For prom night?"

Paige turns bright red and buries her chin in her collar. "I'm not *planning* anything," she squeaks. "I'm just…not ruling it out."

"It's good to be prepared," I agree. I don't care whom Paige screws, much less why. I can hardly judge her for her love life given my track record.

"Any particular brand you want?" I hold out my hand for the money and she slips me a ten dollar bill.

"Um, no?"

"You're not allergic to latex, right?"

Paige shakes her head. "You won't tell anyone, will you?"

"Nope. But take the time to read the directions on the box, eh?"

She nods and wrings her hands. "Do you think I should go through with it?"

How should I know that? I sigh and shrug. "Do you want to?"

"I don't want to go to university totally inexperienced," she says. I remind her that she has an entire summer between now and frosh week, but she seems to find something special about prom night and wants to make an occasion of her cherry.

"Have you ever?" she asks.

"Yeah."

"With Jem?"

"No, before I met him."

"Does it hurt?"

"Not if you do it right."

She gets that fretful look again. "Right? Like, how?"

I have a chuckle at her nerves, even though I know I shouldn't find this so funny.

"Like, don't let him lead. And don't rush. Get yourself on top and make sure you're wet enough."

Paige nods like I'm giving her the secrets of the universe.

I smirk as I tell her, "Make sure you come at least once before taking a run at home plate. You probably won't come during, at least not the first time."

Paige blushes, but smiles timidly. "Thanks."

"Don't screw this up." It's the best warning I can offer her in light of being a horrible influence.

"I won't," she says timidly. "Hey, Willa?"

"Yeah?"

"Why are you with Jem? Really?"

Because he loves me, warts and all.

"Because I love him, warts and all." Paige doesn't really get it, but that's to be expected. She knows what lust and affection feel like, not love. Hell, I didn't properly know what love was until someone I loved was taken from me.

This train of thought only makes me miss Jem more. I have the urge to cook—maybe his favorite sweet potato soup with carrot puree, or peas and spinach with honey. It's a wasted thought, because his food intake is controlled and monitored at the hospital.

But when I stop by to see Jem after school, I take a little Tupperware of sweet potato soup with me, just in case he feels like being a rebel. It's only a small amount, less than the contents of a pudding cup, but it makes his day. Jem can't eat it immediately because he's still hooked up to a dialyzer when I get there, but he makes me set the container on the side table and calls it his 'light at the end of the tunnel.' Apparently soup is a heavenly experience.

He's looking rough today. He complains of joint pain, chest pain, head pain, fatigue, and dizziness. But the doctors insist his condition is improving, so I try to stay positive. He hasn't had another blackout or stopped breathing in the last forty-eight hours, so they've dialed back some of his monitoring equipment;

he's no longer buried in nodes and wires, and those that are present have been consolidated into a neat little bundle.

Jem gets a little self-conscious when the nurse comes in to disconnect the dialyzer because it means his Hickman needs to be exposed, but thankfully he doesn't make a big deal of it. The nurse is barely out of the room before Jem turns to the side table and makes a grab for the sweet potato soup.

"No spoon?" he asks. Crap, I should have thought of that.

"I'll get one from the cafeteria."

I'm only gone for five minutes, but when I get back the container of soup is almost empty. He drank it like a warm milkshake.

"Couldn't wait," he says, and uses the plastic spoon to greedily scrape the sides of the Tupperware.

"At least you have an appetite."

"Feel free to bring more of this," he says, and stifles a cough.

"Don't eat too fast."

"Would you judge me if I licked the bowl?"

I say no, just because I want to watch him do it. Jem gets sweet potato on his nose and tries to lick that off too.

"Don't they feed you here?" I joke.

"All-liquid diet," he says. "It blows. I never feel full."

Eventually Jem has to concede that the container is indeed empty, and sets it aside with a pout. He tries to make me promise to bring more and I tell him I'll have to check with his parents before sneaking any more food in.

"Traitor," he mutters. Jem makes a show of being put out with me, but the food has made him sleepy and content, and he can't sustain the act. He falls asleep while I massage lotion into his hands, and all too soon visiting hours are over. I don't want to leave him.

I kiss his forehead before going. "Goodnight."

Tuesday

My temperature is normal. No swollen glands. No tender throat. Sinuses and breathing are normal. Whatever germ Jem has, I don't. It would have manifested symptoms by now if I were susceptible. I'm so excited about this development that I do a little victory dance in the bathroom and rail my elbow on the doorframe. Totally worth it.

I call the Harper house before school. I meant it when I said I wouldn't bring more food without talking to Jem's parents, and I know he'll be sore with me if I show up sans food.

Dr. Harper is puzzled by my request at first. "Is he not eating at the hospital?" I hear him turn to his wife and ask the same question. Somewhere in the background Ivy says, "He eats, but not enough."

"He's on an all-liquid diet right now," Dr. Harper tells me. I ask of soup is fair game in extremely small quantities.

"I don't think his body can handle something as rich as soup right now, not with his kidneys still so fragile." I'm tempted to tell him how well and how eagerly Jem 'handled' soup last night, and smirk at our little secret.

"I figured I'd have to adjust the protein content for his kidneys and the diary for his lungs. Any other restrictions?"

I think Dr. Harper is mildly annoyed that I haven't immediately backed down on this idea. Behind him I can hear Ivy say, "If she can get him to eat, let her."

Dr. Harper sighs. "Okay, but only a small amount of soup."

Elise picks up the line from elsewhere in the house and puts in her two cents, "See if you can get him to eat his fruit cups."

"I'll give it a shot." But I'll feel bad doing it—packaged fruit puree is gross. Dr. Harper gives me the details of what Jem can and cannot eat right now. A small part of me is pleased that I guessed right with the sweet potato soup—it perfectly fits his dietary guidelines.

"It's nice that you want to do this," Dr. Harper admits.

"It's my pleasure." Anything for Jem.

❧

To hell with homework, I have high-vitamin, low sodium soup to make. I boil carrots, peas and yams with a pinch of garlic, and thin the puree with homemade vegetable stock. A splash of honey and lemon compliments the sweetness of the yams.

I take a thermos full of it to the hospital with a bowl and spoon—I remembered this time—so that his parents can decide how much to allow their son. When I step off the elevator on the third floor, I find Elise sitting in the waiting lounge, reading a book.

"I wouldn't go in there yet," she says.

"What happened?" I flop down beside her on the couch.

"Dad's with him right now. The dizzy spells have passed and he's not a fall risk anymore, so they took the catheter out. He's in a *really* bad mood." Can't blame him for that. It probably mortified Jem to have to put his private parts on display, and there was probably a med student there to gawk—and that's just the mental discomfort.

I go down to the vending machine by the gift shop for a drink and a snack. Elise says this particular machine is least likely to eat my money. As I head back toward the elevators a sign on the wall catches my eye: *Chapel*. I would never have noticed anything religious before Jem and Group, but now I'm curious. I peek through the window in the door and look around. It's just a beige room with benches. Up at the front there is a lectern with interchangeable faith symbols, and along the wall is a bookshelf with various holy texts. The room is empty apart from one guy sitting in the front row.

I think about going in, but I don't want to disturb the guy. Then I realize it's Eric, taking full advantage of the front row to extend his legs comfortably. For a moment I stand outside the door and watch him. He's normally boisterous, but here he's so still and quiet. It's fascinating, watching his sense of connection to this place—or whatever divine thing dwells within it.

I slip in and walk quietly to the front of the room, studying him. Eric's eyes are closed and his face is relaxed. Is that what it is to pray? It looked different in church—boring, zealous, halfhearted, token. This is something different.

I sit down next to him in the pew and Eric slowly opens his eyes. Maybe I had it wrong and he was actually napping.

"Is he okay?" Eric asks of Jem.

"Still in a bad mood, from what I hear."

Eric nods once and closes his eyes.

"Tired?"

"No."

I envy his easy peace. "Teach me."

He looks at me with confusion. I tell him I'm not religious, or even spiritual. Eric wraps his strong hand around my upper arm and tugs gently. I scoot closer to him on the bench, but that's not close enough for him. He isn't satisfied until he's picked me up and placed me down on his lap, back to front. His arms wrap around me and his cheek rests on the side of my head.

"Here," he says lowly, and takes my little hands in his sturdy ones. He makes me press them palm-to-palm with my wrists turned up toward the center of my chest. The posture feels good, like a full heart and a clear head.

I look at Eric out of the corner of my eye and find that his are closed. He has that peace about him again, like he's listening to something I can't hear. I try to tap into it, but it doesn't come easily.

"What do you ask for?" Don't prayers always ask for something? Some blessing, or divine intercession?

"Don't ask," Eric says lowly. "Give thanks."

I don't know how prayers usually start, so I just launch right into it. *Thank you for letting me get away...and for not killing him before I moved here.*

I don't know what to say after that, so I just sit quietly while Eric makes his peace with the divine. When he seems to be finished I admit that I admire him for being able to focus like that.

"I don't know how you do it either," he says. I get the feeling we're not talking about prayer. "You're the only person I know who can just *be* with him. It's exhausting."

"You do it too. You took all those photos."

Eric shakes his head. Maybe taking pictures was his way of avoiding the act of 'being' with his sick brother. He can hide behind a camera and express himself through still images that reveal everything and nothing at once.

"How do you look at him at his worst and not be bothered by it?"

I consider that for a moment. "It does bother me. But...I just become what he needs. He doesn't need bothered people. Forget your own agenda."

"And now, when he's being a whiney bitch?"

I shrug. "I'm gonna go try to see him now."

Eric and I share pretzels in the elevator. He has no intention of really 'visiting' Jem. He's only here because Elise needed a ride to the hospital. Apparently it's Eric's habit to make an appearance, snap a few photos for the album, and then disappear until he's needed. It's how he copes.

When we get to the third floor, Elise is no longer on the couch. Eric sits down in the lounge and calls, "See you later," to me. I head to Jem's room, hoping to find Elise and a conscious Jem.

Dr. Harper is in the visitor's chair, leaning back with his head against the wall and his eyes shut. Tired after a long shift, it seems. Elise is sitting at the windowsill, probably as close as Jem will allow, reading her book quietly. Jem is lying on his side with his back to the door, sulking.

"Hey." I come up behind him and kiss his shoulder. Jem turns his head to look at me and some of that scowl softens. "Word has it you're cranky."

"I'm not cranky," he snaps. I just chuckle. He's lost the hospital gown and is wearing his own pajamas. The dark blue cotton looks a lot comfier than a thin gown.

"You look nice."

Jem gives me a withering look. "If I was a car you'd have sold me for scrap by now."

"Have you seen what I drive? I wouldn't give you up until you couldn't go another inch."

Elise snickers quietly in her corner. Jem shoots her a glare and she mutters, "Shutting up now."

"You're not a fall risk anymore?" I ask. Jem shakes his head and goes back to sulking. "How long has it been since you've been out of this room?"

Jem looks up at me again. He's caught the spark of the idea.

"Want to go to the lounge?"

"My head hurts." He gives a feeble cough.

"Some other day, then."

"I want to."

"Wait till you're ready."

Jem's stubbornness rears its head. He's restless and snappy and determined to get out of his room now that I've mentioned it. Elise suggests using one of the ward wheelchairs to travel to the floor lounge, but apparently that's beneath his dignity. "What am I, an invalid?"

"You're sick," she says. I really think she's going to put up a fight about this, but when Jem asks her to pass him his slippers she does so like a loyal dog told to fetch. Jem stands without signs of weakness, but when he starts to walk to the door I really regret ever mentioning this stupid idea. He shuffles along like an old man and needs his sister's arm.

"You'll need a mask," she says. Jem mutters a few very colorful curses, but dutifully dons a mask to be out among the other patients.

The floor lounge is only twenty feet from the door of Jem's room. We take it slow, and Jem keeps one hand on the wall-rail and the other on his IV pole at all times. Elise takes the excursion, foolish as it is, as license to be chipper, and chatters about her book. It seems almost absentminded, the way she also keeps her hand on the IV pole to prevent it skidding away from her brother.

The pediatric lounge has toys and board games for the young patients, but Jem isn't up for anything more than watching TV, so we park ourselves on the couch and search for something to watch. Jem finally begins to mellow out as he's cuddled from both sides—or maybe he's just too tired from the walk to be snippy.

We're joined in the lounge by another boy, wheeling his meds along with him. He sits down next to Elise and strikes up a conversation. I get the impression that they're old friends on this ward. It's actually kind of cute—I think the boy is flirting with her.

Jem doesn't seem to care. Where the hell did the protective older brother go? He just rests his head against mine and stares blankly at the TV. I tell him about buying condoms for Paige and her high-pitched anxiety about sex. It was a toss-up between ribbed or flavored, since she didn't specify. Laughing at the stupidity of others cheers him up some.

"And I brought soup."

Jem's eyes slowly narrow. "Why are you withholding it?"

"I left it in my backpack, in your room."

"You were gonna let me starve," he accuses, and I think I see a smirk behind the blue mask.

"Fruit cups aren't filling?"

Jem wrinkles his nose. "Are you going to feed me or not?"

I get off the couch to retrieve my backpack. As soon as I come through the lounge door Jem reaches out a hand and makes grabbing motions.

"Jeez, you're demanding."

Jem actually makes the effort, weak as he is, to scoot down the couch to be nearer to the holy grail of soups. I give him the spoon first, but as soon as I hand over the soup the spoon is forgotten. Jem drinks straight out of the lid, practically chugging.

"Easy, you'll upset your stomach."

"I told you I was hungry." Jem stifles a cough and keeps on drinking.

"Why not savor it?" Elise says, and Jem looks torn. He eyes the thermos, trying to judge how much soup is left and how to ration it.

"It'll keep for a few hours with the lid screwed on tight."

"Good." Jem picks up the thermos and tucks it under his arm like a teddy bear. "Cheers."

◦⦵

Jem gets completely food drunk on two cups of soup, and is practically asleep when Elise and I wheel him back to bed. The nurse replaces his nasal cannula with an oxygen mask to give his nose a bit of a break, and then Elise and I are encouraged to say goodbye.

"You get some rest," Elise says to Jem.

"I will. Where'd that thermos go?" Elise helpfully points to the side table and the unused spoon.

"I'll meet you at the elevator," she says to me, and then Jem and I are left alone. I take one of his hands in mine and kiss the back of it.

"Hey, beautiful," I whisper. He tugs on my hand, pulling me in for a hug. I try not to disturb the oxygen mask as I lay my cheek next to his. I tell him I love him, and that he's precious, and under no circumstances will I be selling him off for scrap.

"You made my day," he confides with a contented smile.

"You made mine." I wonder if it's dangerous to rely on someone for my happiness, but by the time I reach the elevators I've decided that I don't care. It's hard enough to be happy without worrying about why.

Jem: June 14 to 15

Wednesday

The devil is five feet tall and carries a suction catheter. She lifts her thumb off the end of the tube and the thing growls at me.

"We can do this the easy way or the hard way."

Never toy with someone who is willing to bully you to get the job done, especially when that job involves a hard rubber tube up the nose. I cough and cough until it feels like my lungs are about to explode, and Nurse Kim jokes that I must be five pounds lighter without all that phlegm. This disgusting routine is what my days have been reduced to: cough up phlegm; cough up more phlegm; piss into a sample container; eat disgusting food; blood draws; more coughing; enjoy exactly four minutes of privacy while shitting; swallow pills; nap; contemplate death by boredom.

Mom is with me for most of the day, working from her laptop while I rest. When I'm awake I'm bored and in pain, so I try to sleep a lot. This plan has the added benefit of keeping me rested for when Willa visits after school.

Today she comes in the company of Eric and his Polaroid camera. "You got mail," he says, and hands me a fat envelope. It's a get well card from my friends in Ottawa, including Celeste.

"You told them I was sick?"

"Cee knew," he says. "She bought the card and got everybody to sign it."

Emily left me a cluster of Xs and Os with her well wishes. Morgan sends me a 'God bless.' Kyle has drawn a picture of what appears to be a clown and written 'get well' in a speech bubble, like I'm five years old. Caitlin has written: *Alright, now you're just doing it to get attention. Kidding, we all love you. Get better.* From Celeste I get a terse, *Feel better soon,* and Ava sends me a whole novel. Most of it is about Willa and me—she's heard we're a couple, it seems—and apologies for 'the incident' last time we saw each other. I let Willa read it and she seems vaguely amused.

"Was it even good?" I shouldn't ask such stupid questions.

"She was enthusiastic," Willa says, and leaves it at that.

Eric snaps a picture.

"Will you knock it off?"

"Nope." He shakes the picture. "We've got to get Willa into the album." I think my brother has delusions of being an actual photographer, because he directs Willa to pose with me by the bed and snaps a few shots of us together. She just chuckles and goes along with it.

"You don't have to humor him, you know."

"Have a little fun."

Thankfully, Eric eventually stops taking pictures. Willa has brought more soup. While I inhale it she opens the tube of cream on the nightstand and massages it into my calves. I'm going to owe her big time when I get out of here.

"You want a neck massage too?" she says, and winks at me.

"You're spoiling him," Eric warns. I stick my tongue out at him. He's just jealous.

Did I mention Willa has great hands? Small and soft and warm, but strong enough to push through the stiff knots. Her fingers rub from my shoulders to the base of my skull, stretching the muscles. Her thumbs work little circles behind my ears, pushing at the edges of my hat. I just close my eyes and relax into her touch.

Willa turns my head in her capable hands and I smile when her lips touch my cheek. "Open your eyes," she whispers. I do, and Eric immediately snaps a picture. Willa helped him set up the shot—had me smiling and everything.

"That's a nice one," Eric says, and holds it out to me. It's a romantic photo, aside from the fact that it was obviously taken in a hospital. Willa and I are cuddled close and happy. I don't look like I'm dying; just content.

"Holy crap, you actually took a good photo."

"Har har," Eric says, and snaps a photo of Willa. He tosses that one at me and says, "Is that a good one?" It's a snapshot of her chest.

"You son of a bitch," Willa mutters.

Eric feigns offense. "What did you just call my mom?"

I whisper loudly to Willa, "He's actually adopted."

"Ah. That explains it." Just to be on the safe side, Willa pockets the photo of her tits so it can't make its way into the album.

Suddenly Eric sits up straight in his chair, petty argument forgotten. "It's Wednesday," he says excitedly.

Willa doesn't get it.

"The gift shop has fudgesicles for half price every Wednesday." He's quickly up and out of the room, but at least has the decency to ask Willa if she wants one too. She declines, and the atmosphere of the room calms by ten degrees once he's gone.

"I have a little gift for you," Willa says.

"Is it more soup?"

"No."

I pout. "When I get out of here I'm going to eat a shit-ton of your soup, just to feel full again. You've been warned."

Willa smirks. "A whole shit-ton?"

"Yes, one shit-ton, equal to two assloads or half a metric fuck-ton."

She laughs and reaches into her backpack. A thermal lunch bag comes out, and to say that I'm excited is a gross understatement. She said it wasn't soup, but it could be something equally delicious.

I tear open the bag and find...a freezer-sized Ziploc with a *towel* inside.

"What the...?"

"The insulated bag should have kept it warm." She cracks the top of the

Ziploc and the warm scent of Gain detergent wafts out. My Willa is a genius. I pull the towel out of the bag and wrap it around my neck and face, enjoying the warmth and the comforting scent of fresh laundry. After so many days of hospital smells, this is heaven.

"God, I love you."

Willa kisses my cheek through the towel. "Love you too." It's an older hand towel, well-loved and soft with use. She rubs the corner of it against my cheek. "I missed that smile."

I am utterly content, even though everything aches and it's hard to breathe. She knows how to make me feel better, what little gestures will bring me comfort.

"Never change," I murmur.

Eric returns with a frozen brick of fudge hanging out of his mouth and snaps a picture. "Aw, aren't you two cute," he coos.

"Shut up."

"Seriously," he slurps his fudgesickle, "I'm happy for you. Now that you're getting laid you're less of a whiney maggot, most days."

"Will you shut up?" It's one thing to be a jackass, but it's entirely another to be rude about private matters in front of Willa. How could he just assume we're having sex? It's a miracle she even wants to call herself my girlfriend and I don't need his help to scare her away.

"Oh, please," Eric says. "Look at you two. It's obvious you've had your fingers in each other's fruit bowls."

Willa tries not to laugh and ends up snorting loudly. Eric takes this as a sign of vindication. "See? She thinks I'm funny."

"You're an idiot."

Thursday

I get sent for another chest x-ray. There's a crying kid in the waiting room outside Radiology, and his wailing is doing my head in. When I get back to my room all I want to do is nap, but Nurse Kim is waiting to take a sputum sample.

"You again?"

"Maggie's on her break. Now hack it up."

"Can't it wait?" Dumb question; it never can.

"Jem," she warns me.

"Satan," I reply in the same tone.

"I'll get the suction catheter."

"Fine, I'll cough; Jesus, woman." I swear, she gets some kind of sadistic satisfaction out of this. That's why she magically appears every time this needs to be done. There's no half-assing the job with this nurse, either. She keeps me coughing until my diaphragm hurts, and when I finally get to lay back and rest she wants to have a *conversation*.

"Where's your girl today?"

"School."

"She'll be coming by later?"

"Yes." She'd better, damn it.

"I like her," Nurse Kim declares as I rinse my mouth. "She looks like she can handle your attitude."

"Because I need your approval."

Kim pats me on the head like I'm five years old. "Good coughing today, smartass." Now that's good bedside manner.

The sun is past my window when I wake up from my nap, tangled in my blanket and over-warm. Mom is working on her laptop near the window and Willa is curled up in the recliner. And they totally let me sleep with my hand down my pants.

I slip my hand out and hope neither of them noticed. Willa appears to be dozing, but Mom looks up when I shift positions.

"Hey sweetie," she says, and gets up to offer me water. "It's almost five. I have to go home and feed the heathens soon."

I nod. It'll be dinnertime here soon, too. Mom asks if she should wake Willa to keep me company.

"No, let her sleep."

Mom packs up her work and gives me a kiss goodbye. She leaves it vague as to whether she'll be returning tonight, and I hope that Dad will insist she stay home and sleep in a real bed. I can stand a night alone.

Mom leaves with a kiss on the cheek, and I calculate. It's almost five o'clock now. Dinner is served around five thirty, and someone will be coming around in the after-dinner hours to sample more bodily fluids—preferably blood, so I don't have to do anything. Either way, I have thirty minutes alone with my Willa.

I swing my legs out of bed and sit up. Willa is curled up in a ball with her feet on the edge of the recliner and her knees slumped to the side. I tow my IV pole over to the side of the chair and ease my hips into the space between her body and the armrest.

Willa stirs. "Mmm, what are you doing?"

"Nothing, love." I wrap an arm around her shoulders and kiss the back of her head. "Go back to sleep."

Willa scoots to give me more room and uses her shoulder to recline the back of the chair even more. "Can you still breathe all right?"

I take a few test breaths. "I'm okay."

She turns the lever to extend the footrest, and I pull her back up against my front. It's been ages since we spooned and I miss holding her.

"Are you warm enough?"

"I'm perfect. Go to sleep, Willa." She snuggles right in, careful of the wires and tubes around me. I don't smell so nice right now, but she doesn't say anything. I fall asleep with the scent of her hair in my nose and the rise and fall of her breath under my arm. Sweet bliss.

↔

"Wandering, are we?"

I crack an eyelid and find Nurse Maggie standing over me with a scolding look on her face. Willa is still asleep with her chin tucked to her chest.

"Uh, I got lost on the way to bed?"

"Good try. You should be in your bed, with blankets. You're still running a low fever, mister."

I reluctantly leave Willa, careful not to disturb her, and allow the nurse to escort me back to bed.

"Have some dinner before you go back to sleep," she advises, and pushes the side table with a meal tray up to the bed. God, I hate hospital food. Tonight it's flavorless broth, Jell-O, and some sort of purée that tastes like baby food.

"Thanks."

I watch Willa sleep while I work through dinner. At one point she wakes up a little bit and scoots back into the chair, looking for my body behind her. I consider calling out to her, but Willa quickly goes back to sleep. I eat as much as I can, eager to sneak back to the recliner. The nurses can give me hell for it, but it's better than if we were caught laying in my bed.

Before I return to the recliner, I have to use the washroom. As I pass Willa, I almost give in and snuggle up to her right away, but I want to cuddle her indefinitely and that means peeing first. I touch her hair softly, just to feel it, and then carry on my way to the washroom. I'm barely past the recliner when I feel a soft smack on my ass. When I turn to look Willa is still reclined with her eyes closed, looking peaceful. I did *not* just imagine that.

"I know you're awake."

Willa feigns a snore.

"Oh grow up."

When I turn around she smacks my butt again. I go into the washroom and lock the door behind me. Willa seems to be in a playful mood, and I wouldn't put it past her to prank me in the washroom. I'm wary of her playfulness because it's changed since we agreed to be a couple. She's been looking at me strangely, especially when we're alone. It's like she's got naughty things on her mind, secret things, and wants to do them with me. And earlier this week, when she saw me bare to the ribs, she had this look of...*lust* on her face. Part of me wishes she wouldn't do that, because I can't fulfill her expectations. That expression contains propositions for things I can't do or am not ready for. The other part of me is stupidly stoked that she thinks well of me. I'm *wanted*, sick as I am.

560

When I come out of the bathroom Willa stretches and yawns, pretending that she just woke up.

"How are you feeling?" she asks.

"Well, my left ass cheek is a little sore. Maybe you could kiss it better?"

Willa just smirks. She reaches over and cups my left cheek in her hand like there's nothing to it. "You've got a cute bum," she says. "Round and soft. Like bread dough."

"Uh, thanks?"

Willa stands up and gives me a hug. I squeeze her ass for good measure and tell her it feels like ham. "Round and springy."

Willa rolls her eyes and says I should stick to peaches, since I'm obviously a breast man. That I am. I tell Willa hers are nice, because I really can't tell her that enough. She gets this smirk on her face and pushes me back into the bathroom.

"What?"

She locks the door behind us and takes off her shirt. Jesus. Willa mutters something about a week being too long to go without touching, and I completely agree. I try to move my oxygen mask to kiss her, but Willa insists I keep it on. She has another method of torture in mind: kissing my neck and ears with her open mouth while her hands move across my back. The stupid heart monitor gives away my accelerated pulse with an annoying beep, and Willa giggles.

I never thought I'd be making out in a hospital bathroom, but since we're here, I enjoy it. The small of her back rests against the edge of the counter and her chest rests against my open palms. The scars on her back—the ones she showed me in the darkness of the shower—are reflected in the mirror. Seeing them makes me feel a little better; she's imperfect too, and I'm one of the few people who know about those marks on her body.

"I missed this," Willa murmurs, and sucks my earlobe between her teeth. Her hands move across my back and shoulders, reminding me how much I missed this too—the holding, the touching, the giving and taking.

Willa licks the shell of my ear and I blurt out, "Touch me." She doesn't hesitate. Her hand goes down the front of my pajama pants and cups me. Her other hand goes to my ass, pulling me closer until our fronts are nearly flush. Her hand is gentle while her mouth on my neck is not. She knows what I need, and it feels wonderful.

Willa's feet bump against mine. "Spread," she says, and I set my feet wider. Her legs slip in between, and the hand on my butt guides me forward again. She sets a rocking rhythm, brushing her legs against my inner thighs and the underside of my penis against her palm. She teases my balls, tugging softly and rolling them around the pad of her thumb. The heart monitor won't shut the hell up.

I start to pant, and then I start to cough. Willa stops rocking and moves her hand up to my back, holding me. I have to spit a wad of yellow phlegm into the sink behind her, because if something horribly disgusting didn't happen to interrupt a sexy tryst, I might forget that this is *my* life.

"Catch your breath," Willa says when I'm done hacking. Her hand is still down my pants, holding my bits.

I want her mouth.

You haven't had a proper shower in days.

My dick doesn't care.

"You look a little pale," she says. Now the fun is definitely over, if she's remarking on that.

"I'm fine."

Willa makes me turn so that I'm leaning my butt against the counter. "Let's screw with the heart monitor some more," she says, and suckles my earlobe. *Shit.* I grab her hand and put it back on my crotch.

Willa chuckles in my ear. "You're so impatient." Her fingers form a tight ring around my privates while she licks my ear, and after a minute I have some semblance of a semi. Her other hand slides down under the head and I buck.

"Too much?" She moves to play with my balls instead.

Just as good.

It didn't feel this good to play with my balls before cancer. Then again, it didn't feel so benign to jerk off or hurt like hell to come, either. Willa pays me exquisite attention, like she knows exactly what will feel best. Am I really that obvious?

There's a knock on the door and Willa whispers, "Shh, shh," like I'm being noisy. Well, I might have been. I wasn't exactly paying attention.

"Jem?" God damn it, time for another sample already? I've got Nurse Maggie until this evening, the one who never shuts up and always has cats on her scrubs.

"I'm fine."

Willa removes her hand from my pants with a smirk.

"You don't sound fine." Once, just once, I would like to get away with selling bullshit to a nurse.

"I'm *fine.*"

I guess I was making some pained noises with Willa, because Nurse Maggie offers me stool softeners. Willa has to cover her mouth and nose with her hands to keep from laughing, and I narrow my eyes at her. Rock hard turds are only funny until you've had one.

"Not necessary."

She takes that to mean that I have diarrhea. Christ Almighty, why now? Why? Just why?

"I'm *fine,* Maggie."

"So what was that groaning?"

"Jesus Christ, woman, let a man crap."

Willa is red in the face and has tears in her eyes from trying not to laugh. I turn on the faucet to make enough noise that she can take a deep breath and calm down without being overheard.

I pull Willa close and whisper in her ear, "I'll slip out. Wait behind the door, okay?" She nods, and I move my mask to give her a kiss. "Thanks for this."

Willa gives me a gentle squeeze. "I needed it too." She steps away to hide her body between the wall and the door. I flush the toilet for the sake of the charade and shut off the faucet. With one last wink in Willa's direction, I take my IV pole and step out of our unlikely sanctuary, back to my sickbed.

"So," I smile at Maggie as she snaps on a pair of gloves, "what fresh torture do you have for me now?"

Willa: June 17 to 19

Saturday

Between sleeping and waking there is a simple place that is entirely physical, where all I notice is whether I feel hungry or if I have to pee. Then thoughts of the day ahead filter in. Jem comes foremost in my mind, and with those thoughts comes a twinge of lust, like some primal drive to fuck in the face of disaster. Humans are a truly stupid species, evolution-wise. While every other mammal has the good sense to stop mating when a dire situation arises, humans are hard-wired to propagate, since the current generation is doomed. It's a dumb instinct, to say the least.

More immediate concerns settle in next, such as the need for breakfast before my opening shift at work.

It's busier at the B&B now that summer is officially here. We're seeing more tourists and there's a wedding reception booked for next weekend.

"You seem better today," Mrs. Elwood says to me. "Chris told me about your boyfriend being sick. Is he feeling better now?"

"Getting there." It's a token answer, vague and terse enough not to invite further discussion on this topic. I like my boss, but I don't want to talk about personal stuff at work.

My shift ends at two, and I go home to prepare for the next one: visiting hours at the hospital. I portion a Tupperware of soup, throw a hand towel in the dryer to warm, and head upstairs for a shower. I'm just about to step into the tub when my phone rings, and I have to rifle through my pile of clothes to find it. Elise is calling.

"Hello?"

"Guess whose fever is gone?" she sings happily, and then switches to her normal fast-paced speech. "And they say his phlegm is looking better. I wouldn't know, because it's all *phlegm* to me, but the staff seem satisfied that he's getting better. And no fever!" She gives a short squeal.

"That's great."

"He was asking when he could go home and Dad thinks that if the fever doesn't come back and his breathing keeps getting better, he could be home to recover within the week."

"Jem must be excited."

"Pretty stoked," Elise agrees. "He hates hospitals—of course. But even if he's home he won't be well enough to do school yet."

I still have the shower running, so I excuse myself and end the call with promises to come over with soup as soon as I can.

I step under the spray and soak myself from head to toe. For a few moments I breathe steadily, riding the same wave of calm sobriety that I've been relying on since Jem first got a cold. Breathe in, breath out; stay calm and collected.

And then something in me lets loose, and I snap. I can't get enough air. I have to sit down in the tub, panting with my head between my knees, and I sob with relief. He's going to be okay. The fears that I've kept locked away in the back of my mind have been addressed, and to calm them I have to actually deal with them. I'm a shaking, sopping mess, crying in the shower because things *didn't* go badly wrong. And I'm filled with regret, because I have so often been the instrument of destruction. The memories I kept at bay around him can no longer be swept back into the dusty corners of the attic. My sister's face, which has haunted my dreams and memories for so long, comes to mind now and I can feel bile rising in my throat. I gag on it, and eventually I vomit on the floor of the tub. The water is running hot, but I feel cold all over. My heart is pounding and my shaking hands are numb from reduced peripheral blood flow. With fumbling fingers I turn the water to cold, and the shock of it brings me firmly back to the moment at hand. The frigid water runs down my neck and back and thighs, making me tremble for a different reason.

I look down at myself, shaking like a leaf and still spitting bile, and the hairs on the back of my neck stand up with the realization of just how right my brother was. Up till now I've refused to think of what would happen if Jem died—what it would do to me. It would have been a hell of a lot worse than a panic attack in the shower, I'd wager.

"Fuck me." I sit back on the shower floor and slowly bring the water back to warm. In the cold water my breathing is fast and shallow, and as I thaw out I breathe easier. I enjoy the oxygen for about thirty seconds, until my lungs choke on fresh sobs. This is pathetic. I shouldn't be this upset when he's going to be okay.

I can't wash, so I just rinse my mouth between hiccups and get out of the shower. Water droplets vibrate off my shaking body like a dog, soaking the mat. I dry myself as best I can and head to my room. I'm still sniveling and sobbing like a moron and I'm glad that Frank isn't home to see this.

Clothes have to be simple right now. Nothing with buttons or zippers—my fingers can't handle it. It's sweatpants and a t-shirt. No socks, because I drop three pairs before I give up, and no bra, because I'm trembling too badly to put one on properly. I hate to look at myself in the mirror and see the mess I've turned into. I didn't cry when he was critically ill; why should I be so upset now, when it's all over? Why can't I be relieved without first dealing with a backlog of fear and pain?

I'm having a Freudian moment, as Mom would say—a stupid phrase gleaned from some therapist or another. That which I repressed is coming back to bite me in the ass, or something. If I knew it would be this hard to function, I'd have dealt with some of the anguish up front.

The dryer buzzes, and I dutifully make my way downstairs to empty it. Embrace the normalcy of mundane things; maybe that will help. Then I open the dryer door and remember that I didn't run a full load, just a hand towel for Jem, and I lose my composure all over again. I slide down to the floor with my back against the dryer. The tears are a little more controlled this time. It's not a spontaneous panic attack, but what Tessa would have called a 'good bone-cleansing cry,' because the emotion runs that deep and by the time it's over a body feels stripped to the core.

I wipe my face with the towel I warmed for Jem. It smells like that afternoon that Frank caught us, when Jem and I were almost like a normal couple for ten minutes.

I didn't trade Jem for normalcy, exactly, I think as I pull myself up on the dryer. In a lot of ways he is normal for me—the sickness, the food, the hospital—and in so many ways he's something better; it's something new with him, different and more whole than any relationship I had in St. John's.

I try to calm myself with a cup of tea. I'm shaking and hiccupping too badly to drink it, so I end up sipping through a straw. By the time I've finished my tea and blown my nose half a dozen times, I feel very tired. Bones don't feel cleansed yet, though, so I hold off on feeling any sort of relief. I drag my feet upstairs and crawl into bed. I'll just take a short nap, enough to center me. And as I curl up under the blankets my stupid mind wanders to cuddling with him.

Jem's affection is something I've grown accustomed to with embarrassing speed. He feeds off little touches and kisses. He's willing to hold and not too proud to be held. I wonder if it was always that way with him, or if long loneliness has made him greedy for affection. Either way, it's one of my favorite quirks.

I put a hand on my chest and count my heartbeats, trying to relax enough to escape in sleep. The rhythm is strong and regular, and I smile at my little secret: sometimes, when Jem is asleep, I watch the heart monitor and notice that our pulses match. It never happens for long, because eventually he'll cough and his heart rate will change because of it, but for those brief moments we're in tune in a way we couldn't have planned.

My short nap turns into a long one. I dream of unsettling things, and when I wake my mood is still fragile enough to allow tears. I don't wake without immediately wishing for sleep's return, and so my rest is prolonged by repeated attempts to escape and recharge my batteries in sweet unconsciousness.

It's past dinner hour by the time I try to get out of bed. I successfully put on socks and feel proud of the accomplishment. I brush out my hair and watch my pale face in the mirror for signs of life. None reported.

The ringing of my cell phone startles me badly, and I sit down again before I answer it. The call is from a number I don't recognize.

"Hello?"

"Hey, Willa?"

"Eric? Where are you calling from?"

"There's a payphone on the third floor. Is everything okay? Elise said you were going to drop by this afternoon, but it's almost evening and no one has heard from you." I look at the clock and notice it's seven. Visiting hours end at eight.

"Uh, yeah. Everything's fine." Apart from my embarrassing tendency to burst into tears at random.

"Jem bugged me to call you. He got worried when you didn't show up."

"Shit. I'm sorry." He doesn't need to be dealing with my nonsense right now.

"Can you come by? I think he needs you. You're kind of the high point of his day."

I have to hold my breath for a few seconds to keep myself from losing face again.

"Willa?" Eric prompts when I don't reply.

"I'm on my way."

When I get to the hospital, Eric is already on his way to his car. He stops to talk to me long enough to say that Jem is pretty much settled in for the evening, and that for a little while he and I have some time alone. Ivy will be coming by in about an hour, and she'll likely spend the night. "Go on," he shoos me. "This is the only privacy you'll get all week." If only he knew.

The distance between the lobby and Jem's room has never felt so short. I round the doorframe into his room without fully remembering how I even got to the third floor, but when I see him I decide that a walking blackout doesn't matter. Jem is on his side with his knees pulled up, fighting sleep. He looks so frail, but the numbers on his heart monitor say different. He's noticeably better than he was yesterday, with consistent blood pressure and oxygen saturation above ninety percent. Jem lifts his heavy lids when he sees me coming and holds out a hand. I give him mine and he cradles it to his chest. I'm not getting that back, now.

"Are you okay?" he asks in a voice thin with exhaustion. Funny that he should be asking me that.

"I'm happy you're getting better." I just happen to express it like a complete twit. I gather Jem close and he tucks his head into the crook of my neck.

"Where were you?" He sounds so sad, and I feel even worse.

"I was having a moment."

Jem tilts his head to look at my face. His tired eyes are tight with worry and he bites his lip to hide its sad downturn. "I'm sorry," he says, and squeezes my hand tighter. "I shouldn't have made you come. It's selfish—"

"Jem, shut up."

He sighs fretfully and touches my hair with his free hand. He has a tender touch, even when he's weak.

"I was worried about you," he whispers. The words echo slightly within the plastic oxygen mask. "I thought something had happened—and no one had told me. Or that Elise had lied, and you weren't coming today."

"I always meant to come," I assure him, and kiss his cheek. "I just got a little held up, is all. You don't need me coming in here and being disgustingly emotional right now. I had to wait until I was calm."

My explanation saddens him again. He gently twirls a lock of hair around his finger. "I wasn't there for you."

"Maybe that's for the best. I had snot bubbles coming out my nose—hardly attractive." I reach over to grab a tube of lotion off the side table and Jem snorts.

"*You're* worried about being the unattractive one?"

"Hush." I put a dollop of lotion on my finger and lift his mask away. The skin around the edges of the plastic is dry and rough, so I gently smooth it with my hand. Jem kisses my fingers and closes his eyes with a sigh.

"I thought that, too," he murmurs as I put his mask back in place and cap the lotion bottle.

"What's that?"

"Why you didn't come today—I thought you were…finished. That you'd had enough." Jem opens his eyes just enough to look at me under his lashes. "I wouldn't blame you for leaving me."

I'd love to smack some sense into him, but I can't, so I settle for flicking the front of his oxygen mask. "You think I'd let you bleed, puke, and phlegm on me, and then turn around and kick you when you're down like some meaningless crush?"

"I'm not easy to be with."

"No shit. I'm not either."

"You don't have to stay with me out of…I don't know, a sense of history or *pity*." Oh, how he hates that word. I kiss the smooth skin between Jem's eyebrows and reach a hand under the blankets. He flinches when I run my fingers over the waistband of his pajama pants.

"I didn't pull you into the bathroom yesterday out of pity," I whisper. "I want to be here, to be with you—but I'm only human. I had a weak moment, and I'm sorry, but I'm here now. No more talk of me leaving you, okay?"

Jem nods, but it's a token gesture. I let it be, rubbing his back and talking to him about ordinary things. Frank spent time with Doug this weekend, so I guess their spat is over. Jem listens languidly and rubs his fingers between mine. His hand is warm now that his fever has abated.

"Do you need anything?" I ask as his smile of contentment grows.

"Kisses." I owe him an afternoon's worth of affection, and I genuinely miss it, so I give him many little kisses. His oxygen mask stays in place while I kiss his cheeks and eyes and neck. Jem revels in it, with small sighs and whispered endearments. He doesn't even complain when I push his hat back and kiss the soft spot above his ear. I nuzzle his hair and Jem smiles.

"I think you lied to Paige," he says teasingly.

"About what?"

"About not caring about my hair. You told her you didn't miss touching it."

"You should let me do it more often," I hint. "The novelty will wear off." Jem surprises me by taking the suggestion seriously.

"When Mom isn't around," he bargains. "It upsets her."

"Are you sure?" Maybe it upset Ivy when Jem first lost his hair, because the diagnosis was still so new and her fears were so fresh. But now that the fight is over, it might comfort her to see that his hair is growing back. He's filling out the image of his old, healthy self. I tell him this and he still shakes his head.

"Not yet."

"Okay."

"It'll be just for us." As if to prove it, Jem slips his hat off the rest of the way and allows me full access to his scalp. The soft hairs are long enough to poke past my fingers when I run a hand over his crown.

"You haven't been wearing gloves lately."

"I know."

"Why not?"

I can only shrug. I'm not entirely certain of my reasons. It could be that I'm finished with hiding, or it could be that I just want to shove my imperfections in the face of bullies like Elwood. Maybe I'm embracing my past. Maybe my reasons change from hour to hour.

"I'm a little jealous," Jem admits. "You're braver than I am."

"Nah, I've been chickening out. Every time someone asks how I got it I lie or only tell half the story."

Jem weaves his fingers between mine. "Doesn't matter. It's nobody's business but yours." Jem points to the foot of the bed where a clipboard and pen are kept with his chart. He wants the pen. When I pass it to him he uncaps it and begins to draw on the back of my hand.

It starts with a leaf growing out of my scar, and then Jem adds another. Where the scar curves around my wrist, Jem inks flower petals one by one, layering them into the image of a partially open rose. The tip of the scar becomes the edge of a petal, and when I bend my wrist the flower 'blooms.'

"There's a real romantic in you, you know."

"Do you mind?" he says sweetly. I smile and lean down to nuzzle his temple.

"It's one of the many things I love about you." And I never thought I could even enjoy it, never mind love it. "You're converting me."

Jem winks. "Love you too."

Sunday

I'm up half the night writing. After I left the hospital last night, it didn't take much reflection on the events of the day before I figured out what I wanted to say for the Soc project. I wrote the whole thing in four hours and wake up tired and cranky. It's a therapy day and I have to go without Jem. I'm not eager to face the firing squad alone, but Frank won't let me I skip two weeks in a row. I make the task bearable by making plans for after Group, which of course include Jem. After breakfast I create a little surprise for him, one that will hopefully make up for worrying him yesterday and banish all idiocy about me leaving him.

Arthur prefaces the group meeting with an announcement about a church picnic next Saturday. The youth ministry is setting up an event with food, games, a sing-along (shoot me now) and prayer for the benefit of parishioners from the local assisted living home. At first I think he means it's a retirement community, but then Arthur goes on this hyper-politically-correct spiel about making the 'handi-capable' of our community feel welcome at the parish.

I'm kind of glad that Arthur is an idiot. Otherwise he'd know what an ass he sounds like right now, and he'd have to feel embarrassed. He ends his enthusiastic speech with an invitation to come out and volunteer with 'our differently-abled brethren.' I'm glad Jem skipped this group session, because Arthur's tendency to alienate people by over-including them is in full force today. Jem would probably have some smartass remark for him, and the thought makes me smile.

"Willa?" Arthur catches me smirking. "Something you'd like to say?"

Might as well exploit the moment. "If we volunteer do we get t-shirts? *Gimps for Christ* or something?" Arthur is horrified at my use of such a derogatory word, and for a moment I almost miss Steve. He had nothing against words like 'gimp.' He tried to own them, because it was better to face a problem than avoid it. Can't say I ever really picked up on that lesson.

I head straight to the hospital after Group. I miss Jem, and I'm excited to give him the little surprise that I hope will lift his spirits, since I worried him yesterday. It's tucked away in my iPod so it will remain between just the two of us, and, personally, I think new and ingenious ways to screw with his heart monitor are fun. I recorded it for him this morning in another fit of fuck-in-the-face-of-death horniness. I know firsthand that dirty talk isn't Jem's strong suit, but I'm hoping that track will *inspire* him. It's hidden in the 'Jem' playlist amongst other easy-listening songs that I thought would be good for his state of convalescence: tracks by Mae, some Stones, a little Joshua Radin and a smattering of Sia.

"I made a playlist for you," I tell him, and hand over my iPod.

Jem smiles at the gesture and puts the earbuds in. It's been awhile since we could exchange music and I

miss it. Evidently he does too. He goes straight for the playlist with his name on it and closes his eyes to focus on the sweet strains. All the tracks in the *Jem* playlist are purposely love songs today, conveying the whispers of my twisted heart much more readily and eloquently than I ever could.

I know he's reached the homemade track when Jem smiles to himself. It starts out innocently: *Hey love, I was thinking of you. You were in my dream last night.* And I know he's gotten to the 'good' part when his eyes snap open and his pale cheeks flush. Jem's eyes flit to his mom in the corner with paranoia, and then he gives me a deep glare. I just smirk and make a naughty gesture where Ivy can't see.

Jem crooks a finger at me, beckoning me closer. I scoot my chair up to the bedside and take his hand.

"I'm going to murder you," he mouths. I wink.

"You know, it has a pause button." I reach over to touch it and Jem yanks the iPod out of my reach.

"*No.*"

"Enjoy," I mouth, and take one of the earbuds to listen. He's not even at the best part yet, just the warm up. I took my time with this little project; set the scene, told him in explicit detail everything I wanted to do to him, and what I would have done if we hadn't been interrupted on Friday. Jem's cheeks are perpetually pink through the whole recital, and it only gets worse when I use his finger to demonstrate the descriptions on the recording. The monitor gives away an elevated heart rate as I give his finger a very slow and sensual handjob.

Jem's fingers grip mine, stopping me, when the track progresses out of description and into something a little different. At first his jaw drops, and then he licks his lips and eyes me curiously. He can't say it out loud without his mom overhearing, so he gestures by curling two fingers.

You were touching yourself?

I wink and Jem mutters, "Jesus." Little beads of sweat appear around the edges of his hat. I wipe them away and he whispers, "Kiss me."

I move his mask and give him a slow, sensual kiss. Apparently it lasts a few seconds too long because Ivy scolds us, "Hey now, no funny business, you two." Jem and I both chuckle guiltily. If only she knew what we were really up to right now.

Jem insists on keeping my iPod when visiting hours are over.

Monday

I think Frank is testing me. When I've put in the requisite number of study hours and come downstairs to pack a serving of soup for Jem, he asks if I'm going over to the hospital soon.

"Mind if I come with you?"

"You want to?"

Frank shrugs uncomfortably. "Kid's in the hospital," he says, as though that justifies his behavior. I never thought I'd see the day when Frank would feel any obligation of kindness toward Jem.

"Alright, but we should drive separately. You'll probably want to leave before I will."

"How sick is he?" Frank asks.

"You'll have to wear a mask around him. He still coughs a lot and he's tired, but his breathing is much better and most of the time he's alert." I sound like I'm talking about an old man.

"I got him something." Frank goes to the junk drawer beside the fridge and pulls out a Get Well card. He hands it to me for approval and I try not to smile cheekily.

"You're really trying hard here, aren't you?"

Frank mutters something that sounds suspiciously like, "It was Doug's idea," and stalks away to the front hall. "Are we going or not?"

⌒

As Frank and I ride the elevator in silence, I wonder if he's pulling some reverse psychology trick on me. Pretend to support my relationship with a former cancer patient, accept him into the fold, and then…what? Ship me off to military school?

I'm not sure what to expect when we exit onto the third floor. Frank isn't good with delicate situations. He even makes me carry the card, since he can't be seen to show any kind of sensitivity or emotional aptitude. This visit with Jem is probably going to be short and awkward.

We sign in at the nurse's station and take masks from the bin on the counter. Elise comes along a moment later, whistling to herself and carrying a can of juice from the vending machine.

"Oh, good, you're here," she chirps, and links her arm with mine. "You've got to see this. It's hilarious." Frank follows behind us, keeping to the center of the hall like he's walking through a correctional facility.

"What happened?" If it isn't a good time to visit, I'm sure Frank would be happy to postpone.

"Some idiot intern turned the drip on his painkiller up too fast," Elise says of her brother. "He's high as a kite."

I remember all too vividly how Jem and painkillers get along. "How's his stomach?"

"Fine now, after he barfed up an entire meal and what I'm sure was his spleen or pancreas or something."

Frank coughs uncomfortably. "Maybe we should come back later, Will."

"No, he's fine now," Elise says cheerfully. "He's very uh…friendly, at the moment."

As we come up to the door of Jem's room a nurse walks out smiling and shaking her head. I can hear singing: "I've got a lovely bunch of coconuts…" Of all the annoying songs to sing. I finish the line as I approach the bed, because I can't let the poor bastard embarrass himself alone. Jem looks at me with such innocent joy and says, "You know the words!"

"Imagine that." I lean forward to kiss his forehead and he giggles like a little

572

kid.

"Touch my face." He grabs my hand and makes me poke his cheek. "It's bread!" Jem finds this wildly funny and carries on laughing, happy as a pig in shit. Ivy just shrugs apologetically, but Elise leans over and bites her brother's eyebrow with her lips.

"You'll eat it all!" he says through giggles.

"I'll save you some," she promises. Jem stops giggling suddenly and goes very still. We all know what that means. Elise clears out of the way and Ivy and I both reach for the basin at the same time. Jem still manages to vomit all over himself and the blanket.

"I'll go ask for a new one," Elise volunteers, and makes a quick exit. She looks a little green from watching the puke show. Frank turns to follow her, but ends up standing awkwardly between the hall and the threshold like he doesn't know whether to leave or help. Jem is so out of it that all he manages to say is "ew" regarding the taste in his mouth, and I help him rinse while Ivy grabs a pair of gloves from the box by the sink.

"Can you sit up, sweetie?" Ivy folds the dirty blanket away and between us we help Jem sit up on the edge of the bed. She helps her son take off his soiled shirt, and then tells him to lean on me for balance while she gets a clean one out of his backpack. Jem rests his head on my shoulder and his arms around my waist. This is the first time I've really got to hold him without a shirt on, and he's too stoned to appreciate the moment. He just hums into my neck and squeezes my sides sporadically. It doesn't occur to him to be embarrassed, and for that I'm thankful.

I look up and Frank is eyeing Jem's back curiously, as though he's some strange and exotic animal in a zoo. I suppose it's natural to be put off by what cancer does to a body, and his paleness and the prominent shape of bones can be shocking at first. Even though Frank is a paramedic, he's not used to having this view of a patient. I don't think of it until someone reminds me that it's not typical; this is just Jem, to me.

"Here, love," Ivy prompts him, and tries to guide Jem's arms into the sleeves of the clean shirt without disrupting the monitor nodes that line his chest and hand. It's a long and delicate process, which Jem resists with childlike whines in his throat, resentful of the fact that his mother makes him lift his head and let go of me. He won't let her button up the new shirt, because he won't turn away from me.

"Come on, Jem, time to lay down." Ivy puts a hand on his shoulder to guide him, but Jem shakes his head slowly.

"I'll stay here," he mutters.

"Give him a minute," I mouth to her over his shoulder. If we let him have his way for a few minutes, eventually he'll become easily distracted again and we can move him. I rub his back and hum what I can remember of the Bach we've played. Jem smiles against my neck and kindly scolds, "You should have shared the scissors."

"Shall I tuck you into bed?" I prompt him. Jem stubbornly tightens his grip on me.

"No." He sounds like a tired, petulant kid.

"Let's do up your shirt so you don't get cold." I shift him in my arms to reach his front, and he doesn't like that. Jem whines wordlessly until I let him back to his original position with his head on my shoulder and my arms around his back. Ivy gives a bewildered shake of the head, and I smile to let her know it's okay.

"Want me to help move him?" Frank offers quietly. It's true that we could probably shift Jem into a prone position without much trouble, but then he would fuss and try to sit up again. Best let him decide when to lay down.

"Hurts," Jem murmurs.

"Where?" He doesn't answer, so I ask him to show me.

"Right there," Jem says. He hasn't moved or pointed, but he thinks he has. I slip a hand under the edge of his shirt to touch his stomach.

"There?"

Jem winces.

"Are you going to throw up again?" Ivy is already reaching for the basin while Frank shifts restlessly. Jem opens his drowsy eyes and looks up at me.

"I don't want to anymore," he says, as if I'm the one forcing him to vomit and he's begging me not to.

"Okay," I agree, and rub his back. "You don't have to. Just relax." His eyes close and his feet start to swing, knocking gently against my shins. "Are you ready to lay back now?"

"I'll stay here."

"Aren't you cold?"

"Soft."

"Maybe he'll fall asleep," Ivy whispers. I nod. "Are you okay like that?" she says even quieter, and I agree. Elise comes back with the new blanket and Ivy drapes it around Jem's shoulders.

"Your breathing sounds better," I tell Jem. He grunts at me in response.

"He coughed up a lot this morning, but he's been better throughout the day," Ivy volunteers. We talk over Jem's head and he doesn't seem to mind it. Occasionally he interjects nonsensical statements and we just roll with it. Ivy tells me that they've been weaning Jem off the supplemental oxygen since yesterday. It started with turning down the flow, and today he's been taking brief breaks from wearing the cannula. It takes added effort to breathe without the oxygen for support, and so he hasn't had much success at weaning while tired and dozy, but there is progress.

Frank tries to make small talk with Ivy, obviously uncomfortable with watching Jem and Ime cuddle. When he's not speaking or sighing into my neck, Jem is tugging gently at the side of my shirt or touching the ends of my hair.

"I like you," Jem declares softly. I give him a squeeze and tell him I like him too. "We're going to be friends," he says with quiet anticipation, and smiles with his eyes closed.

"I'd like that."

We stay wrapped up beneath his blanket for another quarter of an hour, during which Jem says, "Annoying as fucking eggs," for no apparent reason, before he finally starts to doze. We lay him back in the bed and wrap the new blanket around his legs, and he falls asleep with a snuffle and a twitch.

"Sorry he wasn't up to visiting today," Ivy whispers.

Frank says, "We'll let him rest."

I'm mildly annoyed that Frank speaks for me without asking if I'm ready to leave, but with Jem high and asleep, he wouldn't know I was here anyway. I hug Ivy and Elise goodbye and gently kiss Jem on the forehead. He doesn't stir.

Frank tears off his mask as soon as we're in the elevator. "Hell of a thing, isn't it?"

"Yeah." Whatever that means. I'm sure it would make perfect sense if I had a Y chromosome.

"You're very good with him," Frank says.

"Thanks." Jem isn't usually so difficult and demanding when he's stoned, but I didn't mind. It gave me an excuse to cuddle him uninterrupted for almost a full half hour.

"He seems...reliant on you," Frank says as the elevator beeps for the first floor. "That makes me nervous."

"Because you want me to leave him?"

"Because you're young, and relationships don't often last when you're young."

"Aren't you and Doug kind of an exception to that rule?"

Frank sighs and gives me the eye. I'm not supposed to bring this subject up in public. "It's not easy," he says finally. "No relationship is." Frank can't take depressing and personal topics for too long, though, and as we step out of the hospital he changes the subject. "Want to go for dinner at Ger-Bo's?"

The question is, do I feel like cooking?

"I'll meet you there." Call it bonding time, since Frank is in the mood to try today. He made more of an effort than I thought he would in the hospital.

"Love you, Frank."

Frank surprises me by wrapping an arm around my shoulders and pulling me in for a sideways hug. "I'm proud of you, kid," he says lowly.

"Are you sure?"

He looks at me seriously and nods. "You've got your issues, but you're a fine young woman." That's the most personal and endearing thing Frank has ever said to me, and I don't know how to respond except to say, "I'm buying tonight."

"That doesn't mean you can make me order the salad."

"We'll see about that."

Jem: June 20 to 24

Tuesday

A man I've never seen before stands next to my bed, apologizing for some mix up with my IV drip. I have no idea who this guy is, much less why he's apologizing to me, but Dad is glaring at him from the doorway so I guess there must be a reason.

"Uh, sure, we're cool." It's only after he leaves that I find out from Dad who the guy was—some intern who screwed up my painkillers yesterday.

"Maybe he did something right. I don't remember any pain."

"Do you remember *anything?*" Dad says testily.

"Uh...no."

"You were out of your mind and vomiting. If it hadn't been handled right, you could have developed further lung problems from aspirating food particles."

Thanks, Dad—nothing more picturesque than inhaling my own vomit.

"You have to really try to eat well today, okay? You might not feel it now, but you're weakened by what happened."

Actually, I do feel it. I'm just trying not to show it so he'll quit parading around in doctor mode and let me go home sooner. The man watches me like a hawk while I eat breakfast.

"I'll call your mom and ask her to bring some of the soup from the freezer when she comes."

Willa's is better.

"Thanks, Dad."

Wednesday

The attending physician has visited me an inordinate number of times today, and for no purpose other than to check my vitals and assess my respiratory status. It's hard not to get my hopes up, but I suspect he's doing it because he's considering if I'm ready to be discharged. I'm still phlegming, but it's no longer dark green or red and there's much less of it. I can breathe better and go for long stretches without extra oxygen.

At three o'clock, an hour before this doctor's shift ends, he discusses the idea of discharge. I want to go home. I want to be in my own bed, on my own schedule, without the noise and interruptions and smell of the hospital. I want to have privacy again. I want real food and my cello and the sound of Mom singing in her office.

Elise and Eric swing by after school. Dad and the attending are talking in the Family Room at the end of the hall, so Eric goes out to the vending machine to spy on them and see if Dad looks pleased or upset.

Elise fills the silence while we wait for him. She's all aflutter because the grad dance is this weekend, and the social planning committee still has to set up the decorations and tables and stuff.

"Sounds like fun."

"Are you even listening?"

"Of course."

"You're lying."

"Okay, I'm lying."

"I'm trying to talk to you about important things and you just zone out." Prom is not important. It's just another school dance, but with a fancy name and a bigger budget. But it would hurt Elise's feelings if I said that.

"Sorry."

"So can I borrow that fedora you have in your closet?"

"For the dance?"

"Yeah."

"Fine, but I want a favor in return."

"What's that?"

"Don't tell Willa I'm coming home, okay?"

Elise imitates a confused dog, complete with head tilt, low whine and bewildered eyes.

"I want to surprise her."

"Oh. That's sweet." Elise beams and rocks back on her heels. "I kind of have a surprise for you too."

I have a bad feeling about this. Elise doesn't usually announce surprises. She springs them on people in the most violently exuberant manner possible.

"What is it?"

"Well it's not really *for* you, but it is surprising."

I guess that she got her driver's license, since she's eligible now—she's gone long enough without having another seizure—but that isn't it.

"I got a summer job."

"That's great. Where?"

"I'm cooking at a camp."

Jesus Christ on toast. "The same camp that that douchebag is working at?"

Elise winces. "The very same."

"What the fuck, Lise?"

"I'm just cooking; we won't even work together 'cause he's a counselor. And I like cooking." She pouts sweetly. "Not many students get summer jobs doing things they like."

"Tuck that lip in."

Elise folds her arms and huffs. "Eric was cool about it," she says haughtily. I'm not buying it. I know this trick: she pits Eric and I against each other for her love in order to get what she wants.

"Fine then."

"Fine."

"I'm not gonna be happy about it."

Elise sticks her tongue out at me. I know she wants this and that I should be happy for her, but I don't trust that jerk she's chasing, and who am I going to hang out with this summer when Willa isn't available? It's not like I have any other friends, and she knows it.

"You're going to be gone all summer." That gets to her.

Elise drops her arms and gives a long-suffering sigh, as if she knew this was coming and doesn't have a good counter-argument planned.

"It's not that far away."

"You've never been away from home before."

"So it's about time. And you did it for five summers, so how hard can it be?"

I glare at her. Cooking macaroni and cheese for campers and competing for music scholarships are not on the same level.

"What if you get lonely?"

"Ha." She's right; stupid argument. Elise makes friends wherever she goes, and she has that wingnut to keep her company if no one else will.

"I get a weekend off at the end of July," she says, "so quit whining. It's not like you're *never* going to see me, and there are these amazing things called phones."

"Are you actually going to call?"

"Yes," she declares, and pinches my cheek. "Now will you stop being so pissy?"

I'm about to tell her no, I'm not finished yet, when Eric comes in, crunching loudly on a bag of chips. "You two fight like an old married couple," he says. "It's creepy."

"We do not." We say it in unison and Eric struts around like he's right. Ass.

"Did you tell her you were cool with her going away to camp?" I demand. Eric shrugs like I'm overreacting.

"Dude, imagine all the amazing shit we can do with her unguarded stuff while she's gone. I say we make slingshots with her training bras."

Elise gives him a well-deserved kick in the shin for that one.

"Damn it, kid, don't cripple me. I've got to carry his ass into the house to-night." Eric gestures to me, and my hopes rise of their own accord.

"They're letting me out?"

"Yeah. About time, too. You're not even that sick; just lazy."

I give him the finger and he offers me a chip. "Bugger off. And you won't have to carry me in. I can walk just fine."

"We're not supposed to tell Willa," Elise adds. "It's a surprise."

Eric shakes his head at me. "You know, most girls prefer flowers."

⊷

I'm home before dinner and ridiculously happy about it, even though the short car ride has made me a little tired. The doctors sent me home with a miniature oxygen tank and a few new prescriptions. I have to go back next week for a checkup, but I don't care right now because the house smells like home and everything is familiar.

"I'll bring some food up for you," Mom says, and welcomes me home with a hug and a kiss. Dad walks me upstairs with one hand firmly on my elbow and the other around my back. We have to take it slow, but that's okay. I like the feel of carpet under my feet instead of hard tile. Somewhere in the house an open window lets in a fresh breeze. Dad tries to walk me to my bed, but I've had enough of beds. I slip away from him and go to my desk.

"Jem," he says.

"I'll rest. Give me a moment." I just want five minutes of normalcy, sitting at my desk, among my things. A backlog of homework is piled high on my desk, and I'm actually happy to see it. I reach over and touch the edges of the CD cases on my shelf. Behind me, Dad opens the dresser and starts emptying my backpack of clothes.

"Can I have a minute?" I ask when he's done.

"Shout if you need anything," he says, and lets me be. I call Willa, and when she picks up she sounds surprised.

"Are you out in the garden?" she asks. She's referring to the enclosed garden behind the hospital, with benches and paved walkways and low-maintenance vegetation. It's the only place where I could reasonably call her from my cell phone.

"No."

"Where are you?"

"I'm home."

Willa is silent for a beat. "Shut up."

"Well, that's one way to say congratulations."

"Why didn't you tell me you were going home?"

"Come over," I say. "No more visiting hours."

I lay down in bed to wait for her. I stretch out like a starfish, enjoying the room and the soft feel of clean sheets. My sheets. My pillow, smelling of fresh detergent. My comforter, a hell of a lot warmer than a hospital blanket. The only thing missing—and won't be for long—is my Willa.

I accidentally doze off before she arrives. When I wake up the sun has set and I'm being spooned. I clear my throat of sleep and phlegm and murmur an apology.

"Don't worry," she says, and kisses the back of my neck. "We had a nice conversation that time you sort of woke up."

I groan into the pillow. "What did I say?" I feel Willa's lips curve against my skin in a wicked smile, and I know it's bad.

"You can keep my iPod for a few more days, since you like it so much."

Aw hell.

Thursday

To no one's surprise, I've racked up an obscene number of school absences this semester. I'm pretty much screwed because of it. Mom, Dad and I have a meeting with the guidance counselor. I know I've failed at least two of my courses this year, but the others might be salvaged for credit if I can be allowed to make up assignments and have my exams deferred until I'm well enough to sit them. We drive over to the school at one o'clock and it feels like last Fall, when I still had cancer. I'm a freak, thin and weak and wearing a stupid mask to prevent infection. A miniature oxygen tank sits next to me in the back seat, 'disguised' in a little black carrying bag. Luckily, Dad promised not to make me use it unless I have to.

I look around the parking lot when we pull up. It's not nearly as full as it usually is, and for a moment I wonder why. Then I remember that it must be exam week already, and the only people here are kids who are writing their finals today. I suppose that's what Elise and Eric are doing today, since they both went to school. I feel bad that I don't even know what subjects they're in for or when they had time to study in between taking care of my pathetic ass.

Willa didn't burden me with her exam schedule, either. I look around the parking lot for her beat up Toyota, but it isn't here.

Dad asks why my head is on a swivel.

"No reason."

Dad carries my oxygen tank and lends me his arm for the short walk inside. I try to walk like I have strength and energy, but it just isn't there, and I end up shuffling slowly like an old man. Mom holds the door open for us, and once inside I want to turn around and go home.

The afternoon block of exams starts at one-thirty. At five minutes after one, all the students are still in the halls, cramming with their friends and quizzing each other on testable trivia. At first they don't notice us—notice *me*—but then heads turn and people go quiet. They start whispering before I'm out of earshot, and I feel like shit.

I just want to get to the main office and hide from all the prying eyes. Dad tells me not to walk so fast. "Take it easy, don't overdo it." I persist anyway, and soon spots of color appear in front of my eyes. I have to stop entirely and lean my hand against the wall.

"Are you okay, sweetie?" Mom asks, and presses a hand to my clammy forehead. That's a relative question. I'm not dying, but I'm definitely not fine.

"Everyone is staring," I whisper.

Mom doesn't look around to verify. She just smiles at me and whispers back, "Fuck 'em." My jaw drops. Mom only swears like that when she's injured herself.

When I feel well enough to move again Dad directs me to a bench outside the administrative offices and starts to unwind the tubing for my oxygen. Everybody can see us here.

"I don't need that."

"Keep it on during the meeting," he says. "Build yourself back up for the walk out."

As he adjusts the tubing and flow, Hannah Trilby walks up to my end of the bench. She smiles uncomfortably and says hello.

"Hey." I sound like a breathless weakling.

"You're not here to write an exam, are you?"

"No. Here to see if they'll let me." I gesture over my shoulder to the main office. Dad hands me the nasal cannula. I have to take my mask off to put it on.

"Well, uh, I see you're busy so I'll just…" She gestures vaguely and takes a step back. "See you around, Jem."

"See you." Hannah is a sweet girl, and in a way I'm sorry that I made her uncomfortable. The rest of me is irrationally hurt that she would duck and run because I was 'busy' for the five seconds it takes to put on a nasal cannula. I put my mask back on over top and Dad zips up the black bag.

"Ready?"

Elwood walks past us, headed to his exam, and sees me. For a moment he just looks, and then he turns around and moonwalks with this stupid smirk on his face. Asshole.

"Yeah, ready."

⟳

Willa comes over before dinner. I didn't even have to ask—we were talking on the phone and I told her about the meeting and that jerk Elwood, and she just showed up to hang out. It's good that she knows me so well, because I need the company to take my mind off thoughts of Elwood being repeatedly run over by a transport truck.

She brings her French book with her and we relax on the couch while I quiz her on verbs. She's absolutely horrible at this subject.

"Why didn't you tell me when your exams were?"

Willa shrugs. "It's not that important, and French is my last one."

"Yes it is important. Your stuff matters, too."

Willa just shakes her head. "French isn't on par with pneumonia." Her dismissive attitude toward her own issues frustrates me. Just because the goings-on of her life aren't as dire as my medical situation doesn't mean that I don't want to hear about her day-to-day life.

"You should have told me. I could have helped you study for Soc, at least." Not that anyone does study for such a bird course.

"When are you writing the Soc final?"

All of my exams have been deferred until next week, and my teachers have agreed to streamline them. The exams will be shorter, since I don't have the energy to write for three hours, and I'm told they'll cut straight to the core material.

"I should really give some thought to studying."

Willa just shakes her head. "You're such a slacker."

"I could be a bored, under-stimulated genius for all you know."

"Nah." Willa doesn't even look up. "Lazy ass is a better description."

"That's what I said!" Eric calls to her. They share an air-high-five across the living room. Fuckers.

Friday

Elise is gone for most of the day. Exams are over, and prom is the last hurrah before the stuffy grad ceremony and summer vacation. The social planners spend all day setting up the gym. I don't like it. Elise is driving up to that stupid camp tomorrow, so on her last day at home she isn't even *home*.

I'm restless and, if I'm being honest, a little mopey, so I spend the afternoon doing laundry with Mom. We wash and fold as much of Elise's stuff as we can, parceling out what she'll need to be away from home. Are five pairs of shorts enough? Will she be warm in that sweater? I slip one of my t-shirts into her duffle—she can use it as a nightshirt or if she outgrows some of her clothes, and I secretly hope it will remind her to call home. I also hide that pair of obscenely tiny short shorts so she can't pack them.

"Eric and I are going to drive Elise to camp," Mom tells me as we fold socks. "I've called Willa, and she's agreed to stay with you while we're out."

I feel like I'm five years old. "You called my girlfriend and asked her to *babysit* me?"

Mom gives me a withering look, as though to say, *Don't be so dramatic.* "Dad can't take time off right now because Dr. Mathers is on vacation, and Eric wanted to come see Elise off. You need someone to stay with you right now. You're still fragile and tired, sweetie." She's right, but I don't have to like it.

My only hope is that Mom doesn't scare Willa into believing that I'm helpless and weak, so I can actually enjoy some quality time with her. Alone. For hours.

God, I wish I wasn't sick.

⌖

Elise comes home at six and heads upstairs to take a shower before going out again. I shuffle over to the kitchen and put a frozen pizza in the oven. Now she has to stay for dinner. Elise is powerless to resist pizza.

I think I'm annoying her, because when she comes out of the bathroom and finds me studying on her bed instead of my own, she calls me a weirdo and stomps back to the bathroom with her clothes to change. I'm not a weirdo. I'm merely capitalizing on every available second I have with her before she goes to camp.

Elise reemerges from the bathroom in the black dress she wore at her birthday party. I'm a little relieved to see it, because the hemline is decent and though the dress gives her cleavage, at least it isn't displaying her tits on a platter.

"Will you zip me up?"

I do up her dress and Elise fidgets with the seams, tugging them into place. "You look good."

"I still have to do my makeup."

"You don't need that crap, you're beautiful."

"You have to say that 'cause you're my brother," she says, and begins rummaging through her closet for shoes.

"I'm not supposed to say nice things *because* I'm your brother."

Elise sticks her tongue out at me and traipses back to the bathroom to put on makeup she doesn't need. It's stupid, but I like the sounds of her puttering around in there. It means she's home. Her bedroom has lost so much of her presence already. The little objects of life are missing from its surfaces—a hairbrush, her sunglasses, half-empty rolls of Lifesavers…. Her nightstand is actually tidy for once, because almost everything on it went into her duffle bag along with clothes and other essentials. It's zipped and sealed and waiting by the door. I notice her toy wand is still sitting on the dresser and ask if she's not taking it.

"No!" Elise sounds mortified. "I'm not a baby anymore."

I slip the wand into her bag. She'll need it at some point, and it'll be there for her.

The doorbell rings and my stomach drops. "Do you have a *date* to prom? I thought you were just working at it."

"No." I don't believe her, so I make my way downstairs to see who it is. It's Willa, trapped against the coat rack and playing keep-away with Eric and a foil packet of what I assume is food.

"Leave her alone, bro."

"Not until she shares."

"It's not even cooked yet," Willa says of the foil package, and ducks under his arm. She scurries away to the kitchen and tosses the foil into the oven with the pizza. "There."

Eric kneels in front of the oven door like a prisoner looking through bars. "You didn't even let me see it!"

Willa has no sympathy. "Yeah, yeah, life's tough between the wars." She finally turns to me for a kiss and I trap her in a hug.

"I didn't know you were coming over."

"Frank was pestering me about prom. Told me to 'be normal' for once."

"Normal is overrated. We'll do something special," I promise, because I don't want her to regret spending her evening with me. I'm not up for much activity, but I'm sure we can find something to do.

Ten minutes later, the call for pizza brings everyone to the dining room. The foil packet is open for about half a second before Eric devours half the contents (it was a loaf of garlic bread with cheese; may it rest in peace). Mom emerges from her office and notices that we have company, and the conversation quickly turns to how to *babysit* me tomorrow.

I think Mom is losing her mind a little bit. She's typed up a detailed itinerary for Willa as though I'm a newborn with a feeding schedule. It includes all the numbers for the local hospital and the names of my doctors, my medication schedule, information about what I ate today, and how to handle my oxygen tank. The fact that Willa expresses aptitude for handling said oxygen tank isn't so surprising.

"Can you stop embarrassing me now?" I ask Mom when she starts to tell Willa about how often I'm supposed to purge the phlegm from my lungs. We're trying to eat here.

"I'm not trying to embarrass you. This is important information."

"Well, you are embarrassing me."

She takes mercy on me and targets Elise instead. Elise isn't actually *going* to prom, just working at it, but Mom still insists on taking pictures of her baby girl all dressed up for the event. Elise is doing the femme fatale look again. She curled her hair and wears her borrowed fedora on a slant over one heavily made-up eye. The black goes all the way around her eye and onto her cheek, while the other eye is almost makeup-free. She only has one elbow-length black glove on, because it would look dumb if only her face were asymmetrical. Only Elise could pull off something so off-the-wall.

"You need to dress up like that to take tickets?" Eric says.

"Oh come on, it's an occasion," Mom chides, and snaps another picture.

"If you had a boyfriend, this would be the part where Mom takes out the old baby albums and humiliates you beyond recovery."

"I would do no such thing." Nobody buys that. Mom keeps snapping pictures until Elise is halfway out the door and annoyed enough to snap, "Are you giving me a ride or not?" at Eric.

The house is quiet once they're gone. I immediately miss the sense of normalcy our obnoxious family dinners give to this house. Willa stands up to do the dishes. When I go to help her Mom says I look tired.

"Do you want to lay down, sweetie?"

"I'm fine."

"Maybe you should take a little oxygen." That oxygen tank is the bane of my existence. It's annoying and uncomfortable and I hate that I need it.

"I'm fine."

"Go lay on the couch," Willa says, and kisses me. "I'll be in soon." I don't want to lay down. I want to do dishes with her, because that's what normal couples do after a meal and I miss hanging out with her. I stubbornly stick around until the job is done. Willa does a good job of humoring me; I get all the easy tasks that don't require much movement or effort.

"Now will you rest?" she asks as we close the dishwasher.

"I have an idea." I take her hand and lead Willa to the front room. My stupid oxygen tank—I should name it something really awful for effect—is on the coffee table where Mom left it. I hand the carrying bag to Willa, who immediately starts to uncoil the tubing for me.

"How many liters per minute?"

"Hold that thought." I open one of the front windows and turn a TV speaker to face it. Willa looks at me like I'm being an idiot.

"What are you doing?"

"You'll see." I plug my iPod into the auxiliary port on the stereo system and adjust the volume. "Come here." I take Willa's hand and lead her out into the porch. It's the last warm hour of the evening, when the sky turns gold and red before setting. There's a word for this time of day.

"I think it's dusk."

"You think you know everything, don't you?" I tease, and take the black bag from her. I set the tank—I think I'll call him Adolph—on the porch swing and fit the tube under my nose and around my ears. "A Million Dollars," by Joel Plaskett, one of Willa's old standbys, plays through the window screen.

"What are you doing?" she asks when I reach for her hand.

"Come here." I pull her in and guide her arms around my neck. We can make this better than prom: we're both wearing sweats, which are way comfier than a dress and suit; the music doesn't have to be censored by school administrators; no crappy lighting, we have the sunset; every song can be good for slow-dancing, because I'm not letting go of her.

"You can be disgustingly romantic, you know," she says as we shuffle from foot to foot.

"You're so observant."

"What do you want to do tonight?"

"Just this." I nuzzle her temple and Willa smirks.

"No, really." We stay on the porch, dancing and rocking on the swing until the sky is more purple than red, quietly making plans. I want to meet her parents, even if it's just through a phone conversation. We both agree that more time hiking along *our* creek is definitely necessary. I want to cook with her. She wants me to 'outgrow' the hat. I want to go swimming with her. She wants to see me naked.

"Willa."

"Can you blame me?"

I never know what to say when she hints at sex, because on the one hand I'm flattered, and on the other I'm scared shitless.

Willa changes the subject. "I have some things planned for us tomorrow."

"Yeah? What?"

"Let me surprise you." I'm not opposed to that. Willa's last surprise has already been transferred to my iPod...and has an embarrassingly high play count.

"Okay. But be gentle." Willa kisses the corner of my ear-to-ear grin.

"I'll take good care of you."

Saturday

I wake up early to see Elise off, ignoring Mom's nagging to get back into bed and rest. Eventually she concludes that I'm either too stubborn to move or temporarily deaf, because she quits harping on me. Elise sits on my lap during breakfast, crunching on Cheerios. She doesn't have a choice in the matter; I pulled her onto my lap and there she stays. Dad gives her a hug and a kiss good-bye before he leaves for work.

"Be safe, honey," he tells her. I get a look of concern over Elise's shoulder. What's his problem? Everyone has been looking at me weird since Elise told me she was working at that stupid camp. I don't like it that she's leaving, but we've been separated before—every time I went to music camp. The difference is that this time she's the one going away, and I can't protect her there.

"Relax," Eric tells me as they climb into the car. "She'll be fine. You were." What the hell does he know? He never went to sleep-away camp. My mind is a blur of memories that now seem like horror stories—homesickness, injuries, weed, blowjobs behind the cabin after hours.... I hope they never let my sister out of the kitchen.

"Willa called, she's on her way," Mom says, and kisses me on the cheek. "Cheer up. The summer will be over before you know it."

Yeah, right.

They pull out of the driveway and I sit there on the porch like an abandoned dog, waiting for them to come back. I miss her already. I shouldn't have put that toy wand in her backpack—condoms would have been more appropriate. What's the spell for preventing teen pregnancy?

I'm still sitting on the porch swing, stewing in misery and panicking inside, when Willa pulls up. She comes up to the porch with her backpack slung over one shoulder and a full trash bag in the other hand. I ask her what it's for and she says, "You'll see."

I'm fine with spending our day together in the regular living space instead of holed up in my room. Willa has seen me in bed enough this month.

"Do you have the breath to do stairs?" she asks.

"I'd need you to walk with me."

"Okay. Wait here." Willa takes her bags inside. I can hear her walking around in there for a few minutes, and when she comes back to get me she's carrying Adolph.

"So I don't have to explain to your dad how you passed out and fell down the stairs." Willa holds the bag out to me. I take it with a sigh and unwind the tubing. Once I get the stupid thing fitted and turned on, Willa holds out a hand to help me up.

"We don't have to spend the day upstairs," I tell her as we cross the porch.

"I'm not so sick anymore that I need to be in bed all the time."

"Your dad said you'd say that." Willa smirks and kisses my shoulder. I move my arm so she is no longer supporting my elbow and put it around her shoulders. This feels less like an invalid being guided and more like a couple strolling.

Willa works fast. My bed is made up with about six additional pillows—the contents of her mystery trash bag—and a TV dinner tray is set up with fresh sliced fruit and juice. Another short table has been set up near the foot of the bed with a laptop and a stack of DVDs. The window is open to let in the warm breeze.

"I thought it would be nice to spend the day in bed together," she says. "Brought the living room and kitchen in, too."

I kiss her temple. "You're wonderful." We get comfortable on the bed, propped up by pillows. There are four movies to choose from: *300*; *Anchorman*; *Lock, Stock, and Two Smoking Barrels*; and *Ocean's Eleven*. I take back whatever I said about Willa having lousy taste in movies.

We start with *Anchorman*, cuddled close and without risk of interruption. I put aside my oxygen for the time being. I can breathe just fine while resting and I want to be able to smell her. Willa pulls the container of fruit closer and calls it our movie popcorn. She even cut the fruit into kernel-sized chunks and used only what I can eat without hurting: kiwis, raspberries, banana, grapes, and peaches.

"I love you," I tell her, and slip a cut grape past her lips.

"Keep grazing on this," she says of the fruit. "It'll keep your energy up and your stomach from hurting." Brilliant as that plan is, I enjoy this setup for other reasons. For every piece of fruit I eat, at least one is sacrificed to food play with my Willa. I trace bits of kiwi around her lips and kiss the juice away. Some peach juice drips onto *her* peaches, and she lets me lick it off. "Can't have you being undernourished, can we?"

Only half my attention is on the movie, and that's fine, because I missed this holding and touching and teasing. We cuddle as close as possible, twining our legs together and nibbling fruit from each other's fingers. The movie provides humor, and I missed laughing with her about simple things.

Willa is generous with her patience. She holds me when I cough, and every time I have to shift positions because of joint pain she helps me rearrange the pillows and snuggles up to me again. I love how she doesn't fuss.

At the end of the first movie, Willa makes me sit up. I've been coughing more often since the beginning of the third act, and now it's time to hack up as much mucus as I can.

"I can't believe you want to watch this."

Willa just kisses my cheek and pats my back with cupped hands to help loosen the phlegm. "If I was sick, you'd take care of me." She does do a good job of that, I have to say. She stays with me until I've coughed up all I can, and then brings me my noon medication from the bathroom.

"You want a hit?" she says after I'm done swallowing pills, and extends the oxygen tube to me like a stoner offering a bong. I take it from her and give my lungs some rest.

Ocean's Eleven is next, but I'm getting tired. I fall asleep with my head on Willa's shoulder before Ocean has his full team.

Waking up is heaven.

Willa: June 24

Saturday

I turn off the movie when it seems Jem is really and truly asleep. He doesn't stir when I slip away from him, or when I tuck a blanket over his legs. While he sleeps I take the opportunity to get up and stretch; use the washroom; put the fruit in the fridge for later; and when all that is done, I sit against the headboard and watch Jem nap. He looks deceptively innocent in sleep—earnest and soft like a baby lamb. I take his hat off and his hair sticks up in all directions. It only enhances his overall cuteness.

Jem stretches his arm and leg to the side, looking for me, and ends up sprawled like a starfish. The position displaces his nasal cannula. I adjust it and he smiles.

"Looking for me?" I take his outstretched hand and Jem hums contentedly. "You awake?"

"No."

"Too bad." I run a hand down his back and he hums encouragingly. He's only awake so long as I love on him and let him lay there. I pat his bum and his smile grows.

"You've got a cute butt." The goof teasingly lifts his hips, pressing his cheek further against my palm. "Like that, is it?"

Jem nods against his pillow. He hasn't even bothered to open his eyes yet. I think a little fun is in order, so I slip my hand down from the curve of his cheek, between his thighs. That wakes him up. Jem's eyes snap open and his fingers dig into the blanket as I run my fingers around his balls.

"Cool, it's an *On* button," I tease him, and tug gently. Jem lies there like he's afraid to move and end the moment.

"Kiss me?" he says. That shouldn't be a question. I lay down to kiss him and Jem wraps an arm around me. I can't quite reach between his legs from this angle, but I can touch elsewhere.

"You want to play?" he murmurs against my lips. He sounds nervous, and I don't blame him.

"I'd love to play."

"Can we keep clothes on?" By 'we' he means himself.

"I'd rather not."

"But—"

"Relax, love. You don't have to say yes or no to everything up front. We'll go slow. Keep your oxygen on—I have to give you back to your parents in mint condition."

"Give me a minute." He leans toward the washroom and I unwrap my arms to let him go. Jem is gone for a few minutes, and from the bedroom I hear the faint sounds of the medicine cabinet opening and closing. When he comes back the buttons on his pajama shirt are undone, but it's such a loose garment that I can't see much between the gap.

Jem crawls across the bed to me and I immediately slip my hands under his shirt to trace his bare skin. "I knew you'd go straight for that," he mutters against my lips.

"It's a novelty." I run my fingers up both sides of his spine and he arches his back with a sigh. Jem leans down, planting little kisses along my neck and jaw, and whispers in my ear, "I love the way you touch me."

"You should let me do it more often," I tell him, only half teasing. Sometimes the touch of another is the only thing that can remind us that we're alive; I love being able to give him that—to welcome him back to his body after a long dormancy.

As my hands travel across his shoulders the front of his shirt parts and I can see why he needed a minute in the washroom. Jem bundled up the end caps and catheter of his Hickman and taped it all to his chest under a patch of gauze. I pause to look at it and Jem smiles apologetically.

"I didn't want it to get in the way," he says quietly. I push back the sides of his shirt to look at his entire chest, fair and slightly freckled. It only takes a moment for his nipples to react to the open air and they withdraw into tight ovals. Just like in the hospital, I want to commit every inch of him to memory—every freckle and scar and ridge of bone and muscle.

My scrutiny sets Jem on edge again, and he sits back on his heels and begins to close his shirt.

"Hey." I grab his hands to stop him from buttoning up. "Stop that."

"It was stupid," he says to his lap. "I'll put on a t-shirt or something."

"No, you won't." It's ridiculous the lengths to which Jem will go to hide from himself. I'm not done looking at him yet.

Jem glances up at me long enough to see that I'm not going to back down on this. He bows his head again and takes his lip between his teeth. "I'm sorry," he whispers, and avoids looking at me. Intimacy is a careful balancing act with Jem, because even when he wants to touch and be touched, the slightest gesture can make him self-conscious again.

"You wouldn't let me beat myself up like this if it were the other way around."

Jem doesn't quite know what to say to that. He sits there brooding for a few seconds and belatedly tries to cover his chest with his shirt.

"I don't want to argue anymore about how beautiful you are," I tell him, and shift to straddle his lap. I push his shoulders back and part his shirt. "Now pipe down and let me appreciate you properly." And just to level the playing field, I take my shirt off too. Jem tries to continue being irritated with me, but my breasts are quite distracting.

Jem's chest is full of little surprises. His nipples—which are pleasantly sensitive, for a guy—are firm from the open air and tighten further in response to my touch. They're asymmetrical, too; the left one is pointing toward his elbow.

"That's good luck, you know."

"What?"

"Okay, fine, I just made that up." I tug his shirt off and Jem lifts his arms obligingly. "Lay back," I tell him. Jem reclines against the pillows, watching me study him. "Do you remember cuddling with your shirt off when you were high?"

"When was this?"

"In the hospital, that day your painkillers were screwed up."

"I don't remember."

I run my hands up his sides and along the undersides of his arms, spreading them as I reach toward his inner elbows. The new hair under Jem's arms is blond. The hairs on his arms and chest are darker, but only just. I remark on the color and Jem shrugs. "It'll probably change, you know."

I blow across his underarm, watching the new hair tremble, and Jem recoils with a scolding look.

"You tickle me, and I swear to God…"

I take off my bra and the transgression is forgotten. He traces the edges of my breasts with his fingertips, like they're fragile or fleeting and he wants to memorize their shape. I run my hand through his hair and Jem complains about cowlicks. He tries to flatten it with his hand, but it only makes his hat-head worse. "God damn," he mutters. "And this thing is only going to get in the way." He touches his oxygen tube and scowls. "Maybe we should just cuddle."

I trace the outline of his gauze patch. "You didn't tape this up so we could cuddle," I argue, and Jem's ears turn pink. I ask what he has in mind, but he refuses to tell me. "Did you cover it up just so you could hide it?"

"No. I didn't want it to get caught, or be in the way. I wanted things to go smoothly with you." He laughs weakly at himself. "Like I'll ever manage not to screw that up."

"Want to know a secret?" I ask. Jem raises an eyebrow at me and I trail little kisses up his jaw to whisper in his ear: "Sex only goes smoothly in the movies. It's awkward, and messy, and in some positions there's a high probability that you'll fall over, but that's okay because it's still really fucking fun."

"I can't do that right now," he reminds me.

"I know. We're just going to roll with it and enjoy ourselves. And it's likely going to be messy and awkward, and you're not going to get embarrassed because that's par for the course, right?"

Jem doesn't make me any promises, but he does try. It eases his anxiety somewhat when I roll off him and we resume the side-by-side position we used this morning, during the movie. Laying like this, with neither one of his being dominant over the other and with no obvious way to segue into naughtier things, we can just hold and touch and make out—and we do. A lot.

There are things about Jem that I get to discover, now that I can touch him skin-to-skin. He likes nails against his back, gently trailing the ridge of his spine. The stretch of skin between his collarbone and shoulder is sensitive to kisses—

the long, wet kind that make him turn to mush when applied to his neck.

Jem's inhibition recedes as we kiss, and his hands begin to explore on their own. One even explores below the waistband of my sweatpants, cupping my ass beneath my underwear.

I return the favor and Jem murmurs against my lips, "Don't you dare mention bread dough."

I laugh and ask him if he remembers having a face made of bread.

"What?"

"You made me touch your face when you were high. You said it was made of bread."

"I did not."

"Yup. And Elise tried to eat your eyebrow."

"Now you're just making stuff up."

"I am not." I spank him teasingly and Jem bites my lip. "Can I see all of you?" I ask. It's a long shot, but if I don't ask there's no chance at all. Before he can answer I start to shimmy out of my pants. Nudity is a team sport, after all.

"You can keep your underwear on."

Jem blushes. "Um, maybe?" His eyes are locked on my underwear. I decide to test the limits of a 'maybe' by slipping my hands under the back of his pants, touching his bum and thighs over his boxers.

Jem turns shy when I start to remove his pants. First he tries to distract me by making out, and he almost succeeds. I'm waiting for him to say no and tell me to stop, but he doesn't. When making out fails to put a stop to things, he starts to make excuses for keeping his pants, telling me that he isn't aroused yet. That's still not a 'no' or a 'stop.'

"Neither am I." Jem shivers as I palm him through the thin layers of cotton and I ask what he wants to do right now.

"Don't take it personally if I don't get hard, okay?"

"Of course."

"I want you to lay down," he says quietly.

I do as he says, but not before I turn up his flow of oxygen—just in case.

It's his turn to discover. I lay back, exposed except for my underwear, and let him touch and kiss and smell and taste. Jem is fascinated with the curve of my waist and hip. He tastes the skin from my neck to my navel, peppering it with tender kisses. His hands trace the sensitive spots—elbows, collarbones, nipples—testing my reactions. It's slow and languid, and even when he has to take a breather and lay with his head on my chest, his hands never stop moving.

I enjoy watching him look at me. His unguarded looks of interest and appreciation are a wordless compliment. He loves me, and he likes what he sees. Fingertips trace the curve of my pubic bone and the slope between hip and thigh, exploring my shape. Suddenly it all seems very funny, because if I tried doing this to Jem, he would shut down completely.

"What?" he says, and draws his hand away. I put it right back where it belongs.

"I'm enjoying myself. You?"

Jem smiles timidly. "Yeah, I am too." I beckon him closer for a kiss and he happily complies. His tongue teases my lips and I chuckle warmly. I missed that wonderful appendage.

"More?" Jem offers with a smirk. I think he's teasing me. And I think I like it.

"Please...but stop if you can't breathe."

He snorts. "Duh." Jem rests more of his weight against me and cups my neck with his hand, angling our kisses for comfort. I wrap a leg around his hips and pull him in closer. I like feeling him so near.

Jem's tongue tastes like kiwis and grapes. I can't be certain if the pounding against my ribs is his heart or mine, so I reach over and turn his oxygen up a little more. I'd rather the fun not end in a blackout.

"Stop worrying," he says against my lips. He's right; I should let it be. I follow Jem's lead—tongue, and lots of it; hands in hair; fronts pressing closer and closer together.

Jem needs a brief break to cough, so I kiss his neck while his mouth is occupied.

"I'm sorry."

I don't accept apologies in bed. I want his mouth back, now. The easy resuming of our activity seems to please Jem. He doesn't question it, at least, and his self-conscious timidity is forgotten in the midst of having his lower lip sucked.

That tension begins to creep back when I kiss his ears, though. His hands are on my breasts, teasing me gently. I ask if he needs a break to rest and Jem sighs against my mouth. "Can you take my pants off?"

"You sure?"

And then he gives me a pair of quiet, wonderful words: "I'm ready." He doesn't mean that he's hard, because we both know there's a slim chance of that happening no matter what we do, but he's ready to show me everything. Underwear doesn't hide much, but it gives the illusion of being covered. He's not truly *naked* with shorts on.

He's got Pac Man on his boxers. I think it's cute. He thinks my plain black cottons are boring. Since we're teasing, I slip my hand through the fly of his boxers and stroke the skin along his upper thigh. I tease, but touch nothing he wants me to.

Jem's fingers brush against the outside of my underwear. I palm his balls—briefly—before I go back to teasing. He shivers against me, delighted and afraid at once.

"We'll stop if it hurts," I promise him. Jem nods and leans in for a kiss.

"Feels good," he admits softly.

"Can I see all of you?"

Jem hesitates. "You first." I obligingly slide my underwear down and kick them away. I want to take the loving look he gives me, seeing everything, and give it right back to him.

My hands settle on his hips. "May I?"

"Are you sure?"

"Please."

Jem sits up halfway and lifts his bum off the mattress while I push away his shorts. I slip them down past his hips, and he helps kick them the rest of the way down his legs. It only takes Jem a moment to regret his decision to take it all off.

"Lay back."

Jem complies, but he leans on his elbows instead of fully reclining and keeps his knees drawn up, as thoughhe doesn't trust me. I work around that, laying across his lap and kissing his thighs.

Jem sighs and ever so reluctantly parts his knees a few more inches. I take my time with him, making every touch a gentle, worshipful gesture. Jem manages to thoroughly enjoy himself.

"God," he says, and pulls away slightly. His thumb brushes my moist lip and he says, "Give me a minute."

"You okay?"

"Need to breathe." He leans back on the pillows and pulls in a few deep lungfulls.

"You're beautiful," I murmur, and run my hands up his thighs and torso. Jem's skin is pleasantly flushed and slightly damp with sweat.

"Can we work on you for awhile?" he says when he's regained some breath. I tell him to do as he likes, and he shifts down to be face level with my chest. He looks so happy, grinning like a sweet idiot before laying his weight on my chest with an appreciative hum and kissing every inch of available skin. I could get used to this—this feeling of being appreciated. Jem is going to spoil me.

I hear him mutter 'peaches' as he takes my right breast in his hand. He flattens his tongue against my nipple and blood rises to the surface all over my skin. My blush amuses him.

"Like that, huh?" Jem echoes my sigh of pleasure as his lips close around my nipple, sucking it gently. It's one of my favorite feelings—to be flicked between his tongue and lip, and the near-pain of it when my nipple grazes the edge of his teeth. He licks away the stinging pinches of his teeth and moves to the other breast.

"You have the best tits ever," he says between kisses. I wonder if that sounded more eloquent in his head, but decide I really don't care. I like this relatively uninhibited Jem.

He gives my left breast as much attention as the right, in the interest of fairness, and then leans up to kiss me.

"My neck," he says against my lips. I shift to give him what he desires: open mouthed kisses, licks and nibbles along his neck and collarbone. It drives him crazy, especially the skin below his ears.

"God," he murmurs, and moves his hand up my thigh. Jem's hand is shaking, but he's gentle and he knows what he's doing. The first five seconds alone are better and gentler than any other hand I've ever had down there, and then he starts to play with me.

"Damn." I pant against his neck. "Twelve years of music pays off." Jem chuckles at that and stifles a cough.

"Yes?"

"More." I'm not sure what I mean by that, but he does. I bite down on my lip as he changes the tempo, driving the sensation deeper into my skin. It's heaven.

"Inside?" he breathes. How sweet of him to ask.

"Please." So what if I can hardly breathe? He can; that's all that matters. I take him in. We moan in unison and I have the bizarre impulse to call jinx. Jem turns back to my breasts, kissing and suckling at my nipples. He can't hold in a few small coughs. "I'm sorry."

"Don't care." I touch as much of his skin as possible while I rock back and forth on his hand, compounding the pleasure his fingers give me.

"Neck?" I offer. Jem leaves my breasts for the moment to expose his neck to me. He's earned some attention of his own.

Jem's unoccupied hand goes to my knee and makes me straighten it. He's mewling from the kisses I place higher on his jaw, just below his ear, as he straddles my leg and rests his weight on my hip.

"Yes," I encourage him. He's still soft, but his cock is tucked between us, subject to gentle thrusting against my skin as he continues to touch me.

Jem moans into my mouth and I think I heard 'I love you' on the end of that.

"I love you too."

"So good..."

"More?" I should be careful what I wish for. Jem shifts his hand and the room promptly melts away. I couldn't care less about trivial nonsense like breathing right now, arched into his chest, throat open with a soundless scream. He rides the high out with me. Jem holds my gaze and never looks away—I couldn't if I tried.

"Beautiful," he whispers with tender awe, and lies his head on my shoulder. His hand keeps moving slowly while I gasp for breath, giving me a break, but not a rest. He fully intends to make me come again once we both catch our breath—he tells me so in between leaving little love bites on my neck.

He's still moving against me, thrusting gently for his own pleasure. I cup his ass, smooth and lightly sheened with sweat, and encourage him.

"When we can do this for real..." he whispers in my ear. "God, I can't wait to make love to you." I nod in agreement. It's nice to want the same things and have it feel so right.

We focus on him for a little while. He continues to rock against my hip. I kiss his ears and neck, encouraged by a steady stream of half-coherent compliments. My nails across the back of his shoulders make him shiver.

"Feels so damn good..."

A shout snaps me out of the bubble of bliss. It's just a momentary cry, and then the rest of it is muffled in the pillow where Jem buries his face. His groan is long and pained. His back curves with tension and I feel his groin twitching against my skin. There's a feeling of warm wetness as Jem trembles around me.

"Jem?"

He tries to lift his head from the pillow and I can see his face screwed up in pain. His breath comes in short gasps as he tries not to make a sound.

"Lay down." I put a hand on the back of his head and he readily drops back down to the pillow with a moan.

"Hurts," he says into the bedding.

"I know, I know. It'll pass. Just relax." I curl my wrists around the backs of his thighs and feel the muscles tremble. His lower back carries similar tension, and the muscles in his groin are as tight as untried springs.

"Where's your heart beating?"

He lets a shaky breath out into the pillow and doesn't answer. I didn't expect him to.

"Feel it in your fingertips."

It takes ten minutes of this, trying to relax Jem with words and massaging hands, before the worst of the pain has abated. He rolls onto his side and looks us both up and down warily. When he sees the mess he made between us, his cheeks turn bright red.

"Oh shit," he says hopelessly.

"I'll get a cloth." I get up and go to the bathroom. I wipe myself off first and then take a wet washcloth back to the bedroom. I find Jem kneeling on the bed, supporting himself with his arms and looking sadly at the wet spot on the sheets.

"Here." I make a move to clean him and he turns toward me with a pained expression.

"I'm so sorry."

"It was an accident."

"I didn't mean to."

"I know."

Jem closes eyes and hangs his head. "God, I'm fucked up."

I kiss the back of his neck. "You're perfect." He's having a moment, and I let him. I kneel behind him with my front pressed to his back and wrap an arm around his middle. My other hand trails the wet cloth between his legs, tenderly wiping away the mess.

"Are you okay?" he asks hoarsely.

"I'm fine."

"It, um…you may get a rash where I…where my…" He trails off in embarrassment and I squeeze him tighter.

"From your medication?"

Jem nods. "You should wash well." He tries to sound composed, but it only makes him sound distant.

"Shower with me? We both need to unwind." Jem nods his assent, and it's only after we're standing under the spray together that he starts to come back to himself. He insists on washing me, soaping my skin with quiet devotion.

"Let me take care of you."

My back is pressed to his front as he washes me. Every few seconds I feel a kiss on my scalp or neck, shy but loving. His hand lingers guiltily between my hips.

"I don't hold it against you," I tell him. "You're still the best I've ever had."

I look over my shoulder and find Jem trying not to smile. "You're just saying that to make me feel better, aren't you?"

"No, I mean it. You actually paid attention. You were generous. I loved it." Jem rests his cheek on the top of my head. "It shouldn't have ended like that."

"There will be other chances. It won't always be painful."

"I'm sorry."

I extend my arms back to give Jem an awkward hug. "Next time we get you off first, okay? We'll control it, together."

The sigh he blows across my scalp is shaky. "Thank you."

⧢

I ask Jem not to get dressed after our shower. Instead, he opens the front tie of his bathrobe and lays face down on the bed. I open a bottle of lotion and massage it into his skin, trying to help him relax his leg and back muscles. I can still feel the odd spasm under my hands, though Jem insists he isn't in much pain.

"Do you need your oxygen?" I ask as I press my thumbs along his hamstring.

"No, I'm fine." He helps me arrange the bathrobe to keep him warm while exposing new skin to be oiled and rubbed. I spend some extra time on his lower back and bum. Just a little. Jem reaches over and turns on the iPod dock on his nightstand. Classical string music is the first thing that comes on.

"Leave it," I say when he moves to change the song.

"You sure?"

I nod and press the dimples above his hips. Jem hums with pleasure at the gentle pressure and sighs contentedly when I work little circles into his muscles.

"Willa."

"Mmm?"

Jem turns his head to the side and reaches for my hand. His cool fingers twine with my moist ones and he smiles. "I feel beautiful."

Forget the lotion. I abandon the job and crawl forward to lay next to him, cradling our twined hands between us. "I'm happy."

"You're a good person," he murmurs. "You made some awful decisions, but that doesn't make you bad." I don't entirely agree him, but I think it's sweet that he believes in my goodness. I lean in to give him a kiss and make a promise that

I think I can actually fulfill, "I'll be good to you."

"Likewise."

⬥

Jem is playing his cello again. His hands are getting better and the rubber finger sheaths help. Today the music is light and happy. I listen from the other room while I make lunch. No soup on the menu today; it's warm rice with olive oil and pear cooked in honey for lunch.

Jem tells me about his song when we sit down to eat. He was in the middle of composing it when he got sick, and for the past year it's been on hold; he says he wants to rewrite the melody to sound happier.

"Is that so?"

Jem gives me a charming smile and takes my hand on the tabletop. Lunch is a slow affair because Jem has to chew thoroughly and take small bites in between the coughs, but it's time spent together.

Eric and Ivy return home just as I clear away our plates. Eric is disappointed that there isn't any food left.

"Was she okay? Did you guys get her settled?" Jem asks of Elise. He makes it sound like they dropped her off in a war zone.

"Relax, she's fine," Eric says. "She'll be Little Miss Popular by the end of the day." This closes the issue for him. Eric offers to cheer Jem up with a game or two. Playing with the Wii is usually Elise's thing, so it's an understandable sentiment.

"I'm too tired," Jem says.

"It's going to be boring around here without Elise." Eric turns to me and declares, "You're our de facto Elise until she gets back. Crouch down, you're too tall."

I leave the dishes in the sink and give Eric a shove. "Come on, I'll have a game with you." He leaves to set up the system in the living room and Jem mouths "Thank you" behind his back.

"Will you play some more?" I ask, and give him a few soft kisses to sweeten the deal. Playing his music takes his mind off missing Elise, at least. It makes him happy in such a fundamental way.

While Eric spazzes and flails in front of the TV, I listen to Jem test notes beside each other, retracing his steps across bars to alter the tempo and talking to himself when it goes right.

I think I've finally killed him.

Jem: June 28 to 29

Wednesday

"God damn it, Eric." I take out my phone and call him. I get a busy signal. He was supposed to wait at the school for me to write my exam. Mrs. Brett cut it down from three hours to one for me, and instead of an essay I had to do an oral interview about the novel (I think she knows I only read the Coles Notes). An hour is not that long to sit in the parking lot and wait for me.

I walk across the lot to the picnic tables and sit down to wait for him. It's interim week—the time between the end of the regular school year and the start of summer courses—so the parking lot is empty apart from employees' cars. It's weird to look around and see this place so vacant.

I used to hate it here. School was the worst part of my day, with the stares and the fatigue and knowing that I wasn't living up to my academic potential because I was just too sick to work. I have a lot of horrible memories of this place, but there are some good ones, too. Some from this very picnic table, actually. How many times did I stalk Willa out here? We plotted domination of Greenland with an army of seagulls. We exchanged music and talked about inconsequential junk. I had her all to myself for a little while, away from the people who made me feel like a freak. This bench was our little island of normalcy, because even when Willa was poking fun at me, she treated me like a real person.

God, she was a bitch. I smile stupidly at the memory of how much I loved to hate her at first. If someone had told me then that in a few short months, she would have me stripped to the core and teaching me to love myself again, I'd never have believed it. I wouldn't have believed her to be a good person, either, or understood that even the best intentions can manifest in horrible, cruel ways. I couldn't sympathize with a person whose mistakes were too big and too permanent to be fixed before I knew Willa. I still don't understand her pain, just like she doesn't completely understand mine, but we try…and sometimes we reach an understanding.

She was wrong about forgiveness, though. I probably won't ever agree with her decision to help Thomasina die the way she did, but I can forgive her for being that person. She's learning to love herself again too, and I can't have her thinking that I'd withdraw my love and esteem based on something she can't change. It would kill me if she did that, so I won't do it to her. I'll come to terms with why Thomasina's death upsets me, one day at a time.

A car drives by in front of the school, punctuating the silence. I'm alone out here apart from my memories, and it feels liberating in a strange way. I can be here and not be stared at. I'm just me, without context, enjoying the afternoon sunshine on a picnic bench.

The idea makes the hairs on the backs of my arms stand up, as though I'm about to do something mischievous. That thrill is half the fun. I look around first, even though I know there's nobody here, and I pull off my hat. It's too hot for wool, anyway.

I haven't felt a real breeze on my scalp for almost a year. I run my hand over my hair, trying to do something about the hat-head. The strands are thickening and filling out now. It looks almost like a really amateur buzz cut, since there's a bald spot above my ear and my hairline is still lopsided.

A seagull trots past on its way to forage the garbage cans and stares at me. "That's right," I tell it. "It's growing back."

The stupid bird squawks at me and I tell it to go shit on the principal's car. An animal that stupid ought to be good for something, at least.

The bird walks away and I'm bored again. I call Eric again but the line is still busy. I want to call Willa, but she's at work until this afternoon. Maybe I'll go for a walk. Maybe I'll 'forget' Adolph on the picnic bench. Maybe, maybe, maybe. I've been planning for months, thinking about what I'll do when I'm well again. I'm nearly there, and I'd much rather be doing than planning.

This is the start of summer. This is the beginning of me. I get to have my life back, to be myself instead of just another patient. Meira didn't have that chance, and neither did so many other kids I met on the ward. I can't waste this time.

As long as I'm waiting for Eric, I take out one of my notebooks and a pen. I'm not just planning, I'm *promising*. Every item on this new list of goals is a promise to myself, my family, and to my dead friends that I'm going to do something with the opportunities they've given me through sacrifice and encouragement.

This is going to be a long list.

⟿

Eric shows up half an hour late. There are no food wrappers in his car, so I can't assume he went to get a bite to eat while I was at school. He doesn't look bored, so he probably wasn't just sitting around someplace, either.

"What took you so long?"

Eric shrugs and puts the car in gear. "Nothing." He's up to something. His cell phone is on the dashboard. I pick it up and check his call history.

"Put that down."

"I tried calling you twice and you were too busy to pick up." The last person Eric called was Celeste. The time signature on the call says they talked for over an hour.

"What did you have to say to that airhead that took a whole hour?"

"Give that back." Eric reaches for the phone and I hold it out of his reach.

"Watch the road." I want to see what prompted an hour-long phone call, so I pry into his text messages. The last one from Celeste says: *Pink lace.* I don't understand it until I read Eric's message before it. She was answering the question: *Which panties do you have on?*

"Jesus Christ, man, *Celeste?* Seriously? Of all the girls on this planet, you're fooling around with that bitch?"

"Hey," Eric barks at me. "We're not just fooling around, and don't call her a bitch."

"She is a bitch. She used to hold me down at recess and spit in my eye."

"That was like, twelve years ago, and she apologized. It's not like she could kick your ass now."

"That's not the point. That chick has no soul, bro."

"Did she not make you a Get Well card a week ago?"

"After calling me Make A Wish Boy for months and acting like I got sick on purpose to get attention."

Eric shrugs awkwardly. "You make her uncomfortable."

"*I* make *her* uncomfortable? Well, that excuses everything, doesn't it?"

"I don't want to hear it," he says sternly. I dump his phone on the dashboard and look anywhere but at my brother. I'm disappointed in him. Eric's such a good guy. It was okay to put up with Celeste when they were just friends, but she's going to ruin him. She'll suck his soul out like some freaky succubus and make him into a miserable, cruel person like her.

"You can do better," I mutter.

Eric stops a little too suddenly at the stop sign. "Listen, asshole," he says through clenched teeth. "I didn't say anything bad about Willa when she was making you all emo and shit. You don't get to judge me or Cee. I'll knock your teeth in if you do." He gives me a narrow look to let me know he means business. "I've known her since kindergarten—you're not going to change my mind by insulting her."

Oh, but I can try.

⟿

Elise calls after dinner. Mom beats me to the phone, so I hover around her and try to overhear the conversation. Mom tries to assert her personal space with a hand on my chest, but if she wants breathing room she can damn well put the call on speakerphone.

"Hi, sweetie, how was your day?" she coos at Elise while giving me warning eyes. I can't make out Elise's reply, but Mom rolls her eyes and says, "Yes, he's right here." She grudgingly passes the phone to me with the instruction to hand it back when Elise and I are done talking.

"Everything. Spill it." Not that my sister needs much encouragement. Elise launches into an enthusiastic recap of her life since Monday. She likes her co workers. Making macaroni and cheese for two hundred is really hard. She likes the girls she's bunking with. The mosquitoes aren't as bad as she imagined, but still really annoying.

"So how are you?" she asks when my hand is ready to fall asleep from holding the phone.

"Eric is pissing me off."

"What'd he do now? I'll help you plot revenge—just don't tell him I was in on it."

"He's dating that infected gunshot wound of a human being."

"I assume you mean Celeste."

"Of course, Celeste." Who else merits that description?

"You didn't see this coming? You think he drives up to Ottawa every other weekend to play checkers with her? Come on, she has her own ringtone, for crying out loud."

"But she's such a bitch!"

"To you. To him, she's pretty sweet."

"I wouldn't date someone who was mean to you."

"You could try to get along with her."

"No." Basic civility is a stretch for me and Celeste. Interactions were manageable when she and Eric were just friends because we didn't have to talk that much. Now that they're dating and school is out, she's going to be around more often. She's going to be at family dinners and special occasions and I'm going to have to try exceedingly hard not to backhand her.

"You should try. He's nice to Willa, even though he doesn't really trust her." Eric is nice to anybody who will feed him. He's like a dog.

"What do you mean he doesn't trust her?"

"He thinks she'll leave you. Not that there's any evidence that she would, but he's wary. And still, he's *nice to her.*"

"Because Willa is nice to him, dummy."

"You're being stubborn."

"You're being stupidly optimistic about this."

"Are you going to be this mean when I have a boyfriend?"

"Elise, we've talked about this: you're going to become a nun."

She whines my name over the phone and calls me a cheerless bastard. "It's not a blank space down there, you know."

"Don't make me puke." Though, it would be a hell of a lot easier on my stress level if it were a vacant lot between her legs.

"I have to go. We're setting up to do several hundred freaking s'mores at campfire tonight." I let her go with a reminder to take her Ritalin. God knows what sugary s'mores will do to her energy level.

Thursday

Willa picks me up from school after work. I just hobbled through my Soc final. The questions were pretty straightforward and I think I did okay. After I handed in the exam, Mrs. Hudson kept me back to comment on the term project.

"Since you were sick for the oral component, I based your mark on the written components alone, okay?"

"Sure." That's actually more than generous, because the only parts I contributed to the write-up were a paragraph about Ronald McDonald House Charities and the local center for bereavement counseling. Willa did the rest, and I didn't even read it. The subject is too painful.

"Here's the paper." Mrs. Hudson hands me the stapled project with a red A on the cover sheet. Sweet.

"Thanks."

"It was a very good assignment." I can only nod. Mrs. Hudson knows more about this paper than I do. I wish her a good summer and leave the classroom behind.

Willa is supposed to pick me up after work, but not for another twenty minutes. As long as I'm sitting here, I might as well look at the marks Mrs. Hudson made on the project—and *just* the margin notes.

My paragraphs only got checkmarks. It was Willa's work that Mrs. Hudson commented on. I try to stick to reading the red ink, but my eyes can't help but drift to the type.

> The more time goes by, the more I'm convinced that I never really knew my sister and that the memories I live with are just manifestations of my own issues. By wearing black I tell myself that I'm grieving my sister, but some days I'm just grieving the loss of everything that no longer fits into my perfect image of her. This urge to sanctify her, to tidy her life into a series of palatable facts, I think reflects my desire for order at a time when my life was falling apart. This, I believe, is what it is to grieve.

I close the cover on the project. I can't read any more. It's too personal, too raw. Too true. One day she and I have to have a real conversation about Thomasina…but not today.

When Willa pulls into the parking lot I put the paper away and offer a smile.

"How'd it go?" she asks of the exam.

"It was easy." I lean across the bench seat and kiss her. She smells like love.

"Where's Adolph?"

"I only have him to sleep, now. Dad says I can get rid of him by next week." I get a high-five for that. I have other good news for her, too. My bloodwork finally reflects good kidney function. I'm pretty much done dialysis after next treatment, and they're taking my Hickman out by the end of July, provided my kidneys keep their act together.

"Will they have to admit you for that?"

"No, it's an outpatient procedure—if they don't screw it up."

"Congratulations," she says.

"You don't sound so thrilled."

"I'm trying not to get my hopes up."

I really shouldn't, either. A lot could happen between now and the scheduled removal date that would necessitate keeping the damn thing awhile longer. Still, I have plans, and I really don't want to let them float on ambiguous deadlines. I want to try weaning off the painkillers again. I want to cross the first item off my list: *Be healthy.*

"Let's go to my house. I'll make lunch," Willa says. I agree, and because it feels dishonest to say nothing, I tell her that Mrs. Hudson returned our project.

"Did you read it?"

"Some of it."

"Thoughts?"

"I need to read the rest." I don't bother to say that doing so might take a very long time, but Willa seems to understand. She takes my hand and says I can keep the paper for as long as I need it.

It's three-thirty. Frank is due home shortly after four, and at the moment Willa and I are curled up in her narrow twin bed, wearing nothing but one sock and two smiles between us. Willa grudgingly admits that we should get up, but I'm not ready yet. We don't get enough time to do this—spoon naked in her bed, talking of stupid things like what movies to see or whose relationships aren't going to last the summer. I trace patterns on Willa's ribcage under the thin sheet, feeling her skin pucker to gooseflesh. She insists I'm not tickling her. Her arm is drawn back slightly, running her hand over the outside of my hip and thigh. Occasionally her hand dips between us to play with the short hairs below my navel.

"Are you happy?" she asks.

"Very much so."

"Me too," she says. "Let's try not to mess that up, okay?"

I kiss the back of her neck. "Go team?"

Willa rolls out of bed and starts collecting her clothes. I subtly snatch her bra off the rug and throw it under her bed. I try to convince her that she doesn't need one, but that alerts her to my scheme.

"Where did you put it?"

"I have no idea what you're talking about."

Apparently she can't take a joke or put on a different bra, because Willa picks up my hat and throws it out the window.

"Hey!"

"Do you really need it?" she throws my argument back at me.

"*Yes.* Go get it."

"No one needs a wool hat in summer." Willa puts on her shirt, sans bra. I can't find it in myself to really care because all I can think about is my hat *on the lawn.*

"So go get it."

"It's on the front lawn!"

"So it is." She sounds so annoyingly blasé.

"So people will see."

"And then the sky will fall." Willa laughs at me and rattails my bare ass with her sock. I should really consider pants....

"You're getting it back," I tell her.

"Bite me." Willa leaves the room, still doing up her jeans. I scramble into my pants and follow her.

"Your brother is going to be home soon," I hiss.

Willa turns on the landing and affects a horrified gasp. "Do you think he'll realize you had cancer?"

"Shut up."

Willa laughs and heads down the stairs. "My brother's seen you puke. Your bare head isn't that big of a shocker, really."

Back right up. "When did he see me puke?"

"That time you were high. He came with me to the hospital to visit you. You insisted your face was bread, puked all over yourself, and then clung to me like a baby koala for half an hour."

"Oh God." What must that man think of me now? He's probably going to sit his sister down soon and advise her not to date a glue-eater like me.

"Go get your hat. You can be out there and back in less than five seconds."

"You threw it out there."

"I have no recollection of that whatsoever."

"Willa."

"And you can't prove it, either." She smirks and smacks my ass. "Go get it."

I peek out the window before opening the door. None of her neighbors are out in their yards. The street is quiet of traffic. I don't see anyone on the neighboring porches or walking past the windows.

I dart out the front door, cross the lawn, and grab my hat. As I straighten up I realize that in my search for people, I completely missed the pickup truck parked behind Willa's car. It's empty. Frank Kirk is home, and I have no idea where he is.

"Everything okay?" he says from behind me. I whirl around and find him at the side of the house, coiling the garden hose.

"Uh...fine." I sound guilty. I remember too late that I don't have my hat on, and jam it down past my ears. "See you inside." I rush into the house and shut the front door behind me. Willa is already puttering in the kitchen.

"Your brother is home."

"Oh. Good."

"He saw."

"Is the sky still in place?"

"Smartass." I pick up a wooden spoon off the counter and smack her bum with it. Willa just bends over and gives me a taunting look, daring me to do it again. I put the spoon back on the counter before Frank can catch me in yet another compromising position.

"Help me cook?" she says.

"Please."

By the time Frank comes in, we're quietly peeling vegetables for dinner. He looks at me strangely, and I just know he's going to mention my hat or the stupid fluff that is my hair.

The man uncaps a beer and asks me very seriously, "Are you making a *salad?*"

"Uh…yeah."

Frank makes a disgusted sound in his throat and walks away muttering about 'damn rabbit food.' Willa gives me a smug smile that reeks of *I told you so.*

God, I hate it when she's right.

Acknowledgments

I owe thanks to the wonderful people who supported me throughout the writing and editing of this book, especially Dan and Kim. Thank you also to the people who gave me a wonderful education in letters and psychology. You have all given me so much more than I could have ever asked for.

My thanks and appreciation to the artists and bands whose songs I have mentioned in these pages for providing me with inspiration and for being the medium through which so many real people have been able to communicate the things for which there are no easy words.

About the Author

Abria Mattina is a graduate of the University of Ottawa. She holds a degree in English Literature and a certificate in Publishing from New York University. She currently resides in Ottawa, Ontario.

Visit her online at www.abriamattina.com.

Made in the USA
Lexington, KY
26 July 2014